The Second Pearl

by Mike Bentley

The Second Pearl

Printed in the United States of America
10 9 8 7 6 5 4 3 2 1

ISBN-13: 978-1-948035-83-5 (Paperback)
ISBN-13: 978-1-948035-93-4 (eBook)

Published by Defiance Press and Publishing, LLC

Bulk orders of this book may be obtained by contacting Defiance Press and Publishing, LLC. www.defiancepress.com.

Defiance Press & Publishing, LLC
281-581-9300
info@defiancepress.com

Table of Contents

Book II

Book III

Book IV

Author's Foreword

This novel is a cautionary tale, a warning to my fellow Americans and our many freedom-loving friends around the world. Its premise is based on the current reality that there is a massive dragon on the prowl in Asia. He is focused, relentless, takes the long view, has nearly unlimited human capital and financial resources, and is very aggressive. This growing threat is, of course, Communist China, whose leaders view their country as the center of the world—the current manifestation of the vast Middle Kingdom of old. The Chinese Communist Party (CCP) leadership wants its realm to be the world's sole superpower, and their intentions are well-chronicled. Therefore, we need to inform ourselves regarding those intentions, even as we resist them. We need to believe them, wake up to the implications for the United States and our many allies, and develop a relevant and coherent philosophy—and an attendant group of policies—that apply the hard-learned lessons of history.

We are witnessing a long-term series of actions by China in the western Pacific that are eerily similar to those in the 1930s before Imperial Japan attacked Pearl Harbor in 1941.

During Japan's transition from a closed feudal society to a modern one after the Meiji Restoration in 1868, it never abandoned its ancient militaristic bushido code. Even as the country became a fully engaged member of the community of nations, it rapidly absorbed Western technical know-how and, less than 40 years after emerging from its self-imposed isolation, it built a modern battleship fleet that defeated the Russian Navy in 1905. And they didn't stop there. Japan continued to industrialize its economy, modernize its naval and ground forces, and steadily moved out of the home islands into Taiwan, Korea, and Manchuria. Not content with these gains, and nearly unopposed by the international community, Japan decided to keep expanding its empire into east Asia and the western Pacific. The country was temporarily successful in this endeavor in 1941-1942, but could not defend such a vast territory from awakened allies and America's military-industrial output.

An additional example is Germany's long recovery from World War I that included a massive build-up of its military forces before it attacked its neighbors in 1939. Germany had overcome the unfair post-World War I Versailles Treaty and survived the political instability of the 1920s and the Great Depression but, unfortunately, the latter suffering provided the perfect environment for the Nazi message and ascendency. The Nazi Party steadily consolidated its power inside Germany, then became strong enough to bully some of its neighbors into capitulation. And, after absorbing as much of Europe as it could by bluff and intimidation, Germany invaded Poland and began World War II.

Unfortunately, during this era, American leaders and ordinary citizens largely ignored what was happening in Asia and Europe; life at home was, at varying times good or bad, but we were inwardly focused and didn't want to be drawn into another world war. But ignorance plus isolationism is a recipe for disaster in a world of aggressive totalitarians, and we allowed the bad guys to sneak up on us. Seemingly overnight, Americans were fighting for their lives. And one important theme in this book is to describe what happens when America repeats the same mistakes it made in the 1930s by ignoring the comprehensive threat posed by Communist China.

While we've been focused elsewhere—and, as usual, ascribing our values of toleration, friendship, pure hearts, and mutual respect to China—that country's leadership has been busy laying a foundation for taking over the world. If you doubt that, look objectively at the CCP's influence in every country on Earth. Research its Belt and Road projects that are gaining traction in South Asia, the Middle East, Africa, and the Caribbean. Inform yourself as to what the Chinese have been doing in the United States—investing in some of our industries to the point of economic dependency, hacking into our computer systems and stealing our technology, integrating passive spies into our higher education system and research labs, donating copious shiploads of money to win friends—and let's not forget their intentional failure to warn the world of the dangerous Covid pandemic they knew about for at least several weeks before coming clean. And that mea culpa was weak at best—even including a laughable attempt to shift the blame onto the U.S. Army.

Once again, while we've been sitting behind our two oceans and thinking good thoughts about everyone, the CCP has constructed a 350-ship navy—which has components that are larger than the U.S. fleet. And the Chinese navy is mostly in Asian waters while ours is scattered across the globe. American friends, we have an historical proclivity for being asleep at the switch.

However, as we DO wake up and shift our focus to the dangers posed by mainland China, let's not repeat (with our many Chinese American citizens) the terrible mistake of early World War II, wherein we overreacted to the racial aspect of Japan's aggression. We were angry and embarrassed, and poured out unconstitutional and unjustified wrath upon American citizens of Japanese ancestry. Placing Japanese Americans into concentration camps was one of the worst deeds in our history. Yet, to their everlasting credit, Japanese Americans didn't turn against their homeland—they did just the opposite: They volunteered for military service while incarcerated, and their 442/100 Regiment, drawn mostly from Hawaiian and West Coast families, became the most decorated military unit of its size in U.S. history.

Today, let us be thankful for the 300 different ethnic groups that constitute our nation's population—the third most populous country on Earth. Included in this rich diaspora are Chinese Americans who serve in our military with distinction, and who are leaders in every profession and industry in all 50 of our states. In addition, while we should be angry at the CCP leadership for ordering China's entire Uighur ethnic minority into concentration camps and for persecuting the tens of millions of Christians that worship in mainland house churches, we should not blame average Chinese citizens for the sins of their government. The urban and rural population of China is spied on and bullied every day. If you think "1984" lives here in the U.S., spend a few days in the People's Republic of China.

I love Asia and Asians, and have spent half my life traveling and working there—first with the military in 1985 when I was stationed in Korea, and then later when I served as a civilian business and humanitarian worker in Vietnam and Laos. I've made some 60 trips to Asia during the intervening

35 years—including to China. I have been treated very well there—during meetings and social events with provincial and city-level officials, and with business leaders and everyday folks. Chinese customer relations practices are excellent, and family hospitality, in my limited experience, is universal. I have many friends there; however, they have largely stopped communicating with me due to the negative implications for their social credit scores. But the federal government is another story; the CCP wants to conquer Taiwan, and will soon have the ability to push us out of the western Pacific. Technically, they have that power now.

Finally, let me say that The Second Pearl is a story, not an objective scholarly dissertation, and I'm grateful to all of you who are sacrificially investing your time and treasure reading it. I enjoyed creating its fictional characters, but their heroism is intended to inform us about the real political and technological threats posed by modern China. The technology described exists, though I chose the various numbers of weapons and some of their capabilities to facilitate the narrative. If there is one take-away, let it be a warning to remember the passivity that created the power vacuum in the 1930s: Into that void rushed the dictatorial governments that started World War II. Aggressive entities look for weaknesses to exploit, and our isolationism contributed to the war and its 60-70 million deaths.

And please remember our friend Taiwan—25 million people who just want to remain free.

MNB/2021

Book I

Prologue
December 7, 1941

Imperial Japanese Navy Lieutenant Matsuo Matsuzaki flared his Nakajima B5N2 Type 97 Kate torpedo/observation plane in preparation for landing on the carrier *Akagi*, and expertly made tiny last-second adjustments before touching down on the gently rolling deck. With only a slight bump, the plane jerked to a halt after its tailhook caught the middle arresting cable—a routine end to an historic mission. Like every aspect of his flying, Matsuzaki had honed his skills during hundreds of such landings over the previous five years. He was one of Imperial Japan's best naval aviators and was, at the moment, feeling triumphant—exultation probably shared by every crew returning from their raid on the United States Territory of Hawaii. They'd just destroyed or damaged several battleships, plus a host of other military ships, planes, additional facilities at Pearl Harbor Naval Base, plus other targets on Oahu Island. But, as in every battle, their euphoria following the early morning attack was tinged with sadness because twenty-nine of their fellow aircrews would never return to their carriers, or to their homes and families in Japan.

Lieutenant Matsuzaki was the PIC (pilot in command) of the aircraft carrying the mission's overall leader, IJN Commander Mitsuo Fuchida—a veteran aviator who'd been the on-site orchestrator of the 360 dive bombers, torpedo planes, high-level bombers, and fighters that delivered the opening round of Japan's new war against America. But, tragically for Japan, their audacity and tactical triumph had the unintended strategic consequence of moving a reluctant United States—currently sitting mostly on the sidelines as a friend of Great Britain and her allies in Europe—to an economic powerhouse wholeheartedly committed en masse to defeating the Axis threat.

But, at that moment, none of that was known to Japan's heroes, and the Kate trundled slowly across the steel deck as Matsuzaki used his foot pedals to follow the directions of the controller. Finally, he received the signal to stop, and parked the heavy plane and cut the engine. Relieved, and shaking from a combination of adrenaline and fatigue, he breathed a sigh of relief, and called back to PO1 Norinobu Mizuki, his excellent radio operator sitting in the third (rear-most) seat. They exchanged some quick banter about the ten eager young sailors surrounding their airplane—enthusiastic hands that would help fold the wings and push the aircraft to the nearby elevator for its trip down to the hangar deck below. They joked that these kids were more of a threat than the allied flack they'd encountered over Pearl! But these young men had a right to be excited, and the PIC gave them a respectful yet playful salute.

Every returning flight crew was grateful that the *Akagi*'s commanding officer, IJN Captain Kiichi Hasegawa, continued to move the fleet's flagship southward after their dawn take-off. In fact, he was only 190 miles north of Oahu Island when this last plane touched down. His action was especially appreciated by these last three aviators in the mission commander's plane who, by tradition, were the last to land. They had been "bingo" fuel when they'd finally reached the safety of the mother ship, and couldn't have stayed aloft much longer.

However, in sharp contrast to the two younger flyers' elation, Commander Fuchida, occupying the Kate's middle/observer seat, was experiencing conflicting emotions that had just swung from jubilation to gut-wrenching turmoil: The triumph he'd shared with the others upon landing had vanished as soon as his quick scan of the *Akagi*'s flight deck revealed that preparations for the next attack wave—absolutely vital in his mind to finish this initial battle with the Americans—were nowhere to be seen. *No…it couldn't be!* With growing panic, he jerked off his four-point harness, slammed back the overhead canopy, and climbed onto his seat—holding onto the top of the curved Plexiglas surface to steady his tired body. He stared up at the carrier's island superstructure, looking in vain for the impassive face of the task force commander, Vice Admiral Chuichi Nagumo, but couldn't spot him. Fuchida couldn't believe it. *Was that conservative and taciturn old-school cruiser commander going to leave now—just when they had the American fleet on fire, and the whole Pearl Harbor Naval Base in chaos and vulnerable to their all-important third strike?* That additional assault was designed to destroy the extensive fuel tank farm, dry docks, and vital repair facilities that would put the enemy's inevitable counter-attack back an additional six months or more.

Fuchida's eyes were drawn slightly to the left when he spotted Commander Minoru Genda matching him stare for stare as he leaned against a railing high on the Admiral's Bridge. He was the brilliant planner the fleet's overall commander, Vice Admiral Isoroku Yamamoto, had assigned to formulate and develop the raid in every detail. It was Genda who had received inspiration for the raid after watching American military training films demonstrating a successful mock raid on Pearl Harbor a few years earlier. Then he'd received additional conceptual proof from the recent British raid against the Italian fleet moored at Taranto Harbor: There, outdated aircraft sank three Italian battleships and shocked the world's naval community—further convincing the senior commander of the Combined Japanese Imperial Fleet that the Pearl Harbor raid could succeed. And it had—to a point. *Surely Genda would convince Nagumo to stick to the plan and finish the job—they'd never get another chance like this! It was imperative that Japan maximize its time to consolidate its primary gains in Asia and throughout the western Pacific.*

Genda and Fuchida were long-time colleagues, and had agreed during the planning phase that the first two waves of attacking aircraft would destroy as many of the American ships and planes as possible. That destruction would earn Japan a probable six-month respite from an organized, American-led counter-attack against the empire. But a third wave was deemed necessary to destroy the remaining infrastructure, which would buy Japan a full year or more—forcing its new enemy to start the long campaign from San Diego and the other West Coast ports.

Adding further context to Fuchida's frustration, not one of their primary targets—the American aircraft carriers—had been in port. That fact didn't preclude them from being located and sunk at a later date—perhaps during the next few days as the fleet returned to Japan, but at least today they'd escaped. Fuchida searched Genda's stone face in vain, and received a barely perceptible shake of his friend's head. It was a small gesture, but it cut like a knife plunged into Fuchida's soul. He understood its implications immediately: It was not to be—they were going home with the job unfinished!

As the coldness of disappointment confirmed his fate, Fuchida climbed out on the wing and jumped down onto the hard steel deck, barely acknowledging the back-slapping and victorious shouts of the jubilant young sailors celebrating his return. He strode purposely across the heavy plates, feeling the vibration as the ship's engines revved as additional power was sent to the great shafts in the bowels of the ship that would push them home. He reached the island superstructure, stepped across the sill of the open doorway, and bounded up the two flights of steel stairs to the spot where Genda stood alone.

"What is happening, Genda?" he demanded, already knowing the answer. "The American ships in the harbor are severely damaged and the airfields and planes are largely destroyed. Pearl Harbor is helpless to defend against our next wave…we must attack the fuel-tank farm and dry docks now!"

Genda tightened his already white-knuckle grip on the rope-covered hand rail—a passionate professional who was dealing with his own surging emotions. He sympathized with his old friend's dramatic appeal and had, in fact, already earnestly pleaded that very case with the reluctant admiral standing inside the bridge a few feet away. But their task force commander had already issued his orders to the *Akagi*'s captain, so Genda's words had fallen on the ears of a mind made up. Admiral Nagumo believed his first responsibility was to protect the fleet from American counter-attack—however improbable that seemed to the two younger officers at that moment—and he believed that the raid was already successful enough to justify their withdrawal.

Genda knew Nagumo had not been enthusiastic about the raid in the first place, and that the veteran leader wanted the fleet back in the relative safety of home waters to prepare for the long and bloody Pacific war they'd just started. And, at least in that respect, Genda knew the admiral was right. Genda suddenly turned and grabbed Fuchida's arms—not in rebuke, but as a brother in arms. "I made our case with Admiral Fuchida, but he is adamant: He has ordered the fleet to return home."

So the decision was final. Both men could only stand helplessly embracing each other at arm's length as they accepted their fate. Then, after a few meaningful seconds of silent comradeship, they separated and turned to grip the waist-high railing. They watched in silence as the busy aircraft crews wrestled the last of the planes to the waiting elevators. The two veteran aviators tasted the clean salt air and felt the great ship heel to starboard as she turned eastward toward Japan. The smell of exhaust dissipated in the freshening breeze as the *Akagi* accelerated, and together the pilots instinctively scanned the horizon for the enemy planes they knew weren't coming. They watched the distant destroyer screen match the turn and speed of the flagship and, as the bigger ship cut through the whitecaps, the smaller and lighter ships also began to knife smoothly through the low westerly swells.

Little did either man know that military historians generally would agree that the Pearl Harbor raid, though brilliantly planned and executed, only served to bring a reluctant America into the war. In that context, the Pearl Harbor assault was a strategic disaster. The loss of life and damage from the attack provided a severe enough shock to spur the Americans into action, and they enlisted in the military in droves. The naval engineers and civilian workers also made fairly rapid repairs on the Pacific Fleet, and six of the eight battleships sunk or heavily damaged on that fateful day returned to combat by 1944. Genda and Fuchida were right to have lobbied for that third wave: Those famous Pearl Harbor fuel tanks and dry dock facilities played a big role in America's quick recovery from the attack.

Genda never quit lobbying, however, and recommended throughout the coming spring that Japan should not only return and occupy Hawaii, but should also use its extensive military resources to take the battle to the American West Coast. He believed such risky and dangerous actions were necessary to preserve Japan's gains in Asia—the whole point of their Hawaiian aggression in the first place.

Admiral Yamamoto did try to rectify the Hawaiian raid's glaring lack of luck at missing the American carriers: He sent a large fleet back to the Midway Islands (lying just 1,300 miles northwest of Hawaii) the following June. He hoped to lure the American Navy into a trap and sink its three precious carriers, but the reverse happened instead: U.S. Naval Intelligence had broken the Japanese naval and diplomatic codes sufficiently to reason that Midway was the target of a coming attack. They ambushed the Japanese carriers and sank four of them—including the flagship *Akagi*, while losing only one of their own. So, after a mere six months of fighting in the Pacific, the tide turned in America's favor. And, though three bitter years of intense fighting remained after the Battle of Midway, Japan was on the defensive for the remainder of the war.

Finally, in August of 1945, after the Japanese cities of Hiroshima and Nagasaki were devastated by the detonation of the world's first and only nuclear weapons used in combat, Japan unconditionally surrendered. In retrospect, and ironically, the raid on Pearl Harbor, believed necessary by Japan's leaders to keep America out of their way while they absorbed most of Asia into their so-called East Asia Co-Prosperity Sphere, only served to light the fuse of Japan's eventual destruction. From the moment the first shot was fired by the USS *Ward* at a Japanese midget submarine trying to slip unnoticed into the entrance to Pearl Harbor, it was only a matter of time before America's industrial capacity fully transitioned to war production, and its Axis enemies were overwhelmed.

The lives of the four principal Japanese naval men who envisioned and led the attack on Pearl Harbor came to very different ends: Admiral Yamamoto died when his plane was shot down by American P-38 fighters over Bougainville Island, Papua New Guinea, on April 18th, 1943. He was 59 years old, was deeply mourned by the Japanese people, and is still remembered as a national hero. Admiral Nagumo committed suicide (with a pistol shot rather than by traditional dagger seppuku) while on Saipan in the Northern Mariana Islands, thus avoiding capture by U.S. Marines. His death occurred on June 6th, 1944 (a day that was to be ever famous for the Allied landings in Normandy, France). He was 57.

However, in stark contrast to the two admirals, Genda and Fuchida survived the war to great glory: Genda rose to the rank of lieutenant general in Japan's post-war military, and logged 5,000 hours in both Japanese and American-made aircraft (including more than 1,000 hours in the F-105 Star Fighter). He also completed a long second career of public service in Japan's democratically elected national legislature as a member of the (conservative) Liberal Democratic Party. He died in peace as an old man on August 15th, 1989.

And the last of the four—the daring Fuchida—retired as a navy captain, and after the war converted to Christianity and became a prominent evangelist—even working with the noted American minister, Reverend Billy Graham. He died of natural causes on May 13th, 1976, at the age of 73.

Chapter 1

The People's Republic of China
A few years after the successful 2008 Beijing Olympic Games
February 2nd

As a typically vicious northern China ice storm slammed wave upon wave of crystalline snowflakes against the thick windows of her drab office building in downtown Beijing, Miss Lin Po hurried from her supervisor's office nearly in tears. The normally quiet scientist she loved working for had been on a rampage for several days, and the petite young researcher and the rest of her colleagues were beside themselves with worry and puzzlement. Completely out of character in both his foul mood and relentlessness, Ma Tao Qing, Ph.D., had been demanding Herculean efforts from his harried staff, and yelling at anyone within earshot when the data or documents he'd demanded were slow materializing. Nevertheless, the 15 men and 10 women who comprised his immediate staff continued to cut their genius/scientist/team leader considerable slack because they, too, were beginning to realize that his dark mood was driven by terrible discoveries that threatened both their lives and the social fabric of their ancient homeland.

The implications of the data—combined with the fact that Dr. Ma could be executed if the wrong Politburo member took his soon-to-be-submitted report the wrong way—had them all on edge. Bad news was never well-received by those who commanded the highest levels of the People's Republic, particularly when such news portended danger and possible destabilization of the masses. In the leader's case, such disruption meant possible doom for the Chinese Communist Party and for their families—each dependent on the other for continuing dominance over modern Communist Chinese society.

In contrast to this localized drama playing out in Beijing, a similarly talented scholar, Reginald Trammell, Ph.D., was working alone in a drab cubical in Washington, DC, and coming to the same conclusions: The PRC was in real trouble. In fact, when he combined the newly available data he'd secured from the Central Intelligence Agency with that already in his possession from numerous other classified and open sources, he pieced together the fact that the most populous nation on Earth faced dual crises.

First, their ravenous industries had over-exploited reserves of several key natural resources to a greater extent and at a faster rate than even their most conservative scientists had previously mentioned in internal memos. Reg had access to this intelligence because agencies within the United States, particularly the National Security Agency, had acquired and subsequently shared on a need-to-know basis, most of what Dr. Ma was discovering. The NSA had also learned that certain senior PRC leaders had over-hyped the potential of the relatively new oil-shale fracking technology that was a tremendous bonus for the United States' economy. This meant less oil and natural gas would be available to feed China's hungry factories—a situation that would force the decision-makers to choose between either (1) significantly curtailing their rapidly expanding industrial base, with resulting social chaos from millions of laid-off workers, or (2) significantly increasing their dependence on international suppliers who charged considerably more. Politically, both of these options were equally repugnant to those senior CCP members who believed they had the most to lose.

But researchers Ma and Trammell both figured out that the second major problem was equally threatening: Shifting weather patterns were affecting crops along wide swaths of the PRC's arable lands in the north and west, and yields were trending down. In fact, unless long-range production changed for the better, both scholars estimated that starvation was a probability for up to 10 percent of the rural population—particularly likely to happen in the more arid regions hundreds of miles west of Beijing. And 10 percent of 1.4 billion people would produce catastrophic death, disease and, most alarming to those in power, violent social upheaval.

Both scientists also recognized the severe and complex political realities with which their governments would have to deal. Dr. Ma, who worked for the Chinese Ministry of Natural Resources, was deeply worried—his hands even shook at times as he exacerbated his anxiety by daily chain-smoking three packs of harsh unfiltered cigarettes. But he believed it was his patriotic duty to produce an unflinchingly accurate picture of the unfolding crises; it was the reason he'd been pushing his frazzled team to help him distill the massive data load into a concise, yet comprehensive report for his superiors. He was becoming so overwrought by the process that, during the previous evening's grueling hours of compilation, he'd embarrassed himself by weeping in the presence of his sweating colleagues.

But Dr. Ma was descended from a grandfather who had trudged alongside the late, great Chairman Mao during the famous 1934-1935 Long March to Beijing. He drew strength from that example, and decided to produce a report presenting both the unvarnished truth—along with possible solutions—something generally not done at his level. He reminded his soon-to-be readers that China's long-term production contracts with regional and international suppliers were up for renewal, and recommended that new contracts be negotiated as soon as possible to leverage favorable prices. This was advice so presumptuous and sensitive that it could trigger a backlash that could finish him and his family forever; he knew he faced possible wrath when he submitted the finished report three days later—but he did it anyway.

However, China also selectively rewarded those deserving special merit and, after Dr. Ma's supervisory chain recovered from the initial shock at both the boldness of the report and its depressing content, its members too did the right thing and forwarded it with their endorsements to the top echelons of government. This time, Ma's luck held: The powers that be rewarded his technical analysis and political courage with a two-level promotion. His new-found responsibilities included appointment as section head of his entire department (which brought higher pay and nice bonuses for Miss Po and his other researchers—all of whom he elevated and kept on his technical staff). His own accompanying pay raise thrilled his wife to no end: She used part of their windfall to sign up for one of the new credit cards available in the People's Republic, and immediately upon its delivery went on a memorable shopping spree.

But things weren't so rosy for Reg, laboring alone in the bowels of the Agricultural Section of the China Interests Desk at the U.S. Department of State. He was also a patriot with a significant heritage. Reg's grandfather had been a young ensign on the USS *California* during the Japanese attack on

Pearl Harbor—a daring junior officer who'd become a recognized American hero after the public learned that he'd jumped into the water at the high point of the battle to rescue several wounded sailors who were struggling to stay afloat. They were in particular danger of being trapped against the hull of the damaged battleship as a burning oil slick drifted toward them. But just before the fire engulfed the port side of their listing ship, the lieutenant dragged the last man to the safety of a waiting lifeboat. Decorated and promoted after the battle, Lieutenant Trammell served throughout World War II and, afterward, he and his wife decided to stay in the Navy and make a career of it. They had to endure another long separation during the Korean War, but their family service was greatly appreciated by their government, and he rose to the rank of rear admiral in 1961. Fortunately, he lived long enough to inspire his grandson, and Reg spent every chance he could absorbing the elderly gentleman's heroic stories and common sense advice.

Not surprisingly, Reg inherited some of his grandfather's strong character, too. Like his counterpart in China, he decided to stick his neck out by annotating his report with extensive warnings about how the PRC might react to the shortages he was describing. He opined that Chinese scientists would use the same data to come to the same conclusions regarding probable starvation and industrial depression. Reg warned that the PRC might aggressively move against its regional neighbors to seek the resources that could forestall economic collapse—and he drew upon the historical parallels of pre-WWII Japan to emphasize his points.

* * *

However, Reg's immediate supervisor, a Ms. Polly Armstrong to whom he submitted his report, had a ho-hum response to his research and analysis, and only reluctantly forwarded his findings to the minimum number of recipients on the distribution list. Her cover letter was so bland that the various department heads barely scanned the report and, with one exception at the CIA, passed the report to their busy administrative assistants for hard-copy filing or storage in secure electronic databanks for future consideration.

However, Polly went a step further on her own initiative by informing "her" deputy assistant secretary that, though she thought the report was "alarmist," she would yield to his greater experience in evaluating its implications. In doing so, she'd called upon her highly developed sense of "CYA," that is, personal preservation combined with long-term careerist aspirations, to never expose oneself to organizational ridicule. While essentially tabling Reg's report, she also protected herself by withholding any criticism of Reg, whom she wanted to keep on her staff. She believed that he was a talented researcher and that his routine data analysis was, in her limited experience, unusually thorough (and made her look good when she endorsed those reports that she knew the chain above her would like). The DAS, also an ambitious appointee who knew what the chain wanted to hear, accepted her cautious warning and ordered the matter to be placed in the long-term, periodic re-exam file. CYA to the max.

But Polly had one last (and very secret) component to her long-range plans: She also sent a private summary via snail mail in memo form to her (benefactor) senator. She had worked under the man when she first joined the federal government after law school, and he'd been instrumental in getting her the cushy job she presently enjoyed at State. So, after she dropped that letter in her outbox, she enjoyed a moment of reflection to confirm that she'd done all she could to contain Reg's little firestorm. Polly leaned back in her expensive real leather executive chair that she'd finagled at taxpayer expense, rested her chin on steepled manicured fingernails, and was at peace. She was sitting behind her elegant quarter-sawn antique oak desk, and glanced over at her (she had to admit) stunning reflection in the large mirror she kept strategically placed against the closet wall in her spacious office. She winked at herself and smiled as she remembered how literal "working under" the senator had been. She also took another moment to enjoy the related thought that, as long as her senator/sponsor kept getting elected—and subsequently appointed to serve on the Appropriations Committee—she had it made in the shade.

* * *

After learning what Polly's machinations had done to his report, Reg realized that it was going nowhere. He considered resigning and moving to the private sector where many nearby think tanks and government contractors (aka "beltway bandits") were paying top dollar for visionaries like him. But, after due consideration (and considerable unhelpful tut-tutting from his frustrated wife), he decided that the patriotic course of action was to stay at State where he could better monitor the deteriorating situation in China. He rededicated himself to monitoring China's natural resource sectors on his own time, even as other assignments were steadily dropped into his inbox. He remained in his department at the same level and pay grade and soldiered on, quietly using his top secret security clearance to keep an eye on the PRC.

His next assignments included the latest topics that the self-impressed Ms. Armstrong was hot on. Among her concerns were poppy production in Afghanistan, and Reg accepted as valid her premise that cash flow from the poppy's raw heroin sales had terrorist implications. He dug into his new assignment with his usual professionalism, but never forgot his real reason for staying put. Reg's wife, Tipi, however, decided that her scholar/nerd husband lacked the requisite ambition to excel in the super-competitive world of DC government lifers, and that he would never reach the assistant secretary level her friends' husbands coveted. She felt humiliated and tremendously sorry for herself, but determined to invest her time in something self-actualizing: Since Reg was her lot in life (because she feared her social circle's long-term backlash from a divorce scandal), she enrolled their two pre-school age children in a local day care, then used her college sorority connections to land a job as a branding advocate for a regional big-box chain. She believed her husband's once-promising career had tanked, and that it was up to her to bring in the extra income she craved to "keep up."

A meeting of the "Eight"
Beijing, the People's Republic of China, 21:00 Hours

Han Gaoli, General Secretary of the Communist Party of China and president of the People's Republic, stepped out of his whisper-quiet German-manufactured elevator and crossed the room to his waiting colleagues. The floor was covered with an exquisite handmade Tibetan wool rug, and his fellow senior leaders were respectfully standing around his utilitarian yet beautifully polished teak conference table. The rug and table rested upon scientifically designed, sound-absorbing composite material—a security requirement that his architect and protective detail had especially created for this room. In fact, his underground bunker contained many components of a comprehensive electronic cocoon that protected him from prying eyes and ears—both domestic and international.

GS Han had taken particular delight in the table: At his request, a master craftsman had personally selected the boards from a colleague's private stash, constructed it upstairs without glue, then disassembled and carried it piecemeal down the elevator for final assembly and polishing. Now it was the understated yet central feature in Han's ultra-secure underground meeting room, located seven stories beneath his private estate in the gently rolling hills northwest of Beijing.

Han was trying to project calmness, but he was truly worried as he arrived at the end of an unanticipated and frantic week of daily meetings with senior scientists and generals. They'd laid out for him the implications of the report he'd felt obliged to circulate among China's most senior leadership. The subject matter experts had confirmed the terrible threats that the report prophesied, and its sudden descent onto his shoulders had unnerved him to say the least. Tonight, though Han usually enjoyed this special room that had been such a challenging engineering feat, he took no notice of his priceless collection of French Impressionist art that decorated its walls, nor of the equally rare Ming and Ch'ing Dynasty vases that rested in specially recessed cubby holes between the paintings. As he arrived at the head of his special table, he was all business.

He felt safe in his unique bunker: The carefully designed 2,500 square-meter underground complex boasted a dozen smaller outlying storage and service rooms, plus a high-technology kitchen that his personal chef used to produce an amazing array of gastronomic delights for his guests. The complex even had a quarter of a mile-long emergency escape tunnel that gently rose to a cleverly concealed exit and helicopter pad located on the northern edge of his estate. Nestled in thick forest, the structures were nearly invisible from above. The multi-acre complex had been secretly constructed using millions of off-budget Renminbi (meaning "people's money," also referred to as Yuan), yet those in the know had agreed that such an expense was necessary for his (and their) physical security.

As Han sank into the plush red silk brocade cushion resting on his elegantly carved and lacquered redwood chair (identical to the eleven other chairs placed around the oval table), he was in a rare state of emotional unease. He would discuss the alarming news with this hand-picked group of confidants who were nervous, too—feelings heightened from having to wait the better part of an hour for him to arrive. He nodded respectfully and beckoned them to sit, but no one spoke as trusted staff quickly poured steaming bowls of green tea and unobtrusively set out plates of delicate sweet and spicy treats for each guest before vanishing. It was a tribute to the group's collective faith in the engineers that none of those present were concerned that their ensuing conversations would be overheard. The room's walls were completely impervious to any eavesdropping devices yet created, and the architect and chief engineer had assured him that even the United States' newest deep penetrator bunker-buster bombs couldn't reach them. Yet the existence of such bombs was the reason for the side tunnel—deemed necessary in case the elevator was destroyed in an attack, or rendered inoperable if the estate's redundant on-site generator failed. There were no traditional stairs.

Eight was an auspicious number in China, and the reason the planners of the Beijing Summer Olympic Games had decided to stage the opening ceremonies on 08/08/08. The power of the superstitious number had also influenced Han when he carefully selected this particular group of trusted friends and colleagues to be his very private think tank. Their combined presence represented organizations within the complex structure of the CCP that were necessary to create or change the nation's laws, and the Eight, like Han himself, wore multiple hats in their labyrinthine bureaucracy. Between them, they directly or indirectly governed the Central Committee, the Politburo, the Central Military Commission, the 1.5 million officers of the People's Armed Police Force, the Ministry of State Security, the Ministry of Public Security—including its two million domestic police force members, the State Council of the PRC, the People's Liberation Army, and the National People's Congress—each of which had varying degrees of control over the interlocking spheres of modern Chinese government and society.

But in this room, as in every space he entered in the PRC, Han was more than just a "first among equals." He ruled China with the proverbial velvet hammer. Case in point, the relatively small group sitting with him today were there because he wanted an unofficial decision-making body to ensure that his vision cascaded directly down through (and was absorbed and obeyed by) the incredible number of government layers below him. Each layer had its own descending chain of command (and accompanying bureaucracies) that, in turn, exercised command and control over the vast network of CCP functionaries that governed the (nearly) 1.5 billion people who resided in their ancient "Middle Kingdom."

Han had believed since his youth that he was destined and appointed by fate to lead the Great Dragon, and he usually made decisions utilizing only symbolic advice from others. But the current crisis presented one of those rare times when he'd admitted to himself that he genuinely needed real input and sound advice. Accordingly, he'd summoned his team of six elite leaders from the ruling government's most important and influential organizations, plus his two long-time friends, now retired, who comprised his Eight. They were his "kitchen cabinet" and, with their willing collaboration, he'd been formulating and dictating the actual policies of the PRC since his ascension to China's presidency several years before. Philosophically and actually, Han had long ago rejected that hogwash that the modern state was ruled by a consensus of senior CCP leaders: Han ran the PRC his way, and he'd ensured that everyone who counted knew that those who dared defy him did so at great peril.

However, on this cold winter evening, regardless of his own perceptions of "right to power," Han was deeply worried and needed his friends and colleagues to help him find just the kind of traditional consensus solution that would help him solve this newly discovered and impending national crisis. After taking a customary sip of tea to calm his nerves, and theirs, he leaned his five-foot, ten-inch frame forward and fixed his penetrating brown eyes on each colleague one by one. Then he spoke humbly and directly. "Thank you, everyone, for coming on such short notice—and for forgiving me for being late. But I know we are of one mind that fate has laid before us a monumental task—that of formulating plans to deal with the report I had placed in your hands a few days ago."

His statement elicited worried murmurs from all present. They were as alarmed as he was and they, too, accepted that the country was in deep trouble. But now that a serious problem had presented itself, they also accepted that it was up to their small group to find workable solutions. Their goal could be nothing less than finding courses of action that would save their party and people; not only was the future of their country at stake, their personal survival depended on keeping the masses content and themselves in power.

Li Gao Bang, Han's oldest friend and most trusted senior advisor, sat to Han's right in the place of highest honor. Li was two years younger than Han, but shared the same salt-and-pepper hair and nearly unbridled energy. The two of them had worked together since Li's first day as a junior intern in the Beijing headquarters of the Ministry of Heavy Industry four decades before, and they had subsequently risen through the bureaucratic ranks together. They had even married sisters. And it had been Li's son, Li Gao Fu, one of China's notable young architects, with whom Han had entrusted design authority to oversee every aspect of the construction and security of Han's private residence—including the amazing underground room in which they now sat—in perfect, seasonally adjusted comfort. The senior Li was also privy to the fact that they sat in one of only two rooms in the PRC where his old friend felt safe enough to speak without being overheard by any of China's (or Han's personal) enemies—and the only one in which he could (selectively) unburden his soul. The other secure room, also seven stories underground, had been built by another trusted firm, and was located in a neighborhood about 15 miles away in northern Beijing. That site had been selected because its construction would be masked by that of a massive sports complex being built for the '08 Summer Games. The construction chaos from the sports site had worked to perfection, and the Ministry of State Security (MSS) reported that none of the world's intelligence agencies had mentioned its existence. Li met Han's gaze and nodded reassurance to his friend—they would solve this looming catastrophe together.

As everyone set delicate rose-colored porcelain tea cups onto equally exquisite lacquered saucers, Han diplomatically nodded gratefully to each in turn. Then he began his appeal. "As you were no doubt shocked to learn from the report before us, one of our bright younger scientists, Dr. Ma Tao Qing, pulled together data from myriad sources and, thankfully, had the courage to put it into a useable report. He warns us that we face many years, perhaps even decades, of severe food shortages—explaining this situation by turning a spotlight on the changing weather patterns that have negatively impacted our crop yields for some time. He also presented data concerning our rapidly dwindling natural resource production, which forced me to acknowledge what I think all of us suspected: Our mineral reserves are being exploited at unsustainable levels. However, I reluctantly admit to you that I am surprised by the severity of his conclusions…" Han sensed that his unusual candor brought a sense of unease to his worried colleagues. Everyone squirmed a bit, but he knew they felt relief, too: He had to unlock their pre-conditioned cultural reticence against candor if he was going to benefit from their insights.

He continued, "As soon as I saw this alarming report, I immediately asked several of our most competent and trusted senior scientists to review its data and conclusions. They generally agree that the report is correct, and their disagreements are mere nuances that do not alter the basic set of problems it exposes. Let us examine these problems individually: First, our agricultural sector. As far as Ma and his team of climatologists can foresee, a broad swath of our population faces likely starvation within 10 years, and by that he means 10 to 15 percent of our combined rural and city populations—150 million or more—dead!"

He paused, letting them absorb the horror of it. "This fact alone, if true, forces us to make one of three unpleasant choices. The first is to develop additional domestic sources for our current basic foodstuffs—particularly wheat and paddy rice—which will be accomplished by opening new lands in the southwestern part of the country. These areas are apparently being favorably transformed by the changing climate. However, Ma addressed this option and predicts that insufficient hectares of new, suitably arable lands can be made ready in time to replace those that will be lost."

Han glanced around at his intent audience. "The second option is to rely more heavily on foreign sources—a strategy Ma supports because the West, particularly Canada, Australia, Argentina, and the U.S., are predicted to become even more fruitful than they are now. And third, he speculates that we might be able to develop different crops that are suitable to our changing climate. These alternate crops, of course, would have to be palatable to our people."

He gazed around at his most trusted advisors, noting that the faces staring back at him were uniformly aghast, but he pressed on because they had to hear it all. "The second great problem we face is dwindling output from our drilling, quarry, and mining operations. You all know that we need vast amounts of raw materials in the form of 'rare-earth' metals and petroleum to keep our factories running. And, while we have plenty of coal, the other sectors are more important and will be exhausted long before we can effectively shift to nuclear or solar power sources. We will try to discover new rare earth deposits, open new mines, and exploit additional pockets of oil under lands and seas that we now control, but this work takes years." He then lowered his voice to an ominous level and said, "Therefore, based on these three weak solutions, we must discuss an additional and far more dangerous option that Ma didn't mention—that of absorbing our Asian neighbors by force—those wealthy ones who will enjoy decades of increased abundance in every category wherein we are about to suffer loss!"

Han paused again as furtive glances darted among the two factions he'd built into his group—members who he knew held generally opposing philosophies that gave him room to maneuver. "Failure to adopt the correct strategy—or combinations thereof—in a timely manner, will result in the aforementioned starvation and the great social disruptions that will surely follow…" He knew this last statement contained their greatest collective fear: Their privileged positions existed solely because they projected the illusion that they, the elite at the titular head of the CCP (the current manifestation of the historical emperors of the Middle Kingdom), provided food and security for China's teeming millions. But all of the senior leaders sitting around this important table understood the honest truth: If the workers lost faith in their leadership, the CCP could be swept away by massive revolutionary upheaval, and them with it. Even their combined police and military cadres, by sheer brute force, could only contain the active discontent of a few million—but these limited forces could not contain the unfocused violence of tens of millions.

Case in point: Government forces had broken up, killed, hunted down, and selectively executed the several thousand Tiananmen Square democracy protestors in 1989, precisely because they were relatively few in number, and not unified in group or purpose. It had been a straightforward "cleansing mission" for the police and military. But this brewing crisis was potentially far worse: Starving children would embolden the peasants to act with irrational bravery, and they could turn this potential domestic catastrophe into the CCP's downfall.

The loss of food sources, combined with the industrial sector's reduction in urban jobs, was a sure-fire recipe for multi-faceted doom. If factories shut their doors, millions of panicked workers could morph themselves into savage mobs that would overwhelm any deadly force the CCP threw at them. China would turn in on itself and become a self-immolating volcano of social chaos.

This knowledge had rattled everyone present from the moment they read and began to reflect on the implications of Ma's report. Han anticipated their anxiety, and he'd intentionally let them stew while he conferred with relevant scientists. He knew by now that his Eight would be ready and open to discuss any option that would save them. But to be an effective leader at this singular moment, he had to infuse his intimates with enough hope to find (and agree upon) practical solutions that would see them through the threatening crisis. Acute distress could overwhelm anyone's rational decision-making capabilities, and this was one of those very rare moments when Han's nearly absolute power required him to truly inspire his confidants. He had to use his extraordinary position, with its unique trappings of real authority, to genuinely inspire his colleagues to act in concert. Even their founder, the amazing leader/politician Chairman Mao—who enjoyed nearly absolute power at the height of his reign—lacked the military/industrial might that Han now possessed. This was one of those "stand and deliver" moments where the CCP's future—and its multi-generational successes—hung in the balance.

Han allowed 15 seconds of profound silence to stretch to 30, during which the only sound came from the faint hiss of the decorative fake fireplace built into the base of the wall behind him. Then, without warning, he smacked his open hand on his beautiful table with a fearsome crack. They all jumped in their seats! Then he forcefully declared, "This is our moment, my friends—we will save our great party and nation together!"

A jolt of energy shot through the group; they embraced his new-found electrifying confidence by spontaneously clapping. They straightened their shoulders and their eyes brightened. Han had won the moment, and he followed up this initial victory by inviting their insights and opinions. "My brothers and sisters, please share your ideas."

Deeply moved by this dramatic appeal, Han's friend Li appropriately provided context for the others: "General Secretary Han, fellow ministers, this is indeed the gravest threat our party and nation has faced since our struggle for unification prior to 1949. The implications are obvious: Either we develop our own new food sources domestically, or we will have to go as supplicants to our regional neighbors, and to the Americans, Australians, Canadians, Russians, and others to meet our people's needs. This crisis might even delay our long-term goal of becoming the world's sole superpower by 2049!" Li paused as murmurs washed across the room: His summary was repugnant and, with varying degrees of revulsion and derision, they began to voice their objections.

"We will never delay our 100-year plan to dominate the Earth!" proclaimed Senior General Tai Ming, who was the operational commander of the People's Liberation Army—the uniformed military officer who directed the day-to-day activities of all ground, naval, air, and space forces in the PRC.

Han had recently reorganized some parts of the government to reflect his growing power, and one key area that needed upgrading was the military. As chairman of the Central Military Commission, he was the commander-in-chief of the armed forces, similar to the position held by the President of the United States. As such, he believed his soon-to-be largest military on Earth needed a modified rank structure to reflect China's status: He reinstituted the former rank of "marshal" and gave it five-star importance. It was reserved for the one person who held the dual positions of vice chairman of the Central Military Commission and Minister of Defense—meaning it was the number two position under Han militarily. It was also a political position with ministerial rank, and was currently held by the aging Marshal Zhang Sheng. Han also added four-star ranks for those officers who commanded the top-most levels of the fighting military, with "senior general" being the designation for army and air force four-stars, and "senior admiral" for the naval officers. The other flag officer ranks corresponded to those of the United States and NATO militaries. Senior General Tai was Han's hand-picked, four-star who, once Marshal Zhang retired, Han planned to elevate to be the next vice chairman of the Central Military Commission and Minister of Defense.

"Our party and people will never again debase themselves by kowtowing to barbarians!" the senior general ended his declaration. Some were a bit taken aback by the vehemence of the general's statement, but even the more moderate among them hated the idea of sacrificing even a little of their hard-earned sovereignty by going cap in hand to the West.

Following on the heels of Tai's bold assertion, Minister of Public Security Ti Quo Qing (one of the two women present) also expressed her disdain. Han had invited her to join his team because she was the "Top Cop" in the People's Republic—and nearly two million police personnel reported to her. But, unusually, Han had additionally entrusted her with administration of the Central Military Commission's 1.5 million People's Armed Police Force. These cadres were quasi-soldiers, and this combination was an unheard-of concentration of power in the hands of one person. But Han had grown to like this woman's reliability, and she did as he directed without hesitation. She also possessed a broad appreciation for the scope of Chinese history, and was a reliable hawk who aggressively supported General Tai. The two of them provided Han with a useful right wing among the Eight—allowing him to express hawkishness when it suited his goals.

Ti's portfolio included placing and controlling every public camera in China, plus establishing the emerging "Social Credit" system that would further control the population. Reporting to her were the Ethnic Affairs Commission, which was steadily rounding up the Uighur Muslim minority tribes into concentration camps in the far west. She also controlled the Ministry of Civil Affairs and the Ministry of Justice, which rounded out comprehensive control of the social order. In less than three years, she had become Han's principal ally in consolidating power over every man, woman, and child in the PRC.

As Han expected, Ti spoke up and forcefully stated, "Fellow patriots, we have been on a long-term journey to re-establish the People's Republic as the dominant force in the world—the true Middle Kingdom that history remembers with awe. We lost that position two centuries ago when our weak, self-indulgent leaders allowed foreigners to temporarily occupy and defeat us. But our great Chairman Mao inspired us to overcome that shame! I see a silver lining here: This vexing potential disaster might just rattle the cages of those cowardly foot-draggers who timidly serve throughout our current government. Those weaker souls are appeasers, and they are keeping us from projecting our rightful influence over—no, our rightful domination—of our modern world!" She bowed her head respectfully as all applauded—some more forcefully than others.

"Well said, Comrade Minister!" responded General Tai who, like Ti, reported directly to GS Han. Tai had been in the PLA for more than 40 years—reared by a descendant of the Boxers (that super-nationalist group that was anti-imperialist, anti-foreign, and anti-Christian that had raised such havoc with the colonial powers as the 19th Century turned to the 20th). He shared the same distrust and hatred of the West as did his father, and Tai's zeal perhaps surpassed even that of his grandfather, who had actually fought in the 1899-1901 rebellion. "These former vassal states surrounding our Republic have been avoiding their rightful responsibility to pay us tribute for hundreds of years. The time has come for these recalcitrant ones to be 'encouraged' into a closer and proper relationship with our modern and revitalized motherland!"

Encouraged, my foot, he thought to himself...*the PLA was a coiled serpent ready to strike, and they would crush any border state that resisted. Then we will take on and defeat the meddling Americans and Japanese!*

Lee Tuc Chang, the Minister of Heavy Industry (who replaced Li when the older man retired from his official government position to serve as special counselor to the General Secretary), jumped on the bandwagon. "Comrade General Secretary Han, I agree with our colleagues. We have both an unprecedented problem and a modern opportunity here...I am referring, of course, to our great 'Dragon,' into which we have invested trillions of RMB these last years—our powerful armed forces who are now equipped with the modern technology that our engineers have developed—in addition to the impressive bounty that Comrade Minister Wing's intelligence network has stolen from the naïve and vulnerable West!" He paused as those around the table spontaneously clapped in the direction of the Minister of State Security, a squat, rough-looking character with a bulldog's neck, severe crewcut, and a legendary meanness that made him feared throughout the government: Senior General Wing Kang Lo, who also reported directly to GS Han.

Wing was not a formal member of the Eight, but Han usually included him as a kind of "adjunct" member because he had his fingers in so many pies—domestic as well as international. That, and the fact that the man was so dangerous, convinced Han that it was better to keep Wing close rather than to risk losing sight of whatever mischief he might be doing in the shadows. He was charged with the comprehensive spying program that China operated in every country on Earth, and his long-term, deep-penetration agents had been siphoning off a steady stream of intelligence data from all foreign governments and companies. He directed the purchase of businesses that were deemed valuable to the PRC—especially components of every foreign country's media and university systems. They also distributed bribes to influence government and civilian leaders in a host of ways, and ran an especially successful "sparrow" program. And Wing considered it a personal failure if a targeted foreign election didn't go China's way. His sparrows were highly trained women (plus a few men) who would entice their targets with sexual favors. It was rumored that some were so seductive and alluring that even heads of state had divulged useful pillow talk.

Wing and Ti had formed a quiet unofficial partnership, and they worked well together identifying and eliminating China's internal and external enemies. As the group applauded, he accepted this show of appreciation without comment, but beamed like the Cheshire Cat. It was his tens of thousands of computer technicians who'd been formed into effective "Siphon Teams"—constantly hacking into virtually every computer and communications device in existence. He owned the Cloud. So far, they'd been successful beyond the world's comprehension: Their legions of STs had robbed international governments, companies, and even individuals blind.

Chang concluded his remarks by raising his voice another notch to state triumphantly, "Our vast military will soon rule the oceans, the land, and even space! We have been quietly absorbing the world for decades—and now we have an excuse to accelerate our schedule and show them our power."

Han was relieved: The group had turned a corner, and positive vibes were bouncing around like electrons. At Chang's conclusion, everyone enthusiastically clapped in the direction of Marshal Zhang, who sat to Han's left.

Marshal Zhang smiled at Chang's compliment and also slightly inclined his head with appropriate humility. And though the military rank of marshal had previously been discontinued for a few decades, the 82-year old warrior - was pleased that Han had reinstated it and appointed him to serve as China's only five-star general. He never said much during these meetings because the verbosity of the fire-breathing Tai and Ti (not so subtly aided by the menacing presence of General Wing) was almost over the top on the militancy side. But his long service was without parallel in modern China, and he remained unchallenged as Han's number two in the military community. Zhang knew he was very important to his old friend Han—the last of his string of political benefactors who'd kept him at the helm of China's expanding military with its attendant and vast portfolio of commercial holdings that had made him wealthier than the emperors of old. Zhang had a steady hand, and he knew Han wanted him to remain in place for as long as he could. He and Han often spoke in private about the dreams they shared for China's future, and Han had made sure that Zhang understood that his chief duty was to keep General Tai on a fairly short leash. Zhang was also the only member of the "Eight" who, like Han, was a voting member on the Politburo's Standing Committee—the seven men entrusted with the greatest political authority in the PRC.

"Thank you, Comrades," Zhang responded in a quiet yet authoritative voice that belied his age. "I too, am against relying on the West to feed our people, although I am more than willing to buy their grain at favorable terms until we determine that it is an auspicious time to expand our borders—if that proves to be the best option, of course." He noted that this sage comment resonated well—being interpreted by each of Han's factions in their own most favorable way. "But, looking forward, I agree that our 'younger brothers' who border China seem to possess the resources we need. From now on, our task will be to help them 'manage' these resources better—and, of course, in our favor. But I must caution us all that the PLA is in the midst of a long-term build-up: We need a few more years—not to mention several trillion more RMB—to be on a technological par with the Americans. Only then can we fully apply the defensive/offensive strategy and tactics taught by our illustrious founder, Chairman Mao; only then we will be able to deny the American and Japanese navies access to our homeland waters inside the Nine Dashed Line and First and Second Island Chains."

His Nine Dashed Line referenced China's annotation of the maps of ocean areas between the mainland to the west and the Philippines to the east, and between Hainan Island in the north and Malaysia to the south—the four geographical reference points that encompassed all of the East and South China

Seas. The First Island Chain was their imaginary north/south line extending south from southern Japan, around the east side of Taiwan, continuing around the curve of Vietnam, and finally terminating as far south as Indonesia. They would soon have a large and technologically advanced enough navy to deny the Americans and these regional neighbors access to this vast stretch of island riches and ocean expanses that China considered her "home waters." His declaration brought a chorus of cheers that accelerated their rising spirits.

Zhang smiled coyly, knowing he was preaching to the choir tonight—combined with the fact that he was helping Han build the optimism and resolve they all needed to face down this long-term crisis. And, regarding the growing PLA few, even inside this exalted room, knew that the PRC was spending more than triple its published budget on military expansion. And, though he suspected the West believed the real figure was well north of the more modest totals the PLA published in their numerous military journals, Wing's spy network assured him that their enemies were grossly underestimating the real figure. In fact, the PRC had been spending nearly as much as the United States for years and, because of American inefficiencies and the fact that the PLA concentrated its forces in Asia, China would surpass American military might in the western Pacific quicker than the Allies believed. Added to these objective facts was Zhang's subjective belief that ***his*** military was more ruthless.

Zhang had promoted and overseen this modern build-up, and had drawn, like so many international naval and military strategists, on American Admiral Alfred Thayer Mahan's philosophy that military sea power was a vital element of any nation's commercial expansion. Zhang believed this truth nicely dovetailed with Party Founder Mao Zedong's "offensive/defensive" strategy wherein China could, at the same time, selectively build up its littoral, or near-coast defenses, thus gradually denying the western navies of Japan, Russia, America and Australia access to the western Pacific. This access was annotated on their maps using the term "Second Island Chain," by which they meant the imaginary line that stretched from the central Japanese east coast down to Papua New Guinea. It was "defensive" in that it protected China from the dictates of the West, and it was "offensive" in that, by degree, it enabled China to extend its "home waters" hundreds of miles east across the Pacific Ocean.

Additionally, in the rapidly approaching future when they were strong enough—the PLA was constructing modern blue-water surface and undersea fleets much faster than the West knew—they could expand their defensible space deep into their half of the Pacific Ocean. The visionary planners in PLA headquarters had already described a Third Island chain, an imaginary line that ran from the Aleutians down through Hawaii, terminating in New Zealand.

In order for the PLAN to build a fleet that big—meaning bigger than the U.S. and Japanese fleets combined—they needed true budgetary parity. Only then could they take on the American strongholds in the Marianas, Wake Island, and Guam that presently housed strategic U.S. military bases. Yet all this was established doctrine. What was new were the conceptual Fourth and Fifth Island chains: The Fourth envisioned the PLAN controlling all the western half of the Indian Ocean from Pakistan south through the British protectorate of Diego Garcia. The Fifth envisioned control of the eastern half of the Indian Ocean along the coast of Africa. It all added up to a massive and dominating goal, but one the entire Chinese government was working to complete by 2049. These five island chains were just components of the Politburo's plans to become the world's only superpower by the one hundredth anniversary of the founding of the People's Republic. However, Zhang realized this crisis might give them the opportunity to dramatically accelerate their timetable.

In contrast however, not everyone in Han's elite group was a dedicated hawk. Liu Keqiang, party chief of Yunnan Province in the far south (and the other woman Han trusted with this special level of access and responsibility) was continually alarmed at the thirst for war exhibited by the majority of Han's Eight. She was a decided moderate who, though alarmed by the current revelations, knew she had to try to push the conversation back toward a more rational center. She feared a collision with the heavily armed West, and she believed in her heart that open war would bring disaster on her people (despite the hawks' unwavering hyper-optimism).

She spoke up and the others turned to listen. "Thank you, honored colleagues, for your bold patriotism and brave words—and for acknowledging our ongoing transformation and revival started by Chairman Mao. But may I ask that we consider very carefully what is being suggested here tonight? The more peaceful solutions mentioned by General Secretary Han were seemingly brushed over—and I'm sure you didn't mean to signal that you felt they were inconsequential. Surely use of our powerful and dedicated military is not our only solution? Should we not also bring our talented scientists into this discussion? Should we not hear from them regarding their perceived abilities to develop new and better crops that will thrive in our depleted soils and changing weather patterns?" Liu was willing to use the military to defend their republic from attack—and perhaps even to reunite with Taiwan—but she was against the aggressive warfare being not-so-subtly floated by her old friend Han and lustily embraced by Tai and Ti. *What a pair they were!* "Comrades, we have also made great strides with the Belt and Road Initiative begun by our Foreign Ministry in 2013. We have gained the indebtedness of countless nations in developing countries on the continents of Africa, South America, in the Caribbean, and elsewhere. Our loans were adroitly administered to give us the greatest advantage and, in a short time, we have gained incredible financial leverage everywhere—we even own access to ports and other infrastructure hubs across the globe. Soon our reach will exceed that of Great Britain at the height of its empire. General Secretary Han, is this an appropriate time to hear from our illustrious foreign minister, who is managing this peaceful expansion of our power and influence?"

"Yes, Comrade Liu…the perfect time," granted Han, nodding graciously.

Chapter 2

Foreign Minister Wu Yingjie was pleased to be asked for an update on the very successful diplomatic/commercial program he'd dubbed "One Belt, One Road." It was a world-wide comprehensive effort by the PRC to expand its influence over as many of their fellow humans as possible, using infrastructure projects in every developing country to gain footholds and leverage. They offered low-interest loans or asset-backed cooperative projects to eager recipients, and they were constructing actual roads and/or railroads that followed the Old Silk trading routes through Asia and out to Europe. This was the "Belt" half of the program. They were simultaneously implementing overwater routes via greatly expanded merchant fleets and, as part of the program, negotiating lucrative deals to construct ports in Asia, Africa, Central America, and the Caribbean. This was the "Road" half of the program.

Of course, the West criticized them for foreclosing on and taking over the projects if the local country couldn't keep up its end of the bargain, but business was business, and both parties had signed on the dotted line. That these projects had military implications was only a projection of the suspicious U.S. and its allies, and not his fault. But today, Liu was correct that it was particularly important to mention this successful (and peaceful) initiative—hopefully counteracting the militarily aggressive hawks that always seemed to dominate Han's special roundtable.

"Comrades, let us remember the successful promise of our Belt and Road projects—now spreading everywhere with the blessing of the various host countries. Will these not provide the extra trade goods we need to overcome this crisis—without firing a shot?"

Inwardly relieved that this moderate line of discussion was gaining traction, the remaining member of Han's inner circle, Sun Yuanchao, vice president of the CCP National Congress, believed it was an auspicious time to speak. He was Han's hand-picked candidate to succeed him as titular head of the Politburo when Han decided to step down (which, Sun knew, meant Han's death at a ripe old age). Sun understood that he was jeopardizing his future by voicing tendencies toward moderation, but his conscience was strong and he made his appeal as clearly and bravely as he could: "Fellow patriots, our foreign minister reminds us of the comprehensive infiltration represented by the Belt and Road Initiative, and we all know it is rapidly expanding our influence in every geographic region. Our comrade from the South is full of wisdom, and she gives us good warning with her questions. We don't want to back ourselves into a corner by adopting a single solution when others may exist…"

General Tai rankled when he heard this surprise revelation from the heretofore seemingly conservative Sun, and couldn't resist a retaliatory response, "And while other 'theoretical' solutions are sought, Comrade Vice President, more and more of our people will be driven to starvation—and rebellion!" *Oh, how I hate these soft-backed moderates! Did they want their blessed homeland to surrender her hard-won sovereignty again—to become a mere servile dog that the West could kick around as they did in the 19th Century?*

Before Sun could respond, Han headed off an impending confrontation between his two factions by offering gentle support to his friend Liu. His support was heavily influenced by the fact that he had been secretly in love with her for more than 40 years—starting when they had gone through high school together. Their families had been friends during their childhood in southern China, and it had been natural that they would get to know each other and be drawn together. She had always been his better intellectually, while he was the natural leader with the winning personality. Both had been dedicated Party youth workers and, though their parents had never verbalized it, Han suspected that they assumed he and Liu would marry. But it was not to be.

After university she had gone her own way, joining the provincial government at an entry-level position in the personnel department, and she'd subsequently and steadily risen through Party ranks in their home province. He, on the other hand, had excelled in engineering, and had been cultivated for higher service while participating in projects for the Ministry of Heavy Industry in the north. She and Han kept in touch over the years, but they had met other people who were situationally better for marriage, and their family lives matured separately. But when he had finally become General

Secretary, he'd invited her to join his elite inner circle precisely because he respected her moderation (and her strong but gentle character) that was so useful among the others.

"Thank you, Comrade Liu," he said, "your wise counsel is always most welcome at this table…" *And you, Wu and Sun, provide a wonderful moderate counterpoint to my hawks Ti and Tai—not to mention that borderline psycho Wing,* "…please elaborate on your insights…"

Liu bowed her head slightly to her old classmate, secretly wondering as she often did during quiet musings always in his presence, of course, what her life might have been if she and Han had married. But fate had dictated otherwise, and they'd found other life-partners and had gone on to equally productive lives of national service. Yet, occasionally, when she was alone with her quiet womanly thoughts, she remembered that certain evening when the two of them had slipped away from their colleagues during a college Party retreat. They had discovered a place in the forest where they could enjoy a few private hours, and she still treasured his gentle thoughtfulness during their first experiences with physical intimacy. But that was a generation ago and not for contemplation tonight. She focused on the immediate and responded evenly, "Thank you, Comrade General Secretary. I am concerned that we dwell too heavily on our passionate hatred of the West as an enemy of our CCP, rather than on our growing successes in dealing with them on our own terms. Minister Wu outlined just one category—the Belt and Road infrastructure projects.

"Comrades and Ministers, we have faced many adversities during our long history, and since the CCP's founding, we have shown great creativity and resourcefulness when solving our problems—whether fighting for our freedoms in war, or during more ordinary times like the last 20 years of rapid worldwide expansion while the West slept. Let us not forget what we have achieved: We have accumulated tremendous financial leverage over the Americans—do we not own vast amounts of dollar-denominated foreign exchange—and have we not loaned them copious funds totaling nearly seven trillion of those dollars to help them buy our products, which they must repay with interest? We have carefully worked the trade imbalance in our favor, and will their insatiable hunger for our manufactured goods not only increase with time? And have we not used the West's hunger for corporate profits to decimate their manufacturing sector, while building up our own with the promise of cheap labor?"

She saw nods around the table as everyone listened carefully—everyone except that warmonger Ti. That 'she-dragon' was even more radical than General Tai or, as she thought of him, the murderous General Wing. Nevertheless, Liu was encouraged that her points were resonating, so she continued. "We don't have to go 'cap in hand' to the Americans, Canadians, and others to purchase grain for our people. We have the money they crave, and the consumables they can't seem to live without. They've transferred so much of their manufacturing capacity to us—including a substantial percentage of their medical sector—that we almost control their healthcare industry. All their supply chains are significantly under our control, and we can use this combined leverage to maintain a future playing field tilted in our favor. They have been selling us grain, and they will continue to do so because they need us; they will buy our medicines because it will be extremely expensive for them to rebuild their own infrastructure and pay their workers exorbitant local wages; and their constant complaining about our trade practices is largely ignored by most everyone else in their government—especially among their media and the imbedded political elites who really run the United States."

"Good points all, Comrade Liu," responded Marshal Zhang quickly, catching the others off guard (as he intended). *I am not going to let the hawks dominate this meeting, even though I'll probably lend future support to any military solution that carries the day.* "Do we have to rely on a single strategy to insure our future needs? No! It makes more sense to prepare scientific, diplomatic, financial, **and** military strategies to solve this crisis. After careful consideration, we will pick the best option or combination of options that suit our long-term needs." Zhang tended to distrust this moderate woman—really all women, if truth be told—but for some reason Han doted on this one and protected her, and he wanted to be on the right side of every eventuality. Most puzzling of all was why Han even gave Liu a voice at this most special of all tables in China. But Zhang respected Han's wiliness—he was the cleverest man the old soldier had ever encountered, and was the only person Zhang currently feared—far more than the thuggish Wing (though any sane person should fear him with good reason).

Zhang's calculation was simple: People who crossed the General Secretary had a way of disappearing—as opposed to Wing, who had to (at least theoretically) get tacit permission from Han before he 'offed' senior leaders he disliked. It was common knowledge among those in the know that Wing shot ordinary people almost every day. But this was Han's hour in the spotlight, and Zhang and the rest of them would carefully trust his decisions and judgments—unless the fabric of Chinese society began unraveling under his leadership. But **that** eventuality was the Sword of Damocles that hung over them all…

Sun then added his personal support to Zhang's comprehensive suggestion: "Although I hope Comrade Liu's theory will carry the day—and I, too, believe we should exploit our financial and intelligence-gathering leverage over America and the West—I am thrilled with the early promise shown by Minister Wu's Belt and Road program. We should not rely on the power of just one branch of our vast 'river system' to carry us to victory!" He noted that the others were beginning to feel better—enough to smile at their colleague's colorful word picture; Sun could be counted on to introduce at least one noteworthy metaphor into every discussion. "I would like to hear an idea from General Tai's military prospective to add strength and balance to our diplomatic, scientific, and financial considerations. That is," he added tactfully, "if our General Secretary and the rest of you agree." Then he sat back and steepled his fingers to let his suggestion ruminate.

Han had to admit that Zhang, Liu, Wu, and Sun had given him adequate cover to support a reasonable, multi-pronged investigation. He couldn't immediately discern any downside to this approach, so relying on his well-developed political instincts he decided to support it. "I like this line of thinking. How can we develop each of Sun's four 'rivers'?" He was feeling better already. There was no substitute for talking things over with one's peers—even Chairman Mao had sought counsel despite possessing nearly absolute power for decades.

A lively discussion followed, as supporters of each of the options voiced their ideas. It took 90 more intense minutes, but they finally hammered out the basics of their four lines of inquiry. They slipped their handwritten notes into personal folders that trusted aides would soon type—with a copy placed in a secret file all wise leaders in the PRC kept to protect themselves from later misrepresentations. They stood and stretched; then, in groups of twos and threes, they crossed Han's precious rug toward the elevator. The luxurious elevator was spacious enough to accommodate them in two groups, with Han in the first group. They rose to the exit hallway inside Han's residence. There, as dutiful host, he shook each person's hand and, as they departed, Han gave each of them a courteous yet solemn charge to tap into whatever resources they needed during the ensuing week. He wanted them all to return sufficiently prepared to present their preliminary recommendations from their assigned "river." Han knew it would be a week in which the resulting ideas and decisions would be long remembered in China's history.

Chapter 3

General Tai awoke the following morning refreshed and zealously committed to his new mission. He'd arrived home the previous night deeply troubled, and was still reeling from the suddenness of the crises that had surfaced without warning. After arriving home, he'd sat in his study racking his brain for another couple of hours, trying to envision a military solution that could succeed with their current force levels. But a solution escaped him, and he finally admitted that he needed a few precious hours of sleep to recharge his mental batteries. Fortunately, he had trained his brain to shut down quickly when he needed sleep—a blessing throughout his life that helped him glean the most of his always limited downtime. Sleep had indeed done the trick: He was refreshed and ready for a new work day.

He had a quick bite with his wife, knowing the value of keeping his dear Ling-Kun happy with some husbandly attention. Afterward, he walked briskly to his waiting staff car, and his driver whisked him through the double gates of his modest suburban estate. The next 30 minutes were typically hair-raising as they wove in and out of the usual ridiculous traffic to PLA headquarters—the imposing August First Building in downtown Beijing—named after the date when the People's Liberation Army was formed in 1927. It was then that Communist cadres began their organized campaign against the Nationalists—and though interrupted by limited cooperation during China's long war against imperial Japan—the PLA finally achieved a comprehensive victory in 1949.

As they drove, Tai phoned his brother's son, who had graduated from the Dalian Military Academy the previous year. The boy had the smarts to amount to something, and Tai had taken an interest in him when he showed early promise. But, by mutual agreement with his brother (who was a provincial bureaucrat living almost a thousand kilometers to the west), and with the young man himself, no one outside the family knew about this familial relationship. Tai had kept his distance during his nephew's high school and military academy training because, in China, it was often wise to keep one's cards (and one's relatives who could be of useful personal service) close to the vest. To date, it had proved a satisfactory arrangement, and General Tai was more convinced than ever that this was a special young officer who was destined to rise far.

Upon reaching headquarters, Tai's driver nosed the armored limousine down the steep driveway into the underground parking garage, stopping next to an elevator. A waiting sergeant opened the car door, and Tai hopped out. Dashing into the elevator, he quickly rose to the top floor. In moments, he was striding through his suite of offices, projecting his usual air of boundless confidence—barely acknowledging (also as usual) the greetings of his numerous staff officers, senior NCOs, and the legion of administrative secretaries who served him daily without question or hesitation. It was their considerable responsibility to translate his virtual river of orders into proper military documents—and subsequently to disseminate them throughout the military's vast network of commands—including the thousands of commercial enterprises still nominally controlled by the elderly Marshal Zhang. Those businesses enjoyed the incredible benefit of being recipients of government-derived intelligence—a win/win in the PRC that enhanced the profitability of all concerned. The businesses owned by the PLA numbered more than 10,000, and employed millions of workers, and yes, like all his predecessors—and like Han, who currently served at the pinnacle of the PRC's power structure—Tai was becoming one of the wealthiest men in government. He couldn't help smiling, however, when a stray thought reminded him that his official monthly salary of 16,000 RMB was an acceptable paycheck for some of his generals. However, his actual haul of 16,000 RMB per hour, 24/7/365, was more like it.

But Tai had no time for that kind of material distraction today. He focused on the doors held open by two handsome young staff NCOs. He entered his inner sanctum with its spectacular view of the Temple of Heavenly Peace, and toggled his intercom button to summon his chief of staff, Major General Bao Guo, from an adjoining office. Tai then plopped down into his comfortable leather executive chair, placing his thin briefcase on his massive modern desktop made of inch-thick green-tinted glass which, in turn, rested on sturdy mirror-shiny chrome legs. It was not the only luxury he afforded himself, but it was definitely the biggest and most pretentious of the many acquisitions he'd placed inside his spacious corner redoubt. He was the boss here: The hands-on commander of the largest military on earth—an entity that was getting bigger by the day. Marshal Zhang had relocated himself to a ceremonial office with the other ministers a few blocks away and, at this point in his career, only wanted to be consulted on matters with strong political implications. And General Tai, being politically astute enough to do that regularly, kept his mentor happy.

Bao entered, came to ramrod attention, and saluted—a strict tradition that Tai expected and returned. Tai then bid his brilliant COS to take a seat and got right to the point. "Something big has come up, Bao—maybe the most important opportunity of our lifetimes…"

"Yes, Comrade General?" Tai didn't go in for exaggeration so Bao was all ears. He leaned forward with his pen poised above his omnipresent leather-bound notebook.

"It was confirmed to me this week that our county is facing several years of crop shortages—on top of the rapidly depleting mineral reserves we already knew about from our portfolio of companies. This first development—an implication of the world's shifting weather patterns—will force us to buy more grain and other foodstuffs from the West as a temporary fix—in addition to the increases in petroleum purchases that we are already making in the Middle East. But, since it is exceedingly dangerous to rely on the Americans, Australians, Canadians, or even Arabs, in the long term we must create a new independence for ourselves in every key resource area."

Tai leaned forward, his elbows resting on the desk and fingers forming a small steeple. "The obvious context forces us to look at our neighbors who possess an ocean of oil and natural gas under our shared continental shelf and are, inside their own borders, essentially large gardens that produce an abundance of every agricultural product our people favor. So, given this new challenge, General Secretary Han directed our private working group to develop four principal options to solve this dilemma: A diplomatic one, which he entrusted to Wu and those hand-wringers in the foreign office; domestic agricultural and mining options, by which he meant those eggheads in the non-military science labs—and Heaven only knows how long those Brainiacs will take playing with their calculators; and a financial solution (probably tied to any diplomatic one) being pushed by VP Sun and Comrade Liu. But most importantly and practically, we have been entrusted with developing a military solution. We must accelerate our plan to take over Asia and the western half of the Pacific Ocean—in addition to our longer-term plans to dominate the rest of the world. It is obvious to me, and to anyone with half a brain, that our country's only real, long-term solution is aggressive warfare—that is, taking by force what we need from our neglectful and wealthy neighbors!"

Tai paused, settling back in his chair to gauge Bao's response: He needed his visionary staff officer supporting this effort in every detail. He noticed the man's understandable shock—but also sensed Bao's instant surge of pride as well—confirming in Tai's mind that the man would cause him no trouble as they planned this vital gambit. "This is where you come in, Bao: Do some serious brainstorming and do it quickly but quietly. Your job is to develop a comprehensive military solution to solve our future natural resource, mineral, and agricultural needs—meaning the optimum plan to appropriate the resources of our immediate and regional neighbors. And I want this done without interference from the Americans or Japanese. Complete a set of preliminary recommendations in five days. And, Bao…" the general cautioned gravely, "…this is as big as it gets—we'll never have a better opportunity to prove our worth to our people. Select a few trusted insiders and form a working group. Develop a solution that will enable us not only to survive, but to expand our direct influence beyond our region in accordance with our long-term goals. And I can't stress enough that we must be able to carry out our plans without significant interference from the West."

From his chair in front of the huge desk, Bao was glad he was sitting down—and holding his pen tightly. What the general was asking—no, demanding—was his participation in a high-stakes gamble that included certain war against the United States and her allies. It was patently obvious that no other outcome would enable the PLA to accomplish what the general was really suggesting: That China invade and occupy her neighbors without America, Japan, Australia, or Pacific Rim and European friends being able to stop them. And Tai had made it clear that this was coming down from on high—there was no room for negotiation here. And, if that wasn't enough, there was considerable personal risk for Bao, too: Tai had a well-deserved reputation for personally sacking senior officers whom he considered grossly incompetent (by his definition, that meant failure to produce the timely results Tai considered vital to Tai's agenda). Bao didn't wish to be counted among that lot who were now toiling in obscurity—or dead. The general was known to have personally executed senior officers whom he considered traitors (and Tai had to have cover from old Zhang and GS Han to have done so). Plus, there was always the unspoken threat that the truly vile could be turned over to the devilish minister of State Security, General Wing, whom Bao had known as a classmate at the academy. Bao knew Wing was loosely part of that "working committee" Tai referenced so casually at the beginning of his little speech.

Wing had been a bully at the academy—pushing the other cadets whether they challenged him or not, so Bao and most everyone else just stayed out of his way. But Wing had surprised them all when he resigned from PLAN and transferred to the MSS. It turned out to be an adroit move for someone with his skillset, and he rose up the spy organization's ladder faster than any of his classmates did in the navy. Bao kept track of his old classmate and, by mid-career, Bao figured out what was really happening: Wing was used as a club by every supervisor he'd worked for—keeping order for the current boss by any means he could get away with. And, because the MSS had a different rank structure, Wing was now a general instead of an admiral—just like Bao, who had elected to accept his commission in the army instead of the navy.

Bao decided to risk a clarifying question, which his boss always encouraged within reason: "Is every option on the table, my general—including the nuclear option?" *No sense pussyfooting now.*

"Your job, Bao, is to present me with a smorgasbord of ideas. I will pick what I like from that menu. Include what you will..." Tai then gave him that look that usually sent shivers down the spines of his staff—though Bao was made of sterner stuff than them. "Do this with all haste, Bao—our nation's future depends on us! I want the optimum military plan. And, don't forget: We will submit this plan directly to Comrade Han, with history as our judge!"

"Yes, my general!" Bao responded enthusiastically. He rose, snapped to attention, and saluted. When his salute was returned, he hastily retreated to his office with his mind churning. *What a nightmare...and out of nowhere! But what an opportunity as well!* He plunked down heavily in his black leather executive chair, and retrieved the still-smoldering cigarette he'd been enjoying when Tai summoned him. He took a moment to deeply inhale the rich, pungent smoke of his favorite Turkish blend—always appreciating the instant buzz and accompanying jolt of energy that helped him focus. Then he set the cigarette on the mottled green jade ashtray his wife had given him as an anniversary gift early in their marriage, and reached for his Rolodex. He needed an operation-planning genius, and he knew just the man to call.

As Bao quickly thumbed through the names, he reflected that, within seconds of hearing Tai's bombshell, his mind had flashed to the obvious historical parallel of the 20th Century: The Japanese strike against the Americans at Pearl Harbor, Hawaii. The attack had been conceived to give Japan's forces extra time to occupy all of east Asia and the western Pacific Islands—neutralizing the only threat to their Big Plan to exploit regional resources. Tai demanded a military option that neutralized the United States at the outset of this coming world war (and Bao knew this would be the Third World War) and he immediately remembered Japan's attack and subsequent conflict in the Pacific. It was a campaign that had interested him since he was a boy and he knew many of its details well—including the fact that Admiral Yamamoto had relied on a youngish naval staff officer named Commander Minoru Genda—plus some others—to plan the incredibly audacious raid to neutralize the Allies. The plan had both succeeded and failed dramatically, so Bao knew he needed to consider every detail. And he had to do everything absurdly quick. *I need a "Genda" now,* he reasoned. *I will summon my Genda! History can repeat itself—but with better results from lessons correctly learned. Our old enemy Japan made costly mistakes even as they hurt us and the Americans severely...but they had their successes throughout Asia and the western Pacific, too. We will learn from both.*

Bao again retrieved his cigarette after dialing a number on his reasonably secure land line, and swiveled his chair 180 degrees until he could enjoy most of the same panoramic view his commander had next door. The heart of Beijing sprawled below, and he marveled at the 5,000 years of history that had evolved in this ancient place. The only negative was the fact that he had to settle for a limited near-horizon view because, even in winter, the nearly omnipresent smog blocked all distant vistas. Today's visibility was perhaps five kilometers, which was good, and the city was enjoying a break from the snow storms that had battered the capital for days. It was a temporary reprieve, however, because the weather geeks downstairs were forecasting a new storm sweeping down from the Mongolian steppes by the end of the week.

National Defense University, Beijing

Professor Dang Zhi was sitting on the edge of a folding chair in front of his wall heater. He had removed the front panel, and was trying to fine-tune a sensitive adjustment knob. He prided himself on being able to effect small repairs to all things mechanical, but this blasted heater in his office in the PRC's most prestigious military college, where he served as chair of the International Military Capabilities Department, was giving him fits. Then, just as he was making a (hopefully) final delicate adjustment with his trusty screwdriver, he realized the irritating noise emanating from the far side of the room was his desk phone. *Oh, bother!* So, with no little irritation, he reluctantly laid the tool on the linoleum floor and crossed the spacious room to find out who it might be.

Across town, General Bao was getting impatient by the fourth ring when he heard the distinctive click and a tentative, somewhat nasally male voice. Bao recognized the high-pitched tone immediately. "Professor Dang, this is Major General Bao from the Defense Ministry…" They ran into each other regularly so they exchanged the expected pleasantries. Then Bao invited the academic to come over for a meeting "as soon as Dang could fit it into his schedule." Bao knew Dang would correctly interpret his politeness as a request for an immediate audience, and also counted on the academic's natural curiosity to speed his response. He was not disappointed and got the expected assurance from the famous scholar: He would arrive within the hour. Bao noted that Dang wisely didn't inquire as to the nature of the summons—everyone in China knew that someone was always listening.

After politely disconnecting, Bao buzzed his lead administrative secretary and directed her to reserve one of the secure conference rooms in the basement. Then the general settled back in his chair and became introspective as he finished his cigarette. He began formulating relevant preliminary questions and scribbled them on one of the ubiquitous yellow legal pads used throughout the world. He jotted down ideas that needed an expert's clarification and elaboration, and Professor Dang was, without a doubt, the premier military authority on foreign navies and modern naval history in the PRC. Bao and most senior officers had heard his lectures and, if anyone knew what it would take to keep the Americans at bay, it was Dang.

The August First Building

A little more than an hour later Bao welcomed the somewhat frazzled, short, reed-thin, and bespectacled Professor Dang into one of the MOD's secure basement conference rooms. His secretary had placed a service of green tea and small crackers on the spacious table and, as host, Bao politely poured for them both. After they enjoyed a customary first sip, they got down to business: Bao informed the puzzled academic that he needed his informed opinion on a matter of utmost national importance. Therefore, before asking his first question, he formally swore Dang to perpetual silence and had him sign a non-disclosure form. There was an element of absurdity about such a document—people in the PRC who made unauthorized disclosures would probably receive a bullet in the back of their heads—but government HR folks had determined that, psychologically speaking, signing a formal document reinforced any meeting's seriousness and generated better results.

General Bao then spent several minutes summarizing General Tai's bombshell for the surprised scholar. As Bao expected, the middle-aged professor was as stunned as he had been.

"Incredible, General!" exclaimed the profoundly shocked academic. Dang was instantly on guard, too: *This is a very dangerous gambit these soldiers are considering! This is a potential trap for me, too...a very big trap!* He needed a moment to think while his mind organized the relevant facts. He removed his wire rim glasses, and wiped imaginary dust from the thick lenses as ideas and implications flooded his great intellect—now churning a mile a minute as he formulated an initial response. He had adopted spectacles-cleaning as a habitual mannerism to buy time, and he needed it now. He was challenged by the enormity of the topic, but his encyclopedic mind easily downloaded information from his packed mental storehouse, then digested the results, categorized his responses and, within a few moments, he was ready to begin.

"This is a momentous situation, General. Historically, what jumps to mind are the similar circumstances faced by our old adversary, Imperial Japan, before they decided to attack American Hawaii in 1941…"

We're on the same page! Bao was both relieved and elated. He nodded agreeably and said as much, "Professor, the same scenario occurred to me. We're facing a long-term economic crisis similar to what Japan faced during its illegal war against us beginning in 1931. And, if I remember correctly, natural resource-poor Japan's economic problems were magnified when the Americans and their allies imposed an oil embargo on them in July of 1941. For several years now, the Americans and others have been upsetting the established trade relationship and hurting us with their targeted tariffs. And, if we have to abide by their standards, things will only get worse. Do I remember correctly that Japan had been importing 80 percent of its oil from the USA and needed to find alternate sources? Then steel and other resources were also denied—things that Japan needed to continue fighting and expanding their control over mainland Asia?"

Dang agreed. "Yes, General, you are right in every respect. I've been studying the Americans' published concerns about our rising influence over our territorial waters and islands—and they don't understand our long-term commitment to bring renegade Taiwan back into its rightful place as a province of the People's Republic…"

"Correct, Professor. They are unjustifiably of the opinion that Taiwan's rebellion is a natural right. Additionally, our population policy is a constant source of consternation to them—they think they can curb our desire to rid ourselves of unwanted mouths to feed. If it weren't for our large dollar-denominated cash reserves—plus their consumers' relative dependency on our manufacturing sector—they might be tempted to attack us economically with more than just tariffs. They might even try to bring some of their expatriated manufacturing base back to America. If they do, we'll lose some of our leverage—they can't even provide enough steel or medicines for their own people without us!"

Dang smiled in agreement, then responded thoughtfully, "General Bao, I must say that I am saddened beyond words that our nation is facing the severe economic and societal challenges you've outlined. I'd read that our crop yields had been downtrending for some time, but I had no inkling that we faced starvation of such magnitude! However, with great honesty, I'm also terrified that we have to envision a scenario where our forces provoke a shooting war with the United States military—at least a lot quicker than we envisioned." Dang was truly shocked but, by the same token, had electricity shooting up and down his spine as he realized that he was being asked (and trusted) to weigh in on a military campaign that would change the history of the world. If correctly undertaken, a brilliantly planned first strike could start a chain of events that would end with China as the world's undisputed sole superpower.

The diminutive professor was a civilian because his eyesight was so poor that he'd failed the military induction exam. However, government evaluators quickly realized they had a real genius on their hands, and heavily invested in his considerable academic potential. With their enabling, he worked his way into national service by teaching military history. As he progressed through higher levels of academia, he so impressed his instructors that they encouraged him to join the faculty of the PRC's National Defense University (equivalent of America's West Point).

Fast-forward 25 years, and he was still reveling in his good fortune. He'd had the satisfaction of knowing he'd made a difference in China's ability to defend itself by preparing several generations of cadets for the responsibilities they'd face during their careers. And, in addition to undergraduates, he regularly lectured senior officers in his area of expertise: The historical and current military capabilities of American and other international navies. *But this bombshell…this was amazing!*

Dang refocused and elaborated on his initial comments, "The Japanese situation before their campaign in the Pacific is, of course, the obvious parallel to our current plight. And there is much to learn from both their victories and their failures. But the threat paradigm around the Pacific Rim has evolved significantly since those days, too. With your permission, I'd like to start our discussion with World War II and go from there."

Bao congratulated himself for contacting Dang: The man was the perfect sounding board—as well as a fountain of knowledge for all things relating to modern western military capabilities. The little man was also a visionary who could see the "big picture." Bao nodded his approval and leaned back in his chair—the attentive student listening with genuine interest as this amazing scholar settled into his familiar professorial role. He was fascinated as Dang recounted facts and events, and blended them into the incredible story that was the Pacific theater during the 1940s.

Dang spoke without interruption for nearly 30 minutes before summarizing: "America and China emerged from the war as the preeminent players in the western Pacific—particularly after our victorious revolution of 1949. Our control was littoral, while theirs was comprehensive. And the Americans still have a heavy presence on our side of this 'great lake' that physically divides us. Each side possesses vast resources of people, industrial capacity, financial strength, and military power—including nuclear arms. But there are significant differences, too: China has significantly more people to utilize, employ, and feed, while America has enjoyed great technological advantages throughout the same period. However, we are catching up fast. And, of great importance to our current discussion, the Americans are suffering financially due to their expensive social programs—even they admit the undeniable fact that they've been living above their means for 40 years. As a result, they are potentially more vulnerable to external attack than at any time since 1941. They keep about half of their ships and submarines in port at any one time. And I know for a fact that our intelligence community has penetrated many of their business and government computer networks, so we know a lot more about them than the Japanese did before their confrontation."

Dang took a sip of tea, then continued, "By contrast, our greatest—and, as you rightly pointed out—our growing vulnerability, is our dependence upon foreign grain and Middle East oil. Our tankers must transit thousands of miles of ocean where the American Navy still rules supreme. Their 'blue water' Navy has a significant advantage over us in aircraft carriers and submarines, and our superiority in land-based forces means little in an ocean war. However, the islands we have reclaimed from the East and South China Seas provide our air forces with a real tactical ability to counteract those American carriers, which are extremely vulnerable to our rocket and space forces. Our advantages with these truly lethal weapons are significant. From the latest five-year projection I read, we will rapidly catch them in both combat surface ships and submarines—with the positive caveat that we are improving our ship-killing ballistic missiles specifically designed to kill those carriers. And, last but not least, our computer hacking units can not only steal their secrets; at the outset of any war, we can wreak amazing disruption on their technological networks."

The professor was really rolling. "Our 'island airfields' are fixed whereas theirs can move but, if we sink their carriers at the beginning of any conflict, as Imperial Japan tried but failed to do, only their submarines pose any real threat. And to counter-balance that, we are quickly building our own submarine fleet, and our space-based weapons are unknown to the West. Specifically, we are nearly ready to launch and put into permanent orbit our anti-satellite space system that can nullify their canopy of stationary orbiting transmitters. This is extremely important—a game-changer—because they rely almost exclusively on their GPS satellites to target, with astounding accuracy, nearly every square centimeter of the globe. Soon we'll be able to nullify that advantage. They will probably maintain their significant advantage in long-range bombers, but if we can sink those in-port submarines and carriers at the outset, it will help us tremendously. And I know for a fact that we are expanding our drone technology at a pace that will astound the world..."

Dang paused as if searching for another vital fact that he might have forgotten, then brightened when he remembered: "...and let's not forget that our industrial production is roughly on par with the Americans (at least capacity-wise), and we don't have their rats' nest of regulations to strangle our output..." The scholar paused to offer a rare smile, "...and I also think we can transition to a war-time footing quicker than they can."

Bao seized the chance to interject a salient question: "Professor, would you agree that our greatest disadvantage in starting a war with the Americans and their allies is the impossibility of surprise?"

Dang's response was immediate. "Yes, in that I believe you are correct. Japan's initial success was directly related to its surprise attacks throughout the central and western Pacific theater. The element of surprise allowed them great latitude to implement their version of the new lightning warfare that their ally Germany introduced in 1939 against Poland, and again in 1940 against France and Britain in western Europe. That strategy was instructive as they quickly backed the Allies against the English Channel, and it was only the miracle of the Dunkirk evacuation that the whole British army wasn't captured. Then they invaded the Soviet Union the following year, and only Hitler's forgetfulness of the Russian winter stopped them.

"In the Pacific, Japan implemented its own version of lightning warfare in late 1941 and early 1942, and quickly conquered and consolidated its initial objectives. And, though the IJN lost at Midway in June of 1942, it still fought a tenacious island campaign until the Americans' massive industrial capacity was fully converted to military production—and included the development of nuclear bombs. When U.S. output flooded the Pacific and European theaters in the last two years of the war, the tide turned in the Allies' favor and they never looked back. At that point, both Japan and Germany were doomed."

Professor Dang sat forward to emphasize his summary point: "The key here is that Japan could not hold its initial gains—it did not accomplish its key objective of preventing an effective American counter-attack. The attack on Hawaii was intended to buy enough time to consolidate gains in Asia (and everyone knows that Japan never wanted anything else). But, instead, all they accomplished by attacking Hawaii was awakening and motivating the formally sleepy and very isolationist American colossus." The professor paused to let his narrative sink in for Bao, then continued. "Since the mainland United States remained largely unmolested throughout the war, they had plenty of time to get their industrial might onto a war footing and dictate the course of the war. But the Japanese navy didn't catch the key strategic weapon of the day, the U.S. aircraft carriers, at Pearl Harbor and, as a consequence, had to try again at Midway in June of 1942. But the Americans got lucky there: They used their superior intelligence-gathering to give Admiral Nimitz enough information to make a calculated guess about the imminent Midway attack, and that battle turned the tables on the IJN.

"All this to say that when we fast-forward to today, it is evident that the situation in the Pacific is eerily similar: We must deal with the U.S. carrier task forces (and their even more potent submarine fleet) if we hope to keep the territories we take from our neighbors. And, problematically, the Americans are quite less isolationist nowadays—and have even stated that a move by us against renegade Taiwan is the same as an attack on Hawaii. They will be highly motivated to respond to any significant move we make in our region. And, as you pointed out, the intelligence situation is dramatically different than in 1941: They will see all our moves via satellite before we begin our actual attack—if we knock out their satellite system too soon, we will only alert them that something dramatic is underway, and they'll send their entire fleet to sea. Therefore, we have similar challenges facing us that Yamamoto did in 1941, plus this modern, seemingly insurmountable technological one. If we can't find a way to initiate military action without tipping our hand, I believe we will fail. And failure to achieve tactical surprise will doom us: We'll end up the broken ruin that was Imperial Japan in 1945. The only difference is that I don't think the United States would risk a land invasion here where our ground forces are so potent..."

"What about a pre-emptive nuclear strike against them?" Bao interjected. "Not a destructive event such as the atomic bombs dropped on Japan, but atmospheric bursts that would knock out all their electronics in Hawaii and/or on their mainland? That would eliminate any short-term—and possibly any long-term—interference from the Americans while we conquered greater Asia."

"You mean EMPs...electro-magnetic pulse weapons?"

"Precisely."

Dang steepled his fingers and looked thoughtful before replying, "General Bao, the key problem with any nuclear weapon is that, once you go down that road with a superpower like the United States, you open yourself up to retaliation in kind. The U.S. military will not be fully neutralized by any nuclear first strike, because it possesses a significant nuclear weapons-carrying submarine fleet that—apart from targeting their aerial munitions in their home waters—won't be neutralized by EMPs or any weapon in our arsenal except our navy's torpedoes. Plus, they keep all their nuclear stock piles and many other strategic and tactical weapons systems in shelters already hardened against that exact eventuality. Their civilian electronic infrastructure is woefully inadequate; it will be ruined and millions of their people will die, but enough of their military will survive and remain not only lethal but dangerously motivated. Pearl Harbor all over again! We would have to conservatively estimate that they would still have at least 25 percent of their conventional weapons systems intact, and most or all of their nuclear arsenal. They could, and probably would, retaliate against us with their truly awesome array of strategic and tactical firepower—especially nuclear-tipped missiles carried in their 'boomer' submarines." Dang paused before delivering his summary of the nuclear option. "Therefore, sir, in my opinion, the results of our attacking them with any type of nuclear weapon would be as damaging in the long run for our homeland as attacking Pearl Harbor with conventional weapons was for Imperial Japan in 1941."

Bao felt the scholar's emotion, and couldn't disagree with his logic; Dang's argument against the nuclear option was as sound as it was heartfelt. He'd spoken objective truth as he believed it to be—now the problem would be convincing General Tai and his hawkish allies that the nuclear option was as good as suicide. He had to develop and make a pitch for an effective, conventional-only option—without sounding like either a coward or a defeatist. "Good points, Professor. I, of course, do not want to use those awful weapons if we don't have to…"

"No sane person would, General Bao."

Bao let that comment pass without a response, knowing his boss just might gamble with such power. China possessed many nuclear weapons, including those that would be effective as EMPs. But, for now, Bao decided to re-direct the conversation and asked, "Professor, what is your reading of the American political and military psyche regarding retaliation? Would they employ nuclear weapons against us if we attacked them only with convention ones?"

The wiry academic sat up straighter as this question seemed to touch a nerve. "That's the proverbial golden question, General, and I have pondered it many times. As I read them, I doubt that they would use any nuclear weapons unless they felt their national existence was threatened."

Bao was assuming that, too. The Americans were fair, and it was still a point of controversy that they used atomic weapons against Japan—even when they were obviously necessary to hasten the end of a war they didn't start. Military historians in most countries agreed that millions of Japanese lives would have been lost if the Allies had invaded the home islands, and the island campaign had proved they would fight to the last man without surrendering. On Iwo Jima alone, 7,000 U.S. Marines had died killing the 22,000 Japanese defenders. What would be the death total if the Allies had to fight door to door from the southern tip of Japan to the northern tip?

Bao understood that he and Dang had to develop a strategy that froze the Americans in place long enough for the PLA to capture, reinforce, and hold whatever areas the motherland needed in its own backyard. China had to conquer and maintain a blue-water defensive perimeter wide enough to protect home waters east of Taiwan so they could absorb and keep the renegade province. *If we must take those vast gardens and rich oil deposits that lie nearby, we can't rely on initial victory, as Japan proved during World War II.* He then added, "The entire reason for this potential operation is to enhance and maintain the long-term flow of oil, agricultural products, and other resources needed by our people and industries," Bao said. "We have to realize that the flow of oil from the Middle East will end as soon as our military campaign begins, so we will have to store enormous quantities before undertaking such a program of conquest."

Dang digested his pupil's summary: It was thorough and correct. "Good summary, General." Then he asked another key question: "Am I correct, General, in believing that our leaders have no intention of trying to capture the United States, Canada, or Australia outright?"

"You are correct, Professor." *At least I hope Tai and Han haven't taken complete leave of their senses!* he thought. But Bao couldn't voice that kind of rebellious thought in this building, even to an objective scholar like Dang. If overheard and reported—and he was never fully certain whether this or any room he entered in the military/industrial complex (or even any private home) was devoid of Minister Ti's listening devices or hidden cameras. In that instance, Bao's family would be presented with the bill for the bullet Wing would delight in firing into the back of his classmate's head. He therefore responded tactfully, "Our only operations against the American mainland, Japan, or Australia would be to achieve the very thing the Japanese failed to do, namely, to preclude an effective Allied counter-strike. Once we have consolidated our expansion in Asia—and we control most of our half of the Pacific—we can dictate terms during any future negotiations. We need to be able to convince the Americans that it would be too costly for them to force us back to our current borders, as they finally did against Japan."

He had learned over the years that the Allies not only occupied Japan, they restructured their society. Their General MacArthur even lobbied the post-war government to give the right to vote to women—a tangible progressive change from a previously feudal society. "My key worry is that we live in the information age where every school child can view satellite pictures of the whole world. And we know for certain that every industrialized government watches us from their satellites 24/7 in truly real-time…"

Dang nodded thoughtful agreement—it was the modern reality that Japan had never faced. "I must give this potential undertaking much thought, General. The future of our country is at stake."

They spoke for another two hours trying to formulate potential strategies. Then Professor Dang took his leave with a promise to return with the skeleton of a plan before the end of the week. He departed with Bao's encouragement to think boldly.

Bao returned to his office upstairs and began ruminating on their most vexing problem: How could they hide their initial moves? The age of satellites and social media seemed to preclude a cross-ocean sneak attack—either by sea or air. Even a submarine attack would be tracked by the ever-vigilant American Navy. China would have a better chance of victory after employing an EMP device, but that (he hoped) was off the table. How then could they move significant naval task forces throughout Asia—let alone as far west as Hawaii or the American mainland—without being detected? It was a vexing problem, and he and Dang had an amazing challenge before them.

Most important of all, there remained the strategic 800-pound gorilla: Japan's great mistake was attacking the Americans in the first place. And it was worse now: The United States was an interventional-minded global superpower with significant commitments to friends and allies everywhere. If the PRC tried to bring Taiwan into the fold by force, he believed the Americans would feel obligated to send in its Air Force, Navy and Marines to help the Taiwanese repel an invasion. The same held true for his county's moves against Japan, South Korea (where the United States still had 30,000 troops and significant numbers of combat aircraft), or the Philippines, Indonesia and Malaysia, Thailand, Vietnam and Brunei. Therefore, neutralizing the Americans (and at least their immediate regional allies, Japan, South Korea and Australia at the outset) was crucial. He believed Russia would stay on the sidelines because they had nothing to fear from a Chinese move south and east. Russia had massive natural resources, and was more than willing to sell anything to China for a price. The Russians were hungrier for cash than even the greedy Americans.

So, at the end of the day, Bao reasoned that China had only two choices: Adopt a humble strategy of developing good relations with the West—and purchasing or negotiating what they needed—or implementing a military option and taking what they wanted by force. But that choice was political and way above his paygrade. His duty required him to develop a workable military option that would both deliver what his country needed while, at the same time, avoid the devastation that Japan endured when its plans went awry.

Luckily, before the end of the week, Professor Dang had a brainstorm.

April 15th, the following spring

(China Evening Herald) "At noon today, in the historic Dalian Shipyard located on the Liaodong Peninsula in Liaoning Province, a dramatic announcement was made by CCP General Secretary and President of the People's Republic Han Gaoli. During an elaborate and much-publicized event, President Han addressed dozens of diplomats and the accredited representatives from more than 100 international news organizations, informing them that China was simultaneously laying the keels of a fleet of new super-sized and ultra-fast container ships designed to enhance the PRC's current competitiveness in trans-ocean trade. President Han thanked engineers from South Korea and Norway—historically the world's leading super-tanker and giant container-ship builders—for providing much needed advice on previous projects and for early recommendations for this new fleet. However, the General Secretary seemed radiant when he stated that, from this moment on, China would build its own ships utilizing only its own resources. The new fleet will be constructed solely with Chinese know-how and labor—and he further intimated that the project would be done in the spectacular way that China liked to do everything: Big! He stated that, within the next three years, domestic marine engineers and workers will simultaneously construct and launch 14 merchant ships that will be among the largest classes of vessels ever floated. These marvelous 'servants of the Chinese people' will be large enough to carry thousands of containers, fast enough to beat any competition, and have drafts shallow enough to enter most of the world's commercial ports. Comrade Han emphasized that no country had attempted to build such a large number of Panama-Max container ships at the same time.

"President Han's specially constructed platform for the day's address was adjacent to a row of massive wood-frame and corrugated steel dry dock buildings that had just been completed during the previous months—a Herculean effort by thousands of dedicated workers. As he stood on the magnificent viewing stand that faced the harbor frontage—the structure decorated with copious rolls of red and gold bunting—the General Secretary informed the world's press that these buildings had been specifically constructed to build the new ships, one ship per building. The ships would be launched directly into the harbor as was the normal practice at Dalian Shipyard, but would be finished at an unannounced site yet to be completed.

"Chairman Han stated that China's trade with the world was expected to continue expanding at its record-setting pace, and the PRC needed to build a new fleet of high-capacity container ships to help meet the world's ever-increasing demand for China's incredible industrial output. Many dignitaries were present, and everyone seemed to enjoy the conclusion of the ceremony when a group of adorable children released 14 giant red and gold balloons into the azure blue sky. Each balloon signified the friendly spirits that would protect the workers and crews who would build and sail these nautical wonders. General Secretary Han concluded his remarks by reminding every nation that win/win international trade was the keystone to preserving world peace!"

Chapter 4

The Oval Office, Washington, DC
Present Day, November 23rd, 07:00 Hours

President of the United States Spencer Stilwell, Vice President Rebecca Jane Mason, and John Laughton, the President's national security advisor, were sipping coffee as they went over the morning's schedule and discussed the PDB (the President's Daily Brief, prepared overnight by the office of the director of National Intelligence). President Stilwell and his VP had just been elected one year before—supported by a narrow majority of their fellow citizens who hoped they would govern effectively—and swing the ideology of the government back to a left-of-center position. Given the context of the diminishing Covid-19 pandemic and the effectiveness of the vaccine rapidly developed under the leadership of the previous administration—and distributed under President Stilwell's—the national and world economies were almost back to normal. The origins of the virulent flu had been confirmed in the minds of most of the world's leaders—not to mention its billions of citizens—to have been mainland China. A flurry of lawsuits from across the world had begun to fill various courtrooms, and each sought compensation for the families of the more than one million people who had died. Yet the People's Republic was masterfully stonewalling all related legal actions—clinging to various alternative theories for the origins of the controversial pandemic—including one narrative that U.S. Army specialists had developed and planted the original pathogens in Wuhan. No one in the Western world believed that, and President Stilwell had criticized China for refusing to warn the world about their terrible accident, covered up its lethality until it spread worldwide, thus adding to the level of sickness and death around the globe.

The President had become cheerleader-in-chief for American companies who had developed the vaccines to fight the disease, and who were now rolling out millions of doses. He was also leading the charge to encourage these companies to bring back significant percentages of their healthcare-related manufacturing infrastructure to America. These efforts were aided by the fact that the pandemic had exposed national vulnerabilities—especially in medical supply chains. In a phrase, the U.S. had become "dangerously dependent upon China" in many strategic industries. Specifically, the United States had to reclaim its medical manufacturing sector, but this would not be accomplished overnight. At least in the interim, Americans could take comfort in the fact that the current generation of new pharmaceuticals were being developed and produced at home.

Spence Stilwell had won the national election, but he was not one to rest on his laurels; underneath his generally calm exterior he was worried about every conceivable thing most of the time. And, though it was Thanksgiving week, continuing duties did not abate for the chief executive and the federal government he led. President Stilwell placed his cup down on the glass surface of the coffee table, signaling as it did every morning that it was time to wrap up the briefing. Vice President Mason did not usually take part in this daily ritual, but had been specifically invited today because the President wanted her input on the latest North Korean missile launch. The ever-irritating NKs had done it again, this time sending another salvo of missiles into the Sea of Japan. He addressed both his guests, "I have to say I feel for the Japanese—they are fit to be tied! I called Jack this morning (Secretary of State Jack Madrid) and he confirmed both the event and the fact that the Chinese still haven't done anything to rein in the NKs. It's like the PRC has gone tone-deaf as yet another crisis brews in their own backyard."

"Mr. President," responded the Vice President, "did Jack call Ambassador Bang? If so, can you share what he said?"

"He did, Rebecca, and received the same old lame excuses, platitudes, and no promises of action. Jack asked again if they realized how dangerous this situation was and, as usual, Ambassador Bang downplayed the whole thing. He says these launches have been going on for years and that NK technology is nowhere near advanced enough to reach the U.S."

Rebecca responded to that declaration with some exasperation. "Hopefully his government realizes that assertion is false, and that the Japanese are not only darned scared but getting itchy trigger fingers, too—NK missiles can certainly reach Tokyo! The Japanese should lodge another official complaint with the UN Security Council and demand action." She was perplexed by the lack of PRC engagement, wondering privately if there was some kind of internal squabble bubbling under the surface. Something was affecting their historical attempt at leadership in everything that affected Asia. "Mr. President, the Chinese are really something these days—ignoring North Korean belligerence while, at the same time, more vocal than ever that we infected their people with Covid-19!" She was disgusted and the gentlemen couldn't blame her: Tens of millions of Americans had been infected, and more than one hundred million worldwide. Attendant economic disruption had been devastating everywhere—including the most significant drop in the stock market since the Great Depression. *Thankfully the economy had come roaring back!*

John agreed, "They're keeping that fantasy alive, that's for sure, Mrs. Vice President. And the Japanese are as angry as I've seen them." John was mad, too—everyone, everywhere was mad. And exasperated. "I concur that the Chinese are a puzzle these days: They've been very vocal—doubling down on their Covid assertions on the one hand, while on the other they've been overly passive regarding other important international issues. Specifically, they continue to reinforce those islands they occupied in the East and South China Seas, and expand that Belt and Road Initiative they advertise ad nauseam, but they seem content to sit on the sidelines of other world events. But I'd be willing to bet that if the NKs ever lose control of one of their new missiles and it lands on Chinese soil—particularly if it has a working warhead attached—they'll wake right up!"

Rebecca chuckled as the President just cleared his throat and rolled his eyes. There was nothing more to be said about North Korea, but she wanted to make a suggestion regarding the Chinese: "Mr. President, is there any chance a private meeting between you and General Secretary Han might shake something loose?"

"Perhaps, Rebecca, but with the Iranian saber-rattling getting worse in the Arabian Gulf, I'd better put off China for a few more months. Maybe I can squeeze in an early summer meeting? If Iran closes the Strait, we'll be in a shooting war overnight!"

"Yes, Sir…I hope sanity breaks out there soon!" Rebecca was always worried about the Gulf: Her brother had served in Iraq during Desert Storm, and been severely wounded. All of her family were thankful that he'd made a full recovery, and had carried on with a fairly normal life.

The President agreed. "We are fully engaged with all parties, Rebecca. Jack is planning to leave in a few days to start another round of consultations with the Saudis and our other Arab allies, and the Israelis are improving dialogue with everyone, as the regional treaties with Bahrain, the UAE, and others prove. We'll just keep at it…"

John saw the Middle East discussion had concluded, so he raised another concern about China: "Mr. President, though the PRC has been generally ignoring other issues, they're hinting that their new fleet of merchant ships is due to launch. Is this important enough for dedicated monitoring?"

"Maybe—because I worry about everything. We all know they're having economic issues stemming from our tariffs, so maybe they view this new fleet as a necessary enhancement for their export-dependent economy—another cash cow. However, they started constructing this fleet years ago, and our intelligence community has been keeping a quiet eye on them for years. Actually, since we're talking about those Chinese ships, this is a good time to inform you both that the DNI (referring to Edith Carmichael, Director of National Intelligence) briefed me a couple of days ago that the CIA was sending in someone to scout that huge complex where those ships are being completed. She said Director Tide would inform her if anything seems amiss."

"Thank you, Mr. President, that's good news." John trusted the President's team; they were the best at what they did in any administration he'd observed. His studies had concluded that President Reagan's was the best, but that was way before his time.

Rebecca was feeling the pressure of her busy day, so she grabbed the opportunity to excuse herself: She already knew the President's schedule, and hers was equally demanding. The President smiled his usual polite dismissal and both men rose as she took her leave. She made a beeline for the nearest side exit with her Secret Service detail in tow. She tightened her heavy coat against the early morning chill, but still enjoyed the crisp autumn air that contrasted so nicely from the stifling humidity of the DC summer. She climbed as gracefully as she could onto the high back seat of her waiting black Suburban, and was sorry she needed an "up-armored" vehicle that seemed like a tank. She felt incredibly protected as they headed down the long White House driveway, and smiled and waved habitually at the guards at the main gate, knowing as always that they couldn't see much of her through the tinted glass.

Rebecca finally had a minute to think, so she invested her time to mentally review the details of her meeting with the President: The report about the North Korean launch was troubling, and the seeming reluctance of the PRC to rein in its smaller belligerent neighbor was strange. But, from so far away, the United States could only do so much. America had maintained a strong military presence in Japan, South Korea, and off and on in Taiwan since World War II, and the country couldn't do much more until something really hit the fan. *Like one of those missiles hitting Camp Humphreys in Korea!*

Momentarily, she was riding down Pennsylvania Avenue toward the turn-out to Joint Base Andrews Naval Air Facility Washington, usually abbreviated "JBA." She had a Marine Corps ceremony to attend at Camp Lejeune, North Carolina, and it would be a lot more interesting than hanging around the city. She had something planned every day until Christmas, after which she and her family could take a few days off—it would be just her husband and two teenage kids together, away from DC. But, before that respite, she was looking forward to the highlight of her early December calendar: A trip to Hawaii for the annual Pearl Harbor Day remembrance ceremony. This year it would be especially meaningful because her son and daughter had never seen the solemn event in person. But today was all about the Marines.

Chapter 5

On the road above the Dalian Shipbuilding Complex Liaodong Peninsula, The People's Republic of China November 24th on the Asian side of the International Date Line, 03:00 Hours

As Vice President Mason headed for her visit with the Marines at sprawling Camp Lejeune, a bicyclist on the other side of the world peeled off from the heavy traffic and stopped by the side of the road. Nearly invisible in the darkness and drizzle, CIA Clandestine Officer Jennifer Chen (dressed in character as MSS Major Lee Qui Ming) rested her bicycle against a small stand of bamboo that had taken root by the busy roadside. She slowly glanced around as her racing heart calmed, and her conditioned body began its quick recovery from the long uphill pull. For the last ten minutes she had been pedaling through the rough gravel and packed dirt of the semi-improved road—turned overnight into bumpy slop from unrelenting sleet and rain. However, the good news was that the weather was gradually improving and, though the chill of the autumn night was still penetrating, the rain had slackened into an intermittent drizzle and was forecast to blow itself out before dawn. Jen was in top physical shape, so she viewed the ride as good cardio that warmed her for what lay ahead.

She finished her casual survey of the surroundings, and confirmed that she was in the right place. The street corner she'd use was a few yards north, and it formed the top of the "T" of a broad driveway she'd scouted the previous day. It led downhill to the commercial gate on the inland side of the harbor complex—the entrance where trucks delivered a steady stream of smaller items not carried by the shipyard's railroad boxcars or flatbeds.

As her breathing stabilized, Jen confirmed her anonymity: It was clear that the passengers in the few cars churning past—kicking out small sprays of wet muck and pebbles as they went—were paying her no mind at all. The same seemed true of the steady stream of ubiquitous bicyclers who pedaled.

past in both directions. Similar riders clogged every road in Asia, but on this rainy November night, the people on the frontage road were hunkered down in their multi-colored plastic ponchos. The air was clean and wet because the storm was stronger than the smelly exhaust. Even at this crazy hour, shift workers from the massive shipbuilding facility sprawled at the base of the hill pedaled to and from their jobs. Jen had picked this spot for convenience and access, and if her bicycle was stolen it was no great loss. Even with the corner street light and the distant glow from the shipyard that never slept, everything was partially obscured by the weather, and Jen was certain that she blended in. More important, she had not been followed. She'd specifically chosen the three o'clock hour because sentries are universally at their dullest at that hour, and she needed every advantage to pass unchallenged through this checkpoint at the shipyard's western gate.

Continuing with disguised urgency, she shed her own sea-green poncho and exchanged it for a black umbrella that she removed from the back of her "Flying Pigeon" bicycle—a vehicle that was nearly as common in northern China as the roadside grass. The umbrella would look more official than the common poncho, and she'd selected its symbolic authority to aid her passage into the facility below. She snapped it open and enjoyed immediate respite from the slackening storm that threatened to turn her immaculate forest-green woolen MSS uniform into a sodden mess. Dressed as an officer of the dreaded Ministry of State Security—which sometimes conducted operations domestically to back up or keep an eye on the People's Armed Police—she was, in reality, on a recon mission, a "reccee" in Agency jargon, to discover what the PRC was doing to its fleet of cargo ships being completed in a massive cavern bored into the cliff below. They'd hollowed the space out of the coastal cliff just a mile south of her current position, and the government had invested incredible resources to excavate what must be a massive space. They'd bored directly into the face after dredging a wide and deep channel across the beach between the cliff and the harbor. From satellite photos and her own observations, she knew the cavern was approximately 400 feet in height, and more than wide enough to accommodate the huge container ships that had been towed inside.

Before heading down the hill, Jen carefully confirmed that her small Chinese-made .22LR CH-119 pistol was chambered and hot, and she tucked it discreetly inside the back of her uniform's waistband. She smoothed her tunic jacket over it to complete the look, then took a deep breath, shot a prayer heavenward, and began picking her way around the puddles as she headed toward the right-hand turn and her first challenge of the night.

As soon as Jen reached the corner, she couldn't help but be awed by the amazing spectacle below: The sprawling shipyard was a vast open-air workspace illuminated by hundreds of hooded halogen lights. The lights produced a dull yellow glow underneath the overcast sky and, except for shadows, it penetrated every nook and cranny where quiet ships rested amid noisy cranes and an army of workers. Included in the yard were the open dry docks where ships were propped up by networks of iron and wooden beams—exposed so their hulls could be scraped and re-coated with the universally used brick-red and very caustic anti-fouling paint. Others ships were being built from the keel up, while still others were undergoing minor repairs. As the full panorama opened, she looked down to her left and saw the row of impressive covered buildings that jutted out into the harbor; she knew that was where the hulls of China's new fleet of 14 container ships had been constructed. To her right, she could barely make out the huge building that covered the entrance to the gigantic cavern. The hulls of the ships had been towed from the 14 buildings—pulled by tugs along the waterfront until reaching the channel leading into the cavern. One by one they were pushed inside stern first and, after that, the great doors that covered the entrance had been closed to the outside world. What had happened in the interim was the mystery that required Jen's tasking today.

The structure covering the cavern entrance had been easy to study during her daylight reconnaissance, undertaken from a small boat the previous day. The building acted as both a giant doorway and as an additional security barrier to the cavern—denying the world's press access since the fleet had been pushed inside. The powers that be in Langley wanted to know what was so secret about 14 cargo ships hidden in a man-made cavern—requiring excavation work that was so massive that it required a fleet of ocean-going dredges, huge boring machines, numerous land-based scoop shovels, and thousands of workers. What was the PLA hiding? The cave's excavation took two full years to dig and cart away the mountains of rubble the laborers produced, and it was evident to all that the cost must have been astronomical.

The United States RNO technicians (the National Reconnaissance Office—keepers of the U.S. government's satellites) easily noticed and kept track of the steady procession of giant barges that were used to collect and move the debris down the channel, through Dalian Harbor, and finally far out into the Yellow Sea. They took special note of the coordinates where the mountain of tailings was dumped because the underwater pile (which eventually became a ridge) was so large they needed to alert the U.S. Navy. Naval mapmakers subsequently agreed that the man-made sea mount was significant enough to mark on their charts. The cartography section placed a new hazard on their official digital marine charts (paper charts having become mostly passé) as a warning to the U.S. submarines that regularly trolled the shallow sea.

A few interested parties in the U.S. government kept a loose track of the proceedings, but no serious alarm bells went off. It was a giant curiosity that seemed much less important than China's other renowned engineering projects (like the completed Three Gorges Dam complex on the Yangtze River). The PRC had become inveterate shoreline cave diggers, and several known complexes already housed navy ships and submarines. The biggest excavation before the Dalian cavern was the submarine base on the south end of Hainan Island, which lay just south of the Chinese mainland, so the Dalian project was just viewed as a bigger version of that facility. Consequently, the U.S. intelligence community shrugged off threat scenarios until the launching date approached, then suddenly they got nervous and wanted details. There was precedence in modern times for concern: The Germans had constructed fortified submarine pens along the French coast during World War II, and this one was 20 times bigger.

The external building covering the front door resembled a 1920 blimp hangar that had been cut in half and attached to the face of the cliff. During this phase, construction continued inside the cavern, too—simultaneous inside/outside work that took another full year to complete. But, in due time, the answer for why the cavern had been built was revealed: Its massive front doors were opened and the world's press were invited to watch from a distance as the 14 half-completed container ships were moved one by one over a period of 14 days into the cavern. After that, the great front doors of both the outside building and the cavern entrance were shut again, and the media were asked to turn to other stories until the ships were finished. That didn't sit well with anyone in the journalistic community, and endless speculation raged until they got bored. In fact, a few weeks after the doors were closed, a couple of ambitious reporters conspired to launch two small camera-toting drones in an attempt to enter the building surreptitiously. They hoped to get a peek inside the ships' lair, but the drones were shot down by marksmen with shotguns stationed on the beach—obviously, the security folks had thought of that, too. After that, the authorities installed an electrified mesh net over the front of the building that acted like a gigantic bug zapper, and that ended unwanted snooping. No government agency seemed interested in getting an actual person inside, and media organizations moved on. After that, secrecy reigned.

The official PRC publicity blitz also tailed off after the ships were sealed inside the cavern—in sharp contrast to the hull-construction phase when the ships were first laid down. The world's news organizations were always welcome to check on progress then, and even encouraged to report their observations as widely as possible. Many asked why completion of the fleet was strictly off limits, but the government said it was using proprietary technology it wanted to keep confidential. The entrance was heavily guarded behind multiple rolls of razor wire-topped chain-link fence erected on the flat beach, and the trails and roads on the hill above the cavern were patrolled by teams of armed soldiers with snarling dogs. Additionally, China's penchant for electronic counter-measures, cameras, and even badge scanners were in full display. Only heavily screened workers, engineers, government types, and high-ranking military officers with special badges were allowed to enter through the gate that connected the south end of the shipyard to the beach area in front of the cavern. They entered via a small pedestrian door built into the base of the security building, but their comings and goings were only casually scrutinized by the RNO. Even the ever-vigilant Taiwanese Intelligence Agency didn't bother infiltrating the cavern.

Satellites did reveal plumes of oily sludge constantly oozing under the front building's doors, and analysts noted that the pollution was significant enough to foul not only the south end of the harbor, but seepage also worked its way in an easterly direction out into the Yellow Sea. Some even found its way around the Liaodong Peninsula and into the Bohai Sea. Spectral analysis indicated that the sludge was laced with the type of bunker oil that was routinely burned by ships' engines, and by diesel fuel used by trucks, generators, and other heavy equipment. Also present were paint and metals residue—none of which was surprising or sinister in a complex building ships.

Tim Duncan, the CIA analyst who'd read Reg Trammel's report on potential Chinese social unrest, thought the CCP must have a post-launch, multi-use plan for the cavern (perhaps another submarine base); otherwise, the massive cost necessary to achieve the level of secrecy around the project was not only illogical but smacked of a questionable use of public funds. Even the Politburo had some level of accountability to its constituents. Tim knew there was always the possibility that the project might be more than just an incredibly large publicity stunt—that it might be a cover for something threatening: Perhaps they were developing a new shipboard missile system or laser weapon that would vault China into a new dominance of the western Pacific? Or perhaps a particle beam acceleration chamber that needed multiple kilometers of underground space? He'd raised the issue with his colleagues and supervisors, and no one had any answers or any great desire to risk an extremely valuable agent to investigate. The result was disparate agencies within the U.S. government just watching at a distance while waiting for the fleet's eventual launch.

However, as the launch became imminent, Tim's boss, Clive Hanson, DDNCS (Deputy Director, National Clandestine Service), received a directive from his boss, Director Clarence Tide of the CIA, who received his directive from DNI Edith Carmichael. She believed the situation warranted a look-see. The request went down the chain until it reached Jen's supervisor Ken in Beijing.

Everyone in the senior reaches of the Chinese government had been buzzing about the ships for years, but nested agents, including Jen (who, like everyone in her profession, was otherwise very busy) had no insights beyond the surface story. She and Ken designed a reccee that should solve the mystery. The problem with Jen's participation was the fact that it had taken considerable effort to establish her "Lee" legend and, subsequently, to nest her inside the hard-to-penetrate MSS headquarters. The Agency's Beijing team could lose a lot by risking such a vital agent on a side mission—only to discover nothing more than PRC paranoiac nationalism. But after she digested the work of the photo-interpreters at a briefing she received at the Agency's safe house in a middle-class neighborhood in the southwest corner of the capital, she became personally convinced that the risk was warranted. She admitted that the government might be up to nothing more than "Part Two" of its spectacular PR campaign, but great unknowns generated great doubts. All the secrecy and effort didn't make much sense for a commercial enterprise, so Jen lobbied Ken to let her go. He wanted to go himself, but after a lot of creative persuasion he reluctantly agreed.

So here was Jen, in the middle of a night-time storm, carefully walking down a fairly steep and slippery driveway whose darkness was punctuated by a half-dozen street lights fixed on old wooden poles. She was descending toward the shipyard's western sentry point, and she couldn't help but mull over the downsides that her tasking entailed: If she was caught, her country would lose an invaluable source of intelligence inside the heart of the PRC and, because of the physically dangerous entry method she'd been forced to choose to enter the cavern, she was risking her life as well. Still, she believed her investigation necessitated the risk.

Chapter 6

Entering the Shipyard, 03:10 Hours

As she approached the guards huddled in their sand-bagged kiosk, Jen's immediate concern was that, in this most bureaucratic of nations (where pre-authorized visits were the norm even for routine People's Armed Police or MSS investigations—meaning an official of similar rank and status would be waiting to escort her around the desired inspection site), she was arriving unannounced, alone, and with no one to grease the skids into a vital state enterprise. But she had chosen this gate instead of the others, where the mass of shift workers entered via the northwest and northeast corners of the yard, because it was closest to the cavern and saved more than a mile of useless walking and possible questions along the way. And she wouldn't be human if she hadn't considered the worst-case scenario: If she was caught, her method of entry would be indefensible. The local security people would have to suspect her of spying and, if she couldn't talk her way out, she'd be forced to use violence. At that point, the odds of her getting out alive were slim.

As Jen neared the squat, dirty, and yellowing cement-and-sandbagged guard post, she became visible in the pool of harsh yellow light from the dual lamps mounted on the gates, and her feelings of vulnerability heightened. The gates were topped with razor wire, but a chain-link fence allowed her to see through to the closest part of the yard. The entire gate area was illuminated in the muted wash of the lamps, and there were only occasional shadows dotting the several hundred acres between her and the harbor. She could also feel, as well as hear, the thumping and constant din from hundreds of hammers, cutting torches, banging steel plates, and raised voices from many urgent calls between workers. Her senses were assaulted by the pulsing vibration emanating from every quadrant, plus the pungent odors of burned solder, sweating people, and that odd semi-rotting seaweed smell that characterized harbors the world over.

This incredibly busy scene was regularly punctuated by flashes of intense light, followed by a cascade of sparks. These displays were generated by dozens of arch welders' torches that cut the heavy metal plate, pipes, and fittings that were typical of shipbuilding and construction yards everywhere, and the scene stretched as far as Jen could see. Ship masts sprouted from an array of different-sized vessels that rested temporarily in the huge dry docks, or leaned against cement quays as they waited their turn for repairs. All of this controlled pandemonium was spread out under a night sky whose stars Jen could not see. Even the distant glow from Dalian City was mostly obscured—a metropolitan expanse that was home to the six million souls who lived near the harbor.

Dalian Shipyard occupied more than a quarter of the harbor frontage, and nearly half of the adjacent land on the eastern tip of this south-facing peninsula in Liaoning Province—an historically important area in northeastern China. The arrowhead-shaped peninsula separated the Yellow Sea lying to the east, from the shallower Bohai Sea that lay to the west and south. And across the open water 100 miles to the southwest, the northwest-facing peninsula of Shandong Province formed the two great arms that created the Bohai. Its famous ports had been variously occupied by the ancient Chinese; then, during the colonial period, by the British, the Russians, and the Japanese, and finally by a divided China at the end of World War II. Then, since 1949, Dalian, Lushun, and Tianjin Harbors (the latter, especially) combined to provide the principal gateways to the communist capital Beijing, located nearly 150 miles inland from the harbor docks on the mainland side of the shallow Bohai.

Jen knew in her soul where she worked: This was ancient China—still the Middle Kingdom, still the Great Dragon—if you asked most anyone from the ruling Politburo at the top of PRC society, down to the ordinary peasants who comprised the teeming millions who toiled in anonymous drudgery. This was the Han Motherland and, for Jen, her ancestral home, too. But it was also the country that was rapidly becoming the greatest long-term threat to her family's adopted heart-home: America.

However, as Jen approached the guard shack through the palpable damp air, such thoughts were far from her professional focus. Though still in her

28th year, she was a proven operative with the language skills, personality, and inner confidence to have absorbed and lived her Agency legend in a continually challenging environment. She had arrived in the large western city of Shanghai five years before, posing as a "tourist from Singapore." But after a few days wandering around sightseeing, she'd quietly slipped beneath the government's radar. A week later, she presented herself to the local MSS headquarters with documents attesting to her achievements at her first MSS duty station in the far west. Her papers also contained a record of a successful year in the military before her recruitment, plus an excellent report from her (now deceased) supervisor at the MSS Ministry's training academy. Her documents proved she'd served with enough distinction to be identified as a rising star, one who'd excelled during her first assignment near the Afghanistan border. It was a carefully crafted legend—and it was plausible that her supposed specialized training had been done alone and without corroboration from fellow trainees who could dispute her story. Thus, when she presented her orders and portfolio to the MSS personnel office, her documents were accepted with nothing more than a cursory check; the gaining supervisory chain sorely needed an infusion of top young talent.

Jen was assigned to the local MSS district headquarters where she served for two successful years before being promoted and transferred to Beijing with orders assigning her to the MSS's Fourth (Technical) Directorate. Once inside the dragon's lair, she charmed and achieved her way into a lateral transfer to the MSS Second (Intelligence) Directorate. In a remarkably short time, young Jennifer Chen had become America's top operative in the PRC. Yet, on this dark and rainy morning, she was risking all trying to discover what the leaders of this immense country were hiding within walking distance of where she came to a stop under her protective umbrella. Her mission might yield dramatically important information—or might prove to be relatively bland. But, if the PRC possessed a new technology that threatened the United States, her government needed to know now.

Inside the guard post, PLA Corporal Wei Cheung, the sentry supposedly keeping a sharp eye out for truck deliveries or any trouble, finally noticed an approaching uniformed officer about ten feet from his window. The young corporal was startled out of his reverie, and shook his head to clear his mind of the pleasant thoughts he'd been enjoying since his last truck admittance two hours before. Like soldiers everywhere, he'd been passing the boring middle hours of his watch by fantasizing about a post-breakfast liaison with his new girlfriend as soon as he came off duty. But those thoughts disappeared in a heartbeat as he quickly gathered his wits, grabbed his rifle, and stepped out of the narrow doorway to greet the visitor (hastily kicking and startling his shift mate who was really sawing logs in the other chair).

Outside in the bracing cold, Corporal Cheung, in one shocking moment, noticed three important facts concerning his immediate future: The military officer under the dark umbrella was female; alarmingly wore the uniform of an MSS major; and, worst of all, wore one of those dreaded red, green, and gold badges with the words "Special Investigations Unit" above her left tunic pocket. It was a situation that just screamed danger, and he snapped himself to full attention, brought his QBZ-Type 95 assault rifle to present arms, and stammered, a little louder than necessary to cover his shock and fright, "Good morning, Major…I, I wasn't expecting your visit!"

Deadpan, Jenifer replied quietly (using the level and tone she'd discovered through trial and error to be the most menacing), "Yes, young corporal, I noticed that you didn't seem to be expecting anyone…perhaps you were even sleeping on duty?" She noticed that this question caused this young man's eyes—and those of the other young sentry just then stumbling into the doorway of the small building—to widen with considerable guilt. It was obvious that these boys weren't more than 18 or 19—and were justifiably frightened to be confronted with an unannounced MSS visit. But she'd planned and hoped for just this eventuality and enjoyed her first victory of the day.

"No, Major…we were not sleeping!" the corporal stammered. Soldiers could be shot in the PRC for such infractions. Behind him, the second guard had also come to full attention. But he was still a bit blurry-eyed and disoriented after being jolted out of his sound sleep, and was utilizing the door jamb to steady himself. He wisely said nothing.

Jenifer proffered her flip-open badge case with its "Lee, Ming Qui—Major, Second Directorate, Ministry of State Security" identity card, and held it at arm's length in the full light that spilled from the guard's doorway. She raised it to within six inches of the corporal's eyes, almost forcing him to go cross-eyed to read it, and said, "Do you want me to begin my inspection out here, or are you two 'Heroes of the Motherland' going to let me in?"

"No…I mean, yes! Of course, Major!" The title "major" was squawked in unison now that the second sentry had found his voice. Both stepped aside so Lee could walk to the gate, but she remained in place, taking her time to replace her badge and identity case in the left-side breast pocket of her tunic. Then, with a mere raise of her eyebrows—she'd made up her face to appear older with a touch of harshness—she indicated that she expected the men to open the gate for her. Thankfully, the corporal got the message and reached it in a single bound. She also noted that, though it was a typically chilly morning, beads of sweat had materialized on his upper lip.

Corporal Cheung held the gate for the serious-looking officer and tried to look professional. *What bad luck!* He mentally kicked himself. *Nothing good was going to come from this!*

After another brief pause, during which she affixed a quietly evil stare at the two hapless sentries, Jenifer obliged them and walked through the pedestrian gate. Then, needing them to focus on their futures rather than on her presence in the yard, she turned and, in an even softer and more menacing tone, asked, "By the way, boys, what are your names?"

Ugh! thought the two men in unison: A negative report by one of these *witches*—these inspector-demons—could get them transferred to a God-forsaken isolated outpost on the North Korean border—if they lived to see it. The only thing to do up there was freeze! "Corporal Cheung and Private Lao, Major!" the senior man croaked.

"Well, boys, I'm in a good mood this morning so I'll not report you to your sergeant. But you would be wise to keep a sharper watch from now on…you never know how close 'enemies of the State' might be. And one more thing: You will not mention my entrance to a living soul…" She saw them nod vigorously like a couple of squirrels entreating a hungry mountain lion. Then she simply nodded once and headed in the direction of the distant administration building, located just past the line of wooden buildings where the Dragon Fleet's hulls had been constructed in the center of the great complex. She didn't look back until she was fully enveloped by the shadows of the first dry dock that towered in the darkness. Then, feeling relieved, Jen paused to take a couple of deep, cleansing breaths so she could bleed off her adrenaline rush. She used the brief break to scan the area to ensure she'd been unobserved. Satisfied, and with umbrella in hand, she turned abruptly to her right and began making her way toward her departure point at the base of the cliff—just visible in the distance among the diminishing showers.

Half a mile away from the chastised sentries, Jen picked her way through the busy shipyard at a good clip, trying to project an image of someone who looked neither sneaky nor lost in the early morning darkness. Her goals were to avoid drawing attention to herself while at the same time appearing to anyone who might notice that she was a confident official who knew where she was going. She passed several knots of workers heaving on wet cables, or shouting up at crane operators who were furiously pulling and pushing levers inside their cupolas. These large cranes dotted the yard, and moved in their own steady rhythm, lifting both machines and pallets of steel plates up to waiting colleagues barely visible on the decks above. Everywhere people were hustling and bustling in the chilly dampness, but Jen avoided all eye contact and kept her pace moderate as she walked along. She disciplined herself to not rush and took nearly all of the time she'd allotted herself to cover the distance to her goal. She used a non-direct route that was basic tradecraft, employing a technique that precluded bystanders from recalling her path or destination. Some people did take casual note of her in passing but, since she ignored them, and because they didn't want anything to do with someone wearing her type of uniform, they were glad she paid them no mind.

* * *

Jennifer Li Chen of Oakland, California had been recruited by Agency headhunters before she finished her degree in Asian Languages at the University of California, Berkeley. They liked the fact that she was a bit headstrong (actually a real pain in the kazoo, according to her parents, friends, and teachers—but who was also a relentless and talented competitor, according to her soccer and track coaches). They liked the fact that her lifelong record was one of toeing the thinnest of lines that she could get away with, without "time-outs" from her often-frustrated parents, or later, more serious reprimands from (comparatively) intellectually challenged high school and college teachers. In short, she was an independent woman who possessed the perfect temperament/skillset the Agency sought for the unique demands of the clandestine service. Thus suited, Jen began her career with a raw but moldable combination of high intelligence and stubbornness, and her senior handlers knew right away that they had a trainee/candidate that was worth their investment of time and treasure to cultivate. Her instructors subsequently gave her tremendous leeway to develop her potential, and it wasn't long after her grueling academy preparation that these mentors entrusted her with a frontline field assignment.

Jen quickly proved them right as she became an invaluable asset: During her current assignment, she'd already wormed her way into the confidence of several high-ranking MSS officers within her official billet in the investigation division of the Second Directorate. The directorate focused on international intelligence collection, but had a small but highly important domestic arm that looked for high-level government corruption. Her standing gave her access to a bale of important information almost every day, and she employed the remarkable level of tradecraft necessary to live in the dual worlds of a "placed" intelligence officer. But it was her gift with men, particularly the dramatically older Chinese military men that she targeted, that produced the best results. These senior gentlemen took an immediate shine to this charming (not to mention drop-dead gorgeous) young officer and, though she kept her personal distance lest they try to take her to relational levels that her Christian faith would not allow, they genuinely enjoyed in her the warmth that was often lacking in the other women in their MSS sub-culture. But Jen also had the wisdom and tact to de-claw some of her more rapacious female colleagues—the majority of whom were threatened by the upstart from the south (these roots having been necessarily woven into her legend since she spoke Mandarin with her parents' Cantonese accent). She put everyone at ease, and several men and women thought they were fairly close friends.

* * *

However, Jen was not thinking of that greater context when she finally reached her goal: About 100 yards ahead, barely visible between a jumbled pile of scrap steel, stacks of empty wooden pallets and an apparently abandoned double-stack of rusting 20-foot shipping containers, she spotted the parallel rows of razor wire-topped cyclone fence that was her landmark. Even from a distance, the fence's 10-foot height—topped with the ubiquitous halogen lights—made Jen glad that it was just a landmark and not a barrier to be crossed. But what concerned her most was the fact that the lights illuminated a wide swath of sand at the base of the 400-foot cliff—the open space she had to cross without being seen. She was here to climb that towering granite face, and she would be dangerously exposed for the first few yards, even in the relative gloom and daunting weather.

On the far side of the fence, the beach was bisected by the 50-foot-deep channel that connected the harbor and the cavern, a passage that continued inside the massive space. The area on both sides of the bisecting channel was patrolled by roving sentries accompanied by large black guard dogs—from a distance Jen thought they looked like Rottweilers with their characteristic bull necks and blocky shoulders. But it was not the strength of the animals that she feared—she could always shoot them, if necessary, to save her life. Their greatest threat was their heightened sense of smell and hearing that could catch her scent or footfalls—even when their handlers could not. Jen needed to elude both guards and dogs until she was far enough up the bare rock to be hidden by the night.

She found a patch of shadow next to a stack of rolled cable and folded her umbrella, then peered up at the towering face to evaluate its dangers and plot her next move. But since she couldn't see more than the first 50 feet, she felt comforted that she would soon disappear in the gloom. She was also reminded of the precipitous 350 feet she couldn't see. The whole cliff was about 15 percent from vertical, which in dry daytime conditions was just a pleasant challenge for a talented amateur. But, under the current circumstances, she was facing a rough climb with limited time before dawn, so she had to get going. The granite was fairly smooth and a bit shiny—which meant deadly—because its surface was dripping wet and probably slick as glass.

Jen had decided on this approach after rejecting the obvious underwater entrance through the channel. She had scouted the whole area, including utilizing a re-breather to swim up the channel to the entrance building, but the two patrol boats guarding the area were not the reason she'd rejected the route. To effect an entrance, she'd have to use a sled like the SEALs did, and ferry in a marine acetylene torch to cut her way through the steel mesh barrier. But, whether night or day, the cutting flame would reveal her presence. She'd confirmed that both sets of doors were tightly shut, and those heavy steel mesh nets were suspended from steel pillars imbedded on either side of the channel. The nets reached the gravely bottom, and were held in place with lead weights the size of bowling balls resting in a U-shaped steel track. The entire apparatus was so heavy that a large motor had been installed to move the screen out of the ships' way. All things considered, Jen was forced to abandon a channel entrance because it was virtually impossible. There was no getting around the fact that she had to undertake the much more physically demanding task of scaling the face without aides or protection, and then enter the cavern where the building fitted against the cliff. There a ventilation shaft had been cut through the rock that was big enough for her to enter.

Itching to go, and wary of the danger from the fence lights and dogs, Jen inched her way past the cable rolls to the container stack closest to the cliff. There, on a ledge formed between the vertical boxes, she found a good spot to change and stash her unneeded things. The place where she would start climbing was about 100 yards from the fence, but only a few feet from the stack of old containers. From her spot to the fence, the cliff ran nearly north and south, meaning parallel to the harbor but, past the fence, it curved dramatically to run nearly east and west until it met the corner of the cavern's entrance building. That meant she had to ascend vertically, while angling slightly to her left. That route would bring her to the building's roof overhang, which wrapped around the first few feet of the rock it was attached to. There the engineers had chiseled the rectangular vent she'd use, and she guessed it was approximately 10x15 feet. But the size of the opening was not the challenge; two large circulating fans were, and she would have to figure out some way around or under them to get inside. The size of the structure covering the cavern's opening was amazing, and it reminded her of the front half of the blimp hangar she had visited as a youngster, when her dad brought her to the annual air show at Moffett Field in Sunnyvale, California.

As Jen changed, she was certain she'd not been seen or heard, but now she had to become a ghost—a slowly moving shadow among the shadows. She stripped off her uniform tunic, hat, trousers, and sensible shoes, and adjusted the "ninja" outfit she wore underneath. It was a mottled-dark gray body suit made of warm, stretchable, and waterproof fabric that would not only ward off the chill and rain, but would also help her retain vital body heat. She had chosen its particular camouflage pattern to blend into the rock and darkness, and she was counting on it to render her nearly invisible. Up to this point it had made her uncomfortably warm, but she knew that, within an hour, it would protect her from hypothermia.

Jen smiled sarcastically to herself. "All" she had to do was free-climb the treacherous 400-foot cliff without slipping, then navigate the dangerous fans. There was no middle ground here; if she lost her grip higher than the first 40 feet or so, she would plunge to her death. The ground was unyielding packed sand, liberally littered with baseball to boulder-sized rocks. Then, after penetrating the cavern, her actual mission began; she had to conduct a quality reccee that yielded definitive intelligence. After that, she'd hide inside until she could climb back down and exit the following night. And dear Ken had been worried…

She took a moment to survey the visible portion of her route, and prepared herself mentally and physically—mindful of the 10-knot breeze that wafted and parted the weakening curtains of mist still visible in the wash of the perimeter lights. She was thankful for the gloom nonetheless. For the next few minutes, it would be a life-saving shroud that protected the most vulnerable part of her assent.

Jen invested two precious minutes stretching before carefully wiping the sand off her feet and sliding them into her well-broken-in La Sportiva Mythos rock climbing shoes that she'd stashed in her briefcase. She then completed her preparations by clipping a small but well-stocked fanny pack around her waist and then tucking her shoulder-length black hair into the hood of her ninja suit. She stowed her clothes in her case and slid it into the narrow hiding space with the rest of her things. Feeling as ready as she could make herself, she whispered a fervent prayer to her Lord, double-checked that her fingerless climbing gloves were tightly velcroed in place and, in a crouch, crept across the three-yard gap between the container stack and the rock face. She froze in place against the cliff, and then looked around to confirm that she hadn't been spotted. Everything remained quiet, so she lifted her right foot, found a secure nub, felt the cold rock with her fingers, and began her arduous climb.

Jen's climbing gloves and shoes were the best that money could buy, and she was an experienced recreational rock climber. Still, no one who wanted to live long hurried unnecessarily during any assent. She established a steady rhythm, finding good foot and handholds, climbing with her legs while steadying herself with her hands. That was Climbing 101. Jen was a smooth climber and quickly conquered the initial few yards until the darkness closed around her. When she felt safe enough to pause, she did so for 30 seconds to slow her breathing and heartrate so she could listen carefully one last time. She was rewarded with deathly stillness; she'd not been spotted by the guards or sensed by the dogs—she'd won another round!

Chapter 7

A fatal slip? 05:21 Hours

Jen started climbing again. As she moved carefully and confidently, she felt the cliff gradually surrender to her skill. The surface was slick, but the 15 percent slope was just enough off vertical to make the effort a difficult ladder climb, rather than a purely technical one. After a confirming glance downward to ensure that she couldn't see the fence lights or entrance area, she settled into the familiar routine of a long climb. In the darkness, she couldn't identify the small features of the rock face right in front of her nose, but she was experienced enough to use her hands to find the precious nubs, cracks, and crevices that were life and death in her demanding sport. She relied on her feet and legs to provide the power she needed to make steady upward progress, and used her petite hands to find the smallest fissures that kept her safe. She'd brought a fist-sized bag of climber's chalk to keep her fingers dry, but the powder gradually became useless as the wet conditions turned the dry mixture to paste. Her only glances upward were in vain, and she reminded herself to be patient: She wouldn't spot the light emanating from the vent for another hour.

Jen soon found and followed the obvious vertical crack she'd spotted with her binoculars during the previous day's recon, but she hadn't been able to see the surface's looseness and occasional patches of unstable rock in the cliff's middle zone. These places slowed her a bit because of the danger they posed, but she crossed them as they came, and she was soon more than half-way up. She knew the constant drizzle would quickly shift from protective friend to physical enemy. The higher she went, the added slipperiness on every surface magnified the danger of her assent. The risks inherent in free climbing were bad enough, because there were no ropes, pitons, "friends" or artificial protections of any kind. It was just the climber and the cliff. But Jen was not free-climbing for the added challenge or environmental commitment to keeping the rock face clean (though she supported both in the sporting world). She'd chosen this method to avoid the associated noise that would expose her to discovery and death.

After another half-hour of steady progress, the character of the rock face changed for the worse and became her main antagonist. As she climbed out of the middle section, the nubs became jagged and every handhold was painful. Climbers relied heavily on feel when searching for cracks, especially in bad weather where visibility was limited, but during a nighttime assent like this, Jen admitted that the dangers equaled foolishness bordering on crazy. There was also the pervasive and penetrating chill that contributed to her fingers becoming raw and stiff and, by the end of the first hour, a hundred tiny cuts made her life miserable. Every purchase—every life-giving nub—was a two-edged sword: Jen steadily lost her sense of touch and, for the first time, worry began to seep into her soul.

Jen's pre-assent planning included her estimation that the climb's degree of difficulty was about 5.6 (6.0 being vertical), a rating that was straightforward for skilled amateurs like she and her usual climbing partner (her fiancé Tim) attempted on dry, sunny days. However, in the current conditions, every aspect of the assent was significantly more difficult. She rested a minute and calculated that she was about two-thirds of the way to the top. She had crossed that point in her pain threshold where she was just gutting it out. Jen was very tough mentally, and she compartmentalized pain better than most, but underlying worry could lead to a loss of confidence—and that was a snake in the path of every climber that could strike without warning.

After another 25 grueling minutes, she glanced up and was rewarded with a surge of hope: The vent's faint light cut though the gloom and she knew she would make it. She redoubled her efforts and soon the roof's overhang became a discernable shadow—tangible encouragement that she admitted she needed. She couldn't deny that she was in real pain, forcing her to go into that special place in her inner spirit where she could deal with suffering. Her training helped cope with the cumulative effects of the cold and the cuts, but they'd become an honest and dangerous impediment to survival. She'd also had to adjust her footholds as the outer layers of her copper wire-reinforced climbing shoes had steadily shredded from the razor-sharp toeholds, and even that minor adjustment made her grip on the cliff more tenuous. The only good news was that her fingers were so cold that the blood slowly saturating her gloves coagulated quickly. However, in counterpoint, her knees were taking a beating—the thin bodysuit didn't offer much protection from the rock, and she was accumulating bruises and additional soreness, and the fear of deadly cramps eroded her recently regained confidence. She'd suffered two, short, heart-stopping slips and, at more than 350 feet above the beach, she had no room for error. She'd had to dig deep during several significant assents in Yosemite (not El Capitan—that big boy was still on her bucket list) but this one had steadily devolved into the most daunting of her career.

Jen was afraid—only a crazy person wouldn't be—but she was convinced that her country needed her to find out what the PRC was doing inside the cavern, and her certainty of purpose gave her added strength. Pain also tended to make her mad—and she channeled her anger constructively to finish the job. Inch by painful inch, she levered herself ever upward and slightly to the left, willing the beckoning light to draw her to safety.

Suddenly, disaster struck: During a foot transition, her right foothold gave way and collapsed in a shower of small pebbles, and she gasped in terror as she dropped nearly six feet before her foot caught again on a tiny ledge. Frantic, she fought off gut-wrenching panic, and scratched and clawed at the unforgiving rock to find something to hold on to. She even forced her hooded cheek against the featureless surface to gain extra traction—anything to keep from falling into the abyss! The unavoidable surge of adrenaline flooded every cell of her body, but her tenuous foothold held while she hung on for dear life. She nearly wept as she prayed for God's help.

In the middle of her panic, she was struck by the thought that she was immortal until God was done with her and, if this was His mission for her, His mercy would see her through. She initially remained frozen in place, afraid to move, but gradually she began to believe that her small right-foot perch would hold. She clung to her faith and believed that God would enable her to climb on. Her left foot had miraculously found a precariously thin half-inch ledge, and her right index finger had caught on a nub that was big enough to trust. Her violently beating heart seemed like it might knock her off her little perch, but she chided herself that such thinking was irrational. She forced herself to engage her left hand and feel laterally for fingerholds; a second later she found one large enough to hook with her ring finger. Her hummingbirds' heart rate gradually regained its equilibrium, her panic began to subside, and even her breathing returned to normal. She willed herself to calmness even while whispering prayers of relief and thanksgiving. She knew she'd just been preserved through a frighteningly close call.

Jen had never intentionally climbed alone; in recent years she'd relied on Tim's amazing strength to help her as they enjoyed difficult assents together. And even though she was in a real predicament, she thought of Tim and dearly missed him. It was easy to wonder through a moment of fleeting sadness if she'd ever see him again. *This had better be worth it!*

She gradually trusted her footholds enough to push herself upward, gathering enough confidence to release her right hand and slide it above the left until she felt another promising nub. Throughout the process she didn't dare to look up, but in her cacophony of surging emotions, she had to suppress a sudden giggle when she realized she'd almost peed in her pants—*wouldn't that be a heroic entry to add to my post-operation report!*

That tiny moment of levity got Jen going again, and though she had fresh body damage to contend with, she felt enough renewed confidence to finish the climb. On the positive side, the rocks she'd kicked off had been mere pebbles, and she'd heard no tell-tale shouts or barks from the beach below. She had a related thought that all good climbers quickly learned the character of the rock they scaled, and she had, unfortunately, learned the hard way that this section was fairly loose. This meant there was a silver lining: Since any rock exposed to the elements is inherently unstable—meaning that they are always subject to the stresses of the weather and other natural forces—the guards and dogs were no doubt used to tiny rock slides and would pay them no mind. But all that being true, being invisible still helped the most.

Time was now becoming a factor: It was approaching 5:30 in the morning, and she could sense the slight pre-dawn light signaling a new day was almost there. A breeze had blown away the last of the front and the mist was gone, but she had used up her maximum allotment of two hours to complete the climb. She realized that she would soon be visible to the sentries below and on the trails above. Thus motivated, Jen pressed on, and 10 minutes later she slipped under the roof's overhang. She traversed the last few feet horizontally—using a blessedly wide six-inch crack to reach the vertical cement wall—an anti-climactic experience to touch its immensely comforting flat surface. Now all she had to do was reach up and grab the lower sill of the vent.

The architects had hollowed out a large rectangular space so that inside air could be forced out. The passageway had been cemented, and Jen summoned the last of her reserves to grab the bottom sill and hoist her athletic body up and over the roughly finished ledge. She accomplished this with no little effort. Exhausted, she lay face down on the hard, flat surface—nearly overcome with relief. She took a few minutes to regain her emotional and physical equilibrium, then pushed herself to begin moving again. She had made it!

Chapter 8

Inside the cavern, 05:37 Hours

Jen quickly took stock of her surroundings. She was being heavily buffeted by a stream of gasoline-impregnated air being expelled from the building by two six-feet-in-diameter rotating fans, invisible (but logically suspected) during her recon. They were designed to extract dangerous fumes from the cavern, and she surmised that fresh air must be drawn into the space from other locations—probably including engineered gaps around the large front doors that didn't need to be airtight. This mechanism would provide a life-saving circulation loop necessary to protect the army of laborers inside. The sound from the powerful fans was loud but not harmfully so, and the wind they produced was strong but not violent enough to push her back over the sill. The sound and movement combined in her favor because the people inside would be conditioned to ignore the fans—thus providing cover for Jen when she began her investigation. But first she had to get past them without being chopped to pieces.

First, she squirmed 90 degrees clock-wise so that she faced the danger, and immediately confirmed that, because of their round shape and the fact that their blades could not touch each other, there was a large enough triangle underneath their spin path for her to wriggle through. Additional safety was provided by sturdy metal sheaths that protected maintenance technicians from loss of limbs or worse. Jen easily low-crawled through the two-foot gap with room to spare, then she carefully edged forward across the complementary three-foot cement sill on the inner side until she could finally peer into the immense space below.

Just under her level was a sea of yellow-orange industrial light panels suspended from the vast ceiling, but their glare was focused below. The light made Jen wince as she made the transition from night to day, but what was worse was the assault from the stench of the place. Her olfactory senses rebelled against the mixture of paint fumes, human body odor, and that same nauseating rotting fish smell she'd experienced during her earlier traverse of the shipyard. However, she guessed that it would be worse at her level because the naturally rising heat would lift the stench as well. Whatever ventilation system the engineers had installed was barely keeping the cavern habitable.

Jen could easily see between the gaps in the light panels, and she began processing the incredible sight below: Resting in the channel just inside the great front doors, and stretching as far as she could see to her right toward the back of the cavern, were side-by-side pairs of the largest ships she'd ever seen. And, though each of the ships must have been close to 1,000 feet long, the vastness of the cavern dwarfed them by comparison. Jen guessed that the hollowed-out space inside the surrounding ridge was the largest cave-like structure ever made. The Chunnel that had been constructed under the English Channel was certainly longer, and she knew of open pit mines that were bigger, but they had different engineering requirements. In sheer cubic volume, this cavern was surely competitive. Marveling, Jen had to hand it to her "cousins": The Communist Chinese were famous for big projects (like the Great Wall that had been built to protect Beijing) but this one had been completed in less than three years—not 2,000!

After two minutes gawking like a tourist, Jen refocused on her mission. All superlatives begged the immediate and obvious question: Why go to such trouble just to finish a fleet of container ships that the world already knew about? It was the million-dollar question she been tasked to answer, *and for which I almost lost my life scaling that infernal cliff!* Jen began noting details: The immense door that opened into the channel to the harbor was wide enough for only one ship. However, the engineers who hollowed out this immense space had made the cavern more than twice as wide inside—enough to accommodate two ships abreast, plus additional space for broad cement quays bordering each wall, and a third one running lengthwise between the two lines of ships. Jen wondered how the far line of ships could move over into the "exit lane" closest to her: *Perhaps the center quay is hinged or detachable?* Perhaps she'd find out later, but for now she was mightily impressed.

Jen reached around and dug into her fanny pack with her injured right hand, and painfully extracted a pair of small binoculars to aid her study of the ships directly below. She appreciated that each one was a marvel in itself—designed to carry the incredible number of containers typical of modern Post-Panamax cargo carriers. Then she suddenly realized that this first pair was already stacked to capacity with the expected jumble of multi-colored containers (sporting the dozens of different companies' logos and paint schemes that made them easy to identify). These first two looked fully ready for departure, and that made sense time-wise because the government had been promising an "any-day" series of maiden voyages. *But how very strange to load the containers in here rather than at one of the normal and spacious east coast container terminals.*

She shifted her gaze down to the waterline to see how deep the closest vessel was resting in the water and, sure enough, the massive ship was drawing a lot of water, and must be nearly full. She had been briefed that they had entered the cavern empty—in hull-only configuration. Therefore, there must be a back entrance through which full containers were moved into the space. But why load them in secret? It was so ordinary a task as to be quite puzzling, and Jen wondered with renewed interest what the authorities were up to.

She already knew that each ship was identical, and that they had been built to match the largest type that could fit into most of the world's major container ports—including those on the west coast of the United States. But they were intentionally designed to be smaller than the largest ships afloat, like the colossal CMA CGM *Marco Polo,* the British-flagged container vessel which, at 153,000 tons displacement, could carry 16,000 twenty-foot containers (TEU or twenty-foot equivalent units). And there were even bigger ones: Maersk "Triple E" class ships could haul 18,000 TEUs, and the truly monstrous MSC *Gulsun* could carry more than 23,750 TEUs. Those ships could not fit into many of the world's military or commercial ports, and none in the United States—they were simply too massive and drew too much water. Jen was no expert on marine shipping, but she guessed these "Dragon Ships," as the PRC government had christened this fleet, had been built to service the 75 percent of the world's container ports where they currently conducted the majority of their cross-ocean trade. This assumption matched the Day One claims at the fleet's announcement four years before.

Next Jen adjusted her view so she could focus on the fairly narrow main deck that surrounded the container stacks of the closest ship—that is, the space between the bottom of the outside stacks and the safety railing. She was again surprised to see that the deck had dozens of military men milling about—not the civilian personnel one would expect. She quickly identified some uniforms as belonging to PLAN (People's Liberation Army Navy) Marine officers. They stood casually talking here and there, but were interspersed with busier sailors in the expected Merchant Marine uniforms—scurrying about completing normal shipboard tasks like folding ropes, touching up scrapes with paint or polish, or scrubbing invisible dirt off what looked like immaculate surfaces. But, on closer inspection, some of these ratings were dressed in PLAN sailor uniforms and, for some reason, the scene was unsettling beyond its sheer scale. Jen didn't like the presence of so many military personnel on merchant marine ships. *This first pair had been loaded in secret, was covered with soldiers, and was already laden with a full complement of mysterious containers heavy enough to settle the ships to near-maximum capacity. What on earth could these giants be carrying that necessitated such costly secrecy?*

Jen's interest in the amazing Dragons had temporarily masked her damaged physical state, but as she warmed inside the building, her battered body—especially her fingers—started to throb. She resigned herself to investing a few minutes administering basic first aid, re-hydrating, and eating something—she needed to replace lost calories and infuse a spark of physical energy. She carefully slid back from her vantage point, unhitched her fanny pack, and then turned on her side and busied herself with the mundane tasks of extracting lightweight bandaging materials and her plastic container of orange juice. She had to contend with the loud fans, but she was rapidly getting used to their dull roar and the steady but manageable flow of air being expelled outside.

As she worked, she focused on refining the two principal questions she needed to answer: One, the reason(s) for the overall secrecy, and (two) now that the containers were loaded, what were their contents? The government had gone to great lengths to hide this operation from the world's prying eyes, and it didn't make sense. Their existing commercial fleets regularly sailed from container ports dotted all along the Chinese coast, and then openly plied the world's oceans bringing consumer goods to everyone on earth. They had eager buyers and an established logistics flow. *Surely, they hadn't produced enough new and wonderful products to justify this colossal undertaking? The world could only consume so much stuff!*

Jen gently removed and tucked away her bloody climbing gloves, then painfully repaired her damaged hands with some absorbent and slightly sticky medical tape and a tiny tube of antibiotic ointment. Next, she downed four of her eight ibuprofen tablets with several swigs from her pint of juice, and hungrily wolfed down a local-label candy bar—thinking critically that its bland taste and waxy chocolate would never give Snickers Bars a run for their money. Thus fortified, she placed everything back into her trusty pack—careful to not let any of the paper wrappers float away—and then inched carefully back to her lookout point. She was tempted to rest a bit longer, but she accepted that she had to survey the whole line of ships—all seven pairs. Her best-case scenario had envisioned a quick in and out, but that opportunity died during her longer-than-expected haul up the cliff—and her initial discoveries inside necessitated several hours of detailed recon. Her next reasonable opportunity to leave the cavern wouldn't come until darkness closed in again. She felt sorry for poor Ken—her supervisory guardian angel she knew would worry unnecessarily until she came out; she could picture him hovering outside and trying to inconspicuously blend into the local traffic as she had earlier.

Jen took a deep cleansing breath and got back to business: *Start taking pictures.* She extracted a diminutive yet amazingly powerful satellite camera from another compartment in her pack. *Oh, no!* She nearly cried when she saw that it had been severely damaged—no doubt during one of her falls. Its small antenna had snapped off so it couldn't automatically send the pics into space. *Oh, well…no use crying over spilled milk.* She'd planned on carrying it out anyway, so Ken (and everyone else in her chain of command) would just have to wait another day to view her findings. Fortunately, the body of the camera appeared intact and functional, so she wrapped its thin braided hand-loop around her wrist so she couldn't drop it, then raised it to eye level and started snapping photos. It had no flash to give away her position—the brain trust in the Agency's version of "Q" Branch had made sure her little gem didn't need one.

Despite her growing sense of foreboding, Jen couldn't help but admire the beauty of the ships: Their livery was a dazzling Chinese red with gold trim, and it was obvious that the government was backing its comprehensive PR campaign with truly magnificent details. She conceded they would indeed have themselves a publicity splash when they began launching these spectacular new merchantmen. Jen was hard to impress, but she couldn't help being in awe of their size and uniformity. She photographed the man-made wonders from her perch, and noted that she was about 100 feet above the top of the highest containers—space necessary to allow the antennae and radars that were affixed to the tops of each bridge's superstructure—with room to spare for heavy duty loading gantries, attached to the cavern's ceiling. The top edge of the front door was built to accommodate the fleet's exit, so its highest point had to be at least 400 feet, too.

Jen's perch was perfect, and it allowed her a perfect view of the big picture. She guessed from the low set of the hulls that there couldn't be much room between the bottom of the ships' keels and the channel bed underneath. It would be tricky to get them in and out of the world's container ports without scraping bottom, but the designers had bragged to the media that these ships, even when fully loaded, had especially shallow drafts for their size.

Just then a flurry of movement on the deck of the closest ship caught her attention, so she focused on the spot to see what was going on. To her surprise, a great line of soldiers in camouflage uniforms—then she immediately corrected herself—they were PLAN marines carrying assault rifles and full packs, streamed around the front edge of the forward container stack. They'd obviously just climbed a ramp or stairs from the quay that separated this nearer ship from its sister Dragon moored against the far wall. She watched fascinated as they streamed past the vertical stacks, and then she was further surprised when large doors suddenly opened at deck level. The marines walked through previously unseen doors that were evenly spaced along the line of 40-foot containers resting on the deck. *What on earth?* Jen trained her binoculars on that door, then automatically shifted her gaze further along the base of the stack. Sure enough, occasional marines or sailors were coming and going through additional openings in successive containers that she hadn't noticed before. And then she had a revelation: *These are not container stacks at all—they are vertical external bulkheads—carefully constructed and cleverly painted with varying-colored rectangular shapes to look like containers. The stacks were a ruse! Why, you clever guys...you're transporting marines!* Suddenly a shiver ran down her spine, and Jen began to have a very bad feeling about the whole enterprise.

She craned her neck to the right to get a better view of the succeeding pairs of ships that stretched back into the cavern, and it seemed that every ship had its full complement of "containers" fully in place. There was also greater activity and noise farther back in the cavern, so Jen's sense of urgency increased—confirming her imperative to expand her investigation. She briefly wondered how she could accomplish this unobserved, and risked a peek over the edge of her perch. However, she was immediately rewarded with a clear view of a sturdy steel catwalk running just four feet below the sill, just above the level of the suspended light panels. She then glassed the far wall and confirmed that an identical catwalk ran the length of that wall, too. In fact, she noted that four lengthwise catwalks ran horizontally along that far wall, each about 100 feet apart, so she peered through the lattice of the walkway directly below and saw through the gaps in the steel mesh that the same structures also ran lengthwise on her side. She then invested a couple of minutes carefully examining all four catwalks on both walls, and was relieved that there were few workers who could spot her movement. All of them were engaged in tasks on the lower three levels on each side and, thankfully, this spacing permitted her to conduct an unobserved recon to the end of the cavern.

Confident that the shadows above the lights would mask her traverse, Jen wriggled her slender body over the edge and dropped silently onto the catwalk. She had close to two miles to go, but as she moved cautiously away from the noisy fans, she knew she was almost invisible from the ships or the quay. She was so absorbed by her investigation that she didn't notice two gray-haired men walking side by side next to the first Dragon 400 feet below.

Chapter 9

The great deception, 06:00

CCP General Secretary Han and his minister of Defense, Marshal Tai, were animated as they sauntered along, occasionally gesturing up at the ships in obvious delight, and pointing at this or that feature on their immense creations. They both wore simple dark gray Mao jackets and seemed to be enjoying each other's company. They stopped briefly and pointed downward toward something they'd noticed in the water but, after a minute discussing whatever it was, they continued walking toward the rear of the cavern. Four members of their security detail shadowed them a few respectful paces away, and each carried the same Type 95 assault rifles as their numerous colleagues filing into the ship's container/troop areas above. The only notable difference was that these four marines' weapons had full magazines. Also ambling along just behind the military guards were several members of the regular civilian security unit (whose function was equivalent to the American Secret Service). The four military members were all senior sergeants—elite Marine OR-7s of the First Flotilla—that regularly augmented the normal security detail when the president and minister of Defense visited the cavern.

The two CCP leaders were a familiar site to all who regularly worked in the cavern, and they'd enjoyed checking on construction progress since the first day the ships were towed inside. They were justifiably proud of what they had risked to make this vast enterprise happen, and supremely confident that their upcoming operation would confirm their gamble. As they walked, the little procession was trailed by a half-dozen small electric carts driven by other trusted marines. These were always ready to ferry the two men (and their entourage) whenever they tired or just wanted to speed ahead. The pair passed scores of workers and military personnel on the quay, and everyone respectfully bowed or saluted as appropriate.

Han and Tai had thrown the dice four years earlier, initiating a project they believed would save their homeland and vault them into the status of lone world superpower. It had been an incredibly expensive venture, but the growing agricultural and industrial crises threatened the Party's hold on power. Humanly speaking, they were pleased that the unexpected situation allowed them to accelerate their long-term goal of world domination while they were still young enough to enjoy it. They and other supporters had approved "Operation Unity" as developed by General Bao and Professor Dang—a plan that ingeniously provided a hide-in-plain-sight strategy and, so far, everything was on schedule. Even the Covid-19 setbacks had been quickly turned into an unexpected blessing as the world focused on that catastrophe and seemingly ignored the possible downsides of the new Chinese fleet.

The pandemic also dovetailed perfectly with Minister Wing's plan to disrupt every targeted country before the general attack, and he'd already achieved far more than his component called for. The economies of most of the world had been severely damaged but, so far, China had been able to shrug off its responsibility as the nation that had created the virus that had killed so many. Minister Wing's thousands of agents still planned on carrying out pre-attack disruptions, but any positive results from them were now just icing on the cake. America had become inwardly focused again—just a big, fat, sleepy cow.

Han spoke enthusiastically, "I have to admit, Comrade Tai, my old friend, I had my doubts when you first brought me your ministry's remarkable idea."

"But you had faith, exalted Comrade President, plus the courage and vision to support this great undertaking! We are two weeks ahead of our most optimistic schedule, and soon China will be transformed into the dominant power on Earth!" Marshal Tai had recently been elevated to his current position of minister of Defense, a foregone conclusion after his many years of faithful service as Marshal Zhang's number two. When the old warrior had finally retired 15 months before, Tai was more than ready. As had his predecessor, he relished the title of "Marshal" and its five-star rank denoted greatly enhanced authority. Practically, however, he maintained a different style of leadership than old Zhang: He stayed in his regular office, kept a tight hold on the day-to-day operations of the PLA, and attended ministry-level meetings only when he had to. He also enjoyed making even more money from his increased percentage of the military-owned businesses. "Starting tomorrow, and concluding a few short weeks from now, our shared dream will be realized: Our Middle Kingdom will have consolidated, for the first time in a thousand years, all of east Asia under our direct and rightful rule, plus we'll have expanded our control of the western Pacific sea lanes and Oceania—indeed, our half of the Pacific Ocean!"

"And the Americans and their allies?" Han worried as he always did. He just couldn't believe such a strong military power could be destroyed so quickly. "Soon to be irrelevant, as you and Wing promised? And without using nuclear weapons?"

"We have planned every detail to neutralize them, Comrade Han. We will keep them at bay while our forces overrun and consolidate our hold over the entire Asia/Pacific region!"

"And the Russians?" Han had never been satisfied with Tai's oblique statements regarding neutralizing that potential threat.

"As promised, Comrade Han: We have a special diplomatic team in place to assure them they are in no danger from us, and we have already greased the palms of all the decision-makers, with promises of a lot more. We have even removed about half of our normal forces from our shared frontier as a sign of general good will. And, going forward, we will lavish win/win trade on them. Besides, if necessary, our land forces are significantly larger than theirs, and you know that more than a million of our citizens have drifted north over the last several decades to reside in eastern Russia. Moscow's leaders are uncertain masters of Siberia, and have no reason to engage in—or the stomach to begin—a shooting war with us."

Han was again reassured for the moment, and both men continued to walk and talk, and to admire their red and gold "Dragons" named after the mythical creatures of Chinese lore—those ancient beasts that were still powerful symbols reverberating among the people. The Politburo was about to unleash these modern Dragons in the name of conquest, and they'd spread violence across a third of the world. It would be a storm of such magnitude that the Asia/Pacific region—indeed the entire Pacific Rim and world—would never be the same again. For the moment, however, the two long-time colleagues were so lost in their own conspiratorial anticipation that neither they nor their expanded security team noticed the young woman creeping along above the lights on the catwalk above.

* * *

Jen was moving purposely along the narrow maintenance walkway, dutifully trying to ignore her damaged hands, sore feet, and badly bruised right knee. She hoped the pills would dull the pain enough to preclude any interference with her mission but, regardless of distractions or dangers or pain, she was determined to explore the whole complex and get the answers her President needed. If her discoveries today proved that important, she'd accept the difficult decision to leave China, because sometimes actionable intelligence required unusual sacrifices. She'd simply disappear and leave her superiors wondering what happened. But, at the moment, at least she wasn't worrying about the walkway: It was constructed of heavy-gauge steel mesh bolted onto the concrete walls. She presumed the walls were reinforced by acres of inch-diameter rebar, and the structure seemed very solid under her feet. It also had a sturdy waist-high outside handrail with parallel cross wires strung tautly every six inches between the handrail and the base. And, although the whole apparatus was suspended hundreds of feet above the quay and not for the faint of heart, Jen couldn't help but enjoy her current situation a lot more than her earlier hair-raising climb. Psychologically, the catwalk seemed wonderfully safe. She stayed as close to the wall as possible to minimize detection from the occasional worker directly below, and she intentionally moved slowly because the eye is drawn to movement. As she tiptoed along, her heavily damaged climbing shoes afforded her near-silent traverse, and she'd checked them at the outset for any dirt or gravel that could break loose and give her away.

Jen occasionally glanced up at the network of steel girders that supported the cavern's ceiling—wary of cameras but spotting none. She noted that the ceiling's structure was part of a comprehensive grid that included a sturdy-looking metal screen hung a foot below the ceiling's beams. It was an obvious precautionary measure designed to catch the smaller rocks and chips that released and dropped as the previously virgin rock warmed and cracked. From her vantage point, she could see a carpet of such chips had already collected on the fine mesh—some as big as her fist—a notable precaution that must have already saved lives below.

Soon Jen came abreast of the second pair of leviathans—each identical to the first, and resting nearly as deep in the water. She mentally dredged up the relevant fact that the government had bragged that, when these ships were fully loaded, they drew only 39 feet below the waterline. It was amazing marine engineering when considering the tonnage they were designed to carry. This second pair was also a beehive of activity, not because of soldiers streaming aboard, but because giant yellow-colored heavy-duty gantries were raising huge bundles of palletized cargo from the quay, and setting them inside "clamshell" doors that opened at the top of each "container stack." *Wow,* Jen thought, *the practical details thoughtfully designed into these ships is amazing!*

Jen used her binoculars to peer inside the stack and saw a solid-looking deck covered with pallets, and soldiers busily pushing them against the bulkheads or carrying them out of her view. She glanced down to the quay, and noticed for the first time that small electric trains were rumbling along on tracks—heavy steel parallel lines recessed into the flat cement surface. A new train pulled up with several flatcars carrying stacked pallets, and Jen didn't need her binoculars to see workers grab cables suspended from a hoist. Hooks were quickly fastened onto each (she guessed aluminum) pallet whose contents were covered by heavy green tarps. Then, after receiving a wave from the ground team's foreman, the gantry operator deftly lifted each pallet to a point above the clamshells and repeated the process until the flatcars were empty. The whole process was admirably efficient. Each container's clamshells seemed hinged, and Jen could see that they served as two halves of each roof. She presumed they were engineered to interlock and seal the compartments from the elements.

These revelations helped Jen surmise that the entire upper level of each ship was an incredibly large cargo hold for lighter materials—everything needed by the large number of marines on board. However, since the PLAN was supposed to have only about 10,000 marines, either they had trained tens of thousands more during the last couple of years, or the number of "rifle-toters" on these ships included regular army soldiers as well. The regular PLA force was officially listed at about 1.5 million personnel, with another 500,000 reservists, so the large number of personnel on these ships (she estimated about 3,000 each, including sailors) would only be a fraction of their fighting force. Still, when multiplied times 14 ships, 42,000 frontline warriors were formidable, and obviously going somewhere to fight. *Incredible!*

Jen forced herself to move on and presently drew even with the third pair of Dragons, and observed something new: Lines of wheeled trucks and smaller vehicles that looked like American "Hummers" with top-mounted guns were moving up a ramp that had been lowered from the upper side of the hull. She surmised that the ramp must move laterally first, then lower to ground level. The vehicles motored up the ramp without a hitch—one at a time for weight purposes—and disappeared through giant doors engineered into the highest level of the hull. She hadn't noticed them on the earlier two ships, so they must slide into tightly recessed slots. She could see a short way into the inside space—guessing it functioned like a parking garage with acres of space. It would make sense that such vehicles would be stored lower than the personnel and their equipment because of their greater weight. She concluded that the "stacks" above the main deck were barracks—spacious enough to carry the light equipment, food, and sleeping space necessary for about 2,000 marines.

Jen knew the U.S. and other international navies had RORO ships (Roll On/Roll Off) that could take large numbers of tanks and trucks overseas—and this ship was bigger than the largest ROROs in the U.S. Navy's arsenal. Yet, it was a standard technology: The world's auto producers shipped their cars across every ocean using boxy-looking auto carriers with the same basic configuration.

Jen's sense of urgency pushed her onward, but she made herself take photos as she went. She needed to learn more about the "big picture" here, and her pix would help Langley make better sense of every detail. She was doing this in faith—hoping the main function of her camera was operational. She peered through the magnified viewfinder to snap the next photo, and noticed words and symbols stenciled on some uncovered palletized boxes. She squinted and made out the Mandarin characters for "rations" stenciled in green. *Obviously, they needed to carry tons of food*, Jen reasoned, given the slew of people she was seeing everywhere. Switching her focus to the farthest ship of this pair, she could just barely make out the lettering on the uncovered boxes being lowered into it. These boxes were a bit smaller than the ration boxes, but she could decipher similar green stenciling that read, "Ammunition, 5.8 x 42mm DBP87." *That's the standard ammo for the PLA's Type 95 assault rifle!* She looked down the lines of ships toward the end of the cavern and a red light went off in her head. *Okay, boys, where are you going with enough ammo to start a small war?* Then she immediately corrected herself: *If similarly loaded, there were enough men and ammo in these fourteen ladies to fight a really* ***big*** *war!*

Jen was conflicted by her desire to report her discoveries as soon as possible (meaning a quick return to her place of ingress and chancing a daylight climb upward to the level of the road). But that would increase her chance of discovery and negate her completed recon. Two and two were coming together fast: These ships were not big merchies—they were giant assault ships designed to deliver a lot of war materiel and personnel to a combat zone—and ingeniously, they were hiding their master's intentions in plain sight! But where were they going? Perhaps she could discover that, too.

China was not presently at war with anyone, except for the escalating skirmishes along the Indian border, and their continual confrontation with Vietnam and the Philippines over occupied islands. But the PRC had widely advertised its claims within the "Nine-Dashed Line"—that is, the territorial waters of the South China Sea, bordered and shared by Vietnam, the Philippines, Brunei, and Malaysia, respectively. China had placed troops, airstrips, planes, and surveillance stations on many of the region's islands they'd occupied—not to mention significantly engineering upgrades they'd made to the islands—including constructing harbors to accommodate ships, and runways to handle large military planes. Perhaps China's leaders had finally decided it was time to forcibly bring Taiwan into the fold? These 14 Dragons would certainly constitute an impressive vanguard ahead of traditional assault ships, airborne troops, bombers and fighters, etc. But such action would bring the United States and perhaps Japan into the fight—and that was World War III! Was reunification worth it? There were also a host of lingering questions surrounding the Chinese part in the origins of the Covid pandemic, and Jen wondered if this fleet and the disease had any connection. These questions gave her a needed jolt of energy, and she got moving again.

As she continued her silent traverse, different parts of her body competed for which hurt the most. But she had to ignore them, and she occupied her mind by piecing together what she'd learned: The PRC was systematically filling these ships in order—from the first pair nearest the harbor entrance—backward toward the end of the cavern. This enabled each succeeding pair to be a step behind the one just in front. They were also logically loading them from bottom to top to properly account for weight distribution and ballast. Jen again reasoned that, since it was self-evident that the cavern had secondarily served as a finishing yard, it must have been a sight to behold when the necessary army of workers swarmed onto these ships to construct the multi-decked upper levels, and to refine them into effective storage compartments that looked like typical container stacks. She also accepted that the Agency had dropped the ball by not infiltrating an agent at the beginning to ascertain what was going on. Now a launch was imminent—an assumption backed by thousands of soldiers streaming on board the first pair. However, personnel, food, small arms and ammo would not combine for enough weight to lower these big ladies to maximum capacity, and Jen wanted to find out what was.

Glancing down continually, Jen took note of the accouterments of shipbuilding scattered everywhere: Cranes on railroad tracks were now stationary against the walls; giant spools of steel cable were stacked there, too, along with arc-welding machines and a few piles of unused steel plate. Additionally, there was the nearly overwhelming odor of fresh paint. Giant fans and miles of exhaust ducts were visible as she made her way deeper into this hollowed-out mountain, and these measures were evidently powerful enough to drive out most of the dangerous fumes. But, at the height of the operation, the cavern's extensive exhaust system must have been taxed to capacity; she was living proof of the danger because she was developing a slight headache from the residual fumes that still collected near the ceiling.

Jen soon reached the fifth pair, and paused amidships to take note of something different being loaded into the "stack" behind the bridge: These two ships were receiving what appeared to be dozens or more of multiple rotary-wing aircraft— hexagonal-shaped drones about the size of VW Beetles. Each was painted with a camouflage matrix of greens and browns, and sported six small engines—each mounted with three-bladed propellers. Jen was no expert on drones but, as she studied one currently suspended in midair as the crane operator waited for it to stop swaying, she could see that it had 50-gallon-sized drums hanging under two stubby wings, and a bomb-looking thing attached under the middle. She wondered what might be concealed in the drums but, given the size of the drones, there was a lot of something. There were dozens of the drones resting on the flatcars of a waiting train, and the space behind the bridge could hold hundreds of them. *Why does a ground force need several hundred drones? How much observation capability does one brigade-sized unit need—unless these were similar to the U.S. Predators that carried Hellfire missiles?*

She didn't invest much time studying the sixth pair of ships, only noting that numerous tracked fighting vehicles were moving up their own heavy ramp, which was much thicker than the first. This one led up to a middle-level deck inside the main hull. These vehicles looked like the standard ZBD-04As she had seen many times in parades. But there was also a half-dozen of the new export models waiting on the quay for their turn—the VN-17s that were similar to her own country's Bradley Fighting Vehicles. Since the '17s were designed for the international market, she wondered briefly why they would be included in an assault package. Perhaps they were being tested under combat conditions—or to demonstrate capabilities for a future overseas market? *If that was true, it was very arrogant, to say the least!*

Hastening on, Jen finally arrived opposite the last pair of Dragons. She was beginning to wear down physically, but she had gotten the picture she desired of the immense threat these secret ships posed. The lowermost, and surely the most sturdy of the vehicle ramps, was resting on the quay, and of the width of the previously invisible hull doors. She guessed that when the ship was fully loaded, the lowermost ramp would rest nearly even with the dock. And it was impossible to miss what was rolling up it now: A steady line of heavy tanks—Type 99A Main Battle Tanks, she guessed—which were China's most modern and lethal ground weapons, and which packed a real punch. She occasionally hobnobbed with military officers, and one had taken her to a parade and bragged that these monsters sported 120mm cannons. But she was out of her depth now; all she could do was take pictures and include them in her report. The military guys would figure out the rest.

Throughout her traverse, Jen had been wondering how Allied satellites had missed the incredible stream of personnel and equipment that had been funneled here from all over China; the RNO folks from several countries should have picked up on this activity and shared the news. Her alarm had been growing proportionally as she made her way to the back of the cavern, and she had the disconcerting thought that she was the only Allied agent who possessed the absolutely crucial knowledge needed to confront this threat. If ever there was a "clear and present danger" to regional security, this was it! Then she spotted four tunnel openings at the end of the cavern, and the logistics flow became clear. She was thankful that she had decided to investigate the whole space, and now she'd go the second mile and check the tunnels to learn as much as she could. She lingered a minute to watch the huge tanks lumber up the ramp's gentle incline, and had a mental picture of a line of elephants marching along—lacking only the trunk-to-tail grasping she'd witnessed in the circus. She rested on her good knee for a minute as her mind churned, and she used the brief respite to calculate the fleet's enormous capacity: Though each tank weighed more than 50 tons, as long as they were securely clamped to the decks, their weight and bulk were easily handled by the ships' awesome displacement. She did some mental math and estimated that, if the tanks occupied the entire bottom level in front of the bridge, each ship could haul about 100 of the ominous-looking creatures. These assault merchies were true floating islands of destruction. Jen knew she was rightfully worried: Fourteen times the loads in these big babies would deliver a large army somewhere—arriving at their destination without raising suspicion. *This whole operation is bad news!* Though she guessed an invasion of Taiwan was the most logical target, she couldn't be certain: Further investigation might offer some clues, so she painfully rose to her feet and pressed on.

Jen mulled her options for gaining access to the tunnels, but it was going to be complicated. She was curious by nature—a character trait shared by all good field agents—and she could see that there were multiple tunnels feeding into the cavern. She surmised that they ran for miles through the spine and hills of the peninsula, and that transportation networks must deliver everything to central locations. She shuffled painfully to the end of her catwalk where it was anchored against the terminal wall and, craning her neck, surveyed the rock face and its honeycomb of steel beams that, like those against the ceiling, stabilized the end of the cavern. In vain she tried to locate a reasonable route to the floor, but the area was lit up like Times Square with no exploitable cover. There was no way she could climb down without being seen by the hundreds of workers laboring below—not to mention the military personnel scattered throughout. Using her binoculars, Jen spent five frustrating minutes scanning the roof, sides, and end of the cavern, plus the open area above the tunnel openings, but there simply was no promising route. Additionally, she couldn't descend to the quay dressed as a ninja; she needed an alternate strategy that included climbing down the ladder that connected the catwalks.

Desperate for ideas, Jen carefully glassed the workers and confirmed in 30 seconds that they all wore the same baggy outfits that were typical of those engaged in rough factory work throughout China. If she was to continue her mission—which meant blending in—she had to get into one of those outfits. Quickly Jen hit on the obvious: Out of necessity, she'd been keeping track of the occasional men and women working along the horizontal catwalks on both sides of the cavern and, if she could lure one of the females up to her level, she could disable her and take her set of more petite-sized clothing. But how to do so without raising an alarm? She cautiously peered down and back, remembering she'd just passed over a likely candidate.

Chapter 10

Outside Dalian Shipyard, 07:20 Hours

Dressed as a common laborer, Jen's CIA supervisor, Ken Hai Ling (MIT, Chinese Linguistics and History, 1989) pedaled past the top of the driveway that Jen had walked down earlier. Riding his old bicycle, he looked like a tired shift worker heading home to breakfast and bed. Some of his fellow bicyclists still wore Covid masks, though the government had officially declared the "American Military Flu" crisis over. The Agency had estimated that more than a million people had died in China, but the true numbers had been carefully covered up. Anecdotally, Ken encountered average people every day who spoke guardedly about missing loved ones, and he'd learned from his Agency briefings that 20 million cell phones had gone silent during those initial three months when the disease was racing through the people. It was unlikely that all the inactivity could be chalked up to canceled service contracts as the government claimed. Greater Wuhan and the surrounding provinces had lost a lot of people, and unconfirmed rumors continued to circulate that bodies had been buried in mass graves and/or cremated at night and their ashes scattered. At least none of Ken's team had gotten the terrible bug.

The Chinese government had done its best to contain the pandemic inside the country but, in the early weeks of the outbreak, they'd covered up the contagion for as long as possible—a clever strategy enabling them to gobble up every mask and ventilator in the world. They'd also allowed the bug to travel globally, and untold millions had been sickened; nearly 5 million had died. The cover-up of the initial accident seemed more than further negligence—the PRC authorities may have calculated that evolving disruption of the global economy could favor them. The vaccine had brought the pandemic under control, but the long-term damage to the international economy was ongoing. It was evil on a vast scale, and the local perpetrators were still trying to shift the blame to America. Fortunately for the United States, few inside or outside of China believed the CCP.

Ken was making his third pass since his first pre-dawn pull up the hill, and with each passing hour he'd become more and more certain that Jennifer had to spend the day hiding in the cave. He was wracked with guilt that he had let her undertake the dangerous mission in the first place—but, as usual, she had won the argument with her typical "mission-first" logic: She had the better skill-set to scale the cliff, and she was considerably younger and stronger than him, etc., etc. He had reluctantly agreed that she was right, but now she was way past her least optimistic completion time, and Ken was a profound worrier. It was more logical that she'd come out tonight as planned, and he had to cut her some slack due to unforeseen complications, but Jen's bike on the shoulder of the far lane was clearly visible leaning against a small stand of bamboo, and it just made him sad. He gave Jen the benefit of the doubt but, by three o'clock the next morning, he'd be a nervous wreck. He sighed in resignation; it was time to go home.

Ken pedaled a bit farther up the hill to a place where his turnaround would not be noticed, then joined the next throng heading downhill for work. As he slowly coasted along, he gratefully let gravity do the work, and pondered another complicating factor weighing on his soul: Jen had worked for him since she came to China, and he had grown to love her like his own daughter. He had always been a real mother hen to his agents anyway and, as he parceled out requests from Langley, he believed it was his duty to consider worst-case scenarios first and then work back from there. He knew what the shipyard's security people would do to Jen if they caught her—though he also knew how dangerous she could be when cornered. *Oh, Jen...where are you? Are you okay?* He steeled himself against the uneasy feelings that eroded his inner peace, and resolved to resist the temptation to make one more circuit with the next horde of shift workers. He'd spotted a couple of cameras mounted on tall steel poles along his route—an omnipresent reality in every industrialized area in China—not to mention in every nook and cranny in highly urbanized areas. He knew the government was feverishly working to install them everywhere, but he doubted he'd be noticed by the watchers today—he just blended in too well.

Ken had been in the Clandestine Service for more than 25 years, and he knew better than to hover. The rain had stopped, but the remaining grayness fit his mood to a tee. He shivered involuntarily, but not from the damp November morning, and continued toward his shanty as he was carried along with the stream of traffic. An uneventful half-hour later he arrived at the simple makeshift room he shared with his uncle—a real distant relative who would never guess that his nephew was a senior American agent. They did odd maintenance and painting jobs together that required them to move around the city—sometimes as members of larger crews as far away as Beijing—irregular travel that provided perfect cover for what Ken really did. It was now time for the two men to head out for their first job of the day, and he'd kill time painting the inside of a corrugated metal barn a few neighborhoods away. The drudgery would help his nerves.

Suddenly he had a happier thought: When Jen surfaced that night, she'd report to the safe house on the way back to the capital, and she'd be exuding barely contained joy at having pulled off another dangerous assignment. They'd meet for about an hour, then she'd make her way back to her regular apartment, and report for duty first thing the following morning (back after a restful "vacation in the south"). But, for the next 20 hours or so, there was nothing Ken could do to help her. He worried and prayed as he pushed his bike inside Uncle Bi's odd-sized tarpaper-covered board and plywood home.

Inside the cavern

Enough dilly-dallying! Jen chided herself, and decided on a course of action. It was risky, to say the least, but her plan offered a reasonable chance to explore the mysterious tunnels. She'd noticed that the workers on the lower three catwalks on both sides of the cavern were occupied with routine maintenance, with several currently performing checks on what looked like electrical junction boxes, or on the red-and-white fire extinguishers hung strategically throughout. These latter devices were vital because, next to mass suffocation, fire must be the chief concern in this enclosed space. And, given the large amount of ammunition and fuel on every ship, a major fire could sympathetically detonate the lot with a resulting conflagration that would cause the cavern to erupt like a horizontal volcano. Jen knew in her heart that if she confirmed that the purpose of this fleet was to attack America, she'd instigate that very option. But she didn't know, so starting a war with China was not on the table.

Jen focused her attention on the young woman she'd spotted earlier. She was working alone on the catwalk just below, and was the perfect target. Jen moved nearer to the end wall where the catwalk stopped just two meters short of the terminal wall, and carefully examined the sturdy steel ladder. It had the typical attached half-moon protective cage that ran all the way down to the quay, and had been welded to each catwalk level, and also bolted directly into the cement-covered wall to give it strength. The ladder permitted vertical access to all four horizontal walkways, and Jen risked a peek through the opening to confirm that her likely target was just a few yards back, and currently monkeying with one of the junction boxes.

Now all Jen had to do was get the woman to come up to her level by herself, subdue her without creating any noticeable disturbance, change into the woman's outfit, descend the ladder 400 feet to the quay, and begin scouting the tunnel system. *And I was worried,* she thought sarcastically. In truth, she knew she had zero room for error. She examined the two-meter space that was all that was left between the ladder handholds and the sheer rock face. The ladder was constructed so that whoever climbed it would face the wall and would notice someone crouching close by as soon as their head rose above the catwalk. However, because the corner was in deep shadow above the light panels, and because the natural way to glance was to the right, meaning back down the catwalk, Jen had a realistic chance of surprising her quarry. *Well, nothing ventured...* Jen took a deep breath and lay face-down on the heavy mesh, pulled off her hood and shook her hair to look reasonably normal. Then she leaned through the ladder opening and whispered just loud enough to be heard, "Qing wen…Qing Jiuming!" "Excuse me…please help…I have an emergency!" This was Jen's one and only chance: If the woman yelled for additional help from her colleagues farther down her catwalk, the game was up. Jen had her pistol, but how much good would it do? She wouldn't last long in a firefight that was 400 feet above a cement floor with no way out—not to mention that she'd be fighting against thousands of heavily armed soldiers who'd want her dead.

However, to Jen's considerable relief, the woman looked up when she heard Jen's subdued voice and smiled. "Hao de!" she replied at once. "Okay…" The young woman had matched Jen's whisper—two young women with a conspiracy—and she'd immediately set down the pair of pliers she'd been using. Without so much as a glance back down her own catwalk, she walked quickly toward the ladder and began to climb the 100 feet to Jen's level.

Jen was a bit taken aback by this immediately helpful response, and she had to quickly shift her position so that she could crouch in the corner and prepare her assault. She pulled her dark hood back in place, squatted in the limited space, and readied herself to pounce on this nice young person the moment she appeared. Jen had no intention of hurting this girl—she looked like a teenager about the same age as the gate guards she'd confronted earlier. But Jen was confident that she could render her "victim" unconscious without causing the girl any permanent damage. Still, it was a violent act—and Jen hoped it would be the worst thing this young one would ever experience. Jen tensed as she felt the slight vibration from the ladder, and momentarily a head popped into view. *There!* The girl indeed glanced to her right back down the catwalk, giving Jen the single second she needed. She slipped an arm-bar around the girl's slender neck, and with the vice-like power she'd developed during her many years of martial arts strength training, she lifted the hapless girl out of the ladder space before she could start thrashing. Jen held her pinned against her own chest for a few seconds until her prey went limp. Then, with the girl lying unconscious in her arms, she dragged her gently to a safe spot away from the ladder opening where she couldn't be spotted from below.

There was a six-inch toe-kick that ran the length of the cavern-side of the catwalk to keep tools from being accidentally knocked off (hence becoming lethal missiles against the people below) so Jen knew the girl would not roll off when regaining her senses. She laid the girl down and quickly glanced around to see if the encounter had been witnessed, but everyone continued their duties without giving her corner of the cavern a second look. Jen had to move fast because the girl would surface within the half hour. She removed the woman's overalls but left her otherwise clothed in her ordinary work shirt and pants. Jen quickly pulled the overalls over her ninja outfit and tucked her hood beneath the outfit's large collar. To complete the look, she removed the woman's dark blue head scarf and placed it on her own head in the same manner as its rightful owner. She considered the shoes, but decided her own dull gray climbing shoes, though scuffed and a bit worse for wear, were not that much different in appearance from the common sport shoes worn by her inert victim. And besides that, she didn't want to risk additional damage and bleeding to her injured feet.

After a quick check to ensure that the woman's ID tag was still firmly clipped to the pocket, and further confirming that her own fanny pack and pistol were not too obvious inside the loose overalls, Jen zipped them to her neck. The outfit wasn't perfect but would pass casual muster. Her immediate fear was overheating in the double outfit, but she guessed the cavern was fairly cool at floor level this time of year. Jen finished the look by rubbing her hands across the wall to pick up a smear of dusty oil, and rubbed a few streaks over the back of her bandaged fingers and hands—with a little on her face for good measure. The dirt covered her bandages a bit, and incidental workplace injuries would be commonplace in this hazardous environment. Finally, with her heart racing, Jen stood fully erect for the first time, stepped onto the ladder, and began her 400-foot descent to the quay.

Except for the pain in her hands, the first 100 feet to the next catwalk went without a hitch. But, as Jen passed that level, a male workman about 50 yards farther down from the spot where the young woman had been working, called over and asked a bit imperiously what she was doing. Jen figured this was a foreman and, though she didn't slow her descent, she meekly called to him that she was headed for the "little house," hoping it passed for a reference to the bathroom. The man just grunted in apparent indifference and turned back to his own project. The rest of the descent was incident-free, and it wasn't long before Jen touched down on solid cement. She turned around to get her bearings and looked up at the stern end of the truly imposing ship to her front. *You magnificent beast!* she thought to herself as she walked toward the middle of the quay before turning to her right toward the nearest tunnel. Her hands hurt like the dickens from her descent, and a little blood seeped through the bandages but, other than that, she was ready for the next phase of her journey.

The first thing Jen had to process was the general chaos on the quay: The din that had been somewhat remote from 400 feet up became specific as foremen shouted over hundreds of normal conversations, and clanging metal and the whine of giant motors in overhead gantries overpowered everything else. Jen was expecting odors more intense than those wafting around the ceiling area, but she hadn't been prepared for the nauseating olfactory assault she encountered as she mixed with the workers. The level of danger from the combined exhaust fumes was better, but the whole place reeked of human sweat and the murky water where the ships rested. It was a tribute to the laboring ventilation system that people didn't just keel over.

Jen navigated around dozens of workers straining on thin cables that draped down from the closest ship's fantail, and briefly walked between a spread-out line of camouflaged tanks emerging from the closest tunnel. Railroad tracks ran from all four tunnels, and small electric trains were quietly rumbling on each. The tanks she could touch were inching along the quay toward their turn on the ramp, and Jen tried not to rubberneck as she took in the interesting sights. She'd pocketed her camera before leaving the catwalk so photos were out, but her expanded mission was to explore one or more of the tunnels and photos weren't necessary. She fell in with a flow of workers who were skirting one of the slow-moving electric trains—its powerful motor growling and its brakes squeaking in seeming protest from the weight of a gigantic generator on its flatcar. It was organized chaos for sure, but the system seemed to be working: The equipment was being systematically loaded on the ships, and a line of soldiers was emerging from the farthest tunnel and filing along the far wall until they could board their assigned Dragon. Jen was suddenly troubled with a related thought, wondering how many workers had died during several years in this dangerous environment.

The train came to a halt and two dozen technicians swarmed onto the generator's flatcar, dragging heavy-gauge electrical cords with them. Some immediately plugged the cords into the room-sized machine's numerous electrical ports and snapped them in place, while others proceeded to toggle switches and study gauges. Then, a few seconds later, a middle-aged female foreman barked a command Jen couldn't make out, and pushed a prominent red button on the control panel. Jen cringed as the several-ton behemoth roared to life, and she guessed from the line of cables that it had been summoned to provide power to a sturdy-looking sand-blasting machine situated on the quay next to the ship.

Jen tried to take everything in as she shuffled along with the foot traffic, and couldn't help but wonder at the lack of safety procedures throughout. But she wasn't surprised either: During her years in China, she had come to understand that lower-level workers were viewed as expendable by owners and various authorities, and were sometimes provided little in the way of safety equipment. She did note that, at least here, the welders had face shields to protect them from sparks—and that the pair of men standing by the sandblasting machine were pulling on heavy canvas gloves and hoods, and had goggles draped around their necks. This plethora of safety equipment contrasted starkly with several small shops she'd spotted on the outskirts of Beijing, where iron work was done with simple goggles and gloves—with no other "luxuries" such as OSHA standards demanded back home. Consequently, workers' faces had a variety of red welts, burns, and scars that would mark them for life.

Jen peeled off from the first group and blended in with a different one that was taking a direct line toward the right-hand tunnel—careful to avoid being squashed by the line of tanks emerging from the next tunnel to her left. Together her group squeezed past a cluster of men and women laboring to push a large coil of bright blue mooring rope across the tracks behind the generator's flatcar. Then, a few paces later, Jen's group compacted even more and climbed three broad cement steps that led up to a 20-foot-wide pedestrian ramp running inside the tunnel. *Here goes nothing,* she said to herself as she pushed her way into the relatively dark passage.

After the bright lights of the cavern, the tunnel's string of bare light bulbs kept the walkway just safe enough to avoid tripping over other people or falling over the low hand rail onto the cement below. But there was enough light to spot the two parallel sets of heavy steel railroad tracks situated between the wider cement tracks that turned the tunnel into a dual-purpose passage way: The trains used the tracks and vehicles could roll easily on the cement. And, to her immediate relief, there was a steady breeze bringing fresher air from somewhere ahead.

Streams of people moved both ways, so she allowed herself to be carried along by the flow on the side closest to the railing. She shuffled her feet with the crowd for several minutes before natural light appeared ahead. Then she had a revelation: *Oh... it's the first covered dry dock!* When she entered the shipyard in the darkness, she'd been so focused on the cliff rising to her right that she'd ignored the row of large buildings that jutted out into the harbor to her left. As she got her bearings, she realized that the long tunnel had curved slightly from northwest to north, and that the cavern was dug so deep into the bedrock that the tunnels ran under the edge of the shipyard. *The tunnels must run to both sides of the peninsula as well as through it, Jen reasoned, with the middle two extending directly under the spine.* Her rightmost tunnel gradually rose until it entered the first of 14 dry docks where the hulls were constructed. The other three tunnels all ran farther west, and she estimated that the farthest one must be close to the Bohai Sea itself. That's why they were invisible to the satellites. Jen was impressed again.

Chapter 11

Dry-dock revelations, 09:05 Hours

Jen's crowd spilled into the first dry dock, then dispersed in a hundred directions toward various exits or other duties. The buildings had been constructed across the relatively narrow beach between the mountainous spine of the peninsula and the harbor itself, and Jen reasoned that the latter portion rested on wooden pilings sunk into the harbor sand and probably into the underlying bedrock. Each building was large enough to construct one Dragon ship's hull, and the center was deep enough to float the finished hull—making it a giant cement bathtub at least 40 feet deep. Additionally, there were cement quays running parallel to each dock, an impressive feat that required sectioning off the water so that forms could be built and hundreds of thousands of cubic yards of cement poured. The resulting surface area supported the equipment, material, cranes, and vehicles necessary to construct the ships. There were countersunk railroad tracks on each side of the water-filled space that the cranes slid on—presently busy unloading a small freighter that had pulled inside the space. Jen had seen the row of buildings in the distance during her brief off-shore survey of the cavern, and it had been hard to comprehend how spacious they were. But now inside, she noted that each building was, of necessity, much deeper and wider than the awesome 1,000-foot hulls they'd been built to accommodate.

The freighter was currently the center of attention as crews off-loaded quantities of material secured to large wooden or steel pallets—each covered with snuggly-fitting tan or green canvas. Cranes lowered these pallets onto waiting railroad flatcars connected to the same electric engines Jen had seen earlier, and several large forklifts moved pallets apparently off-loaded earlier. She imagined this operation to be identical in the remaining 13 dry docks, though floor-to-ceiling wooden partitions separated each space. Each crane and forklift moved in concert to off-load and move the cargo—an orchestrated dance that would impress the most demanding logistician (or choreographer).

Everywhere a beehive of workers moved with urgency to complete their tasks, and Jen's ears were assaulted by an incredible variety of noises that, though less than what she'd experienced inside the cavern, were still pretty intense. Steel pallets banged onto steel flatcars; crane engines strained under maximum loads; hundreds of people shouted in every direction for an untold number of reasons. It was an immense (and immensely complicated) operation that required an incredibly talented visionary to put it all together. Jen marveled at what planning and resources it must have taken to build, equip, and load the massive ships now nearing completion inside the cavern—not to mention the parallel jobs required in these dry docks that were still being used to bring in supplies. At least Jen had discovered this giant ruse before the dangerous ships put to sea—with no other purpose than to start a war!

Jen had to keep moving to avoid attention, but she soaked in her surroundings like a sponge. She took more than an hour to move past all 14 docks, then risked a glance through a dirty window in the last wall that separated her from the balance of the shipyard just beyond. The Dragon's dry docks effectively cut the shipyard in two. The window was smudged with oil and grime, but she could see enough to confirm that there was nothing beyond except a similar collection of ships and boats like she'd passed through that morning. Jen was nearly exhausted and in continual pain, and she believed she'd gathered enough evidence to sound a coherent alarm. She had to find an alternative way out of the complex, having rejected her original plan out of necessity: When she rendered the female worker unconscious and took her clothing, she could never go back that way. There was also some urgency to leave: That woman would be awake now and security personnel would be searching for her attacker everywhere.

Jen still wanted to scout the other three tunnels, but it really wasn't necessary: Her report would alert the authorities and U.S. Navy and/or Allied submarines would stalk the Dragons until their true purpose was revealed. If aggressive intent was in the offing, the big merchies could be sent to the bottom in an hour. She also believed that the other three tunnel exits must be visible if someone really looked for them, because endless trainloads of tanks, vehicles, personnel and drones being funneled into a limited area couldn't be ***that*** disguised—plus soldiers (a ***lot*** of soldiers) were streaming in from posts all over eastern China. Jen didn't envy President Stilwell, who would have to confront President Han and get him to take a step back from this international adventurism—and she hoped it was really Han in charge of this dangerous gambit because, if it were rogue military types, China was in for a world-class civil war. After what she'd just seen, Jen didn't think any worse-case scenario was an exaggeration.

Jen moved to an unobtrusive vantage point next to a large pile of folded cardboard cartons, and paused to decide on the best way out. She had many thoughts vying for attention, including the revelation that each freighter off-loading cargo sported a different civilian livery. This meant that each was different enough from one another in paint schemes and structure to blend into the general maritime traffic. In fact, they probably *were* the normal maritime traffic. *No wonder our satellites didn't pick this up!* The ports and littoral areas along the Chinese coast were always busy places anyway, so hiding in plain sight was easy. Jen had been observing this place for three days and hadn't taken any special note—shipyards were logically busy places anyway. Then she had a confirming revelation: That was the whole point of the Dragon Fleet! *They'd been constructed amid much fanfare and PR to do just that—**Hide in Plain Sight.** This fleet of super container ships had been announced years before—meaning their planning cycle was also years in the making. The PRC had pulled this whole thing off right under the world's nose.* It was clearly not a rogue operation, but it did have extraordinary compartmentalization. Not one of the rank-and-file Second Directorate folks she worked with had uttered a word, though she guessed only the senior-most echelon knew what was going on. The overall project was a secret tightly controlled by a very few at the top of the government, and now it was up to Jen to get the word out.

But it was not to be.

Jen began picking her way toward the exit farther along the wall of Building 14, weaving through throngs of busy workers, cranes, and small trains. She had spotted an unobtrusive doorway after quickly rejecting the idea of climbing through one of the windows—people were everywhere and they'd simply grab her. And making a run for it and subsequently squeezing through a torn fence on the other side of the vacant lot next door was just suicide. If she could exit with other workers and make it into the main part of the shipyard, she could blend in and leave with the crowd. From there she could make it back to her bicycle and rendezvous with Ken. She'd abandoned the idea of returning to her uniform now—she or someone else would have to retrieve it some other time. And, though it was important because her ID was there, nothing was as important as the information she had collected today—she could even alert her supervisor that the uniform had been stolen…or abandon her previous cover altogether and end her tenure in China—her discoveries were that important. She paralleled the normal-sized coastal freighter docked to her right, and made a beeline for the exit she could see ahead—obviously provided so workers didn't have to walk all the way back through the 14 dry docks after their shifts ended. Jen noticed that a significant queue had formed, and she'd just join the line.

When she got within a few paces of the line, Jen watched the guards checking badges, but she was pretty sure she could use her injured hands as an excuse—her hastily concocted story was that her supervisor had ordered her to use this exit because it was closest to the shipyard clinic. She'd almost reached the back of the queue when she sensed hurried footsteps behind her. She made a subtle sidestep to let them pass, but instead she felt a hard finger tap on her shoulder. She stiffened but turned with eyes downcast in what she hoped was her best submissive worker's persona.

"What are you doing in this unloading area?" an authoritarian male voice demanded.

She looked up and was face to face with a beady-eyed, little ferret of a security guard flanked by two others. He had corporal chevrons on his green coat, but he wasn't military like the two boys Jen had engaged earlier. He was internal security, and obviously full of self-importance. The two similarly dressed guards bracketing him both wore holstered side arms.

"I was directed to this exit by my supervisor…I injured my hands an hour ago," Jen offered meekly and raised her bandaged hands as proof. Her mind now quieted as she considered her options.

"From a section that works inside the cavern? That never happens! You must come with us!"

"But, sir, my hands hurt. Besides, I don't want to get in trouble with my supervisor. He is in charge of more than 100 of us!" Her statement would vault the authority of her "supervisor" several levels above this little rat and his two flunkies. She hoped it would intimidate them into backing down.

The three indeed exchanged somewhat worried looks before refocusing on the scared common worker cowering before them—a little dirt-stained female that, at least, was showing proper deference to their superior positions. And her hands were indeed a mess. But the central figure in this four-person drama had his orders, too: Anyone wearing the wrong badge was to be brought to a security supervisor—no exception! They were all on the alert for a troublemaker of some kind, and his department was in a tizzy. He decided to soften his tone a bit—this peasant girl might be telling the truth and he didn't want to get on the bad side of someone who out-ranked his own sergeant. "You must come with us. No exceptions!" he quoted, "but if your story is true, you will be allowed to proceed to the clinic."

Jen quickly evaluated that it would be easier to make a break for it close to an exit doorway, rather than from a security station deeper inside the complex. So, without warning, she instinctively selected a non-lethal thrust from her martial arts repertoire and drove her wedged hand into the ferret's throat. He gasped in pain and surprise, and dropped like a stone. Jen operated under the philosophy that it was usually more beneficial to temporarily maim threatening people than to kill them: People writhing in pain added complexity to any attempted diversion, and she needed confusion now to aid her escape. As the first man fell to his knees choking and grasping his throat, the man to his left lunged for Jen with his arms outstretched. Her countering move was a blur as she dislocated the man's elbow with an audible snap, and he too screamed in pain and crumpled at her feet. Lastly, she sidestepped the third guard's wildly swinging fist and struck his left lower leg with her right foot, breaking the "tib/fib" bones just above his ankle. All three men morphed into a disorganized heap of screaming, cursing, commotion—chaos she needed to cover her dash toward her only point of escape.

However, Jen instantly re-evaluated her plan because the doorway exit was jammed with workers—they were several layers deep and would block her way. But the harbor's inviting surface was visible through the partially opened door only a few yards farther on, and the 50-foot-deep water offered a better chance than running through the shipyard. She was like a porpoise in the water and it would take time to organize boats to look for her. She fished out her gun as she quickly accelerated, and her purposeful strides had her on the verge of freedom when a gunshot rang out behind her. The impact of the bullet sent her flying and ended her escape; she'd not spotted a fourth guard standing behind the other three, and bystanders later recounted that a little sheet of flame erupted from the tip of the shooter's pistol barrel.

Chapter 12

Central Medical Clinic, Dalian Shipyard
November 24th, 11:35 Hours

Jen slowly emerged from the depths of unconsciousness. Her mind was fuzzy and her soul deeply troubled after a series of nightmarish dreams. She couldn't remember all the grisly details—only that her dreams had been terrible and numerous. In them she'd faced one near-disaster after another, and though she'd called to her parents for help, they always seemed to be mere observers who couldn't rescue her. She also had vivid memories of a pack of ferocious wolves chasing her, but even her beloved fiancé Tim ignored her cries for help. Then she was drowning in pounding surf that dragged her down into darkness—her hands and feet entangled in strands of clinging kelp. Then she was climbing an impossible cliff. When her feet slipped, her clawing hands found no traction as she plummeted into an abyss—extreme panic gripping her as she fell toward snarling black dogs. In some part of her mind, she was certain that none of this was real—but, if not, why couldn't she wake up?

Gradually her mind began to clear, and even with her eyes tightly clenched, Jen perceived a bright light directly overhead. But rather than offer comfort, these beginnings of consciousness brought a new wave of emotional turmoil: She began to recall who and where she was—and the violence that had led to her capture. She tried to think—to gain full control of her senses—but, even as she did so, her training kicked in, and she knew she had to keep from giving herself away. Someone else was controlling her now, so masking her recovery was important; she willed her body to remain limp even as her mind activated and she took stock of her situation:

It was immediately clear that she was tightly and painfully bound—stretched lengthwise on her back on a cold surface with her wrists and ankles squeezed by rope or tape. She was lying on either a table or the floor, with her hands and feet each separated by the width of her shoulders. She guessed that a table was more likely because it somehow felt less solid beneath her than a cement or stone floor would be. Then she had a terrible realization: *Oh, God, I am naked!* She inwardly cringed and felt horribly vulnerable, exposed, and powerless. But even as her heart raced, she also realized that she was, in fact, lightly covered, and felt gratitude to the stranger who had spread a sheet over her body.

As she took stock of her situation, she next realized that she was seriously injured: Intense pain flooded her senses, and she hurt everywhere. Her wrists and ankles were constricted, but her head ached something fierce, too. Then she suddenly and involuntarily flinched as she remembered her last visual experience before blacking out: A short length of metal pipe arching down toward her head, and her mental snapshot of the angry eyes of the longshoreman who had ended her flight.

Men with guns! Memories of her confrontation now flooded her consciousness, but they also reminded her that she was alive. So, with a concerted effort, Jen calmed herself and focused on the present. She decided on a head-to-toe medical self-assessment: *Head...severe headache but I can think. Neck...okay. Arms...pain. Shoulders...oh, the left one was bad!* Severe pain throbbed in her left shoulder and radiated the length of her arm and across the top of her back. This realization caused another flashback: A shot had rung out behind her as she'd fled—her dash for freedom ended after only a few strides. Each step had brought her nearer the promised freedom at the end of a building—the beckoning safety of the harbor's deep water behind the ship—but it had ended abruptly with the shot and its brief aftermath.

Jen remembered the guards, and accepted that the shot was fired from one she hadn't seen. She'd successfully disabled the three men who'd initially confronted her, recalling her brief struggle and her attempt to escape. She'd run, using skills from her high school soccer days, dashing in and out, changing direction to throw off her pursuers, weaving between dozens of startled and even frightened workers who, before her noisy confrontation with the security detail, had been feverishly separating loaded pallets descending from the stern deck of the freighter alongside. She remembered the crack of a gun and her involuntary grunt as the bullet knocked her forward. Part of her mind professionally identified the sound as that of a pistol—probably a 9mm—the standard issue of both the Chinese military and her own MSS organization. But the bullet's impact, combined with her sprinter's speed, had slammed her into the next knot of startled workers with such force that they were knocked in every direction like bowling pins.

She remembered extracting her own compact small-caliber pistol during her run, but the impact of her landing had knocked it out of her hand. She'd watched helplessly as it bounced and skidded across the unyielding cement until it banged against a stack of corrugated sheet metal 10 feet away. She'd ignored her injury and clawed her way toward it—arms and legs fighting for traction on the smelly, wet, and oily surface—scrambling over the people she'd knocked down in her final desperate attempt to elude capture. Hands grabbed at her, but she'd fought them off with her good arm and struck out with her legs, rolling and straining with every fiber to reach the pistol that offered the only realistic chance of escape.

Finally! She reached it and snatched it off the rough surface. It felt cool in her normal shooting hand—an old friend she knew well. It provided a little victory that gave her a surge of energy—a second chance to escape! She'd rotated back toward the shooter, using her injured left shoulder as a painful fulcrum, clenching her teeth against the wound's searing pain, but it was all for naught: A dock worker holding a length of heavy pipe had pounced on her like a lion. She'd noticed the movement in her peripheral vision and seen the arc of the weapon as he swung it toward her, but before she could adjust her position to parry the blow, he'd bashed her in the head and the lights went out. Her present situation was testimony to the fact that he'd hit her just hard enough to knock her unconscious: If he'd hit her any harder, she'd already be dead.

Jen now attempted to counteract the pain in her shoulder by employing a martial arts technique wherein she "went into herself." "Prana" was the term her sensei used, and she hoped it would help her compartmentalize the pain. This line of thinking caused her to have a pleasant memory of the beloved master who had trained her from childhood. His kindly face reminded her of the endless hope that self-discipline offered. It was never intended as a substitute for her Christian faith—but it had helped her develop her God-given skills.

Jen was starting to feel better. The pain was still just as real, but at least its tentacles no longer dominated her thoughts. She used the respite to stabilize her heart rate, and she continued her assessment: Her chest and abdomen seemed okay. A little sore but nothing she couldn't manage. Then lower. "Down there," her grandmother used to say when teaching her about the things a young lady should know. The dear elderly woman had used the cute Asian euphemism "butterfly" when she'd taught Jen and her younger sister how proper Chinese girls from good families should think and act. Then Jen flinched when she realized there was sharp pain there, too. *Oh, God...have I been raped?* That thought was so repulsive that she mentally and emotionally recoiled from it. But even as she resisted that terrible reality, the analytical part of her brain knew it made sense: She'd quickly disarmed the three-person security team's obvious leader and his two underlings and injured them painfully, then fought like a caged animal against violent men she'd humiliated in front of a crowd. An angry bystander or group of them might have taken revenge by dragging her into some corner and assaulting her.

But Jen had to fight off the horror of that line of thinking—her survival depended on compartmentalizing what might have been done to her body. Emotionally she couldn't fall apart now—failure would mean the certain death of her mission. She was thoroughly trussed, but that also proved that her arms and legs were intact, not broken, and that her captors believed she was more valuable alive than dead. They would logically understand that she possessed real intelligence value. Jen knew why she was being kept alive: She faced terrible torture and the very real possibility that she would tell all and expose her known CIA colleagues to equally horrible deaths. So now it was imperative that she formulate a workable plan; if she could somehow get loose, she could still fight. And, in spite of her painful injuries, in any enclosed space against limited numbers she felt confident of her skills.

She hadn't yet opened her eyes, but the overhead light obviously came from a lamp that had been focused directly onto her face—it was powerful enough that she could feel its warmth. She shifted her focus from assessing her physical condition to assessing her surroundings; she listened carefully and began asking herself relevant questions: Was anyone nearby? What kind of room was she in? But before she could analyze her situation further, she was startled by a woman's voice:

"I can see you are waking up, little flower." A pleasant, middle-aged female voice. Words spoken warmly in Mandarin, yet with a touch of authority. "Don't pretend otherwise. I am Doctor Ling, the physician who treated your gunshot wound. I've been caring for you since the policemen brought you to my clinic nearly three hours ago…"

A doctor…that could be very good. Jen considered playing possum a bit longer but logic dictated that it served no useful purpose. Her only hope now was getting loose, and she was so tightly bound that she needed help. With some effort she pried open her eyes until they were tiny slits, but the light was so intense that she snapped them closed again.

"Too bright," she whispered weakly, careful to modulate her adopted Mandarin dialect. At the same time, she suddenly had the awful thought that she might have muttered in English during her earlier delirium.

"Yes, I will dim that. I needed it bright to tend to your injuries…" Doctor Ling Qui Lai stepped to the wall and twisted the round dimmer switch until the overhead circular medical lamp faded to a pleasant softness. Then she returned to her patient's side and regarded the young woman clinically: According to the security team, she was quite a fighter—martial arts training, for sure. And Dr. Ling had no trouble believing them: One of the men carried over from the nearby dry dock building had needed emergency surgery to repair his damaged larynx. This little tigress had reportedly hit him with a flat-handed strike to the throat. The man was lucky not to have suffocated to death on the spot. After Ling stabilized him, she had sent him for more sophisticated surgery in the main hospital in Dalian City. She'd also glanced at the second and third security men: One had a broken shoulder blade and dislocated elbow, and the other had lower leg fractures. They had been treated by staff doctors in another room of the clinic, interviewed by the base security team, and then also sent over to the city hospital.

That Ling had been onsite today was complete luck: Her regular office was in the provincial MSS headquarters, where she was assigned as both a staff physician and (on an "as-needed" basis) as a member of the provincial interrogation team. But, quarterly, her duties required her to inspect the medical records staff doctors maintained in this secure facility within the secret section of Dalian Port. She knew about the special fleet of ships from conversations with many who worked in the space. The MSS had spies among the workers—as did the PAP cadres who were looking for troublemakers—but overall security was the responsibility of the PLA military police and intelligence branches.

Today just happened to be one of Ling's four annual site visits—how fortuitous that she'd been here during the most exciting day that any of them could remember. She could use her skills on this obvious spy—hopefully discovering who she was spying for. Judging by the woman's mumblings, her prisoner's accent was southern—perhaps an agent from a separatist Hong Kong group. This situation presented a real opportunity to advance Ling's career, and she was excited. If she could discern anything of real intelligence value, it would be a feather in her cap. Rather than the boring routine inspection that she'd dreaded when she left her nice apartment that morning, it had turned into the most interesting day of the year. But it was a very bad day that would get a lot worse for the young woman she had strapped to her exam table: Ling had seen first-hand what the MSS boys did with pretty girls like this.

As she stood by the table, quietly watching as her prisoner regained consciousness, Ling rehearsed lessons she had learned through experience and experimentation: The best way to approach a patient (criminal or otherwise) was to use situationally appropriate psychology—and, with criminals specifically, that usually meant avoiding the rough stuff during the early stages of an interrogation. She would apply her psychological skills first—techniques that worked particularly well with younger prisoners. She usually began her sessions in the role of the warm, caring, and benevolent "aunty"...that is, the kindly family doctor most everyone remembered from early childhood. She was that family friend, the one trusted by a child's parents who was naturally sympathetic to a patient's needs and feelings. She had used this technique to extract considerable useful information from the various trouble-makers and law-breakers that came through her district headquarters, and when she was done with her role-playing (which she combined with the prodigious application of a witch's brew of pharmaceuticals), she'd then hand the prisoner over to her colleagues in the nearest MSS detention facility, whose "break" teams would relish applying their traditional array of harsher techniques. In this case, it would be the Dalian headquarters, whose personnel she had not worked with yet. When they were done with a prisoner (if he or she was still alive), a final disposition would be made. That usually meant a bullet in the back of the unfortunate's head, administered by their section chief out behind the main interrogation building. Ling avoided those executions and executioners because they were in a different section, and because they were unrefined and arrogant bullies, to say the least. Just then, Ling's musings were interrupted when the young woman asked a coherent question:

"Where am I?" Jen asked groggily. She knew she had to build rapport with this doctor and extract as much useful information as possible. Every detail could be a vital piece of an escape plan, and she had to get out so she could complete her mission. And, though it was not as important as the big picture, Jen was somewhat relieved that a woman was attending her, and that the two of them seemed to be alone. Men could be manipulated in different ways, and their psychology was less complex. But the hardest scenario of all was when both genders were present—though playing men and women off each other also worked if done adroitly. Jen was hungry for details when the doctor replied pleasantly:

"After your altercation in the cargo area, a group of security guards brought you to our medical facility. We don't treat many gunshots here…" Ling added this superfluous tidbit, part of establishing normal doctor/patient rapport. She wanted this young woman talking and relaxed as much as possible so relevant facts slipped out. After cleaning up this woman's "through-and-through" gunshot wound, Ling had inserted a drip that fed a mild hallucinogenic into her patient/prisoner's arm to keep her off-balance. The initial batch was exhausted so she'd soon hang a new bag if this first conversation indicated it would facilitate the "gentle" interrogation phase.

"Don't worry," she told Jen, "the bullet didn't cause any permanent damage and you should heal nicely. You are probably also wondering about the pain in your groin. Don't worry, little one: As part of my complete medical examination, I discovered that you were a virgin. I had to surgically cut your hymen to make sure that you didn't have anything inside you that was against our rules." Actually, Ling had been quite surprised when she discovered that she had a chaste woman in her care; not only was it rare these days, but the girl's morality could be useful at some point over the next hours or days as she and her team collaborated to extract information. This one was spying for someone, and it was a priority for her MSS team and their PAP counterparts to discover who their petite captive worked for. And, if this one was not from Hong Kong, which the Politburo had recently decided to bring into the fold with appropriate force, she might be a Taiwanese agent—and that would be sweet indeed. Ling, like most government professionals, longed for the day when Taiwan would be reunited with the mainland. And, if the political and military leaders of the PRC succeeded in forcing the rebellious province to surrender, Ling and the rest of her intelligence colleagues would have years of interesting work ahead, debriefing the captured rebel leaders and their families.

Her prisoner today had been carrying a broken yet sophisticated camera with satellite technology, plus a pistol, climbing shoes of western manufacture, and some medical and nourishment items. She had also employed dramatically different levels of violence twice during her sojourn through the complex, and the assessment team was still trying to determine how she entered the site. She must have been the one who overpowered a young female worker in the "finishing grotto" where the special fleet's construction was nearly complete. This assault had happened early in the morning, but for some reason the prisoner had not killed the worker, only incapacitated her. The prisoner had taken the worker's outer clothing to use as a disguise, and subsequently made her way through the tunnels and main cargo-dispersal buildings where the ships' hulls had been constructed. Ling had cut off the stolen overalls and an underlying camouflaged skin-tight body suit to do her medical work, and she was impressed by this young women's obvious conditioning—she was in superb physical shape.

The prisoner's camera was currently being examined by technical experts that had rushed over from the MSS HQ in Dalian City, and it would be interesting to see if they could discover what the woman recorded. How lucky for all concerned that its transmission mechanism appeared broken.

Physically, Ling had discovered that her prisoner's fingers and knees had been badly injured, but not from her fight with the guards or during her brief escape attempt. That fact, combined with that of the climbing shoes, made Ling suspect that this woman had climbed up the rock face near the cavern's entrance to get inside. If that was true, especially given the context of last night's weather, it was an incredible accomplishment. It would also mean she had traversed the entire complex with a satellite camera without being spotted. Ling was fairly well acquainted with the somewhat haughty colonel who was charged with facility security, and she figured he must be sweating bricks at that very moment. She chuckled to herself at that amusing prospect—the man was an arrogant ass.

Ling had also taken note of the woman's dental work that suggested western expertise and materials—a significant clue because her teeth were too good for her to have grown up in the PRC. So, what did it all add up too? Her accent during her drug-induced mumblings suggested a mixture of Mandarin and Guangdong regional Cantonese. This was curious because Ling had confidence in her drugs: When awake, a subject might have enough training to resist the usual doses in the bloodstream and fake it, but resistance was highly unlikely when sedated. Her Mandarin was native-level, too—at least her comprehension was confirmed during the rapid-fire test Ling had just administered. That suggested either confirmation of whatever story her patient/prisoner would claim—or it could reveal significant schooling of a skilled agent by a foreign power. *Fate has given me a delightful puzzle to solve!* Ling had to pinch herself to contain her excitement.

As Jen watched the doctor process her language skills, she admitted to herself that she was relieved at the doctor's news about her medical condition—especially about her "private area" injuries. But Jen remained on guard. This doctor was all sweetness and light now, but she wouldn't be trusted with a class one prisoner unless she was a fairly high level (and probably MSS or PAP) government agent. Jen was intimately familiar with the Chinese bureaucracy, and she had to use that to her immediate advantage. Honesty was a good first approach, "It is a relief to know I wasn't violated by men…" *Just keep the doctor chatting and build a bridge of trust as soon as possible. But how much time did she have?* "My shoulder—how bad is it?" she asked with as much cultural subservience as she could muster.

What a little charmer! Ling thought. *The boys are really going to have fun with YOU!* But she stayed in character and answered warmly, "The bullet went completely through soft tissue, dear…I fear you'll never regain 100 percent use of your shoulder, but you will not be greatly hindered if you pursue a normal life. Are you right-handed?" A neutral question.

"Yes, Doctor," Jen replied politely. Then Jen decided it was time to tip the psychological scales in her favor, and she dramatically seized the offensive by stating: "Doctor Ling, before you question me further, you need to know that I am Major Lee Qui Ming, assigned to the Second Chief Directorate at MSS headquarters in Beijing. I am here on a classified mission. Please loosen my hands and feet immediately; these bonds are cutting off my circulation, and I am in terrible pain." Jen had to get the upper hand as quickly as possible, and turning the scales was as old as tradecraft itself. It had been included in the comprehensive package of techniques "The Farm" had drilled into her throughout the CIA's basic course. This woman seemed like a real doctor, but she was definitely a security type, too, and that meant real sensitivity to politics and careerism. Perhaps her built-in sense of CYA/self-preservation would overcome her hesitation to trust a suspected criminal. If this doctor loosened Jen's bonds, she'd have a fighting chance to escape, but she had to push the right buttons, and fast. She was still a bit fuzzy-headed, and suspected that the doctor had added something to the drip in her arm to make her divulge secrets. But she fought its effects and stared directly into the eyes of the obviously startled doctor.

Uh oh! Ling suddenly felt like she'd been punched in the gut and her momentary joy evaporated. "You are an MSS officer?" she stammered. All sense of her previous superiority suddenly vanished. "But why were you in the top-secret facility?" Yet even as she asked the obvious question, Ling felt the truth of the woman's claim in her soul: Missions like this were always possible in the People's Republic, where government agencies constantly spied on each other. *Damn those quarreling generals!* Ling quietly raged inside. Instant conflict flooded her mind as she was torn between two dangerous possibilities: *What if the woman's claim is true? What if she's lying?* But Ling instinctively leaned toward self-preservation—meaning first avoid wrath from her own MSS hierarchy. If this woman was on a legitimate mission and had discovered corruption, delays, or the kickbacks that were so typical in the construction industry—and innocent Ling was accused of hindering an agent's sanctioned investigation—then Ling's own career would be in jeopardy. Or worse: She could be the next one dragged screaming into the basement torture chamber where her former subordinates would take excessive delight in humiliating her before they tore her apart! The government had been cracking down on corruption these past years, and people had been shot for far less than obstruction.

Ling made a quick decision and said, "So sorry, Major Lee, but you are correct in noting that I had nothing to do with your arrest." Then she snatched a pair of stainless steel medical scissors off the adjacent counter and gently cut the elastic restraints from her patient's wrists and ankles. "Better, Major?" she asked solicitously, even as she hurriedly but gently removed the drip needle from the woman's vein and placed a small bandage over the puncture. Then she massaged the young woman's wrists and carefully folded the woman's arms so that her injured shoulder would not be further damaged. She actually was an accomplished physician, so she did everything with as much focused professionalism as she could muster.

What a relief, thought Jen, confirming in her mind that Dr. Ling was indeed both a medical practitioner and part of the MSS establishment. She then spoke honestly, "Doctor, I ache everywhere!" Jen was cautiously elated that her situation had taken such a sudden turn for the better—the flip side of a police state working to perfection—because the PRC was as paranoid about interagency spying as any regime in history. Now however, she had to exploit this opening and weave it into an escape plan. "Are you the regular physician here, or an MSS or PAP professional from Beijing?" Jen played a hunch as her mind cleared, and she formulated a series of questions to keep her opponent on the ropes. But waves of pain interfered with her thinking as they cascaded through her upper torso and head. When the doctor helped her sit up, Jen nearly fainted.

Ling saw "Major Lee" grit her teeth as renewed circulation enabled frayed nerves to hammer their owner mercilessly, and she quickly hugged her patient to steady her. "Let me give you something to make you more comfortable, Major. I couldn't assess your discomfort threshold properly while you were under anesthetic." It was all she could think of to cover her tracks as she quickly extracted a small bottle of quick-acting, though fairly mild Demerol from a cupboard and administered an injection in her patient's hip. Then she answered the woman's question to help take her mind off the pain. "I come here a few times per year, Major. I am part of the regional MSS team and, as you surmised, I usually work out of our headquarters in Dalian City. I also keep an apartment with my husband in the capital." Ling deemed this a good time to mention that she had friends in higher places than this shipyard—even though agency scuttlebutt suggested that it had become dramatically more important because of those monstrous ships. The powers that be had been constantly frothing about them for years, and they were nearly ready for service. She'd been allowed inside the cavern just once, but even to her untrained eye they had seemed more military than civilian. She'd admitted to her colleagues on the tour that they were indeed spectacular—especially with their breathtaking livery and all seven pairs lined up in a row.

Then Ling remembered her patient's original reason for being there, and tried to ask a few questions that would look good to her boss if "Lee's" story didn't check out. "Please tell me, Major, why is your dental work so good? It would make any doctor think you had grown up in the West."

Jen accepted this question as reasonable and drew on her established legend: "I spent many years in Australia, where my father was part of our nation's embassy staff. As children, we received regular medical and dental care from local doctors." Actually, one of her childhood dentists had emigrated from Australia—however, since that dentist's practice had been in her childhood home in Oakland, California, she didn't need to mention it here.

"Oh, I see…" Ling said, accepting this reply as plausible. However, it could also be part of a well-prepared legend if the woman was a western spy. That eventuality would really stir up a hornet's nest! "And your accent? Are you from the south?"

"Yes. Mother is from Guangzhou and I have a bit of her accent, particularly when I'm tired. Like now. Could you please give me something to drink? I am suffering needlessly here!" Jen carefully altered her tone a bit—harshening it to match that of an important MSS officer who'd been wrongly abused. "And I'm quite upset that you clipped the wings of my 'butterfly'! That was a gross and unauthorized violation of my person." This last was delivered with genuine feeling: Like most young women her age, Jen was looking forward to marriage. She had a wonderful fiancé back home, and they'd delayed intimacy because of their mutual faith and commitment to government service. It was the greatest sacrifice of her career to be away from Tim. As Agency professionals they accepted that mutual sacrifices were necessary, but it didn't change the fact that they longed to be together. And besides, she'd had many well-rehearsed and well-fantasized-about plans for their wedding night the following spring—and this overzealous doctor had altered the sanctity of her body. *At least no men touched my body!*

Genuine worry seeped into Ling's soul. *What an unlucky and dramatically bad turnaround in only a few minutes!* She knew she had to tread very carefully from here on out, to avoid the many-faceted criticism that could knife in from rivals and bureaucrats trying to cover their backsides. And, though innocent, her part in this drama could ruin her. She had to avoid becoming anyone's pawn—or an expendable chip caught between senior officers and politicians quarreling over turf. Additionally, if this woman's father was a diplomat, it made Ling's position even worse.

"I deeply apologize, Major. But hopefully you can understand my responsibilities, too: You were badly injured, seemed like a spy, and you'd almost killed three of the complex's security guards!" She was now embellishing facts to build the best defense she could muster.

"I injured them, yes, but you will not accuse me of trying to kill staff in our secret complex! And now that you understand who I am, please give me proper medical care until my general can send a driver to pick me up…" Jen had two cards to play: If not scrutinized too thoroughly, playing the first card would lead to freedom within the hour. The second card might, too—but it had to be played with finesse because it was far more dangerous and would not stand up to any test. This second option, because of the name she'd have to drop, would get her the proverbial "bullet behind the ear" if her present jailers weren't immediately scared into compliance. And Jen was under no illusion here: She knew with dark certainty that she'd be blessed if that bullet came without her being abused and tortured first. But her duty proscribed her from chancing that: She possessed specific knowledge about her team and organization, and she was duty-bound to sacrifice her life to protect them. And, if circumstances forced that decision, she would not hesitate to do her duty.

The doctor helped Jen get comfortable, but said she could not place Jen's phone call until the shipyard's chief of security okayed her release. The doctor gave her a second shot of Demerol, which she promised would not dull Jen's senses, and it did relieve the worst of her complex pain. During this interlude, Jen was grateful that the doctor fitted her with a proper pad and underwear to stem the seepage of blood from her damaged personal area, and also helped her into a set of cotton hospital pants, gown, robe, and sling for her injured arm and shoulder. The final transition, which was excruciatingly painful, was to slide her off the table to which she had been clinging, and cross the small room to sit in a reasonably comfortable padded chair against the wall. If the doctor hadn't nearly carried her, Jen would have fainted dead away. The doctor then extracted a small bottle of orange juice from a little fridge in the corner, and found a small package of cookies to give her some energy. Jen deemed it prudent to demand again that she speak with her supervisor, but before the doctor could respond, the two women heard some commotion in the corridor outside.

Chapter 13

Dalian Shipyard Medical Clinic, 12:45 Hours

At least two sets of thumping footfalls slowed outside the exam room door. Then, without knocking, two men in military uniforms barged in. When the first man spotted Jen seated against the wall, he abruptly stopped in his tracks and the second nearly banged into him. They were both shocked to see the prisoner sitting in relative comfort with the doctor dutifully standing alongside. The doctor's hand was even lying gently on the young woman's uninjured shoulder.

"What is the meaning of this?" the senior man demanded gruffly. He was wearing a standard PLA uniform with the shoulder boards of a full colonel and metal insignias on his collar denoting the military intelligence branch.

Ling answered quickly, "Comrade Colonel, I made Major Lee of the MSS Second Directorate more comfortable until her commanding general sends a car. I knew that after we learned her true identity, you would direct everyone to help her to the maximum." This not-too-subtle warning was delivered with equal parts defensiveness and indignation.

"What? An MSS officer?" the colonel asked incredulously—standing like a statue and completely taken aback. He then looked directly at Jen and said, "I am Senior Colonel Kang Li Quo, this facility's chief of security. You claim to be an MSS officer?" He nearly sputtered his question, he was so shaken. The fairly short and stout colonel looked like he'd been slapped in the face. He finally took a step forward, allowing the second officer, a younger, taller, and quite handsome army captain (whom Jen figured was the colonel's aide) to enter the room and face her.

Jen noted that he also looked taken aback—but there was something more, too. He looked equal parts bemused and sympathetic at the same time. "Yes, Comrade Colonel." Jen spoke up as forcefully as she could. She'd slightly adjusted her position both for effect and to genuinely relieve the dull but still-throbbing pain in her shoulder. At least the two Demerol injections were mercifully allowing her to function.

"Then, Comrade Major, I ask for proof of your identity and of your mission," he adjusted the tone of his demand by adding a bit more tact and gentleness. He'd quickly regained enough composure to make the demand but, like the obviously nervous doctor, he had a bad feeling about this. If his men had shot an investigating officer of the MSS—and she could only have been assigned here by very senior officers or civilians at close to ministerial level—he could be in serious trouble. *What bad luck! For the last several hours, he'd thought he'd nabbed a spy—which would most certainly put him over the top to get that general's star he'd coveted for the six years since his promotion to full colonel. But, in an instant, instead of a great reward, he could be in real trouble and could even receive a reduction in rank and be forced to retire into the provinces.*

"Colonel Kang, please send someone to check between the storage containers against the cliff face just outside the fence encircling the main entrance to the cavern. There you will find my uniform and identification. My orders, however, are strictly confidential, and require a 'need to know' from the highest level…" She let the last statement hang, and was satisfied that it had the desired effect of magnifying the senior officer's discomfiture.

"Very well, Major." To save face, he turned to the captain and ordered imperiously, "Kai, go check on those articles and bring them back immediately!"

"Yes, Comrade Colonel!" Captain Kai replied politely. He was secretly enjoying this sudden turn of events that made his haughty boss squirm. He also couldn't help but notice that their prisoner was quite beautiful, in spite of her obvious pain and modest and unflattering hospital garb. He hadn't seen her body earlier because the doctor has shooed the men out of the room before tending to her wounds. But he imagined she was really something. He also hoped she was who she claimed because he'd instantly decided he wanted to know her better. As he trotted down the hall, he also couldn't help smiling to himself as he continued to ponder the potential political threat their attractive prisoner posed to his egotistic boss. He'd enjoy any comeuppance that befell his usually self-important and posturing supervisor. He bounded down the side stairs and raced through the complex toward the spot Major Lee had indicated, hoping to find things exactly as the interesting lady said.

Back in the medical office, Colonel Kang gave this now mysterious woman a gentle order: "You must wait here, Major, while we check on your story." He didn't elaborate and merely nodded to the doctor, turned on his heel, and left. He had some calls to make—first to his immediate superior, and then, if directed, to the Second Directorate. But underneath his calm exterior, he'd already begun to worry.

Ling was now in full CYA, and thought it best to offer hope. "Don't worry, Major. If all is as you state, you will soon be on your way..."

Jen just nodded curtly as her character would, even as she tried to cope with the occasional jabs of pain that snuck through the drugs. But her first priority was to anticipate scenarios that might confront her when the men returned, and she invested her time game-planning each one. She almost smiled to herself, however, when she had an unrelated thought that a gunshot wound might be the perfect introduction to the pain of childbirth. She'd be ready if the Lord ever blessed her with that wonderful yet future dream! Meanwhile, she had to get out of her present predicament. As she considered the immediate issue, she accepted the doctor's ministrations. The older woman fussed over her—checking her temperature, which was slightly elevated, and draping extra blankets across her lap and good shoulder to ward off the cool draft seeping under the exam room door.

About 15 minutes later, the women heard clumping boots again. Momentarily, the same two officers entered, though this time preceded by a polite knock. The captain, still in trail position and trying to stifle a grin, was holding Jen's things. She caught his eye and knew instantly that she had an ally—if not an admirer.

"Well, obviously a uniform was there, but your story didn't check out, Comrade Major." The colonel announced this with sarcastic brusqueness that revealed his somewhat renewed confidence in their respective positions. He then proceeded to elaborate without waiting for a response, "General Woo, with whom I spoke at Second Directorate HQ in Beijing, stated he has no knowledge of your being assigned a mission here. Unless you are assigned a specific liaison with the PAP, your duties fall within the directorate's focus on foreign intelligence, not domestic investigation." He raised his voice as the sentence progressed, and finished by staring daggers at Jen, his hands on his hips. "What do you have to say about that? I think you are a spy!"

Jen affixed her own neutral stare at the colonel, but didn't respond for a full 30 seconds. She was carefully letting his impatience build—letting him twist in the wind until his face reddened. But inside Jen felt a slight knot in her stomach; her first card had been played and failed. She was now forced to up the ante and play her second and unfortunately last card. "He didn't know, Colonel…" she finally declared with more confidence than she felt. "…and neither he, nor you, are authorized to know for whom I am working today. In fact, you greatly exceeded your authority by informing a person who had not been cleared for any aspect of my mission—which was to demonstrate, at this critical hour, before our magnificent fleet is launched—the ease with which an enemy of the state could penetrate this complex that **you** are charged with protecting! I demonstrated significant ease during my ascent of the outside cliff to access the cavern. Then I subsequently photographed the entire fleet and facility inside. Could it be that graft among your staff is causing such shoddy protection of these 'Gems of our Motherland' as our exalted General Secretary refers to our Dragon ships? Could it be that security funds are being spent in some other way?" Jen had allowed her voice to rise to an accusatory level before abruptly quieting. She then folded her hands in her lap defiantly, and waited for the startled colonel to absorb the full implications of the outrageous accusations she'd just leveled against him.

Taken aback again, Kang gasped and sputtered immediate denials. "Do you mean to tell me you had orders from someone outside your own department?"

Jen seemed to ignore the colonel's question—another drawn-out pause that added mystery and foreboding to her ominous reply. "Are you sure you want to go down this path, Comrade Colonel? Not just 'outside' my department, but 'above' it by several levels…"

Confound this woman! The colonel felt like a knife had been inserted into his gut. He knew his career hung in the balance: His next action could lead to a favor from a well-placed senior—whomever this mysterious and irritating woman might actually work for—but a misstep could spell disaster. She might be acting on orders from someone at the very top of their complicated government hierarchy who wanted to keep an eye on General Woo's office. Or she could have been sent by his own three-star general who worked at PLA headquarters. Or by someone in the Politburo—wouldn't that just make his day? Or, worst of all (and he nearly lost it at this thought), she might even be working for the diabolical Ministers Wing and Ti, who were known for creating scenarios like this. It was maddening: He could be facing a bullet by the end of the day! What a mess—and not of his own doing. He was on the horns of a dilemma and torn with indecision. As a result, after a full 30 seconds, he did what was ingrained into his soul from birth—he retreated to the security of the group. "I will consult with my seniors and get back to you, Major. So sorry, but you will have to remain here a bit longer." Then he looked at Dr. Ling for help. "Comrade Doctor, please make Major Lee as comfortable as possible until I clear up this misunderstanding." Then he headed out the door with his aide in tow—but not before the latter glanced back over his shoulder and gave her a discreet little smile.

Jen caught the smile, but didn't think the young officer could help her much. She had no choice for the time being but to settle in and see which way the winds would blow—knowing, as always, that her life was in God's hands. She kept shifting her position to ease the constant ache, and continued thinking through the possible scenarios she'd confront when the colonel returned.

About 30 minutes later, a sharp twinge in her shoulder interrupted Jen's thoughts but, more important, she also became aware of footsteps again clumping down the hall. It was no surprise when the door swung open without a knock and the once again stern-looking colonel and his trusty sidekick entered. She momentarily ignored the senior officer and locked eyes with the captain, and almost smiled: If ever there was a Chinese army version of "Captain America," this guy was it. He was impressive enough to remind her of her fiancé Tim, and she momentarily let down her guard and experienced a sudden twinge of sadness as she knew she might not see him again. Then she refocused and shifted her gaze to the senior officer. She didn't have to wait long for his demands:

With more impatience than he intended, Colonel Kang commanded, "Comrade Major, my senior general insists that you reveal the identity of the person who issued your orders. Any hesitancy on your part will force us to turn you over to the MSS interrogation unit. Your people would then have to pick you up there. I don't wish to place you into their hands." *Keep yourself on high ground,* he reminded himself. *This woman might be telling the truth and this situation just screams danger!*

"'My orders, Colonel, since you mention the MSS interrogation unit as a threat, ironically come from one very important man. Most senior members of our government know him because of his well-earned and very dangerous reputation. And let me assure you, he will not be at all happy with your challenge to his authority! So, would you like to contact him yourself…or do you wish me to do it?"

By all the gods! The colonel fumed for a second time. *If she is lying, I'm going to strangle her with my own hands!* "Thank you, Major, and I am not challenging this mysterious person's authority. But please, just tell me who this distinguished person is and I'll make the call." He managed this last bit carefully—modulating his voice to control any subsequent spin as the scenario played out.

"Very well, Colonel. You already know this gentleman's name: Senior General Wing Kang Lo, minister of State Security." Jen was carefully watching for the colonel's reaction and it was predictable—he was shaken to the core! Then, before he could respond, she added, "…and when you speak with him, please use my real name—Lieutenant Colonel Ma. I am very close to the general and have secretly worked for him for years…" And by this bold declaration, Jen would either sleep in her own bed tonight, or be in Eternity. There was no middle ground.

She was also taking another chance: There was a real Lieutenant Colonel Ma, of course, and she was indeed very close to the infamous General Wing. But Jen didn't know if Dr. Ling had met Ma, so she might be caught in an immediate lie. But most bureaucrats—even in the MSS—went out of their way of avoid the horrors of the interrogation cells and the people who plied their trade there. Jen decided to take the chance, but she had another reason for dropping that particular name: That lady was a very bad person and Jen had heard her name whispered several times. Ma had tortured and killed numerous innocent people over the years, including members of various cult groups, the underground Christian church, and others simply because Wing didn't like them. She was also known to have deviant proclivities. Jen had learned these tidbits from a senior MSS general, who shared that Wing had not objected when Ma murdered a rival for the general's carnal affection. It seemed to be a component of the sick relationship they enjoyed, and such stories were universally believed among Jen's colleagues. She also doubted Wing objected to these anecdotes that were floating around because they added to his fearsome reputation. Most everyone Jen knew, including some pretty tough MSS and military officers, were scared to death of attracting his attention.

"The minister of State Security? Lieutenant Colonel Ma?" Kang had to control his voice to keep it from squeaking, which it often did when he got too excited. In fact, his wife regularly cautioned him to avoid using that voice at all costs. *This was the worst possible revelation! Wing was a vicious pervert—and a notorious executioner!* Contacting him would be a career-endangering gamble—like sticking one's hand into a cobra pit! He wished he could shift this responsibility back to his own senior general but, as Kang quickly reminded himself, *that oaf of a careerist wouldn't touch this mess from Tibet—a bleak place where they all might end up (if they were lucky). His general never took any chances, particularly political ones. The man had spent his whole career riding on the back of his wife's brother, who was now transportation minister—and he'd done that all the way to three-star level.*

Kang found his good voice and responded more calmly than he felt. "I'm shocked, to say the least, that such an important national leader is concerned with corruption in this shipyard, Major, ah, Colonel. We have a spotless record here. Are you willing to say why he assigned you to this, ah, mission of yours?" *During which one of my security people nearly killed you. Wouldn't it be great to have that crazy Wing after me for that? I'd kill myself before I'd let his band of thugs arrest and torture me!*

Jen said nothing and let the moment drag out—watching as the colonel's face colored from a blood pressure spike. She had played her last card because she lacked an alternative; it was a creative risk because she knew how much these career-minded bureaucrats feared the dreaded general. She had, in fact, seen Minister Wing twice during inter-agency functions, and she had to admit the man was as intimidating as his reputation, and fortunately, she'd not attracted his attention, which might have backed her into a moral corner. But, for now, she had to be very careful not to overplay her hand—not to look too defiant or proud of herself. She had to let Kang make his decision based on the facts she'd presented, rather than to show her who was boss. She didn't want to push him closer to the edge than he already was, because this career soldier's character would impact her own fate, too. She watched without comment as Kang turned and simply left—head hung down and looking like a man headed for the gallows.

The doctor then patted her shoulder again and said, "I've heard your name around the headquarters, Colonel, but hadn't had the pleasure of working with you." *And I hope I haven't earned your wrath!*

Jen sat still and said nothing.

Chapter 14

A meeting of the Executive Committee of the Politburo
Haidian Qu District, Beijing, same time

Constructed entirely below ground on a tract of land in one of the outlying neighborhoods that had hosted the immensely successful 2008 Beijing Olympic Games, lay the actual meeting rooms where the Politburo Executive Committee conducted its truly secret (as opposed to ceremonial) meetings. They thought it was totally unknown to the outside world and had invested much to keep it that way. In fact, Party General Secretary Han had ordered its initial construction, and it was he who had requested the site for the afternoon's truly historic event. Not only did Han need its security, but its size was essential due to the nearly 500 people that constituted the most senior leadership of the PRC. The designers had ensured that its facilities were as impeccable as they were functional, and its amenities were the best that their engineers' constantly upgraded technology could provide.

The first invited attendees arrived an unnecessary one hour before the start time, but they all made sure they were early, and journeyed either alone or in pairs (with their retinues in tow). Some had traveled across the city in the luxurious chauffeured limousines they normally sported around the capital—accompanied like America's senior leaders by security personnel in shiny black SUVs. These entered a ground-level opening at the base of an architecturally challenged, generic-looking government building, but once inside all could see it was quite different: Numerous security guards met and directed them down concentric rings of broad passages, and the garage itself resembled an immense vault. The vehicles entered a second and even more secure underground garage and, after gliding to an impressive stop, the dignitaries stepped out onto bright red carpet that made their souls sing with pride. Others arrived in equal comfort (and with greater anonymity) via a secretly constructed subway train that whisked them from the private underground station several stories beneath their official offices in the Hall of Ministers building. That special structure was located adjacent to Tiananmen Square—the site infamous to the outside world for the massacre of the students who were demonstrating for greater liberty in 1989.

These elites arrived with an air of expectation, knowing that today's meeting would be recorded as a milestone in the history of the Middle Kingdom. Those in the know anticipated that the General Secretary would reveal the scheduled launch of their Dragon Fleet—the beginning of their impending war of conquest against their neighbors and the ever-meddling West.

GS Han, as usual, was last to enter the most spacious room in the complex. Everyone stood and, also as usual, he politely bid them to make themselves comfortable. He settled himself and then, after the usual pleasantries, got down to business. Catching everyone off guard, he suddenly stood without special introduction—an act no one could remember him doing before. Thus, assured of their complete attention, he commenced his historic address: "Fellow comrades and patriots, we have been considering a course of action—indeed preparing for a specific course of action—for several years. We decided to move up our timeline to become the sole superpower of the world because we were forced by unavoidable long-term circumstances to do so—circumstances that placed our national survival in doubt. But I also believe that these circumstances—continually validated as the years have passed—are a blessing in disguise. We have believed for generations that it is our destiny to dominate greater Asia, and to greatly expand our nation's influence over the remainder of the world. And, make no mistake, our people will applaud this accelerated schedule, and they will greatly benefit from our bold actions!" This declaration was followed by such resounding applause that he was forced to pause. But he didn't mind.

"Approximately four years ago, our natural resources experts warned us of grave consequences if we didn't adopt bold policies to head off a terrible downward spiral in production, one that would lead to starvation for our people and social disruption that would impact our party. At the outset, we were warned that we were rapidly running out of time and other options." He paused so everyone could absorb his not-so-subtle implication that he was building up to an announcement of a favored course of action—and that the policies he was about to outline were, therefore, a fait accompli. He already knew that he enjoyed nearly universal support among the senior-level cadres, and everyone else in this room knew the score: China was in deep trouble and had to act fast. "Our esteemed minister of Agriculture will now elaborate on this situation…"

Han had been laying the groundwork for this final, essentially ceremonial meeting, as his Dragons were being readied for launch. His Group of Eight and others had been in on "Operation Unity" for several years and, though he theoretically remained just an "official title" higher than the senior-most colleagues present, he had steadily coalesced his personal power to the point where he had been easily re-elected to his current five-year term as the Party's General Secretary. He was also China's president and chairman of the Central Military Commission, making him the most powerful titular leader since Mao.

Han's sobering introduction complete, everyone looked over at Ly Hua Tong, the current minister of Agriculture, who'd been prepped to give an appropriately dire report. He waited until the General Secretary sat, then stood himself and began his carefully prepared remarks. "Thank you, Comrade General Secretary. It is my sad duty to confirm what we were alerted to several years ago—that our crops are continuing to suffer amid the new weather patterns and depleted soils. We must anticipate that yields will continue to deteriorate compared to our historical norms: Some areas are wetter and colder, while others are dryer and warmer, but all in the wrong regions at the wrong time. The normal monsoons will continue to bring as much as 25 percent less moisture to our farms in those affected areas, and will result in, as we predicted earlier, additional seasons of between 20 and 40 percent lower yields. Tragically—also as predicted—our people have already begun to starve in some places and, despite the best efforts of our military to truck in thousands of tons of wheat and rice, this awful trend will worsen after this year's inadequate harvest…" He paused to let the first part of his grim report sink in. Then he delivered his most relevant point: "…in contrast, however, in many adjacent countries, crops are being positively affected by the changing weather patterns, and these neighbors actually enjoy bumper yields." Ly hoped that no one blamed him as the harbinger of this bad news—nor as the one sending China to war. Then, without further comment, he simply sat down.

To Ly's instant relief, Han stood and stated the obvious, "There is no blame here, fellow ministers. But facts are facts, and we, the chosen few whom the people count on to feed them and give them jobs, must confirm our next course of action or they will die in great numbers. Therefore, it is incumbent upon us to use our vast military force to envelop and absorb these neighboring nations that are rich in food production and natural resources—those who have existed on our periphery since ancient times—or we watch our people starve and experience their wrath! I know we all share the same repugnance at these thoughts. Minister Quen will now present the next report." He then nodded to Quen Ma Woo, the relatively new minister of Natural Resources, to present her own bleak report.

"Thank you, Comrade General Secretary Han." Quen looked across the room at her anxious colleagues, and sighed inwardly from a heart heavy with bad news. It had fallen to her to add final justification for launching the impending war, and she hated that eventuality; she had always believed, as did a minority of her colleagues, that there must be some other way. But she had to admit that China's back was against a very large wall. Poor stewardship of their once vast deposits of strategic metals and petrochemicals, combined with the negative impact of the treasure they'd spent building the world's largest military instead of plowing the money back into resource expansion, had left them desperate. But now the chickens had come home to roost. The changing weather had brought things to a head quicker but, on top of everything else, the incompetent boobs who ran the biological warfare laboratories had somehow opened Pandora's Box and released a pestilence upon their own people and the world. The central Chinese provinces around Wuhan's bio-weapon laboratories had borne the brunt of the disaster, inflicting sickness and death that may have cost the motherland a million or more of her own people. Additionally, almost two million people around the world had died, and tens of millions at home and abroad had suffered economically. The whole mess had placed her homeland in a very bad light and, though the coming war could solve some of their problems, it would certainly sentence China to suffer the world's indignation as an international pariah—perhaps forever. She felt very bad indeed. However, she was a patriot with a job to do, so she summoned her strength and announced to her colleagues:

"Fellow ministers, our dependence on imported oil and strategic metals—including graphite and rare earth ores—continues to escalate, and our fracking program has yielded far less useable oil than we hoped. As many of you know, the chemical structure of this relatively new source of oil is different from the so-called 'light sweet crude' favored by most of the world's refiners, including our own, and its refinement requires significant retooling of certain parts of the refining infrastructure. Even the Americans discovered this requirement some years ago and export on an exchange basis, all of their 'fracked oil' to international refineries that can handle it. The result for us is less useable oil than we need…"

Han only half-listened to Quen's somber recitation (the contents of which he knew as well as she did). He mainly used the time to scan the faces before him—assessing their readiness to hear, and their commitment to carry out, what he and his inner circle had already decided. He believed there would be little reluctance in this room to adopt the Plan, and all senior members knew the start date (only withheld from the foreign minister whom he did not fully trust). The others had already communicated unswerving loyalty to him and support for his weighty final decision. But there was still a final call to be made—and he wanted it to at least appear broad-based and responsive to this governing body's collective will. He had met with most of them privately, but a wise leader never lets his guard down in politically sensitive situations. He'd decided it was prudent to solicit their combined opinions one last time, and he'd frankly informed every minister-level attendee that their vote today would be on the record. Han watched Quen finish and sit next to Ly. He then stood and risked an historic question: "Ministers, what are your questions and comments?"

Tao Fu Ling, the minister of Finance, rose to speak first. "General Secretary Han, fellow ministers, I'd like us to remember at this crucial hour, the overarching context of our dilemma, that is, the Pacific Rim's outrageous and immoral response to our shortages. Although they know that we have vast reserves of cash on hand, plus abundant stores of bullion gold, plus United States' dollar-denominated foreign exchange with which to legally purchase all the grain and other raw materials that we need—they have shackled us with export quotas and tariffs that are strangling our people. They make outrageous intrusions into our internal policies by haranguing us about how we manage our prison population—not to mention our population in general. They bombard us with continual accusations of human rights violations, and unacceptably criticize us for trying to eradicate the anti-party cults of Christianity, Falun Gong, and others, and they think it is their business how we strictly manage our minority Uyghur tribes! They are also particularly incensed with our naval expansion into our natural and historical ocean waters. They are immorally using our present health crises that **they** caused to accelerate their meddling in our affairs! Do they think they are still our colonial masters who can push us around?" Tao paused as general outrage bubbled around the room. "...and though we own more than seven trillion dollars in American debt notes that we bought to prop up their economy so they could buy our products, they remain ungrateful. Even the historically reliable Canadians have joined the Americans in a concerted effort to undermine us. The Canadians and Australians—plus the Japanese and Filipinos—are hand in glove with the Americans in meddling in our affairs!" He paused to catch his breath, and to let his borderline COPD regulate so he could breathe easier. "And, as you all have been reading, the American government and others are raising issues with our world-wide Belt and Road Initiative infrastructure projects. We are building roads and harbors to improve the trading abilities of the incompetent emerging world. But it is clear that these third world nations who benefit from our projects—and the West that criticizes our funding methods—are not yielding to our ascendancy. They don't understand that we rule Asia, not them! And, as you all witnessed, the Americans have elected a so-called moderate to be their president, but he promised to continue the policies that meddle in our affairs. If we want to jail or kill any of our own criminal classes, that is our business!"

This near rant was merely giving voice to deep concerns shared by most of those present: The Americans had been complaining for decades that China's trade practices were unfair, and they were attempting to "level the playing field" with updated policies. Recent tariffs had shocked China and left her manufacturing sector flat-footed, and the U.S. was even trying to move part of China's manufacturing base back to America. Their Congress just didn't understand its place. Its bonehead policies had been bad and were getting worse. No one had foreseen that the voting population of their chief rival for world influence would support someone from the proletariat—referring to President Stilwell's middle class upbringing—let alone someone who was a defense hawk who would probably try to interfere with China's long-term plans to re-absorb Taiwan (Operation Unity notwithstanding). American voters clearly didn't believe CCP propaganda that their military had planted the Covid germs in Wuhan. Fortunately, they didn't know that the Chinese leadership thought their accident was a mistake gone right: Wing's labs had accidentally unleashed a demon, but China could absorb deaths much better (actually and psychologically) than the United States and the West. Han's political advisors had predicted the American public would turn against their president, but the PRC's massive behind-the-scenes propaganda efforts to destabilize their public opinion had faltered.

At least President Stilwell was a known quantity with whom they would have to deal during the coming war, and the PRC leadership had game-played his predictable responses. Hopefully they'd not overestimated Stilwell's uncertainty in the face of the coming surprise attack, which they were counting on to give the PLA an extra advantage in Asia. Tao drew strength from this known context and the supportive room, and moved to his conclusion: "Comrade General Secretary, fellow ministers, as we all know, the Western powers have grain to sell, but they have publicly announced support for renegade Taiwan's radical rebellion against our motherland, and are trying to hold us hostage to their threats. I want to go on record as fully supporting 'Operation Unity'!" Tao decided he'd made his point, and sat down to watch the fur fly.

Ti Quo Qing, Han's long-term and predictably hawkish minister of Public Security and commander of the People's Armed Police, was so incensed that she broke protocol and jumped to her feet shouting "Those outrageous meddlers! Tao, your ministry should have dumped their debt paper on the world market and ruined them before this! We should have already used the American's debt against them and forced them to sell us the grain we need! However, I am glad that we can teach them and the world a lasting lesson about tweaking the Dragon's tail!"

A chorus of agreement washed over the room like a tidal wave of pent-up rage: Minister after minister jumped to his or her feet to be recognized. They were allowed to huff and puff for Han's usual allotment of two minutes until, gradually, everyone cared more about hearing the heretofore secret details of Operation Unity.

Han waited until everyone looked expectantly at him, then he nodded to Minister of Defense Marshal Tai. The senior military leader solemnly rose from his place of honor at the front table. "Loyal patriots and comrades, please allow me to summarize our plans to extricate ourselves from this dilemma. It is a path that requires danger and great risk to our homeland, but it is also the option for which we have been preparing for years." Everyone listened intently to this highly respected veteran soldier—they trusted him to lead them victoriously (and quickly) through the incredible era ahead.

"The nations on our borders—those whom we have historically controlled to one degree or another for millennia—are virtual gardens, and also rich in a variety of vital on-shore and off-shore natural resources that we need to thrive. I am speaking, of course, about Vietnam, Laos, Cambodia, Thailand, Myanmar/Burma, Brunei, the Philippines, Malaysia, and Indonesia—countries that can provide our food and energy needs for decades. They have vast oil and natural gas reserves—a true bounty of petrochemical treasures in addition to their remarkable agricultural sector." He then paused dramatically, waited for five seconds, then suddenly raised his voice and thundered, "And it is also time to bring our rebellious province of Taiwan back into the fold!"

The room gasped with unanticipated joy at hearing this revelation, and erupted in a spontaneous standing ovation. The veteran warrior raised his arms in victory—they would finally do it! So swept up were these senior leaders in their own euphoria that they blew through Han's preferred two minutes of demonstrable celebration. However, they could see that he was as excited as they were.

After the room finally quieted, Marshall Tai vocalized another sore subject that was bubbling just under the surface of Chinese society, "Let us not forget another vital fact: These 'satellites' also have millions of healthy unmarried women to meet the needs of our men who cannot find suitable wives among our own people." He didn't need to explain that the government's long-term "one-child" policy was the 800-pound gorilla that weighed heavily on nearly every family in China. Restricting families to one child (though recently expanded to two) had led to an incredible demographic imbalance: Thirty-five million more female fetal, infant, and toddler children had been killed than male children (though several hundred million male children had been intentionally aborted as well). Its unintended consequence was an infanticide-holocaust and a catastrophic imbalance between the number of marriageable-age men versus women. For many years, hundreds of thousands of young women in surrounding countries had been actively solicited to come to China as wives for these men—including many who'd been tricked and were now little more than slaves.

Out of the corner of his eye, Tai noticed Ti glaring at the room—daring anyone to look accusingly at her: It was her ministry that was responsible for population control, and she'd only reluctantly yielded to the ground swell of support for the adoption of the new "two-child" policy. But she'd been clear with her colleagues: That was enough new social engineering, and she'd ordered all her medical cadres to kill the rest of the illegal children as before.

"Hear, hear!" chimed in Minister Wing. He stood for effect in support of Marshal Tai's proclamation. "These lands are historic vassal states on the edge of the Middle Kingdom. They owe us hundreds of years of unpaid tribute! Their young women will partially pay that debt—but our management of their economies will pay the rest. We should bring every one of these rebellious provinces back under our direct control—now!" He was practically bellowing as he slammed his fist on the table for emphasis. Then he sat down victoriously and, like Ti, dared anyone to object to his summary.

But this assertion was too radical for some, and the predictably dovish Wu Yingjie, the Foreign Affairs minister, though filled with as much patriotic fervor as the majority, still hoped for a peaceful solution. He rose to try to bring a more moderate perspective to the discussion, knowing he would have to do so without his fellow moderate from the Group of Eight, Liu Keqiang. Her provincial rank did not otherwise qualify her to sit with this larger and more official group. President Han could have included her here as he did with the Eight, yet he evidently chose not to for reasons of his own. Therefore, Wu bravely accepted that this was the eleventh hour and decided to go it alone.

He knew Wing and Ti didn't appreciate being contradicted, but Wu was too old to be continually intimidated by those bullies.

Wing saw Han recognize that "weak pacifist," as he thought of Wu, and responded with a quiet snort. But Wing never challenged Han directly, and he wasn't going to start now.

The Foreign minister stood and began his appeal, knowing it would be China's last reasonable chance for peace. "Fellow patriots, we all know our magnificent history, but let us not forget that we live in a new world with Russia to our north, Japan to our west, and the Americans, with their airplanes and navy, seemingly everywhere. Our military is now largely on par with the West, and we owe a large debt of gratitude to Marshal Tai and the PLA—and to Minister Wing and his legion of industrial spies. But we must be realistic, too." He was immediately rewarded with whispers of support from several quarters. He knew he was not the only one who feared terrible world backlash if they started an Asia-Pacific war. Even if they realized their best-case scenario, hundreds of thousands would die and multi-generational enemies would be made. And, if the military planners were wrong and the PLA was beaten, the death toll could be catastrophic. Their party would lose power and prestige, and they might even be forced into a multi-party democracy, which everyone knew was the death-knell for the CCP. The resulting "new Chinese order" would have uninformed and stupid peasants naturally thinking they were qualified to have a say in government affairs. But at this moment, Wu believed that he was not the only one concerned that underestimating the Americans and their allies could bring disaster on the homeland—even exceeding in numbers the very deaths and instability they were trying to avoid by justifying this war. He remembered all too well Japan's self-inflicted disaster during World War II—and there was always the specter of nuclear weapons hanging over any global conflict.

But General Tai, sensing a weakening in the predetermined outcome, jumped back to his feet without letting Wu finish and declared, "Yes, our knowledgeable Foreign minister has mentioned the obvious. But he may not understand the full capabilities of our new Dragon Fleet of super assault ships that is now ready to sail—nor of our comprehensive plan to utilize them!" And with that, he noticed that Wu just sighed in resignation and sat down.

Accepting the Foreign minister's action as capitulation, General Tai sat down, too, and looked over at General Secretary Han.

From his prospective, Han was happy that the Foreign minister's concerns had given him cover to avoid the appearance of a white-wash, and granted the point with a quiet nod to the elder statesman. But now it was time to get the meeting back on track, so he stood and spoke again—signaling to all that debate had ended. "Thank you, Ministers Tai and Wu. Both of your valued opinions have been carefully blended into our plans. Now let's turn our attention to important details that our minister of Defense and his staff have prepared. Many of you are generally familiar with 'Operation Unity' but some of us are just learning of its scope for the first time." *Diplomatic to a fault,* Han congratulated himself. He then gestured to Marshal Tai to make his presentation.

Tai was ready and stood again. "Thank you, Comrade General Secretary. It has always been a PLA contingency to help restore the peoples on the edge of our historic borders to our full control—that is, to fulfill that glorious destiny envisioned by our Party's founder to enlarge our borders to its fullest possible extent. From the Long March to the present, Chairman Mao and our many generations of leaders have wanted the restoration of a greater China—a China in which everyone with Han blood flowing through their veins would be loyal servants of the Middle Kingdom. This is the essence of 'Greater Hanism,' which has always been a central theme of our Party doctrine." He acknowledged the spontaneous clapping and calls of support from around the room—always proud that his family was of nearly pure Han blood (with some Mongol mixed in, of course). Most of those present were entwined with the long-term flow of Chinese history, and even those more dovish in their outlook felt they had to support this clarion call to honor their ancestral history. Every surrounding country had significant Chinese minorities, and many of them wanted their adopted lands to be directly controlled by Beijing—though he admitted that most didn't. But the MSS would deal with those traitors later.

Another unifying factor was their long wait for reunification with the rebellious province of Taiwan, and even he had a hard time believing they were on the verge of realizing that, too. Tai built his argument for war: "Though we are a land-focused people, we are a sea-faring nation as well. And today, with the help of our comrades in the People's Liberation Army Navy—and with additional help from our maritime construction enterprises—we are ready to begin our campaign of reunification and conquest!" He was warming to the task, and he could be both inspiring and entertaining when the floor was his. "Yes, Comrades, we have developed our amazing military to the point where we are finally ready to dominate any foreign land we choose—even our navy is larger than the Americans, and we are ready to envelop our half of the Pacific Ocean, too. He paused again, this time enjoying the surprised responses of those who didn't know that their navy had matured to this level. They had achieved this goal almost 30 years ahead of schedule, and didn't need to wait until 2049 to dominate the world.

The CCP had won its decades-long campaign against the warlord cabal led by Generalissimo Chiang Kai Shek in 1949, but that generation of leaders accepted that they needed another 100 years to pacify the rest of Asia. The international community would be in awe of what they were going to do—and the barbarians would fear them anew. It took him a full minute to get everyone listening again. "We are going to accomplish in a few days what the under-achieving Japanese could not do during their 14-year war against us! They thought they could expand their so-called 'East Asia Co-prosperity Sphere' by immorally invading us and slaughtering helpless civilians, and again later by destroying the American fleet in Hawaii and taking Singapore from the British. But they were over-confident, and they lacked both the comprehensive vision and the capability to do what was necessary to remove the meddling United States and their colonialist allies from the western Pacific chess board. But we are going to conduct ourselves differently: We are going to defeat the Americans not just in Hawaii, but 2,000 miles east on the American west coast. We are going to conquer and hold strategic parts of the U.S. mainland long enough to consolidate our goals here in Asia!"

This proclamation was mostly unexpected, and it was met by both cries of jubilation from those he and Han had carefully prepared, and by sudden gasps of near-terror from those few who instinctively dreaded such a risky endeavor. The hawks rejoiced that they would see "Mao's Great Dream" fulfilled in their lifetimes—and they could not believe their luck. But the minority who had not been fully trusted with the Plan (those known by Han to be "fence-sitters," who considered themselves to be "prudent centrists") could not believe the potential for calamity that this adventurism could bring upon their homeland. They feared China could lose everything the Party had been building since the epic victories of 1934-1935 and 1945-1949.

Wu was the senior-most of those who hadn't been briefed on the mainland America aspect of the plan, and he jumped to his feet in near-panic. "We don't have the blue water fleet necessary to take on the American Navy in its home waters!" he shouted—clearly acting out of turn and without being recognized. "Attacking the barbarian mainland is crazy, Comrade Marshal! They will counter-attack and sweep our ships from the sea. Then they will invade our precious motherland and destroy our Party!" He realized that he was becoming hysterical and had to focus his objections or he wouldn't be taken seriously. *What madness had these fools concocted?*

"You are weak and an embarrassment to the Party!" shouted General Wing, jumping to his feet, red-faced and shaking his clenched fist at the perceived coward. "Away with all counter-productive and reactionary defeatists like you!" Pandemonium suddenly engulfed the room as several dozen previously dignified leaders began shouting and waving their arms at the same time—pointing fingers at anyone they considered "reactionary."

Appalled at the gross loss of decorum, Han was also shocked at the level of vitriol and disunity: Usually self-controlled ministers were shouting at each other as viciously as in a barroom brawl, and his well-orchestrated gathering was quickly spinning out of control. Personally, he thought Marshal Tai and General Wing had developed a brilliant plan, and he was prepared for only limited opposition. This political body had always looked for a conciliatory path, and he'd already made clear his support for the upcoming campaign. It also rocked his confidence that his own stamp of approval was being questioned—opposition at this point meant nothing less—and he hastened to insert himself into the fracas. He once again stood and raised his arms in an appeal for calm—an unprecedented gesture that he hoped would quell this potentially dangerous rebellion. "Comrades, please…please calm yourselves! We are a unified committee representing our unified Party! General Wing, I demand that you apologize to our distinguished minister of Foreign Affairs immediately!"

Realizing he had overstepped the bounds of propriety, and stung by this unusually strong public rebuke from Han, Wing got his flaring emotions under control. He was thankful that he didn't have his sidearm because he probably would have shot Wu on the spot. But, like everyone here who regularly carried firearms, he was obliged to leave his gun at the door in the care of Han's personal security detail. He was shaking as he sat down and avoided eye contact with both Han and Tai, both of whom were staring at him in disbelief. Wing folded his hands and didn't even look for support from Ti on the other side of the room. He knew she was seething, too, but neither wanted to lose their influence on the eve of launching the first three Dragons. The hawks had labored day and night for years, so losing their positions now would be a tragedy. His "Chaos Teams" were only days away from starting their terror campaign, and Wing wanted to be **the** key operational leader of every detail. Plus, he was one of only a handful in the inner circle who knew that Operation Unity was just the first phase in a larger plan: They'd start with Asia and the western Pacific and, when that region was thoroughly pacified, they could expand the military aspects of the Belt and Road projects and really spread their wings.

The room quieted as Tai waited for Wing to meet his gaze; Wing was brilliant and ruthless, but he could ruin all if he didn't keep a lid on his zeal. Wing looked up and seemed repentant, so Tai nodded to Han that their subordinate was back under control.

Wing knew what he had to do, so before Han said anything more, he spoke up with surprising humility: "General Secretary Han and my fellow ministers, I apologize to Minister Wu and everyone who was offended by my outburst. I can only say in my defense that I have mentally and emotionally transitioned into combat mode, and I am anticipating the great battles ahead. I am sorry for being short—I merely want us to be unified in our full support for the coming war…"

Satisfied with Wing's humble reply, Han spoke kindly to the room. "Thank you, Minister Wing—we all owe you a debt of gratitude for your part in our extensive preparations: Your fifth columnists have been working for years to weaken the nations we'll invade, and your spies have reaped an inconceivable bounty of useful intelligence—both military and technical—to help our businesses, military, and scientists. Even the unexpected Covid virus has ended up being a blessing in disguise." Han was doing his best to sooth ruffled feathers, and get them all back on track. "Comrades, we are in desperate straits now. If our people starve, we will lose control of them."

It was noteworthy that few around the table were troubled, even in their souls, beyond that point: People had always starved in China, albeit not in significant numbers in modern times—and certainly not in large enough numbers to threaten the Party's control. Even widespread panic from the Covid outbreak had done little to threaten the CCP's control over the masses. That was the one thing the Party could not allow to change: After their historical victory in 1949, the Party's number one job was to keep its large population pacified. Social chaos could lead to revolution—the only thing any of them really feared. Its threat was the principal reason Minister Ti's massive police force had established the Social Credit Scoring System, with its comprehensive facial recognition components. She also used her People's Armed Police units to monitor every communication in the land. The Party's ultimate goal was to first control every action of every citizen, every moment—and eventually to expand that to the Asia region and then the world. Failure to do so meant global instability and, especially domestically, uprisings could become tidal waves of uncontrollable violence. If the masses went on a rampage, and became desperate enough to lose their fear of the government (which alone had guns), then the privileged elites were in mortal danger. The leaders would be swept away as surely as driftwood on a stormy beach.

It was obvious to Han that everyone needed an infusion of confidence, so he turned back to Marshal Tai: "Comrade Defense Minister, perhaps this is a good time to share your magnificent plan with our honored senior colleagues? You and your staff have been perfecting it for some years now, and it would be good for all of us to hear its details and gain an encouraging perspective." By this, Han reinforced his earlier message that he supported the decision for war—just in case anyone hadn't absorbed that fact earlier.

"Thank you, Comrade General Secretary. I believe that everyone will embrace 'Operation Unity' as a remarkably practical method to achieve our multiple goals. It will facilitate expansion of our homeland to its rightful borders, by which I mean increasing by millions of hectares the abundantly fruitful lands that will provide for our people's current and future needs. Additionally, it will give us control over millions of square kilometers of ocean, whose sea beds hold rich deposits of vital petrochemicals and other minerals. And, rightly, in all our minds, the meddling Americans, Japanese, and other Pacific Rim powers will be prevented from future interference in our ascending leadership of greater Asia!"

A variety of emotions played across the faces of those focused on his every word. They were listening intently; some obviously impatient to learn more—some hiding doubts and fears—but only Wu seemed genuinely resentful. They were culturally a group that instinctively believed that unity was the way of survival and, typical of all totalitarians, they accepted as their due, their right, and their responsibility to lord it over everyone they considered lesser peoples. They genuinely believed that their power always came, as Chairman Mao famously stated, "from the barrel of a gun."

Chapter 15

Dalian ship yard medical clinic, same time

Jen had played her last card and now watched the colonel make his decision—and seal her fate.

"All right, Comrade Major—or Lieutenant Colonel—I will contact General Wing myself. And I can only hope for both our sakes that you are telling the truth!" With that, he turned on his heel, opened the door and left. His aide just smiled at her quietly, shrugged his shoulders, and took a seat by the door to await the outcome.

"How are you feeling?" Dr. Ling asked solicitously, handing her a paper cup that held an inch of water.

Minister's Briefing Room

Marshal Tai looked toward the left side of the conference room and motioned to an aide. Instantly, the large screen built into the side wall displayed a grainy photograph of a double row of vintage military ships. They were at anchor in a port, and everyone adjusted their seats for a better view. They could see giant splashes alongside several of the ships—a picture from an earlier time. "Does anyone recognize this photo?" Most looked blankly at the screen, though the inner circle had been fully briefed several times.

"Marshal Tai, it is a photo taken from a Japanese military plane as their air armada attacked the United States Pacific fleet at Pearl Harbor, Hawaii, on December 7th, 1941." This from Han who admittedly, was tremendously excited, and also relieved that the meeting was back on track.

But Minister Wu just shook his head sadly; he was terrified for his nation. *What disaster would these militarists bring upon our beloved homeland?* He believed he had to do something to stop this madness, and raised a relevant point without being recognized: "Marshal Tai, our ancient enemy Japan proved that attacking America was folly. Their attack touched off a series of events that led to their complete destruction during World War II. And we of all people understand how much they deserved their fate for widening the war they had first started against us in 1931."

Marshal Tai didn't seem to take offense, and was ready for just this reaction. "It is true that Japan is our ancient foe, and committed terrible atrocities against our people during the Great War. But we are enlightened enough to learn from both our enemy's strategic and tactical successes as well as their failures. I believe our planners have learned the correct lessons from Japan's disaster—to the benefit of our homeland and collective futures. And Minister Wu, not to belabor the point, but I would borrow ideas from the Devil himself if it helped save China from starvation, and our party from doom." He paused as supportive murmurs quietly crisscrossed the room. He'd sensed for weeks that tremendous collective energy was building among the CCP's second tier, and support of the war was nearly unanimous. He'd felt it unnecessary to meet today, but Han wanted one final check to ensure they'd have no back-room undermining or second-guessing once they got underway. He took a moment to extract a handkerchief. Even the state-of-the-art air conditioning system was straining; their accumulating body heat was taxing the system.

Then, before Wu could marshal another objection, Tai shifted his gaze to the back of the room and said, "I'd like to call forward Lieutenant General Bao, my long-term chief of staff, and with him, Professor Dang, our distinguished military historian. They have led the team that developed the specifics of this plan, and they will now brief us on its key points." Tai often utilized this clever sidestep: If any plan proved successful, he was its benefactor. But if it proved less so, lesser lights would shoulder the blame.

Striding purposely up the side aisle, Bao both knew and didn't care that Marshal Tai was using him and Dang. They were fully committed to significantly increasing the landmass directly controlled by Mother China, plus quadrupling their "near-ocean" defensive zones. Bao arrived at the lectern first, but stepped a bit to his right to give equal honor to the slightly built and bespectacled academic who arrived a step later. He and Dang exchanged nods and Bao began his well-rehearsed presentation. "General Secretary Han, Marshal Tai, Comrade Ministers: Commander Genda of the Imperial Japanese Navy was the principal author of the attack you see in this old photograph."

He motioned grandly at the screen, and the audience was fascinated as other photos began to scroll. They showed the widespread destruction the air raid had inflicted on the sleeping Americans—carried out on that fateful morning three quarters of a century before. Bao then activated a red laser pointer as a photo of a foreign admiral appeared. "The overall Japanese combined fleet commander, Vice Admiral Yamamoto, was a brilliant strategic thinker, and he was against further expansion of the war they were already waging so ruthlessly against us. But he also knew that Japan was running out of oil and other strategic materials as we are today—and Japan doesn't have five percent of the natural resources that we do. So, after these shortages were exacerbated when the Americans slapped a painful embargo on them—a failed attempt to force them to withdraw from China—Japan believed that they had no acceptable alternative other than conquering Asia and taking what they needed by force. The decision to absorb their regional neighbors required them to remove the United States and her allies from the western Pacific. Great Britain was severely distracted by the war they were losing in Europe, so Genda formulated a plan that surprised the Allies, and the rest is history."

Wu then took advantage of this pause to jump on that statement. "But don't you see the irony of your words, General Bao? It is evident that we find ourselves in the same situation today: Running short of almost everything we need to keep our industries going and our people fed—while the Americans and their allies are slowing grain sales to us because they don't like our growing influence in the region, nor our severe internal policies. Still, you recommend that we repeat the disastrous decision that Japan made decades ago—starting a war with them rather than negotiating. We still possess money to buy food from them (as well as oil from the Middle East), and their economy is still weakened from the virus-related shut-downs. They are shackled with astronomical debts from their social programs that are only getting worse, and we have the economic upper hand. Let us use our existing strengths and make token adjustments to our internal policies to appease them. Let's not reap the same total destruction that Japan suffered in 1945!" He was appalled that these supposedly brilliant historians learned nothing from the very history they were touting. He knew well the old adage: "Those who ignored the lessons of history are doomed to repeat them."

Sensing an undercurrent of unease in the room, Dang signaled to Bao that he would like to respond to Wu's legitimate points. He stepped to the microphone and appealed for reason with the polished experience of a veteran professor. "Comrade Minister, I too advocate learning from both Japan's successes and from their mistakes…please hear us out." He received a reluctant nod from the Foreign minister, even as several around the table signaled their own desire to hear the whole plan. Dang also noticed that General Wing looked like a coiled serpent ready to strike the irritating defeatist and throttle him. The veins on the general's neck were distended and his hands were digging into the soft leather armrests of his chair. Nevertheless, Dang ignored him and continued. "Japanese officials knew they needed the agricultural and petrochemical abundance of their Asian neighbors, just as we do. And Admiral Yamamoto knew he had to keep the British Empire and the U.S. on the sidelines until the Imperial Army solidified its expansion. Yamamoto's perspective included knowing the American industrial and military capabilities first hand: He'd lived and studied there for some time, and spoke fairly good English. And from this accumulated knowledge he believed that he could only buy his military six months—certainly no more than a year—if their navy attacked and destroyed the American Pacific Fleet that had recently been relocated from their mainland base in San Diego, California, to Hawaii. He candidly warned the Japanese government that, after probable initial successes, things would get dicey. His prediction proved correct because, during the initial attack—the photos of which you see before you—they failed to achieve their number one and number three goals that would have greatly delayed an Allied response. That first goal was to sink America's three fleet-level aircraft carriers, while the third goal was destroying the Pearl Harbor repair and fuel storage facilities. The carriers were not in port on the morning of the attack because they were out to sea delivering airplanes to their Pacific Island strongholds, and the third attack wave that was designed to destroy the base infrastructure was never launched by their overly cautious task force commander, Admiral Nagumo.

"Yamamoto also knew the so-called 'age of the battleship' was long finished, ironically proven by American Army aviator General Billy Mitchell after World War I. This fact had been further confirmed by the British attack on the Italian naval base at Taranto, just one year before Pearl Harbor…" The screen changed to a photo of a distinguished-looking American military officer in uniform. It was titled, BG Mitchell, 1937. A series of photos then showed the "before and after" views of the WWI German battleship *Ostfriesland* that General Mitchell's bombers sank, plus photos of the Italian battleships sunk or damaged by British aviators during their attack on the Italian navy. "Just seven months before Pearl Harbor, the German battleship *Bismarck* was crippled by antiquated bi-planes from a British carrier and then, shortly after the Pacific War began, Japan's bombers sank two unprotected British battleships as they made their way toward Malaya and Singapore without air cover.

"Because the Japanese failed to eliminate the American carriers in Hawaii, Admiral Yamamoto was circumstantially forced to devise a second plan to sink them: He sent his fleet back to Midway Island only 1,300 miles northwest of Hawaii six months later. He hoped this second strike would lure those dangerous carriers into a decisive battle that would accomplish what they failed to do earlier but, instead of ambushing the Americans, the Imperial fleet was itself ambushed and four of its front-line carriers were sunk. This battle proved disastrous and, for the remainder of the war, Japan was on the defensive."

But Wu was not buying it. "This is an interesting history lesson, Professor Dang, but are you still advocating that we attack the most militarily powerful nation on earth? And I believe I am correct in thinking that they are, relatively, much stronger today than they were back then. Plus, they have satellites that can see our fleet of 'special' container ships coming two weeks before they reach the American west coast. They can watch the ships from the second they stick their noses out of our 'special' cavern that cost us trillions of Yuan. It almost seems like you are arguing against attacking the Americans…" The Foreign minister was proving why he'd been a successful diplomat for more than 40 years. *These militarists are so full of themselves—they are going to lead our motherland into disaster!*

Marshal Tai stood to counter this critical argument, and addressed Wu directly. "Comrade Foreign Minister, we have a choice before us and it pertains to your points: The lessons we learned from Japan's mistakes! The answers yield the difference between repeated defeat and overwhelming victory. The Americans won the 'Battle of the Pacific' because they had carriers—the new super weapon of the time—and they had bases, and conquered still more bases from which to fly their airplanes to bomb Japan. Their homeland was free from attack throughout the war—excepting the pinpricks that the Japanese navy inflicted on their Pacific northwest—and the off-shore German submarine campaign that dominated the early part of the Atlantic and Caribbean theaters.

"What we learned—and have included in our exhaustive preparations—is that we must not only surprise and sink the American fleet in Hawaii, but we must take the fight to the three principal U.S. west coast ports of Seattle, San Francisco, and San Diego—plus sink their fleets in their east coast ports as well. This will degrade their surface and undersea fleets by at least half, and truly buy us the time we need in Asia. With their four great Pacific ports in our temporary possession—plus all of their smaller Pacific Island strongholds captured or neutralized within a few weeks, we will win!"

As Tai expected, the room politely clapped as opinion clearly swung back in his direction. He could see that Wu's face was a mask of doubt and disbelief, but Tai was not done, and continued making his points. "Our brilliant scientists have been working with the PLA's rocket forces, and have perfected an anti-ship ballistic missile system that can sink Allied carriers across the Pacific and beyond. We also have incredible new torpedoes and other modern weapons that are ready for tactical use. We are the first nation to be able to accurately target an enemy ship at sea with ballistic weapons because we can make the critical in-flight course corrections that permit us to be accurate to within a few hundred feet. This, Minister Wu, combined with our new space-based weapons, plus our divisions of computer-hacking technicians, plus our greatly expanded submarine fleet, plus the extensive American city destruction campaign that General Wing will momentarily brief us on, gives us the capability to thoroughly disrupt any meaningful Allied response."

Tai and Han exchanged glances—they sensed that they had won enough hearts and minds to carry the day. From now on, Wu and the dwindling group of doves and other "faint hearts" would be isolated and easy to control.

But, to the room's collective surprise, Wu suddenly jumped to his feet again and blurted, "This is an outrageous mistake!" His face was now red going to purple, and he had a wild-eyed look that made him appear apoplectic. "Attacking the American mainland is…is madness! This kind of adventurism will yield only disaster!" Then, just as suddenly as his fury erupted, it was spent. He slumped into his chair in utter defeat, and more than one person in the room thought he'd had a stroke. In his heart, Wu knew he had tried, but he was just as certain that the winds of war were a growing gale he could not stop; he was just an autumn leaf wafting through the air. *May the gods protect us!*

It took one final voice to convincingly negate the Foreign minister's heartfelt warning: The most distinguished warrior in the room was retired Marshal Sheng Zhang, who was still a member of the Eight and special advisor to General Secretary Han. The elderly gentleman stood shakily to his feet and received the total respectful silence he deserved. "We have two options, Comrades…" he declared, "…either we rely on the good graces of the Americans—our financial strength notwithstanding—and adjust our domestic and international policies accordingly—or we chart our own course and take by force of arms what we need from the world. I don't see any middle ground." It was a brief, yet comprehensive summary of the official version of China's options. After that he sat down, but the room remained deathly still.

Finally, after a respectful 30 seconds, Han decided he'd allowed enough discussion and rose to bring this part of his meeting to a close. He spoke kindly to Foreign Minister Wu, who sat slumped in his chair—a defeated old man staring into middle space. It was obvious he'd lost his will to fight, so there was no point in kicking a dead horse. "You are our esteemed colleague, Minister Wu, and it is right for you to help us to think through our options. But, as Marshal Zhang aptly summarized, we have to make our own way in this hostile world…" Han then sat down and looked up expectantly at General Bao to continue.

Bao refocused and proceeded to reveal the heretofore hidden details of their plan. "I know this is a bold endeavor, Comrades, but we have a new weapon and a new strategy to take advantage of history's hard-earned lessons." A new slide appeared and the room hummed with excitement as a schematic of their new Dragon class of immense assault ships appeared on the screen. He used his pointer to systematically explain the ships' features. It was evident, even to the non-military members of his audience, that these wondrous vessels contained an amazing array of lethal weapons systems and overwhelming fire power. Each Dragon was a mothership that contained a flotilla of four Type

726 assault craft that could exit from a stern "well-deck" cleverly disguised under the aft third of the ship. The smaller craft were similar in design to the U.S. Navy's LCACs (Landing Craft, Air Cushioned—whose design the PLA marine architects had largely copied from American journals and, of course, Wing's legion of computer hackers and in-person spies).

The next intriguing feature was located forward of the bridge: In four tubular spaces, two on each side, one in front of the other, were compartments for small submarines. Bao explained that they were nearly silent diesel-electric models, and they could be deployed to protect the mother ship or to sink targets of opportunity. The mothership's outer hulls revealed no trace of the hidden launching doors, and their crews boarded from inside. The subs were launched after their "nesting" compartments had been sealed and then flooded—with the only requirement being that the ship stop and drift prior to launching. Each sub was about 200 feet long and carried 12 of the newest PLAN Yu-9 torpedoes.

Just above the submarine spaces, and forward of the bridge that rose from the center of the ship, was the most heavily reinforced deck of the entire vessel. The space was designed to carry the 100 main battle tanks that provided the brigade-sized unit's main punch. These ground forces were comprised mostly of PLAN marines, with some army battalions mixed in. The tanks were visible on Bao's diagram, lined up in neat rows and secured to the deck with heavy chains. Also visible, because they were highlighted, giant watertight doors concealed laterally deployable ramps that extended from the starboard side of each hull. This design had been adapted from the American roll-on/roll-off ships (ROROs) that effectively delivered an incredible number of armored vehicles to Saudi Arabia during Desert Storm. The tanks and other vehicles could easily motor down these ramps and deploy as the current tactical situation demanded.

Bao explained many of these details to his enamored audience: "Ministers, these high-capacity motherships can carry a full armored brigade, consisting of 100 Type 99A (ZTZ-99/WZ-123) main battle tanks with their 125mm smoothbore main guns. And, on the next deck directly above the tank decks, we have included 100 ZBD-04A infantry fighting vehicles, onto which we've mounted our 25mm automatic cannons that we co-produced with the Americans in the 1980s. Some carry our own 73mm main cannons, plus dual AJ-73 rocket launchers with 20 missiles each, plus eight of our marines.

"Additionally, every ship carries 18 self-propelled PLZ-45 155mm cannons (each with a range of more than 30 kilometers); 10 type 81 MRLS launchers with 122mm rockets; 18 Type-95 quad 25mm AAA guns, and 50 CSK-141 armored personnel carriers. In addition to the personnel needed for the vehicles, we include a combat engineer battalion, a communications battalion, and three battalions of marine infantry. We can all be proud that these armaments are manufactured by NORICO—our own countrymen working tirelessly at North China Industries Corporation—technical experts who are in turn supported by many other quality factories throughout our homeland." He paused for the expected round of applause in the direction of Minister of Heavy Industry Lee Tuc Chang, who then stood and smiled broadly. He waved his thanks and sat down.

"All of this firepower will be supported by an array of the most highly technical capabilities known to man—both offensive and defensive combat systems that we have developed from our own labs. These are aided by our orbiting satellites—some with offensive anti-satellite capability—that constantly downlink precise intelligence and targeting information for each system." Bao then elaborated on various interesting details and answered questions. "The higher decks are loaded with lighter vehicles, while the personnel and their supplies are housed or stored above the main deck—in cleverly disguised barracks and bays in the 'container stacks' located forward of the bridge."

Bao then used his pointer to shift everyone's attention to the levels behind the ship's superstructure. "Here, inside this large area above the well deck—and comprising approximately 35 percent of each mother ship's spatial capacity—are 500 of our new top-secret drones. This is each Dragon's real offensive threat, and how we plan to control each battle space. Though relatively small like an economy car, this is the most important low-level naval and air force on the planet. These drones will rise from their launching positions inside the aft 'container stacks' and then scatter over the target areas. As they fly, they will deploy tens of thousands of mini-drones that each pack the destructive power of a bullet. They will raise havoc with vehicles, buildings, rocket launching tubes, artillery, and personnel. They are the size of honey bees, and can fly into any small space and explode on contact. They can also kill any human target that can't find adequate cover. Each 'mother drone' carries a new type of bomb—a metal-melting shaped charge that will be dropped primarily on ships and submarines. They explode on contact like regular bombs, but release a potent chemical combination that melts down through successive decks. If this mixture hits fuel bunkers or ammunition magazines, they will explode and further sympathetically detonate everything in the space. This technology will render useless every ship and sub in the Allied inventory.

"The aviation decks also house the maintenance bays to service the aircraft, and the middle and lower bridge decks house companies of drone operators, plus some photo-interpreters to analyze the feeds from the drones' cameras.

"All in all, Ministers, each Dragon mothership carries a force that can dominate a limited geographical battlefield under the sea, on the sea, on land, and in the air. Everything is, of course, connected with our Space Command, which is now better than the Americans. We have a secret offensive capability in our satellites, and we will render the Allies' GPS system useless. And, last but not least, we have the world's first operational ship-mounted laser weapons and various electronic counter-measures that will protect our Dragons against any kind of low-level enemy attack!"

After many "oohs" and "aahs," there was a question from the middle of the room: "Comrade General Bao, how can one ship carry so much weight and still maintain a shallow draft of 13 meters?" The man was an engineer, and he could read the simple schematics everyone was gawking at.

"Great question, Comrade Minister! When you see these mother ships on your tour tomorrow, you will wonder no longer! But in short: These ships have been designed to draw no more than a ship two-thirds its size. Our marine engineers have made a breakthrough that incorporates special inflatable air pods borrowed from submarine technology. This breakthrough allowed us to meet our design specs for 13 out of the 14 harbors we've targeted—only Australia's Sydney Harbor is a bit shallower, and that Dragon carries a few less vehicles to compensate." The room started buzzing in anticipation of the following day's tour.

Bao paused to mentally regroup; the enormity of what they were contemplating was almost more than even he could bear. He and Dang had pulled it off, and even the ever-conservative Marshall Tai had praised them. He had been promoted in the interim and now wore three stars, and Dang had been given a significant pay raise. Bao knew the future was filled with uncertainty so they needed luck, but he liked their chances.

The room quieted again so he gathered himself and continued his enlightening narrative: "The 'container stacks' above the main deck are a stroke of camouflage genius: Though constructed to look like any container ship that is fully loaded with those normal-looking steel boxes—or 'stacks' in shipping jargon—they are actually convincingly painted steel bulkheads that conceal several sturdy horizontal decks. There are cleverly designed mirrors included in the camo scheme too, making each stack look separate and normal. These integrated technologies contribute to our principal offensive strategy of 'hiding in plain sight' until we attack. This is why we are not worried about our visibility during the two weeks previously mentioned." Once again, he had to pause as the murmurs of approval became a din of animated conversations. Bao couldn't blame them for celebrating; he and Dang had devised an obviously brilliant plan. He felt a touch of irony that he'd gotten his inspiration from an ancient enemy—Commander Genda and Admiral Yamamoto's team of visionary World War II-era Japanese planners.

"These above-main-deck spaces include barracks that house nearly 3,000 marines and sailors, plus all their equipment, food, and the supporting material mentioned earlier. The command group and the air force sections are housed within the multi-story bridge complex. This force has been carefully selected and trained to overwhelm our enemies with lightning precision—including any electronic or physical counter-measures our enemies throw at us from land, sea, air, or space. And, though our marines don't know their eventual targets, they have been training with compartmentalized mock-ups for more than two years."

Tai could wait no longer, and interjected some dramatic news: "Comrades, we will launch our first Dragon tomorrow night, and all 14 within the next 11 days!" He was not prepared for the collective gasp that followed, nor by the outburst of energy that brought the ministers to their feet, applauding wildly.

Sitting back down proudly next to President Han, Marshal Tai was elated: What they had done was indeed a triumph of military and civilian engineering that befitted the Middle Kingdom. They had watched over their "babies" like a couple of mother hens, and they'd longed for this day when they could reveal their plans to the larger governing body. He could only imagine everyone's astonishment when they witnessed the ships firsthand tomorrow. He then watched with anticipation as Han rose and introduced Minister Wing—last of the scheduled briefers.

Chapter 16

Ministers' Briefing Room, 13:20 Hours

General Wing had just returned to his seat after giving those assembled a 15-minute outline of his "Fifth-Column" preparations—soon to be carried out by thousands of in-place cadres. He explained that their tasks were somewhat diverse but, in essence, they were to initiate disruptive attacks within every targeted country that would focus the locals on everything except the approaching ships. His "Chaos Teams' would also slow any Allied response during the landings. Wing's agents would attack assigned targets based on a pre-established timetable, which would begin a few hours before the Dragons docked. He had kept his remarks somewhat vague because he was naturally reluctant to reveal details about any live operation, but his contribution to the greater briefing had put the lid on most unspoken objections. Wu would never be satisfied, but no one in the higher echelons would interfere with Operation Unity now. Wing's advance teams had assignments in all 14 targeted ports, plus extensive additional small-team operators that he guaranteed would divert attention away from the motherships. All teams were in place and ready, and they would cause comprehensive chaos that would lead the news cycle. Sleeper agents, some deeply imbedded for more than 10 years, had already assisted the CTs, and their local knowledge was proving invaluable to the overall plan.

As he sat down, he was unsettled because he wanted to be monitoring and adjusting his personnel, not sitting around listening to drooling politicians. He was also on the verge of one of his famously dark moods—stewing because he knew more about the upcoming mission than everyone here combined. He resented sitting through another lecture on the ships' minutiae given by Tai's pet underling Bao and his wire-rimmed sidekick. These ministers could celebrate all they wanted, but he had a lot of terribly important work to finish before the first ships launched in just a few hours.

As Wing quietly fumed, a young officer entered the back of the room. She noted the general's dark mood instantly, and it added to her considerable trepidation. Nevertheless, Junior Lieutenant Ki Guo Mau got the "okay" from Wing's adjutant after she showed him the urgent note from the communications center. It didn't help Ki's confidence that this full colonel was not willing to risk the general's wrath and deliver the note himself. She was on her own—this afternoon's sacrificial lamb. She took a deep breath, and walked quietly past the backs of several sitting ministers before arriving at the general's elbow. She bent down and whispered politely, "Excuse me, Minister Wing. A priority message just came through for you with an 'eyes-only' designator…" She saw the general startle at her intrusion—he'd obviously been lost in thought—but at least he didn't scold her. He simply met her eyes, and reached up and brusquely snatched the proffered note from her hand. She was relieved to see that her hand wasn't trembling—the general hated such displays of weakness.

Wing had indeed been surprised when he'd heard the sweet female voice whispering just behind him, and he wondered why on earth some irritating underling dared to intrude on his important thoughts. But, as he focused his blazing eyes upward at the intruder, he saw a very young and homely junior officer who nervously, yet bravely, held a simple note. He'd heard the 'eyes-only' designator and impatiently forgot about the messenger. He grabbed the note and hurriedly scanned its content:

<u>Senior Colonel Kang, Li Quo, Chief of Security, Special Section, Dalian Shipyard, requests that you confirm the identity and mission of MSS Lieutenant Colonel Ma posing as a MSS Major Lee. She claims you assigned her the task of penetrating the restricted cavern where the special ships are being completed, and of reporting back to you if she discovered any irregularities. The woman is currently in the medical clinic and being kept under close supervision. Please advise.</u>

An uncharacteristic chill shot down Wing's spine. *I need to get out of this damned meeting now!* Thankfully, the note offered just that: A credible excuse to leave. He quietly signaled Han that he had to depart and received a polite nod. A jolt of negative electricity now shot through Wing's chest. This was the worst possible news! *This person was an obvious enemy agent! But Ma? She of all people would know not to make any appeal in his name! Had she tricked him these last several years?* He could feel one of his seething rages coming on, but restrained himself by an act of will as he nearly dashed for the door. His startled aide and the young lieutenant raced to keep up.

"The Communications Center, immediately!" he ordered the lieutenant sternly, and she jogged ahead of him to show the way. *This was bad,* he worried. *The whole mission might be compromised at the last minute! And what on earth was Ma doing...Could she have been a plant by those Taiwanese pirates—or worse, the West, all this time? I have to get to the bottom of this within the hour!* Fortunately, his helicopter was always on standby and Dalian was not far away.

Thirty seconds later they were in the secure communications room and Wing was connected with Colonel Kang, the author of the alarming note. His subsequent conversation with the security chief was loud, one-way, and very threatening.

Inside Dalian Shipyard medical clinic, ten minutes later

Jen knew her life had run its course the second Kang threw open the door with such force that he nearly knocked it off its hinges. Both his aide and the doctor jumped at the intrusion, but Jen could see the man was terrified—and he had good reason to doubt his own longevity. Jen also accepted that her earthly sojourn would soon be over, but she was not afraid. She was sad because of the implications for her beloved ones, and that she'd never enjoy the God-given privileges of marriage and children. But she was also in control of her emotions, and was determined to make her last moments of service to her beloved God and country count.

"Well, Ma or Lee, or whoever you really are…your lies have sent the minister of State Security into one of his rages! And you are the one who will scream your life away in his dungeon, not me! You are to be handed over to the very person whose name you used, and you should know that an awful end awaits you for your evil lies and spying!" Kang's stress had caused him to lose so much self-control that his voice squeaked and his face flushed. He was also panting, and it was clear that he was far more terrified of Wing's wrath than he was concerned about any aspect of Jen's identity or mission.

However, Jen was not fazed by the colonel's histrionics: She'd been ready for this eventuality and had peace in her soul. She had devoted her life to God, to her family, to the Church, and to her country, and now, at the end of her mortal life, Heaven beckoned with amazing surety. She said nothing as she measured her respective distances to the three persons staring at her in amazement: Kang shaking with fear and rage, and looking like he wanted to strangle her; Captain Kai looked stern yet impressed; and Dr. Ling looked confused and frightened. But Jen remained still. And, as she drew the seconds out to force her adversaries to act first, Kang's anxiety boiled over.

He had not received what he expected—some normal response from a young woman in peril. He anticipated a gasp, a denial, an explanation, or a plea for mercy—something! Anything except this one's cool, non-committal gaze. This passivity finally pushed him over the top and he lost his temper and lunged for her.

Jen was hoping for this exact response, and she reacted to his clumsy attack with calculated precision. Ignoring the searing pain in her left shoulder, she jumped out of her seat and parried Kang's bullish charge like a matador in the ring. She converted his momentum to her advantage, and propelled him with a tremendous crash into the wall next to her chair. This unexpectedly violent confrontation shook Captain Kai out of his reverie, and he leaped to his superior's defense. But Jen instantly evaluated his posture, and accepted that the younger man was highly skilled. He'd obviously assessed Jen's aggressive martial arts technique, too, and tried to counter hers with one of his own. But Jen's art was truly advanced. She'd been sparring with Tim for years, and he was equally talented but much larger and stronger than she. Kai was simply outmatched: Even severely wounded, Jen was not intimidated by the obviously athletic and agile young officer, and before he could connect with a well-chosen hand-strike, she stunned him with a lightning-fast roundhouse kick to the side of his head that would have pleased the wonderful old mentor of her youth. Kai was totally unprepared for the force of the blow and was knocked back against the cupboards behind him. He crashed against them with such force that he was truly stunned, and in slow motion that would do martial arts movies proud, he just sank to the floor. As Jen intended, he was out of the fight but was not badly injured. She had no desire to deliver lethal blows to her three captors—there was no point.

Jen adjusted her posture slightly to face the doctor, having already seen in her peripheral vision that Ling had backed up and was now pressing herself into the farthest corner. Unnecessarily killing was alien to Jen's Christian faith, and though she understood that China might be planning to attack her beloved America—and certainly was planning to attack some unsuspecting nation—there was nothing more she could do. But she was confident that the very fact that she was missing in action would be enough for Ken to get additional assets involved and sound a general alarm. Poor Ken, she thought in a flash…and poor Tim and their families.

Ling felt like a trapped faun. Her patient/prisoner had exploded from her chair and effortlessly disabled two bigger and stronger military men—and done so while severely wounded. She was terrified of this little tigress who had suddenly transformed before her eyes—a passive patient who was now something almost supernatural. And it had only been a few hours since she'd patched up the woman from a bullet wound in her shoulder—a serious injury with significant blood loss! Ling had perhaps seen something like it in the movies, but never in person, and she couldn't help shaking in fear. She abhorred the thought that she would endure a terrible beating or even death at the hands of this spy. She was shocked, however, when the latter did something astounding—her patient stood her ground and pointed a convicting finger at her and spoke evenly:

"Remember this act of mercy, Doctor Ling…you have shown precious little of it to others! Christ is Lord…not the State!" Then she stepped to the counter next to the prostrate and moaning Kang and grabbed the pair of medical scissors that Ling had laid there earlier.

Jen was emotionally torn as both genuine sadness and spiritual exultation washed over her soul. She understood that her next action would bring pain into the lives of many whom she loved—but she accepted that her duty to God and country came first, and she'd walked onto the shipyard that morning prepared to die. The reality of death had always been part of her training and life in the Clandestine Service, and never far from her daily life in the PRC. But she was still human—a young woman with so much of life's potential in front of her, and for a moment she shuddered as she considered her mortality. She didn't want to die. But she couldn't allow a vicious enemy to extract vital information from her, either. Such information could cause China to step up the timetable of whatever it was planning and cause thousands of innocents to suffer needlessly. She would not be responsible for those deaths, nor of those of her colleagues in the field.

Jen had been reviewing her options as she waited for Kang's charge, and she was now implementing the plan she had formulated using the scissors Ling set on the counter. It was her time. Without further delay, she shot a prayer of thanksgiving heavenward, placed the circular scissor handle in her mouth, and bit down hard on her next to last right upper molar. The tooth split as she had been promised by the Agency dentist, and the latest fast-acting poison secreted inside a tiny ampule was released when it shattered. A powerful and lethal dose of the substance was directly injected into her blood stream. Jen momentarily cringed at the sharp pain. Then, just as fast, she felt immediate relief as the chemicals fulfilled their promise. Her life quickly drifted away and, as she slumped to the floor and closed her eyes—her last conscious thoughts were of her parents, of dear Tim, and of her Sunday school class. She heard her kindergarteners, the only children she'd ever have, sweetly singing the hymn she'd taught them when she was a college-age volunteer. Then Jen's soul released and she passed into Eternity.

Across the room, Ling was stunned by what she'd just witnessed. And though she knew she had to help Colonel Kang—currently moaning on the floor near the apparently dead agent—Ling was paralyzed with wonder as she started to process what was surely a once-in-a-lifetime experience. Her life had flashed before her when Lee had pointed at her—and the young woman's words had bored into the center of her being, exposing everything—every evil thing she'd done in the name of the State. But, perhaps surprisingly, everything good had also been revealed. It was unnerving. Then the woman had suddenly killed herself! Nothing in Ling's long life and training had prepared her for this. She suddenly thought about her conversations with her brother, who was a Christian believer living in their small home village in the mountains in Hubei Province. She had thought him a fool for believing in someone you couldn't see, and had mocked his crazy stories from the Bible he loved—but which the State said were lies. Now, in a flash, she suddenly wondered if her brother was right—could the stories be true?

On the other side of the small room, Captain Kai was shaking off the cobwebs and had managed to extract his sidearm and crawl to where the prisoner lay dead. He'd come to his senses just in time to witness Lee's final words to the doctor, followed by her incredible suicide, and he was amazed. He came to the young woman's side and placed the barrel of his gun against her temple while using his free hand to assess the carotid artery pulse in her neck, but it was clear that she had passed. He replaced his pistol, pushed the dead agent's body gently out of the way, and slid another meter to where his colonel was stirring. At least Kang was still alive. Lee had propelled the senior officer into the cinderblock wall; yet, even as he witnessed the lightning-fast encounter, Kai had the definite impression that the woman had been in control of the moment and wasn't trying to kill him; he believed she could have finished Kang before either he or the doctor could intervene. And when she had kicked him, she had struck the side of his head behind his ear, instead of his temple or neck, which he believed was no accident. For some reason she'd chosen to let he and Kang live—obviously choosing to merely stun them—buying just enough time to kill herself. But why—what did her restraint mean? He wanted to know more about what she said to Ling. Suddenly, he was distracted from his analysis when Kang's eyelids fluttered. The senior officer opened them just enough to reveal dulled and unfocused vision. Then he spoke, "What…What happened, Kai?"

"The prisoner attacked both of us, Colonel…then she committed suicide…"

"What…how?" His senses began to sharpen as he remembered the attack.

"I watched her bite down on some scissors…I don't know why, but the act killed her. I have confirmed that she is dead."

At last Ling found her voice—even as she remained riveted in place. "There must have been a poison capsule hidden in one of her teeth, Colonel. Nothing else explains why she died so quickly…" Involuntarily she shivered at the thought, but this very act helped her regain control of her faculties. She moved unsteadily to Kang's side, and then, with Kai's assistance, helped the still-dazed colonel to a sitting position so they could slide him back against the wall. He was still woozy so she advised him to remain seated until he felt better. She extracted an ampule of smelling salts from a drawer, crushed the capsule between her finger and thumb, and waved it a couple of inches from the colonel's nose until his head recoiled from its powerful odor.

Kang needed a couple of minutes more for the room to stop spinning, then he began to think. He looked over at Major Lee's body lying only an arm's length away and stared at her face. She appeared sleeping, though he didn't doubt Kai's assertion that the woman was dead. *What will become of me now?* he wondered selfishly. It was his task alone to explain to an already enraged Minister Wing why he'd allowed this valuable spy to die before a thorough interrogation could be conducted. That impending confrontation caused a jolt of adrenaline to course though his aching body—and the shock accelerated his transition back to reality. "Help me up!" he commanded the others. With great difficulty, he allowed himself to be lifted onto the chair recently vacated by his now-deceased captive. He had to think fast before facing the wrath to come, wondering in horror if maybe he, too, should kill himself while he had the chance.

Less than 90 minutes later, after ordering tea and regaining their strength, the three loyal Chinese citizens heard the approaching beat of two powerful helicopters. They looked at each other and knew the terrible truth: It was General Wing arriving to dish out wrath. Captain Kai wasn't worried, but the other two were truly terrified.

Wing emerged from the second of two helicopters as several of his personal bodyguard jumped out of the lead aircraft and raced ahead to secure the clinic. They knew something terrible had happened and that their general had come to get to the bottom of a rebellion of some kind. They were ready for his orders—no matter whom he or they had to execute. They held the door as he climbed the short flight of cement steps, and then rushed ahead as he clumped down the hall. Light spilled from an open doorway and, as he entered, he saw two of his men holding assault rifles on two PLA officers and a female doctor in a white smock. On the exam table was a body draped in a sheet.

"All right," he bellowed without preamble, "start talking!"

Prepared but extremely nervous, Colonel Kang stood up painfully and stammered, "Minister Wing, we captured a spy who made claims that she worked for you!" He indicated the draped body on the table.

"Are you insane, Colonel?" Wing shouted. "How did such a spy gain access to our fleet's preparation chamber?"

"She climbed the outer cliff face, General," Kang replied, mortified that his answer was delivered in his awful squeaky voice. "She was shot inside attempting to escape from security."

"Do you mean to tell me that she managed to penetrate the shipyard's security layers, climb more than a hundred meters of open bare cliff, and penetrate the facility before being confronted by your inept security personnel?" *He was just getting warmed up and was sorely tempted to personally shoot these three incompetents before nightfall!*

"I will fully investigate!" offered Kang weakly—finally finding his normal voice. He feared he was finished, not seeing a way out of this dreadful mess. But he had decided earlier not to kill himself. He wanted more time, and hoped he could do it later if necessary. In the matter of a half-day his life and career had gone from promising to doomed.

Turning to the woman in the white coat, Wing recognized one of his MSS cadres. "What's your story, Doctor Ling?" He could see he surprised the middle-aged woman with his address. "Aren't you the MSS staff physician who's an 'expert in interrogation' at Shenyang Province HQ?" He made quotation marks in the air to mock her, even as he enjoyed unnerving her. He had a gift for names, and knew all key regional personnel. "Did you learn who she was working for…?"

"No, Comrade Minister. But I suspect she was an agent of the rebellious province." It was all Ling could muster at the moment. She heard the general's unconvinced grunt, and she knew in her soul, as Kang had, that she had seen her home for the last time.

Wing then moved two steps to the table and flipped off the sheet covering the deceased spy's face, but he was surprised that it was not Ma. It was a pretty young girl who seemed asleep. *What on earth was going on here?*

He turned back to the frightened officers and said, "You three are worse than useless to the country you are supposedly committed to protect!" He then barked an order to his detail: "Take these three idiots to Dalian MSS Headquarters…I will be along shortly to deal with them personally!"

MSS Headquarters, Dalian City
November 25th, 23:45 Hours

This confusing chapter in Chinese history ended that night behind the regional MSS headquarters building: A terrified and bewildered woman in her late thirties, wearing the torn and blood-stained uniform of an MSS lieutenant colonel, was roughly dragged from the basement chamber where she'd been "closely questioned" regarding her role in possible treasonous activities against the State. Specifically, she'd been forced to answer questions about the activities of a deceased enemy agent who'd been caught inside the secure section of the nearby shipyard. That agent had used Ma's name during her interrogation and later, to the great consternation of senior authorities, had committed suicide.

The horrified officer had pleaded ignorance and innocence to no avail, and had been beaten mercilessly by the three men she used to regularly bully and humiliate into obeying her commands. Finally, at the end of the terrible session, she'd cried out her devotion to the man whom she truly loved with all her heart, the man who now, at the end of her mortal life, stood over her with a pistol in his hand. Forced to kneel like many she'd subjected to the same terrible ordeal, her pitiful cries fell on deaf ears. Wing pointed his .32 at the back of Ma's head when she at last looked away in resignation, and he pulled the trigger twice. It was his usual method of execution.

Before midnight brought an end to this ugly affair, the now-disgraced Ma's body was buried in an unmarked grave in an undistinguished cemetery not far from the sordid courtyard where she'd been executed. In an adjacent grave, the body of the enemy agent was also buried without fanfare. Then, early the next morning, Ma's once-proud parents were left alone to deal with their shock and grief after they were presented with a bill for Wing's two expended pistol cartridges. The officer delivering the horrible news whispered to them that they should sell their belongings, move away, and disappear as quickly as possible. Then he arrogantly strode from their front door to his waiting car and sped away in the morning traffic.

However, the three officers who had witnessed the death of the spy, plus the interrogation and execution of their colleague, were surprisingly spared:

Wing occasionally showed mercy when he thought it magnified terror in all concerned. Those who knew they were going to be executed and were not spread the word, and Wing's deadly reputation only grew. Two of the spared went home shaken but grateful to be alive, and were consoled by their shocked but relieved families. The third made a call to a family member. Though sickened by what Minister Wing's interrogators did to the MSS officer, Captain Kai never worried about his own fate: He'd kept certain personal facts secret—an ace he didn't need to show. His strongest feeling was gratitude that the admirable young woman had let him live—an amazing person, regardless of her national loyalties. He was curious about her life and faith, and vowed to learn more when he had the chance.

Book II

Chapter 17

Inside the cavern, Dalian Harbor, Liaoning Province
Night of November 26/27, 18:30 Hours

Vice Admiral Sun Lin Duo stood on his ship's port bridge wing, anxiously watching the slow motion movement that signaled, both symbolically and actually, that the Dragon Fleet's long confinement was nearly over. The cavern's massive front door was gradually sliding to his right. Because the harbor was located in a northern latitude in late November, he could see that it was already dark outside. The moon's cycle had been a known entity when the hulls were towed into the finishing grotto, and he felt fortunate that the waning crescent rising above the harbor was dim. At least during the initial launch, any bit of extra protection from prying eyes was welcome.

Contributing to light discipline, every light inside the vast complex had switched to red 30 minutes before, and the southern one-quarter of the shipyard's outside lights had been dimmed as well. The on-board crews and launch teams didn't need red-lens goggles like the submariners famously wore because the previous half-hour in the "red" environment provided plenty of time for everyone's night vision to adjust. If any of the Dragons had engine problems or ran aground as they left the cavern, the Chinese would look ridiculous in front of the world. There were extra tugs standing by to push the affected vessels back into the cavern for repairs, but that would be a nightmare. The media would be informed the following day after each successful launch.

So many years of preparations, the veteran sailor marveled. Now it all came down to the simple mechanical act of opening a door—a low-tech operation that would release his task force ship by ship for the largest Pacific Ocean war since the 1940s. *Dragon's Claw* was Sun's flagship, and she was second in line on the left-hand (northern) lane of the grotto, and one of three ships scheduled to put to sea before dawn. They had the longest voyages (to the United States' ports of San Diego, San Francisco, and Seattle, respectively) and the entire fleet's departure schedule was staggered to facilitate their simultaneous arrival 11 days hence. The next departures would be the following night, when the ships bound for Sydney, Australia, and Honolulu, Hawaii, would follow. The balance of the fleet would launch alone or in groups according to the meticulously created master schedule, and all would (hopefully) arrive within a few minutes of each other at H-Hour on D-Day. Sun, and most of those in the know, believed that, from this moment on, it all came down to luck.

Waiting impatiently (because he was fundamentally a man of action), the admiral's thoughts once again considered General Wing's promises that the fleet would arrive at countries consumed by debilitating chaos. The MSS minister (and General Bao), who Sun knew well from their academy days together, had created his so-called "Chaos Teams" to disrupt the target countries and hence divert attention from the Dragons' arrival. However, these teams were now just an additional factor after the release of the ironic and accidental flu pandemic. Wing's laboratories had developed the flu, but it had somehow gotten away from his scientists—killing an unknown number of Chinese citizens before spreading around the world.

But Sun admitted that the accident had an unintended golden lining—producing amazing fear everywhere and bringing the Western economies to their knees. Only recently were the world's workers back to something approaching pre-Covid levels, but its disruptive effects lingered on. He admired the pure Machiavellian devilry that prompted Wing, Han, and Tai—utilizing the cooperation of a handful of other leaders—to withhold any announcement of the outbreak until the PRC had gobbled up every mask and respirator they could buy on the open market. They'd kept flights to and from China running at full capacity, and that decision enabled the virus to spread worldwide. It was a two-part decision that cost many lives, but the Politburo considered the results as collateral damage—that is, expendable assets invested in their long-term goals. They never envisioned that the Western economies, especially that of the United States, would succumb to the levels that they did—a related phenomenon that became a pure bonus. Anecdotal reports that Sun and his fellow senior officers kept hearing—that a million or more of their own citizens had perished—were indeed sad. But no one he knew personally had died. Sun and his confidants knew the extent of the lies about the origins and extent of the outbreak, but they drew their own conclusions about domestic suffering. It had helped the PRC's narrative that the World Health Organization and the international media had swallowed the State's media commentaries hook, line, and sinker. The bottom line for Sun was that any ruse that helped their hide-in-plain-sight strategy was gold dust.

Finally! Sun rejoiced as the big door opened to its maximum width with a solid "clank." He was not naturally fidgety, but tonight was a true exception: He had years of pent-up anticipation sending tingles up and down his spine and, like the nearly 3,000 marines, sailors, and air force technicians crammed into every nook and cranny of his wondrous assault ship, he just wanted to get underway. He was the task force commander of the four-ship American component of Operation Unity, and he knew many would perceive weakness in him if he looked impatient. He was trying to project a posture of outward calmness, and distracted himself by forming an image in his mind of the heavy-gauge double towline that would momentarily be attached to the bow of *Dragon's Fire*—the ship closest to the door. Eager sailors would catch the thin messenger line tossed up from the sea-going tugboat that had backed up to within a few meters of the massive bow, and the sailors above would pull it hand over hand until they received the heavier woven 10-centimeter-in-diameter bright blue lines that could take the weight of each 1,000-foot ship. The stanchion team would fit them though dual one-meter ovals in the bow flare that opened directly onto the main deck, then wrap them around the heavy steel posts welded to the deck. Then the tugs would gradually take up the slack and, in a matter of minutes, *Fire* would move down the channel and out into the harbor. There she'd be met by two other tugs that would come alongside and push her into deeper water so she could take on her 726-Type LCACs and mini-submarines.

It was impossible for Admiral Sun to see the tug because of the towering bridge of the first ship, but he knew what was supposed to happen, and he appreciated, imperceptibly at first, that *Dragon's Fire* had begun her journey into world history. She steadily gained momentum, and Sun nearly wept at the sight of his sister ship gliding away in the darkness. He imagined more than saw her slide into the harbor—quite a feat for a ship that, fully loaded, weighed more than 150,000 tons.

Now, with the front space free, the cavern's small workhorse electric railroad engines pulled *Dragon's Claw* forward until she reached her position by the door. Two identical engines provided gentle back pressure until they brought their charge to a stop—preventing the massive ship from bumping the tug. About 10 minutes later, Sun heard the walkie-talkie conversation between *Claw's* captain and the tug's CO, and soon heard the "okay" from the bow team. A few seconds after that, the two messenger lines sailed over the bow, and the process of hauling the two main lines up to the stanchions began again. After another three-minute wait, the admiral felt a tiny lunge and, slowly, *Dragon's Claw* began to move.

Sun's flagship was the centerpiece of his task force—assault ships that would traverse the Pacific Ocean and attack the dangerous Americans where they lived. His target ports were four of the five most distant the PLA would occupy—their mission just a component of the comprehensive and audacious operation that would give them control of a third of the world's surface—land or sea. Sun's Dragons had been ordered to assault and hold the United States' three main West Coast ports, plus the commercial port in Hawaii—each port located adjacent to military bases where the American Pacific Fleet was stationed. They could also attack nearby airfields where combat aircraft posed an immediate threat. The air, sea, and ground forces hidden within each Dragon would sink or damage as many of the enemy's surface ships and submarines as they could, plus destroy the related infrastructure in every location. They'd also hold the captured port cities for as long as possible—buying time for the ground forces in Asia to consolidate their regional gains.

Sun knew that if Operation Unity was successful, China would emerge as the world's undisputed superpower—only a first step to enlarging her dominant footprint even further in the future. The PRC would accelerate its influence beyond east Asia via its Belt and Road Initiative—already established in much of the emerging world. Infrastructure of every kind had been built utilizing clever aid packages agreed to with weaker host countries, and China was already siphoning wealth back to the homeland from dozens of ports, highways, and airfields. And, someday, after the Americans and their closest allies got used to the new world order, bi-lateral trade would begin again. However, China would dictate the terms, the Americans' recent fussing notwithstanding.

As individual targets, the San Diego Naval Base held the largest number of surface combatants on the U.S. West Coast, while the Seattle/Puget Sound region held the largest number of submarines. Several of the precious aircraft carriers (both "big-deck" and "small-deck" types) rotated through their home ports, and destroying them was vital. Additionally, each port's fuel and repair facilities would delay any American counter-attack by degrees. San Francisco was no longer a military port, but it was the gateway to the vast Oakland container terminal and the Bay Area's technology hub, and the PLAN wanted to deny the Allies its potential threat. There were American air force bases nearby, and those would be taken out within minutes of the first attack.

The last of Sun's targets was Joint Base Pearl Harbor-Hickam Air Force Base—America's military command nexus for the entire west/central Pacific. It was the homeport of the U.S. Navy's regional submarine fleet, and headquarters of the United States' Indo-Pacific Command. It and several key subordinate commands were on their target list.

Additionally, Pearl Harbor's home-ported LHAs, LHDs (the U.S. Marine Corp's "small deck" helicopter carriers) plus LSDs and LPHs (the Corp's assault ships similar in purpose to the Dragons) were key targets, along with the usual 10 submarines that were in port between patrols. He also wanted to sink as many of the other surface ships as he could, plus damage their airfields, aircraft, workshops and other vital components of their military infrastructure. Pearl Harbor was still America's key jumping-off point for any retaliatory strike against the People's Republic, so it had to be taken and held for as long as possible. This part of the objective would be accomplished by *Dragon's Tail*'s armor-heavy force, which would nullify any effective response from the U.S. Army's 25th Division, or the locally stationed U.S. Marines and National Guard units. But the real power of each Dragon was her massive drone force that would introduce a new and dominant technology to the world's battlefields. The Americans and Israelis had effectively utilized individual drones for years—both as observer craft and as missile-launching platforms—but no one had used them en masse. China was about to teach the world what real "shock and awe" was all about!

An hour after *Dragon's Claw* first nudged into the channel, she was pushed gracefully through the harbor by her tugs and was soon in water deep enough to take on her four mini-submarines—currently waiting a safe distance yards away as the mothership approached. As had *Fire* before her, *Claw* paused long enough to take on mini-subs, and each one slid neatly into its inner-hull compartment. Then, after the four were sealed inside their chambers, the four 726s slid into the well deck, then its ramp was raised and sealed, making it invisible to any prying eyes. *Claw* then engaged her propellers for the first time, and the great ship moved forward and gradually built up speed. All systems worked like a charm, and she proceeded without incident into the western end of the Yellow Sea.

Admiral Sun, and the rest of the naval and merchant marine veterans, didn't like the unheard-of idea of launching fully laden ships without a shakedown cruise, but they had no choice this time. It was a necessary component of their giant gamble, and crucial to the plan's hide-in-plain-sight strategy. The marine architects and engineers were confident that every one of the millions of parts had been manufactured and installed to perfection, and any deviation from the plan would risk their ruse being discovered. They'd only get one chance at this, so every engineer and mechanic had fussed over his or her charges for more than two years—including ultrasound scans on every individual part at the factories, so there was no reason for any of the ship's main functions to fail. The "bottom line" was simple anyway: All the fleet had to accomplish was one cross-ocean voyage—and any use they got from the ships after that was a bonus.

Chapter 18

The White House
November 26th, 08:30 Hours

As the first Dragons were putting to sea, the President's "gate-keeper," Virginia Ross, had barely disconnected from her counterpart in the Vice President's office, when the VP herself appeared in the hallway. The "Boss" had requested that his "Number Two" come over right away to discuss something in person, and Rebecca Mason was very curious.

She had just finished a briefing with her own chief of staff, so President Stilwell's timing was good. She made an immediate beeline for the impromptu meeting and, as soon as she was a couple of paces from the Oval Office, the female agent tending the door opened it, announced her arrival, and then followed her inside.

"Good morning, Mr. President…" She greeted the most influential human being on the planet. Even though she entered this inner sanctum often, she still felt an emotional zing in the historic room. So much of American and world history had happened in this old and relatively small space, and she appreciated the tremendous heritage she shared with her fellow citizens. She also greatly respected this President, and was committed to supporting him as he served amid a slew of enemies (both foreign and domestic) that criticized him from every quadrant, every day. Fortunately, the man had emotional skin like a rhinoceros and, though he also had his flaws and human weaknesses like everyone else, his national and international vision for America's place in the world, plus his genuine love for people both here and abroad, engendered loyalty among those who knew him best.

"Rebecca, thanks for coming right over…" Spence greeted his Vice President warmly. He motioned for her to sit—personally fond of this exceptional lady. She'd done an excellent job for him and the country, and was an example of a natural leader who'd balanced home and professional responsibilities for a long time. He'd been lucky to have her support: She'd been a successful business founder and owner, a member of Congress, plus her home state's governor—and, in the future, on the same day he retired, he hoped she would be the one who finally broke the world's loftiest glass ceiling. He made his way around the big desk that was a familiar sight to everyone who'd watched televised presidential addresses by several presidents, and settled into his favorite dark brown overstuffed leather chair. Between them was the office's low-set, glass-topped coffee table on which a thoughtful steward had placed a tea service with the VP's favorite blend.

Spence got right to the point: "I just received an unsettling update from Edith Carmichael regarding China; however, she admits it might turn out to be nothing serious at all…" The President regularly received scheduled and unscheduled reports from the DNI, who oversaw the 16 organizations that constituted America's comprehensive efforts to gather, analyze, and distribute intelligence data from the entire world. These organizations included the relevant departments within the six principal military branches (Army, Navy, Air Force, Marine Corps, Coast Guard, and Space Force), plus the Central Intelligence Agency, the Defense Intelligence Agency, the Department of Energy, the Department of Homeland Security, the Department of State, the Treasury Department, the Justice Department, the Federal Bureau of Investigation, the National Geospatial Agency, the National Reconnaissance Office, and the National Security Agency. There was the perception that these 16 agencies knew everything that the nearly eight billion inhabitants of the Earth were doing at any one time; however, in reality, many of these billions were doing all kinds of things that the U.S.'s vast intelligence enterprise wasn't able to discern. And many of these unknown fellow humans were planning evil actions against the U.S.

"Yes, Mr. President?" Rebecca was all ears because her own staff regularly kept her abreast of various news threads from the People's Republic, and she was also privy to the PDB. She was also generally aware that the CIA, in particular, had become more concerned about the secretive aspects of the new fleet of ships that the PRC was readying for launch—a strange situation because the Chinese government had made no secret of its investment of time and treasure to create these merchant ships in the first place. In fact, they'd gone overboard to the point of verbosity to keep the world's media abreast of the fleet's approaching launch—continually reminding everyone who would listen that it was all part of their larger effort to expand win/win cross-ocean trade.

However, none the Allied military and intelligence communities liked the steel curtain of secrecy that had been placed around the fleet's "fitting-out" phase. That phase was being accomplished inside an incredible chamber they'd dug into a cliff adjacent to Dalian Port on the Yellow Sea, adjacent to the yard where the ships' hulls had been constructed. The new fleet's construction was so widely trumpeted by the PRC leadership that everyone eventually got tired of listening to them. The Chinese were famous for big infrastructure projects that had previously been completed in the open but, when the hulls were towed into the massive cavern and a cone of silence descended on the project, many intelligence agencies became suspicious. Could there be an underlying sinister purpose for this container fleet? However, the world was filled with more pressing crises, so concerns over the nature of a merchant fleet were put on everyone's back burner.

"I mentioned earlier that Edith directed the Clandestine Service to send someone to check out that giant man-made cavern where those ships are being finished. The update is that the agent went in almost two days ago and never came out, so she fears the worst. And, hopefully coincidentally, the first ship of that fleet just nosed out of the cavern…"

"Not a good coincidence, Mr. President." Senior leaders didn't want to receive that level of detail regarding intelligence operations, but Rebecca accepted that this case was different because of the timing of the launch. The Chinese state news media had been promising a momentary launch for several weeks, but had withheld the exact timing to stoke the fires of anticipation (or maybe because they hadn't known themselves). Both reasons nicely dovetailed with their usual attempt at controlling the news cycle—and could indicate nothing sinister at all.

The President continued, "According to their just-released schedule, three ships will be launched tonight—the ones heading for our three major West Coast container ports—and tomorrow night they will launch the two heading for Hawaii and Sydney, Australia. The balance of the fleet will sail according to a coordinated master plan that enables them to arrive at ports around the Pacific Rim at the same time, just under two weeks from now. So, on the surface of things, no pun intended, I can't see anything alarming. Just a continuation of the PRC's on-going public relations campaign. But the timing of our agent's disappearance **is** troubling: Edith shared that it's a young woman—a third-generation Chinese-American from California. Edith noted she is a rising star—and that's high praise coming from her." Spence couldn't help worrying about this agent: She was in one way typical of the dedicated professionals the Agency recruited and trained but, in another, she was about the same age as his daughter.

Rebecca was immediately worried, too. "Could her potential capture have forced them to launch early—indicating she'd discovered something they were trying to hide?" Her mind churned with possibilities, and she couldn't help forming a disconcerting mental picture of what this brave young woman might be enduring for America.

Though Spence also hated thinking about the agent's predicament, there was a wider strategic concern that took priority: "Your theory occurred to the DNI, Rebecca, so we'll keep a closer eye on this fleet's maiden voyage than we might have otherwise. The CCP has been dangling the launch date, so everyone knew they were on the verge. And regarding this particular agent, you may or may not know that all deep-cover field personnel carry a fast-acting poison capsule imbedded in one of their back teeth. If this young woman was captured—and able to do so—she wouldn't have allowed herself to be interrogated…" The very thought was repugnant to him, but he marveled at their agents' willingness to endure such incredible risks. And sadly, if she died in the line of duty, her fellow citizens would never know about, or appreciate, her sacrifice. "…it's perfectly awful to contemplate, I admit—especially for us sitting here safely drinking tea—but unfortunately it is necessary in some cases…" Then Spence felt a wave of anger wash over him, and he fought to get his emotions under control. "…I'm going to hold the Politburo accountable if they're up to no good with these damned ships!" He paused as their eyes met—Rebecca's calm exterior was a constant reminder to him not to overreact. Temper flares were one of his weaknesses, and they'd dogged him since boyhood.

"Sorry..." he apologized. "I asked you here because I want you to take the lead on this. Please monitor these ships—keep an eye on them until we're fully satisfied they are solely what the Chinese government claims. I have to lean on you because I am too scattered to add another hot-button issue to my plate. I'm sorry to dump something else on your own full plate, but please do this and keep me informed. And, Rebecca, I told Edith that I want us to get that girl out of there!"

"Yes, Mr. President. I'm happy to take this on—I'll make it a priority."

Spence was grateful to have an "exec" like Rebecca, and he thanked her sincerely. They went over a couple of lesser items, then stood and shook hands as they always did in front of others (more formal due to presence of the President's omnipresent Secret Service agent sitting inside the door). The agents only left the President in peace when he was working alone, with a family member, or if he asked them to step outside—which was rare. And, though this special room was filmed and recorded 24/7, when he assumed the presidency, he'd asked his lead agent to ensure that the "chaperone" was female anytime he had a female visitor—including the Vice President.

Rebecca smiled as the agent opened the heavy door for her, and momentarily she was retracing her steps down the hallway toward her own White House office. Despite the possibly negative news about one of their agents, Rebecca was energized; it was going to be another long day, and she'd just had a doozy dropped onto her (as the President admitted) already full plate.

But she was now hurrying toward something fun: She was scheduled to be at the opening of a new fine arts academy in Ohio. She loved any excuse to participate in education-related functions. Her dad was a retired art teacher, and she'd grown up with a love for the academic life. This morning, her detail would take her to Joint Base Andrews where she'd catch Air Force Two and fly west until they landed in Cleveland. She'd feel incredibly spoiled along the way because she'd been assigned a new state-of-the-art Gulfstream Aerospace G700 for the journey. She'd enjoy the ceremony, visit some key supporters in a nursing home setting, then fly back to DC. She'd finish her busy day by attending the monthly national security briefing that evening. She grabbed her coat and purse from her office and hurried out the door toward her waiting SUV.

The White House Situation Room
MonthlyNational Security Meeting
November 26th, 21:00 Hours

Underneath the White House grounds are several structures that the public never gets to see. They are often creatively depicted in movies and books, but only those who have official reasons to be there know the real layout. Tunnels head in various directions, and many stories of multi-functional rooms occupy levels as deep as 150 feet below the pristine lawns and stately faux and real colonial-era buildings. This evening's meeting occupied the largest single room within the 15th level of the complex—the conference room where President Stilwell, Vice President Mason, National Security Advisor John Laughton, the secretaries of Defense, State, and Homeland Security, and the directors of National Intelligence, the National Security Agency, and the CIA met. These principals were joined by the chairman of the Joint Chiefs, Admiral Simms, the rest of the service chiefs, plus a significant contingent of military and intelligence professionals. The underground complex was believed by its designers to be able to withstand a thermonuclear detonation at ground level.

The President was coming from a press briefing, during which the media had been given opportunity to ask questions about his goals for the new year. They'd mainly focused on domestic issues—especially the administration's (in their minds) mixed successes in helping the country recover from the pandemic. The President hoped that "herd immunity" was starting to take hold after he'd pushed the vaccine program to its limits, and that soon the whole mess would be in the rear-view mirror. He had been honest and direct and was generally well received by the American public. The opposite was true of the "politically objective press," many of whom had an agenda that they injected into every interview and story. But he was thankful that he consistently scored high marks from those who really counted: Working class people from the American mosaic.

Spence didn't have much time to mentally shift gears between the "presser" that afternoon and the current briefing, but he was a sponge and would absorb everything he could in the realm of international security. As he entered the most secure room on Earth (despite what his counterpart in the People's Republic believed about his own private bunker), this space was truly a physical and electronic wonder. He made his way to his familiar chair in the middle of the main conference table, acknowledging, with a word or nod, the many friendly faces that protected the American people. The previous administration's rank and file of the Defense, Intelligence, and Homeland Security departments had, in his mind, done a credible job, and he wanted to give them the benefit of the doubt. As such, he had retained most.

Tonight's briefing was Spence's monthly opportunity for deeper dives into the world's troubled regions—expanding his knowledge of many issues that the PDB and occasional daily follow-ups only highlighted. Those updates usually focused on issues requiring decisions—essentially putting out fires—but tonight's information would delve into any noteworthy changes in current capabilities or dispositions of American and potential enemy armed forces, plus political situations that might be moving in dangerous directions. The glaring problem that Spence's predecessor had inherited was long-term depletion of force levels in every military branch. Either by lack of foresight, naiveté, budgetary concerns, or because of philosophical antagonism to all things military, the previous administration(s) had allowed personnel, equipment, and R&D capabilities to dip dangerously low. Conventional forces had dropped to the point where fighting two wars simultaneously would be impossible without going nuclear. Spence wanted to keep all conflicts conventional—not using nuclear arms unless the survival of the nation was at stake, so he'd kept his own foot on the gas. He believed that conventional forces should be at deterrent strength—meaning a military strong enough to empower the diplomatic corps to the point where negotiation alone would cause all but dedicated belligerents to back down.

An attendant problem of this past erosion—especially for big-ticket items like ships, planes, and tanks—was that the infrastructure necessary to develop and build them was also degraded. These industries were much harder to rebuild, and represented short-sighted thinking that could prove fatal in future conflicts. But at least the recent trend was good: In the last year alone, new smaller and faster carriers were on the drawing boards, and other ships, tanks, and aircraft—not to mention the million other items that contributed to military readiness—were in the hands of the end users, and the military had made a strong comeback. By his estimation, both sides of the personnel/ infrastructure coin were already 90 percent closer to where they needed to be.

As he took his seat, he silently hoped that things in the international realm would be much calmer over the next few months. He wanted to focus on expanding his successes in the domestic realm—creating jobs and bringing industries back from overseas (especially from China). He wanted to redouble his efforts to make healthcare—especially medicines for seniors—more affordable, and he wanted to improve race relations. *Now, if the international malcontents can just leave us alone for a few years, we can achieve a positive domestic legacy that will last generations.*

Spence focused on the largest of the high-tech screens that took up most of the facing soundproof wall. He was confident that what was spoken here would remain secret—the technical geniuses had assured him that no one outside these walls could hear what they discussed. Beyond that, at some point, every president had to trust individual patriotism. He took a sip of water from the glass that someone had thoughtfully placed before him, and scanned the map of the world where eight small white lights twinkled. These always meant areas of greatest concern to his briefers, and he would soon learn what they wanted him to know. Sometimes, when he and his wife shared private musings, he wondered why he had wanted to be President; the pressure to be right on every issue every day was far greater than he had ever experienced as a senator or governor. Spence recognized the Army officer in his late thirties who walked to the podium—Lieutenant Colonel Don Garcia, who had led some of his earlier briefings.

"Good evening, Mr. President. May I begin tonight's briefing?"

"Certainly, Colonel Garcia, proceed."

"Mr. President, the first item concerns our progress in locating the Islamic State-connected cell that attacked our consulate in Dubai two weeks ago. Though their organization is mostly dismantled and their personnel dead, they maintain some isolated pockets of strength…"

And so it went for the next two hours. The men and women charged with updating their commander-in-chief did their best to distill an enormous amount of information into concise packets that he could easily understand. They answered his few salient questions with hard facts, and promised detailed written assessments for his security advisor. The security advisor would study those assessments himself, and then help the President digest additional content as necessary. Everyone had seen President Stilwell in action, and they really liked his "can-do" commitment to everything practical that supported the military, law enforcement, and intelligence communities. It helped all concerned that he was a past master at putting people at ease—being blessed with an enabling spirit and manner that encouraged a wide variety of people to want to share their honest ideas and feelings. He was someone they instinctively trusted.

One benefit of all his goodwill was that the President could count on ever more honest briefings in the future. Spence would be the first to admit he had plenty of flaws, and he was continually amazed at the enormity of the tasks that every president had to navigate. But he had great faith in God, plus the support of a wondrous wife and many friends and counselors; he was determined to be successful and believed "The People" were with him.

After the final briefer had completed her presentation, Spence joked to no one in particular: "So, is it the general opinion among you professionals that the world is pretty quiet…except, that is, for tensions in the Middle East, Africa, Central and South America, the Caribbean, and Asia?" He smiled when he'd finished this light sarcasm.

Chuckling despite himself, Secretary of Defense Baker Halsey answered first and in the affirmative, "Yes, Mr. President, that's about right…"

Secretary of State Jack Madrid then added, "I agree, Mr. President. No immediate crises, but there are many areas on which to re-double our focus…"

"Any immediate recommendations?"

"Mr. President," Jack responded, "I briefed you some months ago that our security footprint in every embassy worldwide needed upgrading. Tonight, I can report that we are in much better shape in every location. Those I deemed most urgent were reinforced first, and so on. In total, we are nearly 75 percent more secure than when you took office."

"Outstanding, Mr. Secretary! That should make things a bit more difficult for the nefarious elements…" He paused to allow quiet applause. "Anyone else?" His question was genuine and not meant as a "meeting-ender." Those who needed to say something important did so, including the Secretary of Defense, who was concerned about China's growing influence in Panama, the Bahamas, and other places in the Western Hemisphere where their Belt and Road Initiative projects had regional security implications. The Chinese had been using the program to increase their logistics and political footprint for many years, and were a continual concern because of the volume of U.S. shipping that passed nearby every day.

Spence then looked over at the Vice President. "Rebecca, would you please give us an update on those Chinese ships? I'd like cabinet secretaries, senior commanders, and my senior staff to stay. Everyone else, my sincere thanks for your usual great briefing." Immediately, those in the room took their cue and exited in an orderly manner.

The Vice President waited until the last person left and the Secret Service agents had shut the door. She figured correctly that the President wanted her to brief any cabinet or senior staff who didn't know about the missing agent's mission. "Mr. President, I conferred with Director Carmichael about the agent we sent in to investigate the ships in the finishing cavern, and she confirmed that the agent in question is still overdue and has not communicated with the in-country supervisor.

"The first ships have left the cavern, and our military and NRO folks are watching their progress as closely as maritime law allows. May I have the first slide please?" Rebecca waited until a slide of the cavern's front building appeared on the screen—clearly a satellite view that highlighted the imposing cliff. "Our agent was sent into this secret military site to investigate the fleet's progress toward completion, and I'm sure you've all seen similar photos over the last few years. The PRC is a prodigious excavator, and they have many such caverns along their long coastline. None, however, are this big, or have a mission that is so mysterious. Specifically, we do know the agent first conducted a two-day reconnaissance before attempting an entry, and decided the best way to gain access to the complex was to climb the 400-foot cliff next to the building shown here. The ascent was conducted under the cover of darkness and during a rainstorm, so it was perilously difficult. At the top of the cliff face, where it meets the sidewall of the entrance building, is an air duct—next slide please."

Everyone scrutinized the photo with great interest, and watched in silence as a series of views scrolled by. They had been taken from various angles in overcast daylight. "Some of these photos were taken by the agent and transmitted via satellite. The supervisory agent assumes the ascent was successful—no evidence existing to the contrary. However, he now fears the agent was killed or captured inside. The first three ships out of 14 sailed last night their time, and two more are scheduled to sail tonight. Therefore, I'd like Director Carmichael to offer any additional facts or opinions that will help us with any necessary next moves."

"Thank you, Mrs. Vice President," responded the ordinary-looking, middle-aged woman who was the overall leader of the world's most sophisticated collection of intelligence gathering networks. Her looks were no accident: She'd invested many years blending in, and had been a rookie agent imbedded in the Soviet Union when it collapsed. She was still nearly worshiped by the five human beings she'd rescued during those dark days—getting them away from the old KGB before they could be executed. The details of the operation were still kept on a "need-to-know" basis, but the five political prisoners had helped the United States in some way, been caught, and were in Lubyanka Prison in Moscow during a particularly harsh winter, awaiting the firing squad. Agent Carmichael had donned a female KGB uniform, used her language skills to bully her way into their equivalent of death row—and presented the guards with (forged) written orders, directing them to hand over the condemned for transfer to a different place of execution.

However, after she led the shackled prisoners and their guards out a side door, an armed colleague surprised the angry guards, and kept them at bay until she and the prisoners jumped into an old panel truck and escaped into the countryside. After abandoning their vehicle, she and the five escapees spent a harrowing month moving from place to place in the cold and darkness, finally working their way west and north and crossing the Finnish border to safety. Other agents transported the group to England for debriefing. The only sad result was that the colleague who stayed behind to cover their escape had been captured, brutally interrogated, and shot in the same courtyard where the five were supposed to die. That agent's name had never been mentioned outside his team, but his parents knew he had a star on the wall in Langley. He had no other relatives.

Director Carmichael spoke in her usual quiet voice, so the others had to concentrate. "As Vice President Mason mentioned, one of our younger, and may I say, very promising agents, is missing. We have to surmise capture and/or death. Therefore, these circumstances force us to ask a hard question: Did the PRC authorities learn something that made them adjust their launching schedule? If that is the case, then the facts are ominous. However, if the launches are unrelated—and they had been in the offing anyway—then there is no additional cause for alarm. We simply do not know which at this point."

The President thanked Director Carmichael, then said, "First of all, I am distressed at the loss of our agent but, based on your summary, Madame Director, we have to consider a worse-case scenario. But what is the worse-case scenario? I need you all to help me understand what is realistic. It seems virtually impossible that the PRC is going to hide nuclear bombs in container ships, cruise across the Pacific, and explode them in our harbors…" The President thought again about the missing agent: He noticed that Edith and Rebecca had been careful not to reveal her gender, but a brave young patriot had risked her life to get her commander-in-chief possibly vital intelligence. He had to honor her sacrifice with good decisions.

Secretary Madrid responded first, "Mr. President, you are most certainly right about that. China would gain nothing by starting a full-blown war with us because they know for certain that we have deployed 'boomer' missile submarines that could quickly rain death on them. Their Politburo is risk-adverse at that level. On the other hand, they are more than capable of engineering regional attacks as we have witnessed in the islands they've occupied in the East and South China Seas. They are also willing to occupy Taiwan by force if they think they can be victorious and bring their cousins back into the fold. They wouldn't risk attacking us in the mid-Pacific or our homeland after the obvious mistake Japan made in World War II."

"Mr. President," added Secretary Halsey, "the very fact that this so-called Dragon Fleet is such a large project creates a different level of worse-case scenario. The ships may hide one or more new conventional weapons systems and, if true, 14 of them can carry an enormous number of whatever that new threat might be. Known systems include multiple large conventional rockets and launching platforms—and these ships are certainly big enough to serve in that capacity. This is, of course, the wildest speculation. We truly don't know the ships' contents other than their announced manifests. Our civilian and military analysts were surprised when the ships emerged from that grotto fully loaded with containers—the implication being that we missed one or more access tunnels that must feed into the peninsula from the mainland. And those tunnels have to be substantial to facilitate that many containers full of stuff—tens of thousands of them. Yet, in spite of the unusual aspects of the fleet's completion and launch, the remaining facts, plus every phase of the ships' existence from announcement through the hulls build-out, was very public and seemed harmless."

The Vice President then interjected, "But, Baker, that just begs the question: If the whole project is designed for peaceful purposes, why invest such incredible resources to hide the finishing phase from the world? None of this makes any sense from a business perspective—especially for such a relatively pedestrian enterprise."

President Stilwell was also puzzled. "Jack, what's your perspective on this? The enormity and secrecy of the project doesn't make sense in our way of thinking." Spence wanted his Secretary of State's input here—he knew the Chinese as well as anyone in government.

"I generally agree with everything Baker said, Mr. President. We know the PRC is having some agricultural and natural resource issues: The changing weather patterns have impacted their harvests in the north and west—plus they have depleted their supplies of oil, natural gas, and rare earth metals at unsustainable rates. But would that make them belligerent to the point of starting a war? Ambassador Gantry in Beijing isn't picking up on anything sinister from his usual contacts throughout their foreign office. And the logical downside for them would be disaster of epic proportions: They'd be pariahs in the eyes of nearly every country on the planet. But if you're asking me if they're capable of aggressive warfare—especially against Taiwan—then the answer has to be yes."

"Okay, everyone, the bottom line here is possible aggressive warfare." Spence was worried. "Going forward, I want everyone to give Vice President

Mason whatever support she needs. She is the point person for our combined efforts to keep an eye on these ships. She needs input from every agency monitoring the fleet's progress toward their intended harbors. Keep our actions legal for the time being, but I want the ships overflown and tracked with satellites and planes. Shadow them with subs and ships, but do not, I repeat, do not harass them. Throughout the launching phase, they will be in their own littoral waters, and in international waters after that, and I don't want our paranoia to spark an international incident. Ask our allies what they think, and share our concerns quietly. I don't want an international incident over nothing. On the other hand, if they are up to no good, we need as much advance warning as we can get. We can't sink them on a hunch, and we can't board them without just cause. However, it will be interesting to see if they pick up armed escorts after they exit the Yellow Sea, or if they deviate from their announced schedules or courses—like suddenly turning and pouncing on Taiwan."

Secretary Halsey was fully on board. "Mr. President, our shop will work closely with the RNO and Director Carmichael. We'll keep an eye on them, and report to Vice President Mason daily." He and the DNI exchanged nods with the VP, then looked back at the President. The other leaders in the room did likewise.

"Okay, any other concerns?" The President saw that there were none, so he thanked everyone and adjourned the meeting. He stayed behind to have a quiet discussion with Admiral Derrek Simms, and with Secretary Halsey and Director Carmichael. When he'd finished that five-minute conversation, he waved goodnight to the Vice President, who was huddled with her chief of staff and Jack Madrid near a side door. She caught his greeting and waved back.

Finally done with the day's schedule, Spence trooped through the small lobby with his usual entourage of Secret Service agents to catch a waiting elevator to the main level. He was bushed and ready to call it a night but, as he ticked off the day's achievements, he had to admit that the previous 14 hours had been a reasonably profitable investment of his time. He'd made it clear since his first day in office that he wanted to hear bad news quickly, and news that threatened the republic immediately, and he felt he was as on top of things as he could be. On the White House main floor, he switched to the stairs to strengthen his heart and circulation as his doctor recommended and, upon arriving at the door to his private quarters, he thanked his protective detail and went inside. Susan was waiting for him—his highlight of every day for the past 32 years. An hour later, after catching up with each other's respective day's events over cups of tea, he and his wife headed for bed. They were asleep just after midnight.

Chapter 19

Inside the Cavern
Night of November 27/28

Dragon's Tail finally moved to the exit point, and her commanding officer, Merchant Marine Senior Captain Fong Qing, was as relieved as his counterparts when the great door opened to its widest point. He was using his walkie-talkie to coordinate the hook-up with the tug, and had to rely on a flat screen CCTV affixed above his station on the bridge to see the action. The TV showed the messenger lines sail over the flared bow 150 meters forward, landing in front of the container stacks where the waiting hands of his stanchion team pulled up the large tow lines. He'd assigned an experienced chief petty officer to handle the attachment, and didn't worry about that small but important task. He **was** worried about scraping the sides of the hull against the door frame and spoke with the tug captain about the intended angle of pull. But it was a straightforward task, and the tug's captain had already accomplished it perfectly the previous evening. Nevertheless, it was Fong's duty to worry. A minute later, the bow team had threaded the heavy tow ropes through the eyes on the bow and hooked them to the stanchions. It was time.

Soon *Dragon's Tail* began to move, her massive bulk unable to resist the unrelenting power of the tug's strength. Within a half-hour, she'd made an incident-free journey through the covered opening and down the channel to the harbor. There, two additional tugs met her and carefully nudged against each side of her hull, about two-thirds of the way back from the bow. Their job was to keep the 1,000-foot container ship from fish-tailing, and to add their own power to her forward momentum. Another 30 minutes later she was clear of the harbor, and drifting imperceptibly as the four mini-submarines were safely taken aboard and locked into their secret compartments. At the same time, four Type-726 LCACs (similar to the U.S. Navy's Landing Craft Air-Cushion vessels, capable of carrying 100 armed marines plus light vehicles, or one main battle tank) powered up the lowered stern ramp and into the well-deck.

Finally, it was time for Captain Fong to issue the order for *Tail* to proceed under her own power. The engineers engaged the meter-in-diameter shafts, and they began turning in exact unison so the multi-ton propellers would push her along evenly. The bow's stanchion crew released the tow lines that were rapidly reeled in by the tug's crew, and the other tugs gradually slid away. His magnificent ship was now underway—next stop Honolulu—where she'd deliver a death blow to the American Navy and its Indo-Pacific Command headquarters. Behind her, *Dragon's Fang* had been towed to the front position in the cavern and was ready for her departure for Sydney, Australia.

At sea aboard *Dragon's Fire*
November 29th, 11:00 Hours

Senior Captain Wei Tsi Fan was the happiest man in the PLAN: His ship was steaming at the assigned course and speed on her maiden voyage, and the engines, shafts, and the rest of the incredible number of untried parts were all working in perfect unison. The two giant low-speed, two-stroke diesel engines were purring like kittens; they'd been copied from a German model by his countrymen, and they'd apparently gotten everything right. He'd done his part, too: His engine room team had broken the bus-sized machines in gradually over several weeks, and they were running smoothly without a hint of overheating. Putting to sea without trials was the one glaring weakness of the entire naval portion of this mission, and doing so had unnerved Wei and his fellow captains from the outset. But, so far, his nearly two years of compulsive worrying—stressful attention to details often bordering on full-blown OCD—was proving unfounded. He had supervised every detail during the massive engines' installation and testing (including ordering additional sonograms of every suspicious component, and replacing those found even slightly defective). He'd gradually broken in every system on the ship except the four main shafts and propellers, but there was no reason to doubt their quality or installation. So far, they were working to perfection—driving his ship through the waves at a consistent 10 knots, and he'd increase that to 20 or more as the weather and arrival schedule dictated.

Wei's crew had been thoroughly trained, so he was not worried about them. And only one brief outbreak of the dreaded flu had felled nine of his men, but eight of them had fully recovered and were currently on board. Unfortunately, that remaining sailor had died but, given the scope of the pandemic, that was certainly acceptable. He'd been fully supportive of Marshal Tai's decision to quarantine the entire fleet—including all naval, marine, and army cadres according to unit or ship assignment—sequestering them for almost two months after the initial outbreak. When the disease first erupted among the general population, thousands of workers in the finishing grotto had been removed and isolated, too, and the entire facility (including access tunnels, loading docks, the massive grotto itself, and especially the ships) had been meticulously disinfected. That put them two weeks behind schedule but, after the protocols became stricter and stricter, and the blood and nasal screenings more and more accurate, the powers that be learned how to quickly identify and remove anyone suspected of having the virus. A few hundred connected with the project had died but, circumstantially, the naval and marine personnel had already been largely separated from the general population during the intensive two-year evaluation and training programs at smaller bases spread across China, so they'd been spared by luck. After several months of worry, the PLA confirmed that all phases of the mission were back on track.

Wei's responsibilities were confined to running the ship, including commanding the relevant civilian merchant marine and PLAN sailors, and getting *Fire* to the correct unloading dock in San Diego, California. However, the entire host of combat-related air, sea, and land functions were under the command of Marine Major General Chun—whom Captain Wei found tolerable enough to admire. He was not only knowledgeable of the ground aspects of the mission, but he had also studiously prepared for his command of the naval and air components as well. In fact, on every Dragon, the general commanded a small but lethal navy consisting of the four mini-submarines and 726s. And, though they were only eight in number, these surface and undersea boats packed a lot of firepower.

But it was the air component that was most formidable, and around which the entire mission was planned: Each ship carried larger mother drones that would drop bombs on exposed ship and sub surfaces, and mini-drones that could be directed by controllers into just-popped missile hatches before Harpoon or Tomahawk missiles were fired. Each mini-drone carried small explosive devices that would cause the Allied missiles to detonate inside their launch tubes or during their launch. Either eventuality would severely damage the ship or ground launcher.

Once the mother drone's minnies were released, the canisters would be jettisoned and the larger drones raised to 500 feet. They would hover directly over a target, and then drop their 250-pound bombs directly onto submarines, ships, buildings, oil tanks, vehicles, or other targets of opportunity. The bombs were shaped charges with newly developed chemical components that would instantaneously mix upon impact and burn down and through the metal inside. Every mini-drone "swarm" had several that carried micro-cameras, and all were controlled by designated operators within special bays located within each Dragon's multi-story bridge. An air force full brigadier general had administrative command of each air wing.

Captain Wei had been briefed on the capabilities of the armored vehicles tightly chained in neat rows on the bottom three decks of *Fire's* main hull. Row upon row of tanks, APCs, self-propelled cannons, and other vehicles would be employed during the assault, and they would be highly intimidating when enemies considered their options. Wei expected this small army to conquer and hold their assigned target areas for at least several weeks—and, if the Americans wisely surrendered, his ship could stay operational for years. He might even move his family to California: He'd been there many times and really liked the weather.

As Captain Wei continued monitoring the ship's functions via digital displays on his bridge, Major General Chun and his full colonel operations officer (G3)—accompanied by each battalion's commander—were currently running a surprise inspection in the tank bay on Deck 1. And, though he couldn't let it show too much, the general was as proud and confident of his marines as any commander could be. Every tank and marine looked combat-ready, and morale was extremely high; his young men were itching to go. The ships had been designed with excellent ventilation systems to permit daily running of every vehicle engine in his brigade and, at this point in the operation, his units were fully combat-ready. They were the pointy end of the spear, and their mission was part of his country's audacious attempt to conquer and hold most of Asia and the western Pacific Ocean. Operation Unity directed them to simultaneously arrive unopposed at their target ports and, in Chun's mind, the planners had devised a brilliant hide-in-plain-sight strategy. The extensive media campaign, combined with a superb camouflage "mask" on the ships themselves, was pure genius, and he gave full marks to his army counterparts and their civilian colleagues who developed the plan in every detail. He and his fellow senior commanders knew they'd be watched by a steady stream of Allied submarines and aircraft, plus other cargo ships and pleasure craft of every kind. But even the constant gaze of the world's satellites would not alert the dunces—Chun was confident they'd never catch on. The Dragon ships were the most deceptive Trojan Horses ever created!

At the moment, Chun was observing a company commander quiz three marines who were standing at attention next to their lovingly cared-for ZTZ-99A main battle tank. It was a thing of beauty—the most modern tank in the world—and Chun and the other senior ground commanders were certain the West didn't know China had secretly manufactured an additional 1,400 of this newest model. The tank crew, like most of the armor crews assigned to the 14 assault ships, had trained together for months to maximize cohesion. The tank itself was in top mechanical condition, and its 120mm main gun and its machine guns were also in perfect running order. Even though some of the tanks were almost brand new, every one had been field-tested for at least a few weeks and were adequately broken in. He hated the phrase "good enough" but, with the limited time he'd been given, it was the reality every ground force commander had to live with.

The general took note of the flexible metal and composite hoses that ran from the exhaust ports of every tank in the bay, including the nozzles attached to the heavy-duty ventilation pipes that forced the dangerous fumes outside. This system was working as advertised, and none of his tankers had become sick. The immense bay held 100 tanks, and it had that familiar oil and machinery smell that "tread heads" loved, but there were virtually no lethal fumes (a health issue constantly monitored and confirmed by specialists). He heard "Good work, Marines!" shouted by the inspecting captain over the noise of the several dozen engines idling nearby. And then the "carry on!" It was the military at its best and he was in Marine heaven. The captain returned the tankers' perfect salutes—young men who were so excited and full of pride that their chests were nearly bursting.

The general then watched with some amusement as the three men clambered up onto the tank's rear deck and raised and propped in place the engine compartment's heavy armored cover. As he walked to the next tank, he glanced back over his shoulder and enjoyed the sight of three happy young men engrossed in something inside the compartment that the general couldn't see. The company commander was already speaking with the next crew, but the general didn't expect anything untoward there, either. He didn't plan to inspect all 100 of his MBTs today, but he'd been perfectly pleased with those he'd seen so far.

The three marines in question were led by their tank commander, Sergeant (E5) Lee, and he and his crew of two privates were whispering to each other as the brass moved out of earshot. "That was pretty scary!" commented one private.

"The general was happy..." responded Lee. "...that meant the colonel and the captain were happy, too. So don't sweat it: Just keep doing what I tell you and everything will be okay."

That elicited a round of relieved chuckles. They weren't actually doing anything inside the engine cover, but they wanted to appear busy. A few minutes later, the engine run-up reached its allotted minutes so they shut it down. They closed and locked the armored engine hatch, climbed on top of the turret, and then dropped into their tank's relatively spacious main compartment. They left the hatches open for ventilation—and began killing time in relative comfort and out of sight of their platoon sergeant. It would take the latter some time before he discovered them slacking but, until he did, they'd make the most of their break.

One level below the tanks, all four submarine crews were inside their "tubes" and lovingly micro-cleaning every surface, running checks on every piece of equipment in the inventory. Several of those working alone sported headsets to communicate with their supervisory chief petty officers, while others worked in teams—twisting wrenches and screwdrivers as submariners had done for 100 years. Undersea boats were an old concept, but the refinements of the last few decades had been remarkable: These four subs were identical to those in every Dragon—whisper-quiet diesel/battery types whose conceptual technology dated back to WWI. When the batteries were fully charged, these boats became ghosts when submerged. They were extremely hard to locate—either by other subs or by the surface and airborne platforms that conducted anti-submarine warfare (ASW) against them. All were sheathed in the latest anti-detection coatings, and had the latest electronics and various "black boxes" to aid every task imaginable.

In the torpedo room at the front of his boat, Petty Officer 3rd Class (OR-3) Zhou Bing Ti was busily replacing and re-calibrating a torpedo's electronic arming switch. "His" three YU-9s rested securely in their vertical rack, and each of the four, three-torpedo racks were manned by identical OR-3 torpedo men who were fussing over their own charges. Zhou had a panel opened about half-way down the 20-foot-long cylinder, and he was replacing a computer chip whose indicator light was trending dull amber from green. Normally such minor changes were left until the light was bright amber because the torpedo would work anyway, but not on this mission: Now the only standard was 100 percent bright green. He finished this minor job, buttoned up the panel, and tested it to ensure that it fit snugly into its recessed watertight space. Then he picked up a small electronic sensor and held it two centimeters above the panel. *All green—perfect again!*

The 21-year-old sailor was in his version of Heaven: He'd been selected for the adventure of a lifetime, and he was honored to be part of a mission that his commander said was vital to the motherland. He didn't know about the big picture of Operation Unity, but everyone had been briefed by the commanding general, who told them they were part of the greatest event since modern China's founding. They were on a mission to save their homeland from the greedy capitalists, and they would bring Party doctrine across the Pacific to distant America. Only the founding of the Communist Party and the victory in 1949 were considered more important.

Initially, Zhou had been terrified when he learned they were attacking the United States. But, after his chief petty officer held small-unit discussions that stressed the superiority of Party doctrine, and that the American Navy was much weaker than previously thought, his confidence increased. He'd given himself pep talks every day, so now he believed they were really going to overwhelm the American military. Most important to this young sailor was his personal responsibility: His three "little brothers," his beautiful YU-9s, would sink three Yankee ships or submarines.

His boat was formally called Xiao Long Yi (Small Dragon Number One), but the crew affectionately called her "Little sister", and she was a powerful little girl: She was 62 meters long and carried 12 of Zhao's YU-9 torpedoes—the latest and most powerful torpedoes in the world. They were 533mm (21 inches) in diameter, had a range of 45 kilometers, and boasted an attack speed of 105 kilometers per hour. The torpedoes acquired targets in three ways: By active and passive acoustic homing, by wake homing, and by wire guidance. On the business end, the powerful warhead employed a new technology that China had developed as an improvement over the YU-7s that they considered an equal of the currently used American Mark 48s. PRC scientists had developed an electronically powered weapon that was deathly quiet—a big improvement over the Otto fuel II engines of the previous generations. The warhead was state of the art, too: It incorporated a sodium hydride compound chemical reaction where, upon detonation (via contact with, or proximity to, a ship or another submarine), the powder would mix with the surrounding seawater to create a nearly instantaneous, 2,000-degree rise in temperature that melted anything nearby. The resulting explosion created a large hole in the enemy's hull that would in all probability sink the vessel.

Zhou didn't understand every aspect of the science, but he was proud of his three little brothers, and he'd help load them into the firing tubes when the time came. He knew his captain was the best sub captain in the PLAN, and that their boat would attack at just the right time. He and his fellow torpedo men had also discussed the great homecoming they'd receive when the war was over. They even had a secret pool going as to how many days it would take before the Americans surrendered.

President Han's Beijing Estate, a meeting of the Eight
November 29, 19:00 Hours

"I'm afraid I have to share some disturbing news, Comrade General Secretary." Marshal Tai announced theatrically after Han opened the meeting. He didn't like delivering negative news any time, but when he received a particularly disturbing back-channel communication a few days before, Tai immediately made an appointment with the only man who outranked him in China, and Han nearly blew a gasket. However, Tai had done the right thing by briefing Han in private because, like most bosses, Han didn't want to be surprised with bad news—especially in front of others. Now the two were seated around the familiar table with their select group, and Tai was delivering the announcement as Han had directed. The news was bad, even alarming, but it did present a rare chance for the two senior leaders to ping the ever-smug MSS minister—who'd conveniently forgotten to mention the incident to his president. Han was going to make the most of the situation by knocking Wing down a peg just before the great battle began, and he'd chosen this time and place for the chastisement.

After hearing the ominous preamble, Han tightened his countenance with as much skill as any actor, and quickly made a 'let's have it' gesture with his left hand. Privately, he'd been worrying anyway—things had been going too smoothly—in fact, until that moment, everything had been going perfectly. But when Tai gave him the troubling report, he accepted the reality that even the best planned mission could experience a few hiccups. He just hoped this one wasn't a harbinger of something worse. "Yes, Marshal Tai?"

"General Secretary Han, fellow ministers, I learned that we had a breach in our security in the Special Area at Dalian Shipyard. I'd like General Wing to brief you on the details of that incident that occurred several days ago…" Everyone then anxiously turned toward the thick-necked minister who looked like he'd just swallowed a bee.

Wing knew he should have informed Han and Tai on the evening of the incident, but he'd chosen not to. Now that omission could take a big bite out of his hindquarters.

"Ah…yes, of course, Comrade Minister…Comrade General Secretary…fellow ministers…" Wing was rarely caught totally off guard, but Tai had nailed him good this time. *How that sneaky Tai had gotten wind of the incident was anybody's guess. Hopefully he could find out and vent his current embarrassment by harshly punishing the offending party. His own security team wouldn't dare divulge such details to anyone, and he thought he'd scared the wits out of the three boneheads who'd debriefed the spy. In fact, he'd mercifully not executed them along with that traitorous tart Ma (whom he'd trusted with his special confidence). If he found out those three had squawked to someone after his benevolence, he'd rope them together and toss them in the harbor!* But, for now, he decided to play it safe and come clean, "…the incident in question was so thoroughly contained by my security team that I didn't think it necessary to invest operational resources with a report to your level. That said, I am always happy to share good news when our security experts display excellent work—in this case identifying and eliminating an enemy agent.

"Specifically, a female agent of unknown origin climbed the cliff next to the external opening of our secure finishing grotto, entered through an air duct and made her way through the facility—including traversing the covered dry dock area where the last of the marine stores are being off-loaded from the feeder ships. But she was spotted and apprehended by our security personnel and questioned to learn her intent, but unfortunately she pulled out a gun and was shot in the process of resisting arrest…" Wing's unease grew as he noticed the alarmed glances between the others. *What a four-star mess on the eve of the greatest operation in China's history—and it's being dumped on me!* "The security team leader rightly did not want to execute her on the spot—he kept her alive so that we could thoroughly debrief her using a variety of our proven methods. She was given immediate medical treatment to sustain her during the planned interrogation; however, when she awoke from the medical anesthesia, she committed suicide.

"She revealed that one of my MSS officers was somehow involved, so I had that officer interrogated that afternoon, and I executed her a few hours later." He intentionally left out a few details, and didn't think any of them knew about his relationship with Ma. Wing noticed that several of his colleagues were horrified at the obvious severity of this security breach—coming as it had on the eve of the first ships departures.

"How could this happen, Comrade Minister Wing?" Foreign Secretary Wu croaked plaintively. "I feared for just such a calamity!"

What a sniveling dog! Wing thought contemptuously. *How I hate him and all diplomats.* But he wisely avoided any defensive response—this was a moment for covering one's tail. He just ignored the man and continued his report as if no one had said a word. "The captured spy had a camera that our technical experts determined to be inoperable beyond simply taking photographs. She'd taken numerous photos of the ships, which was logical, but could not transmit any data. And, in anticipation of your questions, we don't know her country of origin or anything about her. The only vital fact is that she didn't have the technical capability to relay any of the information she'd gathered to outside entities. Therefore, the incident is fully contained."

Wing had been alarmed that the spy had known enough about the dead traitor Ma to use her name. *How could any foreign intelligence agency know about one MSS officer?* This incident could sully his reputation before his seniors in this room, not to mention his thousands of loyal underlings assigned all around the world. When gossip like this leaked (as it invariably did), it could impact his career. He was taking a big chance here by omitting a fact that an enemy knew something his own countrymen didn't. Ma hadn't talked during the interrogation—he'd supervised the whole process personally. If she had, he'd have executed everyone present, including the three officers plus his debriefing team. He'd then questioned every senior leader that the spy had worked with at MSS headquarters, but they all thought she was a rising star.

"This is very serious, General! You don't even know what country this woman worked for?" The Foreign minister was truly worried, but he was also enjoying a rare opportunity to make the arrogant bully Wing squirm. "First, we had to endure the disease that your 'experimental' laboratories released—killing God knows how many of our own people, and now this. Maybe you should revitalize the internal security of your own ministry!"

Of course, Wing realized the man would try to make hay from two tiny rents in the impenetrable security cordon his MSS people had maintained for years. And the Covid disaster, though initially bad—at the time he'd momentarily feared it would be career-ending bad—had ended up being an unexpected enhancement to Operation Unity. It had caused significant disruption beyond his wildest dreams: In the targeted countries—especially the United States—the disease had been incredibly lethal. In addition, the entire developed world was just now recovering from the related financial and economic devastation. Now his Chaos Teams would place an exclamation mark on the Pacific Rim societies—providing just a bit of last-minute distraction to facilitate the Dragons' arrivals. However, at the present moment, though Wing could blow off Wu, he couldn't ignore Han.

"I am inclined to agree with Comrade Wu, Minister Wing…" Han had been alarmed at the eleventh-hour revelation, and he had to signal to Wing and the others that he would not tolerate a further lapse in security. They had dodged a bullet during the flu pandemic—caused by some (never discovered) carelessness in Wing's matrix of biological laboratories. The MSS maintained 17 branches of the Wuhan facility (all rigorously protected by Ti's police forces), and all the branches fed data, and sometimes transported physical samples, into the main Level 4 hub. But some careless idiot had dropped a beaker or something along the way, and they'd been extremely lucky that no important officials had died. He'd not been able to get a straight answer from anyone because most of those responsible had themselves died—and of course he'd stayed well clear of anyone with possible contamination for weeks. But now this! So many precious years of intense and complex planning had gone into Operation Unity and, if it was undermined now, they might be forced to recall the fleet and endure the wrath of the peasants when they starved. "How can you be sure this current situation is contained?"

Considering the source and the setting, Wing felt this question was a stinging rebuke—one clearly intended by Han with the full support of that sneaky Tai. It was also a not-so-subtle reminder that some incompetent jackass in one of his experimental bio-warfare laboratories had released a pandemic on their homeland. He'd interrogated and executed everyone he thought responsible——but he really didn't know if he'd gotten the actual perpetrator. There were still many unknowns but, luckily, it had not only turned out okay, it had produced the most silver of all silver linings: The lethality of the pandemic had validated his extremely expensive biological warfare program.

Nevertheless, Wing knew Han didn't have infinite patience, even with him—and the man could order him executed publicly, or even have him secretly assassinated any time he deemed it advantageous. In this case, truth was the best policy. "Comrade General Secretary, my agents in every target country confirm that there are no defensive measures being enacted of any kind. This is the proof. If the spy's photos had seen the light of day, or if she'd gotten the word out in some other way, the Allies would be raising a general alarm. Everything is business as usual around the Pacific Rim—including in the rebellious province from whence we suspect the spy came. We are constantly monitoring all message traffic between them and the U.S., as well as continuing our relentless multi-pronged cyber information-harvesting campaign against every country and industry on Earth…as we have for years. Also, our unrelenting bribery and honey-pot campaigns continue unabated. The bottom line is that there is zero indication of discovery."

"Well, that is a tremendous relief!" Han replied honestly. He was still troubled by the gross breach of security, but at least there was insufficient grounds to recall the ships. They only needed to keep a lid on things during the trans-ocean voyages—a mere few days until they arrived and commenced their assault. Seeing no point in belaboring the issue, he asked everyone to turn their attention back to the announced agenda. Han effectively ended any questions surrounding Wing's handling of the breach, but the incident was a useful reminder that failures could undermine the whole operation.

The minister of State Security was not happy, however, and he was already formulating a revenge strategy that would unmask whoever had betrayed him. Someone had leaked the embarrassing facts, and he vowed that the guilty party would die badly.

Chapter 20

Washington, DC
November 30th, 12:10 Hours

Tim Duncan held the door for two middle-aged ladies before following them into the normally bustling, and now just-nicely reopened, downtown eatery popular with government workers. He was there for his bi-monthly meeting with Reg Trammell, his friend from the Department of State. Tim had initially sought Reg out some five years before after reading the scholar's classified report detailing China's future problems within their agricultural and natural resource sectors. Tim was a China specialist at CIA—a mission's coordinator in the same clandestine operations section Jen was assigned to. The document had come across his desk as a routine inter-agency share, and he'd been intrigued. His section was one of two dozen such recipients throughout government—each of which kept a fairly close eye on developments in greater East Asia. His clearance made him privy to a lot of related information, and he read a wide range of publications from domestic and foreign think tanks, plus some material from respected individual researchers. He'd been impressed with Reg's work and figured he was a man to meet. They'd hit it off right away, and their association had grown from the merely professional into a real friendship. It also helped that they both had top-secret clearances in the same general field of inquiry, so they could avoid the lies and dance surrounding the question, "So, where do you work?" so common in and around the District of Columbia.

Today Reg had arrived first, and had located a table outside where they could enjoy one of the last sunshiny days of the fall—and where they could speak with a modicum of privacy. He'd been keeping an eye out for his friend and, when he spotted Tim through the glass partition, he waved until he caught his attention. Tim smiled back and pointed to the order counter—he'd join him momentarily.

"You look worried," Reg commented without preamble when Tim arrived seven minutes later with his vegetarian burger and mysterious-looking fruit-and-vegetable concoction. Reg admired the fact that Tim was not only a rock climber and long-distance runner—he was a health nut, too. Not so Reg. He was a devoted foodie who loved anything and everything—though his spare tire belied his recent commitment to better portion control.

"I am worried: Someone is way late reporting in…" Tim knew Reg would understand who the "someone" was.

"Uh-oh. I take it that's out of character?" Reg and his wife Tipi had met Tim's fiancée Jennifer only once socially, because the "overseas travel requirements" for her "international trading company" kept her away most of the time. Reg appreciated that Tim had trusted him enough after their friendship developed to obliquely inform him about Jen's real role in the Big Picture.

Tim settled his lithe six-foot frame into the cool but still comfortable rattan patio chair and met his friend's concerned look. He spoke just above a whisper so their conversation would not reach a group of chatty women who'd just plunked themselves into chairs around two tables they'd pushed together on the other side of the small courtyard. "This is totally off the reservation, Reg, but Jen has never been this late before. Her team leader reported her missing about 24 hours after she was supposed to return from a reccee. And now it's been six days…" He looked really worried and didn't touch his food.

"The usual part of the world?"

"Yes. She was having a look-see at that cavern just before the first ships launched."

"No kidding? Well, Jen is an amazing woman, Tim. She impressed me as someone who can take care of herself…" In fact, Reg thought, she was more than amazing. Tim's fiancée was remarkable: She was a stunning beauty whose looks Reg's wife had commented on, somewhat cattily. And, from his own brief observation, Reg thought Jen was really smart—a gifted woman, actually. She also seemed devoted to the Christian religion she and Tim shared, though that "religious" part of their friends' lives contrasted with that of Reg and his wife, who'd never had much use for church. In fact, they'd made excuses the couple of times Tim invited them to attend his. Nevertheless, their religious differences hadn't interfered with their friendship, and Reg respected them anyway because they were just superior people. And, in regard to the work Tim and Jen did, Tipi had accepted the story that Jen was a businesswoman who traveled a lot, and that Tim was a China expert who worked for an independent think tank across the Potomac River in Virginia. Tipi was not one to care much about such things anyway; since taking her administrative position with a well-known consumer-products chain, she'd somewhat checked out of family life.

Tim nodded his appreciation for his friend's attempted encouragement and, in fact, he'd given himself the same pep talk during the previous days of fruitless waiting. Ken's cryptic message had set off alarm bells throughout their section, and Tim was on duty when the news arrived on the 26th. She was supervised at a higher level than he worked, and he was not in her chain of command, but he was privy to numerous current operations, and had stayed in the op-center to keep watch—nervously hoping for the best. He'd always feared that something bad would happen, mostly because Jen was a risk-taker but, on the bright side, she'd been late before. Yet Tim knew enough of the details of her intended method of entry into the now-famous cavern that he was truly worried. The whole reccee had been fraught with danger.

Jen had been sent in because the Chinese had suddenly changed the M.O. regarding public information about the new fleet—insufferably bragging for years then, in great contrast—dropping a curtain of secrecy over the whole project. They'd moved the hulls of their great new fleet inside their man-made cave, and the secrecy made everyone nervous. Nevertheless, after a while, the decision-makers had chosen to accept the PRC's early explanations, and remained distant observers. Other hot-burner items garnered the attention and taskings but, when the launchings became imminent, Jen's tasking came down and she had pushed off despite the bad weather. Though Tim and Jen were rock-climbing enthusiasts, real "rock nuts," according to their climbing buddies, he had studied the overheads and weather reports, and he knew how high and how wet and how unprotected Jen would be during her ascent. Then, after the news came of her disappearance, he dreaded that she might have fallen and been terribly injured or already dead. By an act of will alone, he compartmentalized his fears, and committed her to the Lord's care. Now, he responded to Reg's comment positively: "Yes, she is very good at what she does…but the downside is very bad, too…" Tim was just glad to have someone with whom he could share his hovering dread.

Reg leaned forward and spoke quietly but with a sense of urgency, "Those first five ships are really moving fast! Did you see the feed from the RNO?"

"Yes, and didn't you find it strange that they emerged fully loaded? That means there is one—or more—access tunnels inside the cavern, which makes sense, but we never spotted them. Jen may have been apprehended because they'd beefed up their security just before the first dispersal. They'd been making noises about the impending launch recently, and the weather had improved since that last storm—you no doubt saw the reports that the Bohai Sea has been calm and devoid of heavy winds for several days now? Plus, it's too early for ice. It was the perfect time to launch." He saw Reg nod in the affirmative. "Last I saw, the three ships heading for our West Coast have passed Japan and are making beelines across the northern Pacific."

Reg agreed and added, "And just a day behind, the one heading for Honolulu is in trail—though going much slower due to the shorter distance, and that fifth ship is making great time heading south toward Sydney. Presumably the remainder will put to sea as announced. Last I saw, the first three were churning wakes a surfer would love!

"I was also surprised to see that every ship emerged fully loaded and riding deep in the water. That means there is a rear entrance, and it has to be huge; if it escaped notice by the RNO, it must be well hidden. It must have entry points well up the Liandong Peninsula. I've been watching the satellite feeds for years and never noticed a thing."

"It is indeed strange. Even our satellite interpretation folks missed it, and they are the best in the world," Tim agreed, "the whole endeavor seems unnecessary. I never figured out why they felt the need to finish them in secret in the first place—particularly after their constant public proclamations during the hull construction phase. And now we find out they've loaded them in secret, too."

Reg grunted a reply, his mind half-focused on recalling the photos he'd studied before coming to meet Tim. He'd never ceased worrying about the Chinese government's unresponsiveness to the alarming data he'd uncovered years before—becoming inexplicitly passive during grain negotiations. He'd expected them to be hyper-focused, but their official indifference had only whetted his appetite to maintain his quiet but steady eye on the PRC. He was glad he'd stayed on at State as a matter of principle. He knew his supervisory chain regarded him as a merely useful functionary, yet he'd maintained his belief that both his day-to-day job and his side interest were important to the country. Emotionally, it had been trying: Everyone else in his section had been promoted, especially his haughty section chief who was now the division chief. No one he knew respected her much, but she apparently had friends in high places—she was the butt of jokes because it sure wasn't her work ethic or accomplishments that had earned her promotions. But at least her replacement fed him interesting and important assignments to occupy the bulk of his time, and Tim's friendship provided real professional satisfaction. Their high security back channel gave him an opportunity to voice his regional concerns, and they'd become an informal, off-the-books two-man "China watch" that kept him sane.

Tim was feeling melancholy too, and looked down unenthusiastically at his lunch plate, sighing because he knew he had to eat to keep up his physical strength. He took a dutiful bite of his veggie burger, but it tasted like cardboard. He reached for the red plastic bottle in the middle of their small table, and squeezed a healthy dollop of Siracha/Mango ketchup onto the center of the questionable bean-and-corn patty. He also took a swig of his iced "Carrot and Celery Swirl" juice-bar offering, grimaced at its salty/chemical taste, and added a squeeze of fresh lemon to the concoction and hoped for the best. Then, realizing Reg was being intentionally quiet so he could vent, he worried aloud, "The rest of the fleet will presumably launch as scheduled. It will be interesting to track their sequence, direction, and progress and compare it with the official version the DFE folks announced the morning after the first launches. We know they've made advance arrangements to drop off cargo at designated ports on both sides of the Pacific, so we'll know soon if they deviate from their advertised routes. At least they're bringing us tons more stuff to sell in your wife's stores."

Reg knew Tim didn't mean to cast aspersions at Tipi, so he just chuckled politely. He'd already wolfed down his basket of fish and chips and wanted more, but decided to put some spine into his diet. He did, however, accept a passing waiter's offer of a second frothy root beer, the justification being that he was one of many who thought better on a full stomach. Besides, this situation caused his antennae to tingle, and Jen's disappearance only heightened his sense of unease. He knew better than any other U.S. government employee just how desperate the Chinese Politburo was. And, though the CCP claimed that increasing trade capacity was normal and mutually beneficial for all concerned, its government hadn't backed off its full-blown industrial devotion to developing new and better weapons systems, or to producing the stuff of war in ever-greater quantities. In fact, their navy was now on par, numbers-wise, with the U.S. Navy, and their 100-year quest to become the sole world superpower, started in 1949, was right on track if not ahead of schedule. Then, surprisingly, when their grain and oil contracts came up for a second set of renewals, they acted as if they didn't care—a glaring difference from previous cycles. But did these contradictory behaviors add up to anything sinister?

On the factual side, Reg had kept his eye on mainland China's shipments of consumer goods, and the totals had fallen steeply during the Covid crisis. That was expected, but continuing American and world backlash directed at the perpetrators of the pandemic (most everyone was giving them the benefit of the doubt on intentionality—especially after Western intelligence agencies leaked to various media outlets that large numbers of Chinese citizens had probably died, too) was hurting them further.

If there was a silver lining for the U.S. in this terrible mess, the pandemic had illuminated supply-chain issues—especially American dependence on a country that was morphing itself into an enemy. That correction was in play, too: The United States, among other Western nations, was systematically transferring essential manufacturing back to their various homelands (a kind of strategic protectionism), and many companies were well into the transition. In the context of a world beginning to heal from the chaos, Reg's long-term analysis indicated that China's food and natural resources situation was worsening, not improving. The PRC's domestic production of all foodstuffs had continued to slip (along with visible strains in their production of oil, gas, and strategic minerals), and he could see related signs of societal unrest. There was growing uneasiness inside China, and food riots had already occurred in numerous areas. Something had to give soon or the "peasant class," as CCP leaders referred to the general rural population, would really be pinched. Reports continued to leak out regarding accelerating starvation in northwest villages near the Inner Mongolian border, and Reg sadly knew this was only the beginning of an avertable catastrophe. The PRC could buy what they needed if they wanted to get along with the West but, because of pride and their long-term commitment to being the Great Middle Kingdom of old, they'd so far chosen not to. They could also leverage their accumulated foreign currency and stock-piled debt to hammer the United States, but they hadn't done much more than rattle a few small financial sabers. Their only real belligerence seemed directed at Hong Kong, whose freedom protests had led to a general crackdown. They were absorbing Hong Kong now, and it had become little more than an occupied province. The PRC had abandoned most provisions of the 1997 treaty, and were forcefully blending the territory into the fabric of mainland Chinese society. Perhaps Taiwan was next?

Oh, well, Reg thought in resignation, *the President will just have to deal with this mess when it comes to a head.* He'd been mostly impressed with President Stilwell—the man was stronger than he'd seemed during his campaign. He had his faults like anyone but, at least in Reg's value system, he'd deserved the opportunity to succeed or fail. If he failed, he'd be a one-term President and the other party would be back in power. After his thoughtful pause, Reg responded to Tim's previous comment, "Yes, let's keep a sharp eye on the whole thing. And, Tim, try not to worry about Jen…she's really got a lot going for her…"

"Thanks, buddy. I'll try to live out the faith I claim…" Tim had been a devoted Christian since childhood, raised by remarkable parents who'd inculcated their strong faith into their talented children. His mother was an American-born Chinese whose parents had emigrated from Hong Kong in the middle of the 20th Century, and who had eventually settled in Philadelphia. However, his dad was a Caucasian from an old line of Pennsylvania Dutch farmers. But these very different heritages hadn't precluded the two young people from falling in love after they found their separate ways into the Wharton School of Business. Both were egg-head economic types gravitating toward academia, and these shared interests gave them common goals. Their love had quickly blossomed after they'd bumped into one another in the library, and they'd married as soon as they graduated. Both had been hired as assistant professors at Penn, and the university must have liked them, for they were still there more than 30 years later. As a result, Tim and his younger sister had grown up in an academically challenging, yet socially accepting, Ivy League culture. The family also avoided most of the country's struggles with racism—and the kids were grateful to have been raised in a tolerant community that accepted a rare mix-raced family.

Tim favored his mother's Asian side, and he enjoyed an easy fit into the culture of his maternal grandparents, who doted on him. He learned passable Cantonese from them and, after high school, decided to major in Chinese history, culture, and Mandarin language at Yale—at the time considered the best subject-school in the world. But, after his undergraduate experience, he'd gotten itchy feet and left the familiar confines of the northeast—venturing west to U.C.-Berkeley to pursue an MA and doctorate in Chinese history and language. There he'd met the wondrous young woman with whom he'd fallen in love, almost at first sight.

But Jennifer Chen, who'd grown up a few blocks from the campus, was no easy mark for the eager beaver who asked her repeatedly for a date—her initial refusals only made her more alluring. Tim thought she was tremendously independent and beautiful—a true flower who always had a variety of men buzzing around her. But he was persistent and finally won her over—or, as she liked to needle him, just worn her down. Jen proved lively—a real bundle of positive energy to be sure—but their underlying religious compatibility, plus their love for their common hobbies of rock climbing and martial arts—and their devotion to country—cemented their relationship. They'd decided to marry, but also to delay family life until she returned from her first field assignment.

Tim had encouraged her to take the job when the Agency recruited her (she having informed her recruiter that she'd told her fiancé of their interest—despite having read the list of do's and don'ts she was supposed to follow during the recruiting process). But Tim had been informed separately that he was on their watch list, too, so future employment just added a measure of practicality to their long-term plans. And, sure enough, the Agency snapped him up two years later when he finished his doctorate. They were now settled in their careers, and had set a wedding date for the following spring. Yet here Tim sat, despairing of ever seeing his beloved Jen again.

Reg glanced at his watch. "Sorry, Tim, I've got to get back. Please keep me posted on Jen, okay?"

"Thanks, Reg...outside of my immediate team and the Agency shrink, you're the only one I can talk to about this..."

Reg left feeling bad for his friend; Tim was uncharacteristically downcast and it made him wonder if he was telling all. These intelligence people were so compartmentalized it sometimes drove him crazy. But he understood the need-to-know mantra that dominated their lives, so he just gave his friend a politically correct arm-bump, put on his mask, and departed. He pondered the rapidly approaching Chinese ships, and wondered again if they were more than advertised. Worry clouded his brisk walk back to his cubicle at State.

Tim departed, too, but headed home, admitting to himself that he was exhausted and needed rejuvenating sleep. He unchained his bicycle from the rack in front of the restaurant, and pedaled home in 15 minutes. There, he set his alarm and literally fell onto his bed fully clothed. He had to make the most of the two hours he had—not wanting to miss his normal shift at HQ that might yield tangible news about Jen. He was asleep in less than five minutes.

Chapter 21

An apartment rooftop overlooking the Randolph Oil Refinery Houston, Texas, December 1st, 16:00 Hours

Like the 1,700 other MSS Chaos Teams waiting in or near the United States' largest cities or major infrastructure sites, Agents Li Fanghe and Hoa Pengyi, male and female respectively, had found a good place to scout their assigned target and prepare their attack. These two were paired to look like a working class married couple, and both were in their mid-twenties. They were also about as radically devoted to the CCP as MSS agents could be, having been thoroughly indoctrinated since young childhood into the ways of the State. Both were equally prepared to kill or die, and both had deadly poison capsules sewn into the collars of their simple worker's jackets. They had come across America's southern border after meeting a colleague 23 miles south and east of Ciudad Juarez on the Mexican side, and he'd easily guided them through a low-risk corridor.

Their MSS guide was Wang Janjua, a sleeper agent who'd been living in Mexico for more than three years. He'd arrived on a tourist visa before slipping below the local authorities' radar. Since then, he'd invested his time identifying several acceptable crossing points for teams of infiltrators, and had purchased arms or received them from the network of fellow agents that were a significant force in Latin America. He was a highly trained sapper and survivalist who'd been recruited by the MSS after 15 years' service in the elite Shenyang Military Region Special Forces Unit Siberian Tigers. He was also a master of infiltration, so crossing the U.S. border was child's play for him. He didn't know why he was smuggling Chinese agents across the Yankees' porous border, but he trusted his orders and had faith that his actions benefited the motherland. He'd dutifully become a master of the desert landscape, and he knew how to avoid his fellow "coyotes," plus other bands of illegals and the U.S. Border Patrol agents they all feared. Fortunately, there were so few of them, and the border wall was still unfinished, that it was easy to avoid detection and cross.

Wang had also established a safe house on a farm he purchased on the American side of the border. He brought every illegal team there first to acclimate and provision—including the special equipment and weapons they'd need before moving on to their assigned targets across the middle section of the United States. Wang had been told before he left the PRC that Americans would do anything for money, but he hadn't believed it until he somewhat nervously spent his first weeks in the U.S. Now he believed he could rent a grand hotel and stuff it with agents, and no one would be the wiser. Renting little safe houses on the American side had been comically easy—case in point being the apartment for this particular team. The owner had initially demanded all kinds of paperwork and references, but when he was shown a nice wad of cash, he abandoned his requests and went away happy—agreeing to not return for three months. Wang didn't know it, but he was one of 35 "coordinators" helping the infiltrating Chaos Teams get settled.

Li and Hoa spent one night at Wang's "nong chang" (farm) before transitioning to their apartment near the refinery. They'd been issued easily concealed pistols with extra sets of loaded magazines and, most important, a soft-bag containing a man-portable antitank weapon with four missiles. Their target was a massive gasoline storage tank just 100 meters inside a razor wire-topped fence on the oil company's property, and any grandmother could hit its massive bulk towering above the flat landscape. It was a full three stories higher than the roof of the couple's two-story building, but it was just the target tank of a row of similar but smaller tanks that stair-stepped down a slight gradient. Between the tanks and the fence was a low berm and a road that curved around a small hill into the refinery proper.

The two agents wanted to scout their target so, after settling into their temporary home, they found their way to the roof—and as advised by their receiving agent—sat openly on cheap folding camp chairs, and studied the area with expensive binoculars. There were no government cameras in evidence—not even any on top of the fence that surrounded this vital State facility (they knew in their hearts that it was not owned by a private company as advertised). But they were quickly understanding that America was, security-wise, a sleepy place. After scoping the site, Li and Hoa agreed that, when the first storage tank detonated, it would rupture and cause a spectacular blaze that would engulf the adjacent refinery. Burning fuel would pour out and follow the gradient downhill and cause the small adjacent tanks to catch fire, too. Then the combined flow of flaming fuels would flow into the numerous acres of cracking towers visible in the near distance. With a little luck, the whole place would go up in a giant fireball and be out of action for months. The two young agents were willing to die if necessary, but they weren't suicidal; if possible, they wanted to escape and continue to fight in some other venue.

They were filled with zealous patriotism, but their commitment to fight on as a team had been significantly impacted after arriving in Mexico. They discovered quickly that they were incredibly attracted to each other, so the week spent moving north through the back roads and countryside of the high desert had been unexpectedly pleasant. And now, on the eve of their life-changing mission, they were keeping a special secret even from each other: Both had begun thinking of marriage and family after returning to China as heroes. They might even get to meet their demi-god, Minister Wing, who sometimes blessed inter-agency marriages.

At sea aboard *Dragon's Fang,* bound for Sydney, Australia
December 1st, 17:30 Hours

PLAN Commodore Xi Quiliang stood on the starboard wing of his bridge, swaying with the gentle roll of the ship and enjoying the last of a beautiful sunset and the end of another full day at sea. They had made such good time after leaving the confines of the finishing grotto that he'd ordered his executive officer to slightly moderate their speed; arriving early would be just as much of a disaster for the overall mission as arriving late. Each ship's captain was closely coordinating with their counterparts to insure they'd dock within minutes of each other. But, since they could really only control what was happening on their own ships, Minister Wing had promised that a slew of his agents would be working in every port to identify and fix any problems that arose on the terminal end.

During that briefing, Xi and his fellow captains met other experienced merchant marine and navy captains, and they discovered that most everyone knew each other personally or by reputation. They were informed that additional experienced crews were sequestered near each port, and they would be available to fly out to any ship impacted by an outbreak of the deadly flu. Those crews were sent ahead as tourists, and were waiting in area hotels under strict personal quarantine. These crews could be airlifted via helicopter if needed in the event of a health emergency, or in the remote event that the crew rebelled. Both possibilities were judged as very unlikely because every crew member, marine, and MSS agent in the entire sea-borne component of Operation Unity had not only been medically tracked even before the pandemic, but all of them, especially among the NCO ranks and above, had been rigorously vetted for political reliability.

The spare crews could also be called upon to board an interfering foreign vessel—accompanied by an MSS assault team—in case a merchant marine or passenger ship's captain tried to dock where a Dragon had been assigned. It seemed to Captain Xi that the planners had thought of every eventuality, and had done as well as could be expected after the surprise health crisis initially threatened the plan.

Darkness descended as the evening bridge watch changed at 1800 hours, and Xi noted that the new watch got right to work monitoring various radar scopes or leaning over the electronic chart tables as seafarers had done for centuries. The principal difference nowadays was that modern charts and other documents were electronically produced, and the chart table was a horizontal flat screen. Yet, some things never changed: Both the electronic charts and the traditional paper ones required just a gentle brush of the hand to move aside.

Xi's quiet reflections in the twilight were gently interrupted by a signalman with the usual clipboard—the expected twice-a-day communication from Beijing. "Thank you, Seaman," he said after initialing the document. Fifteen seconds later, he determined that there was no new news; all was well and everything was on schedule. Then he turned back to the view, and enjoyed the horizon marked by pale pink slivers amid the darker tropical clouds. These last vestiges of the day faded steadily, and the gentle rumble of the great engines deep inside the ship were as soothing to him as were the ocean breezes—enjoyable even in December in latitudes just above the Equator.

Dragon's Fang had crossed the Yellow Sea before turning south into the East China Sea, and both had been navigated without incident. Then she passed between distant Okinawa Island to the north and the rebellious "cousins" on Taiwan to the south, and now was well east and south of the Philippines. The general public thought of the south Pacific as an endless warm and deep blue ocean, but *Fang's* navigators and lookouts maintained a constant life-saving vigilance for other commercial traffic—not to mention the numerous small islands, atolls, reefs, and even fishing boats that dotted the entire region. The ship's sophisticated radars and remote-sensing satellite feeds were essential, but every modern ship still kept human lookouts scanning the horizon with traditional hand-held or railing-mounted marine binoculars. There was just no substitute for the human computer.

Xi was in command of a great mission at sea—life as good as it gets for an experienced naval officer. Like his friend and counterpart (and two ranks senior) Vice Admiral Sun, who commanded the United States' component of the operation, he'd dreamed of just such a day throughout his nearly 40-year naval career. The magnificent setting caused his mind to briefly reflect on those days when he first met Sun at the academy: He'd thought the young man an odd duck, but soon realized that his initial impression of a misplaced "country bumpkin" was not only unfair; it was dead wrong. His fellow cadet was not only brilliant, but he was a gifted natural leader. Their careers had borne this out: Xi, like every competent officer, had made steady progress up the ranks of the peace-time military, but Sun graduated first in their academy class and had kept ahead of his classmates throughout. In fact, six members of that same class were commanding *Dragons* that evening, but Sun was the only "three-star." Their class had been uniquely successful, and their accomplishments were legendary throughout the navy. *Ask any of us and we'd give you an objective answer, Xi chuckled to himself. We were a once-in-a-generation group.*

He sighed contentedly, then guiltily glanced at his watch: Duty called—it was time to make his evening rounds. Seven more days and all the planning would come to fruition. Always a practical man during moments of honest reflection, during the past few weeks he'd begun to hope that he survived at least the first full day of combat. He wanted to know in his heart that his precious ship and assault force had accomplished their mission, and that they were in command of the objective. Then he could die in peace as a hero, with the homeland reaping the benefits of PLAN conquest.

He didn't want his "sunset" moment to end, but he tore himself away. He made his way through the bridge toward the ladder that led down into the lower levels of the bridge's superstructure. He'd make his rounds, then report to the commanding marine general to give his regular end-of-day status briefing. The two men stayed in their "own lanes" as much as possible—agreeing at the outset that, if each did their jobs satisfactorily, neither would bother the other. As he moved from one compartment to another, two husky marine escorts followed along: Flag officers of every navy in the world didn't walk around their ships without their country's version of fleet marine escorts.

The White House
December 1st, 07:00 Hours

"Good morning, Mr. President," John Laughton greeted the boss with his usual morning peppiness. "Did you sleep well?"

"Yes, thanks, pretty well—you know, John, after four years knowing you, I've never seen you down. What's your secret?" Spence was entering his first holiday season as President, and he was finally starting to relax. It had surprised him how much he was looking forward to the break; it had been a trying first year in office and he was tired.

In his heart, Spence certainly felt he had no justification for anything but overwhelming gratitude for his victory the previous year: The economy and most of the domestic employment sectors had continued to rebound after the disastrous hit from the Covid 19 pandemic, and most people were back at work. He'd had to focus on one immediate problem after another, and he hoped that the New Year would bring some relief. In terms of building a lasting legacy, he would continue to work on social programs and hope for the best. He also hoped to get the federal budget under control by reducing the military, which he thought was too big.

John chuckled at the President's question. "I'm just a normally zippy person, sir..." He found his usual chair after the President motioned him to sit.

Spence observed his tall and lean advisor with admiration: He tried to be a 'half-full' type of person, too, but today he'd awakened with a strange sense of foreboding, and wondered if it portended to what his National Security advisor would present in the PDB. Spence settled into his usual overstuffed leather parking spot, and began to scan the brief. It had been produced overnight—a distillation of current information by teams of dedicated diplomatic, military and intelligence folks the director of National Intelligence charged with keeping the President informed about what was important. A great multi-tasker, Spence began to read, but still encouraged his NSA, "Help yourself to coffee, John, and the pastries Chef turned out this morning are dangerous…" The PDB was organized as he preferred: Not more than five pages of five paragraphs each and printed in the 14-point type he could easily read.

John had indeed been eyeing the usual coffee and pastry service set on the end of the low table, and he gratefully helped himself. Then, as was his routine, he relaxed and watched patiently for the expected few minutes, dropping two lumps of sugar and a splash of cream into his first coffee fix of the day. He also munched on a sweet roll that was as yummy as the President promised. The boss took between four and six minutes to scan the brief every morning (including weekends, whether in residence or not), and John marveled how anyone could absorb so much so quickly. He suspected that President Stilwell had near-perfect recall, a widely believed rumor that kept everyone on their toes.

John finished his roll and arranged his notes on the coffee table. These were his personal annotations to the PDB, and were useful when the President began asking questions. Then he helped himself to more coffee. He'd enjoyed his year as NSA because President Stilwell had proven better than advertised: John had signed on to help during the election campaign and then been invited onto the White House staff. But now he felt more genuine optimism about the long-term prospects for the country than he had previously. He believed that centrist ideology held the answers the country needed, and this President seemed to be in full agreement. He had managed to fight off attacks from the radicals in their party, and was getting things done. In general, it had been a good ride.

Then John wondered to himself, *How can we get racially divided Americans to be kind to one another? But, after 250 years of slavery, it was probably going to take another 250 years to fully heal. At least (time-wise) we are 60 percent of the way there.* He believed that only God could accomplish that work of the human heart. John then focused on the present and was ready for the first question when the President looked up from the brief.

"What would you like to highlight or clarify, John? I don't have any specific questions."

"Mr. President, I want to draw your attention to the Dubai Embassy update. The local police have, encouragingly, caught some credible suspects and are extracting information as we speak. Looks like they're one of the few remaining IS splinter groups as we suspected..."

Spence shuddered inwardly as John casually mentioned the fate of these men—however evil their actions had been. Undoubtedly, horrific torture was being applied to extract information, but he was willing to support whatever measures were necessary to protect his fellow citizens from another mass murder like 9/11. Some of his predecessors had given mixed signals to the terrorists in the Middle East—but appeasement was viewed in the region as weakness, emboldening the worst of the lot.

But, despite his real admiration for the history and culture of the Pan Arab and African worlds, Spence was determined to project an image more like that of the stronger presidents of the past. He'd continued focusing heat on the few remaining IS factions—Al Qaeda, Boka Haram, and many others—and they were now dead or on the run. Many of these operations would never see the light of day, but the bad guys knew the U.S. was relentless and would eventually hunt them down. And there were positive results: America's hundreds of embassies and consulates abroad continued to be safer. He and his predecessor had used force (on occasion) to prevent terrorists from creating mayhem, and no American diplomatic personnel had been murdered or kidnapped for years. Case in point: Peaceful Muslim businessmen had gotten wind of an impending operation, and had tipped off the Dubai authorities about a possible terrorist cell. An evil group would now be broken up, and valuable information extracted that could save other lives down the road. Harshness here would also reinforce the Allies' pointed signals to the multi-faceted but loosely-connected terrorist community. Spence had learned quickly that every good president had to be able to compartmentalize well if he or she was to be effective, so he couldn't allow his personal abhorrence for torture dissuade him from supporting their friends in Dubai. He'd continued his predecessor's growing partnership within the peaceful majority of every predominantly Muslim nation, and many leaders and ordinary citizens were starting to trust his methods, too.

Spence listened to John's answers, and asked a few more questions as his NSA systematically ticked off the issues he believed important. Then, after his subordinate had completed his presentation, Spence stated: "I'm meeting with Secretary Madrid later this morning. I'll pass my thanks through him to the Dubai authorities…"

"Mr. President, that will be much appreciated. Now, with your permission, I'd like to address the other major item…" Seeing the President nod, he continued, "…I know the Vice President is leading the China project, but she asked me to mention that about half of those Dragon ships are now at sea. They continue to fan out across the Pacific toward their announced destinations, and nothing seems amiss. They are not escorted by military ships or subs, and are acting like merchantmen should. However, she knows you don't trust anything the PRC does and, as you directed, her working group is strictly monitoring them as reasonably as we can under maritime law."

"Do we have enough assets to keep tabs on them?"

"Yes, Mr. President."

Spence paused to think. The string of facts regarding the ships was unsettling, to be sure. But knowing the PRC's pension for great theater, the long-term facts seemed to support what they claimed—meaning that their fleet's intent was peaceful in every way. However, Spence had never been a "best-case scenario" leader—he was prudent and tried his best to never let his guard down. "As far as I can see, Vice President Mason is working with the Navy, Coast Guard, and RNO to monitor them day and night. I don't see what else we can do."

"I don't either, Mr. President. The Vice President included me in her working group, and I've been checking in every day. She's asked every relevant agency and service to do what they can—short of boarding the ships like buccaneers."

The President laughed at that one. "Good enough. Okay, John, let's wrap up."

John understood that the President had to get on with his busy morning schedule. After the usual thank you, he quickly departed; it was time for him to grind through his own busy day.

Chapter 22

At Sea in the North/Central Pacific Ocean
December 2nd, 09:45 Hours

Vice Admiral Sun searched the endless blue horizon with his powerful 11 x 14 magnification navy binoculars, and continued to worry. His four massively loaded assault ships—days out of sight of each other visually if not electronically—were all enjoying smooth passages across the seemingly endless swells. With no shakedown time, he had fully committed untested ships and men directly into a 6,000-mile voyage, but so far, so good. Every captain had run his Dragon's engines for countless hours to break them in while still in the cavern—venting the exhaust though an elaborate scrubbing system—but nothing compensated for time at sea. And now that he'd finally had some time for reflection, he was carefully evaluating what he'd been tasked to do. Sun had no illusions of returning *Dragon Claw* or her three sister ships to Mother China—his beautiful Dragons would never see home again.

Sun had been skeptical when he first learned of Marshal Tai's audacious plan but, as he absorbed its details, he steadily became a true believer. The planners had learned from the mistakes made by the Japanese in 1941 and 1942, and the PLA's decision to "hide in plain sight," using this fleet of innocent-looking container ships as assault craft, was genius. The mission's cover had been systematically developed over several years—including the constant propaganda barrage that had the world generally ignoring the boldest cross-oceans' invasion in history. The Normans (mostly in secret) crossed the 20-mile English Channel to invade England with 12,000 dismounted infantry, archers, and mounted cavalry. Then, 900 years later, the Allies had reversed the operation and secretly (in terms of day and place) carried 175,000 troops back across the channel at a wider point—one hundred miles to attack Hitler's "Atlantic Wall" in Normandy, France. But now, less than a century after World War II, the Chinese Navy was crossing 6,000 miles of Pacific Ocean in complete secrecy, and bringing with them four combined-arms heavy brigades—in an age when it was impossible to keep anything secret.

Operation Unity's major weakness in Sun's mind was the finishing grotto phase—its required secrecy naturally appeared suspicious to the rest of the world. But, since there was no other way, President Han and Marshal Tai had decided to live with the consequences. The fact that China was already utilizing many coastal caves and grottos as submarine pens and hiding places (none of which escaped the international intelligence agencies' notice) helped. And, so far, the ruse was working to perfection: The world's media only noted the secretive aspect of the cavern, and the tenor of their stories actually added legitimacy to the government's mantra. Only Wing's after-the-fact report of an enemy agent penetrating the lair had caused alarm; Marshal Tai had notified all his senior commanders of the incident, and assured them that it had been contained. The agent was dead and the world's intelligence agencies and governments were none the wiser. In any event, what could the assault force do now? As long as the plan remained a secret, they were fully committed to landing on schedule.

Sun was reveling in his good fortune as he stood on the bridge of one of the world's largest warships—certainly the largest assault ship ever constructed. As a veteran sailor, he loved the smell of the sea, the small whitecaps, and the sparkles as the sun glinted off the uneven surface. Mechanically, everything was working perfectly since they'd left the smelly confines of the grotto. They had done it—at least it seemed that their true intent was still undiscovered. Except for the novelty of the nighttime exodus, the government had overkilled its PR campaign for just this eventuality, and Sun had to give them their due: No superlatives could adequately praise what his chain of command had pulled off. The PLAN was now the largest navy in the world and, though the Americans' equipment was still technically better in many ways, it really didn't matter if they couldn't use it: Unwillingness or destruction were the same things. Sun's Dragons would neutralize a large part of the U.S. Navy's Pacific Fleet—while additional technologies and personnel destroyed the Atlantic Fleet—and those combined operations would buy the necessary time for the Asian component of "Unity" to succeed.

Sun knew the enemy had multiple satellites tracking their progress, and he was certain that the occasional undersea anomalies they passed in the near distance were Allied submarines. Yet he didn't care about these, either: Enemy monitoring had been factored into the plan and all the Dragons looked innocent. Distant fly-overs had commenced, too, but they were so high as to preclude detection of the truth of the secret "container stack" bulkheads—another ingenious detail that supported their story. Sun also loved the camouflage that "cloaked" each Dragon—special brilliant red and gold paint had made the hulls intentionally spectacular while, in contrast, the multi-colored paint scheme and mirrors had made the "stacks" appear as ordinary containers. So far, their luck was holding and the message was clear: Nothing to see here.

Admiral Sun felt reasonably comfortable aboard *Dragon's Claw* because he'd made a recent voyage on a large civilian container ship—at least it was civilian to the extent that any big Chinese company was independent of the government. He'd invested the time to familiarize himself with the particulars of a vessel this size, and directed all his senior officers to pose as civilian merchant marine crew and experience their own future routes. Because of their extensive preparations, they all knew the waters and hazards as they approached the targeted ports. At Sun's recommendation, either the captain or the executive officer on all 14 Dragons were professional merchant marine officers—true veterans of the cross-ocean trade. But the rest were veteran PLAN military ship commanders with multiple deployments in the western Pacific. Only the ground force cadres were unfamiliar with shipboard life, but their two years of intense training included familiarization visits on ordinary merchantmen. Sun was concerned that his marines spent most of their time training ashore—unlike the American Marines who were often stationed aboard Navy LHAs or LHDs (the helicopter-carrying assault ships that looked like WWII aircraft carriers with full flight decks), or aboard the LPDs and LSDs that looked like regular fighting ships with large stern decks for helicopters. The planners had targeted those first two classes of ships because they could handle the new F-35B STOVL/VSTOL fighters—as could the Japanese Navy's two newest "helicopter destroyers," which everyone knew were fully functional aircraft carriers. Additionally, the previous class of Japanese ships of the same type needed only simple deck refits to handle the same fifth-generation fighters. *And that,* thought the Admiral, *is why we're going to sink them, too.*

The admiral congratulated himself for tapping Merchant Marine Senior Captain Ho Quan Loo as *Dragon Claw's* commanding officer. The man had comprehensive experience in mammoth container ships, and Sun's confidence in his flagship's captain freed him to focus on being task force commander. The other three captains in the "American Flotilla," as Sun thought of them, were equally qualified and ideologically pure. Since he valued competent leadership and trusted his captains, Sun quickly approved the other officers that his captains had selected for their ships: All were veterans who'd made multiple trans-Pacific voyages.

As Sun habitually scanned the horizon, he wasn't worried about the occasional distant vessel that cruised by several kilometers away. *Claw's* pace was so fast that they easily skirted any vessels heading east, and there was just enough boy in him to enjoy showing up the competition. So far, everything was going like clockwork—which both reassured and unnerved him at the same time. He was a veteran of many sea commands, and couldn't help but think far ahead of the others on the bridge: He could visualize the ocean beyond the horizon, and turning a big girl like *Claw* took several miles and advanced planning.

Sun was also responsible for the assault force but, as a good commander, he'd delegated all operational decisions to the marine commanding generals. The ground and air assets had been tucked into every nook and cranny of each spacious ship, and even Sun, with his long association with combined arms scenarios, had been amazed at how much the Dragons could carry.

Down in one of those spaces, Captain Loo was currently speaking with his lead engineer in the engine room. After a brief discussion regarding a slight vibration in one of the engine-frame bolts, Loo got the technical answer he wanted, then climbed the ladders back to his bridge. Happiest where he could see the big picture, he raised his binoculars for the hundredth time that morning and scanned the endless horizon. It was his principal responsibility to anticipate course corrections, often as much as an hour before an order was issued to the helmsman, and he knew the admiral standing a few meters away was very good at that, too. He had great respect for the navy man currently glassing the starboard quarter, and appreciated that "his" admiral wasn't a micro-manager. He owed this opportunity to their inspirational leader, and Admiral Sun had accepted his recommendation for the other three captains for the American portion of Operation Unity. He and his fellow captains could handle the immense bulk and operational complexities of these unique ships and, though the Dragons were not the biggest container ships ever built, any ship close to 1,000 feet long took great skill to command and maneuver. Loo loved Claw only slightly less than his wife and son.

At that moment, *Claw's* sister ships, *Dragon's Fire* (far over the southern horizon) and *Sea Dragon* (far to the north) were also deep into their northern Pacific routes. They had all successfully navigated the passage between Japan's Kyushu Island and its smaller islands between there and Okinawa farther south. The three-ship flotilla had been distantly shadowed by patrol boats and aircraft, but they hadn't gotten close enough to discover anything untoward. The crews were tense during the transit through Japan's southern island chain but, as soon as they reached open ocean, the merchant marine and navy personnel relaxed and settled into normal routines.

After remaining in a loose trail formation during the tricky navigation sequences, the three ships had gradually drifted apart. *Sea Dragon* was heading for Bangor, Washington, in the Puget Sound, which was the home port of a rich collection of high-value targets—submarines being the main objective there. *Dragon's Claw* was headed for San Francisco Bay, and would pin down one of the greatest natural ports in the world. And last of the three, *Dragon's Fire,* would assault Long Beach, California, and attack the three prized aircraft carriers currently home-ported alongside nearby North Island in Naval Base San Diego. These included the USS *Abraham Lincoln* which, at least according to the admiral's morning intelligence report, remained in its usual berth; the USS *Theodore Roosevelt*, which was still in port awaiting orders for its next cruise, as the previous year she had been forced to dock at Guam, her crew beached after hundreds of them became infected with the Covid virus; and the USS *Carl Vinson*, which had returned to San Diego after a refit in Bremerton, Washington State, and was also awaiting orders.

Additionally, in San Diego alone, the U.S. Navy home-ported four LHDs and one LHA (the smaller aircraft carriers that could carry a squadron of the new F-35Bs); six LPDs and four LSDs (the Marine Corps' assault ships); 8 cruisers; 15 destroyers; 12 Littoral Combat ships; and many other ships, acres of planes, facilities of all kinds, and personnel. It never ceased to amaze the security conscious admiral that the American government was so loose with what should be secret military information: Anyone could look on Wikipedia or other open sources and see nearly up-to-the-minute information on the location of every capital ship in the U.S. Navy! Chinese common citizens didn't need to know where expensive military assets were located—only the Party leadership and senior military officers needed that vital information. Citizens' responsibilities included paying taxes and obeying the orders of the State; it was the leader's responsibility to decide what to do with resources. America was a strange place to Admiral Sun.

Sun focused his binoculars westward over the folded clam shells toward the distant bow—its safety railing some 500 feet from his vantage point on the bridge. The fake stack's characteristic seams were barely visible, even to one in such close proximity and who knew where to look. It was a small detail, but one of many the marine engineers had woven into the Dragon Fleet's deceptive camouflage. He had nearly unlimited visibility out to the horizon—which at his height above the surface was more than 20 nautical miles. He'd always loved these days at sea with the attendant fresh breezes that were discernably different during each season of the year. The air smelled different in each locale, too, and each ocean had its peculiarities. He was starting to shift his emotional center to the coming battle that would be momentous in world history, and he'd miss these introspective moments, but now China had to demonstrate what an incredible international power she had become. They had snuck up on the world, and would shortly unleash the lightning packed onto the decks below. Those innocent-looking "stacks" and decks held the most lethal ground attack force of its size ever assembled, and the air wing alone would change the balance of world power in less than one hour.

Sun agreed with the priorities of Operation Unity: The PRC's two main tactical targets were the aircraft carriers and the submarines. The Allies' submarines were the new super weapon of the day—in his mind arguably more lethal than the carriers. They were important in WWII—the "Pig Boats" sailing from Philippine bases had led the Allies' early military response against Japan until the Doolittle Raid—but modern attack submarines were dramatically more dangerous. They carried a wide variety of torpedoes, long-range anti-ship missiles, and long-range cruise missiles—and their "boomers," the giant missile boats—even carried nuclear-tipped ballistic missiles. Their GPS satellites and advanced computers enabled these weapons to acquire and destroy targets hundreds of miles away, and the larger missile subs were also stealthy; they could approach his homeland and rain nuclear death on his countrymen if the Americans chose to do so. This was why the PRCs PLAAF Space Forces were going to eliminate the Allied satellite threat, and the Dragons would take out the rest of the nearby targets close to the surface of the Earth.

Behind *Claw*, the horizon was clear as far as Sun could see. In the farthest distance, the dark blue swells and tiny whitecaps merged with a barely discernable mist that blurred the line where sky and sea met. Closer in, the double wakes churned by her four many-ton propellers, drove her through the cold water at more than 20 knots, and she could go faster if needed. He thought about the electronic capabilities *Claw* possessed (probably more important personally because of his son). Inside the lower decks of the superstructure were several compartments housing communications security teams, and specialists whose sole responsibilities were to monitor the array of offensive and defensive weapons systems that were the most modern in China's arsenal. Banks of computers were manned 24/7 by scores of both navy and air force technicians, and most every system was connected to designated satellites in geosynchronous orbit in space. There were also technicians manning sonar arrays, innovatively borrowed from submarine technology and installed into the mothership's hull. This innovation allowed them to "see" into the depths of the ocean, and "hear" for hundreds of miles in every direction—ocean thermoclines and salinity densities factored into every calculation. They could also receive satellite feeds that permitted them to constantly monitor surface traffic worldwide.

If hostilities began when they were still at sea, Sun's only fear was Allied submarines. He received daily updates on the disposition of every Allied military vessel, but when on patrol the newest subs were nearly impossible to locate. At least Sun didn't fear low-flying aircraft of any kind (fixed wing or rotary wing) because China had perfected secret anti-aircraft technology—part of each Dragon's comprehensive air defense matrix.

Sun had discussed the PLA's greatest challenge with Marshal Tai and his operations planning staff—that of developing a method of neutralizing the American naval forces in their East Coast ports. A rough average promised that about half of all potential targets were in port at any one time but, as a bonus, three quarters of the big and small deck carriers were either in port on normal rotations, or berthed for scheduled maintenance or refueling. However, America's newest carrier, the USS *Gerald Ford*, was perceived as less of a threat. It had even become a joke in the world's press because, more than two years after its commissioning, the U.S. Navy was still trying to fix her various overly complicated mechanical systems. The idiots had invested 13 billion dollars in a ship that didn't work! But Sun didn't care: The PLAN had deployed a fleet of smaller (but no less secret) ships along the Atlantic Coast, and they would sink her anyway because she'd be a threat in the future. In his last report, Sun had learned that the *Ford* was sailing up and down the east coast trying to get the kinks out. MSS agents were watching every port and would provide last-minute updates as necessary.

Just then a sailor stepped over the bridge sill and onto the wing. "Excuse me, Admiral, a message from the communications center!"

Sun lowered his binoculars against his civilian merchant marine captain's tunic, and turned to receive the clipboard from the eager signalman standing at rigid attention. "Thank you, Seaman," he said neutrally, and signed for the message. A curt nod dismissed the sailor, and Sun read: Port of Oakland expecting you. All return cargo ready and waiting.

Of course, the surface message was so much gibberish: The real message was an "all is ready" from their advance team—Wing's saboteurs were ready to strike more than 1,000 targets in the United States alone. *Dragon's Claw* wasn't heading for Oakland, either, as the Bay area's residents would soon find out. And, so far, there was no sign of U.S. government or local authorities being suspicious in the slightest. In fact, the Covid 19 pandemic that Wing's scientists had accidentally unleashed upon the world had proved to be an unexpected ally for their invasion: The automobile traffic within the targeted ports had not recovered to pre-contagion levels, and such scarcity made it easier for the MSS teams to clear the streets. These cadres would also act like traffic cops when the tanks and other vehicles roared down their ramps and disbursed among the various neighborhoods.

The admiral picked up his binoculars again. *Dragon's Claw* would not be picking up any cargo either—just delivering a "cargo" that had not landed on American soil since the second British/American War in 1812. The British had burned Washington, DC during that invasion, and Sun was sorry he couldn't do that on this trip. But the planners had decided to limit every hostile act to tactical necessity—thus avoiding future retaliation in kind. But, he reasoned, as he took in a great draught of the fresh sea air, *it will be enough to destroy as many of their military as we can. My four Dragons, combined with Wing's terror campaign, will give us the edge that the Japanese military failed to achieve in 1941.* But he knew that, nowadays, and in their favor as in 1941, the American people were almost as sleepy and internally focused as they had been then.

In the unlikely event that Sun's Dragons were compromised by suspicious allies ordering them to heave to for boarding—or in case of an at-sea disaster—they had an emergency "ace up their sleeve." In the former case, his ships could shred any Allied ship, sub, or plane in seconds and, in the case of the latter, the mini-subs could evacuate all key officers and technicians, and rescue the codes and black boxes deemed too important to fall into enemy hands. To this end, several of Wing's "special" agents, disguised as ordinary field-grade PLAN officers, were ready to carry out the admiral's orders. These fanatical, brutal men would execute any critical personnel that could not be rescued, and once the key personnel were safely away from the mother ship, they would scuttle the ship and die with her. But, just in case, Sun was never without his personal pistol: He never fully trusted Wing nor his MSS radicals.

Chapter 23

At sea, off the coast of Vietnam
December 4th, 14:30 Hours

As *Dragon's Claw* and her two sister ships crossed the International Date Line heading toward the American coast, *Dragon's Fang,* which had sailed the second night, was making great time toward Sydney Harbor (actually the Botany Bay Container Terminal) on Australia's beautiful Gold Coast. She was 10 percent lighter than her sister ships because the local quay where her captain planned to dock only allowed ships that drew less than 13 meters. Since dredging was never perfect, it wouldn't do to chance *Fang* scraping her keel or getting stuck on the coral sand bottom. To compensate, the command group decided to carry a few less tanks and other vehicles, which was not a deal-breaker against the small Australian military. The initial target was the adjacent airport complex, and the ground force would move into the greater metropolitan area six miles north if necessary. General Bao believed *Fang* packed more than enough punch to keep the Aussies busy for months. In fact, keeping Australia at bay was one of the key corrections Bao and Dang had built into their plan: Failure by the Japanese to get past New Guinea and take over Australia's major ports had doomed their southern expansion. It gave the Allies a jumping-off point for the "island-hopping" campaign adopted by General MacArthur and Admiral Nimitz. Australia was a vital springboard for the rest of the Pacific war.

Off the southern Chinese mainland

At that moment, *Dragon's Breath*, bound for Port Klang in Malaysia, was just passing Hainan Island, a full day behind *Dragon's Fang*. She was the last of the four sister Dragons to depart the cavern on December 1st.

Breath's mission was to use the huge port facilities on the Malay Peninsula as a staging area for the southern component of the PLA's multi-pronged penetration of the sprawling capital's urban areas—a strategic landing considered important to distract and divide the Malayan military while the ground attack bore down from the north. As the marine armored spearhead headed inland, PLAAF airborne troops would capture the international airport, and special forces units would assault and occupy strategic off-shore derricks and platforms dotting the peninsula's continental shelf. After the initial objectives were conquered and consolidated, additional special forces would systematically capture all of the region's oil facilities, including the refineries and other infrastructure that China needed to secure its own prosperous future.

Twelve nautical miles abeam of *Dragon's Breath*, and visible through the powerful binoculars that the lookouts used, *Dragon's Eye* was making equally good time toward the Jakarta International Container Terminal in Indonesia. Part of the world's largest archipelago, Indonesia's islands and atolls held extensive petrochemical treasures. The "Dutch East Indies" had been coveted for its extensive and varied resources for hundreds of years, and were a key target of the Japanese military during WWII. Now it was the CCP who coveted this bounty.

The third ship that departed with the December 1st flotilla was *Dragon's Sail*, which was also "on course, on time" toward its own target: Laem Chabang, the largest container port in Thailand, and the 22nd largest in the world. It was located just south of Bangkok, and *Sail's* mission was to assault and hold the strategic area in and around the port while armored pincers struck directly south from the Chinese mainland. Additional ground forces would force their way in from neighboring Laos to the east and from Myanmar to the west. This four-pronged assault was designed to overwhelm the Thai military—which everyone in the know evaluated as capable to the point of being dangerous.

Trailing just a half-day behind her three sisters, *Dragon's Wing* had been making steady progress toward her intended target: Ho Chi Minh Port in southern Vietnam. She too had passed through the Yellow Sea and turned south to cruise along the Chinese coast, and she steamed as if she'd been making this particular voyage for years. But, since her targeted port was just a bit closer than Malaysia, Thailand, or Indonesia, she was able to throttle back, burn less fuel, and place less strain on her multitude of untested parts. Therefore, it was surprising when her engine blew up.

PLAN Senior Captain Quan Zuocheng was on the bridge, leaning over the chart table and conferring with his navigator when he felt two jolts, one right after the other. He felt the ship imperceptibly begin to slow, and he knew immediately that something was very wrong. Before his hand reached the comms button, he heard it buzz loudly. "Captain speaking…report!"

In the engine room, PLAN Commander Luo Fanghe, the chief engineer, shouted into his handheld: "Captain, the port engine just exploded laterally… looks like a piston from the location. Heavy metal pieces shot across the open space and damaged the starboard engine, too. There are two fires raging and I have shut everything down!"

"All stop!" Quan commanded the helmsman. "Any casualties?" he shouted back to Luo, who he could hear shouting above obvious pandemonium in the background.

"Two dead for sure, Captain…half a dozen injured. But, Sir, the halon fire suppression system is working and I'll know more in five minutes."

"Coming down!" Quan responded, then he dashed for the internal bridge ladder. The ship had already begun to slew slightly to port, so he yelled back at the helmsman to compensate. On the way he passed a marine major and told him to notify the commanding general that the engines were damaged. He promised an update when he had one.

Hurrying along the last corridor before he reached the engine room door, he began to smell the dreaded odor of burning machinery oil. He shouted at a group of sailors gathered by the door to make way, and practically vaulted over the sill and into the chaotic scene. Smoke filled the huge space, and everywhere men were shouting and trying to put out the fires. Four sailors were dragging a bloody and obviously dead comrade up a short flight of stairs, and Quan motioned for them to pass before he descended into the haze. He coughed in the accumulating smoke, and noticed the bright yellow hazard light flashing in one corner. A klaxon blasted a pulsing emergency warning and he knew he had to get control of the situation fast. He landed on the heavy mesh grating that formed a four-meter canyon between the two massive engines towering on either side, and ahead through the smoke spotted Commander Luo. His lead engineer was giving orders to several sailors donning silver fire-fighting suits, and he looked as calm as one could hope. He was also using a hand-held extinguisher—vainly trying to douse the flames leaping from a gaping hole in the port engine. Normally hotter than the rest of the ship, the engine room was now more than 100 degrees Fahrenheit and climbing fast.

"Status?" Quan shouted when he reached Luo's side.

"Captain, the halon system suddenly failed, so we're powering up the conventional powder system. It should be working in a few seconds."

"Turn off that racket first…I can't hear myself think!"

Luo shouted to a senior chief who just arrived at the head of several more firefighters, and he instantly shouted into his own hand-held. Momentarily the wailing stopped.

Just then the halon system started working again, and highly pressurized suppressive gas spewed into the space. Twenty men nearest the fires heard its rush, and quickly backed away. The system was designed to fight electrical and Class C fires and, fortunately, the gas was odorless and tasteless, and not harmful to humans. It sought out fires by suppressing the chemical reaction in the combustion process, and also reduced the associated heat. The technology was particularly effective in tank turrets and other smaller spaces, but worked well in bigger ones if the dispensers were large enough. Typically, ships' engine rooms had the largest systems on the planet, but refineries and power plants had huge ones as well. The only downside was that the positive air pressure briefly hurt everyone's ear drums. They all plugged their ears and screamed as loud as they could for a few seconds to counteract the pain, and relief came a few seconds later when the last fire flickered out. Five seconds later, the gas automatically shut off, and huge ventilators kicked in and rapidly expelled the polluted air.

Next, Quan surveyed the damage: There was a large hole in the port engine measuring three meters by two, and from its location, he agreed with his chief engineer's assessment that it was a blown piston head. It had exploded off its stem, blasted through the metal skin covering the engine body, and shot across the open space and punctured the metal skin of the starboard engine. Enough of the piston head had penetrated to interfere with the second engine's mechanism, and hot metal shards and splinters had broken away and forced the engine to seize. He could see that the insides of both engines were scorched, and pools of ruined oil gave off an incredible stench. In summary, the engines were a complete mess. "Unbelievable!" was all the captain could say to his chief engineer.

Suddenly a commotion behind them caused everyone to turn, and Marine Major General Ling Jihua bounded down the ladder, shouting as he approached. "What happened, Quan?" He was barking other orders in great distress, forgetting his courtesies. Then, before Quan could answer, the enraged officer shouted again: "How long before you can get this mess fixed?"

Both the naval officers came to attention and saluted, then Quan answered, "General, a piston head sheared off and exploded through the skin of this engine…" he motioned with his hand, "…and rammed into the other with sufficient force to damage it, too. We'll conduct a precise assessment, but a full day before getting underway is minimal."

"Can we make up the lost time?"

"General, if we lose one day, yes. If more, then no." There was no point lying to the mission commander—he had to make his adjustments based on accurate information.

"Get it done, Captain!" With nothing more to say, the senior officer turned and marched back to the ladder. He had two marine officers with him, and a couple of senior NCOs, and the group had to pick their way around the body of the second sailor killed in the explosion. Knots of medical personnel tended to injured sailors lying nearby.

Quan then took Luo aside. "What do you think…do we have enough steel plate to patch both openings?" He knew they carried a replacement piston for the port engine, and could probably clean out the starboard engine sufficiently to get it going. Neither could operate without the engine housings being sealed and the entire system flushed of burned oil, but he was certain they carried enough fresh oil to do the job.

"Yes, I think so, Captain. I'll get two welding parties organized in a few minutes, and two more teams to replace the broken piston. We have plenty of engine oil so we should be able to get both engines going. I'll have a coherent answer for you in a few hours."

"Very good, Commander. This is when your senior shop ratings will earn their pay…" Luo nodded, and Quan turned away to see to his dead and wounded. Medical personnel were placing the second dead sailor into a body bag and stretcher bearers were waiting to take their deceased comrade up to the morgue. The superficially injured were being helped up the ladder on their way to the sick bay. One sailor's leg was obviously broken, and he would be moved last and taken directly to the surgical ward, which was part of the significant medical facilities on every Dragon. It looked to Quan like the rest of the injuries were moderate flash burns and minor cuts and bruises. He was thankful that just two sailors were fatally close to the blast, and briefly conferred with the ship's senior doctor before retracing his steps to the bridge. His first task there was to inform all hands what had happened and assure them that the ship was okay. They'd be dead in the water for a day or so and then carry on.

Fortunately, no foreign ships would pass by close enough to see through their camouflage scheme until darkness fell, and their secret would remain safe until late the following morning. At that point, a Liberian-flagged coastal freighter they'd been tracking would pass within 1,000 yards of their position and might veer closer to offer assistance. Then the general would have to decide whether to quickly board her, sink her, or just hope for the best. An emergency call would be made to the mainland, and local PLAN ships should be able to reach them before he had to make that decision. Picket ships would form a cordon around their larger sister after dropping off replacement parts, and they'd take the dead and injured home. Quan dashed off a quick report that was encoded in the signals room and transmitted via UHF uplink burst to his chain of command in PLAN headquarters in Beijing. He knew the general was doing the same.

Bangkok, Thailand

As the unfortunate drama unfolded aboard *Dragon's Wing* off the southeast Chinese coast, two businessmen from Shanghai were meeting with two real estate agents in Bangkok's downtown business district. The businessmen were completing a deal to rent the entire ground floor of an almost-completed 10-story office building, and they wanted access to their suite before the finishing touches were applied to the upper stories. The two mid-level executives represented a mainland Chinese company that was expanding into the region—a commercial enterprise in need of additional floor space to accommodate an additional raft of local workers.

The Thai real estate men were more than happy to meet their clients' requests. They liked most business reps from China, and these two met their highest expectations: They proved from the first handshakes that they really knew how to conduct negotiations, and handed over the requested three month's rent in advance. They also demonstrated the fine art of entertainment, insisting on paying for everything at restaurants of the hosts' choice. The foursome visited several swanky bars boasting excellent floor shows, and generally painted the town red. But what put the Chinese bid over the top were thick envelopes of cash—placed into each rep's hands after the final night's festivities. The keys to the rented suite were turned over a few seconds later, and the Thai real estate agents presented beautiful parting gifts to their grateful guests. The generous "tea" money enclosed in the envelopes amounted to a year's salary, so they returned to their homes hoping beyond hope to do business with the same PRC company again.

The following evening, a truck backed into the deserted ground floor loading bay of the Chinese agents' new digs, and several men materialized out of the darkness to help carry heavy five-gallon cans into the space. The cans were obviously full because the men strained to move them inside, but one by one, they carefully manhandled six cans into each corner of the bottom floor. They then placed timed explosive charges amid the cans, locked the door behind them, and drove away. When ignited a few hours before Dragon's Sail docked, 1,200 gallons of gasoline would cause quite a blaze—and gather the full attention of the city's first responders and the national press. Over the next three days, dozens of identical negotiations would be successfully concluded in greater Bangkok and in other prominent cities across Asia.

Dalian Shipyard, Liaoning Province, the People's Republic of China December 4th, 00:45 Hours

Dragon's Armor yielded to the gentle but steady pull of the tugboat, and eased out of the finishing grotto to follow her sisters. She was bound for Manila's main container port and would do her best to tie down the Philippine military until the bulk of the invasion force arrived a few days later. Paratroops would drop on all the major airfields and, once these were secure, a series of heavy airlifts would land and disperse infantry and their accompanying APCs. These units would fan out and gain momentum—buying additional time for heavier transport ships to arrive with the occupation force. It was these latter cadres that were expected to first match the local military, and then steadily wear them down. Beijing believed the effort was worth its investment: There were tremendous oil deposits hidden among the 7,000 Philippine Islands, and China wanted them all.

MSS Headquarters, Beijing 05:30 Hours

Senior General Wing, minister of State Security, was in his office for his weekly visit to catch up on the small amount of paperwork he actually had to do himself. Trusted staff performed most of the routine or tedious tasks, but certain promotion confirmations or supply orders over a certain number of Yuan (RMB) required his actual signature. He'd steadily built up his force to more than 1.5 million agents and support personnel, and his cadres were now the most powerful force in China behind the military and the PAP. But, because of his carefully guarded relationship with Minister Ti, who commanded the two million national police (and to whom President Han—chair of the Central Military Commission—had also given operational control of the 1.5 million People's Armed Police), Wing accepted that he indirectly controlled three vast armies with unheard-of power.

Wing had monitored Ti's career closely during her ruthless rise to become the "top cop" of China, and they had occasional interactions along the way. But, within days of her promotion to minister, he'd requested a meeting with her at their mutual convenience. Under the guise of secrecy that he knew she'd understand, he asked her to come to one of his Spartan safe houses outside the capital for their first private meeting. He maintained a dozen such places, and each was carefully guarded by one of his special units of loyal killers.

Wing was in fact married, but he saw his wife infrequently and she was quite content with their arrangement. She lived in their palatial West Beijing estate, and she shopped in the finest stores in the country. She enjoyed the intrigues of the capital gossip circle with her many friends and peers, and she left her husband alone. She'd been largely responsible for raising their two children—a son and a daughter—and both had graduated from university with honors and were now junior officers working their way up the MSS ladder. All three had something in common: They knew better than to ever question Wing about anything—a lesson reinforced when he'd brought them to a couple of his bi-weekly executions. It was his not-so-subtle message to his beloved ones.

Ti had been looking forward to her meeting with Wing, anticipating his acknowledgement that their playing field had leveled. She brought her own small entourage of experienced policemen, and Wing's chief of security guided them politely to an inner room. But after the soundproof doors were shut, her team was set upon by Wing's elite guards and disarmed. They were tightly bound and Ti was held at gunpoint by two of Wing's female agents. A moment later, Wing entered with his pistol in hand, and shot all 10 of her security team in the head. After witnessing that horror, she was dragged screaming and nearly hysterical into a side room where she was tied down on a bed with her mouth taped. The guards then disappeared for several hours, during which time Wing gave her the closest possible instructions on what he wanted from her in the future, and demonstrated the close cooperation he expected from their two ministries.

After the session was successfully concluded to Wing's satisfaction, Ti was invited to shower and was driven back to her headquarters by his personal chauffeur. As she reached for the handle, the MSS driver reached back and handed her an envelope containing instructions on when and where she was to be available for the next inter-ministerial meeting. Wing had whispered a choice before she left his compound: Complain to the General Secretary—in which case she and her entire family would be executed within a few hours—or she could retain everything she'd worked for, and closely cooperate with her new lover. She wisely decided on the latter, and their two ministries had worked hand in glove since. In fact, it didn't take Minister Ti long before she looked forward to her bi-monthly conferences with Comrade Wing.

During his "reign" as MSS minister, Wing had experienced only one negative confrontation with President Han: Shortly after his "pacification" program began with Minister Ti, he had assigned two of his trusted agents to check out the mysterious provincial leader, Liu Keqiang. He was puzzled about her inclusion in Han's special advisory group, and thought that perhaps he might pacify her, too. But, less than 48 hours after he'd sent the agents south to Guangdong Province to begin their investigation, a car pulled up to MSS headquarters. An insultingly low-level assistant was shown into Wing's office with a directive to come "immediately" to Han's private estate. The drive across town passed in silence, but it was the only time in his adult life that Wing was truly nervous. He guessed, but didn't know, the reason for his summons.

He arrived with no threatening guards present—just Han sitting on his front veranda in a lone deck chair, next to a low table with one glass of clear liquid, and one small plate of crackers. The message in their culture was unmistakable: Wing was in deep trouble and Han was very angry. The minister of State Security knew the drill: He had not been relieved of his pistol, but he accepted as fact that he'd be dead in a heartbeat if he reached for it. Han had the best marksmen in the country working for him and they were no doubt positioned strategically around the grounds. Wing merely walked up the steps, stood without speaking a couple of paces from the little table, and waited to learn his fate. Han made eye contact but said nothing for a few seconds, and then uttered just one sentence in a quiet voice: "If you approach in any way, directly or indirectly, Governor Liu again, you'll be dead before morning."

There was nothing to be said in his defense so Wing simply replied, "Yes, Comrade General Secretary, it will be as you command."

Han's cold gaze didn't change and he didn't speak again, so Wing accepted that he'd been dismissed. He'd used up eight of his nine lives in one stupid move, and remained more puzzled than ever about whatever relationship Han had with Liu. But further speculation meant certain death and he never considered her again. He nodded politely, turned rather stiffly, and retraced his steps to the car that had never turned off its engine. The low-level assistant had disappeared, and he was driven back to his headquarters without any conversation from the driver. Han had scared the living daylights out of him, but Wing was extremely shrewd: He'd risen to the heights of power in the

PRC partly because he'd never made the same mistake twice. He deduced that he had a free hand in his other dealings, but that he had to stay out of Comrade Han's lane. After the confrontation, Han never mentioned it again, and it was if the incident had never happened.

Wing finished his two hours of paperwork undisturbed, knowing his staff would never approach him unless summoned. He suddenly felt contemplative though, and reclined in his comfortable chair to consider if he'd missed any opportunity to exploit America's many weaknesses. He wanted to maximize the destructive potential of his Chaos Teams, and time was running out; Operation Unity was only days away from unleashing Hell on his hated enemy.

Wing admitted that, from the first moment he studied the operational details of the plan, it was comprehensive and brilliant. Tai's sidekick Bao (whom he knew as a classmate at the academy) and the little dweeb of a professor they all knew, had cooked up a remarkable plan indeed. Such admiration was rare because Wing didn't admire much in other people: He was his own god, and he'd pushed the limit on everything and everyone as he clawed his way to the top. He'd outsmarted, exploited, and intimidated every aspect of every opportunity during his rapid advancement, and he believed he did all for the glory of China. He'd beaten, murdered, raped, and bullied his way to the highest position he aspired to. He didn't want Han's position because he'd lose a lot of freedoms in the glaring spotlight of world attention. He wanted only to help establish the Middle Kingdom as the principal force on Earth—and be the power behind the throne. Operation Unity provided the means, and he was fully committed to doing his all to make it successful. As far as Wing could ascertain, the two eggheads had latched on to every successful move that Imperial Japan had achieved in World War II, and they'd studiously avoided every mistake.

The only blemish on his record had occurred while the ships were undergoing their transformation inside the grotto: His own biological warfare laboratory had unleashed a potential disaster on the Wuhan area, and it quickly spread across China, and then around the world. He had briefly sweated bullets that this might be his "ninth life" that provoked Han's wrath, but Han seemed to take it in stride. Fortunately, the facts had been on his side: It was a true accident and, on top of that, all of the need-to-know Politburo leadership supported his chemical and biological weapons research. They also supported the nuclear laboratories run by Tai's scientists in the PLA. As usual, Wing knew the paranoid senior leadership just wanted as many arrows in China's quiver as they could fund.

Han had ordered the lethality of the virus to be kept secret from the world for as long as possible, and the government had taken comprehensive steps to protect the homeland and cover their guilt. The relevant ministries purchased every mask and protective device they could lay their hands on until 51 days after the accident. At that point, they finally felt enough pressure to obliquely fess up and release spotty information to the media. Then, with the tepid assistance of the World Health Organization (into which they'd poured billions of RMB to engender loyalty), they released dribs and drabs of information to stave off full-fledged accusations of intent. It was a masterfully managed international media campaign, and Wing could not believe their luck: The important people in China had been protected, the research continued unabated, Operation Unity was quickly back on track, and incredible health-related societal and economic chaos had erupted in the United States and Europe. People had died by the tens of thousands, but that didn't matter. What did matter was that the world's governments had locked everything down, and shot themselves in the foot so badly that the entire Western economy briefly tanked. The scene was set for America being in a worse state than they were in the early 1940s after emerging isolationist and broke from the Great Depression. The bar had been lowered for his Chaos Teams: All they had to do was exploit this dysfunctional state of affairs with some last-minute diversions, and no one would notice the Dragons until it was too late.

Wing was loath to miss an opportunity to make things worse for their enemies (and better for their assault troops) and he had to pinch himself when Fate intervened and delivered a second gift from Heaven: Race riots broke out in the U.S. after one of their stupid cops killed one of their black minorities, and all hell broke loose. Then there were additional incidents that made things even worse. He was aware of long-simmering racial issues in the U.S.—left from their earlier history of African slavery, and he'd always looked for ways to exploit this tension but couldn't grasp how. But the riots and demonstrations had made everything clear: *He didn't need to do a thing; America was self-destructing.* He'd just stoke raging fires with his Chaos Teams, and the Dragons would arrive in a country more divided than Wing could have dreamed. He had the better part of 1,700 multi-agent teams scattered strategically across America, and they'd just add to the distractions.

Chapter 24

The Finishing Grotto, Dalian Port
December 5th, 00:25 Hours

Three more Dragons were in the process of launching on their maiden voyages: *Roar, Cloud,* and *Shield* had all been moved forward, and the portable sections of the middle quay closest to the front had been moved back and out of the way as designed. The handlers on the left-hand quay had plenty of room to winch the ships into the exit channel, and the powerful little electric engines did the rest.

Dragon's Roar was assigned Yokosuka Harbor in Tokyo Bay—the combined American and Japanese naval complexes that home-ported numerous important ships and other facilities. One of Japan's four precious "helicopter carriers" was stationed there, plus all the attached escort ships, submarines, dry docks, fuel tank farms, and machine shops needed to keep two fleets operational. It was, as the saying went, a "target-rich" environment. Bao and Dang knew before the fact that the USS *Ronald Reagan* would be putting to sea before *Roar* arrived—departing with her escorts to meet up with the USS *Nimitz* and her battle group for publicly announced regional exercises. But Marshal Tai and his team quickly adapted, and assigned several submarines to intercept and sink the southbound task force off the coast of Japan. His battle staff had tasked the PLA's Rocket Force with sinking all the other Japanese targets on land and sea, and to rain death on the southbound American/Japanese task force.

Closer to the Chinese mainland, *Dragon's Cloud* was tasked with one of the two operations most meaningful to the people of China: Kee Lung Harbor nestled on the southern tip of Taiwan Island. She would deploy her assault troops to form the bottom of a powerful vice, while *Dragon's Shield* would assault Kaohsiung Harbor in the north. These two forces were designed to squeeze the "rebels provincial forces" and divide their response. The planners anticipated that the world would watch in awe as staggered missile and bomber attacks rained death on the island's military. This intensive campaign would be followed by full-blown paratroop drops and a sea-borne invasion that would rival the D-Day Normandy assault in 1944.

In the Yellow Sea, December 5th

Two hours after sailing, *Dragon Cloud's* crew and assault force heard the commanding general's dramatic announcement over the ship's public address system. They felt privileged to have been awarded the grand prize of the much larger mission they were just learning about: Attacking and forcibly bringing their rebellious cousins back into the fold. They'd been told since childhood that millions of their countrymen were being held against their will by unscrupulous and wayward Taiwanese politicians—a cabal aided and abetted by the meddling Americans and the ever-troublesome Japanese. Now their distant relatives would rejoice when the marines bravely stormed ashore to free them. They, the People's Marines, were the liberation force that would strike the long-awaited first blow for reunification! Unable to contain their jubilation, everyone on board spontaneously cheered or whooped for more than 15 minutes.

PLAN Marine Major General Wu Ten, the mission's overall commander, placed the microphone back in its cradle after delivering his historic message to his marines and shipmates. But he, too, had been so overcome by the emotion of the moment that he had to fold his arms behind him to hide his shaking hands. He'd addressed these wonderful men whom he'd trained for more than two years—finally permitted to share the treasure/secret he and the captain had been forced to bear alone. He could hear the cheers echoing throughout the ship—even as those near him on the bridge broke protocol and whispered to each other in glowing terms: *They were the chosen ones—the vanguard of the reunification armada that would storm the beaches and docks of Taiwan's western-facing harbors! It had been granted to them the privilege of pushing the rebel forces back into the mountains—where they'd burn them out of their caves one by one.*

He'd been able to truthfully tell his marines they were not alone: He told them that *Dragon's Shield* would storm Kaohsiung Harbor, and then a quarter of a million soldiers—currently prepositioned just across the strait—would join them within hours. He didn't inform them that these units had been slowly moving closer to their jumping-off points over the last two years to avoid suspicion. He knew that the size of this combined force was about the same as the Allied landing force in Normandy, and just like that great undertaking in 1944, the PLAN had scores of transport ships and a host of smaller but seaworthy craft hovering inconspicuously within 50 miles of each concentration of waiting infantry.

Currently dotted along the east coast of mainland China, and lost in the clutter of the normal coastal traffic, the transports' skippers were biding their time, anxiously awaiting their respective signals to dash just after dusk to their assigned embarkation points. The assault troops would quickly clamber aboard, and then the ships would form into staggered waves and cross the Taiwan Strait to their assigned beaches and harbors. Of historical note, the distances from the Chinese mainland to Taiwan was about the same as from southern England to the Normandy beaches: Approximately 100 statute miles (only a few hours' sailing time) spanned both straits.

The troops had been practicing rapid loading techniques for months on mock landing craft, and they could fill these smallish ships and ocean-going hovercraft in less than 30 minutes. They had pre-loaded the infantry fighting vehicles and motorcycles, so only the personnel were needed. The armada would cross under the cover of darkness, and would land as *Cloud* and *Shield's* tanks and marines fanned out and engaged the local forces. Other fast-landing craft would race across the various distances to the smaller littoral island territories long claimed by the independent-minded province. Scheduled for liberation were the islands of Kinmen (aka Quemoy); Penghu (the Pescadores); Matsu Islands (Lienchiang Islands); and Wuchiu (Dagiu).

The rank and file of these soldiers were waiting impatiently, and had been told nothing of their specific destinations. But most sensed they were on the verge of something big. Among the senior NCOs and officers who did know some details, all were highly confident that the Taiwanese military on the main island—as well as the outpost troops illegally occupying the four smaller island groups—would be no match for the PLA's determined combined arms assault. Even if international elements tried to intervene, they'd be no match for the clouds of missiles that would sink every enemy ship or shoot down every plane. In any event, the overall planners had anticipated that most of Taiwan's air force and navy would be destroyed at the outset, and that the visiting foreign combat ships would be sunk at their berths before they could get underway.

Also supporting the invasion were hundreds of fighters lurking at two dozen nearby airfields. Fighters would be aloft and ready to pounce when the attack began, and most were within 15 minutes flying time of the battle space. Various combat squadrons had been gathering for more than a year—every unit conducting recently established (new normal) operational tempos. Every action by myriad individuals were components of the overall hide-in-plain-sight strategy of the plan.

Mainland-based rocket force crews were poised to launch their arsenal, including hundreds of Dong Feng (East Wind) DF-15/16 short-to-medium range ICBMs armed with conventional munitions. These would destroy most of Taiwan's exposed defenses and airfields. Additionally, more than 500 "ship-killer" missiles were dialed in and waiting in their launching sites about 200 miles to the north. Their first target was the Allied task force approaching Taiwan from the northeast. It would be a comprehensive attack: Submarines would launch waves of torpedoes, the dozens of surface ships would launch salvos of sea-skimming anti-ship missiles—then, just as chaos was overwhelming the Allied ships, the land-based ballistic missiles would rain down too close together for the Allied ships to escape.

China's most modern surface ships (the 055-Destroyer Class) had been fitted with the latest generation of sea-skimming ship-killers dubbed the "CJ-10," from "Chang Jian" or "Long Sword." This dart was similar to the Allies' Harpoon anti-ship missile, but it had a longer range, capable of reaching enemy ships up to 800 nautical miles over the horizon. This compared favorably to the previous generation of sea-skimmers fitted on most of the older combat ships in their fleet (including the first destroyer classes obtained or copied from earlier Soviet models—the 52 Class). Their YJ-18s from "Yang Ji" or "Eagle Strike" sea-skimmers, had ranges of more than 300 nautical miles.

After these initial Allied task forces were sunk, later interventions would be summarily blown out of the water, too. Apart from a few subs, no enemy warship could venture inside China's Second Island defensive zone—they'd now control the western third of the Pacific Ocean.

However, the six active Type 094A SSBN submarines, each loaded with a dozen non-nuclear, sea-launched ballistic missiles, were not in the region: They were already on station, quietly hovering in a line a few hundred miles off the American West Coast. Their 72 missiles would provide a vital component to the overall plan—overshooting most of the continental United States on their way to destroying as many of the airfields, aircraft carriers, submarines, and other ships as they could—particularly those stationed in such bases as Naval Station Norfolk, Virginia; Naval Station Mayport in Jacksonville, Florida; and Naval Submarine Base New London, in Groton, Connecticut. They'd also hit other bases and shipbuilding companies where future carriers and subs were being built. After launching their missiles, the Type 94s would slip away and begin their long journey home. Enabling the destructive power of the Atlantic strikes would be drone swarms—launched from innocent-looking, regular-sized freighters. Several of these were currently steaming just 20 miles east of each East Coast target.

And last, but far from least, the remaining attack submarines not assigned elsewhere were just the proverbial "black holes in the water" ringing Taiwan. They formed an additional fan that would sink any of USS *Nimitz*' task force that survived the other attacks, plus additional Allied reinforcements that arrived later from Hawaii, Australia, or Japan. The planners believed that the Allied task forces were worth the investment of as many missiles and PLAN submarines as it took to sink them. After they defeated the Japanese and American navies, the surviving subs would keep an eye on the Russians, too—just in case—in spite of the Politburo's hope that they would stay out of the conflict. The CCP never trusted anything the Russians said.

Regarding the balance of the PLAN fleet, the surface ships were either hugging the coast in normal patrol patterns or waiting in their assigned harbor berths for the go-ahead to sortie. Among their number were more than 100 destroyers and frigates, each armed to the teeth with torpedoes, and ship-to-ship and ship-to-air missiles. These assets were the essence of the "area denial" strategy that the PLA had refined for several decades. Additionally, multiple warhead missile batteries had been quietly placed on islands near the mainland coast—including the manmade islands taken earlier from Vietnam and the Philippines. These "stationary aircraft carriers" were now fully operational air and naval bases, and could control the surrounding battle space for hundreds of miles. Every component of the larger plan was woven together—every plane, satellite, ship, submarine, and person was part of an overwhelming force that no nation could resist. General Bao and Professor Dang had created overlapping fields of fire that would dominate the western Pacific.

Last, but not least, the PLAN also had its own aircraft carriers: The older *Liaoning* and the newly launched *Shandong* were currently steaming with their escorts toward Guam. Their J-15s, plus their significant component of drones, would neutralize enemy aircraft, submarines, and ships at America's big western Pacific naval base. Follow-on landings would secure the island at a later date—after the mainland Asia component was complete. At their leisure, PLAN would turn Guam into its own first-class facility, and would install the PLAAF's newest generation of long-range bombers. These squadrons would control the sea lanes for great distances around their new home. This strategic outpost—and others, which would also be gobbled up later—would do for China what they'd always done for the Americans: Control their interests east of Hawaii.

On Taiwan

General Wing had deployed a bevy of operatives on the island, and they were tasked with destroying and disrupting the electrical and fuel-related infrastructure grids. However, it was always tricky to find the right destructive balance in any invasion: Destroy too little and the enemy could use those assets to resist and prolong the battle—destroy too much and the victor had to bring in its own temporary generators and refueling stations, and then rebuild those expensive assets itself.

The agents watching the harbors reported that eight foreign navy ships were currently making diplomatic port calls. Of these eight, six American naval vessels were joined by two from Japan and Australia, respectively. They were divided between each of Taiwan's three main harbors: One U.S. Aegis cruiser, one Arleigh Burke destroyer, plus an equally powerful Japanese Defense Force Asahi-class destroyer were visiting Kaohsiung Harbor near the southern tip of the island; two American Arleigh Burke destroyers were visiting Keelung Harbor in the north; and, in Taichung Harbor on the central west coast, two Arleigh Burke destroyers had been joined by an Australian guided missile destroyer. All eight ships had just completed a seven-day joint exercise with the ROC navy to test their inter-service communication and ASW (anti-submarine warfare) skills, and all four navies were reasonably satisfied with the results. However, all equally agreed that many future exercises were vital in case they had to defend against a future PLAN attack. MSS agents were watching all eight ships around the clock, and noted that at least half of every crew was ashore and enjoying the local culture—meaning they were doing what sailors always did in foreign ports. In fact, a few of the "ladies" in the brothels were really deep cover MSS agents themselves—trained at Wing's Sparrow School outside Beijing. The bottom line for the Chinese military was to quickly put this foreign flotilla out of action; they posed a threat to the cross-channel invasion and would be removed from the chess board within the first few minutes of the battle.

The main focus of the Taiwan operation was to destroy the rebellious island's principal dual threats: The first was their 130,000-soldier ground force, and the second was their 250 (plus) air force planes. To do that, the PLA had prepared the largest rocket attack in history. The PLA's nearby surface ships were packed with ship-to-air missiles, too, and they would concentrate on rebel planes that managed to take off. PLAAF fighters would take care of the ROC combat air patrols that were aloft at the time of the attack. It was anticipated that those components of the relatively small ROC navy that were already at sea would be sunk quickly, too.

Aboard *Dragon's Claw*, North and East of the Hawaiian Islands December 5th, 17:00 Hours

Admiral Sun headed down a central ladder, having deciding on the spur of the moment to spring a simulation on the CIC—the Combat Information Center situated in the heart of the superstructure four decks below. There was no such thing in his mind as too much realistic training, and he was confident that such drills sharpened his already razor-sharp sailors just a tic more. It was also an excuse to see his only son, an 18-year-old seaman who'd wanted to serve in the ranks for a year before entering the PLAN's Dalian Naval Academy, as his dad had a generation before. Sun's wife had initially been dead-set against their only child embarking on a combat cruise (the importance of which Sun felt duty-bound to tell her in strictest confidence) but in the end she'd relented. She decided that she didn't want decades of resentment from her "only baby," which would be the natural result of her throwing a fit and insisting that he stay behind, thus missing China's "Great War of Pacific Conquest." Sun figured she was probably home crying now—she'd barely stopped for the last two days before they sailed. And, though he wished it otherwise, hers was the burden that all navy mothers had borne since ships set sail in ancient times.

The admiral stepped off the ladder and the marine guards automatically opened the door so he could step into the CIC. There were no bulkhead thresholds here; the engineers had not designed them into these internal rooms. The designers felt that the cocoon of armor plating surrounding the superstructure was sufficient to stop small arms fire but, beyond that, the ship was not designed to fight at sea or to last long once docked. The Plan called for every mother ship to be mostly vacated within a day of disgorging its assault force.

Trying not to appear the concerned dad, Sun nevertheless immediately spotted his son Tan bent over his threat scope and looking intently for enemy planes. The boy couldn't have been happier—nor his father prouder. Sun had established strict standing orders not to call the CIC to attention when he or any of the senior officers entered, so he just caught the eye of the navy commander who had the watch. His look was correctly interpreted as "run a simulation" and immediately the order was barked and the whole center spun into a fresh scenario.

Inside the Cavern, 20:30 Hours

With crews eagerly awaiting their sailing orders, *Dragon's Roar* and *Dragon's Fear* were towed forward; their sisters *Dragon's Cloud* and *Dragon's Shield* had put to sea a few hours earlier, and reports back were all good. General Bao and Professor Dang had originally planned for *Roar* to catch the USS *Reagan* in port, plus the USS *America* (LHA-6), the escort ships of Carrier

Strike Group Five, Destroyer Squadron Fifteen—and the aircraft of Carrier Air Wing Five on the ground at Naval Air Facility Atsugi/Marine Corps Air Station Iwakuni. But, in the intervening months, schedules changed, and the American task force was preparing to sail with the JS *Izumo* (DDH-183), and link up with the USS *Nimitz* for regional maneuvers. That said, it might be the best of all outcomes: If they caught the two big-deck and two small-deck carriers at sea, sinking them in deep water, they'd be gone forever. The carriers were the Allies' principal capital ships in Asia, and General Bao believed it would be ***the*** coup of the first day's regional fighting if they were able to remove them and their air wings from the fight. He'd never accepted that poppy-cock that the *Izumo*, Japan's new "helicopter destroyer," was a destroyer. As everyone in the world could see from photos of Japan's four similar capital ships, she and her sisters were aircraft carriers.

Izumo and her sister ships did indeed carry helicopters but, more important, she and the JS *Kaga* could carry a squadron of the world's newest and best fighters—the Lockheed Martin F-35B Lightning II. Several of these advanced all-weather multi-role V/STOL (vertical and short take-off and landing) aircraft could be assigned to what was Japan's pride and joy of their rapidly modernizing navy. Two "helicopter carriers" of the preceding class (the JS *Hyuga* and JS *Ise*) needed their decks upgraded to handle the F-35s, but it was a fairly straightforward job and already in the next year's defense budget. When fully complimented with their new squadrons, these four ships alone would have more firepower than the combined might of all of Imperial Japan's carriers in World War II. Sun knew that sinking all four would provide a tremendous psychological blow to both the Japanese and their American allies—not to mention the practical loss of a significant portion of their retaliation capabilities. He was pleased that the planners also wanted to get as many of the Japanese submarines as they could but, for the Japanese portion of Operation Unity, they were icing on the cake.

Lieutenant General Bao and Professor Dang came to the cavern occasionally just to enjoy their creations. This evening was such an occasion and they wanted to see the next pair off. The Dragon Fleet they'd envisioned was only 14 ships, but between them they would create more havoc, and begin the expansion of China's control over more of the earth's land and ocean mass, than any power had since the height of the British Empire. And, when this first phase was completed, China would be the undisputed superpower of the world—with Russia and the U.S. relegated to argue about their respective second-tier status. Great Britain, Japan, Germany, India, and France would compete for the third-tier status. And, while most of these had stockpiles of nuclear bombs, they could not employ them without inviting retaliation in kind. It was "mutually assured destruction" all over, but this time China was on top—the Cold War in reverse. Professor Dang, the little genius, had indeed come up with the perfect plan.

Across the western and central Pacific Ocean, the Dragons relentlessly sailed on, their wakes churning smoothly as they closed in on still-unsuspecting prey. At the end of the first ten days at sea, the "great deception" was being validated by the minute.

Chapter 25

December 6th, 00:15 Hours

Dragon's Fear, the 14th and final ship of the assault fleet, received her orders and slipped quietly out of the cavern, never to return. Her destination was the Port of Busan, South Korea, and after she passed through the giant doors, they closed for the last time—at least until one of the most significant human building projects in history could be used for a new and future purpose. The mammoth operation had progressed at a high tempo for years, but had been phasing out as the ships put to sea. Now the cavern was hollow and lifeless with only a skeleton maintenance crew remaining to prepare for whatever was next. During the preceding few weeks as their respective tasks were completed, the workers had been assembled in groups, and transferred in buses out through the tunnels to outlying military bases. There they were being held incommunicado until the first phases of the attack were completed. This isolation strategy was jointly decided by Marshall Tai and Minister Ti—both of whom believed that a month of housing and feeding a few thousand workers and PAP cadres was little enough price to pay for operational security. Every person was carefully checked by Ti's PAP and Tai's PLA military police as they boarded—searched for any means of communication or recording. Then, upon arrival at their holding areas, they were subjected to a second check before being assigned temporary quarters. Most were housed in hangars that were packed with tents and portable field kitchens, and in and around each closed building were dozens of armed security guards with loaded weapons and orders to use them as necessary. However, there had been no incidents of rebellion because the food was generous and the bathroom and portable shower facilities were adequate; everyone just went with the flow as they were instructed—the usual way of doing things in the People's Republic.

Port of Manila, Republic of the Philippines
The South Harbor International Container Terminal (same time)

Port Police Detective Inspector Raul Menendes wiped the sweat off his forehead with a faded red handkerchief—a gift from his darling young daughter three Christmases ago. He had almost worn the fragile cotton cloth bare because he used it so much, but he asked his sweet wife Maria to keep handwashing it because it helped cheer his spirit. He sure needed such pleasant thoughts on what was rapidly becoming a terrible night: The air was dense and humid—typical in tropical Asia—and pleasantly scented with the perfume from festoons of nearby flowers. However, their fragrance wasn't enough to stave off the awful stench that was sickening everyone near an open container, currently resting on the concrete among thousands of other identical steel boxes.

Raul had been frantically summoned to this spot, and he now stood alongside the stevedores witnessing a scene from hell: They'd been off-loading containers and smelled something putrid emanating from the 40-footer they'd just set on the main quay, and everyone's worst nightmare was confirmed when the supervisor broke the seal and discovered a group of dead stowaways. This unfortunately happened about once a year, and it was always so very sad—especially traumatic for the workers who, understandably, never got used to it.

Detective Menendes' duty was to coordinate with the metro police detectives and the coroner to get the investigation completed. After the police were done, the bodies could be removed to the morgue and normal operations could continue. It was a horrible mess, to say the least, and Raul mopped his head and replaced his cap once again. Thinking that this nightmare could not end soon enough, Raul knew from previous situations that he still had another two hours or more to wait until the forensic team finished processing the scene. Only then would the coroner and his assistants mercifully load the bodies into body bags, and transfer them into their refrigerated van for the trip downtown.

The coroner, Dr. Manny Preferia, was also fighting the urge to be physically ill, despite his years of exposure to every manner of human decay. He had processed several of these tragic stowaway attempts gone wrong, and they always sickened him in every way that one human being could feel bad for another. However, his well-developed forensic instincts were immediately on guard when he and his young assistant gently slid out the first body. They spotted several weapons in a rack mounted near the main door, and a large radio mounted against the wall. They carefully photographed everything, then slid out the three remaining bodies. "Hey, Inspector," Manny hailed the detective hovering by his car. He'd enjoyed a long-term working relationship with the thorough policeman, and they'd established good professional chemistry. "There are several weapons in here, plus a big radio and several large boxes with military-looking stenciling on them."

"What?" Raul was jolted into action by the coroner's statement. Temporarily forgetting the gruesomeness of scene, Raul hurried to the edge of the container's gaping doorway to get a better look. Sure enough, as he moved his flashlight beam around the dark interior, he saw that the dead men had the whole container set up like the inside of a cargo airplane. Affixed to one side were several fold-down red jump seats with sleeping bags laid horizontally, and a pallet of food stores rested on the floor. A mostly full bag of rice had fallen over on top of a small table. Also visible was a camping-style gas cooking stove. And, except for the radio set—with its wires leading up to the ceiling at the end of the row of seat/beds, the remaining space was crammed, waist-high, with varying-sized wooden boxes stenciled with Chinese markings. He didn't know what to think. *Maybe terrorists?*

He slipped on rubber shoe coverings so as to not contaminate the crime scene, stepped into the space, and used his heavy-duty Ka-Bar knife to pop open the nearest box. It contained neatly packed kilo-sized blocks of C-4 explosives nestled in Styrofoam peanuts—clearly confirming that these men were some type of cell. They were dressed in normal casual civilian clothes, but who they were was a mystery his chain of command would turn over to the federal government. His mind flashed to the continuing beef the Philippines was having with its southern island's Muslim separatists—a never-ending confrontation that blew hot and cold from year to year. But these men didn't fit that description at all: They looked Chinese to him, and were more likely sent here as part of the on-going dispute with China over the oil-rich islands to the west. This was clearly a big deal that had to be handled right. He looked over at Manny, who was crouching over a body, and asked, "What do you think killed these men, Doctor?"

Initially, Manny had been as dumbfounded by what he saw as had the policeman. Clearly this was not a tragic family or group of workers looking for better lives in the Philippines—people had stowed away, and then run out of water or suffocated, which unfortunately happened almost every year. These were armed terrorists or criminals of some ilk with abundant supplies. But, after spotting the propane stove, their cause of death became instantly clear: "Inspector, these men accidentally killed themselves with carbon monoxide poisoning. The cook had turned off the flame, but didn't fully turn off the flow of gas—it spewed the lethal propane that couldn't escape the confines of the box. They had probably finished their first cooked meal and gradually got light-headed—perhaps even nauseous, which they just chalked up to the roll of the ship—then slipped away into unconsciousness and died. If they'd just stripped away the rubber lining on the edges of both doors—a universal precaution that maintained the container's watertight integrity—they'd have survived. But those seals, though not airtight, prevented sufficient dissipation of the gas. The valve allowed the tank to empty and that was that. But after a week at sea, we couldn't smell the gas over the stench of the bodies. They lay where they fell for the rest of the voyage."

"Gross!"

"Indeed. Now a question for you: What were these men planning?"

"Way above my pay grade, Doc…I'll call the federal police and turn things over to them."

"I figured as much. I'll finish with the bodies and the rest is up to you. I'll send over a copy of my autopsy report in a couple of days but, unless I discover something unexpected, this one is pretty clear."

"Thanks for everything, Doc…as usual." Raul received a polite grunt from the coroner before turning away—grateful for an excuse to put some distance between himself and the horrible odor. He walked back to his squad car thinking about the implications of what he'd seen. He radioed dispatch and asked them to call the federal police and, while he waited for the patch-through, he leaned against his sedan to keep his balance as he yanked off the stinky shoe coverings. He watched sympathetically as the medical team bagged the bodies and loaded them into the coolness of the coroner's special ambulance. This incident was really going to kick over a hornet's nest.

Several hundred yards away, the activity around the open container was being carefully observed by two men in an upstairs office. They'd rented the space for their "shipping company" and had been monitoring the flow of containers, waiting for one in particular that contained a precious cargo, now lost. As they peered through two nearly opaque windows—stained from years of dust, humidity, and neglect—the team leader asked rhetorically, "All dead?"

"No question," replied the second man, also straining to view the scene through his binoculars. "They must have died in transit for some reason. And now all our equipment and supplies are in enemy hands."

"I'll get a message off to Beijing. The minister is not going to like it."

"Not our fault. Maybe we can bribe a local army commander into letting us have some C-4?"

"Very dangerous—and not enough time! Our back-up plan will have to do. A few gallons of gasoline are easy to buy, won't attract any attention, and will be sufficient to start a few fires. It's the best diversion I can think of for now..." He heard his subordinate's assent and that was that. They watched for another 90 minutes as a new team of investigators showed up—some in police uniforms and some in military camo, and everyone proceeded to mill in and around the container before packing everything onto two large military trucks. After that, the two agents phoned the other Chaos Teams who were expecting the supplies, and told them to go to Plan B. Then they gathered up their few belongings and headed out to purchase a few fifty-gallon cans. Nine teams were on station, and would shortly begin their campaign of terror.

Aboard the USS *North Carolina* (SSN 777)
400 miles west of Joint Base Hickam-Pearl Harbor
December 6th, 09:00 Hours (Honolulu time)

Working through a series of targeting drills 350 feet below the placid surface, the USS *North Carolina* (SSN-777) had been tooling along at five knots—maintaining just enough momentum to keep her nicely under way. At this speed, she was quiet as a ghost, even quieter than some of the Israeli

German-manufactured diesel subs she'd war-gamed against in the Med the previous year. After that tour, she'd been transferred to Pearl, and her crew thought they were among the luckiest sailors in the navy. However, at this mid-morning hour, her captain, Commander (Promotable) James (The Shark) Robinson (so named because his striking blond hair and facial features gave him an uncanny resemblance to the famous Australian golfer) was not satisfied with the morning's drills. The previous day's work had been excellent, consisting of long-range firing solutions using the boat's new computer system installed just six months before. The upgraded technology allowed them to find and track enemy subs (even the electric boats that were maddeningly quiet) from great distances. But today the crew had seemed a bit stiff. *Maybe I overdid it yesterday?* the Shark wondered. *Or more likely, they just care more about seeing their families?* He decided it was the latter—given his own excitement about reuniting with his wife Lois. She'd be in "welcome-home mood" and she never let him forget what it was like being a sailor in love. *If the current drill runs smoothly, I'll call it a day.*

The *North Carolina* was in-bound to Pearl Harbor after her 75-day WestPac cruise and, in less than 24 hours, she and her tired crew would be home. They'd arrive in the bright sunshine of a new day, and with spirts even brighter. Both the crew and their families would be in a festive mood but, before the reunion, they had the honor of being the "Pass in Review Boat" for the Pearl Harbor Day Memorial Ceremony. The Vice President of the United States would be there to greet them, and they would be a proud crew, standing tall, and rightfully showered with praise. It was a special honor to have been chosen to participate in the annual event, and they'd do their part to honor the crew of the USS *Arizona*. She was still on duty with nearly 1,200 sailors resting inside her sunken hull.

At the moment, Captain Robinson reasoned that the crew was probably distracted and he couldn't blame them: He was longing for a few months ashore, the Vice President notwithstanding. He looked at his XO, the boat's executive officer, Lieutenant Commander Lawrence Newman, who was holding his stopwatch, and at Chief Petty Officer Ollie Yonis who was monitoring the recessed flat screen of the ship's AN/BYG-1 Combat Control System, waiting for the data to stream in.

"Probable hit, Captain!" CPO Yonis announced with gusto, privately hoping they could secure from simulated general quarters. He and the rest of the crew were ready to kick back and take the old girl back to Pearl. He was desperately looking forward to a long visit with his beautiful wife Deana. Three months in beautiful Hawaii—man, could he think of some great things they could do in paradise!

"Click" went the stopwatch. "Ninety-two seconds, Captain!" confirmed the XO.

"That's more like it! Okay, everyone, secure from drill…" His orders were repeated and relayed per naval tradition, and a quiet cheer rose up as the 134 officers and enlisted personnel (including six female sailors with a PO2 as their senior "in-gender" female rating/chaperone) relaxed, and quickly secured from general quarters. Mentally, all hands didn't take long to shift their thoughts toward the fun they'd have the following day.

However, PO3 Xavier 'Zapper' DeMarco, currently on sonar watch, had been keeping an eye on his three computer screens: There was a rumble out on the horizon picked up by the boat's amazing 360-degree passive arrays—indicating a distant ship. Components of the sensitive system were mounted on all the boat's major quadrants including the bow, the sail, the keel, and the diving planes—plus they had the stern-mounted wide aperture array. This was a major improvement from the bad old days of the Cold War when his dad had to deal with "dead zones" in the baffles (the unseen and usually turbulent waters immediately behind the subs of that era). The *North Carolina* was a Block I *Virginia-c*lass Attack Submarine and, like her sisters, she had both a TB-16 and a Lockheed-Martin TB-29A thin-lined towed array that they could stream out of her stern. Both connected with their onboard AN/BQQ-10 (V4) sonar processing system that was the best in the world. The boat was also fitted with an I-band Sperry Marine AN/BPS-16 (V4) navigation radar. There wasn't much in the surrounding 1,000 miles that the *North Carolina* didn't know about—or couldn't shoot at if necessary. "Hey, COB," DeMarco called over to the Chief of the Boat, MCPO Dennis Cranston, who he could see in the attack center next door, "that big merchie we've been ordered to track is coming over the horizon."

"Lemme look, Zap," Cranston responded, quickly crossing the two steps from the slightly raised command bridge, and stepping down into the smaller sonar room that was filled with sensors and flat-screens. "You're right as rain," the master chief confirmed, as he watched the electronic pattern on the "waterfall" of a computer screen. It was a surface target that Zap had designated "C-100," and it was one of 29 such targets being simultaneously tracked on his master screen—typical of the out-bound/in-bound commercial and military traffic that was business as usual for the busy container and naval ports on Oahu. There was also some lesser traffic around the other islands—fishing and tourist boats mostly.

The container ship they were discussing just happened to be the largest, and they'd been keeping special track of it for more than two days since receiving orders from "on high." Once it came within the 1,000 nautical-mile circle that was their area of responsibility (aided by the look-down feeds from satellites hovering above), they could even hear when the chopped-up garbage was flushed out of the hull's ports. MCPO Cranston picked up a headset with attached mic and spoke to the captain: "Skipper, that ChiCom merchie just popped over the horizon. Distance about 20,000 yards. She's maintaining her announced course and speed, and should reach Hono about 0800 tomorrow." Cranston heard the affirmative reply; if the boat came to periscope depth when that big gal was overhead, it would ruin their whole day.

Unknown to the excited sailors in the attack center, there was another little drama unfolding in the female enlisted quarters: Seaman Melissa Janeway was thankful beyond words that she only had to get through one more day without the tightness in her trousers being noticed by any of her bunkmates, including PO2 Barbara Rawlins—especially Rawlins! Melissa and Seaman Rob Tatter had hooked up the night before they sailed, violating a number of rules and regulations: Even though they were the same rank, they were under the usual Covid restrictions, were not supposed to be romantically involved with a shipmate, and were heading out to sea for a long cruise. But nature had taken its course, and they were expecting. At least she was. She hadn't told Rob about the future blessed event, and she was scared out of her wits that he wouldn't want to marry her. She desperately wanted her baby, but she might end up being an unwed mother, drummed out of the Navy, and be under her disappointed parents' thumbs forever! *Woe unto her when her dad found out!* But, on the other hand, if miracle of miracles happened, and Rob did want to get married, they would have the support of everyone, and a great and long career in the Navy if Rob wanted to stay in. At least they had played it cool (and followed orders) during the cruise. *Just one more day and I'll tell him.*

The home of Dr. Reginald Trammell, Washington, DC
Saturday, December 6th, 22:35 Hours

Hunched over the cluttered desk in his man-cave that doubled as a weekend office, Reg checked the latest declassified satellite feeds, and wondered at the symmetry of the PRC's Dragon Fleet. He'd noted that there was only one laggard: *Dragon's Wing* bound for Ho Chi Minh Port in southern Vietnam had been forced to reroute to Haiphong Port in the north. She had experienced unknown problems off the southern Chinese coast, and she'd been forced to lay to and drift for 36 hours. A repair ship and a half-dozen armed patrol boats from the mainland had quickly steamed out to render assistance, and they'd formed a 10-mile cordon of security around her. Those efforts apparently did the trick, and the big cargo ship was underway again without any help from concerned strangers. The ship was now heading for the narrow passage between Hainan Island and the southern coast of mainland China and, after the change, the Chinese government had announced the diversion to the big commercial port near the mouth of the Hong River Delta.

Reg had to hand it to them: Thirteen of the fourteen ships were still on course to arrive nearly simultaneously at their original ports of call—a vast stretch of the Earth from Japan to Australia (north to south) and from the west coast of the United States to Thailand (west to east). He knew it was a mass shakedown cruise for the fleet—making the feat even more impressive. One was underperforming, but other than the continuing newsworthiness of the larger event(s) themselves, Reg might have been tempted to ignore the whole thing and find a good movie on TV. But Tim's initial anguish (that had turned to sad acceptance of his fiancée's fate) kept him thinking about the context of the Chinese situation he'd uncovered years before. When he combined his suspicions surrounding the intent of these ships, with his own knowledge of the PRC's steadily worsening economic crisis, he just couldn't shake his foreboding. *Am I being irrational?* he wondered silently.

He felt for his friend Tim—and though they had to speak obliquely—Reg was pleased that he could do his friend some good. It was obvious that Jen was in a real jam—meaning she was probably captured or dead—and her fiancé was understandably sick at heart. Reg really admired Tim's stiff upper lip, though, and had to admit the man was trying to walk the talk of his professed faith. He didn't know how he'd react if something of that magnitude befell his own wife or kids. With the excuse of being polite, he had talked Tipi into attending church with Tim in the morning. Reg needed a good excuse to revisit the whole "belief in God" thing anyway. Tipi's response had been tepid at best, but she reluctantly agreed the kids needed some religious training. Tomorrow they'd go together and see how it went.

Reg adjusted his reading glasses as he focused on the tracks of each ship; they were not hard to spot on the open ocean because they were big and he knew where to look. They were all closing in on their destinations at the same time—meaning late-morning West Coast time—except for the straggler. *Too bad for that poor sod of a captain: He must be in a real fix after the authority's long PR campaign.* Tim had mentioned that the fleet's captains were coordinating their arrivals over open channels, and were adjusting speeds so precisely that they'd arrive within a few minutes of each other. It seemed like overkill to both China watchers, but the timing was not suspicious in itself when the PRC was showing off. Those with the farthest to sail—meaning those heading for Australia and the American mainland—were nearing their destinations' various territorial waters at the same time as those approaching the regional ports in Indonesia, Malaysia, Thailand, the Philippines, Vietnam, Taiwan, Japan, and Korea.

Mitigating Reg's worries was the very fact that the PRC shipping folks had made coordinated advance requests for customs clearance and, as part of that requirement, they had included detailed cargo manifests on open channels per normal maritime practice. It seemed every "T" was crossed, and every "I" was dotted. It was only the other (*possibly* relevant facts) that kept Reg wondering if something sinister was afoot. And, if that was true, what could they be up to? *They weren't going to invade their Pacific Rim neighbors with container loads of troops!* They might have nuclear weapons aboard to blackmail the countries involved, but to what end? Every radical or irrational idea he came up with seemed more ludicrous as the ships approached. At least Tim was coming over for Sunday dinner after church, and they'd mutually vent during the football game.

CIA headquarters, Langley, Virginia (same time)

Tim was finally getting his head and heart back to where they should be. Focusing on his job was important for the nation's welfare, and work helped him heal. His supervisor had cut him considerable slack during his days of despair, and he'd been profoundly grateful, but now it was time to "suck it up and drive on," as his military friends said. He was at the end of his second week with no word from Jen—way past the point of hoping she was just lying low in some cubbyhole in the cavern. Now the best-case scenario was that she had been captured and was being held incommunicado. But, in moments of honesty, he knew Jen better than any other human being. She would have fought and died if faced with capture—protecting what she knew about Ken and others in their network. She would value their lives over her own. The only other realistic possibility was the one he didn't want to think about—meaning unavoidable capture—and he'd prayed against that end until his spirit was numb. However, God didn't exist to support Tim's agenda; it was each believer's responsibility to obey God's will. The military had a similar requirement called "command intent": Meaning it was the subordinate's proactive responsibility to know the chain of command's guidance (orders) and to carry them out to the best of one's ability.

This was his first serious test of faith and he felt he'd failed miserably. Yet he also knew that God was patient, and He had a plan for this season of testing. Tim had resolved to redouble his efforts to seek God's strength and get his act together—for the sake of his witness as well as for his own sanity. He'd faced one of the great truths of the Christian faith and come through it on the mend. Even Christ in the Garden of Gethsemane had prayed, "Thy will be done" when he asked God the Father to deliver him from the coming trial of the cross. Tim hoped to get to that point soon.

Like his friend Reg, Tim had kept a close eye on the twice-daily satellite passes over the various ships; the final one had left the cavern and was right on schedule. That Dragon was sailing for South Korea, and would dock just after midnight in Busan, meaning early afternoon in Washington, DC. The rest of the fleet, minus the ship heading for Vietnam, was still maintaining its original schedule. He glanced briefly at the latest shots of the beach in front of the cavern, and noted that the whole area, recently brimming with activity, was deathly quiet. Even the usually busy Liaodong Peninsula—home of the Dalian Shipyard and City—seemed quieter than usual.

Tim momentarily thought about tomorrow: He'd finally get to host Reg and Tipi and their kids in the morning service, and it would be a blessing to spend time with the one person with whom he could bare his soul. His pastor had been great, but Tim was constrained with what he could share with a civilian pastor with no TS clearance. The Agency's shrink had helped a little, too, but Reg's friendship had helped the most. He turned back to the paperwork on his desk. He'd focus for the rest of his shift, then head home for a long sleep before a peaceful Sunday off.

Chapter 26

United States Fleet Activities, Yokosuka, Japan
Sunday, December 7th, 12:40 Hours

The captain and crew of the USS *Ronald Reagan* (CVN 76), America's only permanently forward-deployed aircraft carrier, had waved their good-byes hours earlier, but families, girlfriends, local dignitaries, and tourists on the dock were still waving small flags and generally hanging around. The *Reagan* herself was already an hour into the long process of departing from her home port, and the immensely powerful fleet tugs had her nicely down the Uraga Channel. Most of her 6,000 sailors were aboard—with just the pilots joining them later when the air wing flew out from Marine Corps Air Station, Iwakuni, and Naval Air Station, Atsugi, respectively. The great ship was now several miles away from the adoring crowd, and her captain had ordered her to proceed under her own power. After that, it was a straight 10-mile shot (south/southeast) to exit Tokyo Bay and enter the Sagami Gulf. The *Reagan's* mission was to proclaim and enforce America's sovereign right to sail in international waters, and her planned two-month cruise would, for the second time in the last six months, reunite them with the USS *Nimitz*. The USS *America* (LHA-6), and Japan's JS *Izumo,* and their escorts, had left an hour earlier, and the combined task force had been designated "Eagle" to remind everyone that, in the western Pacific, the Allied navies were a global force for good.

The "*Gipper*," as she was affectionately known to her crew, never sailed alone: She was always the principal ship around which Carrier Strike Group 5 formed. And, as soon as she was in open water, her air complement, the 90 aircraft of Carrier Air Wing 5 (CVW-5) would arrive and begin normal at-sea operations. But, even during her departure, her two Aegis cruisers, the USS *Shiloh* (CG-67) and the USS *Antietam* (CG-54), preceded her down the narrow Tokyo Bay, and all SPY radars and other systems were up and searching the horizons for threats. Ahead of the cruisers, and already fanned out in the Sagami Gulf looking for enemy submarines, were six of the seven ASW Arleigh-Burke destroyers of Destroyer Squadron Fifteen (DESRON-15) that, along with the *Izumo's* screening vessels, would form a circle of anti-air and anti-submarine protection around the bigger ships. Accompanying the *Reagan* this cruise was the USS *Curtis Wilbur* (DDG 54); the USS *John S McCain* (DDG 56); USS *Fitzgerald* (DDG 62); the USS *Stethem* (DDG 63); the USS *Lassen* (DDG 82); and the USS *McCampbell* (DDG 85). The USS *Mustin* (DDG 89) would join them in a few days after some minor dockside repairs. Also meeting Task Force Eagle in the gulf were three attack submarines, always unseen but greatly appreciated as they, too, would search for possible threats far beneath the surface. In fact, under each deployed U.S. aircraft carrier, there was always a submarine gliding along beneath the carrier's keel. The three American boats would listen for other submarines up to hundreds of miles away.

The *Gipper's* power plants were operating smoothly and her propellers steadily turning, so her captain ordered her to increase speed. In the engineering spaces, she had two Westinghouse A4G nuclear power plants that provided steam for the turbines that turned her four drive shafts—and each of these was attached to massive 33-ton, 5-bladed propellers. The result was enough self-generated thrust to outrace almost every big ship in the world. Soon she was making 10 knots and closed the distance to her two protective cruisers. On the open ocean in calm seas, all the modern U.S. carriers could push through the waves at more than 30 knots, and 40 knots was possible at flank speed. But the real top speeds were always kept secret for obvious reasons.

Yokosuka docks

Standing among the thinning crowd that had wished the immense warship bon voyage were two of Minister Wing's MSS spies who, along with several others hidden around Tokyo Bay, were on station to welcome *Dragon's Roar*—currently making her way up Japan's east coast. The *Reagan's* departure had initially caused some consternation in PLA headquarters, but Tai's battle staff had made the necessary adjustments so they could deal with the task force at sea. The two women hurried away from the public viewing area as soon as they thought they could blend in with other departing well-wishers. They had a lot to do.

Aboard *Dragon's Roar*, off the East Coast of Japan

Major General Lo Quen had received the first great challenge of his mission when confirmation of the *Reagan's* imminent sailing reached him in the finishing grotto the day before he put to sea. He'd been juggling training for both options—either the long-planned, dock-side attack, or a coordinated, at-sea submarine attack. He'd received his instructions from Marshal Tai before he sailed, but it remained his tactical decision to decide how to sink the vitally important carriers while also landing his assault force and capturing the necessary ground targets around Yokosuka Harbor. Lo had successfully argued for redeployment of half of the submarines stationed north and east of Taiwan, and they had detached and sailed north to form an eastern bracket that anticipated the course of the south-sailing U.S./Japanese ships. *Roar's* four mini-subs would form a line closer to the coast, and the resulting corridor would be a death trap for the oncoming Allies. The two lines of subs would send dozens of torpedoes into both flanks and hopefully cut the task force down to size. This would also prevent a link-up with the USS *Nimitz* approaching from the west. The remaining PLAN subs would shift south to prepare a new ambush in concert with the subs remaining close to Taiwan. Ballistic missiles fired from the mainland would finish the *Nimitz* and her screening vessels; General Lo thought they had a good chance of sinking every last one.

Overlooking Kaohsiung Harbor, southern Taiwan
Saturday afternoon, December 7th, 13:45 Hours

Sergeant (E5) Jing Po of the Republic of China Army barked at his men and was pleased when they jumped to ramrod attention. He went down the line, taking note that everyone's equipment was firmly strapped in the correct place, every uniform clean and crisp, and that each weapon was shiny clean inside and out. It was time for him to lead 3rd Squad, First Platoon, Company A, Horse Battalion, on its 10-minute jog from its barracks to the cleverly concealed bunker system hidden among the hills above the port. His 10 men, along with the rest of First Platoon, would occupy the same defensive positions that their fathers and grandfathers had in previous generations. They would relieve the current platoon just completing its twelve-hour shift—all of them doing their part since 1949 to maintain continuing vigil against a mainland invasion. Horse Battalion's positions were just above Taiwan's largest container port located near the southern tip of their island nation, and Jing's squad was assigned to a small stretch of the defensive infrastructure. The network was comprised of fortified trenches, tunnels, and firing positions built into the crest of the hill. Their job was to defend the area against anyone foolish enough to try to move inland after attacking the port.

Jing's squad was always on time, confirming his assertion that 3rd Squad was the sharpest in the platoon. Still single at age 31, Jing had made his 10 men his life, his pride and joy: He'd taken a batch of spoiled mamas' boys and transformed them into tough, straight-shooting soldiers. Like everyone in the Republic of China's military, these soldiers didn't know if war would come in their lifetime but, if it did (and it would only come from the PRC), they would make the mainland Chinese attackers pay dearly for every foot they stole. They and their ancestors had listened to CCP threats for seven decades—promises to cross the narrow straits and unify "the rebellious province" by force. If that happened, Po's squad would do its utmost to protect its assigned sector overlooking the 12th largest container terminal in the world. It and the other port up in Kee Lung, plus some smaller ones along the west coast, were Taiwan's lifeline to the outside world. His men were confident that they would do their jobs well, and would hold their sector longer than most. But Jing and his soldiers also knew with obvious certainty that they would all die: There might be some delayed help from the United States or Japan, but it would arrive long after the mainland forces overran as much of his homeland as they wanted. The PLA was simply too massive to stop—if it wanted to pay the awful price in men, treasure, and the political wrath of the world.

3rd Squad was in good physical condition, and arrived with a minimum of huffing and puffing, and generally ignored the line of fellow soldiers who'd already vacated the trench and small bunker, anxiously waiting to be relieved. The early winter afternoon sunshine offered little warmth as Jing's men jumped down into their well-established cement and heavily sandbagged position. They then turned and gave their "squad shout"—the ritualistic salute to the squad they'd just relieved. The departing squad looked beat as always, and they turned without much spirit and began jogging after their own NCO. The new arrivals struggled out of their gear and placed their assault rifles and one light machine gun gently across the sandbags—then gave their special extended squad cheer—their daily reminder to the other squads who would win the monthly "Best Squad" award. This prompted the usual half-hearted rebuttals from the other squads—plus some good-natured soldier banter. It was the life of every soldier in history, and produced bonds that encouraged small-unit cohesion—a key to victory in every war.

Most of the men scanned the docks and cranes in the distance, marveling as always at the size of the cargo ships that unloaded or picked up the goods that comprised world trade. The 10 conscripts didn't much care about where those ships would head next—their whole world centered around Jing, the tough little sergeant who ruled their lives (at least for another 16 days and a few hours) when, at merciful long last, they'd complete their required two months of annual national duty, and could go home to their mothers' cooking! But, until that happy day, they would continue to look sharp for "the little dictator" who hovered nearby.

Five minutes after arriving, as he usually did, Sergeant Jing moved out of earshot of his squad and wandered over to visit his long-time friend who commanded 4th Squad. The youngsters behind him immediately relaxed and began gossiping and telling lies about their girlfriends—the usual time-killing strategy they employed between training exercises. They would clean weapons and keep a sharp eye out for trouble until their 12-hour shift ended. Then they'd be relieved by those "other" guys and jog back to their barracks for some hot chow and sleep—and then repeat the process again tomorrow.

Behind their position rose the hills and distant craggy mountains that formed the north/south spine of the island. Between that landmark and the sea was a fairly narrow western plain upon which most of the population lived, and a much narrower eastern plain that had a few communities dotted along the opposite coast. The quiet sun overhead helped them feel a bit cheerier, but it wouldn't last long this time of year: A cold and dark winter night would descend and they'd relish their return to warm barracks before three o'clock in the morning. Once a month they drew weekend duty, and this was the one; they usually got weekends off to sneak home if they lived close by, but most of them lived in Taipei in the north. That being the case, they'd wander around a nearby town as a group, looking for local girls to chat with. Local parents kept a constant vigil, too, so the guys usually struck out and just grabbed a couple of beers and relaxed.

This afternoon their sergeant took longer than usual returning, so they used the extra time to quietly speculate on what they'd do after completing their annual tours of duty. Interspersed among this serious discussion were complaints that nothing interesting ever happened during annual national service.

Ngoc Xuyen Peninsula south of Haiphong Port, Vietnam
Saturday afternoon, December 7th, 16:00 Hours

Dai Uy (Captain) Ly Truong Nguyen walked slowly past the soldiers standing just below him in reinforced cement fighting positions, not dissimilar to those manned by the Taiwanese soldiers 1,000 miles to the north. Half of Ly's men were just starting their own 12-hour shifts that would take them to 04:00 the following morning, when they, too, would be relieved by their compatriots. They differed from the ROC soldiers in that they lived there in adjacent low-lying concrete bunkers for two-week deployments, then rotated out with another company from their regiment. The regimental headquarters was a few kilometers inland, and that was where they spent six out of every eight weeks training and enjoying (or enduring) normal army life.

Ly's company was defending a costal position 10 meters above a beach that was part of a continual network of fortifications that encircled Vietnam. It was a defensive perimeter that wound along their common border with China, then south along the 1,000-mile coastline that wrapped around the Cau Mau Peninsula, and ran nearly due west until it touched the border with Cambodia. At that point, it turned north to run along Vietnam's common borders with Cambodia and Laos. Vietnam's standing military numbered just under 500,000 personnel, and they had five million reservists. It was a formidable but necessary force, because their neighbor to the north had nearly 1.5 billion people—plus a massive and growing military led by a belligerent government. And there was context to Vietnam's concerns about China: The larger neighbor had come south many times over the last 3,000 years—including the most recent incursion in 1979.

Captain Ly was the commander of 2nd Company, 5th Infantry Regiment, Vietnamese Ground Forces, and he was thoroughly enjoying his third week in command. His men looked well-trained for which, he admitted, he had his predecessor to thank, but he'd also spotted some tendencies that he knew he could improve upon by applying his own teaching methods and leadership style. Ly's infantry company consisted of 120 enlisted soldiers, 12 sergeants, 3 commissioned officers, and 2 cadets. It was a noble command and he'd dreamed about this responsibility for years. He was now 28, had a beautiful wife who was 26, two young children (a girl four and a boy two), and life was good.

Ly hadn't thought much about actual combat when he entered the national military academy after high school, but tensions between Vietnam and their colossal neighbor had been ratcheting up since then. And, every time he visited his father who was a retired army Dai Ta (full colonel), the older veteran reminded him that a "very big dragon" could come south at any time. His father knew of what he spoke: He had fought against the PLA's infantry in 1979 and had been wounded twice in 14 days. The Chinese army had come south in force through several of the passes along their common border, and the senior Ly and his men had fought like tigers to first stop, and then push the larger army back into its own territory. But the cost of that Chinese adventurism had been very high: In just two weeks of savage, close-quarters, old-fashioned combat, each side had lost an estimated 20,000 dead—a horrific number for so short a war. But Vietnam's army was bigger in those days and had shocked the dragon sufficiently to prevail and maintain national independence. But, nowadays, both generations of Lys were worried that the 1979 lesson had started to fade; in fact, a warning order had been issued to all commands the day before—a general alert that the PLA looked like it was coming south again.

Unfortunately, the four decades of peace had been deteriorating for some time: The Chinese navy and marines were problematically imposing their will on the oil-rich Spratly and Paracel Islands that both countries claimed, and

China had occupied many of the islands and invested significant resources transforming them into strategic harbors and airstrips. The PRC wanted the wealth buried in the entire region's continental shelves and seas—and they wanted not just Vietnam's riches, but also those of the Philippines, Brunei, Malaysia, Thailand, and Indonesia—all of which had abundant off-shore oil and natural gas deposits. The bottom line was that the PRC was using its military to steal several smaller nations' wealth.

However, that level of strategic thinking was far above Captain Ly's pay grade, so he compartmentalized such thoughts on this cool and overcast early winter afternoon, and continued his inspection. But, in spite of the Trung Quoc (China's) bellicosity, the young captain never lost his confidence. If they came south in the next few days like Hanoi worried, he liked Vietnam's chances—they'd make their 3,000-year adversary pay dearly in blood and treasure.

Aboard *Dragon's Wing*, northeast of Hainan Island (same time)

Now a day and a half behind schedule, General Ling and Captain Quan—after conferring extensively with Marshal Tai and his staff over their predicament—decided that, since Ho Chi Minh City was an impossible goal, the only reasonable and workable alternative was to change their destination to Haiphong Port. They could still weave the advance PR aspect into the change because they could use the downstream docking area where the water was deeper, and the larger mission could accommodate an assault from the northern location. The Vietnamese port authorities approved the requested change because they had an opening, and it made no difference to them. The Chinese agreed to pay all ground shipping costs, and some of the cargo was eventually destined for the north in any case. The government insisted on a local harbor pilot and inspection team before the ship could proceed into the channel, and Quan agreed. So, after completing enough repairs to get underway, a crippled *Dragon's Wing* headed for Haiphong.

Captain Quan set a leisurely course through the 12-mile wide Qiongzhou Strait between the northern coast of Hainan Island and the Xuwen Peninsula that jutted south from the southern mainland. They'd arrive at their new destination on time and with the mission reasonably intact—if their hasty repair job held up. To help lighten the load, General Ling agreed with Quan's request to release the four submarines before getting underway, and he ordered them to take up stations in the immediate vicinity and wait for enemy targets of opportunity. Quan pressurized the vacated spaces and the entire ship rose more than five centimeters. Every bit helped.

400 nautical miles off the central California coast
Saturday morning on the eastern side of the International Date Line
December 6th, 05:45 Hours

As *Dragon's Wing* was trying to salvage its mission, Admiral Sun was out on the starboard bridge wing of *Dragon's Claw*, watching the sky steadily lighten in the east—a beautiful reminder that this was his last morning of peace at sea. He knew he'd be a bundle of nerves the following day when he'd watch the golden orb rise above San Francisco's hills. Then, shortly after that, his ship would dock and America's long period of domestic peace and tranquility would come to a sudden and violent end. *Claw* had made excellent time crossing the incredibly spacious northern Pacific Ocean, and Sun was grateful that the other three vessels that comprised his immediate command were also on course/on time. He knew that all but one of the sister ships had maintained their strict to-the-minute schedule, too. Only *Dragon's Wing* bound for Vietnam had changed her destination—forced by an engine glitch to shut down and wallow dead in the water for a day and a half. But, with some timely help from the mainland, the onboard engineers had made repairs and gotten her going again. He'd admitted that it would have been a near-miracle if all 14 vessels had crossed such vast ocean spaces without sea trials and remained problem-free.

Sun's ships had experienced no such breakdowns, and were keeping such precise tabs on one another that he expected to give the "go" command exactly as required by the master schedule. It was, so far, a remarkable feat of planning, execution, seamanship, and luck. Sun would give the anticipated command to attack the following morning at 11:00 Hours (local time) on the dot. Hawaii was three hours behind the West Coast, so *Dragon's Tail* would attack after docking in Honolulu at precisely 08:00. Every Dragon in the larger operation would launch its four mini-submarines about two hours before docking, and the LCACs would launch about H-Hour minus one. The timing of the air wing's dispersal depended on the flying time to the various targets. Most would start launching a few minutes before docking, but both central and southern California had inland air bases that took some time to reach. Hopefully the flying drone squadrons would only attract general curiosity and not cause a premature alarm.

Every captain and navigator had greatly benefited from the fleet-wide, open-channel communications protocols they maintained as part of their public relations ruse and, so far, it had worked to perfection. The admiral was in his usual spot—rarely doing anything but moving from one bridge wing to the other during waking hours—the exception being his daily roving inspection to reassure himself that everything was as it should be. And there was always the joy of looking in on his son. Suddenly, movement caught his eye—it was one of the three Communication's Room sailors who routinely brought him messages.

The young man—so filled with pride that he almost shook—stopped the usual two paces from the fleet commander and saluted smartly. "Good morning, Admiral. First signal of the day, just decoded!"

"Thank you, Seaman," Sun responded pleasantly and, as usual, signed the proffered form affixed to the small clipboard. He watched the young man turn crisply to march back into the bridge proper, and wondered—not for the first time—how long these young sailors and marines, and especially his own precious son down in the CIC, had to live. He knew with certainty that many would die tomorrow morning and in the coming weeks during their bold occupation, but he had trained them the best he could. They were as sharp as a razor's edge and were ready to go—most undoubtedly restless in their cramped quarters below. At least the quality of life had been pretty good by shipboard standards: They'd enjoyed the fresh air constantly pumped into every space on the ship, plus great food and fairly tranquil seas, and their chain of command had kept them busy training or working on equipment. Still, it was tough mentally to wait for two weeks, mostly indoors. He only hoped that Wing's thousands of operatives would do their respective jobs and grease the skids for his assault force. He'd promised himself months ago that, if Wing's legion of spies and saboteurs failed in their duties—and caused the whole operation to blow up in their faces—that he'd hunt his former classmate down and kill him, if he survived such an outcome. He sighed in resignation and read the freshly decoded message:

"Congratulations to all Dragon Ships! All China is proud of what our shipyard workers have created, and what our factory workers have manufactured—a combined effort to bring our wonderful goods to the world in a new and glorious fleet! This increased prosperity will greatly benefit our motherland! We await news of your coordinated arrivals, and look forward to your triumphant return!"

The message was signed by the chairman of the newly formed "Dragon Fleet Enterprises." **DFE** was painted in giant letters along the beam on both sides of all 14 Dragons, and at sea, every passing ship could read those letters for miles. But the message was actually from General Secretary Han on behalf of the Politburo. And, though "triumphant return" sounded inspiring, Sun knew it was a pipe dream. They were all sacrificial lambs intended to buy time for the PLA's ground forces to flood across their neighbors' borders on missions of conquest and material gain.

The admiral knew that forward units of the PLA were already creeping out of their staging areas, chomping at the bit before being loosed to surge forward and attack across a 1,000-mile front. It was a gigantic and complex operation spanning a third of the Earth's surface—even containing a space component. He was well-versed in the defense industry's capabilities in "the heavens." The China National Space Administration had its origins in the PLA but, in the 1990s, it was reorganized along the lines of the United States' National Aeronautics and Space Administration (NASA). In the last few decades, it had become part of the Commission of Science, Technology and Industry for Defense, and its long-term goals were bearing fruit. Throughout the program's long history, beginning with Project 714 initiated by Chairman Mao—through Project 921, which currently launched astronauts into space and had plans to reach out to Mars—the PRC's ambitions in space were well known to outsiders.

However, Admiral Sun was confident that the West didn't know that they had been sending highly sophisticated attack satellites into orbit for years—each fitted with special lasers and anti-satellite targeting software. These killers would knock out many of the American and Allied satellites during the early hours of their campaign, and would mitigate the need for a thermonuclear pulse over the United States.

But everything except the ground attack was a sideshow. Every aspect of the larger campaign supported the army's push across the borders of the motherland's neighbors. This part of the operation was supported by transport planes that would deliver thousands of paratroops to dozens of locations. The rocket forces would lead the Asian timetable with thousands of missile salvos, and the PLAAF would employ its bombers to inflict additional damage—always protected by a cloud of fighters crisscrossing the skies looking for enemy planes to shoot down. All were guided by their own array of satellites—dozens pre-positioned during the years of preparations. The massive ground attack would utilize troops and armor columns, supported by advancing artillery barrages—and it would be the largest combined arms offensive in Asian history. All concerned had been practicing for two years, and the battle staff anticipated that these forces would roll to victory in a matter of days.

Sun was privileged to know the big picture. This would surprise many in his hometown who'd known him as an awkward and stocky boy in the northern province of Manchuria. His rank was also a continual puzzle to a few of his academy classmates who'd teased him relentlessly that he looked like a peasant. But, at the moment, he had the most important naval responsibility in the history of China. He had been personally selected by Marshal Tai two years before—entrusted with command of the greatest and most distant offensive operation China had ever attempted. And, if this great expeditionary gamble was successful, he would be enshrined in their pantheon of heroes forever. However, and to his credit, he sought no personal recognition—he only hoped to contribute to his homeland being vaulted to the supreme plateau of undisputed leader of the world!

On the Chinese side of the Hong River, above Lao Cai, Vietnam
December 7th, 22:00 Hours

PLA First Lieutenant Kee Tao Chun lay on the pine straw next to his platoon sergeant—both looking through binoculars at the faint lights glowing in and around the city buildings below. Beyond the city were barely perceived tree-covered hills on the Vietnamese side of the river, but the soldiers knew every fold and valley after studying the area for almost two full weeks. They were lying on top of a forested knoll directly above a large bridge below that spanned the river separating the two old neighbors (and many times bitter enemies). The two infantrymen were the vanguard of a "sapper" unit that would, in 27 hours, race across the strategic span to capture the far side. They'd take out the dual border posts guarding the far approaches, and then disconnect the explosives wired underneath the bridge. They knew that many blocks of C-4 were attached to the underside of the span, and the PLA desperately wanted to capture the bridge intact so their advanced mechanized units could cross and secure the town. Kee's reward for success would be PLA immortality—meaning admission into his country's military hall of fame—but first he'd have to survive the Vietnamese defenders' rifles, mortars, and light machine guns that would cut down every threat in sight.

Today's version of the bridge had replaced an older version that had been knocked down in 2012. That historic structure had been the scene of many battles, including the PLA invasion in early 1979. But, during the intervening and mostly peaceful years, the new bridge had supported an amazing volume of cross-border trade that eager consumers gobbled up in both countries. Lieutenant Kee knew the Vietnamese bought more of these traversing goods than his country did of theirs—logical because China had a larger manufacturing capability than its smaller neighbor. And he'd read somewhere that the current volume of Sino-Viet trade had grown to nearly one million tons per year. But, as he lay scanning the deathly quiet opposite bank, city, and hillsides dotted with tiny villages, Kee hoped his small part of the larger incursion would be more fortuitous than that of his older brethren.

Personally, he had two goals: The first was to survive his initial dash across the bridge, plus any ensuing battle to capture the structure and its immediate vicinity. But his second goal was extremely personal: As soon as was possible after their speedy conquest, he wanted to meet and marry one of the cute ladies he loved to stare at (when he was supposed to be watching for enemy troop movements or police activity). Finding marriageable-age women in China had become problematic and quite competitive in recent years, and he had met a couple of beautiful Vietnamese girls who had immigrated to China as mail-order brides. In fact, all the local girls that he had gone to school with had already married by the time he finished his military training (which included his first deployment to Tibet as a cadet in what the government called "Southwestern China"). There were no single Chinese girls left in his hometown—a fact exacerbated by the pressure of the culture norm that deemed women after their 27th birthdays were beyond the pale. There was even a well-known term: "Leftover women" that meant something like "spinster" in the West. So it was understandable that, as young Lieutenant Kee gazed intently across the bridge during the last hours of peace, his mind was occupied with his regular fantasy. Somewhere on the far side was his future wife, and their happy life together would be his own long-term personal destiny. He wanted to be garrisoned there, marry that local beauty, and live out his life in one of the quiet villages after his term of military service was complete.

However, the lieutenant's musings were interrupted when his ever-sober sergeant commented on the quietness below. Sergeant First Class (OR-6) Ting Sang was a worrier—in his lieutenant's mind, a real black cloud to have around—an NCO who believed it was his duty to remind his boss how badly things could go "on the morrow." The sergeant had a good grade-school education and an inquisitive mind, and he had read everything he could find on the internet about the last time his nation had come south in force. But what he discovered had shocked him to the core: His own government teachers had omitted several crucial details about the short war—like the fact that they'd been forced back across their own frontier. "Sir, I was just thinking about what happened when my grandfather's unit attacked here in 1979..."

"Thank you, Sergeant Ting, that's just what I need to think about..." But he knew his sarcasm was wasted on the serious Ting. He, too, knew all about the 1979 incursion from studying the internet when his seniors weren't looking. He'd learned that, in early 1979, in retaliation for the 1978 Vietnamese move into China's ally Cambodia, the PLA had launched a significant "punishment" attack across the valleys that rolled away from the hills where the two soldiers were watching quiet Lao Cai below. Sixty thousand PLA soldiers had swarmed across the old bridges that spanned several other rivers and valleys along the border. These soldiers had been supported by some tanks and armored personnel carriers, plus a few combat aircraft and lots of well-aimed artillery fire, and they had created an immediate dent in Vietnam's northern frontier. However, the Vietnamese military was very large in the immediate aftermath of its long wars with France and America, and they'd swiftly counter-attacked by throwing every soldier they could muster against the Chinese "bulge." The Vietnamese regular forces in the area (who were not with the balance of the army in Cambodia), augmented by an even larger number of local militias, had been so fierce in defending their homeland that, after just two weeks of bitter and bloody combat—much of it conducted by old-fashioned dismounted light infantry—that the PLA withdrew and carried out (or left behind) an estimated 20,000 dead. They had also killed a similar number of Vietnamese soldiers and civilians, but it had not been enough to carry the day. Kee had learned about the debacle from open web sources, but hadn't pursued the issue long enough to learn (ironically, at least to the Americans) that the Vietnamese incursion into Cambodia had kicked Pol Pot's murderous regime out of all but the remotest northern areas bordering Laos. This campaign had effectively ended the so-called "killing fields" era of Pot's Khmer Rouge Maoist genocide. His bloodthirsty regime had murdered nearly 25 percent of the Khmer population before the Vietnamese military forced them to flee.

But tomorrow will be different, Kee promised himself. He had been given the honor of leading the advance element of sappers across the bridge—ahead of the 10th Battalion, 139th Mechanized Infantry Regiment—themselves just the vanguard of an incredible combined-arms force that would quickly subdue China's many opponents across Asia's 30 percent of the world. Without taking his eyes off the area abutting the far side of the bridge, he whispered to

Sergeant Ting, “We’ve got to get across the span fast—we’ll be sitting ducks until we can secure that far side!”

“Sir, be assured that the men are ready—and we’ve both heard the newest intelligence report that the enemy is weak and unprepared in this sector.” At least the 21-year-old sergeant hoped the O3 and NCO-level intelligence briefings were accurate. His grandfather had crossed this same spot, and had told him that his company had been wiped out with only three survivors out of 120 soldiers. And, after that admission, he’d sworn his grandson to perpetual silence. The young sergeant was also aware of the rumors floating among junior NCO circles that his regiment had been infiltrating commandos across the river for weeks, and that many spies had been sowing discord among the local population for months. He fervently hoped those rumors were true, too.

Chapter 27

The Embassy of the People's Republic of China
Washington, DC, December 6th, 13:30 Hours

Ambassador Bang Li He was as nervous as the proverbial "cat on a hot tin roof." He had been hoping that someone in Beijing would come to their senses but, with less than a single day remaining before he had to deliver his historical declaration of war to the intimidating American President, he despaired, knowing his hopes remained a pipedream. The leaders of his country wanted war, had prepared meticulously for it for years, and were set to release chaos throughout his assigned country after darkness fell that night. Personally, he was absolutely against every aspect of Operation Unity; in his value system, it was pure selfish adventurism.

The fretting diplomat eyed his chief of mission, Pu Tao Ning, a man Bang suspected was a stooge for that odious bully Minister Wing—sent to ensure that he carried out his duty. Pu was the most conniving little weasel the ambassador had encountered in his 40 years of public service. He detested the man, but was stuck with him, and he wouldn't give anyone the satisfaction of seeing him display an unprofessional lack of courtesy toward a subordinate. And, since this meeting in the embassy's ultra-secure basement communication's room would finalize the next day's schedule, Pu had to be present.

"Well, Pu, are we fully confident that Beijing is going forward with tomorrow's commencement of hostilities?"

"Yes, Mr. Ambassador. All is proceeding according to the master plan agreed upon at the highest levels." Pu could hardly stand to be in the same room with this weak, "talkie-talkie" diplomat who clearly valued the niceties of diplomacy over the iron certainty of comprehensive military victory. Bang could talk paint off a barn, but he was clearly waffling and nervous about delivering the incredibly powerful opening shout of Mother China's surge to world domination. General Secretary Han had agreed with Foreign Minister

Wu to leave the veteran in place—a recommendation Wu believed necessary to give the impression of widespread unity among the Politburo. And Pu admitted to himself that Bang's standing with the Americans would add prestige to their formal declaration of war. But Minister Wing had made it privately clear to Pu that a timely delivery was one more important way that China was going to avoid the mistakes that Japan had made in the last century—when their ambassador had allowed a slow typist to delay his meeting with Secretary of State Cordell Hull until after the attack began. That mistake added to America's rage and contributed to the empire's eventual downfall. Wing had given Pu secret orders: Ensure that the weak and reluctant ambassador carried out his responsibilities at precisely one-forty p.m., Washington, DC time on Attack Day, *"or execute the man and deliver the message yourself!"*

"Okay, Pu, we will do our duty as commanded by the Politburo. I do not relish war, as you know, but I am as much a patriot as any party member, and I'll do all for the motherland..." Bang sighed in resignation and stood, signaling that the meeting was over. He would do his duty, and then suffer the wrath of the Americans who would rightly toss him and the rest of the embassy staff out of the country. He did not fear for their lives—the United States Department of State didn't operate that way—but his team would have to leave everything else behind and be treated henceforth as international pariahs. His life-long devotion to peace would be down the drain. "I am going upstairs to check on the destruction of our documents and files, Pu. Please attend to all but the last bit of communications equipment yourself. We will send one last signal home before we are forced out tomorrow night or the following day." Then, without so much as a "by your leave," he headed out the door, passing the guards who were monitoring their sophisticated white-noise, anti-eavesdropping device inside a recessed nook. It was their job, similar to embassies worldwide, to keep the whole room—and, to a lesser extent, the whole complex—protected from host country snooping.

Pu simply mumbled his assent and waited until the door closed. Then he moved to the opposite end of the room and opened a hidden panel that housed encrypted tapes, removed a CD and replaced it with a fresh one, then shut the small door with a satisfying click. Then he too headed upstairs. He had been making separate and very secret weekly reports to his superior on Gen.

Wing's staff via a dead-drop in a nearby park, and it was his responsibility to read the ambassador's spirit. The MSS minister had entrusted him with determining whether Bang had the nerve to carry out his orders, but so far, Pu didn't think there'd be a problem the following day. But he knew his judgment had to be right, too: There was no coming home if the ambassador chickened out and he, Pu, didn't catch the failure in time to carry out his alternate duty.

The White House Situation Room
Saturday afternoon (same time)

Vice President of the United States Rebecca Jane Mason had requested a meeting with the relevant leaders of her "Dragon Ship" committee—one last gathering to consider the implications of its arrival the following day. After the President appointed her as his point person on the issue, she'd had daily phone calls with everyone physically present that afternoon: secretaries of State, Defense, and Homeland Security; directors of National Intelligence and the National Security Agency, and the President's national security advisor. At present they were assembled around the large conference table, while the extra-wide, wall-mounted TV screen displayed a still photo of *Dragon's Claw*, the ship scheduled to dock late morning at the Port of Oakland, California. Apart from the truly stunning bright red and gold livery decorating the main hull, the stacks looked as generic as hundreds of other containers piled on the decks of giant merchant ships worldwide.

Rebecca knew these leaders would rather be somewhere else—in fact, she wanted to get out to JBA to catch her flight to Hawaii ASAP—but first she wanted to make sure she hadn't missed something before the ships arrived. "Thanks for coming, everyone, and for sacrificing part of your Saturday afternoons. But I wanted us to confirm to one another that these ships pose no threat to us or our neighbors around the Pacific Rim. Let's go around the table and share what each of you has discovered since our last in-person meeting the day before yesterday." Rebecca looked to her right where Secretary of State Jack Madrid was sitting, so it fell to him to go first.

"Mrs. Vice President, we at State haven't had a hint of anything untoward. Our Commercial Desk has been in regular contact with our counterparts in our embassies in the relevant countries, and all is quiet there, too. Just a lot of low-level, horn-honking by the PRC government as has been their pattern of late." The Secretary thought this meeting was overkill on the part of someone he considered a highly ambitious VP trying to prove that she was worthy of being president in three years when Spence stepped aside. His old friend had picked her to be his running mate over other more-experienced candidates, but it was the President's prerogative to choose, and they seemed to work well together. Both were squeaky clean, and there hadn't been a whisper of impropriety between them before or during the first term in office. *To each his own,* he thought. But now he wanted to get home so he could offer last-minute support for his wife Debbie—currently making last-minute preparations for their first party of the Christmas season. She'd been fussing about it since Thanksgiving.

Baker Halsey went next. "I concur with Jack, Mrs. Vice President. We've been keeping a particularly close eye on all PLA activities, and while they continue unabated in their long-term defense increases—both in numbers and tempo—they aren't doing anything different. They've been training closer and closer to their neighbors' borders for the last two years, and we concede that they are a constant threat to everyone in the region—but there are no particular signs that these activities are linked with the ships' schedules. They always look ready to attack, and they have fortified and placed combat airplanes on the island groups they've occupied in the East and South China Seas, as we've discussed before. The only action that looks questionable at all—and certainly not provocative—is their two-aircraft-carrier task force. It is the first time they've ventured out of home waters and into the western Pacific."

"Where are they now, Mr. Secretary?" Rebecca didn't like coincidences.

"They're about a day's steaming time from Guam. The carriers have the same type of screening vessels that we typically group into a task force, but there are no troop ships that we can discern." *And, when I think these second-rate carriers look dangerous, I'll let you know.* He thought the VP was pleasant enough, but he'd be long-retired before he had to follow her orders as commander-in-chief. In fact, he wanted to sit in the Big Chair himself, and he might have to run against her to do that. That sweet job would be his if all went according to plan and, to that end, he'd been quietly building alliances with insiders, media, and money people for more than ten years.

"Thanks, Mr. Secretary. I assume you have conferred with Guam's command group?" Rebecca saw his affirmative nod, then asked a follow-up question, "What is the status and position of their submarine fleet? They are certainly not up to our standards in quality but, from a paper I read recently, they do have more than 80 of them."

"Same answer as their ground and air forces, Mrs. Vice President—they are mostly hovering in home waters. The only notable exception is that their six missile boats have been on maneuvers in the Eastern Pacific for two weeks, and are now a few hundred miles off our West Coast. We've been shadowing them with one of our attack boats, but they are making no attempt at being evasive or aggressive. Currently they are moving in a line about 100 miles apart, stretching from northern California to southern Washington, and seem to be practicing squadron-level maneuvers. They are essentially doing the same thing we do when we steam between Taiwan and the mainland. They are a concern, but we're doing everything we can except torpedo them." He had to watch himself—that last phrase sounded a bit sarcastic. *And please, have mercy...we have families and need to get home!*

"Great, many thanks, Mr. Secretary." Rebecca ignored the sarcasm, and looked at the next person: "Anything suspicious from your folks, Mr. Director?" Her question was for Robert Gainsfield, civilian director of the National Security Agency—the electronic ears of America.

"Just the usual chatter, Mrs. Vice President. No increase or decrease in levels that might signal something's up. However, they are excellent at signals intelligence, and really know how this game is played. But all embassy-to-embassy, embassy-to-Beijing, and ship-to-ship communications are using low level codes we can easily read. They know we can read their mail; therefore, it means they're allowing us to. Everything is regular, expected, and bland. Same can be said of their ground forces traffic, which is always busy. However, there is always the possibility that they're playing us..." *I like this gal. Sure hope she is up for the presidency in three years—or, God forbid—if Spence kicks the bucket. She's sharp, friendly, well organized, and a good leader—and, best of all, she's not Baker, who wants the job so badly he'd jail his own mother to sit in the Oval Office.*

Rebecca smiled. She really liked Robert—he was like the older brother everyone wanted. "Thank you, Mr. Director. We know they've stolen everything not nailed down hacking-wise. Any change in that tempo?"

"None at all, Mrs. Vice President. We catch them trying to sneak into one of our government systems or commercial enterprises almost every day."

"Fair enough." She next turned to Edith Carmichael, the director of National Intelligence sitting directly across the table. "Edith?" They'd known each other for years from shared membership in the Women's Forum, and Rebecca was thrilled when Spence tapped her for the directorship. But it wasn't until she'd obtained the necessary security clearance that Rebecca had learned that Edith had been a first-class spy in the dying days of the old Soviet Union. Yet, to this day, her friend hadn't offered any hints about her experiences, and Rebecca hadn't asked.

"Mrs. Vice President, the only relevant fact we have pertains to the clandestine agent we've discussed before. Sadly, there is no change in that status." *How wonderful, Rebecca, that you made it—I knew you would! What a blessing you are for our country—a model for ambitious and highly competent women everywhere!*

"I'm sad, too. And the disappearance is a red flag—but so far, it seems to be a stand-alone. Your people in all the intelligence agencies risk so much for us. I hope they know how much we appreciate their sacrifices…"

"They know, Ma'am. But I'll pass along your best wishes as opportunity affords…" They exchanged a quiet smile. *Yeah, for our team.*

"Looks like it is up to you, John; send us home feeling sanguine about this incoming fleet…" Rebecca was truly grateful for John Laughton—a man blessed with a positive disposition—and who provided strong, accurate, and loyal support for the President. She knew Spence found him indispensable.

John was sitting at the left-hand end of the table so it would look to an outsider like he was chairing the meeting. But, in most government settings, the senior person sat in the middle chair—especially if there was a central viewing screen mounted on an opposite side wall. But it suited him just fine to be the junior person on the totem pole—he got to work closely with a great President every day, and believed he was doing something to help the country in his generation. "Mrs. Vice President, I can see the blandness of everything we've discussed, except for the missing agent. Taken in total, no one thing points to anything sinister. But, on the other hand, everything could be a carefully crafted prelude for a move in the western Pacific. Perhaps we can send a low-key heads-up to our Pacific Rim neighbors about our suspicions?"

"But do we actually have suspicions, John?" Defense jumped in before Rebecca could answer. He knew everyone wanted to get home, and his colleagues would cheer his boldness. "DOD, RNO, and NSA watch and listen 24/7 and there's nothing new. What can we tell anyone?"

John saw that the Vice President was allowing him to run with this, so he answered with a question of his own. "Mr. Secretary, is there any message we can send that is between alarmism and nothing?" He wasn't going to let the hyper-ambitious Baker roll him.

"No. From my perspective, anything we do sends alarm bells, and we don't want a worse relationship with China than we already have. If we send out some kind of warning order, their agents in every country will learn of it in minutes. They'll always fuss with India over their common border, but they seem content for now with those island groups they've occupied in the South China Sea. The PRC knows we're not going to invade little islands World War II-style—risking a shooting war just to give them back to Vietnam and the Philippines. The status quo in the western Pacific is a fait accompli, and the PLA has actually reduced troop levels on its border with Russia. I just can't see them packing troops into cargo carriers, or flooding an army over their southern border. We have to be realistic…" *John is an egghead with too much influence on Spence—the President should return him to academia and get someone more practical—like one of my DOD civilians who could feed me the inside stuff.*

"Mr. Secretary, not to belabor the point, but where did those troops from the northern border get redeployed?"

"Half were transferred to the People's Armed Police units stationed in the southern province of Guangdong. The balance was disbursed among their army corps stationed near the North Korean Border."

"Sir, were those PAP troops part of the force that was moved into Hong Kong?"

"Yes, I believe they were…" *Give it a rest, man!*

Rebecca felt it was time to intervene; she didn't like the uncertainties, but there were no significant alarm bells ringing, plus she had an important trip to make and had to get going. "Okay, everyone. It seems like things are reasonably stable for now. We are all aware there might be a downside to every current event, so let's not let our guard down. I have to leave for Hawaii shortly, so let's call it an afternoon. I'll actually see the Dragon ship that's docking in Honolulu in the morning. If time permits, I might take the kids over to look at it up close and personal." She looked around the table to give a last opening if anyone wanted to say something, but they all seemed anxious to leave. So that was it. "If anything changes, let me know…" The Vice President and the senior cabinet leaders rose and headed for their Saturday afternoon activities—all of them with agendas important to their families. Everything seemed as peaceful as the always turbulent world ever got, and the entire U.S. government had skilled professionals constantly watching and listening for danger. At least to their personal credit, the Vice President, the National Security advisor, and the director of National Intelligence were privately worrying about a young agent missing somewhere in Dalian, China.

Botany Bay Container Terminal, ten miles south of Sydney Harbor, Australia Sunday morning, December 8th, 01:00 Hours

Geoffrey Palmer, senior superintendent of Port Operations, had come on duty at midnight, and was settling into his routine in his well-lit top floor office. The incredible man-made port was spread out below and, when he got the chance, he never ceased to admire the efficiency of the dock workers and their machines. But as usual, his first order of business was to re-confirm the manifests of inbound ships scheduled to dock over the next 24 hours—and three of them required specific quays due to differing lengths and hull configurations. After that, he would assign harbor pilots to meet the newcomers a few miles out to sea. First up was a Liberian-flagged passenger ship carrying 2,344 tourists—the first two-thirds-full passenger ship since the Covid-19 pandemic eased. She had a Norwegian captain and command group, and a mostly Filipino crew; nearly 3,000 passports that Health and

Immigration Services needed to check. The ship was being diverted down to his commercial container terminal because the passenger terminal adjoining downtown Sydney was fully booked.

Next up were two smaller vessels: An Australian passenger liner that catered to the locals (and never ventured farther than Fiji), and a Russian yacht that was so big its billionaire owner had booked it into the passenger terminal. However, she was refused for lack of space, and she was coming his way, too. *What it must be like to have that much money*, Geoffrey thought in no little envy. He reached over and hung his clipboard on a slightly rusty bent nail that served as a makeshift hook. Then, in the same motion, he unhooked the next one that listed the in-bounds that his port was actually prepared to host. He had been planning for the first one—a Chinese Pan-Max on her maiden voyage—due to arrive in three hours. She was one of the big gals that could easily swamp every small boat in the harbor, so he needed a pilot who really knew his stuff. He'd already decided to send out old Harry Longworth for the job—his most senior pilot who'd ensure that she came in slowly and exactly mid-channel. Harry would take along another veteran with him—these huge ships could always use an extra set of eyes. Of critical importance was managing the height of the bow waves they pushed—sometimes rising more than two meters if they weren't careful. Such waves could resemble a small tsunami surge in an enclosed harbor—enough to smash the aforementioned Russian's yacht against the dock. *What a sweet international mess that would be!* Geoffrey re-hung the second clipboard and picked up his walkie-talkie and called over to the harbor pilot's lounge—confirming that Harry was prepared to arrive in plenty of time to be ferried out to his ship. Geoffrey admitted to himself that he was curious to see what the Dragon ship looked like. It seemed like the Chinese government had been crowing about her for years.

* * *

Though the entrance to Sydney Harbor and its famous bridge was about ten miles north of the container terminal, the actual drive downtown was a bit less. And among these business districts and neighborhoods in greater Sydney were 20 Chaos Teams, currently putting the finishing touches on small blocks of explosives that would draw most first responders away from the southern harbor. These agents and their counterparts in every port and country were nearly ready to unleash their campaign of rolling disruptions. Everything was planned to the last detail, including blocking roads to ensure that the assault ship's armored units could move swiftly to their assigned positions. The plan estimated that, once each assault force was burrowed into civilian neighborhoods and business centers, the military and police authorities would have a devil of a time digging them out.

The senior leader of the Sydney CTs was standing with two colleagues in the nighttime shadows of a nondescript building in an outskirts industrial area. Each man was wearing typical working men's-stained clothing and smoking quietly. He was committed to doing his level best to obey his orders to the last detail and, though he was as fanatical as the rest, he'd admitted to himself that he wanted to see the outcome of the battle, and to enjoy his memories of victory for years to come. In short, he hoped his desires didn't make him any less of a patriot. Tempering this hope was the certain knowledge that General Wing would execute his extended family if he failed or turned traitor and ran.

The Harbor Master's office, Port Klang, Malaysia (same time)

Manfred Singh, the senior docking clerk, was the product of an unlikely marriage between an Indian father and a hippie German mother who'd been "finding herself" while taking classes at Delhi University. Yet the young couple's infatuation blossomed into lasting commitment, and they subsequently moved to Kuala Lumpur for employment. This interesting background also explained Manfred's useful set of languages that helped him in his politically sensitive job. However, at the moment he was so perturbed that he was going to scream in pidgin Mandarin if one more hysterical Chinese customs agent burst into his usually sedate office and yelled at him in poor English! A large group of media people and employees of the DFE shipping company had arrived in force a few hours before, and had, so far, demanded special tugboat assistance, special docking privileges, and re-assignment of other ships (that weren't running a mere 10 minutes late like theirs). They had generally made themselves intolerable, and Manfred finally had enough and told them off!

The last irritating dolt had left in a huff about 15 minutes ago—escorted down the stairs by his equally perturbed port police.

He'd known for months that this new Chinese-flagged ship needed docking space commensurate with her size—and that an exact time was part of the parent company's Pacific/Asian marketing scheme—so he'd professionally accommodated them by making all the usual arrangements. But it was not his responsibility to juggle other nations' vessels, inconveniencing them in the process, just to accommodate one commercial ship on its maiden voyage. An hour's deviation in arrival time here or there was a normal occurrence to which any ship's master could attest. *What was the big deal anyway?* Upon reflection, calling for port police backup via his office landline had been a strong move, and Manfred was pleased with himself for doing so.

The Hale Koa (U.S. Government) Hotel, Honolulu, Hawaii Saturday night, December 6th, 23:45 Hours

Vice President Mason and her family had touched down at Hickam Field about 11:30, and they'd been met with minimal fanfare per her wishes. Tomorrow was going to be a very busy day of remembrance and ceremony, and she needed to recharge her batteries. She, Bill, and the kids had been offered rooms in the Governor's Mansion or in the historic Flag Guest Quarters at the Pearl Harbor Naval Base, but they wanted to stay on Waikiki Beach where the kids could have more fun. They were now safely ensconced in the top floor suite of the old military hotel, and were enjoying the amazing experience that only Hawaii offered. The tropical air wafted the curtains with the hint of plumeria blossoms and, from their balcony, the sight of flickering tiki torches in the distance confirmed that they were in America's Pacific paradise.

Rebecca showered after the kids sleepily disappeared into their bedrooms—exhausted due to the six-hour time difference between Hawaii and Washington, DC. She collapsed on the monstrous king bed and had just started to soak in the wondrous setting when she perceived that sleep would have to wait: Bill materialized with flutes of champagne (aka California sparkling wine) and had that "look" in his eye—his big hint that she had another pleasant duty to perform. She never said "no," and he never asked when she was trending sick or in the middle of a crisis, and that component of their relationship was still sweet and fresh after 26 years of marriage. After a few sips and some small talk, mutual desire had its way. She was dead to the world and dreaming when her alarm went off at six am.

Chapter 28

Aboard *Dragon's Tail*, 25 nautical miles southwest of Honolulu December 7th, 04:00 Hours (H-Hour minus four)

Captain Fong Qing had ordered the ship to dead slow so they could release the four mini-submarines before dawn. The crews had been sealed inside their tubular vessels for just over an hour—enough time to check every system and bring the vessel to full operational status. Especially important was confirmation that the air conditioner/scrubber was fully functional, because it kept the crew alive. As *Tail* slowed to a near-drift, all four subs' nesting chambers were flooded simultaneously, a simple feat that kept the mothership perfectly trimmed. Then, counting on the theoretical rather than the practiced, the hull doors were slowly opened and the four subs released in a pre-determined order: Port front position and starboard rear position, followed by port rear position and starboard front position.

They gently glided down and away from the mother ship, and all four engaged their electric motors without incident. The single shaft/propeller mechanisms worked perfectly, and they moved in near-silence in four different directions until they reached their assigned stations in a rough semi-circle about five nautical miles apart. There they would wait for targets of opportunity—just in case any ships or subs broke out of the death trap that would soon be Pearl Harbor. They'd hover at 100 feet; when they had to raise their periscopes and ESM antennas to attack or communicate, it wouldn't take long to rise to firing depth. There they would wait in absolute silence, hoping the new war would force out targets for them to sink. They relied on passive sonar detection only—coiled hunters waiting for unsuspecting prey.

As soon as the subs were well away, the hull's chamber doors closed and sealed, and then the four chambers were emptied with pressurized air to add compensating buoyancy to the mother ship. When the captain was satisfied that all was well, *Dragon's Tail* resumed her established course and speed.

The whole operation had taken less than 30 minutes—time programmed into the master schedule almost 18 months before.

USS *North Carolina* (SSN-777)

"Hey, COB, can you take a look at this?"

"Sure, Zap. What's cookin'?" MCPO Cranston moved from the attack center into the sonar station to see what his lead sonar petty officer wanted. The crew was in a jovial mood and already dressed in their white uniforms for the ceremonial homecoming. They were part of the Pearl Harbor Day celebrations, and would "man the rails" as they cruised along Battleship Row in front of Vice President Mason and at least one four-star admiral. No one really wanted to delay their family reunions at the submarine base, but duty called, and being cheered by the VP and the brass wasn't so bad. Captain Robinson was slowly making rounds between duty stations—thanking everyone for a quality cruise. The exec had the conn and, in only a few hours, the boat would enter the main channel, bear to the right into the East Loch, and then respectfully pass by the USS *Missouri* and the USS *Arizona* Memorial exactly at 07:55. The navigation team was being especially diligent at the moment: This was not the time to be late. Thousands of well-wishers, their own families, and half the Pacific Fleet would be watching.

"Master Chief, I've been keeping track of that Chinese merchie, and she suddenly stopped and drifted. Then I heard a bunch of weird sounds for a few minutes, then she started up again. But, during her drift, we've moved ahead of her by several miles." They'd gotten orders to shadow the DFE container ship all the way to the break-off point—where the merchie would divert to Honolulu Harbor, and their boat turned into the Pearl channel. They'd matched speeds with the giant ship since yesterday, and remained on her port beam about 20,000 yards to the northwest. Both vessels had been adjusting their courses from due east to almost due north to enter the south-facing Oahu Island harbors, and everything had been uneventful until the 1,000-foot ship suddenly cut or lost power.

"Okay—I'll tell the XO; he may want to slow down and let her catch up."

Cranston moved back into the attack center and conferred with the XO and captain who had just arrived. "Sir, that merchie suddenly stopped for 30 minutes and we've pulled ahead. However, she's underway again and regained her base course and speed. Do you want to slow and let her catch up?"

"That's weird, COB. What did Zap hear?" The Shark relied on his crew for those kinds of technical evaluations; trust on a boat this size was essential for efficiency and morale.

"Sir, he says there were mechanical sounds for 30 minutes, then business as usual."

The Shark decided to step into the small sonar room to see for himself. "Zap, run the tape. I want to see what's going on."

"Aye, aye, Captain!" Zap reached over and depressed a button on his console and immediately the DFE ship's sound track scrolled on a side computer screen. It was a simple waterfall display and showed four divergent lines moving away from the center.

"Gentlemen, I've never seen this before," commented the captain. Then, after another minute studying the screen, he added: "Looks like four low-level screws. Maybe they deployed some scientific equipment—or underwater drones. We know they've been experimenting with various designs like we have. Truly puzzling. Okay, Zap, continue to monitor everything, but make a copy of those drones' signatures—I'll give it to a friend of mine at Pearl. And, as hard as it is to believe, my friend might be even smarter than you, Seaman." Zap and everyone within earshot laughed at the captain's good-natured jibe.

"Aye, aye, Skipper!" Zap loved serving on this boat—but not as much as getting home. *Hang in there—only three hours more.*

The Shark moved back into the attack center and announced, "We're on a tight schedule today, everyone, so we'll maintain our present course and speed."

Overlooking the oil refinery, Houston, Texas
Sunday morning, December 7th, 10:58 Hours

By pure chance, MSS Agents Li Fanghe and Hoa Pengyi fired the first shot of World War III: Each of the 1,700 Chaos Teams that General Wing had sent into the Continental United States—plus the few hundred CTs he had scattered in target countries around the western Pacific Rim and in Asia—were in position and ready to go. All had been assigned certain targets, but all orders had built-in flexibility, giving them freedom to adjust their attacks as circumstances warranted. Granting such independent decision-making was unusual in PLA operations, but Wing did things his own way.

It was late Sunday morning and the neighborhood was still mostly deserted. On the couple's rooftop was a scattering of folding deck chairs and a couple of collapsible umbrellas for people to enjoy the fresh air but, since it was winter, and their apartment was so close to the refinery, the air wasn't that good. Most of the locals worked at the refinery, and the current shift was already on duty. Everyone else was enjoying a lazy pre-Christmas Sunday off, or were heading down to the malls with their Covid masks to fight for gifts. Some were in church enjoying the beginning of the holiday season.

Wing's timetable was definite, however: Begin all attacks at noon, Washington, DC time. Every agent in the world was ordered to use that objective standard as their point of reference. But, as human frailty goes, Li's watch was two minutes fast, so he and Hoa fired off their 40mm RPG-69 rocket-propelled grenade just a bit earlier than their fellow saboteurs. The two of them had been issued the lightweight weapon by their contact after arriving in the Texas safe house, and had carried it unobserved into their apartment in a worn-looking soft bag. The rocket system was old, but proven, and elsewhere in the inventory had been relegated to surplus third-world status. Regular PLA units had been issued the newer and more powerful 80mm PF-89s, but the '69 was still very lethal. The two agents had trained on its use before deploying, so they were familiar with the shoulder-held weapon, which was simple to use. They had three extra missile/grenades just in case, and they quickly prepared the weapon to fire at the large fuel storage tank rising only 200 yards to their north.

Without further delay or fanfare, Li rested the tube on his shoulder, confirmed the elevation and sight picture, and depressed the trigger. They were ready for the loud "whoosh" as the rocket shot over the roof tops and exploded against the middle of the huge tank, but they were totally unprepared for what happened next: The projectile was a shaped charge and, when it exploded against the cement, it not only punched a hole through the exterior, but continued through the inner metal skin, and then through the heavy rubber "bladder bag" that held the gasoline itself. Rather than just start a raging fire that would spew molten froth over the immediate area and down the road into the adjacent forest of cracking towers, the 1.5-million-gallon tank detonated with such force that the resulting shock wave leveled the narrow earth berm, blasted across the open ground, knocked the perimeter cyclone fence flat, crossed the frontage road and parallel street, and leveled the first three rows of apartment buildings. The two agents barely registered shock, and never had a chance to say good-bye to one another. They were blown away like two insects in a tornado—their bodies smashed and instantly dead when they impacted a small hotel across the next street. Their dreams of marriage and family ended along with the hundreds of innocent residents they'd just murdered.

The fireball that followed the shock wave consumed the three apartment buildings and started fires among two farther blocks of small stores, houses, and other buildings, then rose into the air as a towering column of smoke and falling debris. The pillar shot heavenward for thousands of feet, and survivors recounted that the blast was so extraordinary that they speculated a nuclear bomb had been dropped on their city. The row of smaller storage tanks also shattered when the shock wave hit them, and the fuel inside them caught fire and spread the conflagration east and north into the first acres of the refinery proper. A quick-thinking engineer in the central control station frantically closed many pipes and saved the balance of the yard. He diverted various fuels and lubricants to safer areas, and undoubtedly saved many lives, too, but when the last of the metal cooled 72 hours later, a third of the refinery lay in ruins.

This was the first and largest of the attacks: Within minutes, Chaos Teams across America set off charges at electrical stations and other infrastructure centers, and fired long-range 50-caliber sniper rifles at military aircraft sitting in vulnerable locations. They started forest fires in nearly a hundred national and state parks, and destroyed control stations at more than 100 dams. Most of the damage was more cosmetic than catastrophic, but the combined effects of such coordinated efforts accomplished most of what General Wing hoped: Every news organization in the country was flooded with emergency calls, and radio and television stations began non-stop updates as developments overwhelmed them. Speculation went through the roof: The lower 48 American states—except for the West Coast—devolved into unorganized chaos. Alaska and Hawaii were also spared.

Every government agency spun up its emergency management plans, and employees reported for work as soon as they got the word. The Houston area oil fire turned out to be the worst of the civilian disasters, but active duty military was beside itself because several of its multi-million-dollar bombers and fighters were holed by long-range bullets. Every B-52 and B-2 was grounded until extensive inspections could be completed and any damage repaired. A few civilian airports were attacked and most airlines grounded their fleets immediately. It was worse than 9/11 in scope and breadth, but similar in that first responders everywhere did their heroic best to bring local situations under control. All governors mobilized their National Guards and the airwaves were filled with high-level government communication.

General Wing had accomplished his mission: The Dragon ships were temporarily forgotten as America turned in on itself.

Home of Dan Robinson, the Secretary of Homeland Security

The director picked up his phone as he and his family were nearly out the door for church, and listened in shock as he was informed about the Houston explosion. He was patched through to the local office and spoke with the watch officer. "Do you know what caused the blast?" he asked.

"No, Director," the officer replied with emotions torn between anger and grief. "Can't tell if it's spontaneous, an accident, or a terrorist attack! There is so much devastation that it looks like a nuclear bomb went off."

"Okay, I'll send a team over to you ASAP, and I'll also call the governor and ask him to ready a request for disaster relief. You know he'll get that immediately!"

"Thanks, sir. There are many, many dead here…pray for us…"

Dan promised to do so, and they disconnected. He sat down and looked over at his wife and teenage children who were standing in the door with looks of concern. He mouthed, "Go without me" and they understood: Dad had another crisis. They closed the door and left.

Soon a steady stream of alarming reports began pouring in, so he slipped on his headphones, ran out to his own car, and headed for the office. He needed to be in the headquarters command center so he could better manage his resources. It was an obvious terrorist campaign—but much larger than 9/11. He speed-dialed the President as he drove, and recommended that key government leaders be given a heads-up in case they had to move to designated shelters.

Both the President's regular 747 and his "low-tech" Kneecap version used in wartime were made ready for immediate take-off. The First Family would remain in residence at the White House for the time being, but the Secret Service was always ready at a moment's notice to move everyone to safety.

The Department of Homeland Security
Main Headquarters, Saint Elizabeth's
West Campus, Washington, DC
Director Dan Robinson's Office, 12:45 Hours

"Any clear intent or culprit, Dan?" he heard the President ask as their second conversation began.

"Sir, the attacks are nationwide, are clearly coordinated, and limited to the lower 48, but we don't know who the culprit is yet. Those responsible apparently left timed devices in selected locations, then fled the scene of every attack. There are two unverified gun fights with local law enforcement, plus several incidences of shots being fired at civilian and military aircraft, but I don't have the details yet. I can tell you that the incidences we know about—with the exception of the Houston refinery explosion—are not individually significant. More like a thousand pinpricks. There are no large groups of terrorists in any location, and only soft targets have been hit so far. Doesn't seem like people are specifically targeted, either all deaths and injuries are collateral damage. Baker will have to fill you in on the military side, but reports are coming in about bombers parked in the open being hit by high-powered rifle rounds. Many aircraft are not routinely in hardened shelters or even hangars—just parked on curtains where they make easy targets for bullets fired from a mile away. However, in the case of our B-2 Spirits, one bullet hole in a cockpit window or engine is enough to ground a billion-dollar plane."

"Any pattern to the civilian targets?"

"Mr. President, reports are pouring in regarding local gas stations and forested areas. Some explosions are caused by charges alone—probably C-4 or the like—but most are attached to containers of gasoline. They create a heck of a fire, but at least we have the winter weather on our side. All attacks are low-tech, but very effective in destroying property. The bad guys targeted county electrical stepping stations, and other local infrastructure—you name it. But, strangely, everything quieted down after a half-hour of violence. Looks like Islamic State-type of activity, but that is just natural speculation. I'm surprised that they could mount such an extensive campaign, given their degraded numbers over the last few years…"

"How many incidents so far?"

"More than a thousand separate ones, sir. But more reports are coming into our communication centers by the minute. But, again, every report describes attacks occurring in the original 30-minute time frame."

"Casualties, Dan?"

"Hundreds for sure, Mr. President—more likely low thousands. Most of the early confirmations are from the Houston explosion: The tank that was hit was gasoline rather than oil, so it blew up rather than just catching fire. The blast leveled three blocks of apartments, with the initial shock wave doing most of the damage. Nearby oil tanks ruptured, too, and a river of burning oil moved down a slight grade and into the main part of the refinery. My military advisor said that so much gas went up at once that the blast was the equivalent of a fuel-air bomb, the most powerful weapon in our conventional inventory. If there is any good news, it's that we haven't experienced an EMP attack—something that could only come from a large government. Attacks occurred in every state excepting Hawaii, Alaska, and the West Coast. They are peaceful and quiet."

"Okay, Dan. Just keep me updated. I have a call with the governors in a couple of minutes…"

"Yes, sir. You should probably discuss cross-leveling the Guard units—moving them from lightly hit states into the most heavily affected ones. And everyone will need disaster assistance."

"Agreed—I'll discuss that along with everything else. Some country or terrorist organization really laid the wood to us today…"

The two men disconnected, and Dan walked out of his office and took the elevator down to the large Command Center—a cavernous room in the basement of the DHS building. Hundreds of personnel were streaming in and taking their places behind the quarter-acre of computer screens. America might be at war, but he didn't know with whom. He glanced up at the clock: It was a quarter to one DC time—45 minutes since the explosion in Houston started one of the most chaotic days in U.S. history. And, to add to his worries, he had no idea if this was the extent of the attacks or only the first wave.

Home of Reg Trammell
13:15 Hours, H-Hour minus 45 minutes

Church had been surprisingly pleasant. Despite Tipi being ill at ease in the main service, the kids had enjoyed their Sunday School class, and Reg had enjoyed the pastor's sermon about salvation: He said it was a gift from God—given to those whom He chose. Reg liked hearing that—except for repentance, it really took the burden away from the sinner. He knew he could not earn his way into Heaven. He'd heard the message as a teen, but his interest in spiritual things got choked out by the world and forgotten. He hadn't heard hymns for many years either, and they had a nostalgic quality that took him back to his childhood. But, most important to his personal agenda, Tim seemed more content than during the previous two weeks of suffering.

They had attended an early service because of Tim's schedule (he'd volunteered to take a colleague's weekend shift so he could continue his vigil for Jen—and he also wanted to eat Sunday supper with Reg). They'd attended the nine o'clock service and the ten-thirty Sunday School—the adult component of which had been labeled "community hour." Several age-related groups met in different rooms in Tim's rather large suburban church on the Virginia side of the river, and Reg was surprised that so many people were interested in religion.

Afterward, they'd driven over to his place, and he and Tim were sitting in the living room watching TV when amazing news interrupted the Ravens' pre-game: A wave of terrorist attacks was sweeping the county! The kids were in their rooms playing video games, and Tipi was in the kitchen preparing Sunday dinner. Cooking for Tim was her way of balancing the "obligation scales" after he invited them to church. So the men were alone, staring open-mouthed at the news. Then they looked at each other, and both were thinking along the same lines.

"This can't be a coincidence!" Tim declared forcefully.

"Agreed—and the authorities don't have a clue!" They stared at the broadcast in silence, each man privately trying to make sense of the chaos. Then Reg suddenly had an idea that hit him like a hammer. "Hey, Tim, I saw that you have your briefcase with you. Any chance you have yesterday's fly-bys?"

"Sure. They're not classified so I took them home last night. I never leave my case in the car, so you can look at them, but I have to take them back." He sat on the couch and snatched up his case. Sensing his friend's urgency, he fumbled with the combo lock, then got it open and handed over a standard buff-colored folder. "What are you thinking?" he asked, curious.

"Something jumped into my mind…" He extracted the first two colored photos—clearly taken with a powerful telephoto lens by a low-flying plane or drone—and Reg separated out several of the same views of different ships for easy comparison. The pix were taken from 1,000 yards off the Dragons' starboard beams, and the dominant feature was the giant gold color DFE company letters painted on the bright red hull. The first two shots were of the two ships inbound to Hawaii and Seattle, respectively. He laid them side by side on the couch between them, then he extracted the next two photos of the ships closing in on San Francisco and San Diego. As he scanned the four photos, his heart suddenly jumped!

"What do you see?" Tim whispered, noting Reg's reaction.

"Look at the variety of the containers' color schemes—the patterns as they are arranged on the ships," he stated excitedly. "They are supposed to be carrying the normal—meaning random—assortments of containers like every merchantman!" He could hardly breathe. Everyone knew that each of the world's container companies painted its containers distinctive colors to differentiate themselves from their competitors. It made sorting (and branding) throughout the entire shipping industry easier.

Tim flipped the four photos to face him, and was initially baffled until the truth also hit him like a lightning bolt: Each of the four ships' container stacks—the maze of small colorful squares that randomly represented the loading process—had the exact color scheme pattern stacked in the exact same place! Thousands of supposedly random containers were arranged identically on four separate ships—a nearly impossible coincidence. "Oh, my God… you're right! They look random, but that has to be a color scheme painted by unimaginative workers. They were given a pattern for the first ship and just kept repeating it!"

Both men just stared at one another, and their collective brains nearly exploded as they processed the implications. "These are not individual containers," Tim proclaimed. "They are external bulkheads just painted to look that way…they're camouflage!" Then he noticed something else. "Look at the supposed spaces between the stacks; if you focus on them alone, there is no real separation. It's just part of the illusion!"

"This is cause enough to stop and board!" Reg declared excitedly.

"Agreed," said Tim. "You call your chain of command and I'll call mine. We've got less than an hour before these 'container ships…'," he made quotation marks in the air, "…dock in American harbors!"

Both men hurriedly fished out their cell phones as a news broadcaster announced: "This station has an update on the catastrophic explosion at the south Texas oil refinery just outside Houston: Authorities now believe that at least 100 people have died, but many more are still unaccounted for." Then the reporter paused as if listening into her earpiece. "Wait, everyone, I'm getting another update. Yes…Yes…Okay. We can now relate that the EMS director is estimating that multiple hundreds of people have been killed in this accident or attack. We'll stay with you as events unfold…" The TV screen then cut away to wobbly live film of a distant raging fire. In the background, the audience could make out the familiar shapes of refinery towers engulfed in flames, while secondary explosions here and there shook the handheld camera.

Reg and Tim were now on a mission, and started speed-dialing. Reg decided to phone his original supervisor, Polly Armstrong, who'd been promoted in the interim. She didn't know he had her number, and he knew she was going to be mad. But he didn't care: This was a national emergency and he needed her quick cooperation to run this right up to the Secretary of State's office. Those ships would dock in 40 minutes and he needed the Coast Guard all over this. He was hoping she'd connect the dots in the right way when he heard her pick up. "Hello, Ms. Armstrong, this is Reg Trammell. Remember me?" Silence. Then he heard a response that was equal parts sleepy and irritated. He cautioned himself to speak calmly if he expected her to hear him out.

"Reg, for crying out loud! How did you get my private cell number, and why are you disturbing me at home on a Sunday?"

"Ms. Armstrong (she didn't like subordinates calling her 'Polly'), I have an urgent request for a Coast Guard 'Stop and Board.' Those PRC container ships approaching our West Coast and Hawaii ports are not carrying actual containers—the above-main deck structures are just bulkheads, painted to look that way!"

"Really, Reg! That old crazy fetish of yours? You have been on this China kick for years now. You are going to lose all credibility in the department if you don't back off!"

"But they might be a real threat! They might have some offensive capability hidden in the fake containers or in the holds. It's important that we check this possibility right now! Have you seen the destruction on TV? These attacks may be related to the ships' arrivals!" He was starting to raise his voice and cautioned himself not to alienate her any more than she was already.

"Reg, the President already ordered fly-bys this week. Dozens of folks in several departments already looked at the photos. I've seen them, too. What did everybody miss? And what are you talking about on TV? I haven't turned on my set yet." She was starting to regret keeping this small-time analyst on her staff—his obsession with China had obviously eroded his other usefulness. She had even received reports that he was using official resources to continue his unofficial line of inquiry, but she'd ignored the notifications because his usual work was useful. "I am only going to say this once: Drop this China kick or I will rethink your position on my staff! I'm not going to initiate an international incident because of your radical ideas! And I don't care what's on TV on Sunday afternoon!" Then she hung up.

Reg fumed when he heard the dial tone in his ear—what a gross lack of accountability! He glanced over at Tim, who was deep in his own conversation, and it didn't look like he was having much luck, either.

"Will you at least take a second look at the sequence of photos of the four ships approaching the U.S. terminals?" Tim had contacted his immediate supervisor, Blake Reynolds. He knew the man thought his judgment was clouded because of Jen, but that was no excuse to blow off legitimate new evidence. Tim then heard what he had to accept as a final decision: "I'm sorry, Tim, but I can't send this up the flagpole with these terrorist attacks overwhelming the country. We have more than 1,000 reported now, and I can't justify an emergency stop-and-search request from Homeland Security—assets that are probably needed elsewhere. Besides, we don't need an international incident on top of the current crisis. I can't move on your hunch—or expect law enforcement to do so, either. I remain very sorry about Jen—you know that—but I think you must admit that you've lost some perspective. And, believe me, I'm fully sympathetic!"

"But what if these domestic terrorist attacks are related to the ships? Possibly distracting everyone from their sinister purpose?"

"Sorry, Tim…just too far-fetched. That would mean Communist China declaring war on the United States! Your photo evidence is intriguing and I'll look at it later, but right now I have to focus on the immediate. Drop by my office when you come in later…" After that they disconnected politely. Now the question was: What should they do?

"No luck?" Reg asked.

"He's too focused on the terrorist attacks. Doesn't think they're related. Coast Guard is busy. Doesn't want to cause an international incident, blah, blah."

"Same with my supervisor—I even went a level above my actual supervisor to speak with my old one. She says I'm 'obsessed with China issues!' She's barely tolerated me for years…"

"Well, we can't just give up." The two men were standing in Reg's living room just staring at each other. Then Tipi appeared in her apron, obviously curious about the noisy conversations. It didn't sound like football cheering to her.

"Gentlemen, is there a problem?" *It had better not interfere with my special meal!* She'd been preparing since the previous afternoon—shopping for a perfect leg of lamb to roast with all the trimmings. This was her special way of starting the Christmas season right.

"I'm sorry, darling. We just realized that those Chinese ships I mentioned might pose a threat—something connected with the current wave of terrorist attacks. They might be hiding offensive arms in their containers!"

"Well, do you have to deal with it right now? Can't it wait until after lunch?" *I am going to blow up if Reg has spoiled my sacrificial preparations for his friend! He can be so selfish sometimes...and after I went to Tim's church to appease him!*

"This may be war, Tipi…we have to make some phone calls now…"

"Fine!" She retorted with great frustration, and stomped back into the kitchen to see if she could salvage her serving time. *Really! Reg will sleep on the couch tonight if this roast is ruined!*

Back in the living room, both men were frozen with indecision. Then they had the same thought at the same instant: Reg spoke first, "You mentioned that you were friends with someone on the Vice President's staff—a senior admin of some kind. I saw on the news that the VP is in Hawaii for today's annual Pearl Harbor Day celebration. Will your friend be here or there? Will she take your call?"

"If you believe in coincidences, I just had the exact thought—my friend is Becky Peters, Mason's deputy chief of staff!" A jolt of electricity shot up Tim's spine: once in a while he got that tiny supernatural tingle. "You know there'll be a serious downside if there's no connection between these attacks and the ships—the end for both of us if we're wrong…"

Reg nodded and agreed. "I know, Tim. But what other explanation do we have for the false bulkheads and paint schemes?" He had a lot less to lose than Tim did, but it was a sobering moment for both. Patriotism won out.

Tim announced, "I'm going to make the call."

"Okay. Mention my name—we're in this together!"

"Okay, buddy. Here goes," Tim scrolled through his contact list until he located the right number, and then dialed. It was now past 7:30 in the morning in Hawaii.

Washington, DC (same time)

Ambassador Bang nodded nervously at his two deputies who were trying to light a fire under him: Their three-person delegation had arrived at the State Department, and had to exit their SUV and move upstairs for their historic appointment with the American Secretary of State. Both of his deputies were dismayed that the ambassador believed their preemptive strike against the American mainland was a grave mistake. They had been placed into their assignments at the behind-the-scenes behest of the minister of State Security, and both had values that were in stark contrast to the life-long diplomat whom they, at least superficially, worked for. Deputy Counsel Cheung Mai and Chief of Mission Pu Tao Ning had been thoroughly briefed about the drastic mistake the Imperial Japanese ambassador had made on the afternoon (Washington, DC time) of Japan's planned raid on Pearl Harbor. Their ambassador had not trusted a competent secretary to type out the final (and 14th part) of Japan's ultimatum—their equivalent of a declaration of war—and, as a result, the document had been delivered to Secretary of State Hull after the attack began. More than 1,000 Americans had already died by the time the ambassador arrived for his historical appointment. This late arrival meant the raid was viewed as a "dastardly attack…unprovoked," as President Franklin Roosevelt deemed it during his famous speech before a stunned Congress the following day, December 8th, 1941. This fact alone heavily contributed to American outrage that propelled the reluctant industrial giant into full commitment to enter and win the war against Japan. A few days later, German Chancellor Adolf Hitler stupidly declared war on the U.S., and Americans embraced the two-front conflict. That relevant history underlined the urgency propelling the diplomats forward. They now had only minutes to make their declaration of war; timeliness would mitigate the intensity of America's response.

"All right, gentlemen. I'm ready. Let us attend to this odious business." Ambassador Bang had steeled himself to endure the next hour. It was going to be the greatest shame of his life, and a sad way to conclude decades of diplomatic service. General Wing's so-called Chaos Teams were already wreaking havoc throughout an unsuspecting America, and he was certain from the news reports he'd listened to on the drive over that at least hundreds of innocent citizens had been killed or injured. Added to that, the total dollar amount of the damages would be staggering. He shuffled toward the elevators in the underground parking area reserved for diplomats, and momentarily was headed upstairs to deliver his fateful message.

Office of the Secretary of State
Sunday, December 7th, 13:35 Hours

Secretary of State Jack Madrid was not happy. He'd been formally asked at the last minute to receive the PRC's ambassador at this specific day and hour, and he'd had to cancel a golf date with three of his regular partners. A standing foursome was considered nearly sacrosanct in his social circle, and their having to recruit a fourth at the last minute was a real faux pas. The PRC's embassy underling who called on Friday afternoon wasn't able (or willing) to share the reason for the appointment, but Jack figured it had something to do with zealous staffers in their foreign ministry getting a head start on some unknown Monday morning issue in Beijing. He was also pretty sure that the meeting wasn't so important that it couldn't wait a few hours until **his** Monday morning. *First Rebecca's unnecessary meeting interfered with my Saturday afternoon, and now this Chinese meeting is interfering with my Sunday afternoon! What was wrong with people?* Then, on top of everything, a wave of dreadful terrorist attacks was sweeping the country. *Dammed terrorists—what's next?*

Jack's assistant toggled the intercom to announce the ambassador and his party, and momentarily he heard a polite but firm knock on the door that admitted high-ranking visitors directly from the VIP lounge. He stood according to protocol, but waited until the ambassador and his two assistants were ushered into the office before moving around the desk. "Good afternoon, Mr. Ambassador!" he greeted his principal guest warmly as was professionally correct. But for all Jack's personal frustration with the terrorist activity and his missed golf date, he was highly attuned to diplomatic nuance: He immediately picked up that Ambassador Bang's face was ashen, and that his eyes were downcast and almost closed. The man looked like a zombie who wouldn't make eye contact. He quickly glanced at the two deputies, but they were staring at him with an almost, what, defiant look? Smirking could be interpreted, too. Alarm bells went off in Jack's head, but he had to continue as protocol dictated. "Please, gentlemen, make yourselves comfortable."

"We will not be staying, Mr. Secretary," Bank stated with difficulty. His breathing was becoming labored, and feelings of lightheadedness had crept in. But he drew on his lifetime of diplomatic experience, and raised his eyes to focus on the man who had always been fair and correct with him during their many encounters. He assumed the correct posture of a senior diplomat, and began the brief statement he'd strenuously hoped to avoid: "Mr. Secretary, the Politburo of the People's Republic of China has ordered me to deliver to you this document. It is a formal Declaration of War against the United States of America. However, my government stresses that we will conduct all military operations using conventional munitions—we will not be the first country to use nuclear weapons…"

Stunned at the words, Jack couldn't believe his ears. He instantly abandoned his diplomatic persona and lashed out: "Has your country lost its mind, Ambassador Bang? This is an outrage!" His voice ascended to heights he'd never used in this, or any, government office before. "What good can possibly come from millions of deaths?" He saw the ambassador was as stunned by the force of his words as he'd been in hearing the declaration against his country. Suddenly, the senior citizen cried out in pain and grabbed his chest, and stumbled sideways toward a chair but never made it: He crumpled to his knees and toppled in slow motion onto the carpeted floor.

"I am so sorry, Secretary Madrid…" he croaked, as life seemed to slip out of him. One of his two deputies quickly knelt next to the stricken diplomat to offer assistance, but the other just stood his ground.

Then the man suddenly spoke defiantly: "Now, Mr. Secretary, your people and the world will learn the power of the new China! We have stood up, and you will not rule the world any longer!"

"We don't rule it now, you fool!" Jack retorted forcefully. Then he moved quickly behind his desk, and reached under the near side of the middle drawer to locate the emergency button that he'd never used before. Within seconds, three tough-looking agents burst into his office with handguns drawn—security officers on constant standby from the Diplomatic Protection Service (State's equivalent of the Secret Service). "Agents, escort these two gentlemen back into the VIP lounge and hold them incommunicado while I get medical help for Ambassador Bang! Keep them safe but restricted to the lounge until I speak with the President. And get a doctor in here quick!"

The DPS agents gently but firmly relieved the two assistants of their cell phones and frisked them for weapons and took their attaché cases. Then they gently pushed them into the VIP room and shut the door.

"You can't touch us!" screamed the defiant diplomat. "We have diplomatic immunity!"

Jack heard the commotion, but ignored it and punched the direct line to the President's private cell. His heart was pounding so hard that he felt a bit faint and dropped into his chair. Five long seconds later he heard a somewhat scratchy series of clicks, and then the voice of his obviously concerned President.

"What is it, Jack?" President Stilwell asked without preamble. Any use of the "emergency line" would be serious.

"Mr. President, the PRC just delivered a formal declaration of war!" Jack was still in shock—his whole world was suddenly upside down. Just then the doctor on duty barged in from a side door with another DPS agent, and Jack motioned with his hand toward the man lying on the floor.

"That's insanity!" the President reacted forcefully. "A formal declaration, you say—is there a timeline for hostilities to begin?"

"Sorry, Mr. President, I didn't look at the document—just called you immediately! Please hold on, sir." He could almost envision smoke pouring from the President's ears. Jack grabbed the formal red folder he'd dropped on his desk, and flipped it open while cradling the phone between his cheek and shoulder. He quickly scanned the diplomatic language: Yes, there it was in the middle paragraph on the first page! "Two this afternoon, our time, Mr. President. Eighteen minutes from now!"

"Okay, I rushed back to my office from Congressional Country Club when the terrorist attacks began earlier. Did the Chinese say they're connected?"

"No mention at all, but it seems obvious now. There is one vital point: They are stating a commitment to no-first-use of nuclear weapons."

"Okay, noted. I've already spoken with Dan, and Homeland Security is ramping up its response to the terrorist attacks. Get over here as fast as you can, and make a beeline for the Situation Room. I'll call Baker and get him sending out a general alarm to the military."

Jack had to give the man credit: Spence was thinking fast under the greatest stress anyone would have to face in a lifetime. "Yes, sir!" he responded obediently, and disconnected. Then he heard the doctor shout to Jack's assistant in the next room to call an ambulance. Apparently, the ambassador was still alive. He opened the door to the VIP lounge, and spoke with the agents hovering near the diplomats: “Agents, escort these men back to their vehicle. Then escort the vehicle back to their embassy.” Then Jack turned to the diplomats who were glaring at him but not speaking, “Your government is responsible for what happens next. I can only warn you that your Politburo has brought calamity on much of the Earth!” He held up his hand to silence the belligerent one. “Per international protocols, you will not be harmed in any way. You will spend the night in your embassy and we will post guards outside for your protection. Sometime tomorrow you will be contacted with instructions for leaving America. Ambassador Bang will be treated with our best medical care, and your staff physician and his family may remain with him if they choose. They will all be sent home when he is able to travel. Good-bye, gentlemen, and may God have mercy on your souls!” Then, without waiting for a reply, he turned on his heel and slammed the door behind him. It was the rudest thing he could think of.

Book III

Chapter 29

The Underground Bunker of General Secretary Han December 8th, 01:30 Hours (Asian side of the International Date Line)

The polished steel elevator doors opened with their usual whisper, and GS Han and several of his “Eight” crossed the room and sat in a semi-circle around one side of the special table. A tallish PLA general of marshal rank was waiting for them, standing next to a large TV screen displaying a dramatic live view of a maritime panorama. Calm seas, dramatic hills rising steeply from a nearby shoreline, and an impressive dark orange/red bridge loomed overhead. It spanned a distinctive gap between two spits of land, and tall buildings were visible beyond the bridge on the right-hand side of a large bay. It was one of the great vistas of the world—but for these leaders, San Francisco Bay was just a target.

“Is that the famous Golden Gate Bridge?” one of them asked Marshal Tai.

“Yes, Comrade, and the view we are seeing is from the bridge of *Dragon's Claw*. She will arrive at her appointed docking space in less than 30 minutes to commence our attack.”

General Bao and Professor Dang were standing on the opposite side of the dominant screen, and they would give the play by play as their war of conquest unfolded. On either side of the main screen were banks of smaller screens that provided similar views from cameras on each assault ship's bridge—each closing in on its respective points of attack. Farther to the left on the same wall, a huge interactive map of the Pacific Rim was firmly mounted, and it was marked with dozens of different colored arrows and quietly twinkling lights. There were murmurs of anticipation among these powerful leaders who had voted to start World War III but, to their lasting credit, two of them—a man and a woman—had frowns that could not disguise their worry. Senior General Wing, minister of State Security, was not in attendance—preferring to command his Chaos Teams from his own secure headquarters a few miles away.

Aboard *Dragon's Claw*
December 7th (same time)

Vice Admiral Sun, now dressed in his PLAN military uniform, hadn't even glanced toward the bridge when the ship's captain had earlier ushered the harbor pilot through the far door. It was the pilot's job to provide detailed navigational knowledge and instructions to ships entering their harbors, and the Chinese couldn't deviate from that regulation without raising alarm bells—followed quickly by unwelcomed visits from the local Coast Guard. So far, they were doing everything by the book and the pilot hadn't noticed anything amiss. He was ignorant of fact that four 726-Type LCACs had launched from the mother ship earlier—hidden by the regionally typical morning off-shore fog bank. Those four were now approaching a broad stretch of beaches—one fairly close and the others a few miles down the coast. He also didn't know about the four mini-subs that had been launched before the hovercraft, or the formations of drones just then crossing the low hills toward distant targets. The pilot seemed quite pleasant to those on the bridge, and all were confident that he'd offer no resistance when subdued.

"I've been looking forward to seeing one of your magnificent new ships, Captain," Mr. Turner commented magnanimously.

"Honored Pilot, it is our privilege to enhance positive trade between our two nations," Senior Captain Ho Quan Ren replied diplomatically. He'd been a merchant marine officer for most of his career and, like the admiral standing on the port bridge wing and staring through his omnipresent binoculars, he spoke English fairly well.

"Very good, Captain…please bring *Dragon's Claw* to a heading of 90 degrees, and slow to six knots…"

"Ninety degrees at six," Ho relayed to the helmsman, and momentarily the men on the bridge felt the great ship make a slight course correction so it could pass under the bridge exactly midway between the center tower and the southern shore where Fort Point, the old Civil War structure, still held silent sentinel after more than 160 years. *Claw* was scheduled to arrive at the Port of Oakland within the hour, but that was not where she would dock; when the great ship heeled to starboard in about nine minutes, it would be too late for anyone to raise an alarm.

Ashore, near the southern boundary of the City and County of San Francisco

During the preceding hours, San Francisco had been the scene of significant activity on the part of several MSS agents and PLA commandos—most were infiltrated as tourists, but some had recently moved across the southern border. These men and women had joined some two dozen MSS agents who'd been working tirelessly throughout the Bay Area for more than a year, in addition to the three couples that were "imbedded permanents" who spied for the motherland on a long-term basis. There were other informants who were working throughout Silicon Valley—not spies, just technical experts who sent home a regular stream of useful technology. There were also graduate students learning throughout the United States who were even more passive—many who didn't care about their government one way or the other. But they, too, would be debriefed upon their return home; everyone learned something the state could use.

The CTs had begun their attacks across the balance of the United States, but the West Coast had been spared to delay local government or law enforcement interference. As hoped, local police and other first responders were enjoying their usual Sunday morning routines in quiet California—most just becoming aware of the attacks farther east.

Over the past few months and weeks, Wing's agents had conferred on traffic patterns, police coverage, local politics, physical infrastructure and, of course, the location and content of regional armed forces—anything that could impact their mission. Part of this research had been used to prepare target lists and, as the mothership bore down on its landing dock, swarms of previously launched drones were steadily bearing down on their sleepy prey. After extensive study, the agents surmised that this famous city, which had grown up during the Gold Rush in the middle of the 19th Century, was a "soft" target that would be both easy to conquer and easy to hold. The local population was generally considered liberal in the American political sense of the word, and, as such, possessed fewer personal weapons than most Americans. Knowledge of the U.S. 2nd Amendment had caused many countries, including the PRC, to confiscate their own citizens' guns: You couldn't dominate your own population if they had guns, too. The agents figured the locals would not be hard to intimidate into quiet submission. At any rate, the PLAN marines were going to turn the city and county of San Francisco into a fortified "island" of hostages—useful when blackmailing the regional and national governments into reluctant cooperation.

As *Dragon's Claw* passed underneath the engineering wonder that was both a landmark and a symbol of the Golden State, the soldiers and agents of the advance teams moved into their final positions. During the night, one team had taken control of the large pier on the Embarcadero where the giant assault ship would unexpectedly and violently dock—as close to 11:00 as they could. Additionally, other teams sat waiting in rented gravel trucks, each filled to capacity with construction-grade two-inch rock. They would dump these loads on pre-selected freeways at strategic points across the southern boundary of the city and at strategically located city intersections to stall traffic and provide uncluttered lanes for the assaulting tanks and troop carriers to navigate. It wouldn't take long for units to move to their assigned positions and lock down the population. Marine infantry would then fan out to complete the first phase of the operation; the goal was to turn their objective into a giant prison camp where the civilian population would become an effective deterrent against aggressive counter-attacks. All 14 Dragons had the same mission: Tie down each region's military—old-fashioned "divide and conquer" techniques still applied in the 21st Century.

Utilizing identical, off-the-shelf, hand-held Motorola RMV2080 walkie-talkies, the teams easily coordinated their actions. They'd completed several dry runs during the past two weeks and their diligent practice ensured that this morning's real thing would go like clockwork. During the average weekday, San Francisco's normal population was just under 900,000 residents, but this number swelled to more than one million people as more employees streamed into city businesses than left to work elsewhere. The planners incorporated the weekend's reduced congestion (and mouths to feed) when estimating the useful lifespan of their occupation.

PLA Lieutenant Colonel Ton Ning Lee was the officer in charge of "lane closures" and at the moment he was riding in a beige suburban just ahead of a heavy-duty "long-boy" dump truck loaded with tons of heavy gravel. He reached his pre-selected spot—Highway 280's northbound lane where it converged with Highway One—and ordered his driver to slow and begin his drop. He was in constant radio contact with both the driver behind him and the one approaching from the opposite direction and, when he gauged the moment correct, he depressed the talk button and gave the order: "Drop, now, now!"

The agent driving the heavy truck behind him braked and slowly veered to his right, then opened the tail gate and engaged the powerful hydraulic arm that gradually lifted the bed. Tons of loose gravel poured from the back, and then to the consternation of the frantically honking and skewing traffic, he slowly veered back to his left. The result was a two-foot-deep berm of heavy rocks across all lanes, including the inner and outer shoulders. Cars screeched their tires as they rammed on their brakes in both terror and anger—and while those at the front were able to slew out of the way before crunching against the berm—those farther back had no warning and crashed into the next skidding car. Soon all lanes were halted, and it took only a minute before 200 cars were jammed behind the rocky barricade.

The scene was repeated in the southbound lanes at the exact same spot, and both lines of rock formed a nearly constant line across the entire freeway. The waist-high cement center divider provided a useful solid wall in the middle. Both gravel trucks gunned their engines when the beds were empty, and chased after their respective Suburbans. As they rumbled away from the chaotic scene, they left behind two accumulating logjams of cars and frustrated drivers—plus several who were injured and needed immediate medical care. Just out of sight of the pile-ups, the drivers pulled to the side and abandoned the trucks. They jumped into the SUVs and the teams raced off to their next assignments.

A lone California Highway Patrol officer was trapped in the middle of the northbound pile-up, and he extricated himself from his own damaged cruiser by crawling through the driver's side window. He ran forward to find out what had happened, and when he saw the lines of deep gravel on both sides of the highway, he quickly diagnosed the situation and called for massive police, logistical, and medical back-up. Initially, he was puzzled why there were no gravel trucks on their sides, which sometimes happened in roll-overs, but then the light went on: The officer correctly figured that this must be part of the terrorist attacks erupting across the country, and called dispatch again. His watch commander got the on-duty CHP teams vectored toward the accidents, then ordered his team to phone all off-duty officers' homes and get them heading back to work, too. The liaison officer at the California National Guard office in Sacramento was notified next, but the governor had already been mobilizing his troops; he'd been on the earlier call with the President and was trying to get ahead of any attacks in the Golden State.

LTC Ton's teams soon had all the relevant roads and highways blocked, including the secondary ones, and traffic arteries to and from San Francisco were closed. Highway 35 was blocked where John Daly Boulevard branched off to the east, and Highway 101/1 north of the GG Bridge was blocked north of the Robin Williams Tunnel, effectively preventing incoming traffic from Marin. Even the side road down to Fort Baker was blocked, but the plan called for opening that later if needed. The ground force commander would send an armored column across the bridge as soon as possible to take up positions on the north side of the tunnel, and they'd occupy the Marin headlands, too. One batch of drone controllers would man the site 24/7 and protect the city from any low-level northerly attack. But, until the tanks were in position, the deep lines of gravel would have to do.

Within 15 minutes, the city was effectively sealed off from the outside world: Both ingress and egress were impossible except by water, and all internal freeways and major streets were clear of vehicles and ready for the marines. The ferries were ignored for the time being because they were only a small portion of the traffic, and armed agents had been quietly riding them for days to assess their part in the big picture. The MUNI trains were stopped in place, but the under-bay BART tube was merely monitored until its usefulness was clarified. San Francisco International Airport was south of the barrier line, and would be ignored until the PLAAF air wing commander knew how many of his drones returned from their attack on Travis Air Force Base near Sacramento. The eventual goal was to shut all California airports until their usefulness could be determined—but the primary targets were the Air Force and Naval Air units located inland. Some of these would be attacked by drones, others by PLA snipers, but until a post-D-Day assessment could be digested, the planners had given instructions to let sleeping dogs lie.

Aboard the PLAN Type 94A Jin-Class Ballistic Missile Submarine *Bohai* 400 miles off the coast of Oregon, 10:45 Hours

All six PLAN missile submarines had been on station off the West Coast of the United States for two days—running gentle race-track courses and hoping they presented a non-threatening signature to the American Navy. They were free to operate in international waters, but guessed correctly that they were being shadowed by U.S. submarines and being tracked by any means the Americans had. Their orders were to maintain a silent vigil until receiving the low-frequency "GO" signal from naval headquarters in Beijing. The signal would be transmitted across thousands of miles of ocean, and received by special antennas contained in the "boomers" sails. The anticipated signal would order them to launch depth, and they'd fire their missiles toward targets across the United States. They maintained normal noise discipline while avoiding the appearance of being overly sneaky. They were under no illusion that they'd escaped notice when they put to sea several weeks previously, and it was prudent to calculate that they'd be followed throughout. To avoid unwanted company and appear non-threatening, all six had departed one-half day apart and then maintained their intervals so they were never within 100 miles of each other.

After their lengthy voyage, all six boats arrived without incident, and now formed a north/south line that stretched for 500 miles—from northern California to southern Washington State. The estimate from the senior admiral who planned the mission was that the Americans would assign no more than two of their attack submarines to follow along, and after the 94As began firing their missiles, the U.S. boats would not be able to sink more than two of the PLAN boats in the opening moments of the war. Between them, the six Chinese subs carried 72 of their latest ballistic missiles, and Bao and Dang hoped that at least 52 would be successfully fired. Each missile was programmed to follow a standard arching sub-orbital ballistic trajectory, and they'd destroy vital targets located mid-continent and on the East Coast.

The Jin Class submarines carried the JL-2 "Giant Wave" (CSS-NX-4) SLBM (submarine-launched ballistic missile) that used a solid fuel rocket that could propel it 7,200 kilometers (or 4,500 miles). From their resting spot off the West Coast, they could easily reach the East Coast of the United States, and each missile was armed with a conventional warhead.

Traditional ICBMs were guided only in the initial stages of the flight, but the PRC engineers and scientists had developed an enhanced capability that enabled them to guide the missiles in the latter portions of the flight, too. This upped the percentage of targets killed—even when they took evasive action—normally expected by enemy aircraft carriers at sea.

Each of the 12 missiles on the 94As were massive: 13 meters, or 43 feet long, and weighing 42,000 kilograms or 93,000 pounds (45 tons). When utilizing a nuclear munition, one missile was considered a "city killer" but, when armed with a conventional munition, they were considered "carrier killers" that could destroy airport runways as well. For the present mission, per the assurance contained in the PRC Declaration of War, all munitions would remain conventional unless the U.S. or its Allies went nuclear at a later time. After that, all bets were off when the boats returned to their home ports and reloaded.

The Jin-Class captains received the "Go" signal with just enough time to come to firing depth at the announced start time of the war. They brought their boats to just under the surface according to the strict schedule issued before they put to sea, and each boat finished the complicated countdown procedure while waiting for the clock to tick down. The missiles could be fired 15 seconds apart, and the subsequent flights to the East Coast would take between 12 and 14 minutes.

Aboard the *USS California* (SSN-781)
On station 11 nautical miles west of the *Bohai*

The *California* had shadowed the *Bohai* and her sisters throughout their leisurely transit of the north Pacific Ocean. Following enemy boats—particularly ballistic missile submarines—was routine duty, and this crossing had been good practice for the crew. But it was also boring because the *Bohai* never did anything interesting. Her captain had established a predictable course after putting to sea from their base north of Shanghai, and their boomer had followed a predictable easterly route as the Americans routinely did themselves. She stayed on a fixed course and speed all the way across the north Pacific until she was about 100 nautical miles west of her current position. Then she slowed to a crawl. The passage had allowed all the California's junior officers to practice targeting and navigation skills, and several enlisted sailors earned their Dolphins (the prized badge that proved the submariner's qualification level). The relevant teams plotted firing solutions on their singular target twice a day for weeks, and the skipper figured that after 100 or so projected hits, they could do the job in their sleep.

Captain (Commander, promotable) Richard Crandell Marsh, skipper of the *California*, was small in stature and so bald that he shaved off the rest just to keep things uniform, but he'd been first in his NROTC class at UCLA, and chose the "Silent Service" because his Military Science instructor was cool (and wore the distinctive Dolphins of a fully qualified submariner). "RC" had earned his undergraduate degree in Physics, sailed (no pun intended) through sub school at Groton, and then through the advanced nuclear propulsion course at the Naval Postgraduate School in Monterey. After that, his career was fast-tracked but not unusually so, and he'd received his cherished command of the *California* after 18 years' service—just over a year before.

RC appreciated the training opportunities that tracking the *Bohai* presented during its cruise, but once it took up station (along with her sisters, who the *California* had also kept track of), the captain was well and truly focused. They were within easy missile range of the entire United States—including Hawaii and Alaska—and this increased the focus factor significantly. The *Bohai* was southern-most of six Chinese missile subs, but they were strung out of target range, so the careful American skipper requested back-up. Answering the bell was the *USS Connecticut*, which was home-ported in Kitsap Naval Base in the Puget Sound. She was a Seawolf Class attack boat with 8 torpedo tubes and 50 munitions divided between Tomahawk missiles for use against land targets; Harpoon missiles for use against surface ships; and Mark 48 Mod 7 torpedoes for use against other submarines or ships. She arrived on station a day after RC's request, and was similarly loitering 20,000 yards from the northern-most ChiCom boat off southern Washington State.

But there was a tactical problem: The two U.S. subs could keep tabs on all six ChiCom boats, but they could only readily engage two of them with their torpedoes. The four in the middle were a minimum of 100 miles distant from either American sub and, since the effective range of the Mark 48s, even with the advanced Mod 7 guidance package, was under 30 nautical miles, the middle 94As could launch all 12 of their ballistic missiles with ease.

At the moment, RC's executive officer, Lieutenant Commander Jim Barrett, had the conn—allowing his skipper to catch up on the omnipresent paperwork in his stateroom. Therefore, he was the one who received the urgent call from the chief sonar man:

"Sir, Target Charlie One just popped a missile hatch!" That woke the boat up.

The XO grabbed the overhead mic and hailed the captain. "Skipper, Charlie One just popped a hatch!"

RC nearly choked on his coffee, flung his logbook to one side, and raced forward to confirm the dreaded news. Sure enough, the Combat Center threat screen glowed red. "Chief of the Boat, all hands to battle stations!" The COB was standing in front of his own screen three paces away, and depressed an orange button that sent three quick electronic buzzes permeating every space. The crew raced to battle stations and were ready in less than 45 seconds—some a bit bleary-eyed from having just fallen asleep, but all could function as needed. Hatches and water-tight doors were closed and dogged, and 100 other little things happened at once. "Status?" RC asked the XO.

"All green, Captain!"

"Get me a firing solution to the ChiCom boat now!"

"Plotted and ready," came a quick reply.

"Load all tubes!" That order was relayed to the torpedo room forward, and hydraulic rams gently pushed four of the Mod 7s out of their cradles and into the four tubes. The outer doors were opened, tubes flooded, and gauges set. The actual firing would take place in the Combat Center forward.

"Conn, sonar: More hatches popping, Captain!"

Now RC earned his money: He had to decide whether to wait for a launch, or shoot based on the obvious threat-intent of opening missile hatches. Given the proximity of the six enemy boats to his country's coastline, and the fact that the missiles could all carry nuclear warheads, his choice was easy. "Match bearings—fire tubes One and Three!" Less than two seconds later, the boat rocked a bit as the powerful compressed air system ejected the first torpedo, and then three seconds later the second torpedo followed the first. The best heavy torpedoes in the world were underway, utilizing their own motors to drive the nearly two-ton fish through the water at more than 60 knots.

Aboard the PLAN 94A *Bohai*

Senior Captain Loh Sang Jun, PLAN, was not surprised when he heard the frantic shout of his chief sonar man warning of enemy torpedoes in the water. He had been similarly warned just seconds before that the enemy sub had opened its torpedo doors as soon as the *Bohai* raised its first missile hatch. Loh was prepared to die, but hated the same fate for his good and mostly young crew. But his duty was clear: Any of the six missile boats could be targeted, but it was the *Bohai* that would take heat off the others.

"Fire One!" he commanded, and the boat rocked in a different way than the enemy boat had. The ballistic missile was forcefully ejected from its vertical tube, and powered through a few feet of water until it burst out into the clean late-morning air. After a moment's seeming hesitation in mid-air, the solid fuel motor ignited as designed, and the large missile quickly roared into space. Its target was a small deck aircraft carrier under construction at Ingalls Shipbuilding in Pascagoula, Mississippi.

"Fire Two!" he commanded, feeling lucky that he could get this one away, too. Again, the boat rocked satisfactorily—any more launches were now considered bonus.

"Fire Three!" he commanded, and the next giant missile was ejected from its tube.

"Fire Four," he commanded, barely able to contain his amazement that he was still alive but, before that missile cleared its tube, the end came: The first of the *California's* Mark 48s impacted the hull amidships and the *Bohai* was blown in half. The fourth missile had not yet armed, but it was loaded with volatile propellant that exploded sympathetically. The second Mark 48 had been superfluous, but it detonated just feet from the slowly turning propeller. At best, it mercifully killed any sailors who survived the first explosions. The rest of the sub was now just pieces, drifting slowly to the bottom with the bodies of its crew.

All the Jin Class subs were now launching missiles as fast as they could. But the northernmost 94A came to the same destructive end as their sister: *Shanghai* exploded and sank with all hands when the *Connecticut's* first Mark 48 hit it just aft of the sail. The second torpedo struck four seconds later just aft of the forward torpedo room, and killed those few sailors still alive in the flooding spaces. The pieces of both boats took several minutes to sink to the ocean floor thousands of feet below. Now they were the scattered remnants of previously lethal fighting machines, but had instantly become war graves—hopefully left there to be respected and undisturbed for as long as sailors cruised the seas.

The remaining four boats launched all their missiles and turned for home—quickly accelerating to their maximum sustainable speeds. The two U.S. attack boats also turned and took up the chase at sustainable full power. The ChiCom subs headed for a pair of their own attack boats that had arrived on station a day earlier, so the only question was whether the faster American subs could overtake the fleeing "Boomers" before the rendezvous, about 200 miles west. Behind the six racing submarines, 54 missiles were now steaking along their pre-programed parabolas toward nine targets in the continental United States.

Chapter 30

Estate of GS Han (H-Hour)

Han and the others watched with fascination as General Bao switched the main screen's view from San Francisco to Honolulu, where *Dragon's Tail* had just docked. Tall cranes were visible alongside the right-hand side of the ship, and the audience could almost feel the gentle bump as another of their Dragons snuggled against the long, sturdy-looking cement quay. She'd docked against the first right-hand space at the entrance to the commercial port—one of only two spaces that could accommodate *Tail's* 1,000-foot length and incredible bulk. From the camera's elevated vantage point at the top of the bridge, they could see the huge vehicle ramps settling onto the quay, and the first of the men sliding down their own ramps similar in construction and concept to those in playgrounds everywhere. On the left-hand side of the screen, a large explosion in the middle distance suddenly caught everyone by surprise, then others followed rapidly, one after another. Suddenly, however, a secondary camera inside the bridge showed men fighting. What on earth? Han thought, staring incredulously at the screen. Suddenly a man ran out of the space and onto the bridge wing closest to the dock. And the man was waving a gun!

Lao Cai, Vietnam, on the Chinese side of the Hong River Bridge December 8th, 01:00 Hours (same time)

PLA Lieutenant Kee Tao Chung and Sergeant First Class Ting Sang had earlier crept with their sappers down the hill to a point where they could take up positions behind a low berm, crouching there until the attack began. It was just 50 meters from their side of the bridge, and both men, in their very different ways, were feeling the weight of their mission. They were the pointy end of a very large spear: Behind them, and stretching for several kilometers up over the hills and down through the valleys on the Chinese side of the border, waited (in order) the rest of their Sapper Platoon, then Company A, still hidden in the trees on the hillside immediately behind them, then 10th Battalion at the top of the first ridge, and the rest of the 139th Mechanized Infantry Division descending in their echelons down the far slope and into the darkness. Even farther north, the rest of the 72nd Combined Corps waited for their orders, hoping the invasion would proceed quickly.

Kee looked around and gave a fist pump to his men crouched in the darkness—helmeted figures just visible in the faint light cast by the street and bridge lights ahead. He could see some nervous grins—young men on the verge of glory—or at least glorious deaths, and he had little hope they'd all see the dawn. He had learned over the last few months that some were secret followers of the Christian cult, but he wasn't a political officer, and he never begrudged a man his religious beliefs—so long as he was an excellent trooper. His sappers were a tight-knit unit, and he believed they'd fight as one.

As the seconds ticked down to H-Hour, Kee didn't need to glance at the luminous dial of his military issue watch: They would all hear the distinctive sound of the first artillery shells arching overhead and landing on the scouted positions of the nearest Vietnamese army camps. There were two of them on far side of the small city of Lao Cai and, as those shells began to destroy the enemy soldiers, he would blow his whistle and lead the charge across the bridge. There! He heard the low rumble of the cannons firing in the distance, and could almost see the artillerymen pulling the lanyards. Over his position arched the shells but, before the first one landed, all hell broke loose on the Vietnamese side:

A well-camouflaged line of berms on the far side of the river had been concealing lines of waiting soldiers, and they popped up and opened fire with their AK-47s and light machine guns. At the same time, dozens of mortar men began lobbing rounds across to the Chinese side of the river and, farther back in the hills and valleys, artillery cannons opened up with a rolling thunder that sent chills down the backs of Kee's men as they dove for the ground.

The noise was deafening, and a shock to Kee and his sappers who'd been expecting a one-sided battle. "Let's go, men!" he shouted in defiance of his fear, and two years of hard training produced its own reward: His men jumped to their feet and followed him over the berm. They sprinted toward the bridge, but their bravery was met by withering small arms fire from the two guard posts at the far end of the span. Many of Kee's men were cut down, and the survivors were forced to dive for cover and then low-crawl across the road and seek shelter behind a waist-high cement barrier lining the approach.

The whole timetable was thrown out the window, and the entire advance backed up. Kee and the rest of the PLA chain of command didn't know that the Vietnamese general staff had been suspicious of the creeping Chinese ground forces, and their spotting cameras, hidden motion sensors, silent high-flying drones and, above all, human intelligence assets, had warned them that something big was afoot. Rather than being caught by surprise, they alerted the local regimental commanders who'd quietly moved troops forward. For 48 hours, armored and infantry divisions farther back were gassed and ready to go, and were fully manned by active duty personnel. Quiet alerts had also been sent out to reserve forces, too, and a general call-up could be enacted quickly if the PLA attacked. Hanoi estimated that a new ground war was coming soon, and cautioned their border forces to appear as normal as possible—but to keep a sharp eye out for enemy agents or infiltrating soldiers. It had been a nerve-wracking cat-and-mouse game, played by two experts who'd been at each other's throats for 3,000 years.

Numerous MSS agents and PLA infiltrators had indeed been caught and interrogated, and networks were being rolled up and jailed. Vietnamese intelligence units that specialized in Chinese dialects used the Chinese agents' information to confuse and placate the cadres on the north side of the river. The end result was a general failure by the ChiCom intelligence community to notify their chain of command that their surprise attack had been detected.

Kee hadn't dashed five steps before he hit the ground and, when he reached the cement barrier, he quickly peeked his head up and saw, to his shock, that the entire ridge on the far side of the small town was covered with a thousand sparkling lights. Instinctively, he knew they'd been had: His unit was being raked by continuous volleys of light machine gun fire from the sandbagged pillboxes guarding the far side of the bridge and its approaches, and obviously the Vietnamese had been alerted that they were coming. Heavy machine guns were thumping everywhere, too, and a steady stream of green tracers tore up the hills behind him, and he could hear the sickening screams of the wounded.

Kee and his sappers were well and fairly pinned down. He looked around, trying to decide what to do next, and could only confirm that thousands of soldiers were blasting away at each other—some as close as 100 meters—while battery and counter-battery fire destroyed buildings, equipment, forests, and people in ever-greater numbers. Light and heavy mortars added to the general din, and soon the accumulating dust was so bad that he could barely make out the far bank, let alone the buildings of the small city. He had been in practice maneuvers many times—including live fire exercises—but he never imagined that the noise of a full-on pitched battle between regiment-sized combined arms units would be so intense. Within three minutes of the first shot being fired, the four-kilometer-wide valley had become an amphitheater of noise.

Kee's men had been mowed down as they scrambled over the berm and across the street, and he noted that several brave warriors were risking their lives to crawl out and drag their wounded comrades to safety. Heartsick, he took stock and accepted that he hadn't even made it to their end of the bridge! Sergeant Ting had landed next to him, thankfully unhurt, and shouted at the men to return fire. He raised up and loosed a burst from his own assault rifle—blindly firing at nothing in particular. The endless concussions shook the soldiers to the core, but it was time to press on. Kee inched along the wall toward a point where he could peek around the cement barrier down the length of the bridge, and was relieved when his radioman suddenly crawled up with a shouted message. Kee grabbed the offered mic and yelled at his counterpart in the heavy weapons platoon, "I need more fire on the far side of the bridge—get those guard posts first!" He looked around and guessed that 50 percent of his platoon was already dead or dying. Low moans, interspersed by high-pitched screams, emanated from every point on both sides of the river. The war had just begun and already its carnage violated the darkness—hidden from sight but not from hearing.

Missile Warning Center, Peterson Air Force Base, Colorado Headquarters, North American Air Defense Command (same time)

Peterson is the headquarters of the United States Space Force and the NORAD/NORTHCOM Operations Center, plus it hosts several other significant military commands and research units. However, on this cloudy and cold Sunday lunch hour, First Lieutenant Cynthia Drake, USAF, was the person tasked with keeping an eye on the designated missile threat screen for the western half of the United States and Canada. Satellites communicating with computers did everything except raise their arms, so when her flat screen flashed emergency red to indicate an off-shore missile launch, she performed the human act and raised her arm. USAF Brigadier General Cecil Adams, OIC of the watch, instantly came to her side. "General, satellite confirms multiple submarine missile launches off the coast of Washington, Oregon, and California!"

"Okay, Lieutenant, this is the real thing!" BG Adams confirmed. He was authorized to flip up the clear hard plastic cover that protected the "Alert" button on Cynthia's console, and he depressed it forcefully. This caused the 100 x 80-foot screen above the front stage to instantly display an outline of North America, and the missile tracks were represented as red dotted lines that were already arching toward the West Coast of the continental United States. An air horn simultaneously pulsed three sharp blasts, and an electronic voice proclaimed: "Launch detected—this is no drill." The general wore a headset and keyed the four-star USAF commanding general upstairs: "General Miller, we have multiple submarine missile launches approximately 400 miles off our northwest coast. They have separated into multiple sets of arches—the closest being four groups heading for mid-America targets. A second set is heading for six targets on the East Coast. None are heading toward DC or New York City…"

General Miller came out of his second-floor office and onto his balcony that overlooked the big operations center—looking all the world like an admiral on the bridge of his ship. He surveyed the big screen for a few seconds then depressed a speed-dial button on his console that connected him with the direct line to the National Command Authority (the military term for the President). He heard the correct voice answer seven seconds later and said, "Mr. President, General Miller at NORAD. We have approximately 50 submarine-launched ballistic missiles heading for various targets in the central and eastern United States. They were launched from submarines several hundred miles off the West Coast, and we have about five minutes before the first wave impacts."

President Stilwell had just begun to digest the incredible news relayed by Secretary of State Madrid regarding the Chinese Declaration of War, and he was preparing to rush down to the Situation Room when the red phone rang. His earlier calls with Dan at Homeland Security had hit him hard, and the bad reports from the governors had knocked him down further. His blood pressure didn't have much more capacity to absorb stress, and now this. "What? Did you say ballistic missiles, General? Are they nuclear?" What madness was this? It had to be the Chinese!

"Sir, we do not know, but we can see from our computer-generated calculations that the targets are all military installations—mostly Navy and some Air Force—but none are heading for civilian population areas."

Spence sat back down. His mind was reeling but he forced himself to focus: "Can we shoot them down, General?" Five minutes wasn't much time.

"Sir, the Navy will launch a wave of the RIM-161 Standard Missile 3s that are designed to intercept ballistic missiles, and they will intercept some but probably not all. We are notifying every targeted base and port, and they will have time to launch a few with no warning. It will be the East Coast ships that get their missiles off. I'm sorry to report that some folks in the open will make it to shelters, but most won't."

"I'm afraid I'm aware of context for this attack, General: The mainland Chinese just declared war on us—guess they wanted to give us a short heads-up. Homeland Security called the Pentagon, but I haven't spoken with Admiral Simms yet."

"Mr. President, I can see on my screen that Admiral Simms is speaking to my deputy, and I'll follow up with him ASAP. We're automatically notifying the entire command structure about the missiles; and we'll get some of them for sure."

"I just remembered something, General: The Chinese ambassador mentioned specifically that they would not employ nuclear weapons first. Guess we'll know for sure in a very few minutes…"

"Yes, Mr. President—and we'll take their promise for what it's worth; I hope it's true. Oh, wait one, Sir…Okay, I have just received a message: We had two attack subs shadowing the six Chinese missile boats that fired the missiles. Our guys have already sunk two of the enemy boats, but all six got at least some of their birds away. We knew the ChiComs were loitering in open ocean, but our subs couldn't make pro-active moves earlier."

"Understood, General, and I agree. Now I have to issue an order: There will be no retaliatory missile strikes of any kind against the Chinese mainland until I confer with the Joint Chiefs and key Cabinet secretaries. But engage our anti-satellite defense system immediately and destroy as much of their space-based military infrastructure as you can. I'm sure they'll attack ours if they have that capability. Please call the Situation Room when you have updates." The general acknowledged the President's order, and they disconnected. Spence then raced toward the elevators with his Secret Service agents leading the way.

While a moving ship at sea, like an aircraft carrier going 30 knots and turning, is a challenging targeting problem for in-bound ballistic missiles—ships at anchor, planes parked on runways, or huge buildings—are just a computer's firing solution removed from easy destruction. The USS *Bougainville*, the LHA (small-deck carrier) under construction at the Ingalls Shipyard in Pascagoula, Mississippi, was the first such stationary target destroyed. The descending missile hit her dead center on the flight deck, just forward of the "Island" superstructure, and the explosion ripped down through several decks, melted steel beams and miles of electrical cables, and blew rivets out of joints and welds out of alignment. It also killed 24 civilian workers and injured 15 more. The reason for the high death-to-injury ratio was the fact that the 24 workers—a cross-section of the local union members who were building the ship—had gathered at the beginning of their one o'clock shift to remember a colleague killed in a freak accident two days before. The missile impacted one deck above their employee-led gathering and they all died instantly.

Peterson Air Force Base

Lieutenant Drake noted from her console screen that the first impact in Mississippi indicated a conventional munition, and she fired the data off to all relevant commands. Everyone in the Missile Warning Center were working on consoles rapidly computing targeting data, and massive amounts were being forwarded to the naval ships in and near the East Coast bases.

She and her colleagues watched as part of the 53 missiles still flying descended on the mid-continent's two active duty B-52 bases: Barksdale,

Louisiana, and Minot, North Dakota. She didn't know that sapper teams had already shot holes in those bombers sitting in the open parking areas, and 29 of them were now at least temporarily out of action. But the runways themselves were important, too, and three of the ballistic missiles blew huge craters in the main runway of each base. The damage could be repaired with low-tech engineering, but both bases were out of commission for some days at a minimum—just the time needed to support the Asian portion of Operation Unity.

The most important of the ChiComs three targets was Whiteman Air Force Base in Nebraska, home of the B-2 Spirit bombers. Eight missiles were dedicated to the hardened shelters where the stealth bombers were kept, and three others landed on the main runway. The shelters were sturdy, but not sturdy enough to protect the planes against direct ballistic missile hits. Eight Spirits were damaged enough to keep them out of action for months. Two of the invaluable bombers had been sitting in the open, and they were holed by sappers with .50 caliber rifles using armor-piercing bullets. PLA snipers had infiltrated onto adjacent farmlands a mile away, but close enough to get clear shots at America's frontline bombers. The cockpit and engine areas were targeted by the snipers, and the damage was enough to keep them grounded for between ten days and two weeks. All three bases were fully locked down when the distant missiles arrived, but there was nothing they could have done to protect the precious planes. The air police were actively engaging the snipers, and running fire-fights broke out near each of the three bases. But the damage had been done.

The rest of the missiles had longer trajectories, and gradually honed in on their six East Coast naval targets. No civilian leader's homes or American landmarks were on the list: General Bao and Professor Dang believed them to be much less important, and GS Han had specifically forbidden any such attacks. Personally, he didn't want his homes or the country's sacred sites targeted by acts of revenge. Bao and Dang focused on six targets: The Groton, Connecticut Submarine Base, and the General Dynamics Electric Boat shipyard; the Norfolk, Virginia Naval Base, and the nearby Newport News shipbuilding facility; the ballistic missile-carrying "Boomer" submarine fleet in Kings Bay,

Georgia; and Naval Station Mayport in Florida. These six targets contained most of the Atlantic seaboard's inventory of big-deck and small-deck carriers, plus attack and boomer submarines. Other vessels were secondary targets, and many of those were destroyed, too.

Off the Atlantic Seaboard

During the previous week, six older, moderate-sized Chinese-flagged veterans of the international cargo trade put into the PRC's new port facilities in Jamaica-Freeport. Part of the Belt and Road Initiative, this port was just one of eight the CCP had negotiated in the Caribbean region. The six merchies refueled, but did not offload any cargo. Instead, they had used the cover of darkness and strict security to load hundreds of large wooden crates containing "tractors." When their holds were filled, they departed for ports along the American Atlantic coast. The first to refuel and depart was heading for New England, while the others headed for ports further south. Their actual cargo was heavily armed drones and the technicians to guide them.

At a carefully calculated pre-determined time, all six merchies were about 25 miles off shore from their target ports. There were a few American and international ships and boats around, and two attack submarines were on station a few hundred miles farther into the Atlantic Ocean, but no one paid the ordinary ships any mind. Therefore unopposed, they launched their drones precisely at the designated time, and guided them so well that they overwhelmed the destroyers and cruisers trying to launch missiles at the incoming SLBMs.

These U.S. Navy ships had all received the emergency messages, and all had time to focus their incredibly powerful tracking radars on the incoming missiles. However, just before they could get their first SM-3 anti-ballistic missiles airborne, they were overwhelmed with clouds of bumble bee-sized drones that flew into every opening on every ship. Each had the explosive power of a rifle bullet, and they raised havoc with every radar, antennae, missile launcher and exposed crewman, and more than 200 SM-3 and RAM missiles exploded in their launchers. The American Navy was in the early stages of installing laser weapons on its ships, but they were not yet produced in adequate quantity, nor mounted in useful numbers. A minute after the drone swarms destroyed the ships' ability to defend themselves or the precious carriers and submarines, the big SLBMs began to arrive.

The White House Situation Room, 14:15 Hours

Senior members of government had been hustling to the White House since they got the word, and many arrived in the SR panting after dashing across parking lots and down hallways. All were feeling the effects of acute stress. The afternoon was quickly turning into one of the darkest in American history, and they all knew their decisions and actions over the next few hours would be scrutinized for as long as there was a United States.

The first thing everyone noticed was the big screen on the side wall—subdivided into four quarters with raging fires visible on all four. The Houston refinery fire was still spewing smoke miles into the quiet winter air, but the forest fires shown on the other screens were being overflown by tankers showering red retardant to douse the flames. It was raining in the west and the ground teams racing to the scenes viewed the weather as a gift from God.

Ten different conversations filled the room as the new arrivals streamed in, but everyone hushed when the President disconnected his call with the premier of Japan. "Okay, everyone, here is what I know: Just after 1:30 local time, Ambassador Bang delivered a formal Declaration of War from the PRC. It was in the name of the Politburo. Jack Madrid received the delegation in his office per an appointment made on Friday, so it's official in every way. Of great importance, the ambassador declared the PRC's intent is to keep the war conventional, and that they were committed to avoiding the first use of nuclear weapons. Take that for what it's worth but, in this evolving nightmare, I'll hope for the best. It also shows a high degree of confidence on their part, and that they have been planning this for some time.

"The missile strikes across the lower 48 so far bear this out. Baker confirms that he sent the war announcement to every U.S. and Allied command—and the Operations Center at NORAD has been tracking those inbound missiles from the first seconds they were fired. I've been in discussions with leaders of Japan, Australia, Taiwan, and Vietnam, and will connect with the other relevant world leaders as soon as possible. Jack has spoken with his counterparts in

Canada and Mexico, and with several European friends. I'll speak with the Indian prime minister when his call comes through, but our ambassador there—as well as in every embassy in the world—has been informed. All of our Asian friends are under attack, and are fighting for their lives.

"The ChiComs gave us less than 30 minutes before the commencement of hostilities so we did the best we could, but we have to assume that the previous chaos across our heartland was part of their larger plan—though they didn't state that in their official documents. As such, the more than 1,500 attacks were unprovoked, conducted without warning, and hundreds of people were dead before we received the official notice. I expect our entire nation, as well as the balance of the free world, will be outraged—their so-called before-the-event declaration of war notwithstanding. I have spoken with the Senate majority leader and he's instituted their notification system, as has the Speaker of the House. They will join us when they get their own institutions organized. Many in Congress may opt for transportation to the big bunker, but those details will come later. Knee Cap is standing by, but I'm staying here for now.

"PRC submarines launched a salvo of some 50 missiles off the West Coast, and the first of them hit three of our Midwest bomber bases and the shipyard in Pascagoula. The rest targeted our ships in our East Coast naval bases. As promised in their declaration, the missiles carried conventional warheads only. And, regarding our first response, Space Command initiated our "Spotlight" anti-satellite offensive, and we can assume that the first space war is under way. Okay, that's what I know. Comments?"

Just then Jack Madrid arrived with a senior aide, and Dan Robinson and his deputy followed in trail. They quickly found their usual seats, and the Secretary of State asked to be recognized. "Mr. President, Ambassador Bang is alive, thanks to the quick ministrations of our staff doctor. He is on his way to Walter Reed Hospital and his chief of mission has been informed. We will escort his wife to the hospital with their staff doctor as soon as they are ready. His delegation was escorted back to their embassy, and the building is surrounded by DSS agents to ward off any angry protestors that may gather as the facts come to light. I spoke with Ambassador Gantry in Beijing, but he says the city is quiet as a mouse, and he assumes, as I do, that they will treat all of our diplomats and their families with kid gloves. Visiting tourists and scholars will no doubt be detained, but this should be temporary and I don't think they will be harmed in any way. That's all I have."

"Okay, good. All you can do for now."

Baker Halsey spoke next. "Mr. President, our two carrier groups centered around the *Nimitz* and the *Reagan* are still on course to rendezvous north and west of Taiwan, but it will be at least a day before they hook up. When they do, they will be a significant force, and well-positioned for operations in defense of Taiwan. They are protected by their own aircraft, screening vessels, and submarines, but they are vulnerable to attack from those damnable 'carrier-killer' ballistic missiles that hit our Atlantic bases—though they do carry significant numbers of SM3's that are designed to intercept them. They also have CIWS Gatling guns and SeaRAM missiles to defend against sea-skimming anti-ship missiles, but large numbers could overwhelm these systems, too. And there is the threat of their 80 submarines, many of whose precise locations are not known. Around the world, all commands are recalling their personnel to their units, but it will take time to get the whole military on a wartime footing. I heard you mention Space Command, and it is fortuitous that we implemented our Spotlight program when we did. I've already been notified that our new attack satellites are performing as designed: They are maneuvering as designed and getting kill shots on the ChiCom birds."

"Excellent! Looks like today is the pay-off for the X-37B program—it turned out to be gold!" The President was referring to the secret reusable space vehicle that had been the subject of much speculation in the media and scientific communities for years. The nature of its DoD mission required as much secrecy as any program in U.S. military history, but it had been placing small highly maneuverable satellites in orbit near every threatening foreign satellite, and each U.S. "kill-sat" had lethal laser guns that could be fired by Space Command from the ground. All modern countries used satellites for targeting and to guide their long-range munitions, so knocking out these vital systems had become a priority for every high-tech military on Earth.

Spence then turned to the Chairman of the Joint Chiefs of Staff and issued his first order of the war: "Admiral Simms, please give Space Command our gratitude for a job well done!"

"Thank you, Mr. President. I'll let them know. We learned in the first few minutes of the war that they had some offensive capability, too, but it looks like we more than held our own in the first battle in space." The 40-year Navy veteran was grateful: He'd been pushing the idea of arming satellites for decades. *How lucky we were to have consecutive good presidents who understood the looming threat!* He'd been thankful to serve under decisive commanders-in-chief.

Dan Robinson spoke next. "Mr. President, we have arrested three sets of Chinese agents fleeing the scene of earlier attacks, and an additional five teams of agents were killed fighting it out with various law enforcement agencies. The air police also killed several snipers who'd shot at our bombers. Various agencies are hunting for other perpetrators across the country, but it is clear that we are dealing with PRC military personnel or highly trained spies. None of those arrested are talking, but their identity makes it clear that they are a diversion. And one more thing: I admit I dropped the ball on those so-called Dragon merchant ships—they are part of this, too—they are not merchies, but extremely large assault ships."

Chapter 31

Aboard *Dragon's Tail*
Honolulu Port, 07:45 Hours

For the last half hour, *Tail* had been under the control of an experienced harbor pilot named Don Yamaguchi—a fourth-generation Japanese-American whose grandfather had served in the fabled 442nd Regimental Combat Team in World War II. That unit had given fits to the German and Italian armies in Europe, and returned home as the most-decorated unit of its size in American military history. Don had enjoyed stories from this living hero growing up—though the senior citizen preferred to share stories from the family's ancestral history rather than delve too deeply into his wartime experiences. By the time Don was in high school, he stopped asking because he figured Grandpa had experienced some pretty bad stuff.

Don had been born and raised in nearby Pearl City, and loved everything about the ocean: Fishing, snorkeling, surfing and, when he reached his teenage years, the girls that flocked to the beach. With such a background, it was natural after high school to seek a life at sea. He was accepted into the United States Merchant Marine Academy and, after graduation, served on commercial ships in various capacities for 20 years. He was away more than he wanted, but the professional satisfaction was wonderful, and his wife was as supportive as anyone could be. One day, however, he received the terrible news that she had contracted MS—necessitating his resignation from his company. Nevertheless, it proved a blessing as he quickly transitioned to harbor pilot and was home with her and their teenage kids every day. That was 15 years ago and, since starting his second profession, he'd guided hundreds of commercial ships into the historic Hawaiian port that he'd known all his life. He'd had the responsibility of piloting several of the newest generation of Post-Panama Max vessels—similar in size and maneuverability to the Chinese one he was bringing in today, and they were always challenging, to say the least.

Don admitted that *Dragon's Tail* was a real beauty—even if he didn't like the Chinese maritime officers who commanded her. There were four of them on the bridge today, two senior officers and two junior ones—plus four enlisted sailors. He thought their uniforms looked a little more on the military side than the typical merchant marine variety he was used to, but he was too busy for anything but a cursory glance. And, as much as he tried to like them, these mainland officers had so far proven quite typical of those he'd encountered since he'd become a regular pilot: They exuded a veneer of politeness, but underneath he got the impression that they looked down on most everyone. But at least this group was not as arrogant and brusque as some he'd encountered, and there was irony in this: Don had more years and miles under his belt then most of the captains he advised, and he didn't appreciate being dissed by lesser lights. He just sighed in resignation; he'd be done with this particular group soon and would move back outside the harbor to meet the Indonesian freighter that was due in next. He knew that captain personally, and the man was a jovial fellow who always had a funny story or quip.

But first things first. Don had to ensure that this big lady didn't damage herself or the quay; he and the other harbor professionals were dedicated, and they protected everyone with equal skill. He spoke constantly on his walkie-talkie—giving a series of gentle instructions to the three harbor tugs nudging the huge ship against the sturdy hard rubber 'barrels' hanging down from a hundred cleats on the near edge of the quay.

As soon as they bumped the quay, he was surprised to see three huge ramps slide laterally from the starboard side of the ship and lower their big "feet" onto the cement. He'd never seen standard container ships with heavy duty vehicle ramps—similar in design to the car carriers the Japanese and Koreans used to transport their multitude of Asian-built cars around the world. The ramps were evenly spaced along the hull, and Don wondered what kind of cars they had in the holds. He hadn't noticed any on the manifest but it didn't matter to him; he had to make a notation on his paperwork and looked down at his notes.

He glanced at his wrist watch and saw that the time was significant: He dredged up from somewhere that 07:53 was the exact minute when the

Imperial Japanese Navy commenced their famous attack on the airfields and ships around Pearl Harbor. The big navy base was still there, located just five miles west of his present location on the southern edge of Oahu Island, and today thousands of people had gathered there to remember the sacrifices of all concerned. Don was a history buff and had wondered, growing up, what it must have been like for both sides in that battle that committed America to World War II. He loved visiting the historical sites around the area and had taken his kids to most of them.

Don returned to the present, and spoke into his radio, "Secure all lines—ship is fully docked. Tug masters release and return to base." He was pleased: He'd shown these cocky foreigners what a perfect docking sequence looked like. Now it was up to the crew and local stevedores to unload whatever they'd brought to American consumers. The union longshoremen here were outstanding, and they could really move an amazing tonnage when they got going. He turned to hand the captain a copy of the docking certificate and was shocked to be facing the business end of a pistol aimed directly at his head.

"Good job, Pilot," said the officer brandishing the pistol. He was dressed in camouflage fatigues and Don hadn't noticed his arrival. Two enlisted men were with him, holding assault rifles at port arms. "Now sit down against the bulkhead and keep quiet. The People's Marines will take it from here…"

The officer spoke with a smirk and this simple discourteous act, more than the threat itself, caused Don to lose it. His father had passed along traditional Japanese jiu-jitsu training—that his dad had learned from his father—their own family's version of what Pat Morita's character had passed along to his young disciple in the movie *Karate Kid*. With surprising speed that belied his middle years and salt and pepper beard, Don knocked the weapon out of the marine's hand and sent it clattering across the thinly coated steel deck. They both lunged for it but Don's strike had given him downward momentum and made him a bit quicker. He grabbed the pistol in a fluid roll and fired a snap shot into the man's thigh. The marine officer howled in pain and screamed at the two enlisted men who were staring, open-mouthed, as their officer wrestled with the suddenly violent civilian. But his screams startled them into action and they both loosed deafening three-shot bursts toward the disobedient harbor pilot. The shots sounded like cannons in the enclosed bridge and the other men ducked and hit the deck as the bullets ricocheted off the bulkheads and broke some of the windows.

Don wasn't hit by either blast, but he couldn't give them another chance, so he reflexively leveled the pistol and shot both soldiers center mass. They were knocked backward , but the jolt caused one of them to fire a single round. That bullet also ricocheted harmlessly without hitting anyone—a near miracle considering the number of people and the size of the enclosed space.

The two senior officers present were obviously shocked by the unexpected turn of events, and had ducked, but the two younger officers and the sailors had the presence of mind to dive for cover, and then to scramble behind the chart table in the middle of the room. A momentary impasse resulted and Don's mind raced for a way to escape.

Self-preservation won the day; Don grabbed the nearest assault rifle abandoned by the wounded guards, and yelled at the captain to have everyone move to the portside corner of the bridge. The captain barked an order in Mandarin and the four sailors grabbed the three gravely wounded men and dragged them to the corner. Then Don heard shouts and footsteps coming up the interior ladder a few paces away, and knew he had to act fast. He had no chance of winning a fire-fight with whomever he was dealing with—either military professionals, which didn't make any sense—or more likely pirates of some kind. But that begged another incomprehensible question: What would either hope to gain docked in Honolulu's vast container port? He realized he had to warn the civilians on the dock because the heavy glass and steel bridge would have muffled the shots from outside ears. Don jumped to his feet and raced out the door and onto the starboard (quay-side) bridge wing. Outside, everything was calm but, when he looked down, he saw everyone below just staring at the incredible sight of a row of giant tanks coming down the lowermost ramp. Other vehicles and dozens of soldiers were descending, too.

Don kept one eye on the men inside while he leaned over the chest-high railing to raise the alarm. To his dismay, the several dozen stevedores seemed frozen in place. Don raised his newly acquired assault rifle straight up and fired off two three-round bursts. The terrible noise had the desired effect and the workers scattered in sheer panic.

Dockside

As the dramatic events unfolded on the ship below, Tom Bonaventure was sitting in the cupola of his 15-story dockside crane, sipping coffee and enjoying the best view in Honolulu Harbor. He always arrived earlier than his shift demanded, allowing himself a few minutes solace before his busy day began. He was killing time this morning watching the big merchie dock, and she was definitely worth getting up for. As he enjoyed her immense size and her brilliant red-and-gold livery, he popped the last of his "potato puppies" in his mouth—his usual fast-food treat picked up on the way to work. He munched happily and enjoyed his bird's eye view over Honolulu's commercial harbor toward Pearl Harbor to the west. He knew Vice President Mason and many other dignitaries were there for the USS *Arizona* Memorial ceremony, and though he couldn't see the dignified white building that hovered over the ship's grave, he knew she still lay where she'd sunk more than 70 years before. However, he could clearly see the superstructure of the USS *Missouri* rising majestically in the early morning light, and the *Arizona* was just a few yards farther along Ford Island.

The special day put him in a reflective mood, and he thought about his grandfather, also "Tom," who had fought in the Pacific Theater as a soldier—volunteering for the Army rather than the Marines. He was an artilleryman and was fortunate to have survived four island campaigns without a scratch. No heroism and no medals, other than the ones everyone received, but he'd only wanted to contribute to the victory and never forget his friends that died. He was proud of his Good Conduct discharge, and its framed certificate still hung in his den. He married his high school sweetheart who'd promised to wait for him, and they wasted no time starting one of the "Baby Boomer" families. Their first-born son "Tom Junior" also married a local girl, and they had "Tom the Third," which provided never-ending family humor. But then it happened: He and his wife Tammy had two daughters. Oh well…two angels were better than many sons. In fact, Grandmother Bonaventure commented after the first girl came along, "About darn time!"

As Tom III waited for his foreman to give him the signal to lower his gantry hooks and latch onto the highest container of the stack, something curious caught his eye: Three huge ramps had been deploying from the side of the ship as she got close to the dock, and these settled onto the quay between the cranes as soon as she stopped. Then, to his amazement, three more narrow ramps that looked like slides from a children's playground protruded from the main deck level, and they also lowered to the dock. Doors then opened from the lowest level of the stacks, and soldiers poured out and began sliding down the three small ramps to the quay. Soldiers! What was going on? They had backpacks, and held assault rifles across their chests, and Tom craned his neck and watched them hit the cement, spring to their feet, and fan out everywhere like ants! Next, tanks and other vehicles rumbled down the heavier ramps. *Was this some kind of military drill?* No one had told him about it. Maybe it was part of the Pearl Harbor Day celebrations?

Aboard *Dragon's Tail*

Captain Ho had stood his ground on the port bridge wing when the shooting broke out inside—shocked that one middle-aged harbor pilot had taken over the whole space. But then his attention was diverted to the west when loud explosions erupted at Pearl Harbor, followed by wailing sirens. His air wing had started its attack, and he could just make out the squat forms of the mother-drone formations circling above the harbor. The bigger ones looked like a large flock of birds, but he could not see the tiny drones from this far away. He glanced down at his watch and noted the time: It was 07:55 so they'd almost made it—just five minutes early. He had been briefed before departure that their ambassador in Washington, DC was to present the official declaration of war 30 minutes before H-Hour, and he hoped they'd fulfilled their part of the master plan. Ignoring the shooting inside the bridge, he hit a speed dial number on the bridge wing phone, and spoke to the commanding general down in the CIC. "Sir, I have visual confirmation that the attack has begun. Good luck to your units, and glory to our motherland!"

In his command chair inside the fairly dark room, Major General Shi Zouming, the mission commander, was relieved and elated at the same time. He reached up and toggled a switch that sent three short blasts from a klaxon horn echoing throughout the ship—his encouraging signal to the dozens of young airmen who were piloting the drones, and to his marines just beginning their assault. The airmen had already released the clouds of mini-drones over several principal target areas, and were also dropping lethal bombs onto dozens of exposed decks. Every ship and submarine in the harbor was on the target list, and he was sure they'd be successful against a fleet of sitting ducks. Within five minutes, the selected camera feeds confirmed that every military vessel in the harbor had received at least one hit—and that every exposed plane or helicopter had been suffocated by a cloud of mini-drones. Imagine it, he almost laughed to himself, I am destroying America's great Pacific Fleet with no more than a company-sized unit of kids with joysticks!

As the general gloated below decks, Don was still on the starboard bridge wing. He had done his duty by warning the dock workers below, so now he had to focus on his own survival. He glanced back inside the bridge and spotted two soldiers pop their heads and guns above the ladder and open fire. Rounds poured out the door and ricocheted off the wing's steel grating and hand rails, but Don was unharmed and poked his gun around the doorway and loosed a few shots of his own. He knew it was time to bail: He had only a few rounds left in the large banana clip that protruded from his appropriated assault rifle, and he couldn't wait for help to arrive. Just then a grenade clattered onto the wing near his feet and, in pure instinctive panic, he grabbed it and lobbed it back inside. He followed this with three rapid-fire shots from his weapon—he'd flipped his selector to "single-shot" to preserve ammo—then ducked back just before the thing exploded inside with a tremendous flash, ear-splitting bang, and the distinctive whine of a hundred ricochets banging off bulkheads, flying out the door, and shattering windows.

Accepting that this was his last chance to retreat, he jumped up, slung the rifle over his neck and shoulder, and frantically bounded the two yards to the back of the bridge wing where the top of a ladder protruded above the railing. He clambered over its curved handles and slid down the ladder without using the rungs—just like he'd seen in the movies—and hit the main deck between the bridge superstructure and the container stack behind him. The impact caused him to wince in pain as his right ankle turned over, but he couldn't give in. He hobbled to the edge of the stack and peeked around its corner. Suddenly, several soldiers raced around the harbor side of the bridge and opened up with multiple automatic weapons, but Don was close enough to dive around the corner and landed at the feet of dozens of soldiers queuing for their turn to slide down to the quay. He painfully got to his feet and stumbled, mostly on one leg, toward the stern of the ship and the crowd of startled men just got out of his way.

As he raced through soldiers parting like the Red Sea, he realized the stacks were a ruse—just bulkheads with open doors—and, as he wove his way along, he heard shouting behind him and ducked into the nearest space. Everyone continued to get out of his way, and he guessed, because he was also Asian, that they figured he was a compatriot and part of their assault.

These are not pirates—they're Chinese soldiers! He was shocked on many levels, but had to keep going. He raced through a maze of corridors as he continued to work his way aft, and finally came to a huge open door and ducked inside. He received another shock as he entered a cavernous space and instantly realized it was an aircraft hangar. He was nearly deafened by the high-pitched whines from several Volkswagen-sized drones that were warming their circle of powerful, top-mounted engines. About 20 yards away, some were rising toward the open ceiling. Remarkably, the dozens of technicians working everywhere ignored him as he crossed to the far side of the ship, and his chief worry shifted to being chopped to bits by the six spinning blades on each drone. Full daylight illuminated the space and, as he ran for a doorway on the far side of the space, one drone after another lifted straight up and disappeared.

He reached the opposite side of the hangar and stepped onto the main deck's narrow walkway, then dashed along it toward the stern. He was on the harbor side now, and the deck was deserted because all the action was on the inland side. To his right was the channel that separated the main container loading area from Sand Island, but he didn't want to expose himself by jumping into the deserted waterway and swimming for it—estimating that the beckoning back railing offered a much greater chance of escape. He surveyed the area and winced every time a noisy drone launched. They seemed to be heading northeast—he guessed toward the logical target of Marine Corps Base at Kaneohe on the far side of the island. He could see a large barrel-looking container hanging under each of the two stubby wings of the hexagonal drones, and a bomb-looking thing attached to the center. Their six spinning, top-mounted propellers sounded like angry wasps.

Don heard a series of explosions and glanced over toward Pearl Harbor, and was saddened beyond belief: His precious homeland was being attacked again! *Did our leaders not learn anything in the last 70 years?* He reached the stern railing, slipped off his rifle and tossed it away into the harbor, then climbed over and hung on the lowest rung and let himself drop. It was a long way down and Don hit the water hard enough to send a searing jolt of pain up his injured leg, but he'd jumped off higher rocks as a teen, showing off at various island diving spots, and still remembered how to tighten his gut to preserve some air. Without surfacing, he swam toward the dock, knowing he was safe from the now-motionless propellers, and surfaced when he reached the back corner of the ship.

He looked back toward the channel, and spotted the harbor tugs that were now nearly to the end of Sand Island. Apparently, they hadn't drawn the ire of soldiers, and were getting away as fast as they could. Treading water, he was under the overhang of the stern, and figured he was safe from firing from above. He hoped his pursuers would not want to risk damaging the propellers or rudder by dropping hand grenades to kill him. He took several deep breaths, ducked under the surface, and then swam underwater until his lungs burned. He surfaced against the quay about 100 yards behind the ship and, not stopping to tempt fate, repeated the process until he had to surface again. He didn't see anyone on the stern that looked threatening, so he rested in the shadow of the large hard rubber bumper that rested against the cement, and clung to the reassuring barnacles of a vertical cement pillar. His lungs were burning, but he was a long way from the ship and apparently forgotten. With no one above paying him any mind either, he decided to press on.

As Don quietly breast-stroked toward the end of the quay, he could hear the sounds of war: Closest was the continual high-pitched whine of the drones heading in various directions. In the intermediate distance were occasional bursts of automatic rifle and machine gun fire. In the far distance, nearly continuous explosions emanated from the direction of the naval anchorage. Columns of smoke towered into the sky, and he dreaded what was happening to the thousands of military personnel and their civilian family members and tourists who'd gathered for the annual Remembrance ceremony. Most troubling of all was a deeper rumble that vibrated through the water, a sound Don had heard before. It was the movement of many heavy vehicles—tanks and armored personnel carriers, which he'd seen in action when he off-loaded the First Armored Division in Saudi Arabia before the ground phase of Desert Storm in early 1991.

Feeling very lucky to be alive, Don stroked away from the chaos until he'd rounded the end of the 1,000-yard dock. There he could climb up the seaweed-covered jumble of large rocks that formed the last breakwater before the main channel, and then low-crawl for a while along the uneven cement chunks until he felt safe enough to rise and stumble along. He dragged his injured leg through the forest of containers waiting for future dispersal, and finally made it to a warehouse area where he could look for a phone. His cellphone had disappeared, and it felt odd to be without constant communication. *So, this is how World War III starts!* He heard several sets of booted feet running toward him and he hid himself behind a door in the first warehouse, feeling the continual vibrations from the explosions in the distance.

Chapter 32

Aboard the USS *Arizona* Memorial (earlier that morning)

Senior dignitaries had been ferried out to the memorial early because there were several speeches scheduled before the official Moment of Silence at 07:53—the generally accepted time when hostilities began. A Navy chief was standing by to ring the honor bell at the precise moment of the attack, and the fleet chaplain would offer a prayer for peace as the haunting tones of Taps drifted away. Vice President Rebecca Jane Mason would then bring greetings from President Stilwell, after which she'd drop a wreath into the still-oily waters above the sunken ship. And, in a show of modern solidarity and hopefulness, the Consul General of Japan would offer condolences from the emperor. It was one of the most solemn ceremonies on the American calendar, and thousands of citizens and international spectators had gathered at vantage points around the harbor. Several hundred were standing near the small footbridge that crossed over to the USS *Bowfin* Memorial, and an equal number waited on the docks of the submarine base where the USS *North Carolina* would soon arrive. The general population knew about the terrorist attacks on the mainland but, because there were none in Hawaii, Alaska, or even the West Coast, the Secret Service reluctantly allowed VP Mason to continue with her plans. The crowd was respectfully quiet yet cautious, and an uneasy mood hung over the harbor's many guests.

Just southwest of the *Arizona* Memorial, the USS *Missouri* rested at anchor on old Battleship Row, now a museum ship that honored all Americans who served in the Pacific theater during World War II. The two historic battleships symbolically represented the beginning and end of America's full participation in the war: The *Arizona* had been sunk on the morning the war began, and the *Missouri* hosted the peace treaty signing the day it ended. Today, the morning was cool and beautiful—signaling to many that God was present—and, indeed, across the spectrum of Oahu's military chapels and civilian churches, services had already begun. Mothers had roasts slowly cooking as families left for church, and it was just another restful Sunday in paradise.

Becky Peters was standing at the back of the memorial with the dignitaries' supporting staffs—about 20 senior aides who carried speeches and generally helped their respective bosses as necessary. Vice President Mason's COS couldn't attend because her husband was home, self-isolating from ordinary flu, and the VP couldn't take a chance that it was a random bout of Covid-19, so she'd asked her to stay behind. It was a blessing for the deputy COS, Becky, however, because she, her husband, and their two grade-school children could go. Her husband and kids caught a MAC flight a day earlier—*an early Christmas present for sure*—while Becky accompanied the VP on Air Force Two the following day. The kids had been given a reprieve by their school—with the proviso that they return ASAP after the ceremony to "enjoy" the end-of-semester exams.

At the moment, Becky was listening to the four-star admiral who commanded the United States' Indo-Pacific forces, but she startled when she felt her cell phone vibrate in her coat pocket. She hated when this happened because she was caught between ignoring a call that might be important to her boss, and the possibility that she'd disturb a very important and solemn public ceremony for nothing. She decided to ignore it and, thankfully the irritating vibration stopped after five or six awkward seconds. Then it vibrated again once—a sure sign of an incoming text. Figuring it was important if someone reached out twice, she decided to check—but she was going to skin the person texting her if it wasn't life or death. She was behind a line of people and positioned off to one side of the large center wall that bore names of the crew who'd died on the *Arizona*, so she surreptitiously extracted the silenced phone and thumbed the message button. She read: "Becky, this is Tim Duncan from CIA. The large Chinese container ship currently docking at Honolulu Harbor may be carrying offensive weapons and/or troops. It is probably connected with the outbreak of terrorist attacks here on the mainland. Please notify the Secret Service immediately—the VP's life may be in danger!"

Becky's eyes widened and her life flashed before her: If she raised a false alarm, her career was finished. But she knew Tim well as a classmate from

Yale, and they'd kept up over the years. She recognized his number and, from some oblique comments he'd made after getting his doctorate, she suspected that he served in the intelligence community in some capacity. But this text was an overt admission of such and added gravity to his warning. She looked to her right out the open side of the Memorial—over the rows of navy ships parked on the far side of the harbor—and, sure enough, in the distance, she could see a massive container ship docking at the commercial port. She also noticed a submarine gliding her way past the battleship *Missouri* as part of the scheduled "Pass in Review." She was faced with a decision that required selfless moral courage, but Tim had given her cover: Contact the Secret Service Agents. She felt a rush of urgency and acted accordingly.

She scanned back to her left toward the inside of the Memorial, and was startled to lock eyes with one of the female agents on the VP's detail. Wow, these gals must have danger radar! With a simple raising of her eyebrows, the agent asked whether there was a problem. Becky mouthed "Come here," and the agent quietly materialized by her side. Becky placed the phone in the agent's hand, and watched a real professional read and analyze a possible national crisis. The agent raised her sleeve containing her whisper mic and notified the detail.

Instantly, the agents interrupted the ceremony in a dignified way: Becky's message was credible, and it ignited an emergency evacuation of the Vice President and the Japanese Consul General. The admiral's gig started its engine as the American and Japanese protective details surrounded their charges, and the two senior leaders were hustled aboard the 30-foot wooden boat. The admiral and his aide jumped in, too, and the small boat surged toward the open harbor.

However, Chief Petty Officer Larry Jenkins, the U.S. Navy coxswain manning the boat's tiller, calculated that the USS *North Carolina* was too close for them to cross, and yelled at his passengers to hang on as he pushed the boat into a radical right-hand turn. He needed every one of his 15 years piloting small boats to save his passengers from being crushed by the massive submarine's bow—a life-saving move that allowed his little boat to pass between the submarine, which couldn't turn—and the Memorial next to Ford

Island. Something was spooking the Secret Service, and he hoped they could still dash across the harbor after the sub passed.

Then a tremendous explosion made him change his plans again: Everyone else ducked, but he merely flinched. He glanced across the harbor and spotted a swarm of small car-sized aircraft flying over the naval anchorage. These machines (obviously drones in his mind) were dropping bombs that exploded on every open deck. Many heads then popped up and those with sharper eyes could see that the large barrels that hung under the aircraft were spewing clouds of small objects. The bigger aircraft hovered a few hundred feet over the ships and submarines when they dropped their bombs, and the knowledgeable among them correctly guessed that the aircraft were a new kind of drone. In less than 30 seconds, several of the helpless ships were on fire, and the sailors in their white uniforms who'd been "manning the rails" were running in every direction. Thousands of civilians on the far bank began screaming in terror and, en masse, scattered in a hundred different directions to get away from the sudden danger.

The lead Secret Service agent, Manuel Acosta, looked back at the coxswain and shouted, "We'll never get across the harbor!"

CPO Jenkins agreed, and shouted back, "Sir, I recommend your party shelter on the *Missouri*!"

"Agreed!" responded the agent. His team had their automatic weapons drawn and they were ready for most anything, but a passing nuclear sub was a first. However, there was a gap between the bow of the *Missouri* and her dock that was affixed to Ford Island, and the space was wide enough for the small boat to hide there. The admiral yelled his approval and in a few seconds, they passed into the shadow of the *Missouri*'s bow. Agent Acosta spotted a ladder that led up to the pedestrian level of the flat dock, and from there they could run to the foot bridge that passed overhead to the huge warship. He knew the Vice President could easily climb the ladder and, if they could make it across that bridge and into the safety of the battleship before the enemy drones reached them, the thick armor plating would surely save her life. He heard another Secret Service agent call for the VP's helicopter—currently waiting on the other side of the harbor—but it was under attack and delayed for the time being. He knew they would explore all options later, but for now the detail had only one job to do, and they'd willingly sacrifice their lives to save hers.

Everyone on the little boat ducked each time an explosion sent shock waves across the harbor but, after a few more seconds, they gently bumped against the dock under the bridge. The VP was helped onto the metal ladder, and she climbed without assistance. Then they all raced for the stairs.

Becky had not gone with VP Mason, and had laid down on the deck of the memorial as soon as the first explosion rocked the harbor. But she wanted to know what was going on, and snuck a peek through the railing to watch the chaotic scene unfold. Not knowing what else to do, she just waited. The air above the harbor was choked with noisy clouds of what she guessed were tiny drones released from the larger ones, and she could see bombs falling on every ship in sight. A few dozen of the larger drones zoomed overhead on their way to somewhere else, and she guessed they were heading for the other Navy anchorage behind her. It was obvious that the sailors had no defense against these machines—their bombs were landing everywhere and exploding with tremendous force. Fires raged in dozens of places, and a hundred columns of black oily smoke curled into the air above the wounded fleet. Tiny specks in pulsating clouds rammed into the upper structures of every ship and building in the harbor, and she could see sailors in white uniforms running everywhere on burning ships trying to get away. Some were bravely hauling hoses from open doorways to douse the flames, but the tiny specks just cut them down. She figured these were drones, too, but they were too far away to really tell. Many sailors jumped into the harbor to escape certain death, and sadly, she could see many white uniformed bodies lying on decks or floating in the water, apparently dead.

Just then, a tremendous explosion and searing heat rocked the memorial, and Becky and those around her were blown back from a center point where the VP, Consul General, and the admiral had been sitting earlier. She was on the edge of the shock wave, and was stunned but otherwise okay, but those closer to the blast were clearly dead—a horror of mangled bodies and broken chairs. With her ears ringing, Becky still had the presence of mind to remember Mrs. Mason, and rose on one elbow to catch sight of her little boat. There! It was parked against the *Missouri's* dock under the foot bridge that allowed tourists and volunteers to visit the old ship. Her boss was clearly okay and running toward a ladder, with her Secret Service detail covering her dash for safety.

Becky was suddenly overwhelmed with emotion and remembered Tim's call: He had saved the life of the Vice President of the United States! The spot where she had been sitting was directly under the roof area where a bomb (she guessed) had punched through. The deck of America's sacred *Arizona* Memorial was now a smoldering hole surrounded by the dead and dying.

USS *Missouri*

Rebecca was in a state of shock, but not so much that she couldn't function. She was not worried about her own safety, but was terrified that her husband and children were in harm's way across the harbor. That whole side of the channel was just chaotic, with continual explosions everywhere and a mass of screaming people trampling one another. During the brief time between the passing of the submarine and their ducking into the shelter of the old battleship, she had chanced a glimpse at the Navy piers and saw that the ship and submarine decks were a living hell. Fires were everywhere and those helpless young sailors were being massacred. *Someone is going to pay for this, she vowed to herself.*

She clambered up the slippery ladder, protected by her dear agents—and she had the related but seemingly insignificant thought that her choice of sensible shoes that morning was paying off big time. As she reached the stairs with her agents shouting at visitors to clear the way, she had the terrible thought that, though they'd hate to do it, her detail would club or shoot anyone that tried to impede their progress toward the ship. They made it and raced up the stairs as fast as they could. Fortunately, the Japanese consul was keeping up, but she noticed that the admiral and his aide had peeled off once they reached the *Missouri*'s main deck.

"Escort the Vice President to the Number One turret!" the admiral shouted over his shoulder as he sprinted toward the ship's still-working communication center. His intention was to connect with his Indo-Pacific HQ and get into the war.

Agent Acosta obeyed the directive, understanding why in a split-second: The armor on the turret was designed to withstand a direct hit from a battleship's

16-inch shells (perhaps even the 18-inch shells of the Yamato Class battleships) and was, at the moment, the safest place in Pearl Harbor. He quickly guided the VP toward the thick hatch hanging down under the back of the turret, and helped her climb the metal ladder into the surprisingly spacious room. The men strained to pull the heavy hatch up and lock it behind them and, panting, accepted that they were sealed off from the world. Within 20 seconds, VP Mason, the Japanese consul and his aide, plus their eight agents, were all protected by 19.7 inches (500 millimeters) of the best steel ever made. No drone could penetrate that.

Aboard the USS *North Carolina* (SSN-777)

The Shark and his crew had been proudly "manning the rail" and facing the USS *Missouri* and Ford Island as they slowly sailed along Battleship Row. They were on schedule to pass the *Arizona* Memorial at precisely 07:53 as ordered—closely matching the timing of the first Imperial Japanese bomb dropped in a different era. But, as he stood in his command position atop the sail, his attention was drawn toward a peculiar high-pitched whine: He knew it was the sound of electric motors—the kind that powered the heavier drones the Navy had been experimenting with for years. He turned slightly to his left, and spotted a large formation of hexagonal drones about the size of small cars flying up the main channel—most headed for the far shore anchorages, but some following the submarine's wake. They veered directly toward the neatly parked rows of destroyers and cruisers—the Pacific Fleet at anchor and decked out in red, white, and blue bunting. Every ship's company was manning the rail in sparkling white uniforms, and the pageantry combined to form a spectacular and patriotic sight. The Shark's first thought was that the massive drone fly-over would add a high-tech touch to the festivities but, just then, his attention was drawn farther to the southwest, where the distinct sounds of gunfire accompanied by green tracers crisscrossed the skyline above the commercial port. Suddenly, something almost spiritual hit him like a medicine ball! Electricity raced up and down his spine and instinct born from years of training took over.

His head jerked back toward the USS *Arizona* Memorial, and he spotted a commotion among the dignitaries. Several people raced to the admiral's gig and practically leaped on board. Then the chief manning the tiller gunned the little boat, and the Shark tensed when he realized they would cut across *North Carolina*'s bow—an act of suicide. Thankfully, the gig's coxswain realized the danger in time and veered back to starboard to run between the submarine and the island. Then the Shark and his crew flinched when, without warning, a tremendous explosion erupted from the stern flight deck of the nearest Arleigh Burke destroyer across the channel. He bellowed at his crew to get below, then called down to the helmsmen and ordered the boat "all ahead one-third" and "right full rudder." He watched as the crew safely dropped down into the forward and rear hatches, then he followed the XO off the sail. The boat had to make an emergency circle inside the narrow harbor that would point them back down the main channel toward the ocean—their only escape from the "mouse-trap" that Pearl Harbor had always been. Safety for *North Carolina* was in deep water in the open sea.

As the last of the sailors dropped down into the attack center, the Shark followed and drew the sail's hatch behind him and dogged it—all the while issuing a string of orders. Everyone in the center grabbed something solid and hung on for dear life as the boat leaned into the tight right-hand turn. The Shark guessed that *North Carolina* was executing the fastest turn a submarine had ever made in Pearl Harbor, but they had no choice: In deep water they were the most dangerous $3 billion-dollar machine in history but, on the surface, they were sitting ducks and an easy target with no defense at all.

Air Operations Center, *Dragon's Tail*

Down in the PLAAF Attack Center, Airman First Class (OR-2) Peng Qinghua had already experienced one success and one failure: He'd successfully released his "mother-drone's" attached drums of mini-drones, and they were flying in multiple three-meter-in-diameter clouds toward the retired small-deck aircraft carriers anchored in the Middle Loch. His clouds would disperse and hit the ships with hundreds of tiny explosions in just under a minute and, while they'd only cause superficial damage to the vessel itself, they would eliminate all air defense weapons, radars, communication antennae, and any crew caught in the open. He and the other controllers would drop bombs a minute later and destroy the ships. Then something dramatic happened: He spotted a submarine passing the old battleship memorial, and made a snap decision to abandon the small-deck carrier that was his primary target so he could sink the moving submarine directly below. His mother drone carried an incredibly powerful bomb that would easily penetrate several centimeters of marine-grade steel armor, and he reasoned that, if he could sink her, it would be a greater victory than his assigned primary. Those reserve carriers weren't going anywhere; someone else could get them later.

He hit the auto-pilot that took control of the mini-drone swarms, and then drew his joystick sharply backward so that his mother-drone rapidly ascended to 500 feet. He watched the altimeter's numbers spin rapidly and, when it reached the desired height, he released the munition and its fins deployed. He was above the sub's inviting midsection—just behind the prominent sail. But one of the four fins suddenly malfunctioned, and the bomb veered to the left and exploded through the roof of the small white building covering an old sunken ship.

Seaman Peng was horrified: He'd gone against standing orders and changed targets—which was tolerated if his decision yielded a better result—but instead he'd wasted a precious munition on no target at all! He looked around the attack center guiltily, but none of the officers were glaring at him. He hoped he'd dodged a reprimand and, turning back to his screen, reacquired the mini-drone swarms, propelling them against the small carriers a bit farther north. Thousands of tiny explosions raked the length of both carriers, sparkling like firecrackers, and they'd surely destroyed the ship's ability to defend itself. He tapped a button on his keyboard and requested another loaded mother drone. Inside the hangar, another six-bladed aircraft zoomed up and out of the confined space.

Bunker of GS Han, Beijing (same time)

"What has that fool done?" Han suddenly screamed at no one in particular. He'd just witnessed the drone attack on the USS *Arizona* Memorial from a camera feed that General Bao was running on the main screen. Instead of going after a moving submarine just a few meters away, some idiot had just desecrated one of the enemy's military shrines. He was fully aware of the psychological importance that all such memorials meant to the American people, and a needless attack would infuriate them even more than they already were. His goal was to stay on the moral high ground, and his standing orders had stated as much. "Our forces were specifically ordered to limit their attacks to military targets." *Nothing good will come from this!* He looked over at Marshal Tai for an explanation.

"General Secretary Han, it must have been a malfunction of some kind! The entire assault force has been specifically ordered to avoid such targets." He'd also reacted to the attack on the Memorial, fully aware of its special place in America's pantheon of heroic locations. Such places meant more to the Americans than was rational, but China had its sacred sites, too. Bao had planned this operation for four years to avoid the mistakes that Japan had made—and preventing a galvanized United States that was focused on revenge was essential. The fact of starting a shooting war with them was bad enough—but needless acts of desecration would incite visceral hatred. Tai would get to the bottom of the Memorial attack when time permitted. However, on all other counts, he was elated: In just the first five minutes, the air attack had successfully targeted every ship and submarine in the harbor—plus destroyed every plane in the immediate area, and several key headquarters buildings and infrastructure hubs.

Their newly-developed shaped-charge aerial munitions had cut through the steel decks like butter, and had exploded in the confined spaces beneath. The bombs were designed to create super-hot gases on impact, and these would expand in a micro-second and melt steel decks and ignite anything flammable. So far, the results were as impressive as the live fire tests he'd witnessed in their proving grounds in Inner Mongolia. The American fleet was overwhelmed, and raging fires were burning out of control on every LHA, destroyer, cruiser, and submarine in Pearl Harbor. Reports were also pouring in from their attacks on Kitsap Navy Base in Washington State, and from the enemy's biggest West Coast naval base in San Diego, California. He hoped the news from the ballistic missile and drone attacks on the Atlantic ports would be as favorable.

Once again, because the Americans were more relaxed on a Sunday that was fairly close to their emotionally important Christian holiday of Christmas, two-thirds of their fleet was in port rather than out on patrol. Today, six of the nine home-ported destroyers were alongside in their normal berths, and those had all sustained multiple hits and were afire; the lone cruiser, the USS *Port Royal*, was a raging inferno; two small reserve assault carriers in the Middle Loch had been hit by thousands of mini-drones and could not defend against the wave of larger drones headed their way. And, most important of all, each of the ten submarines secured against their piers were holed and afire. Eight were *Los Angles* Class boats, and two were the even-more dangerous *Virginia* Class. Marshal Tai was confident they'd all been sidelined for the duration.

Just then, as Han's group watched from what was essentially an extremely expensive home-entertainment system—they exclaimed as aerial views from selected drones showed one of the submarines in Pearl Harbor suddenly explode in spectacular fashion. A fireball rose over the harbor, and only one of the Eight thought about the young sailors they had just murdered. Then an Arleigh Burke Class destroyer exploded, too. It was quite a show.

However, there was one alarming problem: Another screen showed a submarine racing down the exit channel toward the open sea. "What about that one?" yelled Han anxiously, pointing like a student in secondary school.

"The local commander should spot it, Comrade General Secretary!" assured General Bao. At least they better.

Air Operations Center, *Dragon's Tail*

Sure enough, PLAAF Senior Colonel Ning Lao spotted the Yankee submarine making a run for it. "Section Five, concentrate all your available assets on the submarine in the main channel!"

In the space occupied by the Air Wing's Section Five, Captain Liu Gang moved her mouse and clicked on the channel map. A visual from a master drone above that sector filled her center screen, and she sent a command that overrode five of the nearest NP-20 mother drones. They veered from their flight paths and converged as a group on the fleeing vessel, but it was moving faster than she was used to, and her first bomb-drop missed to the right. The enemy boat was still accelerating, and the captain had not invested enough training time practicing on fast-moving targets—a weakness she'd add to her after-action report. Her next NP-20 fell 40 meters short of the stern fin protruding above the water, and before she could bring her next drone to bear, the sub reached deeper water and submerged. It was still a shadow under the beautiful blue ocean, but her munitions were ineffective in more than three meters of water. She watched the sub streak away and turn to the right before it was lost from view. That one had gotten away. "Sorry, Colonel," she apologized over her headset, "I couldn't attack in time. The enemy submarine submerged and escaped. Perhaps our mini-subs can get her?" *And hopefully take some heat off of me.*

Aboard the USS *North Carolina*

"Helm, hug the contours until we get in deep water, then level out at 400 feet!" The Shark was not surprised that his crew had transitioned quickly into full combat mode. Many were no doubt worried about their families and loved ones, but they had managed a really narrow escape, and had to trust others to protect those left behind. Pearl was a great port to shelter in, but it was a death trap when under attack.

"Hugging the bottom, aye, Captain!" repeated the senior chief sitting behind the two planesmen. The three of them had been on duty when they'd entered Pearl and were perfectly placed for their emergency dash back down the channel.

Oahu is a steep volcanic island and its underwater geography dropped away quickly in a series of stair steps toward the abyssal plain. The *North Carolina* leveled out at 400 feet and the Shark brought her to dead slow. He had to think. *I need to speak to the crew before I do anything else.* He pulled down the mic and said, "All hands, listen up: You all did your duty as well as can be expected! We were in a real jam and managed to escape without a scratch. Now we are a combat vessel at war, and the most lethal machine that ever sailed under Old Glory! We didn't start this, but we're going to fight back and bring pure hell against whatever stupid saps killed our countrymen!" He heard a cheer echo though the boat—he never doubted the combat worthiness of his crew or their heart or their training. "I want to mention first of all that I looked over at our sub pier before I came below and our families were running away, and were well clear of the boats alongside. I saw the first explosion there and it didn't affect the civilians. Whoever is attacking us—I'm assuming it's the Chinese—is only targeting combat vessels. We all have our individual beliefs, so this is a time to trust God and believe that our loved ones are okay. That said, our blessed land is under attack, we are at war, and we have capabilities the enemy has only dreamed of.

"We were tracking that big ChiCom merchie before the attack, and everyone missed her true intent: Those drones had to come from somewhere, and hundreds of them require a large delivery system. Others will have to deal with her, so let's focus on what we can do: We are an American ship of war on a combat patrol. We have provisions for a few days and we can fight hungry!" Another cheer. "I know each of you will do your duty!"

He replaced the mic in its overhead cradle and asked the XO and the COB to join him in the sonar room. He remembered Zap's "funny sounds from the merchie" and they now took on a whole new meaning.

Chapter 33

The White House Situation Room, 14:20 Hours

Twenty minutes into World War III, the President of the United States was exhibiting remarkable self-control: For a man with borderline hypertension, he was keeping a pretty cool head as he witnessed the comprehensive and systematic destruction of his Pacific, West Coast, and East Coast Naval bases. He was actively listening to his Cabinet secretaries rather than raging, but everyone there was in the mood for revenge. It would come—and to the eternal regret of the murderous PRC Politburo. "What's the latest, Baker?"

The Secretary of Defense was standing next to a hastily procured white board where one of his aides with headphones was scribbling ship names in vertical columns. "Mr. President, damage to our in-port fleets of carriers and submarines—both Pacific and Atlantic—is nearing 100 percent."

Spence's jaw muscles tightened at the news, but he had to be cold-blooded now—he could rage against the perpetrators later. "None of our ships or submarines are able to fight or escape?"

"Sir, the *North Carolina* was already underway inside Pearl Harbor: She had just entered the East Loch as part of the *Arizona* ceremony, and her momentum enabled her to return to deep water. The rest of the fleet was at anchor, and it now looks doubtful if any of the them are able to contain the raging fires. The ChiComs are using large aerial drones that release clouds of mini-drones about one inch in diameter, and these smaller ones explode against any surface they hit—machine or human. They operate like tiny hand grenades that explode on impact against radars and antennas, or missiles in open launch tubes—and they can penetrate vents on ships or buildings before exploding inside. The larger drones also carry a bomb that they drop onto the thinner steel of exposed decks. We all sadly remember the tragic fire on the *Bonhomme Richard* in San Diego some time ago: The conflagrations started by these incendiary munitions are causing similar damage. First reports indicate that they first punch through the relatively light deck plate, then explode and seemingly melt their way through one or more additional decks and start chemical fires. Every crew is fighting to save its ship, but many sailors have been forced to jump into the harbors to avoid incineration." The SecDef was stunned to say the least; *how could they have been caught so unawares in the modern age?*

"Same situation everywhere?"

"The same, Mr. President. We now know that those Dragons were assault ships containing an extremely large number of drone aircraft. They just overwhelmed the onboard and local air defenses. Additionally, they are off-loading what we think is a brigade-sized unit of main battle tanks, troop-carrying infantry fighting vehicles, self-propelled artillery, and thousands of troops…" He paused as a naval aide walked into the room and excused himself: He was red-faced with rage. "Yes, Captain Withers?" asked Secretary Halsey.

"Mr. President, Mr. Secretary, I'm horrified to inform you that the USS *Arizona* Memorial has been attacked and heavily damaged. There are casualities but we have no numbers yet. We don't know if the Vice President was hurt." His anger bled off rapidly and he just looked sick at heart. He had no one to fight, but hoped his chance would come soon.

"An outrageous violation of civility!" shouted the President, but he got ahold of himself just as quickly and regained his equilibrium. "Okay, Captain, we all share your well-founded anger. We'll strike back when the time is right." Then he turned to the agent standing against the side door—his lead agent was topside coordinating the President's possible linkup with Knee Cap, his airborne command center: "I need word about Vice President Mason ASAP!"

"Yes, Mr. President." He whispered into his sleeve mic, then gave a welcome report: "Sir, we just got confirmation that the Vice President, her Secret Service detail, the Japanese Consul, and the Commander of our Indo-Pacific forces have all reached safety. They headed for the *Missouri* before the explosion, and are sheltering there."

"Thank God for that!" Spence needed some good news. Everyone applauded and relief swept the room. However, during their exchange, the tally on the white board kept growing. He watched the officer manning the board create a new header and write Puget Sound. As information came through on his headphones, he printed the names of vessels sunk or damaged, and he was printing as fast as he could jot down the names.

That good news about Rebecca gave everyone a shot in the arm. The agent informed everyone that she was sheltering inside one of the USS *Missouri*'s gun turrets, and had escaped after her detail received a warning from an unknown source. The wonderful old battleship was built to withstand 16-inch shells, so she was impervious to the aerial munitions being used by the ChiCom drones.

Spence wanted Baker to continue his summary, but he had to pause to take a short phone call from his lead agent upstairs: The first family was okay and had been successfully moved into the presidential shelter. Thank God for that! He then refocused on his SecDef. "Okay, Baker, please continue."

"Mr. President, the Kitsap numbers are as follows: The submarine *Connecticut* is at sea chasing the PRC ballistic missile subs that launched missiles at the continental U.S.; the *Ohio* is on patrol in the western Pacific; and we have attack boats with the *Nimitz* task force, now steaming some 500 miles west northwest of Taiwan. They still plan to hook up with the *Reagan* task force heading down the east coast of Japan. But the other nine submarines in the Puget Sound area have been severely damaged or sunk at their berths. The Everett numbers are better: Only one Arleigh Burke destroyer was in port, and is severely damaged. The rest are at sea."

"Okay. What about San Diego?"

"The reports are equally grim, Mr. President: The four small-deck LHDs are heavily damaged—and the *Bonhomme Richard* was attacked again and is afire. Apparently, they didn't know she was out of service. Of the nine LPD and LSD assault ships, the *Anchorage* is at sea with the *Nimitz* group, but the remaining eight are damaged or sunk; of the cruisers, the Chosin and Lake Erie are at sea, and the remaining six are heavily damaged; of the Arleigh Burke destroyers, the *Stockdale*, *Spruance*, *John Finn* and *Rafael Peralta* are at sea with the *Nimitz* group, but the remaining nine all are heavily damaged or sunk. Both of the Zumwalt destroyers are at sea; of the littoral combat ships, the *Kansas City*, *Cincinnati*, *Charleston*, and the *Tulsa* are at sea, but the remaining nine are all damaged or sunk. Various other supply and countermeasures ships were in port and all are sunk or damaged. The worst news regards our big-deck carriers: The *Lincoln* has been holed by at least six direct penetrations of her flight deck and is ablaze. The *Stennis* is heavily damaged and afire. The *Theodore Roosevelt* is inbound, but still about 100 miles off shore, and her group is at battle stations awaiting your orders for a possible reassignment to WestPac. That's the West Coast report for now, Sir."

"So, in summary, Baker, our entire in-port West Coast and Hawaiian fleets are either heavily damaged and burning, or already sunk?" Spence didn't know how he'd get through this day. It would take supernatural help to make rapid and coherent decisions—but his faith was strong—and God was stronger.

"Yes, Mr. President." What could he say? The most devastating attack in U.S. history had just occurred on his watch.

"And San Francisco?"

"The assault ship there launched long-distance drone strikes against every military target within 100 miles. These drones destroyed all of the planes and most of the infrastructure at Travis Air Force Base near Sacramento, and another cloud descended on NAS Lemoore at the same time—but the local commander thinks they were not launched from the San Francisco or San Diego motherships. He suspects they came from another ship—possibly a small freighter we've spotted loitering off the California coast. We have no defense against the clouds of mini-drones that punch small holes in aircraft engines and kill people—they have the power of bullets and operate in great bunches. There are also reports of hovercraft full of soldiers landing at every location. These are big ones like our LCACs, and carry a mixture of a couple of hundred dismounted and motorcycle infantry, and small vehicles. As mentioned, we also have to contend with heavy armor units supported by mobile infantry."

"Tanks and infantry?" the President asked incredulously. "How could we have missed that?"

"Yes, Sir. That giant cavern in Dalian was more than a finishing grotto—it served as a loading chamber, too." Even Baker thought his answer sounded lame.

"You think?" *Be cool, Spence, everyone missed this.* "And our East Coast ports?"

"The same, Mr. President. The totals are coming in now." The white board had been abandoned in favor of the main (live) screen, which earlier had been experiencing some technical glitch. Someone was typing ship names—annotated by clear-text commentary on type and extent of damage. The font was big enough for everyone to read the bad news easily.

"Was our East Coast fleet sunk by those submarine SLBMs?" the President asked. "The PRC really caught us with our pants down. They accomplished all this conventionally—not a single hint of radiation weapons anywhere. But how can we strike back with more than half of our fleet destroyed?"

"Only partially, Mr. President: They managed to get an estimated 54 missiles in the air, and some struck the Midwest and South, while the rest flew to the East Coast. But these potent missiles were augmented by clouds of drones launched from smaller, harmless-looking tramp steamers that were only a few miles outside our territorial waters off each targeted port. They directed clouds of mini-drones against every radar and missile battery, which eliminated our anti-missile capability, and finished off every ship and submarine with those aerial deck penetrators. All our in-port subs are damaged—but at least we have four at sea in the Atlantic—two *Los Angeles* Class and two *Virginia* Class. Ships and subs under construction in various yards are similarly damaged.

"Regarding the active fleet, in Mayport, Florida, all the in-port helicopter carriers are afire and the cruisers are afire or sunk. But most of the destroyers survived—apparently not targeted. Half of the littoral combat ships are afire or sunk, as are a third of the larger support ships. Two destroyers and two LCS's were at sea. In every case, Navy fighters are hunting down those smaller ChiCom cargo ships and one is reported sunk."

"At least Navy Air got in a few licks! What is the report from Norfolk?" But Spence already knew the answer.

"The worst news of all, Mr. President: All three of our in-port, big-deck carriers—the *Truman*, *Ford*, and *Bush*—are afire, and the *Washington* is in long-term overhaul and was hit, too. About half of the remaining in-port fleet is sunk or damaged, but at least many of our destroyers were at sea on maneuvers. The *Eisenhower* task force is in the Gulf and awaiting your orders."

"At least that's something. Worldwide, how many big deck carriers can still fight?"

"Sir, the *Eisenhower* can be brought to the Pacific in a few days, and the Nimitz and Reagan are planning to link up between southern Japan and northern Taiwan. They are maneuvering with the LHA *America* and the Japanese small deck carrier *Izumo*, and this combined task force will share multiple fast attack submarines. Plus, the *Roosevelt*'s task force as we discussed. So, the total is four big-deck carriers, Mr. President."

Spence felt it was time to address his War Cabinet on a higher plane—his senior leaders had automatically transitioned to that unfortunate status 30 minutes before. "Okay, everyone, let's sort out our options: The Middle East has become a sideshow for now; we have little choice but to concentrate our remaining naval forces in the western Pacific. Our Air Forces, too. Any disagreement?"

"Mr. President," Baker spoke up, "I concur as long as we leave enough air assets in the Middle East to keep the bad guys under control."

"Agreed. But it is obvious that this war won't be won with a crippled Navy. We have only four active big-deck carrier groups, and all are vulnerable to those ChiCom ballistic missiles we've been studying for years. Our land-based air power will have to lead this fight—this will be an Air Force and Space Force show to start—and the Navy, Marines, and Army will join when they can."

Everyone around the table was silent for a few seconds. Morosely, some noted that the tally of damaged and sunken ships continued to grow.

The Republic of China, Taiwan
December 8th, 02:00 Hours

3rd Squad was beginning to lose interest in the big fire burning downtown; it had started a couple of hours earlier and had lit up the Kaohsiung City skyline. In the interim, the men's interest had shifted to the big red DFE container ship that had been pushed against the nearest quay; it was massive but not the biggest ship to dock there, even during the previous week. However, it was now time for Sergeant Jing's sleepy squad to gather their things and climb out of their sandbagged trench. They'd kept their homeland safe for another day and it was time to hit their racks. They pulled each other up the steep five-foot bank, and stood in a neat line waiting to jog back to their barracks.

At least the fire and giant ship had helped pass the usually boring last two hours of their shift.

Suddenly, an earth-shattering explosion rocked the right-hand side of the port where the foreign navy vessels were moored, and then that first blast was followed a second later by another and then another. In seconds, numerous explosions detonated in rapid succession. As the concussions rocked the harbor area and beyond, Sergeant Jing barked at his men, and they jumped back down into their fixed fighting position, and mixed in with 1st Squad, 4th Platoon, who'd just relieved them. Every other unit along the line did the same, and the old trenches and mortar pits were instantly doubly manned and alert. Jing peeked above the sandbags and guessed that they were under missile attack because he knew bombs sounded different. He couldn't see all the explosions, but every foreign ship was afire and, on some, dozens of secondary explosions indicated that their magazines were penetrated and cooking off live rounds. The local reserve armory off to his left took a direct hit, and then his own country's military ships began exploding before his eyes.

The devastating barrage continued for five solid minutes, and then abruptly stopped. The 20 men in his trench were a tangle of bodies and rifles lying on top of one another at the bottom of their fighting positions, but slowly they gradually rose to survey the scene below. The area between the soldiers and the port was partially illuminated by weak lights from the docks, but settling dust obscured most of the details. All the military ships were on fire, but the container ships alongside the rows of cranes were untouched. Suddenly, all 20 men suddenly started pointing and exclaiming when they noticed tanks and soldiers descending down numerous ramps from the huge red ship. The ROC soldiers didn't know who they were, but they could see them fanning out and heading in their direction.

Sergeant Jing got it first: "Okay, men!" he shouted, "we've been ready for this our whole lives. Don't waste your ammo! Lock and load, but don't shoot until I tell you!"

One of the privates called out in a fearful voice, "Sergeant Jing, what is happening?" He could see the tanks and soldiers, but hoped it was their own forces drilling.

"Mainland tanks and troops are invading, men! Hopefully our air force gets them before they get to us. Just be calm and wait—they'll take about 15 minutes to get organized, and another 15 to get up here." He picked up the field phone and dialed the closest heavy mortar position to ensure everyone in the pit was thinking straight and had broken out their cases of live rounds. *So, it's tonight—after more than 70 years!* Then he gave one last order to his men: "Fix bayonets!"

Throughout the port and surrounding area, sirens blared and announcements poured from the civil defense speakers; the government was mobilizing the ROC military reserves for the fight of their lives. Sleepy civilian/soldiers dashed from their homes amid the settling dust from the missile barrage, and they all headed for their armories or civil defense posts. For many, it was their last few minutes on earth because they encountered a new and vicious weapons system that no one had trained for: Without warning, hundreds of tiny drones appeared out of the dust and darkness, and cut down people in the open—running or stationary—and tiny explosions destroyed or disabled every antenna, engine, air-conditioning unit, and anything mechanical with openings. Glass windshields or windows in buildings were shattered—anything deemed a target by the controllers inside the mother ship. Local technology ground to a halt. There was no defense from the horrible drones except taking shelter in buildings or vehicles that couldn't be penetrated. Outside was awful carnage.

Sgt. Jing's hope for air cover was a pipe dream: All the military air fields had been targeted with intensive missile barrages, and all the planes, hangars, and runways were destroyed. The few planes that survived the missiles were enveloped by the mini-drones and their engines destroyed. Those fighters that happened to be airborne responded aggressively, and flew to pre-assigned positions closer to the central mountain chain to wait for the PLAAF bombers they'd been trained to shoot down. They didn't have long to wait.

Aboard *Dragon's Armor*
Port of Manila, the Philippines

PLAN Marine Major Huo Zeman barked a command, and his tankers scrambled onto their ZTZ-99A main battle tanks—considered by military professionals to be one of the top ten tanks in the world. Huo was the youngest marine tank battalion commander in the 62nd Division, and he had been promoted ahead of his peers for a reason: His company had won the "Best in Brigade" award five months straight and, with the expansion of forces for Operation Unity, he'd been given command of 58 tanks—plus the supporting vehicles, personnel, and multitude of other equipment that filled out a front-line armor battalion. He confirmed with his executive officer that his NCOs and junior officers had checked everyone's equipment, and that all the marines had their ear protection in place. Their helmets helped, but they all needed their specially designed protectors to deal with the overwhelming din in the confined space—and during the active battle outside. The master exhaust system was being red-lined to keep up with the fumes, the air was dense with local humidity, and it was the best day of Huo's life.

Along with the other battalion commanders, he had joined the betting pool the veterans had going: Each participant had to predict how many hours it would take for them to roll the Philippine army. Believing that the locals would fight hard for their homeland, he gave them the benefit of the doubt with a generous estimation of 72 hours. But he didn't really care—he just wanted to be part of the larger victory.

Just then the main door opened and the first tank rolled out onto the ramp and disappeared.

White House Situation Room

As the last of the secretaries and senior staff hurried back from necessary breaks and took their seats, the President began his remarks with a surprisingly steady voice. "Thank you for assembling so quickly, everyone—we've gotten onto a war footing as fast as could be expected. To summarize, our big and small deck carrier fleets have been reduced by about 75 percent—as has our submarine fleet. Additionally, two-thirds of our B-2s, and 29 of our B-52s are completely destroyed or will take various amounts of time to repair. Several of our B-1s were also damaged by long-range snipers, and that fleet was having some maintenance issues before that. The key factor in this early stage is that no nuclear weapons have been used against us. They could have used an EMP against us and chose not to—probably a decision made with retaliation in mind. There is a new kind of war raging in space, but advanced planning has helped us tremendously and we are more than holding our own in the heavens. Now we need to discuss appropriate levels of response against the ChiComs. Baker, please give us your summary."

"Mr. President, the enemy is landing what we think are brigade-sized armor units at our two West Coast naval bases, plus at Pearl Harbor and San Francisco. They are exiting their motheships and dispersing rapidly, are clearly well-organized, and we all know now that they've been planning this operation for some time. All of the PR activities surrounding their so-called Dragon Fleet have been revealed for what they are—a long-term deception campaign to facilitate conquest. However, the size of these four units indicates that they have no intention of trying to conquer us—it must be a calculated side show of their comprehensive moves in Asia—no doubt to slow any help we might give to our allies.

"Reports are streaming in regarding massive movements of troops across the ChiCom's entire southern border—an overwhelming projection of force against their neighbors from Vietnam to India—plus against the North Koreans. They have plastered Japan with missile strikes, and have docked Dragon ships in Sydney and two places in Taiwan. Attacking us and our Pacific allies is an effective strategy because they have destroyed much of our individual retaliatory capability, and we can't mount a counter-attack to help our mainland Asian allies if we are fighting here at home."

"How about Russia?" asked Secretary Madrid.

"Jack, we have no reports of them moving north."

The President confirmed as much. "I spoke with President Kumatov a few minutes ago, and he said they are monitoring the situation, but will not fire unless fired upon. And since we know the Chinese moved several of their frontline divisions away from their common border six months ago—and subsequently placed most of them on the North Korean frontier—I am naturally suspicious of what the Russians and Chinese may have cooked up between themselves. But I agree with you: So far, the Russians have not hinted at a move against us, Japan, or Europe and, if they stay out of it, things will be better for all concerned."

"Yes, Sir. Now, Mr. President, I'd like to shift to Japan. They are coping with the same type of comprehensive attacks that we are: Their military is rushing forces to the Yokosuka area where 'their' Dragon ship is off-loading the same offensive package they're using against us. And, like us, the Japanese military suffered devastating ballistic missile attacks throughout their home islands and Okinawa—including hitting of our many bases there. But unlike the submarine-launched missiles that hit us, all Asia-region strikes were land-based. Drones are hammering targets around Tokyo Bay, and clouds of mini-drones are destroying the engines of every plane in every target country's inventory. All key Japanese military installations, and all of their in-port, small-deck carriers and submarines, have been severely damaged or sunk."

"Okay, pretty grim everywhere," Spence summarized, then turned to his Secretary of Homeland Security. "Dan, please give us an update on our domestic situation."

The urbane former director of the FBI responded smoothly, "Yes, Mr. President. May I have the first slide please?" The main screen switched to an interactive map of North America, including Hawaii, and showed more than 1,500 tiny red dots superimposed across the eastern three-quarters of the country. Four twinkling orange lights indicated foreign troop interventions. "These are the attack points, and they focused almost universally on local infrastructure—gas stations, power stepping stations, water purification plants, airports, train tracks, and the like. But they have not targeted civilian centers where people might congregate like schools, churches, shopping malls, or playgrounds. They did start many forest fires, mostly in the western states because of the early snows in the east, but they avoided areas near cities or towns. And, though the number of attacks is very high, with one glaring exception, the level of damage is relatively low. That exception is the Houston area oil refinery fire that is still out of control and has caused significant casualties."

Spence responded evenly, "Do you have a theory for this MO—seemingly wide and shallow, rather than narrow and deep?"

"Sir, since 1,700 attacks could have caused significant damage—such as what they accomplished when targeting our naval forces—I can only guess that they were diversions as part of a greater gambit. They effectively drew our attention away from those Dragon ships as they arrived at our ports.

They've been very successful if that was their end, but that's pure speculation on my part."

"Makes sense, though," Spence admitted, and many heads nodded concurrence. "Baker, what can you add?"

"Mr. President, the missile attacks have ended—at least for now—and all utilized conventional munitions. The drone swarms have switched their tactics to supporting the landings, because all but the major targets are already destroyed. Essentially, they are acting as area-denial weapons—keeping any of our low-flying aircraft away from their troops. The motherships are rapidly unloading their ground forces—essentially unopposed because any weapons system we bring against them is set upon by the drones. The tiny ones attack any personnel using hand-held rockets or even rifles or machine guns—but ignore civilians just running away from the action. Local commanders guess the drones are controlled by technicians and/or trained pilots in the motherships, and they obviously have extensive visuals throughout every battle space. I'd like to recommend that we get a bomber in the air to sink those motherships as soon as possible: It will help our counter-attacks and also send a strong message to the ChiComs and to our people."

This did not sit well with Jack Madrid, and he signaled that he wanted to speak.

"Go ahead, Jack," Spence encouraged.

"Mr. President, we don't want to rush ahead with a military option if a diplomatic one exists. We haven't spoken with their foreign minister to see if we can negotiate their withdrawal."

Spence felt a coldness in the room, but he had to be polite to his chief diplomat if he were to retain the man's long-term usefulness. "Jack, they've just destroyed three quarters of our Navy and killed thousands of our citizens. I don't much feel like negotiating now." *Jack can really miss the larger context sometimes.*

"Why don't we just apologize for existing, Jack?" Dan asked sarcastically.

"Very funny, Dan. But may I remind you that we have more than 2,000 personnel in our Beijing embassy alone. Thousands of American citizens returned to the mainland after the Covid restrictions lifted, and they are scattered throughout China."

Spence had heard enough of this side discussion and nipped it in the bud before it went down a rabbit hole. "Let's get back on track, gentlemen. Jack, when your staff escorts the PRC delegation to their airplane tomorrow morning, send along a request for a similar escort to the nearest international airport for our citizens. Assure them that all their citizens here are under our protection and will be sent out of the country as soon as safe flights become available. Now, Baker, I want to know all our options for conventional military responses."

The Secretary of Defense looked over at the chairman of the Joint Chiefs. "Mr. President, I'd like to defer to Admiral Simms."

Spence nodded, and the admiral stood. "Mr. President, Mr. Secretary, I'd like to address the bombing option first—plus the implications of the space war raging overhead." He looked over at General Clyde Potter, the Air Force chief of staff. "General Potter?"

The four-star aviator had a noticeable scar on his right cheek, and silver command pilot wings above his many rows of multi-colored ribbons, and he had a ready response: "Mr. President, we've already learned that the motherships have sophisticated connections with their remote sensors in space, so I would like to brief the cabinet on our X-37 program."

"Yes, General, no sense in keeping it under wraps any longer."

Potter looked farther down the table at the new four-star Commander of Space Operations, Air Force General Donald Teague. "General Teague, please share our capabilities with the War Cabinet."

"Mr. President, ladies and gentlemen," General Teague began, "we are doing well in our first space war because of decades of real forward thinking by key leaders in this room, in Congress, and in our many technical laboratories throughout the country. We developed our secret X-37 program to place anti-satellite orbiters within striking distance of every military and militarily useful international satellite in space. We've also placed small charges on those specific satellites that we believed existed for no purpose other than to attack the United States. The Chinese have attempted to do the same thing but, unbeknown to them, we knew about their attempts and have dismantled most of those "mines" that they attached to our satellites. This explains why we have been doing so well in our first space war. We believe they were ignorant of our work, which gives us a vital strategic advantage. The bottom line is that we'll maintain our ability to guide our cruise missiles and other smart munitions. We initiated our lasers and exploded our prepositioned charges as soon as NORAD confirmed that the SLBMs were from Chinese boats.

"Unfortunately, the ChiComs knew a lot about our much-publicized ground-based anti-missile programs, and sent drone swarms from an off-shore cargo ship that destroyed our missiles in their silos at Vandenberg Space Force Base in California. The large missile system in Alaska was too far away to launch against the SLBMs, so the Chinese ignored them. I'm sure everyone knows that our proposed East Coast anti-missile system has experienced delays and has not been built. They could have intercepted the missiles targeting our eastern naval bases unless drones overwhelmed them, too." *Looks like another case of Congress being penny wise and pound foolish.* But the general couldn't say that out loud.

There were knowing looks from many around the table, but a couple of gasps from those just learning of this dramatic XB-37 weapons system. However, predictably, Secretary Madrid was alarmed. "Mr. President, by destroying the PRC's space platforms, we've inviting strong retaliation—possibly nuclear EMPs!"

Heading off strong responses from around the table, Spence spoke somewhat forcefully, "Jack, you raise a valid point. However, we are only destroying their military-related satellites—after they launched ballistic missiles against our homeland. This is war, and we are going to use every non-nuclear arrow in our quiver to beat the living hell out of these aggressive so and so's. They have killed thousands of our fellow Americans!" Spence knew Jack was a good diplomat, but he had true pacifistic tendencies. It had always been Spence's belief that pacifism—regardless of the good intentions of those promoting the philosophy—empowered aggressive individuals and governments. He had dear friends who held such beliefs—they just agreed to disagree.

"With respect, Mr. President, I am very wary of their nuclear options…"

"Fair enough, Jack. But now is the time to limit their conventional capabilities while also keeping a close eye on their nuclear threat. They are extremely frightened of our nuclear arsenal—remember the strong assurance in their war declaration? We are going to focus on a conventional military victory—but we will always listen to what their diplomats have to say." Spence saw that his statement effectively ended Jack's objections, and he turned back to the military discussion: "Okay, General Potter, what was the second item you wanted to discuss?"

"Mr. President, B-2s are the best option for the assault ships. Unfortunately, our only available Spirit is at Eglin Air Force Base in Florida—apparently escaping damage by chance. She was temporarily assigned to provide some multi-platform familiarization for the 96th Test Wing, and thankfully missed the Whiteman missile barrage. We can have her up—meaning fueled and armed—in about two hours, Sir; just give us the order!"

"Okay, everyone. I am inclined to utilize our B-2. Your opinions, please."

A lively but overwhelmingly one-way discussion ensued. After ten minutes of positive responses, Spence issued the order: "General Potter, proceed with the B-2 attack."

"Very well, Mr. President!" Both General Potter and General Teague rose and headed for the communications center with their aides in tow.

"Baker, please give us an update on the balance of our B-2 fleet."

"Certainly, Mr. President. Worldwide, we started with 18 operational Spirits: Twelve were in Nebraska, but only the two in closed maintenance bays on the edge of the runway complex were missed by the missile and sapper attacks. They were in a normal maintenance cycle—meaning unavailable for combat—but will now be given top priority to return to the flight line. They were largely disassembled so my best guess is a few more days. Sniper attacks holed the two that were sitting in the open, and they are out of action for a week or so, and the ballistic missiles got the remaining eight that were sitting in their special environmentally-controlled, B2SS Shelter Systems. One operational Spirit is in England; one is in Scotland; Diego Garcia in the Indian Ocean was hammered by more than a dozen ICBMs that destroyed four of our B-52s and the one B-2 stationed there. Additionally, we had four B-52s and one B-2 stationed at Royal Australian Air Force Base, Darwin, and all five bombers were destroyed when that base got plastered. Guam has not been attacked, so the B-2 stationed there is okay, but the two operational

PLAN carriers are headed that way and may attack at any time. That leaves the Florida bird as your quickest option."

"All right, let's get that B-2 out of there now and bring it back to the States. Anywhere safe. How long before the crew from the Florida Spirit can drop their first bomb?"

"Sir, we can have her in the air in two hours, and the flight time to San Diego is about five hours. So, seven hours is reasonable. We can drop four 2,000-lb. bombs on each assault ship; one B-2 can easily carry 16 JDAMs, refuel in flight as needed, and move from one target to the next. The second ship will be hit approximately one hour after the first, and the third an hour after that. Then it's a few hours to cross the Pacific to Hawaii. All four should be sunk before morning."

"Excellent!" Several minutes of discussion followed, as implications of sinking the four motherships led to other ideas and suggestions.

Chapter 34

USS *Missouri*
Inside Number One Turret, 09:00 Hours (H-hour plus one)

"I feel useless sitting in here while our whole fleet is being massacred! And those poor people we abandoned on the Memorial!" Rebecca was beside herself with anger and guilt: Anger that the Chinese had used the subterfuge of civilian ships to cover their dastardly attack on her country—and that they'd compounded this evil by attacking on one of America's sacred days. But, more galling than that, was their murdering of hundreds of young American sailors, many just college-age kids minding their own business in their own home port.

Rebecca also felt a heavy burden of guilt because she had been the President's point person to watch these ships. And, on top of everything else, she was now the safest person in a war zone, while others—maybe her own husband and children—were being slaughtered outside. She felt like screaming and crying at the same time—but that was not how vice presidents conduct themselves. She was a leader—if at the present—only for the Secret Service agents and the Japanese diplomats who were all suffering in their own private ways. She was also sure the irony of taking shelter in the *Missouri* was not lost on Consul General Sakamura. *At least the admiral and his aide had raced off to do something useful!*

Waikiki

Just a short distance from Rebecca's hiding place, four heavily laden 762-Type LCACs had earlier off-loaded hundreds of Chinese marines onto Waikiki Beach. The few early-morning tourists were puzzled at first—most just coming from or going to breakfast on a lazy Sunday morning. Several had come outside to watch the commotion over at Pearl Harbor—hardly believing the first news hour reports that an attack was under way. Many figured that the newsies just got things mixed up with the annual Memorial ceremonies.

The four sea-skimming hover craft had glided slowly up onto the beach so the few people there could get out of the way, then the marines just walked across the sand and divided their platoons among the hotels along the strip. English-speaking officers announced to every front desk that they wanted to speak with the manager and, when he or she arrived, they informed them that the guests had to vacate the first floor and the two top-most floors. No one who cooperated would be hurt. It was still in the post-Covid era, so there were enough rooms in the middle floors to accommodate the displaced guests.

The balance of the marines went out to the front and cleared the sidewalks of shopping pedestrians, while teams assembled at each end of the long blocks between the beach hotels and the Ala Wai Canal. Those private citizens and taxis already driving were waved forward until they left the area. The 726s also carried 20 motorcycle troops each, and these 80 riders took up strategic positions around the cordoned area. A few drones arrived overhead and assisted in reinforcing the new restrictions. Two policemen realized these soldiers and riders were part of the unfolding attack and drew their weapons, but both were quickly cut down. The rest of the patrolmen were allowed to move back, and told via bullhorns to stay away from Waikiki.

Camp H.M. Smith, Honolulu

One of the first on-shore priorities for the drone operators was the headquarters of the Indo-Pacific Command. This four-star command had responsibility for 52 percent of the Earth's surface, and was viewed with increasing importance by successive American administrations. The United States was in a long-term process of shifting its focus from Europe and the Middle East toward Asia, and the IPC commanded the pointy end of the spear. The admiral in command had been part of VP Mason's party that reached the *Missouri* earlier, and it had been he who directed her protective detail to seek shelter in the spacious forward gun turret. Camp Smith was considered vital by the Operation Unity planners, so ten mother drones flew the five miles from *Dragon's Tail* and unleashed hell on the premises. Within five minutes, the buildings were blazing infernos, and dozens of key personnel were killed or wounded. Much of the command center was underground, but penetrating shaped charges found their way into several elevator shafts and the overall effectiveness of the headquarters was nearly destroyed. And adding sorrow upon sorrow, the admiral was killed trying to return to his command.

Aboard the USS *Reagan*, Flagship of Task Force Eagle 300 miles Southwest of Tokyo Bay December 8th, 04:00 Hours

Rear Admiral Seth Jones was both the allied senior officer afloat and commanding officer of the combined task force that had more front-line ships in one armada than at any time since Desert Storm. In addition to the *Reagan*, which was protected by Carrier Strike Group Five and Destroyer Squadron 15, they were accompanied by the LHA USS *America* and Japan's JS *Izumo*—Japan's lead ship in their modern aircraft carrier fleet. They'd been included to provide all participants invaluable inter-Allied training, but now they could bring more than 100 aircraft to the defense of Taiwan. The two small-deck carriers carried the new F-35B Lightning II fighters and, depending on tactical requirements during the unfolding war, additional helicopters currently on board both ships could be switched out in favor of additional fighters.

Since receiving the war notification an hour earlier, Admiral Jones had ordered the task force to spread out and begin zig-zagging—still the gold standard for presenting a more difficult target for lurking enemy subs. The picket destroyers were actively pinging, and their sonar-dipping helos were up and spot-checking the forward and lateral areas. Every carrier had doubled its combat air patrols, and every radar and sonar was on full alert. There was vast power in these 42 ships and 3 submarines, but Task Force Eagle was vulnerable, too: They were relatively close to the Chinese mainland, and they presented a massive footprint for missiles, surface ships, bombers, and submarines. However, being at sea was dramatically better than being tethered to their docks in Yokosuka—currently being pummeled by *Dragon's Roar*, the PLANs Trojan Horse in Tokyo Bay.

Jones was receiving moment-by-moment updates from both Washington and 7th Fleet headquarters in Yokosuka and, like every American, he was outraged that a foreign power had suckered them so badly. Japan had done it in the last century, but with such a powerful historical precedent to warn them, plus every nation's incredibly improved satellite technology, a surprise attack should never have been possible again. Yet the Pacific allies had let their guard down, and the PRC had exploited the opening and adapted to modern realities.

Standing a few feet to the admiral's left, (the carrier's captain had a separate bridge one deck above) and in close to total darkness, was JSDMF (Japan Self-Defense Marine Force) Navy Captain Izo Takakura, the liaison officer representing the Japanese admiral on Izumo. His range of feelings had dramatically undulated over the previous hour from joy in the last seconds of peacetime at sea, to rage, then worry, then frustration. But, to his credit, he'd been a rock of focus and clear thinking amid the swirling implications of ChiCom aggression. His ancient homeland was being brutally attacked without warning or provocation, his emperor was in danger, his family was in quarters at Yokosuka Naval Base where heavy fighting was expanding by the minute, and he had life-long friends who'd almost certainly been killed when the other three helicopter destroyers had been severely damaged by the ICBMs. It was a lot to process, but he spoke with measured calmness to the senior task force commander, "Admiral Seto just checked in, Admiral Jones: The Izumo is on station, zig-zagging, and all counter-measures are in place."

"Thank you for the update, Captain Takakura. Any more news from your countrymen?" Admiral Jones really felt for the Japanese captain he'd met many times during his current and previous tours in Japan. The two navies worked closely with one another these days, and joint tours were the norm.

"Thank you for asking, Admiral. Nothing new since the first wave of reports. It does not seem that China is trying to conquer Japan—just keep us from interfering with their wider moves on the mainland. And may I say, Admiral Jones, the irony of the situation is not lost on me: My country attacked America to keep her from interfering with our wider goals on the Asian mainland, and now the tables have been turned on us. It seems the Chinese have learned some lessons from our experiences long ago, but not the most important one of all: Avoiding aggressive warfare in the first place."

Jones was shocked: He'd never heard such an admission in person or in writing in 40 years of studying Japanese history. It had taken a lot for this honorable officer to offer such a humble summary. "I'm honored that you trust me enough to offer your opinion, Captain Takakura. Let's hope we can draw from the best of our varied experiences and defeat this common aggressor as quickly as possible." The admiral's staff was in the next room so the two men were temporarily alone: His international subordinate had shared his visionary admission in private, and Seth would protect it as a cherished confidence.

Overhead, the speakers relayed occasional chatter between the helicopters dipping their sonars about 25,000 yards ahead of the lead ships. Then their voices suddenly changed and they sounded excited, they'd picked up some anomalies to the west and were starting to drop sonobouys in a U-shape that favored that side. The immediate echo returns trended inshore. Additional helicopters lifted off the carriers, and began sniffing around the western side, too. Then the two officers heard the loudspeakers declare: "Got a strong return on number eight—about 15,000 yards west!" That helo was opposite the *Reagan*'s inshore picket—the USS *McCampbell* (DDG-85). She was an Arleigh Burke Class destroyer, designed and ideally suited for anti-submarine warfare. She could locate and destroy enemy subs miles from the carriers she protected, and she used a variety of on-board sensors and her helicopter to detect a lurking enemy. Once confirmed, the destroyer or helo would select the correct munition, depending if the Mark 46/50/54 torpedoes were launched from the ship (via the Mark 32 triple-tube launching system) or the aircraft.

The mini-sub "wolf-pack" just west of the USS *Reagan*

Inside the stealthy mini-subs that *Roar* had left behind, the pinging of the hated sonobouys overhead was the signal that the crews had run out of time and had to launch their salvo of torpedoes. The four of them had been hovering in a silent northwest/southeast line, separated from each other by half-mile intervals, and the northern-most boat was logically detected first. The subs carried 12 torpedoes each, and they were waiting to volley-fire on the word of the first boat to launch. The convoy had sailed within 15,000 yards of the sub's stationary position between Japan's Kyushu Island and the west side of the task force, and the PLAN skippers had shown great patience waiting for this prize to come within range. Their passive sonars revealed TF Eagle's changes in speed and their zigzag maneuvering, so they'd readied themselves accordingly.

Now it was the mini-sub's turn to add to China's opening victories: "Fire one!" barked the northern-most sub's captain, and the smallish boat rocked as the huge J-9 torpedo was ejected toward the big carrier in the center of its task force. The ships were traveling in total blackout, but the subs had advanced night vision technology built into their periscopes, and the torpedoes honed in on their targets using passive sonar. When they got within range of a target, they'd begin active pinging and were extremely difficult to evade.

"Two! Three! Four!" came the commands, as each of the four boats got off their initial shots. "Fire at will!" came another command from the first sub, and they continued launching their "fish" as quickly as they could empty their tubes. The boats had four tubes, so it didn't take long before 16 torpedoes were powering their way toward the Allied task force. But neither did it take long for the helicopters overhead to pounce on the hidden enemy. Each Sea Hawk helicopter carried an advanced air launch-capable Mark 54 Lightweight Torpedo and, once they confirmed the location of the nearest enemy sub, the crew dropped its deadly weapon in a matter of seconds.

Each helo had the four standard crew members: A pilot, co-pilot, tactical sensor operator (TSO), and an acoustic sonar operator (ASO). Between them, they'd fly, locate, and destroy the subs that threatened their carriers and other ships. The first sub managed to reload once, and fired eight of its torpedoes, but that was all: The American's torpedo acquired them, then started pinging rapidly, and in seconds exploded under the sub's narrow keel. It blew the mini-sub in half and all hands went to the bottom. However, before the other subs could be destroyed, they'd launched additional torpedoes, too, each homing in on the closest target available. In total, the 4 subs fired 24 fish at the task force before they were themselves destroyed. Each boat had set one torpedo to run deep in the hope that they'd either kill an Allied sub, or at least disrupt the inevitable return shots, and all of them were "fire and forget" types—meaning they didn't need further guidance. Every Dash Nine torpedo began actively pinging as they closed in on their various targets.

It takes a tremendous amount of courage for a destroyer to protect its carrier—especially when there are multiple torpedoes bearing down from 60 degrees of the compass. The three western-most destroyers all surged ahead to intercept the incoming fish—sacrificing themselves to give the carrier time to turn. It was the most difficult order the three destroyer captains had to give: Their sailors would die so that the carrier could live. The destroyers bought enough time for the *Reagan*, the USS *Blue Ridge* (LCC-19), and the cruisers to turn 90 degrees to port to offer minimal silhouettes, but seven and a half miles of ocean doesn't offer much transit time for a torpedo traveling at 65 miles per hour. The *McCampbell* and her two sister destroyers on the west side of the task force were hit immediately by three torpedoes each and torn apart. They sank in a few minutes with half their crews lost.

The USS *Key West* (SSN-772) was the western-most *Los Angeles-c*lass attack submarine of the three protecting the combined *Reagan/America/Izumo* task force, and she turned into the four deep-running torpedoes. She got off two snapshots of her own—sending Mark 48 Mod 7s into the path of the oncoming enemy fish. Both homed in on the southern-most PLAN torpedoes and their proximity fuses mutually detonated with a tremendous combined explosion. This severe disturbance in the surrounding water disrupted the northerly deep-runners, so they by-passed *Key West* and continued forward until they acquired the next American *Los Angeles-c*lass submarine, the USS *Oklahoma City* (SSN-723) cruising underneath the middle of the task force where the *Reagan* was frantically steaming east. *Key West*'s accurate firing had bought *Oklahoma City* enough time to run east at flank speed, effectively doing her part to lead the enemy torpedoes away from the carrier. She then deployed noise-makers to confuse them, and the tactic worked as designed: The two enemy fish circled the frothing canisters until they ran out of fuel and sank harmlessly to the bottom.

On the surface, the *Reagan* and the rest of Task Force Eagle was quickly gaining speed but just didn't have enough time to escape. Two of the carrier's four spinning propellers were struck with such force that both were sheared off, while the other two were knocked out of alignment. The bottom of the hull directly above the damaged and missing propellers was also torn open, and thousands of gallons of water flooded the machinery spaces and killed many of the sailors serving there. The giant ship rapidly lost way and, slightly down by the stern, began to drift to port.

The Arleigh Burke Destroyer USS *Barry* (DDG-52) moved in to assist the stricken flagship, but she too, was struck by two of the remaining torpedoes.

She was so badly damaged that her captain ordered the crew to abandon ship, and she sank in less than 30 minutes. Last to be struck was the cruiser USS *Antietam* (CG-54). She received three torpedo hits and immediately began to list. All things considered, it was one of the worst engagements in American naval history—perhaps only rivaling the night-time battle off Guadalcanal in 1942, when four U.S. cruisers were sunk by the Japanese Navy.

The destroyer's helos quickly located and sank the three remaining mini-subs, but that wasn't much consolation for the loss of four destroyers, a cruiser, and a big-deck carrier so badly damaged that she would need a tow to the nearest large dry dock. Of the nine squadrons of Carrier Air Wing Five, only the Marine F-35 Lightning IIs and the helicopters could take off, and they headed for the nearest civilian airfields. The small-deck carriers were so far untouched, but they had no room for additional aircraft. The FA-18s and the other planes needed catapult-assisted forward momentum to take off, so they had to remain on board the stricken carrier. Aloft, the beefed-up combat air patrol aloft circled as long as fuel allowed, then they too had to head for the shore. The USS John McCain (DDG-56) bravely moved alongside the Reagan and rigged a tow line, then the two of them, two of the remaining U.S. destroyers plus one of the submarines turned almost due west in the hope of reaching Nagasaki Harbor. There the carrier could be dry docked and repaired—adding additional irony to a war already filled with pain.

However, any hope for the *Reagan*'s long-term survival was soon extinguished by the PLA's Rocket Force: Using precise satellite targeting (from platforms that survived the space war earlier), the mainland-based batteries launched 20 DF-26Bs toward the wounded carrier. The *McCain* had just gotten the *Reagan* nicely underway when the big carrier killers came streaking down from the heavens. Every destroyer in the task force loosed its anti-missile inventories at the in-bound threats—especially counting on the SM-3s specifically designed to intercept ballistic missiles—but the remaining vessels just didn't have enough combined capability to destroy that many ICBMs. Three of the six ChiCom missiles hit the big-deck carrier and blew giant holes down through her flight deck and into the spaces below. In seconds, raging fires rapidly spread laterally into adjoining spaces. The firefighting crews did their best, and the halon fire-suppression systems that weren't destroyed worked as advertised, but there was too much damage to contain. Within a half-hour, remaining aboard became suicidal.

Admiral Jones and the ship's captain were killed when the first missile struck near the bridge, but Captain Takakura had just walked down into CIC to get an update from Admiral Seto, and he survived. He was the senior Allied officer onboard, and eventually dove into the water when there were no more sailors to help. He was picked up by the *McCain*, who'd released the tow line and moved alongside to rescue as many of the stranded sailors as she could. Other ships helped rescue the large crew, and 90 percent survived. Forty-five minutes later, the sailors and air crews watched helplessly from the ships' decks as their beautiful carrier settled and gradually rolled onto her side. Then she was lost from sight and began her long glide to the bottom.

The next threat came from three PLAN destroyers and ten of their missile boats that were cruising about 100 miles closer to northern Taiwan. They fired several dozen SY-2B advanced sea-skimming anti-ship missiles at the dwindling Allied task force, and it didn't take long before they started hitting their targets. The close-in anti-missile systems on the remaining ships knocked down several of the wave-hopping enemy missiles, but 20 of them got through and blew holes in the hulls of many targets. Three more ships were sunk and five were afloat but burning out of control.

The PLA Rocket Force selected DF-21Ds for their next barrage, and fired eight missiles at the two small-deck carriers, the USS *America* and the JS *Izumo*. Two '21s hit one carrier and another hit the second, but both were out of action. They could still function and had a chance to survive until they reached a friendly harbor, but Task Force Eagle had ceased to be a fighting force. Not knowing what else to do, the remaining ships rigged tow lines to those ships that had a chance, and they rescued as many of the crews as they could from the ships that were doomed. They fired torpedoes into the burning hulks to keep them out of enemy hands, then the survivors turned back north for the slow and perilous journey home.

Aboard *Dragon's Wing*, ten miles southeast of Haiphong Harbor

Senior Captain Quan Zuocheng got the final word: There was no fixing the second break-down; the engines had died again and they had no more spare parts. The welds on the patched engine housings had failed, and boiling lubricant oil had spurted out under force. The chief engineer had ordered the engines shut down to keep them from burning up, and they were now off-line for the foreseeable future. Quan pulled down the overhead mic and relayed the news to Major General Ling, and asked the general to come to the bridge for an urgent meeting.

"Okay, Captain, what are our options?" asked General Ling, using Bower binoculars to peer through the darkness. The shoreline was only a thin ribbon of white where small waves rolled up a nearby beach. He had to make critical decisions fast if he had any hopes of saving his mission.

"General, we are drifting now, and with hostilities underway in two dozen locations, there is little hope of getting a tow into the port. They know we are mainland Chinese and that this is one of the Dragons. I assume you want to put your force ashore, so please let me show you on the chart exactly where we are so you can select the best option for your landing." Quan led the way to the large table that took up a quarter of the bridge space, and pointed to the small Ngoc Xuyen Peninsula jutting south from the mouth of the Hong River estuary. "This is the closest shore—about two miles southwest of our position, and we are ten miles south of the channel."

General Ling was an expert in analyzing beaches that could handle marines, and there were three possible sites along the small peninsula. But he saw that the ship's captain was correct: There were no other likely landing spots. There were small towns in the area and, more important, roads, so he could ferry 800 marines on the four LCACs at a time, and it wouldn't take that many round trips to bring his brigade ashore. They could bring some motorcycles and the lighter vehicles, too, then assemble their force and move inland as a mostly dismounted brigade. He'd target the southern approaches to Haiphong that occupied the banks of the Hong River, and they could still accomplish a tremendous amount of good under the worst of circumstances. He'd draft most of the sailors and airmen, too, and form a combined force of more than 3,000 foot soldiers with small arms. Combined with the drones that could still be useful, he'd keep a large number of enemy soldiers occupied, and form the useful pincer similar to their original plan.

The general wasn't aware of any large military installations in the immediate area—probably just some light coastal defenses—so he didn't think they'd encounter much resistance when they came ashore. They were marines, and they'd carry their equipment into battle. He stabbed his finger on the middle of the three beaches. "We'll land here, Captain—get the LCACs ready!"

"Yes, General!" responded Captain Quan crisply, but the general was already walking away. Quan admired the man for pivoting so fast—he could only imagine the range of emotions the general must have experienced since they'd first broken down.

After circumstances had forced his hand, General Ling believed he had done what he could; he'd deployed his four mini-subs south and east of the mainland to catch any stray Allied shipping. Then he'd ordered the captain to set a course through the Qiongzhou Strait—the narrow channel between Hainan Island and the mainland's south-facing Leizhou Peninsula. Now he would utilize his air wing to support his ground force as they moved inland. They had received numerous reports of the great successes the drones were having everywhere, and he was counting on them to provide his marines with protection from enemy ground forces or low-flying aircraft. As long as they had the mothership, the controllers could maneuver the drones and keep them harassing the enemy. His great sadness was the loss of his armor—sitting useless within sight of the enemy shore—and he still couldn't believe his bad luck: The other 13 Dragons were docked and off-loading vehicles and troops according to the master schedule, and initial reports indicated they'd all secured their targets. Very frustrating to say the least!

He'd just ordered his aide to gather his battalion commanders for a strategy meeting when he felt a tremendous jolt and the whole ship seemed to jump. He and the major were knocked to the deck. *What now?* he thought, as he gathered himself and rose unsteadily to his feet.

Aboard the Vietnamese Navy Kilo-class Submarine *Haiphong*

Lying in wait for a full day, the *Haiphong*—one of Vietnam's six Kilo-class diesel-electric submarines—had been tracking the PLAN's *Dragon's Wing* since she emerged from her passage though the 22 kilometer-wide Qiongzhou

Straits. There were three Chinese hunter-killer subs in the area, but they were out in deeper water, and the captain had managed to skillfully maneuver undetected through the familiar and shallower littoral waters to their present position. They'd waited in absolute silence as the big ship crossed the 150 miles between the Strait and the Hong River estuary before striking.

Senior Captain Lien Nguyen Thu had been skipper of the *Haiphong* for 18 months, and knew her subtleties about as well as any submarine commander could know his boat. The Kilo was at her best when silence was needed—she was very hard to locate and extremely deadly when waiting for unsuspecting ships or other subs. He'd certainly needed all his skills and the experience of his crew to creep through the relatively shallow near-shore waters. As they'd made their approach, his sonarmen had detected the Chinese subs lurking to the south, between the big ChiCom base at Sanya on southern tip of Hainan Island and the Vietnamese coast. But, so far, they hadn't moved in his direction and apparently didn't know he was there.

He'd been ordered to maneuver to his present position because his country's general staff was suspicious of a possible PRC move against their homeland. And, since the *Dragon* ships were a mystery to everyone, they were also a potential threat. Then this one bound for Ho Chi Minh Port had diverted north, and the *Haiphong* was tasked to prepare for war, but not to start one. However, the theoretical vanished when artillery shells sailed over the northern border at Lao Cai a few hours before, and everything Chinese became fair game. He'd been puzzled when the big container ship stopped and drifted, figuring it was part of their tactics, but when she continued to wallow in the gentle tide, he decided it was time to strike. He sent an intermediate pattern of three torpedoes into the exposed port side of the big ship, and when they exploded in rapid succession, she seemed to jump in the water as if startled. She settled again lower than before, and three large holes were visible at the waterline. But her back was not broken. He decided to wait and see what happened before firing another pattern. In less than five minutes, something strange happened: First one, and then three more, large military-style hover craft exited from the ship's stern and headed for the beach. *She has a disguised well deck!* He watched fascinated through his night vision-enabled periscope as the hover craft raced shoreward. He couldn't sink them: His torpedoes would just slide harmlessly underneath the surface-skimming boats.

Above Ngoc Xuyen Beach south of Haiphong Port, Vietnam
The fighting positions of 2nd Company, 5th Regiment, Vietnamese Ground Forces

In the darkness, Dai Uy (Captain) Ly Trung Nguyen and his soldiers watched the tremendous blasts and flashes coming from the container ship they'd been monitoring a few miles offshore, and he figured correctly that their submarine had decided to sink her. All was quiet for a few minutes as the resulting flames grew and silhouetted the big ship, but then he heard the distinctive noise of several motors approaching from the sea. There was also a kind of buffeting sound that shallow draft boats made when they skimmed across the water, but the engine and water sounds were heavier, like they were coming from bigger vessels. Whatever they were, they were heading for the shore a few meters directly below his position. Suddenly the cause of the noise became clear, when four giant hovercraft loomed out of the darkness—obviously intending to land below his trench line strung out along the low bluff. He'd seen photos of LCACs before, but up close they were bigger than he imagined and faster than he'd expected.

Ly put two and two together: His navy did not possess such craft, and he'd been notified to get ready for anything, so he shouted at his men to prepare to repel invaders. Every soldier in his command had been ready for some time, and the mortar men lifted the heavy rounds out of open boxes in their tube pits, and cradled them, ready to go. Ly picked up his field phone and gave his platoon leaders some last-minute guidance, then he called regimental headquarters and, in a voice as calm as his racing heart allowed, notified the XO that Vietnam was being invaded from the sea. The Quan Doi Trung Quoc (Mainland Chinese Army) was coming south again.

Aboard *Dragon's Wing*

Emergency klaxons were blaring unnecessarily and Captain Quan ordered them shut off. His sailors were in the process of launching the first of his four Type-726 LCACs when the explosions holed his port side, and he knew instantly they'd been struck by multiple torpedoes. He looked up at the threat board—a schematic of the ship that showed damage in the various compartments—and he knew immediately that his ship was in mortal danger. She would die from uncontrolled flooding—a situation exacerbated when the massive weight in her holds began slipping toward the listing side. Just then, General Ling raced back up the ladder to see what was going on. Quan spoke first, "Sir, three massive holes have been blown into and through the mini-sub compartments on the port side, and water is entering the tank storage bay. The holes are too big to seal off. If we counter-flood the starboard chambers now, the extra weight will bring the ship down. We have no choice but to abandon ship and make for shore ahead of schedule!"

General Ling wanted to scream at the navy captain, but it would be a waste of valuable time and energy. Now he wanted to save as many of his marines as possible and inflict at least some damage to the enemy. Any of his force that reached the beach could draw some attention from the northern border. "Do we have enough time to wait for the four LCACs to make two deliveries?"

"Probably not, General."

"All right, Captain, jettison all rafts, and launch the two power boats. I'll deploy ropes from them, and they can pull many men to shore that way. We'll fight as dismounted infantry." *What more can I do?* He headed for the main ladder again, shouting a series of orders to his hovering battalion commanders. They raced away to get the men off the ship and into the rafts. What the general had in mind would get hundreds of men to shore—armed only with rifles—but at least it was something. Unfortunately, his air wing was finished, too: The middle torpedo had exploded directly beneath the controllers' work stations in the bridge's lower stories, and most of them were dead and their computers destroyed. The drones had no default mechanism; without guidance they'd simply drop from the sky, so there was no sense launching them.

Dozens of canisters containing inflatable rafts shot off both sides of the stricken ship, and as soon as they hit the water, they broke open and were automatically inflated by gas cartridges. The marines had all practiced rescue floating and all could swim as part of their training, so the rafts were quickly pulled against the mothership and filled with men carrying rifles. The two powerboats had inboard 400 cubic-inch engines, and ropes were strung along from the aft stanchions, and passed down the line. In under 15 minutes, hundreds of marines were ready and the improvised flotilla headed for shore. Unfortunately for them, they'd arrive at a beach engulfed in a deadly crossfire.

Ngoc Xuyen Beach

Captain Ly's 2nd Company was giving a good account of itself: The four large LCACs had discharged 200 marines each, and all of them carried an array of small arms. They also had at least eight QBB-95 5.8 mm Light Support Weapons (light machine guns with high rates of fire) but Ly's men had the advantage of good cover and elevation, and they possessed both light and heavy machine guns of their own, plus mortars. The enemy soldiers were essentially trapped on the open flat beach between the water and the steep sand dunes and, even with the support of the twin 12.8 mm twin machine guns firing from the four 726 Yuri Class LCACs, they could not suppress the well dug-in Vietnamese infantry. The Vietnamese mortar men obviously knew the distance and elevations necessary to target the beach, and within seconds they walked round after round across the four giant boats. Within the first minute, Ly's men had fired so many rounds into the 726s that they could hardly back off the beach and, within a hundred yards, all four began to founder and sink. Ten minutes later, half the first wave of Chinese marines were dead or dying.

Just then a bullet grazed Captain Ly's right arm, knocking him down, but after briefly wincing in pain, he willed himself back into the fight. Adrenaline carried the day for all those not seriously injured, and the medic who watched him fall practically had to sit on him to apply a simple bandage. "I need air support!" Ly barked into his radio at the regimental air liaison officer, but all he got was a neutral reply: All air assets were involved in the massive fight developing on the northern border. Yet the air force promised to try. Ly then took stock of the unfolding battle. He was proud of his men; they were inexperienced in real combat, and many were wounded, but they were dropping enemy soldiers on the beach and no one had run away. So far, they were holding their positions and had driven off the big LCACs, but Ly had to accept that more waves would come out of the darkness soon.

Chapter 35

Aboard *Dragon's Claw*, docked at The Embarcadero, San Francisco, California December 7th, 12:30 Hours (H-Hour plus 90 minutes)

Admiral Sun was more relieved than anything else. All four of his Dragons had docked where and when they were supposed to, and did so unopposed, as planned. They'd all deployed their four mini-subs about 40 nautical miles off the entrances to the target harbors, and all four sets of 726 LCACs had launched in plenty of time to be well away before the various harbor pilots were taken on board. And, somewhat surprisingly to Sun, the omnipresent American satellite watchers had ignored this dispersal of what should appear to be hostile water craft. He'd received a terse message that the space war was progressing, but that made him suspicious that something had gone wrong. He'd make more pointed inquiries later in the day, but for now his four operations were unfolding as planned.

Most important of all, 100 percent of their air wings had deployed and were wreaking havoc on their comprehensive list of enemy targets. The drones were overwhelming the enemy's defenses, and were proving to be the key new weapon of the war. In the three targeted military bases, first reports indicated that all of the ships and submarines were burning or sunk, and that the related infrastructure was also severely damaged. Additionally, the ground forces had deployed without a hitch, and enemy opposition had been lighter than expected—unable to cope with the clouds of mini-drones they had not trained for. The combined blanket of large and small drones was performing above expectation, and potential threats within the four larger regions were non-factors. His mission had been a total success and, if he died today, he'd accomplished his two primary objectives: His assault forces had nearly vacated the motherships, and all 14 were ultimately expendable anyway. If higher-ups could negotiate something for the survivors of this multi-pronged raid, great, but at this point every exit strategy was a big "if." He'd lived to see his mission succeed, and even the Americans' East Coast fleets were in ruins. Sun could rightly argue that, next to their victory over the Nationalists proclaimed on October 1, 1949, this was the greatest day in Chinese military history.

Docking at the Pier 27 complex had gone off without a hitch. The MSS agents on the ground had ensured that the space was ready, and they'd even rented forklifts to move some boxes and equipment out of the places where the ramps would set down. The only surprised person was the harbor pilot, who almost had apoplexy when the helmsman went hard-over to starboard when *Claw* passed the North Beach/Fisherman's Wharf piers. *Claw* had been proceeding slowly toward the Port of Oakland when she'd suddenly rounded the northeast corner of the San Francisco Peninsula and headed for the first set of civilian piers. The tug captains had both screamed into their radios and backed away, but Wing's agents had commandeered two tugs of their own and these smoothly intervened and pushed *Claw* the last mile to her berth. The ramps had deployed as designed and the vehicles and troops quickly disgorged and fanned out to their assigned positions throughout San Francisco. The four LCAC 726s had landed at their assigned spots, too: One came ashore at the aptly named China Beach just outside the Golden Gate Bridge on the Fort Point side—and its 150 marines on foot, plus an additional 20 mounted on motorcycles, had moved up and into the old Presidio grounds. The other three hovercraft had spread themselves out a bit farther south, landing along Ocean Beach from just below the Cliff House Restaurant to Fort Funston near the city's famous zoo. They were the western containment force comprised of nearly 600 marines and 60 motorcycles—more than enough manpower to handle any random acts of rebellion or non-cooperation from the local citizens—or from interference by their lightly armed police force.

Ngoc Xuyen Beach
December 8th, 02:30 Hours (local)

Captain Ly nearly wept with relief when two heavy-duty army trucks roared to a stop in the darkness, just 50 meters behind his beleaguered men. His men had been fighting alone for 90 minutes, and were just about out of small arms ammo, grenades, and mortar rounds. Out jumped 20 reserve soldiers who'd been dispatched from the local armory, and each struggled up the slight incline with two heavy cans of everything Ly's soldiers needed. They even had belts of machine gun ammo draped around their necks. These replacements were just a small part of the massive reserve force that was in the process of being mobilized nationwide—most of whom the general staff was sending north—but Ly's regimental commander had managed to peel off these precious 20—plus what each could carry.

"Hurry, men!" Ly called to the new arrivals straining under their heavy loads. They were just in time; Ly had already spotted two power boats returning with another batch of soldiers riding in towed rafts. They had earlier dropped off hundreds of enemy soldiers just outside the surf line, and then disappeared in the darkness. These new arrivals didn't have any weapons, but there were hundreds of rifles and several machine guns lying on the bloody sand.

From the water's edge to the base of the low sand dunes where his sand-bagged trenches had been dug years before, it was a scene from Hell. Dead enemy soldiers were piled on top of each other, and these were visible in the constant flashes from the guns of the combatants, from the star shells Ly's men shot from their mortar tubes, and from the growing fires raging on the giant ship sinking just off shore. Ly had to remain detached from the horror as he and his men fought for their country and their lives, but in some part of his soul he knew this was the turning point of his life. He watched the latest line of rafts speed by about 20 yards beyond the small waves, and the soldiers rolled off and stumbled though the knee-deep water toward the beach.

"Shift fire!" commanded Ly, and his men began to rake the advancing Chinese marines. Those who survived the small arms fire crawled over their fallen comrades and found weapons and ammo among the dead. They began firing up at Ly's men—only half of whom could still fight. "Illumination!" Ly yelled at his mortar crews and, within a few seconds, the beach was bathed in yellowy light as new star shells burst overhead. At least half of those already on the beach were lying still, and the rare sections of open sand were covered with dark patchy stains. The enemy had run into Vietnamese troops that were well trained and as highly motivated as any troops could be. They held the high ground, had reasonably good cover, an adequate supply of ammunition, and knew the terrain well. The enemy marines fought well, but without the equipment they'd trained with, and without their clouds of drones to protect them, they had little chance. Not many would leave the beach alive.

Eglin Air Force Base, Florida (same time)

Major Pete Randall and Captain Lenore Streeter jogged from the pilots' lounge with their helmets in hand—both elated that they'd been chosen by circumstances to be America's first warriors to strike back at an invading enemy. They'd been happy enough to fly down to Eglin AFB from Whiteman because flying was flying, but since their arrival the day before they'd just been shooting the breeze with the F-35 Lightning II trainees, who were happy enough to learn a bit about the famous B-2 Spirit. Cross-familiarization was as old as military training, and the Air Force familiarized its pilots and ground crews with a variety of American and foreign aircraft. The bomber pilots thought it might be fun to take a spin in the new fighters, and the base commander promised they could ride in the back seats of the F-35 trainers. Randall and Streeter enjoyed sharing the capabilities of the B-2 with the young trainees—especially the fact that the Spirit could carry 80 500-pound bombs.

But, for the combat sortie today, their B-2 would carry 16 2,000-pound JDAMs (Joint Direct-Action Munitions), essentially a dumb bomb with an attached guidance package that made it maneuverable. The B-2 had the APQ-181 synthetic aperture radar system, plus other targeting and navigation systems, and four of the JDAMs would be dropped from miles away onto each of the stationary ships. They'd been assured by their briefing officer that the best Chinese ADA systems could not detect the Spirits flying at 50,000 feet.

Today's mission would be the first retaliation against the CCP aggressors, and regaining home ground was the first task in this new war. Once that was accomplished, the United States would join their many allies and systematically roll back the enemy forces. However, the longer the U.S., Japan, and Australia had to contend with their domestic situations, the harder it would be to dislodge the PLA from their ill-gotten gains.

Sitting in the afternoon sunshine, the Spirit was a lethal beauty: A "flying wing" that looked like a creature out of science fiction, she was nonetheless real, and the world's enemies were right to fear her because the stealthy radar signature was so small as to be nearly undetectable. The pilots strapped in and went through their check lists before taxiing toward the main runway. When the tower released them, they took off over the Gulf of Mexico, and turned west toward San Diego.

Wheeler Field, Oahu, Hawaii (same time)
4th Squadron, 4th Cavalry
(TDY to the 25th Infantry Division's Aviation Regiment)

Ninety minutes after the first shots were fired in Honolulu Harbor, the nightmare of the mini-drone aerial attacks had somewhat dissipated around the U.S. Army garrison at Wheeler Field. CW2 (Chief Warrant Officer 2) Gaston Mackenzie was (1) thankful to be alive, and (2) thrilled that his AH-64E Apache Guardian attack helicopter was intact and ready to fly. Half his squadron had not been so lucky: Non-flyable Apaches were sitting in neat rows, but holed in dozens of places or burned into smoldering wrecks. The entire area was a complete mess: Windows had been shattered in every building, work bays blown up and, tragically above all, cavalry troopers were lying everywhere either dead or badly wounded and being attended to by brave medical personnel. The drones had descended on them without warning, and the tiny things had destroyed everything of military value—exploding like thousands of mini-hand grenades on the loose. After that, the bigger drones had climbed a few hundred feet above the carnage and released deadly bombs onto the hangars and barracks inside the fort's acreage. Some of the munitions had penetrated sturdy roofs and exploded inside maintenance bays and killed everyone there.

4/4 Squadron's 12 Apaches were visiting tropical Hawaii on a two-month training exercise—a thorough preparation for future attachment to the 25th Division. Gaston's unit was normally stationed at Fort Lewis in Washington State, and had been flown over in six C-17 Globemaster IIIs. And, until this morning, Hawaii had been all they'd hoped for: Training was hard but fun, and they got to fly a lot. But they'd had plenty of free time, too, and everyone had really enjoyed the beach and the food (and the married guys had flown over their families, while the single guys like him had enjoyed the local social scene). Most of the troopers were hoping they'd be stationed here permanently—but after the drones descended on their post, he and the surviving crews were all business.

Gaston and his co-pilot/gunner, CW2 Bobby Wells, waited while the ground crew pushed the machine out of its hardened shelter and onto the pad, then they hopped in. They warmed up the engine and completed their pre-flight, then took off with three other Apaches to kill as many enemy tanks as they could. Gaston/Wells were third in line out of the four, and the flight plan called for them to first head southeast toward the ocean then, after they were well out to sea, to swing around and attack from the south.

Gaston moved his stick slightly as he followed the others and heard a click on his headset when the fourth Apache took off behind him. Each attack helo was ideally suited to kill armor vehicles of all kinds, and they could carry mission-dependent mixes of rockets and Hellfire missiles. Today the four helos each carried 16 of the tank-killing Hellfires—and 4/4 were the bad boys of anti-armor warfare. Their plan was to come in just above the waves, pop up over the south end of the container port, and then unleash a barrage of the lethal missiles at the ChiCom MBTs. The heavy tanks were currently queuing to exit the huge parking lot so they could merge onto the H1 Freeway to Hickam Field, lying only a couple of miles west. However, the merge ramp was a bottleneck, and an off-duty SEAL with a cell phone had hidden himself on the edge of the lot in a clump of scrub palms and was giving the aviators the play by play. Visibility over the ocean was perfect, but the harbor area was heavily obscured by smoke from the numerous fires burning in Pearl Harbor, and from planes destroyed on the runways at Hickam Field.

The Apache crews had been given a quick briefing on the layout of the container port and where to zap the tanks. They'd also been informed that the 25th Division was rapidly mobilizing—moving its Stryker Infantry vehicles and soldiers down Oahu's central valley toward the harbor. If they could dodge the drones, they would begin duking it out with the ChiCom armor within the hour. However, that was problematic for the time being and their advance had temporarily ground to a halt. It was shaping up as the biggest battle in Hawaiian history—including those between the ancient Polynesian tribes that had fought one another for centuries.

The 25th had far more men and vehicles than the ChiCom invaders, but they were essentially a light infantry division with mobile Stryker cannons. They were going against a heavy armor brigade that had 100 heavy tanks, plus an additional 100 infantry fighting vehicles. The enemy enjoyed nearly complete air superiority, and the Air Force F-35s at Hickam that attempted to take off at the beginning of the battle just belly-flopped at the end of the runway after honey bee-sized drones were sucked into the engines' air intakes. When the engines blew up, the fighters skidded along the runway like dead birds. The FA-18s at Marine Corps Base Hawaii (at Kaneohe) had fared even worse: All had been destroyed on the ground within a few minutes of hostilities, and even the one ready-bird never got airborne. It was a new kind of warfare and the American military had no answer.

The Apache mission was the Army's way of trying to adapt. They came in low over the water, and popped up at the last minute to punch off their missiles. The southernmost Apache got off two good shots, and two tanks on the merge ramp blew up. He peeled off to make another pass and, one by one, the other three AH-64Es executed the same maneuver with similar success. Then, before any of them could line up again for additional shots, four streaks of brilliant light shot out from a small turret attached to the upper side of the Dragon mothership and killed all four Apaches' engines. The helos were close to the ground, so they just dropped like stones and bounced and rolled. Their rotary blades hit the cement of the huge container storage area and disintegrated, and deadly shards scattered everywhere. However, the Halon fire-suppression systems worked as designed inside the cockpits, and all four crews survived. Gaston and Wells were shaken, but they managed to extricate themselves, and ran as best they could back toward the shoreline. But they and their mates didn't get far: They were immediately surrounded by ChiCom soldiers and, just like that, their war was over. The eight pilots were led off to a warehouse on the edge of the lot and told to sit with the longshoremen and the other civilians who'd been rounded up an hour before. One pilot had a broken arm that a Chinese medic put in a splint, and he also gave him a shot for the pain.

"Lasers!" Gaston whispered to his gunner. The two aviators settled next to a crane operator named Tom who was whispering with a harbor pilot named

Don. But their whispers were overheard, and the nearest guard gave them a dirty look and shook his head. From then on, the prisoners just kept quiet and hoped for the best.

Aboard the B-2 Spirit

Flying almost due west at 50,000 feet, the two pilots monitored their navigation systems and spoke quietly as if the enemy could overhear. They would reach their first target in just over two hours, and estimated that they'd drop on the second mothership about an hour after that. They were confident that four JDAMs were sufficient to settle the big ships into the mud.

Chapter 36

White House Situation Room, 18:00 Hours

As afternoon turned to evening, Secretary of Defense Baker Halsey received a particularly startling report among the constant stream of updates that had been pouring in from myriad sources. Most of the key cabinet officers had been coming and going as the dynamic situation ebbed and flowed, but everyone was in the room when he interrupted the President, who was currently engaged in a side conversation with Edith Carmichael, Director of National Intelligence. The CIA was one of 16 intelligence agencies that reported to her, and she'd been updating the President on some recent developments.

President Stilwell saw the SecDef's hand and knew it had to be important. "Yes, Baker?"

"Mr. President, some more bad news: The *Reagan* and several of her escorts have been sunk by multiple torpedo and ICBM strikes."

Spence was sick at heart to hear the tragic news, but he was psychologically adjusting his expectations downward to accommodate the steady stream of negative information. The country was in a real jam and, though he had no doubt they'd eventually eradicate the ChiComs from American soil, the lives lost and the accumulating damage to the U.S. military could take years to repair—possibly longer than after World War II. He'd visited the *Reagan* in Japan and met many of her sailors and Marines—young men and women who might be dead now—and that was the greatest loss of all. He felt impotent, and lifted a silent prayer heavenward: *Holy Father, I need Your supernatural wisdom.* He then responded to Baker as professionally as he could, "She was 25 percent of our remaining big-deck carrier fleet…" He sensed that Baker had more to report, and didn't want to take out his anguish on him. "…What else?"

"Sir, most of the crew from the carrier, four destroyers, and one cruiser were picked up. The remaining destroyers from DESRON 15, plus one of the cruisers and one of the submarines, have them on board and will off-load them ASAP. The ASW teams got the four subs that sprung the ambush but, at one point, the fleet intelligence officer estimated that there were more than 20 torpedoes in the water. They're using the same tactics that the U-boat packs did decades ago. Unfortunately, that was not the end of the battle: The next attacks came in the form of sea-skimming ship-to-ship missiles similar to our Harpoons. They sank or damaged several additional vessels, including the LHA *America* and Japan's *Izumo*. They are still afloat but limping back toward Japan."

Spence felt overwhelmed again, and just walked to his chair and slumped. "Okay, Baker. Just keep the news coming—good or bad. But we can't keep trading our carriers for enemy subs. That math won't work!" *I need to hear it all.*

"Yes, Mr. President." Baker replied. *I wonder who's more depressed: Spence or me?*

USS *North Carolina*

The Shark's sixth sense had his spine tingling again—usually a prescient warning that trouble was near. They'd escaped destruction inside Pearl Harbor, but now they were fully engaged against the enemy in the one environment where the U.S. Navy still excelled. After a brief time at 400 feet, he'd ordered the boat to 800 feet—and they were now running at dead slow with enforced silence. He wanted to give his best-in-the-world sensors a chance to expand the threat picture out as far as possible. Part of his tingle was just circumstantial, but Zap's tape of the possible drones dropping away from *Dragon's Tail* earlier was worth a thorough investigation. He crossed the attack center to the sonar room and got the ball rolling: "Zap, run that tape on the possible drones you heard when the Chinese merchie stopped—I want a full analysis ASAP!"

"Aye, aye, Skipper!" Zap hit a couple of buttons and the computer selected the relevant data. The captain left him to it—the computer would take about five minutes to make sense of the information.

Back in the attack center, the Shark was willing his silent boat to hear any enemy—surface or submerged. They were simultaneously plotting several ships that had been inbound for Pearl—but since hostilities began, all were obviously hovering—just cruising in slow circles until the local situation clarified. All U.S. military ships and subs in port were presumed damaged, and the civilian merchies and passenger ships inside the commercial port were too afraid to move. His boat was also listening for the low-level messaging alerts that would send them to the surface to receive orders or updates, but that sensor was silent, too. Yet, he had that unsettled feeling, and Zap would have something for him shortly—the kid was almost supernatural in his abilities to hear and analyze noises, almost like he was another sea creature himself. Right on cue, the young sonar man popped out of his little room. "Whatcha got, Zap?"

"Captain, there were four distinct propellers, and electric boat machinery noises. As soon as I knew what to listen for, I nailed them!"

"Don't keep me in suspense..." Several folks were listening to the interesting revelations.

"Skipper, they are about 30 miles southwest, bearing one nine seven degrees. Just hovering in a loose formation about 5 miles across—at about one hundred feet. They are new boats, Sir—not previously in the computer."

"Good work, Sailor!" Then the Shark addressed his tracking party: "All right, everyone...let's close in real slow. Silent as a ghost. Take us down to 800 feet at 5 knots—one nine seven degrees." Excitement shot through the attack center, and then worked its way throughout the boat. Now they were hunting—and no enemy sub in the world could hear them coming.

Aboard *Dragon's Wing*, just off Ngoc Xuyen Beach December 8th, 05:00 Hours

Since there was no point in his sailors or the few remaining marines dying for nothing in the uncontrollable fires, Senior Captain Quan pulled down the bridge mic and ordered his crew to abandon ship. "Clear all engineering spaces immediately! All crew into the water. Put on your life jackets and swim for the beach; the ship will roll to port so get away as fast as you can!" He then replaced the mic, and reached over to a covered button and flipped open the covering cap: It was a special siren that would sound throughout the ship—an alarm signaling that the ship was going down. *I will go down with my Dragon, but I will not murder my crew!*

Major General Ling heard the announcement from the tank garage where he was personally supervising the evacuation. He wanted his marines to fight and, if necessary, die with honor on the beach, rather than to drown like rats in this big tub. "All ranks into the water!" He bellowed at the 300 marines still waiting for their turns on the rafts. "Drop your rifles, men; there are many available on the beach. Just get to shore and fight!" He stood aside as the lines of men pushed through the opening—the sill now at water level—and just stepped into the calm water and stroked away. The ship had a decided list to port, and he knew it was only a matter of time before the weight of the vehicles in the hull tipped the scales. Half the vehicles had been unchained hours before in anticipation of the harbor landing, and they would slide first. It was only 200 feet to the bay's shallow bottom—just enough to nicely cover the ship. *What a waste of an entire armor brigade!*

USS *North Carolina*
Thirty-five nautical miles southwest of Pearl Harbor

The Shark had that tingling feeling again. They'd been closing in on the four ChiCom subs, but he wouldn't fire until they were so close that the enemy boats couldn't get off more than one snap shot apiece. He had to assume they were armed—otherwise why place them in a tactical formation? And he had to assume that they were manned boats with well-trained captains and fighting crews.

North Carolina had crept toward the enemy quartet during the intervening hours. It had been painstakingly slow but, when outnumbered four to one, you had to get it right the first time. They'd maintained their deep approach so that they could come up under the four as quiet as a mouse, and the amazing combination of factors (tight construction, whisper quiet engines and reactor, scientifically designed propeller blade, anechoic tiles and skin covering the outside metal of the hull, and the discipline of the crew) all contributed to the *Virginia*-class submarines being a generation or more ahead of the competition. The result was life-saving quiet, combined with unparalleled sonar, enemy tracking, and multi-weapons systems lethality that should intimidate every (potentially adversarial) navy out of the water. But intimidation had failed this time, so the Shark and his crew would have to scare the world again.

The tracking party had locked firing solutions into the four forward-firing torpedo tubes, and each was loaded with Mark 48 Mod 7s. They were programmed with the Common Broadband Advanced Sonar System (CBASS) and only needed the captain's order to fire. However, patience was the order of the day, and everyone onboard wanted to get as close as possible to avoid an enemy counter-attack. This far from Oahu, it was a long way to the bottom.

The *North Carolina* continued to creep until she was within one mile of the two middle enemy boats, which worked out to just over two miles to the two on the edges of their formation. The Shark didn't want to press their luck further, so he simply looked over at the Weapon's Officer, whose hand was poised about the firing button, and said: "Fire one! Fire two! Fire three! Fire four!" Each order was given about three seconds apart. He waited for another three seconds, then gave his next order: "Diving Officer, all ahead full at two-seven-zero. Make your depth 1,200 feet!"

"Full ahead to 1,200 feet," came the repeated order. The big boat surged straight forward, and her steep angle of descent rapidly separated her from the four targets above. Since the Mod 7s were capable of fire-and-forget homing, and quickly reached their top speed of nearly 65 knots in seconds—the shocked and hapless enemy subs had " none-chance." The first fish exploded ten feet under the keel of the nearest mini-sub that was just starting to turn away from the sudden threat and, before the *North Carolina* reached her desired depth, the other 650-pound warheads exploded within feet of their respective targets. The force was so violent that the smaller boats shattered into a thousand tiny pieces. The fourth target's captain had just enough time to order a snap shot, but that fish was only a few feet from the boat when it was nearly vaporized, too. The larger pieces of the first mini-sub were about half-way to the bottom when the last one's broken hull started its long descent into the abyss. By then, the Americans were three nautical miles west and two thermoclines down.

The Shark was happy for the kills, but he never forgot that his enemies were fellow human beings. At least those sailors died quick. But this was war and their side started it. He'd been wondering how many American sailors died a few hours previously—brutally attacked while peacefully preparing for a Sunday morning in port.

"They never heard us until our first shot, Skipper." This from the XO. He was as pleased as the CO that the crew restrained their celebration. It was grim business they were about and, like their captain, they'd all quickly transitioned into rather cold professionals.

The Shark pulled down his mic and addressed the crew: "Excellent work, everyone! I'm proud of you—this was a first-class job against a dangerous enemy. But this war is just beginning, and we'll take the fight to them until they surrender! Secure from general quarters and relax a little while we come to the surface and report in. I'll get as much information about our families as I can. That is all." The he looked over at his Diving Officer, "Stan, bring us up slowly." Then he called over to sonar, "Conn, sonar. Any contacts, Zap?"

"Sonar aye, Captain. The closest contact is a large civilian tanker at 45 miles, bearing two-eight-four."

"Very well." The angle of the deck gradually changed as the helmsmen pulled back on their yokes and the diving planes responded accordingly. It took about 15 minutes to rise 1,100 feet before the sub leveled off for an additional scan with their subsurface sonar systems. Then they raised a bit more until the AN/BLQ-10 Electronic Warfare Mast went up to sniff the airways for any activity—threatening or otherwise. The *North Carolina* also had two photonic masts that replaced the traditional periscopes, two communication masts, a radar mast with a AN/BPS surface search and navigation radar, plus a high-data-rate SATCOM mast for SHF (super high frequency) downlinks, and an EHF (extremely high frequency) mast for uplink communications. After confirming they were safe enough for a scan, the Shark made a quick traverse of the horizon. No ships, no planes. Good. Then he used the uplink and fired off an encoded burst that went both to Pearl and to the Pentagon. It was a calm early winter afternoon at sea, so he decided to tool along the surface until he got a reply. He didn't expect a rapid response because the war was still expanding over a third of the Earth.

Aboard the USS *California* (same time)
500 nautical miles west of the Oregon Coast

RC had driven his boat fast in pursuit of the four fleeing PLAN missile boats and, along with her sister submarine USS *Connecticut*, had steadily reeled them in. He'd ordered his boat to drift twice to clarify the sonar picture, and they'd been able to identify two more enemy boats waiting about 50 nautical miles farther west. It took a bit of deduction, but he was pretty certain that the ChiComs were racing directly for a rendezvous with two attack boats—and it smelled like a trap. His chief sonar man nailed their machinery noises as certain signatures of known Type-093 nuclear attack boats (very similar to the venerable Soviet/Russian Victor IIIs), and they were subsequently tagged Charlie One and Charlie Two. There were no surface or airborne contacts in the vicinity.

"All ahead full," he ordered, and the *California* resumed her chase. He'd learned during his first drift at communication depth that the six ChiCom missile boats had rained death and destruction across the American heartland where they'd severely damaged Air Force bases and the Gulf Coast's principal ship-building company. The rest of the missiles had flown east and severely destroyed ships and submarines in six major naval ports/marine construction firms on the Atlantic seaboard. RC and his crew believed it was their duty to ensure that this ChiCom attack was a "one and done."

Aboard PLAN Type 94A Ballistic Missile Submarine *Shanghai*

"The two American boats are closing on us, Captain" the XO worried aloud. He knew the crew understood their predicament and was nervous, too.

"Have faith, my friend," answered the captain jovially. He never wanted to display stress in front of his subordinates, but he also felt reasonably confident that their rehearsed ambush would work; he was a gambler and liked six-to-two odds. When they drew even with their own waiting attack boats, all four missile boats would turn and form a line of resistance six abreast against the oncoming Yankees. They'd volley-fire four torpedoes each, then turn and continue their run west at flank speed. Twenty-four of their best Y-7s would give the American boats something to chew on, and he doubted that two Yankee boats could dodge 24 torpedoes at once.

Chapter 37

On the South Korean side of the DMZ
December 8th, 08:00 Hours

After nearly 70 years, the long-simmering pause in the Korean War had come to a violent end. However, this time it was not the resumption of the hot war between the original belligerents—brothers with different philosophies of government. The peace was broken by 300,000 PLA troops crossing the North Korean frontier just after midnight local time. The dozens of infantry battalions were supported by ten heavy tank divisions, massive artillery and missile barrages, and paratroop drops in several key locations. Fifth columnists had been extensively operating in selected areas for months, and the North Korean military and civil defense cadres were confused into total dysfunction.

Farther south, the Republic of South Korea (ROK) had been hit by wave after wave of ballistic and cruise missiles, and both their own military, and that of their long-term American guests, had been seriously degraded. They were also under attack by the small but potent force that disgorged from the cleverly camouflaged assault vessel, *Dragon's Fear*, which had landed a heavy armor brigade at the Busan Container Harbor. It hadn't taken the Chinese armored force long to brush aside the light defenses around the port, but their attack slowed down after a few hours when the ROK army gathered itself and counter-attacked in force. These South Korean ground forces were supported by their own surviving air force planes and helicopter gunships, and were aided by a few sorties from the few American Air Force A-10C Thunderbolt II (tank killers) from the 25th Fighter Squadron. These few had survived the plastering the ChiCom missiles had given Osan and Kunsan Air Force Bases. The entire Korean Peninsula was being squeezed between iron jaws trying to crush the two warring "cousins."

2nd Combat Aviation Brigade Commander Colonel William "Bill" Greenbaum had flown up from the ruins of Camp Humphreys to scout the

DMZ. The 8th Army commander had asked him to personally scan the border area for any noticeable threats, because everyone was unsure of the effect the Chinese invasion would have on the always unpredictable North Korean military. They might move south in hopes of escaping, or might fully commit to stopping the PLA advance. So far, satellite photos showed the latter: Every tank in the NK arsenal was pushing north to meet the rapidly advancing ChiCom divisions.

Personally, Colonel Greenbaum was greatly concerned that widespread panic across many sectors of NK society would prompt thousands—perhaps millions—to try their luck in the extensive mine fields that formed a patchwork of death on both sides of the long-disputed border. Not only would it be a humanitarian disaster of epic proportions, it would interfere with U.S. B-52 bomb strikes that would clear the minefields if the Allies decided to move north, too. But if the Allied high command decided to fight a strictly defensive campaign, the minefields became a tactical advantage.

"What do you think, JP?" the colonel asked his brigade XO, Lieutenant Colonel Jackson Pruitt. "Will the ChiComs try to drive the civilian population ahead of them to clear the fields—or will it just evolve circumstantially?"

"Probably the latter, Sir. But there's a third possibility: The NK civilians may receive the ChiComs as liberators and just get out of the way…"

The colonel had to chuckle despite the fact that his country had just found itself in the middle of a fresh world war. "Hard to wrap my head around a regime that is so bad that a ChiCom invasion is an improvement!"

"Know what you mean, Sir. I was just thinking about the Ukrainians who welcomed the German advance in 1941."

"Too bad they didn't know about the Einsatzgruppen SS killing squads that came along behind the regular troops, and executed civilians." The colonel was Jewish and many of his relatives had been murdered in the Holocaust. He knew that history well.

"Yes, Sir. Pretty sick." The two of them stood in the early morning light and watched and waited, listening for anything out of the ordinary. They were familiar with the area, because one of 2nd Aviation Brigade's missions was to cover the South Korean military's defense of this key corridor on the western side of their country. Libby Bridge and Freedom Bridge crossed the

Imjin River here and, if the ChiComs couldn't be stopped, the ROK combat engineers would blow the bridges. When the dust settled from the blasts, those soldiers surviving on the north side of the river would have to swim for it—hoping to link up with Allied forces in the south. Not too many American or ROK civilians knew the expectations of the generations of U.S. and ROK soldiers serving in Guard Post Ouellette, Camp Liberty Bell, Camp Kitty Hawk, or Camp Greaves, but when war broke out, they were the most dangerous outposts in South Korea. When your life span is measured by the number of minutes you can hold off a massive invading army, you wrote letters home before settling in. And it had been that way for almost 70 years.

"Better get going, JP…"

"Yes, Sir. Still a lot to do." The two men walked a few paces back to where heat from the Brigade Commander's Blackhawk helicopter was still condensing in the freezing morning air. Though keeping their own counsel, both men were thinking the same thing: The rice paddies had hardened enough for tanks to cross with ease. The Allied military units had taken quite a beating in the missile attacks, and much of their equipment and infrastructure was gone. They could still fight but, realistically, there wasn't much to stop the PLA tank divisions from driving all the way to Busan Harbor.

USS *California*

RC was another skipper with highly attuned danger antennae, and the trap scenario was really tingling his sixth sense. He ordered another "drift and listen" and, after the boat had glided through the cold water for a few seconds, the sonar picture cleared and he was correct: Six enemy boats were waiting in a north/south line about 25 nautical miles west. The two American boats were close to the edge of the ChiCom torpedoes' effective range, so the U.S. skippers had to game-plan the rest of their approach with tactical care.

"Okay, everyone," RC addressed the attack center, "let's move in silently to insure we get off the first shots. We're going to use our advantages." All four tubes had been loaded and the main computer was automatically calculating the diminishing ranges and updating the firing solutions. He hadn't communicated with *Connecticut*, but he knew Captain Randy Cummings well and the logic of the situation just screamed splitting the targets down the middle. They were like an experienced quarterback and wide receiver who had played together for several years; the former would just throw to the open area and know his receiver would be there. *California* would take the southern three boats and RC knew Randy would attack the northern three. Sweet—except it was still two against six—and anyone could get lucky.

"Conn, Sonar: Skipper, it looks like Captain Cummings read your mind."

RC and the XO both stepped into the sonar room, and saw on the waterfall that their colleague had stopped and drifted, too. *Connecticut* would see the *California* creeping forward and they would sneak in together. "Great minds…" RC stepped back into the attack center. Everything was ready: He'd shoot four fish, and Randy would shoot eight because the Seawolf class had eight torpedo tubes instead of four, and twelve '48s would make quite an impression on the six waiting ChiComs. But he also knew the enemy boats would be planning to volley-fire their own fish, and their Dash Sevens were pretty good. He'd shoot his four, wait until the tactical picture clarified, then probably go very deep, very fast, and let any enemy torps cruise past overhead. Then he'd listen and fire four more 48s if necessary. *Am I missing something?* It was the common question that haunted every good commander in every navy: Submarines fought in a three-dimensional world that demanded a certain kind of mental gymnastics. *In theory, I'm doing everything right.*

Now things got really tense: RC knew that everyone who could see him was glancing his way. But command required that he alone would give the order to fire their torpedoes. He was relying almost entirely on instinct because his total combat experience was the one engagement a few hours ago. But the Silent Service trained and fought in a unique environment and, after more than two decades in attack boats, RC knew what he was doing. He'd absorbed as much as he could. *If I guess wrong, a hundred and twenty young Americans will be dead in half an hour.* But he was a cool customer, and he let the minutes tick by until they were within 5,000 yards of the southern-most enemy sub. Then he had that moment of certainty: "Match bearings and shoot!" he commanded.

"One fired!" came the reply, and the boat rocked.

"Fire two! Fire three! Fire four! Close outer doors, and reload all tubes!"

"Captain, all outer doors are closed!"

Sonar called out: "All fish running hot, straight, and normal, Captain!"

"Okay, everyone, let's sit tight and see what the bad guys do." He had moved back into the sonar station to watch the waterfall again. He was looking for indications that the six subs were taking evasive action, and/or firing their own weapons.

"There goes the *Connecticut*'s fish, Skipper," the sonar chief confirmed excitedly. *Splitting the enemy's focus will take a lot of heat off us!*

"Okay, the ChiComs are launching rapidly!" the chief sonar man announced. There were few civilian-world comparisons to the life-and-death tensions of submarine combat.

"Yes, I see them…" RC confirmed out loud. "Ah, but they only launched one fish each—and they're turning tail again." He stuck his head back into the Attack Center. "Diving Officer, take us down to 1,200 feet. Two-seven-zero degrees at flank speed!"

"Aye, Captain. Depth twelve zero zero feet—two-seven-zero degrees at flank speed!"

The boat surged forward and sharply downward, as the planesmen pushed their yokes forward. The maneuver was a tried-and-true one that would slide the U.S. boat under the oncoming enemy torpedoes. Sonar called out that three enemy fish had been fired at each American boat, and both U.S. subs were propelling themselves deeper as fast as they could dive. The U.S. subs were about ten nautical miles apart, having closed the original gap during their several-hour pursuit of the fleeing enemy. They'd vectored closer as the ChiComs had bunched together: The enemy attack boats were about six miles apart, and the four surviving 94As had squeezed between them. The Americans had used their superior quietness to get the drop on them, and had rattled their cages badly. The ChiCom ambush had failed so badly that they were the ones in a kill box—once again, the prey instead of the predator. *California* and *Connecticut* were hundreds of feet below the ChiCom torpedoes when they sped overhead in the opposite direction, and their own torpedoes were just minutes from catching their fleeing targets.

PLAN *Shanghai*

"Many torpedoes!" shouted the chief sonar man in horror. "High speed screws coming from both Yankee vessels!"

"Fire one!" the captain ordered. "Right full rudder, flank speed!" The *Shanghai* and her sisters all did the same thing as per their training, and the four missile boats and two attack boats surged into tight turns away from the threats. Everyone not seated grabbed whatever railing or handhold was closest and, as soon as the boats straightened out, all six rapidly gained inline momentum and headed due west as their power plants quickly red-lined. Their makeshift "wolfpack" was now an anxious string of goats fleeing certain death. In terms of survival, it was every boat for itself.

USS *California*

"Twelve hundred feet, Skipper!" called out the chief of the boat—the key player charged with carefully monitoring the technical board with its incredibly accurate digital depth and speed gauges. "Flank speed obtained…" That was north of 40 knots so they were rapidly closing the distance to the fleeing enemy boats. The danger from the enemy torpedoes was rapidly diminishing.

"Conn, Sonar: The enemy fish passed west to east, and have not turned to follow!" The chief sonar man's voice indicated the relief they all felt.

"Very well…all ahead full, maintain course two-seven-zero." RC was playing it cool, but inside he was about as tense as he could get. His tactics were working so far and, if they could create enough distance between his boat and the enemy torpedoes—before their electronic brains figured out what had happened and turned to chase them—they'd escape. Slightly ahead and several hundred feet above, the six enemy subs were in full panic as the American torpedoes closed. But *California* and *Connecticut* had additional torpedoes if necessary, and they would not stop until they sank all six ChiCom boats. What a coup that would be!

"Conn, Sonar: Enemy fish turning, Captain, but not actively pinging. We are still separating."

"Very good, Sonar…keep those ranges coming".

"Aye, Skipper! Our first fish is closing on the closest ChiCom boat—there, it just started pinging!"

The tracking party was focused on their four torpedoes closing on the fleeing ChiComs, and no longer worried about the enemy fish: It would run out of fuel before catching them. The XO held up his stop watch and counted as the seconds ticked down. Then they all heard the powerful rumble as their first torpedo exploded—followed by one more a few seconds later—then two more quickly after that. "Three confirmed hits, Skipper!"

"Good shooting, Tracking Party!" RC exclaimed. He then stepped back into the sonar room and picked up a set of headphones. Sure enough, he could hear the break-up noises as the enemy boats died. It was sickening in one sense because they'd just killed an unknown number of fellow sailors, but it was their dirty job to do, and their country depended on them to do it. The Silent Service was entrusted with command and operation of America's submarines, and they were an elite fraternity—they could shoulder the responsibility and shake off the strain. He stepped back into the attack center. "Okay, set up the next shots and we'll nail any survivors!" The tracking party had anticipated that order and had already crunched the numbers and set up the computer-aided vectors. The tubes were already re-loaded, so the computer sent instructions to the 48s. They were ready to fire when the skipper gave the order.

"Conn, Sonar. The *Connecticut*'s fish just made multiple hits on two distinct targets!"

"Okay, that's cutting them down to size! Sonar, what's the distance of that fish on our tail?"

"Conn, Sonar: About 1,500 yards, Captain, and it has not acquired us."

RC decided it was time to bring the boat up. "Chief, all ahead two-thirds; make your depth 400 feet. Release a noisemaker!" The CPO manning the weapon's computer released a canister that spewed a massive cloud of small bubbles, and the disturbance confused the torpedoes' seeker head. Since his sub would be 800 feet higher than the sinking canister when the enemy fish arrived, it would provide an effective diversion until the torp ran out of fuel and sank. By then, *California* would have risen through two distinct layers of differing salinity and temperature, and those thermoclines would help mask them as well.

RC then got contemplative. He and *Connecticut* had killed five of the six fleeing ChiCom subs, but it was not enough: If even one missile boat escaped, they would return home and were capable of re-arming with nuclear-tipped missiles. The outcome of the war and millions of lives might depend on killing that one last boat. "Sonar, Conn. How far to Charlie 4?"

"Conn, Sonar: Just under 9,000 yards, Captain, bearing two-eight-five at 400 feet."

"Sonar, who's closer, us or *Connecticut*?"

"Skipper, we are 2,000 yards closer."

"All ahead one-third. Weapons officer, match bearings and shoot tubes one and two."

"Shooting tubes one and two, aye, Captain!" The late-twenties lieutenant checked the lights on his weapon's console, confirmed that they were all green, and depressed the red master switch that fired the torpedoes. He allowed three seconds between each shot, in the sequence the captain ordered. The boat shuddered with each launch as it took a tremendous amount of compressed gas to fire the 3,500-pound weapons. The *Connecticut*'s fish were ADCAPS, which were even bigger and required more energy. "Tubes one and two successfully fired, Captain!"

"Conn, Sonar: Skipper, that torpedo followed the noisemaker and it's headed for the bottom!"

"Good news, Chief!" RC had nearly forgotten about the enemy fish, but he was relieved nevertheless. News like that traveled like lightning from the attack center to the other compartments, and everyone took a collective breath. Now the U.S. boats were the lone hunters, and RC followed his speeding torpedoes with great anticipation.

Bunker of GS Han
December 8th, 11:10 Hours (local)

Late morning tea had been served by the nearly invisible staff, and Han and most of his trusted "kitchen cabinet" remained around the conference table sipping their favorite drink and munching on sweet and savory crackers. They were all watching the screens with great interest, but Han had one concern: "Marshal Tai, what is happening with our advance into Vietnam?" He understood that Dragon's *Wing* had foundered due to engine failure, but that had nothing to do with the meager results coming from their common border. The battle screens were clearly visible and the PLAs green-colored arrows had barely dented the frontier.

"General Secretary Han, that front is the only one giving us trouble. Our other 13 Dragons have fully occupied the targeted ports, and the land forces are making expected progress across their respective lines of advance." Tai was pleased: Thirteen out of 14 ports were under their control, and the overland armor spearheads were advancing rapidly. Even the rebellious province of Taiwan was thrashing ineffectively against his overwhelming power. Yet, he could not blame Han; Vietnam was closest to their southern military district headquarters, and the temporary stalemate stood out like a sore thumb.

"Did the military not budget enough forces to swiftly crush all the southern foes?" Han didn't like glaring mistakes, and so far, the whole Vietnamese theater was looking as bad as it had when China invaded in 1979. He was a young man then, but later, when he became privy to the facts, he came to believe it was a PLA failure. Could Tai and his battle staff have been as overconfident as the previous generation had been?

"Comrade Han, the PLA has ten armor divisions attacking all along that one common border, plus they're supported by massed artillery and significant PLAAF air sorties. However, we have received numerous reports that the enemy seemed more prepared for our assault than Comrade Wing led us to believe." Better to start shifting the blame in case this battle goes sideways.

The Foreign Minister then chanced an interruption, "Marshal Tai, what about the airborne forces you mentioned in your briefing? You said they would drop behind enemy lines, link up with your infiltrated commandos, and take control of the rear areas. What is their status?" *I hope our forces succeed, but this is just the kind of nightmare I've been dreading for months. Obviously, these soldiers learned nothing from their 1979 adventurism!*

"Good question, of course, Comrade Wu, but things do not always go according to the best plans. Unfortunately, the Vietnamese Air Force planes were not destroyed on the ground by Comrade Wing's Chaos Teams, and some of them also escaped our initial missile barrage. They were able to attack our planes carrying the airborne forces and shoot them down."

"So, what does that mean in terms of our airborne attack?"

"I am sorry to report that none of them reached their drop zones."

"All of them dead?" Han joined the conversation, alarmed. *I need to ask more questions!*

"I am afraid so." *Better change the subject fast.* "However, let's not overlook the tremendous success we are having against all our American targets! Both their West and East Coast naval bases have been overwhelmed by our drone and missile strikes, and their in-port fleets are nearly 100 percent destroyed!"

"That is commendable, Marshal Tai," responded Han. "But can you please tell us what is happening with the armor columns advancing across our southern border? Before we move on to discuss other battles, I want to understand why things are so far behind schedule on our very doorstep!" *I'm not going to let Tai snow me again—I sense he's hiding something.*

"Comrade Han, the enemy forces are putting up stiff resistance with their artillery and armor vehicles. But we've now shot down most of their air force, and it is just a matter of time before we wear down their ground forces. A delay in this front won't hurt us elsewhere..."

Then Comrade Liu spoke up, "Marshal Tai, I also noticed that we are behind schedule on the Indian frontier. Is there an unexpected problem there, too?" *I was against this radical strategy from the beginning! What will happen to us when the Americans strike back?*

Tai noticed Han's immediate acceptance of Liu's question, and wondered for the thousandth time what shared history they must have; they were both from the south so maybe they had secret family connections like he did. Well, as long as it didn't impact his defense ministry or business profits, he could not care less. "Comrade Liu, you are very perceptive. We are moving slower than our battle plan called for in the Indian Theater. It is due to the fact that they are a massive force. They have a lot of hidden artillery, and their air force is very strong. Plus, they rival us in infantry soldiers. However, I remain confident that our numerical superiority in tanks—plus our better armor technology—will prevail and carry the day. Additionally, we had not planned to advance much further—we just wanted to expand our buffer. These delays are inconsequential." He saw Comrade Liu's neutral nod—she was willing to accept his answer.

Han then decided he'd heard enough for the time being. "Okay, Marshal Tai, I think we'll take a break to attend to some other business, then return for a late lunch. Maybe you'll have some better news for us then?" Han rose and the others followed him to the elevator. Everyone had lots of calls to make.

USS *California*

RC moved back into the sonar room to watch the waterfall: His torpedoes were humming along so it wouldn't be long now. *Connecticut* hadn't even fired; it wasn't necessary. The enemy boat was going at flank speed—probably red-lining its reactor—but Mark 48s were relentless and would pursue at twice the speed of the fleeing target. Just then they started actively pinging so further enemy efforts were futile. Rapid fire explosions destroyed the last ChiCom sub, and the first "Battle of the Pacific" had ended with a decisive Allied victory.

"Great work, *California*!" RC called out to the crew, and was pleased as cheers reverberated throughout the boat. "Secure from General Quarters, maintain speed and bring us up to comms depth. Plot, get me a bearing for Guam!"

He heard the relayed orders and leaned back against a railing. They had done it: Eight enemy submarines would never kill another American. *California* had sunk five, *Connecticut* three—so now it was time to proceed west, restock with torpedoes from Guam's armory, and re-provision for the next patrol. The two U.S. boats could get in and out in one night, and then proceed as ordered by COMSUBPAC. RC ordered the helmsmen to edge closer to their sister boat so he could converse on the Gertrude—the underwater telephone that allowed them to communicate without surfacing. After that, RC had to update his Patrol Report—it would definitely have some dramatic entries.

White House Situation Room, 22:30 Hours

"Mr. President, we have some positive news!" Baker was glad to relay something good after the U.S. Navy had taken a terrible drubbing. He expected a lot more bad news in the coming days, but this was the first indication that they were fighting back. "The *California* and the *Connecticut* teamed up to sink all six of those ChiCom missile boats that attacked our Midwest and East Coast bases, then they nailed two attack boats that were apparently on station to escort the boomers back to China."

"Well, that is good news..." Spence agreed. "...message our gratitude and congratulations when you can." He didn't mind the brief cheer that filled the room—they all needed a lift.

Chapter 38

The 55th floor of the Sales Force Building
San Francisco, California, 19:30 Hours

Admiral Sun had relocated his battle staff to the highest point in the city, and his confiscated suite of offices had a spectacular view in every direction. The Americans hadn't turned off their lights yet, and they twinkled around the perimeter of San Francisco Bay and diminished into the distance. He figured that most of the local citizens were unaware of the gravity of the new war, and real combat hadn't visited this land for a century and a half. On his order, the marines had cleared out five floors of offices for their use, but had ordered the few people above, and the many below, to remain in place until further notice. He believed that his staff would be safer from attack if the building was teeming with civilian workers. They were indeed hostages, but would be treated as well as their captors could manage. After some days or weeks passed, and it was clear that his force was no longer needed in California, he'd pull his force out and head home. But he was a realist and couldn't count his chickens yet.

Sun's first order of business was to deliver a broadcast to a wide audience—on the surface directed at the people of the City and County of San Francisco, and to the greater Bay area. However, the larger audience included the President of the United States and the country and world as a whole. Sun would read from a carefully prepared script that incorporated the MSS's very latest analysis of the American psyche, their past and current historical values, and specific profiles of President Stilwell and some of his key leaders. It had been created over several months with many re-writes and, in the context of the PLA's overwhelming victories, it was still timely in every way. The PRC had achieved 100 percent of its goals in the United States' portion of Operation Unity, and more than 90 percent of its goals elsewhere. However, Sun didn't like the tone of the proclamation, and he knew it would not achieve what the Politburo wanted. He'd told them as much, and they'd told him to stay in his lane.

The White House Situation Room

President Stilwell returned to the conference table after nearly an hour in the secure communications room. He'd had three different calls with his international counterparts—the last with the leaders of all the countries currently under attack by the PRC. Another of the calls had been with friendly leaders whose countries were not directly involved and, by mutual agreement, they would sit on the sidelines for the time being. But they all offered passive help including fly-over permission and emergency landing rights that were invaluable in war. Now it was time to reconvene his war cabinet and receive updates. He found his seat and spoke without preamble, "Who wants to go first?"

"Looks like it falls to me, Mr. President," Baker offered. The Department of Defense was definitely in the crosshairs today. "There is actually some good news: Our *Virginia*-class attack submarine USS *North Carolina* escaped Pearl, and immediately started a combat patrol. And it seems her captain remembered some unusual sonar signals reverberating through the water when they passed the Dragon ship that was inbound to Honolulu. Turns out it had deployed four diesel/electric mini-subs, and our boat sank all four! We had to assume the same capability from the other motherships, so we've warned all relevant commands and Allies accordingly."

"Great news, Baker; three cheers for the *North Carolina*!" responded Dan Robinson.

"Indeed!" added Robert Gainsfield, who'd stopped by to give the President an update from the National Security Agency.

"We needed that, Baker!" added the President. "If my calculations are correct, our three Pacific subs sank 12 enemy boats. Plus, those that attacked the *Reagan*. What else do you have?"

"I can confirm that our earlier optimism regarding the first space war was conservative: Our anti-satellite network performed splendidly and most of our GPS system is still intact. This one victory may have the greatest long-term impact going forward."

"Excellent!" Spence and his predecessor had invested significant political capital—not to mention large expenditures of "black funds"—to place an anti-satellite system in orbit, but it had paid off big time today. Who said successive administrations couldn't cooperate for the common good? "And the situation in our four ports?"

"Nothing new, Sir. The PRC ground forces have fully discharged their large armored brigade from the motherships and have taken over all four port areas and immediate vicinities. All our low-flying aviation-related attempts to attack the vehicles on the ground and the motherships have largely failed due to their comprehensive drone force. We discovered the hard way that those motherships have anti-air laser weapons, too. Case in point: Four of our Apache helicopters attacked and destroyed a half-dozen of their main battle tanks in Hawaii, but within seconds of commencing their attack, all four were shot down by that laser. We are still counting on our B-2 strikes, but I have to admit that we were ignorant of the magnitude of both the ChiComs' drone force and their deadly laser weapons. Speaking of the B-2s, Mr. President, the Spirit's first strike is almost upon us; may we watch it in real time?"

"Yes, I think that will be both edifying and instructive." The President and everyone in the room looked anxiously at the center screen as it came alive with a somewhat blurred view of a large ship that was miles away and not directly below. They were receiving the feed from the bomber's targeting system, and the view included both the crosshairs and some sight picture data. They could also hear the pilot and mission commander speaking in low tones as they made a series of tiny adjustments before releasing their bombs. The enemy ship might guess that they were there, but their air defense radar would only "see" the cross-section of a threat the size of a pie-plate—flying 50,000 feet above their ship and several miles to the east.

The B-2 pilots weren't excessively worried about air defense missiles, or even about the ship's lasers: They were simply too far away. They reached the drop point and, in a calm professional voice, the command pilot simply said, "Bombs away…"

Everyone in the Situation Room noticed the screen wiggle a bit, then stabilize when the bombs released from the RLA (the Rotary Launcher

Assembly). The President wondered if they'd missed but, a few seconds later, four distinct explosions erupted along the top of the container stacks. If the targeted ship had been divided into four parts, the bombs hit within an arm's length of dead center within each quarter. The giant ship shuddered from the fearsome explosions, and tremendous eruptions of fire and smoke shot heavenward. The room was entranced by the live screen but, within 15 seconds, it became less and less clear as the plane flew away to the north. They looked forward to a repeat performance in one hour when the Spirit reached San Francisco.

"Good shooting, Baker!" exclaimed the President. "This is what the American people expect from their military! Can we make this feed available to our media outlets?"

"We can, Mr. President, but it will reveal a capability."

"Our people witnessed this kind of video in Desert Storm three decades ago. It is nothing new. They deserve the encouragement, and I want the ChiComs to know we are awake and on the move!"

"Certainly, Mr. President, we'll make it available ASAP. And, as you said, Sir, 'one down and three to go'…"

Dan Robinson was suddenly summoned by an aide and excused himself to take a call, but returned in less than a minute. "Mr. President, there is a live feed coming in from San Francisco: A ChiCom vice admiral is preparing to address the local area, but networks across the spectrum have been notified, so his message is for us, too. This is clearly intended to be China's message to the world."

"Okay, Dan, let's see what they have to say—but I am so angry I can hardly stand to listen. Jack, I assume this is not an admiral speaking off the cuff, but rather delivering a carefully tailored official communique?"

"Almost assuredly, Mr. President," the Secretary of State responded. In spite of the overwhelmingly bad news, he was professionally curious, and would be fascinated to hear what Beijing might reveal.

The room quieted and everyone focused on the center screen where a test pattern appeared first, then an office view of a modern desk with a rather squat-looking Chinese military officer sitting with a sheaf of papers in his hand. He was not smiling, but not frowning either, just a senior professional doing his job.

Office of Vice Admiral Sun

Sun watched the young TV director give him the five, four, three, two, one hand signal and then he was live. He looked into the camera as he had rehearsed many times and began his address to the world:

"Good evening, people of San Francisco, California, USA. I am Vice Admiral Sun, commander of the four-Dragon Ship task force that has occupied the ports of Honolulu, Hawaii; San Diego, California; Seattle, Washington State and, as you local residents know by now, here in the Bay Area. I am addressing you to share four points: First to provide a general overview of our actions today; second, to explain why the People's Republic of China is taking these steps; third, to explain the level of destruction that has already been visited upon your fleets; and fourth, to explain what we expect from you over the next weeks and months of our occupation. And yes, there is an exit strategy in the not-too-distant future.

"Although this has been a violent assault by the military forces of the People's Republic of China on the armed forces of many countries, our leaders hope you have noticed that it has also been a measured one. We have not targeted any civilian infrastructure, apart from some very small disruptive targets before our landings. We are sorry for any civilian casualties—especially the ones near Houston, Texas; there our agents were attempting to destroy some refinery infrastructure with military implications, and the explosion far exceeded our estimates. We have taken note of the damage and deaths within the adjacent neighborhoods, and we will provide restitution in the months to come. But, given the scope and goals of the People's Republic, we hope you can see that every attack could have been much worse. The same is true of the four occupations of your West Coast and Hawaiian ports—our goal was to sink your military's ships and planes—not to inflict civilian casualties. And please take note of something that is very important: Our Washington, DC Ambassador to the United States of America specifically delivered our Declaration of War ahead of our first ship's landings, and before the first missile was launched. We also specifically stated that we will not be the first combatant to use nuclear weapons. If your government uses them against us, we will use them against you. But we offer this commitment with the hope of avoiding any unnecessary escalation.

"Now let me turn to explaining the reason for our actions: Some of you may know that China was once the great Middle Kingdom of the world. However, we became internally focused over some centuries and allowed ourselves to be invaded and occupied by various colonial and religious powers during the 15th through 19th Centuries. This was a black time in Chinese history that will never be repeated. Our efforts to regain our proper Middle Kingdom status began at the turn of the 20th Century with the famous Boxer Rebellion—the era when we began expelling occupying foreign powers. That process included our long war against Imperial Japan, and the founding of the modern People's Republic by the legendary and visionary patriot, Mao Zedong. He founded the Communist Party of China, led us to victory over the Kuomintang, and in 1949 created the unified nation that you see today. The lone holdouts were the pirates that fled to Taiwan and some smaller islands near the mainland. There were some long-term holdovers from the colonial period in Hong Kong and Macau, but you have noticed that we have already re-absorbed them back into the motherland. Taiwan is being overrun by our forces as I speak, and it, too, will be fully absorbed within a few days.

"The PRC needed many decades of development to overcome the many weaknesses that we inherited, but the world has watched in awe as we transformed ourselves into an industrial and military superpower, and now those weaknesses are a thing of the past. That brings us to today: We are proclaiming our return—we are now the titular head of the world—a reclaiming of our rightful place as the Middle Kingdom between heaven and hell. We are the most numerous of all peoples on Earth, and the center of world population and culture, but we pledge to be a benevolent and merciful leader that will benefit all cooperative peoples everywhere. We will bring peace and stability; we will eliminate crime and criminals; and we will equitably distribute the earth's resources so that starvation and other calamities cease. Average citizens of the United States and the world, it is up to you what you do with your governments: If you rise up as we did against our oppressors, we will do our best to partner with you to free you from their oppression. But you must also know that those who resist us will be quickly eliminated.

"Thirdly, I promised to inform you about our military progress over the last few hours—that is, the developments since the landings here in America and around the western Pacific Rim. We have largely eliminated the American navy ships and submarines that were in their Hawaiian, West Coast, and East Coast homeports—plus a few more in Asian waters—and we estimate that about 75 percent of your military ships and submarines were destroyed at their berths this morning. Those few at sea will be hunted down, too: The USS *Ronald Reagan* aircraft carrier and most of her task force was sunk off the coast of Japan a few hours ago. Additionally, the small-deck carrier USS *America* and the Japanese small deck carrier *Izumo* were heavily damaged and are heading away from Taiwan. The balance of the Japanese fleet has also been similarly destroyed, along with her remaining three cleverly named 'helicopter destroyers.'

"Our ground forces have begun occupation of all our former provinces that we currently recognize as independent nations, and their special status will continue even as they are brought back into the motherland's fold. They may retain a degree of autonomy—as long as they fully cooperate with our comprehensive assistance in re-ordering their economies and societies.

"Important to Chinese people everywhere, the rebel government of the Province of Taiwan is being hunted down as we speak, and they will be eliminated. All foreign military ships visiting the island have been destroyed—including those visiting from the U.S., Australia, and Japan. Our naval forces are landing thousands of troops on the island; two of our Dragon ships off-loaded more than 400 armored vehicles, and our air force and missile commands have eliminated 90 percent of their military and related infrastructure. In addition, we completely control the 100-mile strait between the mainland and the island. Once Taiwan Province is fully under our comprehensive control, we will liberate the captive Taiwanese people and they will be re-educated in the ways of our Party. It is a great day for us after 70 years of patient forbearance. Our ground, air, and sea forces are overwhelming every target area, and even our space forces are fully active in the heavens above.

"Now let me turn to a more pleasant topic: Mutually beneficial cooperation in the future. The key to avoiding unnecessary injuries and deaths is to obey the directions of our military and police forces in your various areas. We have very limited objectives in terms of geographical occupation of the four American ports, and have taken this step only as part of our necessary program to eliminate the U.S. military as an existential threat to our new order here in Asia. As long as America and her military allies mind their own business and stay away from the western Pacific while we absorb our region, we will not fire another shot in your direction. However, any military assault on any of our forces in the occupied areas—or providing any military help to those regional peoples we are absorbing—will be met with the kinds of massive conventional force you are witnessing today. The People's Liberation Army directs that all international military forces of the U.S. return to American soil. You are not wanted outside your borders, and there is little need for a big military inside your borders. China had been preparing to replace you with our every-expanding Road and Belt Initiative—which builds infrastructure and creates local jobs everywhere in the world—but we do not bomb our Middle Eastern or other international hosts. America is no longer the world's superpower—Fate has transferred that responsibility to us.

"Now, what kind of occupation can you expect in the four port areas we entered today? That is a fair question. As I mentioned, the absolute key is simple cooperation with your neighborhood military police forces. Gun ownership is not necessary and is now illegal. Turn in your pistols, rifles, shotguns, crossbows, and any other dangerous weapons. Simply take them to any street corner, unload and disassemble them as much as you can beforehand, and just pile them there. We will pick them up and destroy them at our leisure. It is a capital crime to own a firearm in the four occupied areas and, if you are caught with such a weapon when we conduct our house-to-house searches, the disobedient criminals will be executed. Also, if there are any assassinations of our soldiers—our military police, under the guidance of the Ministry of State Security Agents in that area—we will destroy ten structures closest to the incident. Any military age males in that area who show a rebellious attitude will be executed. Sorry to be so harsh, but we insist on obedience. Since we have announced a peaceful occupation going forward, the same rules apply if there are any military strikes on our forces within the occupied areas. We will choose ten structures at random and destroy them. Plus, we will execute any adult males who show a belligerent attitude while our local authorities are giving instructions.

"Now, let's discuss the longer term. We want to establish a healthy and mutually beneficial trade relationship with every country on Earth. Our goods and services are coveted by everyone, and we all want to do our part to create the good jobs that lead to peace and security. The People's Republic commits to that end. And, in terms of the exit strategy that I mentioned before, we do not want any American territory. As soon as our forces have fully absorbed all of the Asian lands that we do want to re-include in our New Middle Kingdom, we will begin to relax certain restrictions. We pledge to withdraw from American ports as soon as we are certain that our goals have been accomplished. I expect that fulfillment within a few weeks.

"In summary, you have only one good option: Cooperate and enjoy our peaceful presence for a limited time, or resist and face our wrath. We are declaring full martial law in the four port areas for at least the next month and, after that, we hope to announce adjustments from time to time. Stay in your homes and consume the food you have. When you run out of necessary supplies, proceed to your front sidewalk and wait to be recognized by the nearest policeman. He will give you a pass and you can proceed to your local stores to purchase food or medicine. Larger delivery trucks will be allowed into the occupation zones under strict supervision, beginning a few days from now. All medical emergencies should be reported to the nearest soldiers who are scattered throughout the occupied areas and, of course, many of them speak English. Hospitals will remain fully staffed over the coming days and weeks, and all medical personnel must remain at their posts. Be patient, American citizens—this is a new experience for all of us. Our soldiers want to be peaceful, but they all have automatic weapons, and are expertly trained to use force if necessary. That is all for now. Good evening." Sun then watched the TV camera's light fade to black and sat back in his chair to think. *I have never heard so much cow dung in my life—the Politburo's chosen speech writers are totally ignorant of the American psyche. I warned Marshal Tai that they are going to be incensed at this insulting drivel, and will fight like the angels of god to exterminate us!*

Admiral Sun folded his sheaf of papers, then barked an order for his staff to assemble. He anticipated long and dangerous days ahead. He was right to be worried, but didn't realize that America was already fighting back.

The White House Situation Room

To say that the room was stunned would been an understatement. The President just leaned forward in his chair and asked a rhetorical question: "Have any of you ever heard anything so outrageously arrogant? Whoever wrote that speech—and I'm sure that admiral wasn't the culprit—doesn't understand us or any freedom-loving people!"

Jack Madrid was shaking his head. "It's beyond irrational, Mr. President. I can't believe they are so ignorant of us after all these years. We all knew they had a long-term strategy to become the lone superpower by 2049—which is the hundredth anniversary of the founding of the PRC—but this is way ahead of schedule. For them to accelerate their political timetable like this is beyond comprehension."

Robert Gainsfield then added, "Mr. President, we've known for some time that they wanted superpower influence via their numerous Belt and Road projects in Africa and the Caribbean and elsewhere, but we never got a hint of anything so bold. I am shocked, too."

"Well, the good admiral should be getting the word momentarily about the extent to which we've all been intimidated…" This from the Secretary of Defense.

Office of Vice Admiral Sun

"Admiral!" Admiral Sun's senior aide rushed in with a message clipboard. "*Dragon's Fire* in San Diego has just been bombed and sunk alongside its dock!"

"Did this happen before my speech?" Inside he fumed. *I knew it was a mistake to try to intimidate the Americans.* He'd made several trips to the U.S. over the years and knew many of their Navy officers personally. They were a proud and warrior-like people, and his speech would have made them angrier than they were already. *I warned Wing and those idiots he dotes on in the MSS!*

"They struck just as you were starting your speech, Admiral."

Then it is not an overt act of defiance, Sun thought without much comfort. But the next one will be. "What kind of bomber was it?" he asked, already suspecting the answer.

"A very high level one, Sir. The ground force commander said the air defense computers didn't even register it. Our ADA didn't fire a shot in self-defense or retaliation."

"Probably a B-2 bomber: They fly at 50,000 feet and give off almost no radar return. They're nearly invisible…" *Now what?* Sun then did the only thing he could: "Contact the captain aboard *Dragon's Claw* and the other Dragons. Have them on high alert for a very high-flying but nearly invisible aircraft. Have them launch missiles at any blip on their screen, regardless of how small!" He knew the stealth bombers flew above and beyond their missile and laser range, but they had to make a show of trying. "Have them emergency evacuate all key personnel—particularly any remaining drone pilots or technicians and their equipment!"

"At once, Admiral!" The aide ran into the communications room where the technical staff was setting up next door. At least they had radio communications with the three remaining ships.

Then Sun did what most any father would: He pulled out his personal cell phone and speed-dialed a private number—the next bombs were certainly coming, and he would not allow them to kill his only child.

White House Situation Room

"Larry, I need to address the people ASAP! Set it up with the networks for 45 minutes from now." Larry Thomas was the WH Director of Communications.

"Yes, Mr. President!" Larry turned and made a bee-line for the communications office down the hall.

To his assembled war cabinet, Spence said, "Ladies and gentlemen, we need to counteract this load of filth with American resolve! I want to coordinate my address in the Oval Office with the next bomb strike. That will send a very pointed message to all concerned." There were numerous supportive comments around the table.

I can't believe the Politburo is this stupid—or, perhaps, this desperate. With that thought, President Stilwell got up and headed for the elevators. He would deliver this speech from the Oval Office.

Residence of Reg Trammell, Washington, DC

Reg was stunned as he leaned back on his couch to consider what the Chinese admiral just said. The President would have to respond soon, and Reg wondered if he understood the level of desperation that forced the CCP leadership to move up their long-established timetable. He decided to call the Secretary of State's office—after partnering with Tim to call the VP's aide, he had nothing to lose. He dialed a number that only long-term employees knew, and got through to Mr. Madrid's office on the third ring. The young voice that answered sounded frazzled, and he couldn't blame her. "Hello, this is Dr. Trammell from the Asian Interests Desk. Please patch me through to Secretary Madrid." Sometimes boldness conquers all. A second later Reg heard a number ringing, and he braced himself for an historic conversation:

"Secretary Madrid…"

"Mr. Secretary, this is Reg Trammell from the China Interests Desk. I saw the admiral's speech and assumed the President will address the nation soon. I have information he needs beforehand…"

A little alarm bell went off in Jack Madrid's head—he'd heard the name Trammell before—somehow connected with China. And, though this employee's jumping several layers of the supervisory chain was terribly out of order, the man was correct in his assumption about President Stilwell's speech. He felt in his soul that he needed to listen. "Yes, Dr. Trammell, isn't it?"

"Yes, Mr. Secretary. I wrote the analysis on China's crop failures a few years ago, elaborating that the data indicated long-term famine. The report included evidence of their accelerating depletion of natural resources, too, but the report was tabled as alarmist. However, I still believe these factors led the Politburo to move up their 1949 timetable to overtly control greater

Asia. The President could benefit from this context when he formulates his response to their aggression."

Jack was struck by the scholar's boldness, but he vaguely remembered a paper that crossed his desk when he first took office. Seemed far-fetched at the time, but now seemed prescient. "Okay, Reg, I remember your report. We were wrong to ignore it. What are two or three points the President should be aware of? He is going to address the nation shortly, and his audience will be everyone on the planet. He has to pin the PRC's ears back and let them know he is aware of their underlying weaknesses. The right tone and content will have a powerful psychological impact…"

Reg anticipated the question. "Mr. Secretary, the President should inform the world that China's leaders maintain their vaunted stations in society because they have the trust of the people. If the perception of the Politburo's benevolence is broken, the masses may rebel and overthrow them, the power of the military and police forces notwithstanding. This is the real fear driving the current timetable: Crops have been diminishing for several years, and people have been dying at an accelerating rate. The Covid-19 virus may have increased the people's anxiety, but it is clear that the assault ships ploy preceded that; certainly it has been in the works for years. The Politburo is terrified that starving peasants will take up their pitchforks and storm the ramparts—and, if my projections of 100 million or more dead by starvation are true—the leadership's fears are fully justified. Once the people become crazed by hunger, they will lose their fear of the MSS, the People's Police, and the military combined.

"And a final point, Sir, is that President Stilwell should mention the rapacious hunger of their factories—currently vacuuming natural resources at unsustainable rates from their homeland and from countries affected by their Belt and Road loans. If millions of laborers lose their jobs and are put on the street without incomes, they will join the agricultural unrest and become thousands of unwieldy mobs. They will riot, looting and killing anyone they blame for their children's deaths. I think the world needs to hear that context for this war, and the Politburo needs to know that we know."

"Well, that's a concise summary, Dr. Trammel. And, though I know these things in general, I admit I haven't conveyed as much of it to President Stilwell as I should have." This was a time for sacrificial patriotism, not CYA. "Thank you for contacting me directly. Just watch the President's speech and see if any of your wisdom gets through."

"Thank you for listening, Mr. Secretary…"

"We'll speak again…" Jack disconnected and paused to stare at his phone. Then he dialed the President's direct line.

Chapter 39

North Korean Presidential Bunker Complex #9
December 8th, 11:30 Hours

PLA Special Forces Colonel Jiang Hu was prepared to be surprised, but he couldn't help but be amazed at the sight before him: Supreme Leader of North Korea Kim Jong-Un "KJU" sat on a seriously expensive Chippendale couch with two of his doubles, and Jiang couldn't tell them apart. Ultimately it didn't matter because his team would extract all three, but it was a curiosity nonetheless.

Jiang was the leader of a combined PLA Special Forces operation: Groups "Oriental Sword" and "Siberian Tigers" had extensively trained for this unique mission to capture the NK leadership, and their far more important nuclear, chemical, and biological arsenals. They'd prepared for this special mission for more than a year—all the while receiving vital intelligence updates from deeply placed MSS agents. These agents always kept a close eye on the NK president and his powerful family anyway, plus the senior generals and scientists that developed and controlled the dangerous weapons. Jiang didn't like the MSS very much, but he had to give them credit that they had accurately pinpointed the exact spot that KJU would be today, and where his commandos could parachute in or land with their helos. Jiang received confirmation the previous night that KJU and his entourage would be in Complex #9—one of 11 such bunker systems that the MSS knew about. Some were in and around the capital city of Pyongyang, while others were scattered throughout the country. Paranoia had run deep in the Kim family for three generations, and Jiang and his men knew they needed extraordinary intelligence to nab this character before he could escape or deploy any part of his NBC weaponry.

By PLA estimates, North Korea had about 75 working nuclear warheads—some as small as suitcases—and many could be detonated in a matter of minutes. The NKs had some of their ballistic missiles tipped with a variety of NBC contaminants, waiting in silos and requiring only an hour to launch. Other nukes were set in sea mines in harbors along both coasts, and he had underwater specialists disarming them within the hour. They also had buried five along each of their borders—those shared with China and South Korea respectively. On the positive side, when the PLA commandos grabbed KJU, he ran such a centralized military that only he could give the order to launch or detonate the weapons. He also controlled the NK's considerable stockpiles of conventional weapons and the storehouses of food siphoned from the peasants to feed his army. Now the entire apparatus was under PLA control.

Colonel Jiang gave a quiet order and his men (and six women) who were part of this mission to extract the Supreme Leader's entire family, including his wife, his sister, and their families, gently released the zip-ties that they temporarily placed on the prisoners' wrists. The female soldiers were present to mitigate ruffled sensibilities. The snatch team gently but firmly helped the Kims' 20-some family members—along with eight principal NK generals, scientists, and their families—to their feet, and hustled everyone to the main elevator so they could rise to the surface.

Jiang's commandos had stormed the area quickly just minutes before the general attack, and had captured the Kim family en masse before the first artillery rounds and missiles crossed their common border. Advanced knowledge meant everything, and they'd not wasted precious resources or time with the other ten bunkers. They emerged from the low building into the cold morning sunshine, and the prisoners were separated and walked to five large PLAAF helicopters for their trip north to Beijing. The helos rose in perfect trail formation, and stayed just above the tree line until they crossed the coast, then headed out over the Yellow Sea for the trip north. They'd be taken to the capital for gentle debriefing, then held incommunicado until the powers that be decided what to do with them.

Finding the location of the NBC weapons stashes had been a priority, and Colonel Jiang only had to shoot two senior generals to get the captured dictator and his chief scientist to reveal all. Those shots were the number two general in charge of Kim's special security, and the number two weapons scientist. They were executed in front of the assembled prisoners and, after that, the information poured forth like fine wine. Jiang then dispatched his surface teams to locate, defuse, and transport the entire NK NBC inventory from their current storage areas to the secret PLA bunkers 500 miles southwest of Beijing.

As Colonel Jiang lifted off in the trail helicopter, he received the welcome news that the NK military had obeyed the orders of their supreme leader and surrendered. It had taken just a few hours since the first shots were fired for the whole NK army to capitulate. Now the PLA armored pincers could move south unopposed until they were within artillery range of the still-potent South Koreans. The ROK army was trapped with ocean on three sides, so Jiang knew they would fight to the last. The PLA would pause briefly at the north/south border to consolidate their advance, then launch the second stage of their Korean campaign. All concerned accepted that the ROK army and its American allies were weakened from the missile barrage, but that they were far from beaten. At best, it would be a bloody victory.

The Oval Office
December 7th, 23:00 Hours

"Good evening, fellow Americans. As you have seen from the terrible footage continuously streaming from various media, our nation was brutally attacked today by the military forces of the People's Republic of China. They delivered their Declaration of War approximately two hours after a murderous campaign of terrorist attacks—and more than 1,600 of those have been confirmed so far. This evil attack stems from an incomprehensible decision by the Chinese Politburo to strike not only the United States, but every one of their peaceful neighbors as well.

"Not only has the CCP attacked our military installations and civilian construction yards, they have attacked hundreds of civilian targets, including our oil refinery in Texas that is still burning as we speak. Tragic in the utmost, thousands of our citizens have been killed or injured. The Chinese agents also set fire to our forests, and destroyed many electrical and other infrastructure targets across our nation. They have landed tanks and troops in four of our most important ports, including Honolulu, San Diego, San Francisco, and Seattle, and they have destroyed our Navy ships and submarines in 12 of our bases and shipyards, and destroyed many of our bombers in the heartland of America. The number of lives lost grows by the hour, and the seriously injured are more numerous than the dead. This is an unprecedented atrocity rivaling the worst of any unprovoked, aggressive military actions in history, and there is no purpose that justifies this travesty.

"Additionally, the Communist Chinese have attacked Japan, both Koreas, Vietnam, the Philippines, Malaysia, Indonesia, Australia, Taiwan, Thailand, and India. They have launched an incredible campaign of uncivilized barbarism—and, by its sheer scale, such as has not been seen in the world since World War II. As we view such unprovoked evil, we must ask why. Let me share what we know:

"For decades—really from the founding of the PRC in 1949—Chairman Mao and his successors have wanted to bully their own Han majority into submission, and to subdue the minority peoples within their own borders. But they were never content with controlling their own citizens; they wanted to dominate their Asian neighbors as well. As you heard earlier in the PLAN admiral's speech, they not only want to be the world's sole superpower, they expect everyone else to pay tribute to them and to cooperate passively as they overrun the planet. They have made no secret of this long-term goal, but they had planned on achieving it by less aggressive means by their 100th anniversary. So why did they move up their timetable so dramatically? Let me share what we have learned about the real bind the Politburo finds itself in—problems they brought upon themselves:

"First, their agriculture sector has been negatively impacted by the world's changing weather patterns, and their crop yields have been steadily diminishing. They recognized this truth years ago, and could have purchased grain and other foodstuffs from many countries—and they had the cash to do so. They could have shifted their production to more bountiful areas positively impacted by the weather, but also chose not to. Because of willful pride, and the desire to retain personal power, the CCP leadership refused to take simple positive steps, and these mistakes are causing their own people to starve. And may I emphasize that civil unrest from starving farmers is one of the few things the central government of China fears. That being the case, they felt pressured to look for radical solutions to keep themselves in power.

"Secondly, they have been poor stewards of their ample natural resources, and have depleted them at alarming and unsustainable rates. As a result, their factories are experiencing a natural slow-down, and they'll soon be forced to lay off millions of urban workers without pay. This would only compound the unrest of those hundreds of millions of people whom they consider peasants. They could have entered into trade relationships on a fair basis with the rest of the world, but massive egos intentionally ignored peaceful solutions in favor of the awful violent one you see today.

"To prove our commitment to fighting back against this unparalleled aggression, please watch the following video—a real-time airborne view of our first response against the massive assault ship that landed troops in San Diego. This ship was advertised for years as a peaceful merchant vessel, but this was lying propaganda. It was, in fact, a military vessel filled with hundreds of tanks, infantry fighting vehicles, attack drones, mini-submarines, and assault hovercraft." The TV feed then switched to the B-2s targeting view, and the four explosions were clearly visible.

"We all watched the PRC military commander's broadcast a short while ago, and he promised to destroy our buildings and murder our people if we fought back. But I know you join me in rejecting this blatant blackmail technique that will never work against our freedom-loving people. Not only will we fully commit to utilizing our military to remove these invaders, I am asking all of you with weapons—the true militia of the Second Amendment—to take up your arms and utilize them in defense of your country! Our Constitution guarantees us the right to bear arms for the preservation of our individual and collective freedom, and it was written by our Founders, who had experienced a foreign occupation like today. Our patriot ancestors had to use their individual weapons to fight to win our freedom and then retain it; they fought as best they could, and many died. But they prevailed! So, I say tonight: Rise up, fellow Americans! Don't throw your lives away, but do invest them in our liberty! Take up your individual weapons and shoot as many of these invaders as you can. Your National Guard and full-time military will fight, too, but they need some time to get organized.

"Let me tell you what you are up against: The PLA forces consist of about 100 tanks and another 100 smaller armored vehicles in each port. These will be targeted by our advanced military systems, but will be nearly impossible for you to attack. However, any exposed enemy soldiers are vulnerable and can be killed or put out of action with the everyday rifles and pistols that we have in most of our homes. There are about 3,000 enemy soldiers in each ship—not a large number in each location. Their mission seems to be to buy time for their colleagues in Asia to overrun their neighbors, but we will do our best to resist their evil work here. You just witnessed one of their motherships being destroyed, and we will soon destroy the rest. Do your best, fellow Americans—the enemy has made itself our enemy without cause, and this mistake will be to their long-term regret. They have underestimated you; now show them how Americans fight! Give your lives dearly—and may God bless you all."

The screen view of the President sitting behind the reassuring desk in the Oval Office faded away. He had just told the local populations that they were on their own for a while—and that he expected them to make the invaders pay. Then, on everyone's TV screens, there appeared another live feed: The B-2 was preparing its second bombing run of the day.

Reg just sat back on his couch and said "Wow!"

San Francisco, California, 20:20 Hours

John and Matty Benigni were sixth-generation Americans by way of Sicily and Pittsburg, PA. The first two generations were grocers in Pittsburg, but one of the sons in that second generation got itchy feet and he picked up and moved to California. The next four generations were West Coast commercial fishermen catching sardines, salmon, or albacore in their own boat, but then spent a few weeks every summer in Alaska—catching salmon during the massive runs up there. It had been a good living and their family had thrived. However, during each fall for decades, these succeeding generations of fishermen had transformed into hunters, and they were good at that, too. They bagged deer and wild pigs with their long rifles, and they got a host of game birds with their 12-gauge shotguns. Those harvests helped them eat better than most of their fellow citizens.

Now John and Matty were in their forties; they had never served in the military, but they heard their President's clarion call and decided what they needed to do. It was the tail-end of the hunting season in the west, so their aim was honed, and they had all their equipment targeted in and shiny clean.

Without hesitation, they hurriedly dressed in woodland camouflage outfits, left the orange caps in the closet, and said emotional goodbyes to their nearly hysterical wives and pre-teen children. Their Remington 700 rifles had excellent scopes and, with extra .30-06 ammo in their pouches, they made a quick plan: One would go up to the roof of the building across the street, while the other would hide behind the cars parked against their front sidewalk. They'd spotted a patrol from an upstairs window and decided that would be their first target. They got the family into the back bedroom and left quietly.

The nearest large intersection was three blocks down their typically steep San Francisco hill, and the six PLAN marines assigned there were just quietly waiting for something to happen. Around the city there had been a few confrontations with the local police, but nothing in the immediate vicinity. The marines were on guard, and their patrol had a CSK-131 vehicle with them (similar to an up-armored U.S. Humvee with a mounted machine gun). One-hundred 131s had disgorged from the mothership and were scattered everywhere. The Dragon now sat empty and resting quietly against its waterfront pier, and the men figured that, when their occupation was finished, they'd cruise back to China as heroes. In the interim, the marines figured the local population was terrified of their presence and would cause no trouble.

John bent over and moved quickly across the street and climbed the inner stairwell of their neighbor's apartment building roof. He'd played there as a kid and knew it well. It was dark now, but his 2.5X x 8X Balvar 8A scope could lighten and magnify any target out to several hundred yards. In fact, he had killed an elk at 800 yards in fading light a couple of years before, and shooting enemy soldiers 300 yards downrange was fish in a barrel. He didn't like the idea of killing fellow humans, but he didn't care that much either. He peeked over the edge and spotted Matty in prone position, peeking around a car's back tire, and caught his attention with a little whistle and wave. He received a "thumbs-up" response and, with almost no preparation or training at all, a new generation of American patriots was ready to drop enemy soldiers on home ground. John worked the bolt, thumbed off the safety, settled his breathing, and aimed at the soldier behind the machine gun. Then he squeezed the trigger.

The Chicoms were just chatting quietly among themselves and cracking small jokes when a tremendous crack echoed between the corridors of buildings. Instantly, the gunner in their 131 was knocked back, and a split-second later a second crack flattened the marine at the edge of their group. Everyone else dropped to the intersection pavement looking for targets in the faint light of the occasional street light. How could the American military get here so fast? They had drones up and scouting everywhere, but none had spotted an infiltration. Bang! One of those on the ground was knocked to one side. Bang! Another man was hit, scaring the remaining two, who got up and dove behind the stationary vehicle. None of them had fired a shot.

The building that John was shooting from contained the second-story home of the Chong family, who had immigrated from Hong Kong and lived there for three generations. They owned a little grocery store on the first floor that met the family's needs, and they had scrimped and saved enough to send two kids to college. Bill Chong was over 70 now, but quickly dashed to the window to find out what was going on. It took just a few seconds to spot Matty Benigni lying behind a car, and he guessed John was the one shooting from their roof. Bill had seen the enemy's threatening speech too, and appreciated the President's defiant one, and he decided to join his neighbors.

His wife Helen put down the magazine she'd been reading before the commotion. Then she watched with growing alarm as Bill walked to the living room closet as fast as his arthritic knees and hips allowed, and jerked open the heavy door.

"What are you doing, dear?" Helen demanded.

"Searching for Dad's old hunting rifle." He had learned to shoot with it when he was a boy and, after rummaging for a minute, he felt its cool metal surface and pulled it out from behind a stack of coats. Then he took down the key that hung on a nail just inside the door and located the old trunk shoved into the other back corner. He got it open and found a box of rifle shells. He heard but ignored his wife's scolding behind him.

"Matty and John are shooting Communists—I can shoot, too!"

"You old fool, you'll just get yourself killed!" Helen exclaimed in panic.

"Well, do you want me to walk down to the intersection, and yell at them in broken Cantonese that they don't understand?"

"Just stay here. The army will come soon!"

"That's not what the President said. They need us to buy time. I'm sorry; I must fight for our neighborhood!"

Helen was crying now, but the war had come to their doorstep. There was a time to fight—the Bible said so. He gave her a hug, and an admonition: "Please stay away from the windows and turn off the lights. There will be a lot of fighting here soon." Then he hobbled toward the front door, pulling on his heavy jacket. With rifle in hand, he closed the door behind him. Helen just turned off the lights and sat in the darkness, praying quietly.

Across the street, Matty heard footsteps coming down the apartment stairs, and turned to see old man Chong stepping onto the sidewalk. He had a rifle. "Get behind a car, Mr. Chong! Do you know how to shoot that old gun?"

"Yes, I can scare them a little..." Matty was grown up now, but Bill remembered the days when the two boys played with his kids—and now all of them had children of their own.

Matty watched "Uncle Bill" lay down stiffly behind the old sedan they kept parked in front of their store. The Chongs' grandson came by sometimes to start it, but it was more valuable today as a bullet stopper than as a mode of transportation. Suddenly, a couple of bursts of automatic machine gun fire ricocheted up the street and Matty refocused on the Chinese vehicle. He took aim and his powerful hunting rifle kicked again. A satisfying snap of the head confirmed he'd killed another enemy soldier. Only one left now, plus whatever crew was in the vehicle. Another shot rang out across the street and he looked over at old Mr. Chong: He'd just fired, too, and his bullet bounced off the APC with a loud "clang." The driver must have gotten the message that they weren't wanted in upper Sacramento Street, and he gunned the engine and started backing down the hill. The soldier on the ground jumped up and then dived into the back of the 131 to keep from being squashed, hanging on for dear life as they disappeared around a corner.

Both guys at street level heard John yell from the roof: "They're running away! The Sacramento Street Irregulars have chased them off!" Soon other neighbors came out cheering—some carrying rifles and pistols. The Americans had begun to fight back.

Chapter 40

Office of Admiral Sun

For the second time that evening, Admiral Sun's aide rushed in without knocking, highly agitated—unusual for the naturally calm staff officer. He also looked scared.

"What is it, Captain?"

"Admiral, all over the city we are taking small arms fire. Many of our marines have been killed or wounded. The American Army must have infiltrated soldiers into the neighborhoods when we were focused elsewhere!"

"Are their attacks organized?"

"No, Admiral—random, as if there is no coordination. How could our drones have missed them?"

"Then it must be ordinary civilians using their personal firearms as their President requested…"

"Their government permits ordinary citizens to own rifles?" *How could that be?* "How does their government keep control of the population, Admiral?"

"They have a different system of laws here, Captain; the people are quite free and independent. That's why they have so much crime. I warned the general staff of this before we sailed, but they scoffed at my data on massive gun ownership. Now our marines are dying. How sad and unnecessary."

"Should we start executing groups of civilian men, Admiral?"

"No, Captain, I believe that would be counter-productive. The Americans are angry already. Please inform the commanding general that I want our marines to return fire, and to get our drone swarms clearing the streets and rooftops immediately—but our troops are to commit no other acts of violence!" Sun saw his subordinate's dubious look, but he knew the man would follow orders. His commanders wanted to use tank rounds instead of mini-drones, but that was not how to fight Americans. The marine general would cooperate, too—he knew that if he disobeyed, Sun's MSS cadres would execute him without hesitation.

The White House Situation Room (midnight)

President Stilwell opened his last war cabinet meeting of the day: It would be thorough, but it would end the longest day of his life with quality preparations for the next. All the key decision-makers needed rejuvenating sleep, but first they had to hear the latest updates so tomorrow's actions would be as efficient as possible. *Lord,* he prayed silently, *what will the world look like from now on?* He turned to his Director of Homeland Security for the domestic update: "Dan, what's the latest on the home front?"

"Mr. President, the oil refinery fire is about 50 percent contained, and the fires in the city are out. Really great response from the civil population, and the first responders in greater Houston are magnificent! Everyone pitched in and there was a lot of neighbor-helping-neighbor spontaneity. It's the only good that came from this disaster. People are still wearing Covid masks, but taking greater risks to help others. Homelessness is non-existent: Neighbors just took people in that had no place to stay. The National Guard mortuary teams have already moved into the area, and are helping local funeral homes process hundreds of bodies. They are providing temporary cold storage units until bodies can be identified. The Guard is also enforcing the mayor's curfew and looters are being shot on sight with rubber bullets. Crime has slowed to a trickle."

"How many civilian casualties?"

"Six hundred thirty-seven dead so far, but that total will rise once we get the full Houston number. The shipbuilding companies don't have all their dead accounted for, either. I'm estimating 1,000 dead. About twice that injured. Property damage will be in the billions."

Why does it take something like this to pull the country together? "Ladies and gentlemen, it took half a day to get us unified again. Why did it require another world war to overcome our divisions?" The President's question was rhetorical, but everyone shared the same emotion.

Dan then asked, “Sir, have you decided to act on our recommendation that you declare martial law? Most people will understand and support such a move.”

“I’ve decided to wait, Dan—it’s not necessary at this time. Everyone’s doing the best they can and that won’t help.” There were mixed comments around the room, but everyone had to accept the President’s decision; it was a conservative move and could be changed if necessary. “Okay, Baker, what’s DoD’s update?”

“It’s pretty grim, Mr. President: The munitions used in the drone and missile strikes have done a complete number on our in-port ships and submarines. Most are still burning and several have sunk in place. Some can be salvaged in the long term, but most will be out of action for months. The important secondary concern is nuclear fuel leakage from damaged reactors in the carriers and submarines, and there is some. But the hazmat teams are doing their Herculean best to contain all. None is airborne that we can tell from our monitors, and the contamination in the water should be considerably less than Fukushima.”

“Let us know how we can help, Baker,” said Dan Robinson.

“Thanks, we are going to need plenty—especially over the next few days. We have specially trained divers over the side monitoring leakages near suspect reactors, but so far, none have damaged cores.”

“Well, that’s something,” the President interjected. “Okay, Baker, what about military casualties?”

“Just awful, Sir. We have about 8,000 sailors and Marines killed or missing, another 15,000 injured. Many more at sea. Hospitals are overwhelmed on bases, but we are receiving amazing support from local civilian facilities. Several have dispatched ground ambulances and life-flight helicopters to transport our wounded up to 100 miles from each location.”

“The ChiComs are going to pay for this!” Spence lashed out angrily. “This is several times worse than Pearl Harbor and 9/11 combined!”

Admiral Simms then added, “Mr. President, our B-2 has completed its third successful bombing run, and all three West Coast motherships have been sunk in place. They are burning wrecks and of no further use to their landing forces. The Spirit will now head for Hawaii and will shortly complete a mid-air refueling. The final mothership will be sunk in less than five hours and, fortunately, they have no defense against it except threats. After Hawaii, the bomber will return to the States and find a safe place to land. The B-2 from Guam has already landed in Alaska, and will be ready for combat within a few hours."

"Great news on both! Please give the crew of the Eglin Spirit our 'job well done,' Admiral."

"Yes, Sir, I will."

Baker then added another update: "Mr. President, our two *Virginia*-class submarines within striking distance of the ChiCom mainland have successfully launched their complements of Tomahawk and Harpoon missiles. They hit ten different land targets—including scattering sub-munitions across airfields, while the sea-skimmers hit seven surface ships supporting the Taiwan invasion. A satellite pass confirmed that all seven are burning hulks. Additionally, the Japanese got off a half-dozen Tomahawk missile strikes of their own and inflicted significant military damage. And, as we discussed before, our first space battle between satellites went in our favor. May General Teague give us that update?"

The President and everyone else looked over at the Air Force general who commanded the U.S. Space Force. He stood and walked to the main screen. "Mr. President, ladies and gentlemen, here is the list of satellites involved from both sides." He used a green laser pointer to indicate two lists among several that suddenly appeared on the big screen. "This screen is a little busy, but the two columns that are most important are these two here." He indicated a long list of orbital locations. "These are the 19 U.S. GPS sats that are out of action, meaning the ChiComs degraded our network by about 20 percent. However, this next column is the list of their GPS sats we destroyed. It totals 63, which is about 80 percent of their capability. For a first battle, it is highly successful..."

Spence couldn't help applauding, and the other 35 people in the room spontaneously joined in. "This could mean the outcome of the war, General. Well done to all concerned!"

General Teague couldn't help but look pleased. His team had probably saved the country. "Thank you, Mr. President—I'll pass that along to my spacemen!"

The group then spent about 30 minutes discussing other details and finalizing plans for the following day. They agreed to meet again at 06:00, knowing that many subordinates would keep watch after the senior leadership headed for a few hours of critically needed rest.

The Ward Room, USS *Missouri*
December 7th, 18:00 Hours (same time)

Vice President Rebecca Jane Mason's Secret Service detail had moved her from the safety of the Number One Turret to the admiral's suite when they deemed it safe. An hour later, they moved her again to the Ward Room to prepare for her escape from the ship. She had been notified that her husband and children had been rescued and taken to the North Shore in a civilian SUV, and then via civilian sightseeing helicopter to Hilo on the Big Island. Darkness would give her cover to move there, too, and then the family would fly back to the states. Her "Air Force Two" for the trip to Hawaii had been her usual Boeing C-32—a modified Boeing 757—but it had been destroyed on the runway at Hickam Field. However, a Gulfstream G-650 owned by a real estate developer on holiday had been offered by its patriotic owner, and it was standing by to whisk her home. If all went well, they'd be in DC in nine hours.

Weighing heavily on everyone's heart was the death of Admiral Lawson, the USINDOPACOM commander who'd been killed when he tried to drive away from the *Missouri* in a Navy staff car. He thought he could outrun the drones, but a vigilant drone pilot had seen the inviting target and pounced on the lone car with a mini-drone swarm. His driver and aide were killed, too, and the car was currently a bullet-ridden wreck about 500 yards from the old battleship on the far side of Ford Island. Rebecca's Secret Service detail would not make the same mistake with her, and had arranged for a SEAL team to escort her and her agents around the west end of Ford Island on foot. The commandos had brought in a small ridged inflatable boat to ferry them north across the channel, then past the naval station to a canal where they could sneak into the outskirts of Pearl City. From there, she and her detail would travel by civilian van to the North Shore, and then by civilian helicopter eastward to Hilo.

GS Han's underground bunker
December 8th, 22:00 Hours

Han had called in the entire eight members of his special advisory council—plus General Wing, who'd been begging off for the two previous days. This time Han insisted on his attendance, and everyone arrived on time and appeared optimistic. Even the Japanese and American missile and Harpoon strikes had not dampened the attendees' spirits. "I wanted everyone here to receive a comprehensive briefing from Marshal Tai and his team. Marshal, please proceed."

"Thank you, General Secretary Han. Since the good news greatly exceeds the bad, I thought it would be helpful to address the bad first so we can move on to the positives. The worst news is the limited missile strikes from Japan—several of their J-1 rockets escaped our own comprehensive missile barrage, and we were not able to shoot them down as they descended. Several struck our northern cities, including ten here in Beijing. Military targets were hit in all cases, but the damage is limited. The August 1st building was struck but the warhead did not penetrate to the subterranean levels where we have our operational staffs and equipment. The strikes will no doubt give the Allies a morale boost, but caused little more than cosmetic damage to us. A few hundred Ministry of Defense personnel were killed or injured, but no one above the one-star level, and the injured are being treated at local hospitals. We also sustained several cruise-missile strikes at military installations, and we believe they were launched from American submarines operating in the East China Sea. We know they always have one or two of their boats in our waters, so it is no surprise. The damage is contained. They also sank seven of our warships working in the Taiwan Strait.

"The second negative is partially confirmed, partly deduced: Our six ballistic missile submarines and their two escorting attack boats are all missing. Two of the missile boats were sunk before they completed their launches against United States' mainland targets, and this was confirmed on the spot by the four survivors. However, those four were able to complete their launches, and then head west at full speed toward a rendezvous with the pre-positioned escorts. The six of them hoped to spring an ambush against any pursuing Allied subs or ships—and indeed, two American attack subs did take up the chase. But something went wrong and we assume all six were sunk. It is logical that the Americans had other subs in the area that escaped our attention, because it is improbable that two enemy boats could sink all eight of ours.

"The third negative is the sinking of *Dragon's Wind* before she could reach Vietnam. I briefed you about her mechanical problems off our southern coast, and they were temporarily repaired, but the repairs didn't hold. The mission was diverted to Haiphong Port instead of Ho Chi Minh Port to salvage its diversionary support for our cross-border thrusts, but she stranded ten miles south of the Hong River estuary, and about two miles from their coast. The mission commander decided to launch an attack against the nearest shore, but before he could get underway, the ship was torpedoed by a previously undetected enemy submarine. About half of the ground force were ferried to the beach with their weapons, but the four transporting hover craft were sunk, too. After that, the mothership settled in place, and the rest of the marines and crew made it to the beach without arms. From our last communication two hours ago, they were fighting bravely, but the ensuing silence indicates that most are dead or captured. To be frank, that mission is a total loss."

"What about our cross-border operation?" asked Han. "Have we gotten a larger percentage of our forces across the Vietnamese frontier?"

"Admittedly, Comrade Han, the crossings there are going slowly. We are facing stiffer resistance than anticipated. However, our great advantage in numbers will soon wear them down. I've already replaced the corps commander in the sector and I'm monitoring the situation personally!"

Lee Tuc Chang, the Minister of Heavy Industry, then interjected a critical question of his own: "Comrade Marshal, how is it that ten armored divisions cannot penetrate lightly armed militia? Weren't we told that their regular army was stationed more than 100 miles from our common border?"

"That is what Minister Wing's agents told us, Comrade Minister. Perhaps he can explain this inconsistency?" Tai was grateful to deflect the responsibility of answering the unanswerable. The whole Vietnam operation had ground to a standstill. His men had only moved two kilometers after a full day of heavy fighting. They'd barely established a beachhead on the far side of the Hong River, and were bogged down under constant artillery barrages. From his last conversation with his senior general on the scene, it seemed that every tank in the Vietnamese ground force had come out of nowhere. Wing's intelligence agents had completely failed their mission—they'd missed an entire army moving within ten miles of the front.

Sitting a few feet away, General Wing was furious; that incompetent Tai had neatly passed the buck to him after his bloated ground forces had been beaten to a pulp by a few Vietnamese tanks and cannons. Tai had airpower, armor, unlimited soldiers, massed artillery, rockets, drones—an entire combined-arms inventory at his disposal, and all he could do was sack one incompetent general. *Now everyone is looking at me!* "Comrades, our worldwide intelligence-gathering activities have produced a bounty of information for our attacking forces, and Vietnam is the only failure. Somehow our agents missed the moves forward—perhaps undertaken long before my cadres arrived. Regardless of the opposing forces, Marshal Tai's vast invasion force should be able to overcome any regional army. They seem to be doing well everywhere else!" *I'm not going to take the blame for Tai's failures!*

Han could see a useless feud breaking into the open, so he decided to intervene. "There is no sense hurling accusations at one another! Marshal Tai, continue to press your advantages—the slower timetable won't matter in the long run. The Allied forces are largely destroyed, and that has bought us the extra time we programmed into the master plan. General Bao and Professor Dang have indeed developed a great strategy, and their plan is proceeding. Now, let's shift our consideration to reports about what is going right…"

"Thank you, Comrade Han," said Tai, relieved. He didn't want to get into it with Wing now. "The best news is from America, the location where Comrade Wing deserves special praise: His cadres delivered timely and excellent information on the exact location of each ship, submarine, and plane that our missiles destroyed. We had the general layout from our numerous satellite passes, but his on-the-ground agents gave us the exact positions of every target. All are out of action for months. That part of the mission is a triumph!" He paused as the assembled rightly clapped enthusiastically for the MSS minister. He'd been red-faced a minute before, but after Tai's fence-mending, he seemed mollified and ready to move on.

"Thank you, Comrades!" Wing responded. "We had more than 3,000 agents dispersed across America, and they did their duty. Several are dead and missing, but we hope the rest can make their way back across the Yankees' southern border into Mexico, and then eventually home." *Phase One did go well, didn't it—despite Tai's earlier attempt to discredit me.* "Comrades, my agents are in place for Phase Two: They will move like a wave across conquered lands here in Asia, and arrest those thousands on our target lists. I can hardly wait to get some of them in my own 'debriefing cellars!'"

Marshal Tai smiled neutrally at his colleague—inwardly aghast at anyone who relished torturing another human being. But that was Wing, and he served a purpose in the big picture. He continued his updates. "The second phase of the American operation goes well, too, but as expected, the Yankees are pouring resources into all four occupied areas. There is significant fighting in the three ports near their military installations, with both active duty and reserve units heavily engaged against us. However, our drone clouds have given us complete domination of the air war—except for the high-level stealth bombers that attacked our Dragons. We are not sure, but a single bomber may have sunk all four motherships—probably the one in the United States that was known to have escaped Comrade Wing's saboteurs. Those four Dragons are now destroyed, but going forward they weren't projected as vital. All our drone controllers and their containers of computerized workstations were safely offloaded in the first few hours of each assault, and they are now fully operational and carefully concealed in local buildings. Each command group is also established in local high-rises, and all of the other equipment and every vehicle was onshore and fully dispersed when the bombers struck. Only a few sailors were killed, and only one of the captains.

"Of great significance, none of their low-flying aircraft can get close enough to engage our troops: Every fighter, bomber, or helicopter that tries to approach under 1,000 feet is pounced upon by a swarm of our mini-drones—magnificent little beasts that are sucked into their engines. And every aerial threat within 100 miles of our four Yankee containment zones has been neutralized. We've essentially established a no-fly dome over our four occupied ports.

"However, we are facing unorganized civilian opposition—plus some professional military infiltration. It seems that every U.S. household has a gun and they are sniping at our marines. We return fire in every instance, and we've killed many, but there are tens of thousands of them in each location, and the attrition rate is taking its toll. Their president's inhumane call for insurrection against our forces has had a dramatic effect on his citizens. But that is to be expected—and it puts an exclamation point on our policy of prohibiting gun ownership here! It also reminds us to confiscate every gun in every country we conquer! Comrade Wing funneled copious amounts of cash into several American political races in support of candidates who advocated gun confiscation, but so far those monies have yielded precious few results." Just one last dig at Wing for good measure.

Han didn't appreciate Tai's slight of the brittle Wing, but he was pleased that his MSS boss didn't take the bait. However, he saw that Ti wanted to weigh in and he had to recognize her. There was significant support for gun confiscation in the room, and Minister Ti couldn't help but address the issue: "Comrades, this is exactly why my People's Armed Police operate the way they do. I keep the people unarmed and afraid so we don't have to put up with this kind of rebellion!" She was getting agitated and Wing gave her a look. She saw it and quickly quieted.

"Yes, quite so, Comrade…" responded Han sympathetically, "…now let's continue our updates."

Tai saw he'd gotten away with his comment, and pressed on: "Of vital importance, the liberation of Taiwan Province goes according to plan!" He was prepared to pause here and just bask in the applause because reunification had been a long time coming. "Our forces have been completely effective. The initial missile attack hit every target—each one carefully scouted by Comrade Wing's agents." *I love keeping Wing off balance*. "The rebels' military infrastructure was quickly overwhelmed, and is now 90 percent destroyed. All their navy ships are sunk, as are the eight visiting foreign military ships. Their air force suffered the same fate as the Americans, with runways and standing aircraft destroyed in place, and the few who tried to take off were fully engulfed with mini-drone swarms. At this time, nothing of theirs is flying. Those few planes already aloft were pounced upon by our squadrons of attacking fighters and, though we had some losses, we shot down every rebel.

"Regarding our ground forces on Taiwan, the two Dragon brigades faced little resistance, and the general mobilization of the rebels' reserves was systematically destroyed by the missile barrage. The 1,000 large drones launched successfully from the motherships, and they subsequently released their swarms. Everything of value to the rebels was rendered useless. Untold thousands of their active duty and reserve military personnel are dead or wounded, and there is a lot of civilian collateral damage."

"How long before the island is secure enough for my PAP cadres, Comrade Marshal?" asked Minister Ti. She could hardly wait to get her police forces over there to work with Wing's agents to establish mainland law and order. She was also looking forward to working with Wing to identify unmarried women and young widows who could be brought to Beijing and subsequently parceled out to deserving men. She had a lottery system in the works, and would perfect it within the next couple of weeks. War heroes would be among the first to receive these brides, and they would greatly help rebalance their population problem.

"Minister Ti, we seem to be generally adhering to the timetable suggested by the master plan. It will take about ten more days to chase down and kill or capture those rebels who've already fled into their mountain strongholds."

Foreign Minister Wu then asked a question that had been on all their minds for years: "Marshal Tai, have our airborne troops captured the sacred objects held in the hillside treasure vaults? I so hope your missile strikes didn't damage the irreplaceable!"

"Absolutely, Comrade Wu! Our designated paratroops landed there in the first minutes of the airborne attack and quickly overwhelmed the defenders. Our troops escorted several specialists inside the vaults and caves, and they have confirmed that all our ancient artifacts are intact! Additional experts will fly over when the fighting stops and box them up and bring them home." Tai had been relieved when he received his field commander's report: The historical porcelain and metal sculptures—the treasures of ancient China—had been taken by the rebels when they fled the mainland for Taiwan in 1949. They'd never been returned, but now they would be coming home to the people of China. So far, Operation Unity was yielding one notable achievement after another.

"Such wonderful news, Marshal Tai!" Han was relieved, too: Retrieval of the ancient treasures would form part of his legacy when he passed on. He would be credited with their repatriation.

Tai continued, "Thank you, Comrade Han. Now I'd like to report that the rebels' four in-shore islands are in our control and their garrisons killed or captured. The survivors will undergo strict re-education training under the guidance of Minister Ti's cadres, and I'm sure they will be universally grateful for reunification."

"Thank you for that encouraging summary, Comrade Marshal." Reunification had been a long time coming. "What's next?" Han was feeling much better: The negative psychological impact of the long list of failures had initially gotten him down.

Tai was finished with his portion of the presentation, and stepped aside so his subordinates could use the dais. "Comrade Han, I'd like General Bao and Professor Dang to provide updates on the Japanese theater of operations." Tai's chief of staff and the diminutive academic knew the country-by-country details better than he did.

The tallish lieutenant general stepped to the podium, and a map of Japan illuminated the central screen. "Comrade General Secretary, distinguished ministers, we saturated Japan with our missiles—striking them harder than America because of their geographical proximity. Our missiles and sappers did a first-class job on all the Japanese ships, submarines, and air force bases, and most of their military aircraft were destroyed. Only one of their aircraft carriers was at sea, but it was severely damaged in the same barrage that sank the American aircraft carrier *Ronald Reagan*. Both of their smaller carriers were hit with sea-skimming missiles, and two-thirds of the escorts were sunk by the combined arms operation. We believe the four mini-submarines from *Dragon's Roar* sacrificed themselves to accomplish the first phase of this stunning victory, but it is our rocket force that should receive the greatest praise." He paused while the assembled clapped politely. They were all justifiably proud of their warriors' heroic patriotism.

"Were all of them destroyed?" asked Provincial Chairman Liu Keqiang. *These generals were so blasé when discussing the lives of hundreds of young men lost to their families forever. This awful war is going to cost us so much!*

"Yes, Comrade Liu, we believe so." *At least she cares about the sailors—most of the others just see them as expendable pawns.* "We will remember them with monuments in their home towns and villages."

"What's next, General Bao?" Wing was getting impatient with this sentimental drivel.

"Comrade Minister, I would like to discuss our Philippines campaign next. We successfully off-loaded our contingent from *Dragon's Armor*, and they quickly established control over the container port and immediate area. Then our special operations unit 'Black Sword' landed and captured the main airport in Manila. Following that, a full airborne brigade arrived via several air transports and they are now engaged in heavy fighting against the Philippine military. But their navy and air forces were dispatched with missiles, and they have no heavy armor units to resist our main battle tanks. It is a big country that will take a few weeks to fully subdue, but we are actually ahead of our original schedule." That earned a grunt from the squat Wing. About as much praise one could expect from that oaf.

"Good work, General Bao." This from Foreign Minister Wu, who couldn't pass up an opportunity to take a contrarian view of anything Wing said.

"Thank you, Comrade Minister. Next I'd like to turn our attention to Sydney, Australia." A map of eastern Australia appeared on the center screen, with some photos on the side screens of the famous Sydney Harbor Bridge and the unique clam shells of the Opera House jutting into the harbor. "Our ground force made a smooth and only slightly opposed landing—exiting *Dragon's Fang* as scheduled. Our numerous missile strikes across the country destroyed many of their ships, submarines, aircraft on the ground (including some American bombers in Darwin), plus military infrastructure and, of course, Minister Wing's Chaos Teams did their jobs well, too. However, there have been some rather rapid responses by the Australian military ground forces, and our battalions have been delayed from moving from the Botany Bay Container Terminal into the city proper. We may have to content ourselves with current gains—all to accomplish the same thing that we are successfully doing in America. Our goal is to keep the Australian military at home, rather than linking up with other Allies to become an expeditionary task force that interferes with our mainland operations. Our larger drones damaged all their military aircraft and ships in the immediate vicinity, but two of their submarines submerged just outside Sydney Harbor and got away. Our mini-drone swarms are taking care of everything else—effectively lethal against exposed infantry and small vehicles."

"I sense there is bad news, General," commented Han.

"Yes, Comrade General Secretary. A few of their SAS commandos managed to evade the drone swarms, and penetrated the layers of marines protecting Major General Lo. They killed him and his battle staff, and a significant firefight ensued. Our forces killed some of the infiltrators, but some escaped. A marine full colonel has taken command for the time being but, if he is not up to the task, we may send down a replacement via submarine."

"Well, at least that's a sideshow, General. I hope we don't have similar setbacks in our mainland operations." Han was being diplomatic, but he didn't like this kind of failure: Senior leaders of all stripes had to be protected. Underlings didn't know the big picture, and might not have the same level of ideological commitment to Party doctrine. *How could a colonel command a heavy brigade without a general or Party boss telling him what to do?*

"Yes, Comrade General Secretary—we've sent out a cautionary warning to the other mission commanders, and they will tighten security. Now I'd like to give more succinct summaries of the other campaigns, as there is nothing noteworthy to report. They proceed on schedule and there are no setbacks. Our northern Indian operation already achieved our end goal of penetrating an additional 30 kilometers across our common border—and this space will give us the buffer zone we've been wanting for some time. There is no sign that India will retaliate with nuclear weapons, and our land-based drones have done a magnificent job of neutralizing their feeble attempts to attack us with low-level airplanes and helicopters. Their artillery is effective, but our massive counter-battery fire has eliminated all but the most well-concealed batteries.

"In Southeast Asia, our operations against Thailand, Myanmar, Malaysia, and Indonesia proceed as planned, and we should have them enveloped in a couple of weeks. They've all put up stiff resistance, as would any military defending their homelands, but our forces are just too advanced and too large to resist. Having no outside interference is key, and I'd like to thank Professor Dang at this time for devising the overall strategy that has led us to this point. Eventual comprehensive victory belongs to him as much as anyone else."

The little professor was quite taken aback when the room erupted in resounding applause—not just perfunctory politeness, but genuine appreciation. He was nearly overcome with emotion. "Thank you, great patriotic comrades, this triumph belongs to us all—especially you, General Secretary Han, and you Ministers in the senior leadership. General Bao and I are grateful for your belief in this greater mission, and you had the courage and vision to reach out and force the world to acknowledge that we have become the sole superpower."

"The people of China owe you a lot, Professor Dang. You will be remembered!" Han didn't offer high praise very often, so it was gratefully received. "Okay, Marshal Tai, I think that is enough for the time being. Just be prepared to do this once a day. We'll assemble here again tomorrow evening." With that, the briefing adjourned.

Chapter 41

Aboard USS *Ashville* (SSN-758), ten nautical miles north of Guam December 9th, 02:15 Hours

Commander (P) Jim Kraft, skipper of the *Los Angeles*-class submarine USS *Ashville*, had always thought it better to be lucky than smart. He'd had that reinforced the previous night when he'd put to sea at 03:30 hours—boats usually slipped away from this homeport under the cover of darkness—but it was a half-hour earlier than usual, and that 30 minutes enabled his boat to escape the two-squadron attack by PLAN J-15s that had swept in from the sea at 04:00. The tugs were ready, and he knew they appreciated finishing early so they could get back to their families. *Ashville* slipped her moorings without incident and was well outside the channel when the first ChiCom VTOL fighters roared in just above the waves and strafed and bombed everything in sight. One squadron of 12 aircraft tore apart the Navy's side of the base, including everything important in the harbor—including the Air Force's sitting aircraft and buildings. The second squadron dropped sub-munitions over the runways and adjacent areas and, between the two formations, they'd rendered the Allied aircraft and submarines ineffective for weeks. The *Ashville*'s three sister boats were severely damaged, and Kraft was sure this first carrier-plane attack by China provided "proof of concept" for the Chinese navy. The one silver lining was that the B-2 had flown out a few minutes earlier and was well away when the attack occurred.

Captain Kraft was up on the sail when the first jets swooped in from the west, and he saw their tail-fires in the pitch-black darkness before they spotted the *Ashville's* phosphorescent wake. He ordered an emergency dive and waved off the tugs. *Ashville* dove and headed for deep water, and he kept her at 400 feet until they were safely away from the island. After two hours he came to communication depth, contacted the sub base, and was told to wait for orders.

Those came through quickly after that, and Commander, Submarines, Pacific (COMSUBPAC) in Hawaii gave him details regarding the big picture. But the key sentence in his orders read: Proceed at best speed to intercept ChiCom aircraft carriers retiring due west. Satellite confirms location. Coordinates provided. Godspeed.

"Diving Officer, submerge to 200 feet, and proceed at heading two-six-five degrees, at two-thirds." His orders were relayed and the boat rapidly increased her speed. Then Kraft addressed his crew: "Gentlemen, we are at war with China. They have attacked us without warning, and have badly damaged our homeland. But we have trained for this our whole careers, and we have the best boat in the Navy!" He heard the cheers—they were a good crew, and had excellent cohesiveness after being together for 14 months. Out of the 120 officers and crew that were present when he had taken command, only one officer, one chief, and three enlisted men had rotated out. He had no women in his crew yet, but figured it would become normal as the culture adapted. He didn't worry about the female sailors' competence, but the close proximity to one another in a submarine would present challenges. "War has come to us in the most brutal way, and many of our friends have been killed or wounded. However, Pearl sent us word that all of our family members are safe and accounted for.

"Additionally, today's raid on Guam looks like a raid, and satellite imagery shows no follow-on force heading this way. If it comes in the future, we'll be ready, but for now the Asian mainland is the target of a large ChiCom offensive operation. Attacks against us are their attempt to keep us out of the war. Several of our West Coast ports and Pearl Harbor have been attacked with seaborne ground and air forces for a similar result. Pearl reports that our people are holding their own. Now we have been given a clear mission for which we are ideally designed: Our orders are to chase down and sink the two ChiCom carriers that launched this morning's raid. We'll sink them and as many of their escorts as we can!" More cheering. "They have made a terrible mistake attacking the United States without provocation, and we will teach them and the world what happens next. Every sailor will do his duty, and we will make our country proud! That is all." After some good-natured comments and high fives, they settled down: From now on, it was grim determination. At least their families were okay.

Captain Kraft gave his tracking party a course to plot, and they all had certain knowledge that they'd be in Harpoon range by early afternoon. He would send eight of the sea-skimmers into the screening ships first—launching from 30 miles out, then reload and send a second salvo into the carriers. Then he'd stalk the task force and use his torpedoes to pick off any stragglers. The crew was incensed at these unprovoked attacks, and they'd fight like crazy until the whole ChiCom task force had been blown out of the water.

The Capitol Building, Washington, DC
Chamber of the House of Representatives,
December 8th, 12:30 Hours

"The Joint Session of Congress will come to order!" The Speaker of the House was number three in line of succession to the presidency of the United States and, as a side note in history, two of the top three leaders in the country were women. Vice President Mason and the Speaker were somewhat different in their political ideology—not to mention in their views about most everything—but today everyone was about as unified as was humanly possible in the "checks and balances" system of a republic. "Will the Senate chaplain please lead us in a moment of silence and invocation?"

A distinguished-looking and solemn African American gentleman stepped to the microphone, and he offered a simple and humble prayer for the dead and wounded—military and civilian—all the victims of the previous day's attack in the United States and around the world. He asked the Almighty to give wisdom to the decision-makers, to provide protection for all the innocent as the conflict progressed, and for hearts that would be more attuned to His love. Then he quietly exited to his left. Then the Speaker and Vice President stood respectively to await the dramatic announcement by the Sergeant at Arms of the United States House of Representatives:

"Madam Speaker, the President of the United States!"

President Spencer Stilwell entered the chamber through the famous back doors but, at his request, you could hear a pin drop. There were no cheers or stopping to shake hands. This was a time for serious business only, and he and everyone there were well and truly focused. He strode purposely to the raised dais, shook hands with the Speaker and handed her a copy of his speech, then did the same with his Vice President. Then he turned and faced the assembled leaders of America and, via television, his fellow citizens and as much of the rest of the world as wanted to tune in. He knew the Politburo was watching—even as they were busy conquering a third of the world. It was a rare moment in human history, but Spence had faith that God had set him apart for the task at hand, and he'd prayed for Divine guidance before entering. He asked everyone to be seated, and began his address:

"Madam Speaker, Madam Vice President, members of both Houses of Congress, distinguished visitors, fellow Americans, and our many allies and friends around the world: Yesterday sadly mirrored an event that took place more than seven decades ago—in fact, there is considerable evidence, both confirmed and emerging, that the People's Republic of China tried to apply lessons they'd learned from an attack against us at Pearl Harbor, Hawaii, in 1941. Our current friend and ally Japan made the fateful calculation that sinking our Pacific fleet would give them a free hand in Asia and the western Pacific but, in reality, all it did was bring a reluctant America into World War II. China apparently believes a version of that premise: That sinking both our Pacific and Atlantic fleets will keep us from helping our many friends and allies in greater Asia. But they have badly miscalculated: Almost immediately, we began fighting back in many small and large ways, including sinking the four deceptive assault ships they sent against us. We have also sunk all of the missile submarines that fired those ballistic missiles at our Midwest and East Coast bases. Additionally, we have sunk many of their other submarines, and several of the smaller disguised cargo vessels that launched drone swarms against both coasts.

"The Chinese military has killed thousands of Americans and our allies—both military and civilian—and destroyed billions of dollars of our ships, submarines, and civilian property. But these terrible losses will not deter us—rather, such suffering only strengthens our resolve to eliminate this evil from the world. Our peace-loving Pacific Rim fellowship of good neighbors can count on us to join them if they so wish, and we will do our best to help.

This desperate attempt by the Chinese leadership has also killed thousands of military and civilian citizens in Japan, Australia, India, Myanmar, Thailand, Vietnam, Taiwan, Malaysia, Indonesia, and the Philippines. They have also attacked Guam and several islands controlled by Taiwan that are near the Chinese mainland.

"The United States recently completed one of its usually contentious elections, and outsiders might interpret multiple parties as a weakness in our system. But this freedom to express a variety of beliefs and values is one of the cornerstones of our republic, and it makes us stronger. We are all patriots, and today we are fully united in our commitment to, in the words of President Franklin Roosevelt those long decades ago, 'win through to absolute victory!'" Spence then paused as several hundred leaders—joined by those in the balcony—jumped to their feet with thunderous applause. It took a full minute for them to sit back down, but they had provided a very loud message to the world.

"Next, I want to speak directly to our Allies: We are your friend, and an attack on you is the same as an attack on us. We are fighting a determined foe here in our own country, but we will soon join any of you that request our help. We see much evidence of effective counter-attacks across Asia, and we are confident you will repel your aggressive and greedy neighbor who lied to all of us about the peaceful nature of their so-called Dragon Fleet. We now know they were disguised military ships that delivered only death and terror.

"I also want to speak directly to the Chinese people: We know that you, the average citizens of China, did not know about this evil plan hatched by your dictatorial leaders. We know that you want to live peaceful lives as part of the family of nations. But your leaders have started a world war and your casualties will be great. It saddens me to say that thousands of your countrymen have already been killed in battle. We are 11 countries, and we are going to defend our homelands—just as you would do if attacked. We know you are listening—let your government hear your voice.

"Fellow Americans, I want to caution you to remember that we are a society made up of more than 300 different people-groups—we are literally from every country and ethnicity on our planet. Do not single out any group—Asian Americans, for example—to express your anger at Communist China. We are all equal under the law here and every group is to be respected. We have sons and daughters from every ethnic group in our military—including many of Chinese ancestry—and many more will be volunteering in the coming days. I also feel it necessary to express this thought in another way: Any hint of retribution against your fellow Americans—specifically those of Asian ancestry—will be met with swift justice. I want every good citizen to watch out for this kind of sin—there is no other way to accurately describe it—and to intervene on the spot or report it to police authorities. I have to mention this because of the context of the great injustice that was done to our Japanese population at the beginning of World War II: More than 100,000 peaceful citizens were arrested illegally and placed into concentration camps—a clear violation of their Constitutional rights. This regrettable evil will not be repeated.

"Now I must ask our Congress to issue a Declaration of War against the government of the People's Republic of China. And may God have mercy on us all. Thank you." The room erupted again, but Spence just stood quietly for a minute, making eye contact with many here and there, and then up into the gallery where the First Lady stood quietly applauding. Then, in quiet acknowledgement of those assembled, he retraced his steps out to his waiting limousine.

White House Situation Room
December 8th, 14:05 Hours

Spence walked into the functionally large underground room—emotionally drained in one sense, but steeled for the coming fight in another. He needed updated information after asking Congress for the Declaration of War—which, after some procedural moves, passed with unanimous consent. Every member who wanted to be reelected (meaning 100 percent of them) voted "aye." The war would be fought whether they confirmed the formal declaration or not, but everyone wanted to get on record that they supported the young warriors who would represent them in battle. Besides, it was the right thing to do. Spence had felt the steadying hand of Franklin Roosevelt on his shoulder and, like his predecessor, he kept his speech short and sweet. But now he was back in his familiar chair, and was ready to concentrate on winning the war.

"Are we all here?" he asked, just to get everyone focused. Seeing that was the case, he asked his Secretary of Defense for a comprehensive update.

"Thank you for an inspiring message, Mr. President." Baker had to give Spence his due: The man was following in the footsteps of the greatest war-time presidents. Everyone around the small room applauded quietly—it was appropriate for the moment. "Let me defer to Admiral Simms for the first portion of the update, then I will elaborate after that."

"Mr. President," began the Chairman of the Joint Chiefs, "our counterattack against all four landings has begun in earnest. Sinking the four motherships was crucial because each possessed that surprise anti-air laser weapon we discussed before. Many of our aircraft were shot down by those weapons, and eliminating the threat is a godsend. However, the key anti-air weapons they possess—and which they apparently off-loaded before the ships were sunk—are the drone swarms, plus the controllers and equipment that make them go. The bigger drones drop bombs and release the smaller drones, but it is these clouds of 'minis' that give fits to our aircraft. They're sucked into the engines and explode, and they render any engine useless—worse than the bird strikes that down aircraft every year. Any motor with external ports is defenseless, and they are terribly effective against personnel, too. They work like bullets but explode on contact—maiming or killing like a tiny hand grenade, rather than by kinetic force. Obviously, we need to improve our capabilities in this area of warfare." He saw the President was listening intently, and jotting down the occasional note.

"Military units of all kinds are tightening a cordon around the four occupied areas, but the offensive package off-loaded by the ChiComs is comprehensive. They brought 100 main battle tanks, and we don't have any of our own in those four immediate vicinities. We typically kill tanks with our attack helicopters that carry Hellfire missiles, and with our A-10 Warthogs that chew up almost any vehicle with their 30mm Gatlings. But both low-flying aircraft are very susceptible to the mini-drone swarms. We have several squadrons of higher flying fighter-bombers dropping various munitions, but these are limited in scope because the tanks, infantry fighting vehicles, and self-propelled artillery batteries are dispersed in civilian neighborhoods or military housing areas.

The civilian populations are sheltering in place, and ChiComs are ignoring everyone that doesn't seem threatening. Those folks who do are immediately targeted by the drones or by their soldiers that are broadly dispersed. The bottom line is that the civilians are hostages in place, and we'd have to accept a lot of collateral damage if we went after the major ground weapons systems with our fighters.

"In addition to the above, their artillery has a potent counter-battery component, and there have been several bloody exchanges. They are clever in all their tactical moves, and it looks like this is going to be an old-fashioned war of attrition."

"Very unsatisfactory, Admiral," commented the President, but he didn't say it in a condemnatory manner. "They planned their assaults well, and they know they can use our love of human life against us. Please proceed."

"Yes, Mr. President. The only positive is that we estimate about ten percent of their force has already been killed or wounded by our militia. Additionally, our infantry can use shoulder mounted anti-tank weapons at close range, and they work very well in urban settings. The key is dodging those terrible mini-drones." A series of air and ground photos appeared on the screens, and then scrolled by to give the President a clear picture of what his troops were facing. It was obviously bloody and costly. "At least we have great medical facilities in every location and hundreds of doctors and nurses are volunteering various emergency services outside the battle areas. The PLA commander required all our medical personnel inside the zones to stay in place, and they are patching up anyone—military or civilian—who are brought into the various clinics or hospitals. Our armed civilians are making a real difference, and we've been able to infiltrate several special forces operatives into the occupied neighborhoods. They have sophisticated communications equipment and are both instructing the local volunteers in tactics and giving us timely intelligence on the disposition of enemy forces. The militias will only become more effective with time."

Spence was pleased, "Well, that is good news! Desperate times call for desperate measures and, right now, these armed citizens pose the greatest immediate threat to the enemy. They know their own neighborhoods infinitely better than any outsider—friend or foe. So, in summary, it is just a matter of time?"

"Absolutely, Mr. President."

"Okay, Admiral, many thanks." Then Spence made eye contact with his Director of National Intelligence. "Edith, what are your people picking up?"

"Mr. President, our NSA technicians have picked up one consistency that we can call a fact: The ChiComs are clearly frustrated with their stalled invasion of Vietnam. The Dragon ship bound for Ho Chi Minh Port had mechanical problems off the Chinese coast, so the PLAN decided to divert it to Haiphong and land there. But the ship apparently broke down again, and then was subsequently torpedoed by a Vietnamese submarine. The forces on board the mothership made a piecemeal attempt to land on the nearest beach, but the chatter indicates that they've been torn to pieces. The cross-border land invasion has also bogged down—it really never got rolling—and both sides are slugging it out inch by inch. PLA intercepts indicate their suspicions that the Vietnamese knew they were coming."

"That is interesting—three cheers for the Vietnamese! How times have changed... Fifty years ago we were killing each other, and now we're friends. Same with Japan and Germany a generation earlier. There has to be lesson there somewhere." President Stilwell turned back to Edith. "Many thanks, Edith—and many thanks to Robert and the NSA. Your whole team is invaluable!"

"Thank you, Mr. President." Edith didn't need praise, but she agreed with the President's assessment of her 16 incredible organizations.

Spence then turned to Baker to finish the tactical update.

"Mr. President, the other theaters of operation are proceeding according to a predictable military timetable: Japan was pummeled by missiles like we were, and one Dragon assault ship landed its package in Yokosuka Harbor. But it doesn't seem that the PLA wants anything more than to eliminate Japan's military as a threat to their wider ambitions on the mainland. The Japanese Defense Force still has some submarines, but all four of their small-deck carriers are destroyed. They have several squadrons of F-35s in shelters, and they are ready to deploy them when we can mount a coordinated counter-strike.

"For now, Australia is being treated as a sideshow—like us, they're focused on getting the PLA out of greater Sydney. They're also internally focused, and aren't much use to their regional neighbors.

"India is the same: The PLA sent several mechanized units 30 miles south—preceded by an overwhelming artillery barrage and supported by significant fixed and rotary-wing air. Then they just stopped—it looks as if they only wanted a wider buffer zone.

"The real land grab is in Southeast Asia where the PLA is seriously attempting to overrun both the mainland and island portions of Myanmar, Thailand, Laos, Vietnam, Cambodia, Malaysia, and Indonesia. We don't yet know what their intentions are in the Philippines, but they have more assets there than seems necessary for a diversion. The good news is that every country is putting up a good fight, but the numbers arrayed against them are just unprecedented."

Edith Carmichael then added, "We have been analyzing their senior leader profiles, separately and collectively, for many years, and their mindset is dramatically different from ours: As indicated by the Chinese admiral last night, they think they are the center of humanity—picture a circle of nations like a bulls-eye target. The Han Chinese are at the center, and other nations are in ever-farther-away concentric circles around the Han. Those ethnically and geographically closest are considered cousins, while those of us on the periphery are considered barbarians. The Party also espouses 'greater Hanism,' which is their term for anyone of Chinese descent. They want to re-connect them with their ancestral ties to the Middle Kingdom."

Robert Gainsfield agreed. "Mr. President, Edith and I are on the same page here: We have been monitoring this kind of thinking for decades—and they really believe it. It has become a policy—much like their goal of funneling young women from the conquered countries back into China to be wives for their eligible young men. For those who don't know, their one-child abortion polices have yielded a great imbalance, and marriageable-age men outnumber women by tens of millions."

"Mr. Director, did you say tens of millions?" This from Karen Jones, the Assistant Secretary of the Treasury, who was sitting in for Secretary Thomas, who had fallen the previous evening and broken his leg. She could hardly believe what she'd heard.

"You heard correctly, Karen," said the President. "It is important that you and every freedom-loving citizen in the world know this. Robert, please elaborate."

"Yes, Mr. President. Sadly, Karen, the Chinese had a 'one child' policy for decades. The authorities required mothers to abort most second pregnancies. Since male children were preferred due to the ancient custom of sons being responsible for their elderly parents' welfare, girls were selectively killed. Even after birth, millions of baby girls mysteriously died—most, no doubt, murdered. This horrific practice left an imbalance wherein millions of men cannot find Chinese women to marry. Therefore, they search for wives in other lands. They've been reaching out to their neighbors for years, trying various means—fully honorable or truly deceptive—to entice young women to come to China and marry."

"That's sickening!"

"Indeed."

Spence didn't want to belabor the topic, and everyone had things to do. "Great update, everyone. Now please excuse me. I have several calls to make upstairs. Let's reconvene at ten o'clock tonight." They all stood as the President headed for the door.

USS *Ashville*

Commander Kraft brought his boat to firing depth just after 14:30 hours. The *Ashville* was only 40 miles behind the two PLAN aircraft carriers he'd been stalking for hours, and his crew was ready for the fight of their lives. His torpedo men had already loaded four Harpoon sea-skimming missiles into the four tubes, and the satellite data had been fed into the smart munition's electronic brains. There were still sufficient GPS platforms to guide the missiles in route, and they'd come at the fleeing PLAN task force from several points of the compass. He gave the order to fire the first salvo, then ordered a second salvo fired five minutes later.

Aboard the PLAN aircraft carrier *Shandong*

Vice Admiral Sen Ming heard the klaxons begin their alarming wail and yelled at his senior staff officer for clarifying information. The man pulled down the nearest mic and was instantly connected with the CIC several decks below. The admiral was commanding the two-carrier task force that had just successfully raided the Yankee outpost on Guam Island, and he was bringing China's only capital ships back to home waters.

"Admiral, there are several in-bound anti-ship missiles! They are just above the waves and nearing our southeasterly destroyer screen. They're coming in from 180 degrees of the compass. There must be multiple submarines attacking us!"

"Calm down, Commander, our lasers and other counter-measures will splash them!" The admiral proclaimed this with much greater confidence than he felt. How could the enemy—it had to be those damnable Yankees—have multiple random boats out in the middle of nowhere? "Turn on the speaker—I want to hear what's happening!"

"Immediately, Admiral!" The staff officer reached up and toggled a switch that let everyone on the Admiral's Bridge hear the chatter from the combat air patrol, and the ASW helos that were being launched from both carriers and the screening destroyer. There was chatter from several locations.

Suddenly there was terrible commotion, with many voices shouting conflicting reports. Then a clear voice overrode the others: "Three of our pickets have been hit, Admiral!" This from the *Shandong*'s captain from one deck above. "Three of four missiles hit our destroyers, but the fourth missile was destroyed by a laser. The three will have to fall out of formation to attend to repairs. I recommend proceeding at flank speed in case there are additional threats." The man seemed cool in spite of the shocking turn of events.

"Concur, Captain. Order the remaining picket ships to move closer to us and the *Liaoning* and to accelerate to match our fastest sustainable speed!"

"Aye, aye, Sir!" The captain relayed the admiral's order, and soon all hands felt the big ship's engines rev and steadily gain speed. The captain hoped his four remaining destroyers would protect the two carriers from the lurking danger. He lifted his binoculars and watched the four smaller ships gradually converge to provide a closer protective cordon behind the two massive flattops. Both were trying to double their combat air patrols, and those aloft fanned out and looked for targets. The aviators knew they were unlikely to find an enemy submarine cruising on the surface.

The admiral hoped these many platforms might spot additional anti-ship missiles, and any advanced warning would help him maneuver his task force. He shifted his position to look back and was saddened to see smoke pouring from the three destroyers he was leaving behind. But they would have to fend for themselves: Saving the precious carriers was the admiral's first responsibility. The crews of all lesser vessels were expendable. The carriers also had two submarines protecting them, but they were 10 miles from each other, and almost 20 miles in front of the accelerating task force.

The klaxons had just stopped their wailing when they started blaring again. "Turn off that racket!" Sen ordered a nearby lieutenant, and momentarily there was blessed silence. "What now?" he demanded of no one in particular.

His aide was already speaking with the CIC, and he quickly relayed the bad news: "At least four more in-bound missiles, Admiral!" He grabbed the armrest of his chair as the big ship heaved over to port—the captain on the deck above trying to make them a more difficult target.

The comms bell rang and Admiral Sen grabbed the mic. Then he jerked his head around to look at the screening destroyers trying to close ranks to protect the carriers. There! Sea-skimming missiles were racing in from the east but, before he could blink, first one, and then another hit his two closest escorts just above the water line. Flames shot up from the explosions, and both ships fell away quickly.

"Admiral, two more of our destroyers are hit—we have no protection on the port side!" The man was frightened.

Sen couldn't blame him, but it was unprofessional to show open fear in front of the ratings. "We can still escape, Commander." He felt additional vibration as the captain brought the ship to flank speed, and the *Liaoning* matched them as they accelerated. The two ships would have to make a run for it while the remaining two escorts tried to intercept any other missiles.

USS *Ashville*

"Great shooting!" The skipper was elated, having watched the camera feeds from the eight Harpoons sent into the five ChiCom destroyers. Now the two carriers were pulling away from the remaining two escorts and would soon be alone. However, a Harpoon missile travels several times faster than any ship and his four torpedo tubes were ready to launch.

"Fire One!" he ordered, and the familiar compressed air jolt shuddered through every compartment. "Fire two, three, and four in sequence…" Every three seconds the boat rocked again, and everyone in the attack center watched the live feeds from the racing missiles. Soon the big ships were visible on the camera's horizon, and they looked almost pathetic as they tried to outrace certain death.

In the attack center, the men watched the destroyers vainly shoot missiles, lasers, and rotary cannons at the streaking Harpoons, but they easily skirted the two pickets and honed in on the fleeing carriers.

"That's who we want!" declared the Chief of the Boat when all four screens went blank as the missiles hit. Two each hit just above the waterline at the stern of the ships, and the power of the warheads did a tremendous amount of damage to the propellers, shafts, and stern engine spaces. A cheer went up from the ten sailors who could see the screens and the news echoed through the boat. They all had some sympathy for fellow submariners, but none for enemy surface ships.

PLAN Shandong

"Admiral, we and the *Liaoning* have been struck in our engine compartments!" Sen's aide was speaking with the captain, who'd relayed the dreadful news.

"Does he think we will sink?" asked Admiral Sen.

After a brief conversation, the aide looked relieved. "No, Admiral. But we are adrift with serious damage to our propellers. And the *Liaoning* has lost a screw and the other is bent. But our two screening vessels can tow us."

"Have the nearest submarine come alongside: I'm going to transfer my flag!" The admirable was not going to stay on his drifting carrier while the Yankee boats closed in like sharks. He was important to Mother China and she needed him to return safely home to fight again.

USS *Ashville*

"Let's close on the carriers. Plot, give us a course to move well around to the north for an intercept in three hours. I want to get ahead of them and wait. Their escorts will rig tow lines and troll right past us! They have two subs that we know of so let's keep on our toes." He was as happy and relieved as his crew: Everyone on board was high-fiving and talking animatedly. They rightly felt pretty good after participating in one of the most successful submarine engagements in American naval history. Now they'd give the four ships and two subs a wide berth and set up a textbook ambush. He'd nail the subs first, then put fish into the four surface vessels. Only then would they return home.

Chapter 42

Aboard the PLAN mini-submarine *Xiao Long Yi* (*Little Dragon One*) 97 nautical miles west of San Diego

Captain Yao Fu and the other mini-sub commanders were following prescripted orders: After remaining at their drop-off point for 12 hours, they were to conclude that no ships or submarines escaped the initial assault. Following that, in the case of San Diego, they were to proceed directly west at five knots until they reached a spot 100 miles west of the U.S. Navy's North Island anchorage. There they would remain on station for the next 48 hours and, if they encountered no enemy military ships or submarines, they would disengage from the American West Coast and make their way back home to reprovision and wait for new orders. They'd keep a lookout for targets of opportunity along the way. They carried a month's supply of food and a high-tech desalinization unit, and they could recharge their batteries as needed.

However, at the moment, Captain Yao and the other three mini-sub skippers were focused on something dramatically more exciting than returning home: A large U.S. Navy task force was heading their way, and would pass in front of their line of boats at point-blank range. He and his fellow captains would each volley-fire as many of their twelve torpedoes as they could, shooting them into the flanks of the passing ships. They also knew they would be vulnerable after launching their first Dash Nines, because *Los Angeles* or *Virginia*-class submarines were part of every U.S. carrier task force. Additionally, every screening destroyer, cruiser, and carrier carried helicopters equipped with dipping sonars that could detect them, and aerial torpedoes that could destroy them. It would take great bravery to stand their ground, but they were silent and had surprise on their side. Yao, as group commander, got on their Gertrude and ordered one of his boats to a position 10 miles north. It crept away in complete silence and, once the ambush was set, she would fire first to draw the attention of the defensive screen. The Yankee ships would then turn south to escape and they'd be caught in a deadly crossfire. The oncoming task force was about 20 nautical miles east north east when Yao's little squadron was ready. Now they just had to wait.

USS *Theodore Roosevelt*

The *Roosevelt's* task force had been nearing its homeport of San Diego when the war started but, for safety and strategic reasons, they'd been ordered back to the western Pacific. They would replace the *Reagan* task force, and rendezvous with the *Nimitz* several hundred miles east of Taiwan. The remains of Task Force Eagle were still moving back to Japan, and they were out of the war for the foreseeable future. The revised plan called for *Roosevelt/Nimitz* task force to launch air strikes in support of the Republic of China—hopefully buying precious time for the beleaguered nation while others rallied to help.

Rear Admiral Bob Zimmerman, commander of Carrier Strike Group Nine, and his deputy commander, Captain Ben Jarvis, were joined in the task force commander's stateroom by the *Roosevelt's* commanding officer, Captain Roger Sinclair, and the commander of Carrier Air Group Eleven, Captain Russell "Bulldog" Terrier. All four were very worried.

"Gentlemen," said the admiral, "multiple reports have come in from our people and our allies that those motherships carried mini-submarines—perhaps as many as six. No one has seen hide nor hair of them near the container terminal on North Island, so they are probably out here waiting for strays or breakouts. I want assurance that we are doing everything possible to protect our ships."

"Admiral," responded Captain Terrier, "We've got every helo that can fly out on our perimeter, and we've doubled our combat air patrol. The pickets are sprinting and drifting and the subs are listening. What else can we do?"

"Nothing! I'm just worried." Zimmermann had been worried for 24 hours, and awake for 33 hours, and he knew he needed some sleep. But that was easier said than done: His entire task force had been at battle stations since the outset, and sections were only now beginning to rest in shifts. He had awesome firepower under his command, but also the lives of more than

10,000 sailors and Marines; if he screwed up, they'd all be facing the same disaster the *Reagan* experienced. If the ChiComs hit him with two or three of their torpedoes that each cost only a few hundred thousand dollars, his ten-billion-dollar carrier was dead. The difference between his flagship and the *Reagan* was that he was thousands of miles from the Chinese mainland, and they could "see" ballistic missiles coming for a long time. But this mini-sub threat had them all on edge. That left them with traditional anti-submarine warfare that the American Navy had practiced for generations—and, if they were masters at anything, ASW was it. "Ben, notify the task force that I want us to increase our speed to 22 knots until we're 1,000 miles from the coast. I want zig-zagging, too."

"Aye, Admiral!" responded the group's XO. All three subordinate officers stood and hustled out, headed for their respective duty stations. There'd be time for sleep later.

PLAN *Xiao Lon Yi*

Captain Yao couldn't believe what Fate had delivered into his hands: An entire Yankee carrier task force would pass within five miles of his ambush. He knew all torpedo tubes were loaded on his four boats, and that their Yu-9s would do a proper job on the pride of the American Navy. The sonar men could hear the ship's screws churning the water, and every sailor accepted the fact that the enemy's deadly helicopters, with their dipping sonars, would pass overhead. He knew there were enemy submarines about, too, but he couldn't hear them and distance was a guess. It didn't matter: The crews of his four "little Dragons" were all volunteers, and they would sacrifice their lives for the motherland. They would fire as many of their 48 torpedoes as they could before they, too, were torpedoed and sunk.

Forward, in the torpedo room, OR-3 Torpedo man Zhao Bing Ti had earlier activated the hydraulic ram that pushed his first Yu-9 "little brother" into its waiting tube, and then his shipmate had shut the circular breech door and set the dials. The powerful 533mm Dash Nine was sealed inside and, when it had been fired, he and his colleagues would load the next one. All four two-sailor teams had worked together for a long time and, though they were scared of the approaching Yankee ships, they were committed and confident that they would make their captain and families proud. All was ready; they were just waiting for the Weapons Officer to fire the four torpedoes. After that, reloading was a race against time.

Aboard the USS *Alexandria* (SSN-757)

"Combat, Sonar!"

"Combat aye. What's up, Larry?" Commander Bud Walsh was the captain of the *Los Angeles*-class boat, and had been warned about possible ChiCom mini-subs lurking off the California coast. They were on the southwestern edge of the task force, and on the lookout for enemy boats that might be in the area.

"Skipper, I've got three anomalies in a line starting about 10,000 yards south, southwest. Might be those mini-subs…" Petty Officer First Class (PO-1/E-6) Larry Brown was the leading sonar man of the boat. His shipmates joked that having telekinetic powers helped but, on the level, he was pretty good at sniffing out other submarines in concert with his sophisticated BQQ-5 suite of active and passive sonars. He believed his BQS-15 detecting and ranging sonar had just been added to the boat for good measure. He and the machines were a good team.

Captain Walsh had gotten the word from the flagship to be on the lookout for the enemy boats, and intelligence suspected that those near the Japanese coast played a role in the sinking of *Reagan* and her task force. "Okay, Larry, give us the numbers."

The tracking party had something to focus on after cooling their heels during the four hours it had taken the task force to circle around from an easterly to a westerly heading, and they were now more than 80 miles from their homeport. Real action uniquely motivates, and they frantically worked on firing solutions and fed the data into the targeting computer.

"Captain, the targets are stationary, and I can barely make out revolutions. I'll designate them Charlie One, Two, and Three."

"All ahead two-thirds. Track possible targets Charlie One, Two, and Three beginning at 10,000 yards, bearing one-nine-five degrees." The orders were relayed and the *Alexandria* came even more alive than normal.

"General Quarters!" A nearly silent buzz sounded in each compartment, and all hatches were shut and dogged. The boat was always ready to fight, but now she was mean. They were cruising at 400 feet, about 5 miles in front of the Cruiser USS *Bunker Hill* (CG-52), which itself was one mile ahead of the flagship. The USS *Cape St. George* (CG-71) and the replenishment ship USS *Whittaker* followed in trail, and the six destroyers of Destroyer Squadron (DESRON) 23 were guarding the flanks. They all had their ears on—listening with their onboard systems, but only the ships on the surface could hear the helo chatter as they dipped their sonars and searched for threats on the perimeter. The helos would drop patterns of sonobouys if they detected the enemy subs and then pounce on any positive returns.

Xiao Long Yi

Captain Yao had not brought his boat to the surface yet—it was unnecessary and risked being spotted. His weapons officer had pre-programmed a direct northerly path for all four torpedoes, but he'd set one to dive deep in the likely event that an enemy sub was close, too. Given Yao's knowledge of the composition of U.S. task forces, such a presence was guaranteed.

Silently they waited, counting the seconds as the ships came into range. They would volley-fire according to their doctrine—a tactic that had worked successfully against the *Reagan*. However, Yao didn't know about his colleagues' success: *Dragon's Fire* hadn't passed along the information before she was sunk, and the mothership's communications masts had been destroyed in the attack. It didn't matter. The four little boats were observing strict radio silence, and the crews had just under 15 minutes to live. They would die not knowing that their mothership was already dead.

Eight minutes later, the mini-sub on the north flank of the *Roosevelt* Task Force began firing her torpedoes in three-second intervals.

USS *Alexandria*

"Combat, Sonar. Torpedo in the water about ten miles to starboard! Now more high-speed screws! Four fired, Captain!"

"Right full rudder! Zero, zero, five degrees, all ahead full!" Captain Walsh had to ignore the possibility of suspected targets to his south, because he and the USS *Pasadena* (SSN-752), currently cruising on the north side of the task force, had to protect the carrier from actual launches first. The boat surged to the right, and when she'd straightened her course to face just off due north, she rapidly increased speed. "Ready tubes one and two. This is going to be quick, people!" The tracking party received continual updates from the chief sonar man, and the computer updated the firing solution automatically.

USS *Roosevelt*

"Skipper, we have active torpedoes bearing three-five-five degrees!" the lieutenant commander on the Captain's Bridge who had the watch shouted.

"Left full rudder, all ahead flank!" ordered Captain Sinclair. The giant ship responded as quickly as her massive bulk allowed, and her four screws plowed the water white. It took only seconds before her incredible wake lacked only a rooster tail to mimic a jet ski. The *Roosevelt* was executing a hard left turn to put her tail to the enemy and reduce her vulnerable area to the oncoming torpedoes, and she would head directly south while her escorts covered her retreat. Air operations were temporarily suspended until the turn stabilized. An FA-18 on final was waved off and the pilot would return to 1,000 feet until he could land.

Covering the north flank of the task force, the USS *Preble* (DDG-88), USS *Paul Hamilton* (DDG-60), and USS *Russell* (DDG-59) instantly coordinated with their helos and surged to full power. As with the battle between the *Reagan* and *Dragon's Roar*'s mini-subs the day before, these escorts were willing to sacrifice themselves rather than lose the carrier they existed to protect. Reverse azimuths were easy to compute, and the sonar rooms aboard all three destroyers vectored their helos toward the launch position of the submarine. They pounced on the hapless sub in less than a minute and two of the helos dropped sonobouys, while the third dropped a Mark 54 air-launched sub-killer. At 1,000 yards, the third helo was nearly on top of the sub, and their fish began actively pinging as soon as it broke the surface and leveled out. A massive explosion tore through the quiet water a few seconds later, and a giant plume of oily water erupted skyward. Then a second explosion added to the carnage when one of the sub's next torpedo volley sympathetically detonated inside its launch tube. The mini-sub had time to launch six torpedoes, and all were racing toward the north flank of the convoy undeterred.

Preble had been patrolling the northwest quadrant of the task force and didn't have enough time to race back toward the torpedoes: She had to keep her patrol pattern to guard against other threats that might be waiting in her sector. But her helo got half credit for a confirmed kill.

Paul Hamilton was patrolling directly north of the *Roosevelt*'s beam and was closest to the oncoming torpedoes. Her skipper had to repeat that awful decision to run across the weapon's path, and he chose the dangerous way. He shouted over the intercom for the crew to brace for starboard-side impacts and the *Hamilton* saved her carrier from two of the enemy fish. She was blown up and out of the water by the two heavy torpedoes, and immediately upon settling, her captain ordered abandon ship. Her back was broken and he knew she would sink fast. Seventy-three of her 281 crew were killed outright, or were later missing in action and presumed dead.

The USS *Russell* had been patrolling the northeast quadrant and had sped ahead to help, but all she could do was rescue the *Hamilton*'s crew who were clinging to life rafts or treading water in the choppy sea. Many sailors were helping injured shipmates, but some were terribly injured and would die before they could be flown to Naval Medical Center, San Diego.

The two cruisers and the supply ship had turned south with the carrier to maintain their protective screen, but their helos joined the hunt for additional threats. The *Alexandria* launched two torpedoes toward the remaining fish—hoping a proximity explosion would send the others off course.

All attention on the *Roosevelt*'s bridge and lookouts was aft, and many witnessed the impacts of the two torpedoes that struck the *Hamilton*. Then the *Alexandria*'s two fish detonated next—only 20 feet from the closest enemy torpedo, but close enough to the next one to detonate it, too. The result of three full-sized torpedoes exploding near each other at the same time created a tremendous underwater shock wave and memorable above-surface eruption. The remaining ChiCom torpedoes sped past the other ships and soon ran out of fuel and sank. Unfortunately for the task force—maneuvering south to avoid the northern threat—phase one of the battle played into the hands of Yao's three remaining boats.

Xian Long Yi

Captain Yao couldn't believe his luck: The entire task force had turned and raced toward his boats and, after sinking his sister boat, turned again and resumed their due west base course. They were cruising fast and zig zagging, but were as close as any sub skipper could hope for. The picket destroyers were 3,000 yards directly north of his position and, in the excitement of the northern attack—and probably also because of the great disturbances in the water—their helos were now searching south of his mini-subs and hadn't detected them yet. That meant the massive carrier and her cruiser escorts were 6,000 yards directly in front of his boats. If there was ever a target-rich environment—"a line of ducks" in his navy's slang—this was it. A submariner served his whole career for this one moment, and Yao would not waste his chance. He let the lead destroyer pass, then hit the lever that sent his small targeting periscope above the surface. It was the most magnificent sight of his life: Enemy ships were everywhere and close, but the carrier filled the center 50 percent of his viewfinder. He hurriedly gave the greatest command of his life: "Fire one!" Then, in successive three-second intervals, he ordered firing of his remaining three torpedoes.

Overhead

"Lieutenant, they're just north of us!" shouted the sonar operator on the nearest helo.

"Dropping, now, now!" His pilot responded into his headset, and the helo's Mark 54 released straight down with its little drogue chute flying out the tail to ensure that it entered the water nose first. In less than three seconds after breaking the surface, it started rapidly pinging.

Xian Long Yi

Yao had the satisfaction of knowing that 12 heavy torpedoes were racing toward the Yankee task force. The enemy would immediately perceive the threat, but it takes an 1,100-foot aircraft carrier some time to turn and, at 60 miles per hour, a torpedo can travel four miles in a hurry. The USS *Pinckney* (DDG-91), the USS *Rafael Peralta* (DDG-115), and the USS *Kidd* (DDG-100) were the southern picket destroyers, and the *Peralta* had drawn the short straw. She was directly between the mini-subs and the *Roosevelt*, and was blown apart by 3 of the 12 torpedoes. Only half her crew survived.

Captain Yao watched this dramatic scene with professional coldness. Then his life, and that of his crew, ended: The helo's torpedo detonated directly amidships under his keel, and his smallish sub just blew in half. She sank away to the bottom with no survivors. Young OR-3 Torpedo man Zhao died a few seconds later, but he experienced the greatest moment of his life when he heard his little brother strike a Yankee ship and explode.

Eight torpedoes from the first volley continued to race toward the three ships in the middle of the task force. One of the first four Dash Nines had been aimed deep to kill any U.S. submarine that might be lurking there, and they'd detected one Yankee boat as it raced north. There were no destroyers in the immediate vicinity of the carrier or cruisers now, and the first or western-most fish quickly covered the limited distance between the now-dead mini-sub and the USS *Bunker Hill*. It struck her on the port beam just aft of the bridge as she turned away, and exploded with such force that it opened a 30-foot hole to the sea. Her quick-thinking captain ordered evacuation of the lower starboard-side compartments, and began counter-flooding those spaces, and the ship responded well and stabilized, but she had to slow to effect repairs. The next torpedo missed aft of her stern, and ran out of fuel before doing any additional damage.

USS Alexandria

In the American submarine's attack center, Captain Walsh had done everything by the book, but now he was racing back to his normal station to face the southern threat. The ChiComs had executed a perfect ambush—including sending one torpedo deep against naturally suspected submarines. He was an experienced skipper and used to the three-dimensional chess board that was historical submarine warfare, so he was ready for the next attack. He ordered an emergency full-speed left turn—trying to face the oncoming threat and minimize his signature, but he just didn't have enough time. The Yu-9 struck the *Alexandria*'s rudder, and blew most if it off.

"Emergency blow, Chief!" Walsh commanded the senior NCO manning the ballast and trim tanks, and he shot compressed air into the correct spaces to achieve positive buoyancy. The boat was moving fast at about two-thirds power—and she responded quickly as the helmsmen pulled the yokes controlling the diving planes back into their laps. *Alexandria* raced toward the surface—and she was far enough from the ships to avoid ramming them from below. "Damage report!" he called over to the lieutenant monitoring the large schematic of the sub that indicated any internal fires or breaches in the hull.

"The hull is intact, Skipper! The rudder is damaged, there are no fires, and the planes are functional!" Like everyone after a close call, he was sweating bullets.

Walsh then pulled down the mic to reassure the crew, "Attention, all hands, our hull is intact and we are surfacing. We will do a thorough damage assessment and make a decision about next steps. Everyone just do your jobs and we'll be okay." His assurances were necessary, and allowed everyone to relax and focus. They'd get to the surface; then, if necessary, he'd get everyone off quickly. But he didn't think the boat would sink: Hull integrity was everything to a submarine. If it came down to it, suffering the indignity of being towed to port was one all hands could live with.

While this drama unfolded on the *Alexandria*, the eight remaining torpedoes closed rapidly on the remaining targets. The first one passed harmlessly between the *Bunker Hill* and the Roosevelt, but the next three struck the carrier along her port quarter; she was unable to turn away in time and her flank was just too exposed. The final four fish from the salvo had the same result. The next one in line missed—passing between the stern of the stricken carrier and the *Cape St. George*. But the next three hit the cruiser on her exposed flank—with the last of the three striking her propeller. She, too, was holed at the waterline, and her port propeller blade was blown off along with half of its shaft. All in all, it was extreme disaster or success, depending on your international point of view. The helos dropped torpedoes on the remaining two subs and blew them apart before they could fire another salvo, but the aviator's success was too little, too late. The USS *Roosevelt* and Carrier Strike Group Nine were out of business.

Chapter 43

White House Situation Room—Last Presidential Briefing of the Day December 8th, 22:15 Hours

President Stilwell walked in looking a bit haggard. He'd caught a 30-minute nap between calls with world leaders, meetings with his staff, and a Congressional delegation, but the strain was taking its toll. Nevertheless, he smiled at his war cabinet and took his seat, beckoning them to do likewise. "Good evening, everyone. I'm sure you are all more exhausted than me."

"Thank you, Mr. President, but I doubt it," said Baker Halsey; his admiration for the commander-in-chief was growing by the hour. "May I begin the briefing?"

"Yes, please do. I got the word on the *Roosevelt* task force—how bad is it?"

"Bad, Sir. The task force was ambushed by four ChiCom subs. The carrier took three torpedoes and is listing badly enough to halt catapult-assisted take-offs. However, the air wing commander got about half the fighters off before the list became problematic. They weren't sent to their home base at NAS Lemoore in California because of the drones in the area, but now that the disguised freighter that launched and controlled them has been sunk, they can return when the mess there is cleaned up. The planes made it to Fallon Air Force Base in Nevada, and the squadrons will hole up there until the situation stabilizes.

"The bigger problem is what to do with the Roosevelt herself; she has no ready port to put into that's out of the range of the drones. And, honestly, it is touch and go whether she and the two cruisers—which were also heavily damaged—can remain afloat until we get better control of the battle space. The three of them are being towed by their remaining destroyers. One of her two escorting submarines is undamaged, but one is on the surface with a busted rudder and is under tow as well. Two of her escorting destroyers were sunk, and several hundred sailors have been killed or injured. But, as long as the carrier is stable, her amazing medical facility will care for all but the most serious cases. The most seriously injured can be flown via helicopter to mainland trauma centers."

"I'm sickened beyond words at the loss of life, and the suffering of our sailors and Marines, but we have to press on. The glaring reality is that we are now down another taskforce, so we need to discuss moving the *Nimitz* east out of harm's way. Opinions?"

Admiral Simms signaled he'd like to field the question. "Mr. President, the *Nimitz* task force offers the only help we can give Taiwan. If we pull back, Free China is fighting alone and will be overrun in two or three days. *Nimitz* is 500 miles east of the island now, so she can't move too much farther away and still contribute. We had two attack subs in the area that were operating independently of the task force—the boats that fired their Harpoon and Tomahawk inventories at the ChiCom mainland and invasion fleet. They only have their torpedoes left but they can join the three currently assigned to the *Nimitz*. There are two boats from the *Reagan*'s task force that we can break off from the retreating *America* and *Izumo*, and they can join the *Nimitz*, too. We know the enemy has numerous subs surrounding the island, but seven of our boats, soon to be joined by three others—the *Ashville* was the lone survivor of the four boats that home-ported at Guam, the one that single-handedly destroyed the PLAN two-carrier task force. Plus, the *California* and the *Connecticut* have re-armed and re-provisioned at Guam, and the *North Carolina* is in the region, too. That gives us an 11-boat fleet that can both protect the task force and unleash serious hell against the ChiCom navy!"

"Okay, Admiral, that's quite a potent force." Spence had to make a decision: The best he could do was buy some time for Taiwan. The United States had a commitment to that outpost of freedom, and she had existed since 1949 under the shadow of CCP invasion. "Let's hit the PLAAF with everything that can fly, and get our submarines tearing apart their sub and surface fleets. We'll take a stand and force the ChiComs to pay for every inch of ground they gain on Taiwan!"

"Yes, Mr. President. I'll pass the order to attack with every available squadron and boat!" Admiral Simms couldn't help but admire the President's ideals and courage. He knew the American subs and planes had distinct technological advantages, but the numbers arrayed against them were staggering. But he still liked their chances. He'd order 9 of the 11 subs forward and leave 2 to protect the *Nimitz*. And he'd get the carrier's squadrons, plus those Air Force and Japanese units still functional in the southern half of the home islands, fighting, too. He excused himself and moved to the communications room.

Spence then turned back to his Secretary of Defense. "Baker, how are the four domestic battles progressing?"

"Very slow, Sir. The PLA thought this one out carefully and we're boxed in. We'd have to destroy half the civilian populations to get those embedded tanks. They are entrenched in literally hundreds of civilian neighborhoods and populated business districts around the ports, and they are protected by armed infantry fighting vehicles, thousands of troops, and the suffocating drone swarms that have given everyone fits. Driving them out is going to cause unimaginable damage to the metropolitan areas."

"Have we moved in our own troops yet?" asked the President. He'd never imagined something like this could happen to America in this modern, supposedly enlightened world. He'd never fully trusted the PRC government, but he now kicked himself for being too civilized (perhaps too naïve?) to anticipate what they were capable of.

"Yes, Mr. President," Baker answered. "We have parts of several active-duty divisions already inside the original perimeters, and the balance of our units are within six-hour striking distances when needed. The 25th Division in Hawaii is on the move, and we've brought the 10th Mountain, 82nd Airborne, and 101st Airborne Divisions into eastern California. I-Corps at Fort Lewis has numerous ground and helo units standing by to move into the Puget Sound region when we get the drones under control, and the Marines at Camp Pendleton are pushing into the outskirts of San Diego. Special Forces detachments of all kinds have infiltrated all four areas, including SEAL Teams from both coasts, the Delta Operators out of Fort Bragg, and our numerous Army Special Forces and Ranger units. We have lots of troops and firepower, and they can fight house to house and win, but it's a matter of deciding how much collateral damage is acceptable." He couldn't help wondering how the President was going to play this...so far, in Baker's opinion, the President had done everything right.

"How are the Chinese treating our civilians? I assume they are in active fire-fights with the local population that's sniping at them?"

"I'd like to field that question, Mr. President," requested Dan of Homeland Security. His department had steady communications coming in from all relevant local law enforcement and first responders, and they knew some of the battle spaces better than the military. "There is a lot of sniping by our civilians, and the special operators are providing invaluable guidance for the spontaneously formed militias. But the ChiComs are definitely fighting back, and usually fire tank rounds into any buildings or general area from which they receive fire. Yet the people are undeterred and keep harassing the enemy units, and many are showing amazing bravery. Thankfully, we have not received any reports of local citizens being molested. In fact, the occupying Chinese marines seem measured in their responses and gentle with the locals who cooperate."

"Very disciplined then...well-trained troops. They've obviously had a long time to plan this, and are led by leaders who know their business."

"Yes, on all counts, Mr. President."

"What do we know about Admiral Sun?"

Admiral Simms had just returned and fielded the President's question: "Mr. President, I actually know him a little: He's been here for conferences, and I've met him in China when our militaries briefly trained together. He is highly regarded in military circles, and is a kind of Yamamoto in the sense that he is capable of fighting with creative bravery but favors peace. First in his Academy class, and would likely become their equivalent of Chief of Naval Operations if he survives this crazy attack on us."

"What a waste of a good warrior and diplomat... Okay, Admiral, thanks for that."

Spence hated what the enemy had done, but it was never too late to begin planning for the future. He turned to his Director of Homeland Security to wrap up his report. "Dan, their strategy seems to be well-calculated—I'll give them that. That house-to-house campaign you mentioned would be bloody for both sides. They are here to buy time, and they are trying to force us to play their game by our own values. Pretty clever." Spence was disappointed; he knew his forces were really stuck, and he could do virtually nothing, here or overseas. He saw the nods around the table—they had to rely on the militias for the time being. "Okay, Baker, please finish your update, then I'll ask for Jack's diplomatic perspective."

"Mr. President, I'd like to discuss Korea next: We have about 30,000 personnel there and some family members. Two-thirds are Army, mostly in the Second Infantry Division, plus some corps-level independent brigades, and the balance are Air Force, mostly at Osan and Kunsan Air Bases near the west coast. If the ChiCom armor unit that landed in Busan breaks out of its perimeter as our troops did in 1951, we'll be caught in a real vice. However, the Chinese commanding general of the northern invasion force got word to General Barry, Commander of Eighth Army at Camp Humphreys, that U.S. civilians would be allowed to leave on civilian aircraft and fly to Japan. I'm sure they think they are being magnanimous but, strategically, it seems like they just told us they are done sending missiles across the Tsushima Strait."

"Maybe they are so over-confident that they don't care about strategic messages," replied the President. "We've got to find a weakness to exploit pretty soon, or they will solidify 100 percent of their goals and get away with it!" Spence felt his blood pressure rising again and utilized some breathing techniques to calm himself. It was going to be a long war.

"Mr. President, if we can effectively utilize them, the Japanese army is largely intact, and the situation is already clarifying regarding a full ChiCom invasion there. We'll see if they'll be willing to move over to Korea. The Japanese navy had some subs at sea and they'll join ours to support the ROK and U.S. forces on the peninsula. We'll coordinate with Camp Smith in Hawaii since the Indo-Pacific Command has operational control over the WestPac theater of operations—sadly without Admiral Lawson. I believe you heard that he was killed at Pearl, but his deputy is fully capable and they'll drive on."

"Yes, I was very sorry to hear about Admiral Lawson. He was one of the great ones…" *A real loss—Dick and Kathy had been friends for years. Poor girl.*

"He was killed in a drone strike as his car tried to race from the *Missouri* to the far side of Ford Island. He wanted to get back to his headquarters." Baker could see that the news hurt the President; he was aware that the two families had known each other when both were just starting out.

But Spence couldn't dwell on this or any loss—he would mourn for everyone later. "Okay, Jack, what's the news on the diplomatic front? I've talked to every G-20 leader except President Han."

"Mr. President, the Vietnamese indicated that they are open to international assistance in the form of tactical air support. I explained our situation and they are sympathetic—but they are fighting for their lives and have slowed their part of the ChiCom advance to a standstill."

Spence liked the Vietnamese, and signaled his full support: "Baker, if you have anything to spare, let them know…"

Admiral Simms caught the SecDef's glance, and spoke up, "Mr. President, when we get our B-2 inventory set, the Air Force can send them via the southern route to Alaska. There is little chance the Spirits will be shot down so it's worth the risk. However, the B-52s and B-1s will have to use the northern route and reach their bases in Alaska via Canadian airspace. They are much more vulnerable to ground fire. The Spirits can drop their full loads on the ChiComs near the Vietnamese frontier then fly over China, Korea, and Japan on their way to Alaska without entering Russian airspace. After that, we'll have to focus the 75 percent of our fighter assets flying out of northern Japan, plus the bombers, on stopping the enemy advance on the Korean Peninsula. The rest of the fighters flying out of Kyushu and the few survivors from Okinawa will focus on Taiwan. The initial missile barrage missed a large airfield on Hokkaido, and we can operate C-17s out of there in a couple of days. The bombers will round-trip from Alaska, and the fighters can fly top cover as well as attack directly. Our C-17s will form an air bridge to fly in bombs for continual re-arming as needed."

"Many thanks, Admiral. That will be a big help."

Baker then added, "Obviously, the Koreans are fighting a two-front war—facing the Dragon ship in Busan Harbor, and the much greater threat descending from the north. They are currently moving 90 percent of their assembling army up to their border with North Korea, and are taking missile strikes along the way. The air battles near the DMZ have been fierce, but the Chinese ground force brushed aside the NK military after they capitulated, and will breach the DMZ in a matter of hours. It is shaping up to be one of the greatest artillery exchanges in history. It's a moot point, but any NKs that join the Chinese might even slow them down." He paused to let Jack reclaim the floor.

"Mr. President, the Indian ambassador told me an hour ago that they think the enemy advance has reached its climax. Now their government is debating whether to live with the extent of the advance, or to go all in and try and push the Chinese back to the original border. It will cost them so much in lives and treasure that they are deeply divided on how to proceed."

Spence was sympathetic, "It's the old cost/benefit equation, Jack—made far worse when factoring in lives. Just let me know what they decide. Okay, Baker, continue please."

"Sir, many of the off-shore oil wells throughout the Malaysian and Indonesian fields have been captured by a variety of PLA special operations units, and their airborne battalions are landing additional troops throughout the region. They don't have a large airlift capacity, but they do have enough to fly back and forth to load up troops in southern China. They've confiscated several dozen international commercial airliners, and forced the pilots to join the airlift. As it stands, the ground forces are hooking up with the airborne units and overrunning every mainland country except Vietnam. We can only speculate that seaborne troops and supplies will arrive soon in every area: We are tracking numerous commercial ships heading from Chinese ports toward the various occupied countries. We are tracking several suspicious civilian cruise ships, too, but we don't have any subs in the Gulf of Thailand or off the Vietnamese coast. And God help us if we sink a boatload of innocent passengers."

"Not a very good state of affairs…"

"No, Mr. President, it is not."

Spence had to focus their efforts on what they could do: "Okay, everyone, let's use our bases in Alaska as best we can—given winter weather restrictions—and form a bridge from there to northern Japan, and then gradually stage into Korea. Focus our cruise missiles on the mainland ICBM silos and mobile batteries. We'll resupply Korea across the Tsushima Strait. Continue the submarine surge west, and find repair facilities for the *Roosevelt* and the other ships that need help—perhaps they can make it to Vancouver, British Columbia. Fortunately, the Canadians are all in. We have to assume there are at least four ChiCom submarines off the coast of San Francisco and Seattle, so let's hunt them down before they attack our wounded carrier. Continue to infiltrate special operators into our four occupied cities, but hold off on any general offensive until we have a better strategy. I don't want massive and unnecessary civilian deaths because we weren't patient. And get those B-2s and other heavy bombers repaired as quickly as possible—they are vital.

"We all saw that the Japanese missile strikes got the enemy's attention, and our Harpoon and Tomahawk strikes piled on, so let's exploit our technologies as best we can. Our allies and friends throughout Asia are pretty much on their own but, if we can make even symbolic contributions, it will yield a lot in general morale—plus it will give the enemy more than a few headaches. Jack, what's the latest regarding our civilians and diplomats in China?"

Jack replied, "Sir, they are seemingly being ignored, and our embassy communications are not being interfered with. High quality fresh food is being delivered daily to the diplomatic compound and, other than that, everyone is under a kind of nebulous house arrest. People's Armed Police personnel are hovering everywhere, and gently rounding up tourists and local Western residents as they surface. But these are confined to their hotels and homes, and nothing aggressive is being done to anyone—not even threats. The ambassador believes the embassy and consulate staffs, plus their family members and the general tourists, scholars, and students will be allowed to leave as soon as the first phase of their operation is complete."

"Have we finished expelling their respective embassy and consulate staffs yet?" Spence was worried about reprisals, but so far it seemed the Chinese were following the rules.

"Ambassador Bang is recovering from emergency heart surgery at Johns Hopkins Medical Center, and his wife is with him. We asked their staff physician to stay with him, and he has agreed to every phase of the treatment plan and has been freely communicating with their headquarters in Beijing. Diplomatic Security is hovering 24/7. It's probably just an historical footnote now, but I got the feeling from the couple of minutes we had before he keeled over that he was against the war. Just a feeling. His wife is stoic, but polite. The outlying consulates have been vacated under my order and they and their families have been put on planes to England. Their government can pick them up there and, as we would expect, the British are cooperating. All other PRC nationals who want to leave are being processed for transportation to Europe as well, and every one of their graduate students and professional workers here are being expelled whether they want to leave or not."

"Okay, that's all good. I just want our people out of China ASAP—as soon as it's safe."

"Mr. President, we haven't heard of anything untoward—either in Beijing or out in the provinces. Everyone inside China seems to have been caught off-guard—including, I suspect, low-level government folks who are trying to catch up to the new reality."

Just then everyone got a welcome surprise when Vice President Mason walked in. The President was so overjoyed that he sprung out of his chair and gave her a warm hug. "How wonderful that you made it, Rebecca! Please sit down and give us high points."

"Thank you, Mr. President—I'm so grateful to my Secret Service detail and to the Navy SEALs who snuck me and my family out of harm's way!" She then spent a few minutes giving everyone a first-hand account of both the attack and her extraction.

The President listened with great interest, then shifted gears and led his war cabinet in an hour's discussion of next moves and options. At one o'clock in the morning, he finally excused himself, and he and VP Mason left for their respective quarters. He went upstairs and she rejoined her family. Neither expected much sleep.

Chapter 44

The George Bush Center for Intelligence (CIA Headquarters) Langley, Virginia December 9th, 01:35 Hours

Miss Betty Morgenthau Pipes never married, having decided early on that her passion was serving in the intelligence community and that her trusted colleagues would be her family. She wanted to contribute to the hedge of protection that America needed (whether average citizens knew it or not) and that would be her life's work. She was an Ivy League graduate and had many early suitors, but she was just not interested. Her stance caused some speculation in other areas, but she just ignored all and dug into the profession that had been so ably modeled by her dad: He was first-generation old-school, one of the World War II Skull and Bones boys that General "Wild Bill" Donavan (recipient of the Medal of Honor, and confidante of President Franklin Roosevelt) had recruited into the Office of Strategic Services (OSS). After the war, Mr. Morgenthau decided to stay on during the organization's transition into the CIA, then returned to practicing law after the agency matured. However, he saw in his daughter the gifts and zeal that it took to be an effective analyst, and he worked the system to ensure that she was properly discovered by the right people.

Now 70, Betty was a legend in her department, but had rejected the political ladder—she wasn't interested in the highest echelons of leadership, either. She had found her niche, and wanted to continue doing what she loved: Solving puzzles whose answers meant Americans lived and bad guys died. She had invested 20 years combating the old Soviet Union—a typical cold warrior of that era—but, after its collapse, she gradually shifted her interest to China, which she believed was the most significant long-term threat to the free world. She'd been one of the first to take the CCP at their word that they were on a long-term (meaning 100-year) journey to become the Middle Kingdom again. She believed their benign response to American overtures from 1972 onward were just masking their underlying intent to a naïve West. She remained focused even as her country lived from one election cycle to the next.

She became a photo interpretation savant, and was a stunning silver-haired beauty who every five years or so "adopted" one of the younger, up-and-coming professionals who showed promise. This decade's lucky candidate was Tim Duncan, and they had a "thing," that is, a very special relationship based on mutual respect, mentorship, and admiration.

At the moment, she was working non-stop revisiting a puzzle that she'd discovered some two years before; it was one that had suddenly become dramatically relevant after the ChiCom's surprise attack. She felt this puzzle's solution held promise, so she punched the button on her phone that speed-dialed her currently favorite number: "Tim, dear, please come to my cubicle."

Tim was always happy to get a summons from Betty—the organization's prized "Aunty" to a lucky few, and he'd drawn her attention because she liked him. Recently she'd helped him cope with Jen's disappearance, and was generally a great blessing in his life. But she was principally a unique pro at what she did, and nobody, not even the director, gave her any grief. "Cubicle" was one of her euphemisms—she had a corner office with an amazing view of the Potomac River Valley—and it was hers as long as she wished.

"Hi, Betty," Tim greeted his mentor and friend warmly. It was late for her, and mid-shift for him—but it was the life they'd both chosen.

"Look at this tidbit," Betty advised after Tim knocked and entered. She had been concerned about him for weeks—ever since his girl went missing. She'd instantly twigged to his change in demeanor, and wormed the truth out of him within hours of Jen's disappearance. She had even spoken on the QT with her old friend Edith, who was now the Director of National Intelligence. The clandestine world they shared was a very personal and personnel-driven one, and necessary back-channeling was the grease that kept the human side thriving. Edith shared what Betty did not want to ask the director about, and the latter learned the wider story of Jen's mission and disappearance.

Now she focused on Tim, and patted the extra chair by her desk—a seat of honor that she kept for him and a very few others. Tim dutifully sat to see what had caught her attention, and looked first at the left-hand computer screen of the three she had spaced out on her big desk. There was no worry about eavesdropping here: The glass was essentially one-way, containing fine wires that blocked signals coming in or going out—part of the whole complex that was electronically closed off from the world. "This screen is the current satellite pass over Beijing—last night their time."

Tim noted it as a routine infrared view of CCP Party Boss Han's estate. They'd known about it for years, and he'd seen it many times before so it was not news in itself. "Yes, Betty, Han's estate."

"Correct. Now look at the center screen." She loved watching this boy's wheels turn. He was brilliant but also a real person. She just hoped his girl would be found alive and unharmed. And, during Betty's discreet inquiry, Edith had nearly gushed about the young woman's talent and potential. This high praise was extremely rare from Betty's old colleague and friend. But both women were also realists and, after learning of her predicament, they accepted that any optimism for the young agent was tenuous at best.

"Lots of activity. Many fancy cars—a gathering of big-wigs for sure."

"Again correct. Now look at the right-hand screen."

Tim looked expectantly but nothing registered. It was a night-time scene of an evergreen forest, with a small building, circular driveway, and fairly narrow road leading off the screen. Oh, wait a minute: There was a poorly camouflaged circular helo pad just a few yards north of the driveway, with a helo sitting there under some netting and still warm: The infrared showed the glow from the metal engine. Then he studied the other side of the drive, and he identified a small structure partially hidden in the tree line. It looked a bit like a cement pillbox. There was a well-defined path between it and the helo pad closer to the woods. The whole scene was nestled in a grove of mature evergreen trees, and covered with snow from the recent storms. He still didn't get Betty's interest: He'd glanced over such photos and films before and they were common. "Okay, there's a couple of small structures with both vehicle and helicopter access."

"Good boy! Now let me show you where it is." She used her mouse to pan back on the screen until he saw it was part of Han's estate—less than half a mile from where Han and his family lived. "The building inside the tree line is an outbuilding about a quarter mile north of Han's residence—and I'll bet my retirement that it's the entrance to a tunnel that connects his house to the helo pad!" After five decades on the job, the thrill of discovery was still the highlight of her life. "Because of the small valley in between the house and the pad, the tunnel has to run at a fairly step angle, deep enough to pass under the valley. It is probably connected to an underground basement—several stories below the main residence!"

"Wow, how did you find this?" Tim asked in genuine amazement. The whole northern acreage just looked like snowy forest to him.

"Every senior leader, including ours, have escape tunnels in case of attack. Han has got to know we are aware of where he lives, so it's logical that he has a surreptitious way out in case anyone ever went after him. He's got to have an underground complex of some kind to hide in—it would be illogical not to. And, if the normal stairs or elevator are blocked, how would he get out? If bad guys came in the front door, he must have a back one."

"You are amazing, Betty! Now what do we do with this information?"

"Well, let's put on our thinking caps and figure something out. Our job is to get information to the President that he can use."

They talked things over in Betty's cubicle until they had a brainstorm.

Washington, DC Apartment of Tim Duncan
December 9th, 07:00

Tim had returned home after his incredible meeting with Betty, exhausted but energized with her discovery. They had discussed the implications until their heads hurt, and had finally agreed that sleep was essential. He was deep and dreaming when the phone rang, and when he finally roused, he saw that he'd been under for only two hours. Nearly incoherent, he picked up and heard a cheery voice, "Tim, dear, it's Betty. Have you had breakfast yet?"

"No, Ma'am, but I'd love to have breakfast with you!" He enjoyed schmoozing Betty, even though he knew she had a serious reason for calling.

"Great, get over to the Vice President's quarters by 08:00 to meet with her and Edith Carmichael. I want us to present our idea to them right away."

The Vice President and the Director of National Intelligence? Yikes! He was suddenly fully awake. "Yes, Ma'am, I'll be there!" They said their good-byes and disconnected. Tim got ready fast and headed out into a cold and overcast DC winter morning.

Book IV

Chapter 45

Joint Base Andrews, Prince George's County, Maryland
December 10th, 11:50 Hours

Ten men wearing generic army camouflage uniforms, all without identifying unit patches, ranks or nametags, exited a U.S. Air Force C-17 Globemaster III transport and hustled several boxes of equipment into two waiting vans. They drove quickly inside a nearby hangar, and ground support personnel closed the door behind them. They were met by seven men in similar uniforms, including one who was clearly in command. He bid the group to climb aboard a waiting Gulfstream G-700 with simple white livery and no identifiable markings other than the FAA-required tail numbers. The plane had already been warmed and pre-flighted, so it was towed onto the curtain, restarted, and was airborne ten minutes later. The 17 men would devote the next several hours getting to know each other, confer only in Mandarin Chinese, and refine details of their leader's hastily planned operation. At some point on the long flight, they'd pause for several hours of deep-REM sleep—aided by special pills provided by the unit's medic. Tim Duncan, the mission's commander, had needed the pull of the National Command Authority to gather this elite force in such a short time, but the context was war, and red tape had been non-existent throughout the previous 28 hours.

While the G-700 was flying to Alaska, two men boarded a small civilian jet on Okinawa and, 15 minutes later, two men boarded a similar plane near Melbourne, Australia. All three aircraft would rendezvous before dawn the following day at a small commercial airfield outside Nagasaki, Japan. This hybrid team would invest a day studying and refining the OP, then, at twilight, they'd board helicopters for a hop to Incheon, South Korea. The plan had been designed on the fly by Tim and a special team from the CIA and, if it proceeded as outlined, he and his 20 commandos would land in Beijing a few hours after that.

GS Han's Subterranean Bunker
December 11th, 08:00 Hours

Han decided he needed an extra briefing this morning because he was experiencing a lingering uneasiness from the previous night's presentation from Marshal Tai. He'd had a long-term and mutually beneficial relationship with his distinguished supreme military commander, but the man was a soldier first and tended to bend every fact to make "his guys" and, of course, himself, look good. Han also wanted the freshest facts to take with him to his working lunch with several senior CCP leaders—and that meeting would be followed by another with an even larger group of Party officials during the afternoon. All would expect the latest updates from the front. Han planned to conduct both meetings at the "Olympic venue" that hugged the ring road a few miles north of downtown Beijing.

Marshal Tai begged off Han's breakfast meeting because he was busy with his battle staff (which was reasonable) so he sent General Bao to deliver the good and bad news about the war's progress. Professor Dang was also committed elsewhere, so Bao was on his own.

Han got things started with a salient question, "General Bao, have our forces broken through in Vietnam yet?" Han was tired of the double-talk he'd received the last three days, and hoped his directness would head off any waffling. He was getting impatient with the obvious lack of progress against their southern neighbor, and Tai's excuses made him suspicious. Perhaps the PLA had been overconfident of their replay of the 1979 cross-border "punishment" attack.

"Comrade General Secretary, the front has been extended three kilometers farther south in the last 24 hours: The reason we remain behind schedule is that the enemy had more assets in the region than we thought, and also mobilized its reserves quicker than we calculated. If there is any fault here, it is mine."

"That's noble of you, General, but I'm not looking for recriminations—I want results!" *At least the man is honest and loyal—obviously trying to deflect heat from Tai.*

"Marshal Tai reassigned the theater commander, Comrade General Secretary. And he moved the reserve Combined Corps forward. The additional forces should accelerate our momentum toward Hanoi." Bao was covering his own incredulity: The Vietnamese Ground Forces (VGF) had been so well dug in that the PLAAF's hard-won control of the airspace had done little to dislodge the hidden tanks and artillery. His planes continually attacked targets that survived the first day's bomb and missile attacks—and VGF units alone had killed nearly half of the PLA's initial ground force. Additionally, the enemy's older-model tanks were using modern ammunition obtained from who knows where, and Wing's intelligence estimates had been essentially useless. A few of the PLAAF paratroopers (those whose planes were not shot down) had survived, but seemed to be hiding in the forests rather than coordinating with the advancing infantry. Then unknown bombers had plastered the 4th Tank Army funneling into the passes at the border, and a third of their first line tanks were destroyed. It had to be the American B-2s because no one knew they were there until the tanks blew up. So far, it was a fully stalled invasion.

Han heard Bao's early optimism, but decided he had no other conventional options—he wasn't going to order the use of tactical nuclear weapons under any circumstance. "General Bao, let's hope you are right. How about the other fronts?"

"All continues well, Comrade Han. The rebels on Taiwan are heavily degraded, and our forces are pushing the remnants up into the mountains. The island should be ours in a few days."

"That's more like it! I want progress, Bao, not a lot of excuses."

"Yes, Comrade General Secretary. Now, Sir, if I may shift to Japan?" He got the nod and continued, "The Japanese continue to launch occasional cruise missiles at our military installations, and we retaliate with counter-missile fire. But their launching sites are cleverly disguised and difficult to locate. We also estimate that eight or ten of their submarines—a mixture of the *Soryu* and *Oayshio* Class boats—escaped the fate of their comrades during the first hours of the war. These all carry U.S. Harpoon missiles that have been used effectively against us—plus they carry 30 Type-89 torpedoes. Our spies are keeping a close watch on their ports so we can call in missile strikes when they return to re-arm. They are operating around the Korean Peninsula and several of our submarines in the region are missing. Our captains report six kills, but these are unconfirmed." *And most likely overly optimistic.*

"Our landing force is slugging it out with Japanese ground forces in Yokosuka, but *Dragon's Roar* was sunk this morning—probably by another B-2 stealth aircraft—the type we suspect destroyed our four Dragons in U.S. waters. We knew a third of that aircraft type would survive our initial attack because they were stationed abroad—these in addition to that one in Florida that General Wing's Chaos Team missed. However, the good news is that every one of our Dragon's equipment has been successfully off-loaded, and every piece of hardware and all relevant personnel are now hidden among nearby buildings.

"Specifically, regarding Yokosuka, the Japanese have brought up their tanks, and infiltrated numerous special forces personnel. It has become a war of attrition, but we expected that, and our forces are giving a good account of themselves. They are sacrificing their lives to hold on, but all will be dead or captured in a few days."

"Acceptable, Comrade General. Now, what about Korea?"

"Our armor and mechanized spearheads have breached the old mid-peninsula border and are making gradual progress toward Seoul. We are facing increasingly ruthless aerial combat against the surviving South Korean and American Air Forces—and it is clear that the Yankees have mobilized their air arm—drawing in assets from the rest of the world. They are now believed to be staging their bombers out of Alaska and their fighters out of northern Japan. Going forward, this will be our major obstacle because they have hundreds of fifth-generation fighters that are better than our best. Additionally, we have used up most of our missile inventory to destroy other targets, but our factories are working overtime to rectify this lack. Unfortunately, our drones can't reach the bases where the fighter squadrons are hiding.

"Secondly, the Allied submarines have become problematic: They are launching cruise missiles that are destroying our ballistic missile batteries on the mainland, and they re-arm at their ports in Okinawa and Guam—both surprisingly intact after our two-carrier raid on Guam and our heavy missile barrage on Okinawa. We believe it was several previously undetected U.S. boats from Guam that attacked our retreating carriers and destroyed that task force. These boats are also using their potent anti-ship missiles to raise havoc with our surface vessels concentrated in the Taiwan Strait.

"Lastly, *Dragon's Fear* in Busan has been severely damaged by Korean missiles, and she is out of the fight, but the ground force is holding its own for now—fighting under the effective cloud of drones that remain our greatest advantage. We accept that it is only a matter of time before those forces are overrun—an unfortunate possibility if our northern invasion force can't draw off more South Korean armor—or reach Busan sooner than I am currently projecting."

Han was shocked: This was a much more somber outlook than he'd heard before. "What about the DMZ's mine fields and the hundreds of physical obstacles blocking the roads between the border and Seoul?" Han had been worried about breaching such a well-established defense since he first read Professor Dang's proposal. "How long before you clear paths through those mines?" Han was learning to ask specific questions.

"Comrade Han, we have breached several places along the border after comprehensive missile and artillery barrages heavily degraded those mine fields. And we are preparing another barrage for tomorrow. We still have a strong inventory of mobile launchers and missiles for the Korean theater of operations, and we are moving the batteries forward now. Our updated plan calls for cutting three additional breaches through the DMZ's obstacles on the south side of the border. The might of the PLA is gaining ground against the weakened South Korea and American forces who always work together. We have an approximate 2-1 advantage in every area except light infantry, but our combined arms pincers have already degraded their in-country armor and air capabilities by at least 50 percent."

Han then voiced another concern he'd been pondering, "Did any NK soldiers come over to our side as we'd planned?"

"Very few, Comrade General Secretary. After the surrender, most threw down their arms and melted into the countryside. They didn't seem eager to join us, and wouldn't have been much help during our advance south. We've interrogated many and they just want to go home. They are tired, need medical attention from a variety of illnesses, and lack food and other essentials."

Foreign Minister Wu then asked related questions. "General Bao, are we winning the air war over Korea? How much impact is the U.S. Air Force having on our advance?" He knew they thought him weak for firmly opposing this giant gamble, and he was still worried that the aggressive military types had overstepped their resources. Yet, he was grateful that Han had kept him on as Foreign Minister, and invited him to continue as a member of the Eight.

Bao paused a bit, raising red flags in the minds of several present. "We are winning, Comrade Minister—in the sense that they haven't stopped our ground pincers from advancing south. But we are up against tremendous aerial technology: We think that most of their operational F-22 Raptor fighters are in theater, plus we believe that at least half of the ROK and American F-15, F-16, A-10, FA-18 and F-35 squadrons survived as well. Plus, we have to contend with those B-1, B-2, and B-52 bombers that I mentioned earlier. These harass our ground advance without mercy—and we are not yet fully engaged by the Allied tanks. We think they are waiting until all their aerial forces are massed and can strike in force. When we close on Seoul, the ROK and U.S. resistance will stiffen considerably. They also have significant artillery that survived the initial attacks. So, in summary, Minister Wu, things may proceed slower than our initial estimates, but in the end we will win."

The room quieted after this sobering assessment—General Bao's positive ending notwithstanding. Bao was not used to obfuscating like Tai, and he believed Han and his advisors needed to hear the truth.

Han was troubled but grateful. "I appreciate your candor, General Bao—I can't make good decisions without the facts. Now, what about Taiwan?"

"That continues to be a bright spot, Comrade Han: Our forces have overrun about three quarters of the island and we have nearly completed the house-to-house clearing we had to effect in Taipei and the larger cities. We have a continual airlift bringing in fresh troops, plus we are using our somewhat limited sea-lift capabilities to both ferry troops in and to transport the wounded and dead back to the mainland. We have brought over additional tanks and other fighting vehicles, and we captured their refineries before they could destroy them, so we have plenty of fuel. We have a lot of our submarines in the area, and no foreign surface ships have penetrated the Strait. Only the Allied submarines remain a problem, as I mentioned earlier. But these numbers must be limited due to our destruction of a significant portion of their undersea fleet at the outset. This prescient strategy may end up being the key to victory after all.

"Most of the fighting outside the cities has shifted to the mountains, but the rebel forces have constructed tunnels and bunkers there for 70 years, so it will take considerable time to drive them out. Comrade General Secretary, the PLA needs your permission to inject poison gas into those tunnel systems. We believe the technology is necessary to keep on schedule." Bao saw his request caused eyes to dart from one colleague to another—everyone seemed surprised.

Liu Keqiang was appalled. She'd generally remained silent during these briefings because she'd stated her reluctance to begin this endeavor in the first place. But she was extremely loyal to her old friend Han, and now that they were in this war, she felt obligated to support his efforts. And, like everyone present, she was a patriot and wanted her country to win. But this request from Bao was just over the top. "I want to go on record as warning against use of this technology, Comrade General. This escalation would cause all our enemies to respond in kind with terrible results. I've read what evil poison gas caused in World War I!"

Han was a bit taken aback by his old friend's passionate objection, but he was also wary of using gas if they didn't have to. He would head this off quickly: "I agree with Comrade Liu, General. We will not use gas unless there is a self-defense emergency on our mainland. Do not move our stockpiles of either gas or biological munitions out of their secure storage areas. Is that clear?"

"Yes, Comrade Han, no chemical or biological weapons!" *But how many PLA soldiers would die fighting in those caves and tunnels?* BAO felt for the troops—the kids on the ground that got killed or maimed while he sat safely in Beijing.

Han then thought of something else, and turned to his Minister of the Interior. "Minister Ti, how are your People's Armed Police units faring in arresting rebel leaders on Taiwan?"

Ti had been dreading this question all meeting because neither her PAP officers, nor Wing's MSS cadres, were having any luck apprehending any significant rebel leaders. She was also feeling depressed and cranky because Wing had been ignoring her since the start of the war. Nevertheless, she gathered her wits and responded cautiously, "Comrade Han, we have arrested many low-level functionaries, but the top leaders are being hidden amongst the population or have escaped into the mountains. I am working closely with Minister Wing, and we are transporting prisoners to the mainland where my cadres can properly interrogate them."

"But I thought you and General Wing had agents in place to track the senior rebel leaders and arrest them at the outset?" Han was getting impatient again. He was sick and tired of broken promises, lame excuses, and inflated projections.

Ti looked sheepishly at Han and replied, "Yes, we were watching them closely, but they escaped in the opening minutes of the missile barrage." Even she thought her answer sounded weak.

"Well, keep at it! I am tired of these failures!" Han then turned back to Bao. "What's next, General?"

Bao resented Tai for abandoning him this morning. He was today's sacrificial lamb—put on the spot to answer the unanswerable. He and Dang were planning gurus, not the operators who led the soldiers in battle. But a subordinate usually took heat for the boss—it just came with the territory. He pressed on as best he could. "We have completed our advance in India, Comrade Han. As we expected, the Indians anticipated our moving farther into their territory and dug in and reinforced a line 50 miles south of our line of advance. They are just sitting there and our air force is more than a match for theirs. They have not counter-attacked, and our spies tell us their government is divided as to next moves. It seems like a finished outcome."

"Okay, that's good news. What's next?"

"The news is not so good in Australia, Comrade: Their army brought up armor units with surprising speed, and they are driving our forces back toward the mothership. *Dragon's Fang* is barely functioning, having been damaged by their bombers but, as in every location, we moved the personnel and equipment off the ship and into safety. We expect further attacks throughout the day."

"Seems like your estimates were inflated, General. Didn't you say our forces there could hold out for weeks?"

"That was our goal, Comrade General Secretary, and we still have significant fighting capability. But every Dragon was just a measure to give our forces on mainland Asia time to consolidate their gains. That will be done before the Australians can neutralize our troops around Sydney and release their forces to assist their allies. It will be too late for them to make much impact on the regional fight."

The Minister of Heavy Industry, Lee Tuc Chang, then asked a clarifying question, "General Bao, our landing force was very strong in Australia. How come our other forces are doing so well—even in America's ports—while in Australia we are being pushed back rather quickly?"

"Comrade Minister, we knew we could not hold off the Australian military for long because they had armor units in the vicinity. The Americans don't have much armor in the western half of their country—even their Marine armor unit in California near our San Diego operation has been dismantled, and the tanks assigned elsewhere. Additionally, their big southwestern desert training site was between cycles—essentially shut down for their holiday season. But, at least for now, we are successfully keeping the Australian tank units at bay. And, as everywhere, our drone force is having a devastating effect against their personnel and lighter vehicles. That is the success we planned for."

"Seems like a lot of trouble and expense for a short-term gain. I'm not criticizing the soldiers on the ground—it is always easy for us to do so from our comfortable room here, but I expected a longer fight." Lee had also been skeptical of the optimistic forecasts made in the other components of the Operation Unity Plan. He thought the PLA had better conquer its smaller mainland neighbors fast, or the Allies would get involved and complicate the war.

Han reasserted himself, "Specifically, how many of our operations are ahead of schedule, on schedule, or behind schedule?"

Bao hated this kind of question; any answer could really come back to bite him. He opted to be transparent—no one except Tai could fault him for that. "Comrade General Secretary, we are behind schedule only in Vietnam—our troops are fighting for every centimeter there. All the rest of our operations are on schedule. We are not ahead of schedule anywhere—India was completed on time."

"Okay, General, we all know a theoretical plan doesn't always equate to actual fighting on the ground." He let Bao off the hook because he knew Tai had dropped his subordinate into the lion's den. Besides, he had other important meetings and had to get going. "Thank you for coming, Comrades," he said to the others. "Please return for tonight's briefing at the usual time." Soon everyone was in their cars and heading for various offices downtown.

Chapter 46

A civilian airport outside Nagasaki, Japan
December 11th, 18:15 Hours

Tim Duncan had programmed the long flights to Japan into his operational timetable, and when the American contingent arrived at the designated hangar, they were met by a Japanese Self-Defense Force Special Operations colonel. Four other men were with him—two Australian SAS commandos and two Republic of China Special Forces operators who'd arrived earlier. The combined contingent of 21 commandos were all of Chinese ethnicity. Though none had been born in mainland China, all spoke passable Mandarin Chinese. Six were fully fluent.

Tim was commander of the unit, not just because he was the originator of the plan (with the majority of the credit going to Betty at CIA), but he'd previously served in the agency's Special Activities Division (SAD), and knew the special operations world personally. Lieutenant Colonel David Chen was his executive officer (XO), drawn from the 1st Special Forces Operations Detachment-Delta ("Delta Force"), considered the best "specific-task" commandos in the world. Dave had brought the only other Chinese-American member of his team, and had helped recruit several operators from the U.S. East Coast SEAL Teams (especially Seal Team 8, which was stationed in Virginia Beach, Virginia); two Marines from the Force Special Operations Command's Raider Battalions stationed at Camp Lejeune, North Carolina; two members of the CIA's SAD; and one member of the Air Force Special Warfare, Pararescue commandos. The men greeted one another casually as they sized each other up; they represented a number of elite units, but had been pulled together hastily for the current emergency. They constituted the entirety of the ethnic Chinese serving in the American and Australian special operations units.

"Welcome to Japan, Gentlemen," greeted the Japanese colonel in British-accented English. He didn't identify himself and, other than his rank, wore no identifying patches or insignias on his own plain green fatigues. However, the group immediately sized him up as a colleague in their unique fraternity: Japan's special operators had a well-earned reputation, and they had been operating effectively in WestPac for more than 15 years. "You have been brought together with no cohesive training or orientation, and we all know that is a weakness of this mission. However, the operation itself is straightforward, and all of you have extensive training and field experience in what you are being asked to do. We are in a desperate war against a massive foe, and we need a unique operation to turn the tables on this regional menace. Please step this way; we have a room set up for you. There, Mr. Duncan will brief you, and you will pick up uniforms that meet the operation's parameters. From now on, speak only Mandarin Chinese. That is all," he finished his remarks in that language. He watched the men file into a large room accessed from the hangar bay. His own men were in charge of security and, at that moment, it was the most secure place in southern Japan.

Takeo Gota was, in fact, a colonel in Japan's Ground Self-Defense Force. But more important for this operation, he was the commander of the elite commando group of special operators known as the Tokushusakusengun, "Japan's Delta Force." They had been formed in 2004 to combat terrorism—domestic and, to a lesser extent, international—wherever Japan's interests needed them. Trained by and modeled after their American counterparts, both the U.S. and Japanese units owed their lineage to the British SAS commandos who'd taught the Americans how to create such a force decades earlier. Colonel Gota wished he could take his own 300 men along, but this OP called for a small force—plus his unit was currently exterminating PLA forces in Yokosuka. He was proud of his modern day "ninjas."

Everyone found chairs and desks arranged in classroom style, and Tim led the team in two hours of chalkboard work and Q&A. The plan was audacious but, if they pulled it off, it would turn the tide of the war. Tim finished answering the last question, then noticed a "high-sign" from the colonel. He wrapped up the meeting and led the way back into the hangar where two large helicopters—previously covered with tarps—waited with the distinct blue and silver camouflage livery of the People's Liberation Army Navy. Both were identical Changhe Z-18s, and were a sobering reminder that the team would soon ride into the heart of the Dragon. It was dark outside, and Gota's men had ensured that their chances of being spotted by MSS agents was remote. The pilots were Japanese, but spoke Mandarin well enough to (hopefully) fool the air traffic controllers they'd confront in Chinese airspace. Tim looked at Colonel Gota when he saw the helos, but the senior man just said, "Don't ask…" That was good enough for Tim.

* * *

Tim and Betty's brainstorm had gained serious traction after she shared their idea with her long-time colleague and friend, Edith Carmichael. The women brought Tim to a meeting with the ladies' mutual friend, Vice President Mason, and she'd been so impressed that she personally interceded with the President. Spencer Stilwell was desperate enough to try anything creative—much as President Roosevelt had been willing to approve the Doolittle Raid in early 1942.

That operation had been unconventional, to say the least: A bombing raid on Tokyo and other cities just four months after the Pearl Harbor disaster. The strikes were mere pinpricks in terms of actual destruction, but the raid gave the American people a psychological shot in the arm, and put the over-confident Japanese government on notice. Lieutenant Colonel James H. Doolittle recruited and trained the B-25 bomber crews to take off from an aircraft carrier—something the men were neither trained to do nor the planes designed to do. After pulling off that difficult feat, they had to fly at wave-top level until they popped up and made their bomb runs over Japan. But by then they were low on fuel and, when they reached mainland China most had to crash-land. The survivors linked up with local friendly Chinese Allies, but sadly some of the Raiders were captured and executed. Overall, the mission was a dramatic success and the reason Tim christened the plan "Operation Raider."

He had carte blanche from the President to raise his small but uniquely qualified force, and it took just over a day to identify the limited number of Chinese Americans who served in the close-knit special operations community. There just weren't that many phone calls to make, and no red tape or foot-dragging slowed the process. Australia donated two Special Air Service commandos, and Taiwan had two men currently training on Okinawa that could sneak out in a small plane. The Japanese government was only too happy to help with logistics, and they informed Tim that they had the perfect insertion tool. So here they were—a small force of volunteers willing to carry out a plan with far less preparation time than those other heroes had needed in 1942.

* * *

Colonel Gota's men provided the team with uniforms of the "Siberian Tigers"—the PLA's elite special operations unit headquartered outside the large northern city of Shenyang. Their barracks and training area was located north and east of Beijing—about 100 miles west of the North Korean border—so appropriating their identity was a natural fit. Japanese intelligence confirmed that the Tigers were fully involved in the Korean campaign, and would not appear at an embarrassing time to interfere with the mission. Tim was dressed in the uniform of a People's Armed Police full colonel. The team stowed its gear on the two long-range high-capacity helicopters, then settled into fairly comfortable seats for the first leg of the trip. Tim and Dave Chen thanked Colonel Gota for the helos and the pilots, then buckled in. A minute later, the two aircraft rose in the predawn darkness—all aboard hoping the jumpy South Korean air defense artillery units had gotten the word on two Chinese Navy helos landing near Incheon.

An undisclosed safe house in Beijing
December 11th, 20:00 Hours

Han decided it was time to shake up the Korean campaign with a special news conference. Though he enjoyed being the star of every news broadcast in the PRC, tonight he surely would be. The six people on the couch to his left would generate dramatic worldwide news. Most important of those was the Supreme Leader of Korea (and Marshal of the Republic) Kim Jong-Un, currently sitting quietly in a row with four of his most senior North Korean generals. The sixth person was his sister, who was considered the real number two in the Kim regime's power structure. All looked worried. Han was obviously displaying them as a prize but, in so doing, he was also sending a message to other world leaders—particularly those government officials and senior military leaders in the crosshairs of his invading military. He had debated displaying them in handcuffs, or even publicly executing them, but he decided the respectful approach would win more hearts and minds—and would also undermine the propaganda storm being put out by his enemies. His Special Forces units had pulled off a text-book snatch-and-grab, and he felt it was time to crow a little. It also sent a strong message to his troops that he appreciated what they did—and that their achievements would receive the republic's highest level recognition.

Han would broadcast his remarks on open airways, but specifically address the people of both Koreas. He could take the high ground here, and it would help sway world opinion. He received the countdown from the director, and then the red light went on, "People of North and South Korea, as you see before you, our skillful Special Forces units have rescued the northern leaders from the dangers of the warfare circling around their capital of Pyongyang—and we will soon do the same in Seoul." Han paused as the translator rattled off phrases in Korean—a language he'd never taken the time to learn.

"We did not want anyone harmed by the South Korean military—or by the American squatters and interventionists in your ancient homeland. I want you to know personally that we come as friends and liberators. In a few days, we will overwhelm the South Korean and Allied forces, and the end result will be a unified peninsula that so many have dreamed of for more than 70 years. As we liberate and unify, we want you to know that China's administration will be fair and equitable to all sides. We will replace rebellious functionaries with loyal Koreans who will work with us to create a mutually prosperous future. Therefore, all Korean military cadres on all sides, please lay down your arms and accept our unifying efforts. I now call upon Supreme Leader of North Korea Kim Jong-Un to personally address all Korean-speaking peoples worldwide."

Kim Jong-un looked as out of place as anyone could under the circumstances, and he was still in a state of shock that the Chinese commandos had so easily overpowered his elite protective details—layers upon layers of trusted soldiers who were the sons and grandsons of those who'd protected his father and grandfather before him. But he'd been educated in Europe and was a practical man, and he accepted that, if Han had wanted to kill him and his family, he would have done so already. He'd been given a script to read, and he proceeded to do so in his best-educated Korean: "People of the North Korean Workers Party, and all who love Korea, we thank our older brother and neighbor, the People's Republic of China, for helping us liberate the South from the fanatics that have bullied half of our people for decades. We support this unification and liberation, and look forward to governing with Comrade Han and the Chinese Politburo in the decades to come. Since we no longer need to rely on our own nuclear weapons or missile programs, I have ordered both inventories donated to the People's Liberation Army. I will address you again when the liberation is complete." He then looked over at the CCP chairman whom he'd met several times over the years, and received a respectful nod. But he was not fooled: He would live under the Chinese sword for the rest of his life.

"Thank you, Supreme Leader Kim Jong-Un. Your heartfelt words will unify our two peoples into an unbeatable force for good. People of all Korea, please join us and work for a unified peninsula. You in the southern half, please lay down your arms so you can live in perpetual peace." Han paused to let the translator finish, then he switched to English: "And you American and other foreign military personnel, let your leaders know you wish to return home and not be involved in someone else's war. If you lay down your arms, you will be treated respectfully and quickly sent back home. Now we must continue our liberation efforts on many fronts until the job is done. For now, I merely say good night until I am able to address you again." The camera's light dimmed and Han knew he was off the air. Then he just walked out with his staff in tow, and left the befuddled Koreans to contemplate their fate. His security would politely escort them back to their separate rooms. Husbands and wives were politely kept together, and they would be well cared for until Han figured out how best to use them in the future.

The Oval Office, Washington, DC
December 11th, 07:00 Hours (same time)

"Well, another surprise from Comrade Han." President Stilwell had been alerted to the imminent broadcast from Beijing, but hadn't known what to expect. Everyone in the room was equally surprised. "He just informed us that the PRC now has the NK nukes!" That was profound.

"Quite a coup for Han and company, Mr. President." Jack Madrid was rarely impressed. Sharing their working breakfast was VP Mason, John Laughton, and Baker Halsey.

"The only good that has come out of the war," added the VP. "Another irony that the ChiComs are more stable than the NKs."

Spence agreed, "You are right there, Rebecca. But now it will be interesting to see how the South Koreans respond. What's your take, Jack? Will any Southerners obey Kim and Han from a TV broadcast?"

"Mr. President, I believe there will be a few. Some radical pacifists might cooperate, but the majority of South Koreans will fight like the angels of God to protect their hard-won freedoms!"

"I concur, Mr. President," agreed Baker Halsey. "Just a few radicals. Their army is first-rate and they fight well. They are great allies."

"Is our airpower having any effect yet?" The President was looking for any encouraging news.

"Yes, Sir! Our fighters are rapidly taking control of the skies, but it will be another week or ten days before we can claim we have control of the airborne battle space. Unfortunately, the ground war may be over by then, and we'll be relegated to harassing the ChiComs from Japan. And we certainly have not ventured over China's airspace yet."

"So, we're in a race against time." It was a statement, not a question. Spence read updates twice daily, and they weren't good. He realized he was hoping beyond hope that a lone agent and twenty commandos could pull off a miracle.

Fourth Subterranean Level, August 1st Building, Beijing December 12th, 06:50 Hours

Captain Kai arrived early for his appointment, as was expected of a company grade officer meeting the senior commander of the People's Liberation Army. He had been summoned by his uncle, Marshal Tai, and he wondered what was up. His current assignment as Colonel Kang's aide had become truly boring since the Dragon Fleet sailed, and he felt that the war had passed him by. The colonel was still relieved to be above ground, and the doctor had headed back to her clinic in Dalian City, so there was nothing much to do. Kai desperately wanted a combat command, but so far nothing had come his way. Then he received an urgent message the previous evening telling him where and when to report. At last! Uncle will give me a front-line company command!

Right on time as expected, Kai saw Marshal Tai marching toward him through the large underground office complex—currently home to most of the command staff that had moved underground after the Japanese missiles destroyed part of the upper floors. Other than the somewhat claustrophobic labyrinth, things seemed otherwise normal in the roomy subterranean spaces. Kai had visited upstairs a few times in the past when tagging along with the always self-important Colonel Kang, but they'd never had reason to reach the top floor. And certainly none to visit the "dungeons."

"Good morning, Comrade Marshal," Kai greeted his commander professionally. There was never a hint between them of the close family relationship.

"Morning, Captain. Come into my office." Kai had spent enough time under the thumb of that boob of a security officer at Dalian. Now it was time to move him up the ladder. "Shut the door."

Kai came to attention in front of the ordinary gray military desk and waited to learn the reason for his summons. He knew Uncle Tai was mad at the Japanese right now: One of their missiles had shattered his favorite glass desk. Fortunately, he and Lieutenant General Bao had been away.

"Sit down, Kai. I want you to learn new things now. You've done well serving as a colonel's aide after your platoon command—and I know you want to join the fighting as a company commander. However, I want you to serve as my aide during the war so you can learn what to expect in the future. After that, I'll send you for a year's service on the Indian border—the first six months as a company commander, and the second as executive officer of a battalion. Then you can come back here as a major and attend the National Defense University. You have promise, Kai—make the most of every opportunity!"

"Yes, Marshal Tai! It is an honor to serve anywhere in the PLA!" It was a standard answer. But he was disappointed to have to be his uncle's errand boy when there was a rare war on. Oh, to have a company command at the front in Taiwan or Korea.

Tai knew the boy was disappointed. What young officer wouldn't be when the prospects of command during one of their wars was so limited. But he'd promised his brother that he would manage Kai's career—and not get him killed in the process. He'd learn a lot over the next few weeks as the war wrapped up, and it was a great time to see the view from the top. "Go next door and speak with General Bao—he'll have some things for you to do. I have paper work until lunch, then I'll introduce you to the staff."

Kai sharply saluted and properly executed a textbook about-face and left his uncle's office. He then turned left and headed down the hall to the chief of staff's office. *What a dismal turn of events!*

Ngoc Xuyen Peninsula, Vietnam (same time)
On the bluffs above the beach

Captain Ly was exhausted. His men had fought for 47 straight hours before subduing the last of the invading enemy. The vicious fighting had left half his command dead and an additional third wounded. He'd been grazed by bullets three times and bayonetted in the calf once, but his medic was good and just kept patching him up. But, most important, his company had made its stand on this little stretch of dunes, and the enemy had died where they landed. One failed desperation charge near the end had reached the edge of his own fighting position, but he and his men had beaten them back. Afterward, the few remaining Trung Quoc soldiers hobbled off the beach when they surrendered, but the majority were carried up in body bags.

He took a moment to enjoy the early morning vista across the bay: In the near distance, the shattered remains of the four 726s wallowed in the slacking tide. It would take marine engineers some time to figure out what to do with the hulks—they'd probably try to temporarily float them and drag them into deeper water for sinking. Farther out, several small boats were moored to a barge anchored to the assault ship's protruding mast. It was the only visible reminder of the massive threat she once posed. Divers were inspecting the wreck—mostly trying to figure out if her valuable military cargo could be salvaged and used. A marine engineer had come ashore the previous day, and told him the ship had initially rolled to its left as it sank, but then righted itself when it hit the shallow bottom. The top of the (fake) container stacks were only a few meters down and, unless they figured a way to cut it up and drop the pieces in deep water, the ship would be a marked hazard for the next 100 years. He described the deception of the stacks, and row upon row of new tanks and APCs lining the spacious insides of the hull.

Captain Ly didn't know what the regimental commander would do with his surviving men. There were only nine who were unscathed, plus a few more who could be patched up and sent back to the front lines. The rest of the living were walking wounded like him. News from the border was grim, but the high command had committed its full complement of reserves, so the future of his nation hung in the balance. But at least the news in the dispatches he'd read earlier gave a needed surge of pride: The army had given some ground, but for five days they'd held off the largest army on earth. It would be noted in Vietnam's history along with the legendary feats of the Hai Ba Trung Sisters who fought the Chinese with elephants 2,000 years ago, and with General Tran Hung Dao's famous victory over the invading Mongol army at the battle Bach Dang in 1288. The general had placed sharpened logs in the local river that trapped the enemy boats at low tide and, with the enemy thus corralled, his soldiers had swooped down on the invaders and crushed them. The French and the Americans came much later, but every foreign power eventually left—Vietnam was the Land of the Blue Dragon, and had always resisted outsiders well. Yet, for all that, he was glad the Americans were on their side now and he'd heard a rumor that their Air Force had bombed numerous enemy targets on the border. They were also starting to shoot down Trung

Quoc planes in Korea. They were doing whatever it took to win! At least his family had escaped south and was staying with relatives in Da Nang. A couple of years before, he'd visited the nearby historical site of Camp Eagle—the old headquarters of the Americans' famous 101st Airborne Division that had fought in the area for years. *Yes,* he thought, *it was much better to have the United States as a friend.*

Just then a sergeant walked up and saluted, and handed him a note. He was ordered to report to regimental headquarters immediately for another assignment. He was to leave his highest ranking subordinate in command of the remaining troops until events sorted themselves out. He sighed: He'd been in command of his company for less than a month, and wondered if he would ever experience command again. So many of his soldiers had died—and he felt responsible. *Could he have done things differently?* His company had won the battle, but he would gladly have sacrificed his life for theirs.

He moved a bit stiffly back to the sand-bagged trenches where his men had fought so bravely, and called to Sergeant (E-6) Truong. All Captain Ly's junior officers had either been killed or were so badly wounded that they'd been evacuated to the 226th Field Hospital on the outskirts of the city. He gave his sergeant the correct order and reminded him to secure more food and ammo. Then they shook hands and saluted each other—brothers bound by the strings of battle that outsiders would never understand. Then he went down the line one last time and thanked his soldiers who'd help save their country.

Chapter 47

San Francisco
December 11th, 17:00 Hours

Matty hadn't been home since the war began. He didn't want to any reprisals against their family and, though the ChiComs weren't murdering civilians, none of the militia wanted to press their luck. All of them had sniped as targets presented themselves, and then they'd moved to the next block, and then another. Without any training, he and many others had engaged in classic urban warfare. But for the last three days he'd also been emotionally numb: John had died after being struck with automatic rifle fire on the second night of the war, and Matty had barely escaped death himself. He couldn't even hold his brother while he died; they'd waved to each other as an enemy patrol closed in on his side of the street, and his brother had fired into them at point-blank range so Matty could slip away.

In modern times, he and most Americans had felt safe behind their two oceans and, aside from a few incidences of domestic terrorism and 9/11, enemy soldiers had not invaded since the skirmishes with Pancho Villa and earlier with the British. Old Mr. Chong had also died—but Matty suspected a heart attack. The elderly man was lying behind a car, shooting at a patrol, when his head just lowered to the ground. Matty was close enough to reach him, but there was no blood, just a quiet old man who'd died fighting for his friends. Matty had read about such people in the early days of U.S. history when war was closer to home, and he vowed to visit Mrs. Chong and tell her what happened. If he survived the war.

One positive development was the arrival of a Navy sniper. CPO (E-7) McMurtry was the real deal—just like the guy in the movie. He was not there to take the militia's place, but to provide some professional leadership for a bunch of fellow citizens. His SEAL Team had infiltrated from the coast and had fought it out with the ChiCom marines who'd landed in the LCACs. But they'd disengaged after a half-hour and just melted into the urban areas to link up with the unorganized civilians. "Chief," as he like to be called, had gathered several of the irregulars like Matty and gotten them off the streets. He led them into an abandoned store front where he introduced himself and briefly taught them how to coordinate their ambushes. Chief McMurtry was an inspirational leader—and the man could shoot, too. His little unit of seven civilians had killed or wounded more than 50 enemy soldiers, and Matty and the Sacramento Street Irregulars had killed or wounded 10 or 12 before that.

Currently, the chief had the seven of them in an "aerial V formation," meaning they were concealed on rooftops and alley ways—an ambush tracking a ChiCom reccee team working its way up California Street near the top of the hill. Matty could see them move from one doorway to the next, carefully scanning every quadrant in the waning light for telltale movement or glints of light off weapons that threatened danger. Matty would have shot the first one already, but Chief had instructed them to shoot the last one first—and make sure he was not a decoy for a hidden tank or APC with big guns that would tear them apart. The group had to wait until Chief shot first, then the rest of them could blast away. It had proven an effective strategy: Chief killed them back to front, and the seven of them killed front to back. It was lethal and they were getting good at it.

Slowly the enemy marines advanced, dashing in short sprints from doorway to doorway, alley to alley. There were some taller office buildings interspersed with the apartments and occasional single-family homes, and there were plenty of places to hide. Matty's team could hear the rumble of a tank engine somewhere, but the canyon-like echoes between the buildings made it hard to locate. Everyone could also hear sporadic firefights in many parts of the city. There were hundreds of people fighting now—every neighborhood had men and some women who'd killed or wounded enemy soldiers—but the militias had paid a huge price, too, losing many friends and family members as they slowly gave ground to the ChiCom professionals.

At the moment, Matty was aiming at the nearest soldier on his side—he looked like he had sergeant's chevrons on his sleeve—and he would squeeze the trigger once Chief shot the trailing man about half a block further down. San Francisco was all hills, so Chief had taught them always to get on ground higher than their enemy. He taught them to scout points of egress so they could escape to fight again. He had lots of funny or colorful sayings to describe what he wanted them to do, like "shoot and scoot" and, when they were holing up and resting before the next patrol, he shared a lot of his hard-earned wisdom. He'd served overseas many times, and Matty was greatly impressed: SEALs were really something.

"Crack!" boomed Chief's .50 cal. sniper rifle, and the man farthest down the hill just flew backward and tumbled until he crashed into a dumpster.

"Bang!" Matty loosed his first round and knocked his target back against the stone façade of a commercial building. Then, from their rooftop vantage points, the team rained fire on the ChiComs. The Chinese soldiers returned fire, but not accurately. They just sprayed bullets everywhere with their powerful automatic rifles, and broke most of the remaining windows with shattering effect. The sound was deafening inside the vertical walls, but the enemy patrol was pinned down for real. It looked like they'd hit 10 out of the 20 men in the patrol, but the officer in the middle was yelling into a hand-held. Soon a tank or APC would appear, and the little band of patriots would be destroyed.

There! A tank rounded a corner about 10 blocks down and elevated its main gun toward them.

"Crack!" Chief fired another round, and the radio flew out of its user's hand.

"Withdraw!" Chief shouted, and the three street-level guys jumped to their feet and dashed down the side street they'd scouted earlier. As they ran for their lives, side doors of the connecting buildings burst open and the four "roof team" members chased their friends, with Chief hot on their tails. They'd made another successful ambush with no casualties.

Port Klang, Malaysia
December 12th, 09:10 Hours

It was now morning on the fifth day since the Chinese ship *Dragon's Breath* had brought surprising violence to his peaceful adopted land. Manfred Singh had been rounded up within the first hour of the landing, and he was still being held prisoner by the soldiers who'd caught him speaking on his office phone. He'd been trying to reassure his frantic wife that he was okay, but also warning her that he might not be home for a few days. As he sat there, a morning rain storm beat down on the metal roof and it was already hot, but he couldn't complain about his treatment: The PLA soldiers had herded the dock workers into the handy warehouse and kept them under guard, but had not bothered them otherwise. They were issued two army-type rations daily, plus all the fresh water they wanted, and there was an adequate toilet that still functioned. Wooden pallets had been stacked in one corner, so everyone had claimed one and slept on them instead of the dirty cement floor. It was stifling hot during the early afternoons, but they were all locals and used to the heat.

However, what had everyone worried (including, the prisoners guessed, the rotating shifts of four guards) was the sound of the distant battle that was inching closer. He sensed nervousness in their captors, and he assumed that they'd expected a much quicker victory. But the Malaysian military was well-trained, and they were obviously giving the PLA a run for its money. The Dragon ship still docked nearby had been targeted by artillery shells several times, and planes had dropped bombs, but the pilots were being conservative and none had hit Manfred's temporary jail. They had all peeked out at the waterfront, and saw the mass of drones, big and tiny, that were flying everywhere but, beyond that, the prisoners could only guess at the big picture and hope their families were safe.

Honolulu, Hawaii, December 11th, 15:10 Hours

All the military infrastructure and units on Oahu had been carefully scouted by General Wing's MSS cadres, and Dragon Tail's drone force had heavily damaged and harassed every one of them from the moment the battle began. So far, the drones had proven decisive, dominating the skies above the port and surrounding areas, and greater Pearl Harbor was even more vulnerable than the stateside harbors due to its relative lack of size. But neither the four American ports, nor the international ones, had an answer for the mini-drones.

Even destruction of the motherships in U.S. ports had done little to degrade the ChiCom capabilities: They had modular control stations set up in transportable containers, and these had all been off-loaded before the B-2 dropped its four deadly JDAMs on each Dragon. *Dragon's Tail* had settled into the mud, and she was still smoldering four days later. Damage to the Navy ships and submarines was so extensive that none would be of service for months at the earliest. Buildings everywhere were gutted—caused by fires that had raged through the second day. All were out now, but the atmosphere was choked with dust and lingering smoke; it pooled in the basin between the ocean and the volcanic mountains inland, interfering with the usually spectacular views.

Every active and reserve military unit on the island had mobilized and attempted to reach the front lines established by the enemy armor units. But as they tried to engage the ChiComs at the edge of the ground force battle area that had firmed up as a rough semi-circle on the edges of Hickam Airfield and Honolulu Harbor, the drones just cut everyone to pieces. The combined arms of the PLA heavy brigade helped keep the Americans at bay, but there were no M1A2 tank units stationed on the islands.

The 25th Infantry Division's commanding general, frustrated that his Stryker and Apache units were ineffective against the drones and heavy ChiCom tanks, decided to get creative and called for volunteers to infiltrate the controlled areas with FGM-148 Javelins. It proved to be a brainstorm: The man-portable "fire and forget" anti-tank missile system worked like a charm—if the volunteers could sneak in close enough. The system was the perfect tank-killer, and the Javelin teams began killing one tank and APC after another. Unfortunately, creeping close enough to get off shots made these near-suicide missions. The attrition rate was horrible because they were terribly exposed, and only a third survived the dangerous gauntlet of aerial drones lurking in every quadrant.

Typical of American military personnel everywhere, hundreds of soldiers, airmen, sailors, and Marines volunteered for the dangerous duty anyway, and there were so many of these brave warriors that rosters had to be created in every reporting location. But, by the fourth day, there were more Javelins than operators because a civilian airliner had snuck into the small airport on Maui loaded to the hilt with replacement missiles. Small boats had ferried them onto Oahu's north shore at night, and the inventory was full. Dozens of military personnel risked their lives just to report to the designated issuing stations, where volunteers were given simple instructions on the missiles' operation. Then two warriors were paired up and issued the deadly weapons.

At the moment, Corporal Ted Grimes and Private First-Class Kathy Newberry were stalking a tank that was hiding in an Air Force enlisted housing area. Ted's previous partner had been badly wounded during their approach the day before, and Ted had abandoned both the mission and their two missiles so he could drag the man back to safety. Around midnight, he'd reported to the command bunker and asked for another chance, and the Army master sergeant issuing the Javelins agreed. There was only one issue: The only potential partner was a female Air Force helo mechanic.

Kathy saw the men exchange "that look" and got mad. The ChiComs had wounded several of her friends, destroyed all her unit's helos, and had invaded her country. Now she wanted to kill somebody! So, before the two dimwit males rejected her outright, she walked over to the missile system lying on the table, fitted her arms into the harness, and swung its 50-pound assembly onto her shoulders—mimicking the two previous teams she'd watched gear-up earlier. The men exchanged shrugs—she was in.

That little drama had taken place several hours earlier, and Kathy and Ted had been closing in on their assigned target since. Presently they were inching through a green belt in their assigned neighborhood, all the while keeping a close eye out for the deadly drones. A couple of times they'd heard the high-pitched squeal of a mother drone less than a mile away, but they'd frozen in place and trusted their camo to protect them. Each time the noise faded, and they'd jumped to their feet and dashed into the nearest open door of an abandoned home. They'd kept this up for hours, and now were getting close. As long as they weren't spotted, they had an excellent chance of knocking out a tank.

Both combatants wore heavy fatigues, plus the usual helmets and headsets that kept them in contact with their maneuvering NCO. He was running a few teams from a bunker near old Wheeler airfield, and they could also receive the downlink from the only American Predator drone that survived the initial attack. The U.S. drone had been aloft on a training mission over the Kaiwi Channel between Molokai and Oahu, and had relayed usable information down to the ground troops from the first minutes of the attack. The only problem was the Predator's lack of landing sites to rearm with Hellfire missiles. Its Air Force pilots had nailed two tanks after the mothership was sunk (which ended the anti-air laser threat) but its usefulness as an unarmed spotter was dramatically more important. The Predator is truly excellent at trolling along for 24 hours at 25,000 feet—quite invisible from the ground—and it was able to "see" everything, day or night. Its handlers established a landing site at a remote field near the Disney Hotel on the west end of Oahu where a fuel bowser was hidden. There, the ground crew gave it a quick check once a day during refueling. It took on 600 pounds of 100-octane aviation gas and, after a 30-minute going-over, it was airborne again. Four days after the start of the war, the military's "eye in the sky" was still undetected and fully operational.

Whatever secret doubts Ted might have been holding about Kathy had disappeared after the first two hours of their approach: She seemed less fazed by the frightening prospect of being zapped by the mini-drones than he did, and he soon forgot his earlier prejudice and focused on the mission. He'd learned something during the previous day's failed approach, and those lessons contributed to their stealthy approach. After sneaking unobserved along a narrow bushy canal between two housing areas, they had their target in sight: A main battle tank sitting under a carport awning about a mile away. They paused and talked it out. "What do you think?" he whispered. "Want to try a shot from here?"

Kathy looked around. She knew they had a good chance of hitting the tank, but they were terribly exposed, and she wanted to live long enough to at least use their second missile later. In her mind, it was better to work their way into some heavy shrubs near a corner house about 100 yards closer to the tank. Mini-drones would search for them, but they'd be hard to spot in the dense cluster of bushes. If the "minies" found them, they could kick a door in and hide in an inner room until the danger passed. Word had gotten around that the mini-drones could fly through glass, but not through doors or walls. Therefore, inner bathrooms were heralded as the safest place to hide. She shared her idea and her partner agreed.

Ted could see ten dismounted soldiers guarding the tank, but they were close enough to it that he figured most of them would be killed or disabled when it blew up. That depended on a good shot. "Okay, good idea. After the shot, we can hide in that corner house if necessary." He led the way, crawling out of the ditch and across the heavy grass toward the bushes silhouetted against the lighter sky. It had gotten darker as they moved through the afternoon, and a few undamaged street lights still dotted the neighborhood. Ted kept a steady low-crawl, and he could hear Kathy doing the same about two yards behind.

Ted had a male ego like every guy he knew, but his life was more important than insisting on his idea when a better one would get the job done. So far, they'd avoided the deadly drones and arrived at a good spot to launch their first missile. He and his partner struggled out of the heavy harnesses, and assembled the Javelin system together. It was quick and easy—really a user-friendly weapon—and a quality upgrade from the old Dragon system he'd learned about in basic training. He was glad to have this modern one: You just punched off a Javelin and could leave the area, whereas the old Dragon system was wire-guided and left the operator exposed for several seconds. With clouds of deadly mini-drones about, those precious seconds were already saving lives.

Kathy assisted her partner by turning on the unit so it could cycle and warm up, then she helped him heft it onto his shoulder. He held the laser range-finder with his two hands and sighted through the sophisticated scope. "Twenty-one-ten," she heard him say quietly. Just over 2,000 yards.

"Got your ear protection in?" she asked.

"Yes. Okay, here goes." Ted got the correct warble tone in his headphones, then depressed the "fire" button and felt the jolt as the powerful projectile shot out of the launch tube. The back blast emitted a small stream of fire out the rear of the tube, and the missile shot straight out, then angled steeply up as it raced toward its target at tremendous speed. The missile quickly reached altitude and plunged straight down through the flimsy carport roof and directly into the top of the tank's vulnerable thinner top armor. The insides of the tank instantly heated to 8,000 degrees. It caught the tank crew and accompanying infantrymen completely off guard, exploding through the tank's turret and igniting the ammo rack inside. It exploded with a giant roar that killed every soldier inside—plus everyone within the blast radius outside. Ted lingered a few seconds to check for survivors but everything was still. Good, no one to call in a drone strike!

"Great shot, Corporal," Kathy praised quietly. That would teach those ChiCom so and so's not to invade the U.S.!

"Thanks," Ted said, "let's boogie." They picked up the spent launch tube, tossed it through the nearest open window, and raced into a grove of trees that separated the housing area from a small park just beyond. They quickly established a steady pace, and 30 minutes later reached a likely spot to climb down into their original canal. They reoriented and began stalking their second target. Along the way, they came across a culvert to rest in, and invested time for a break. They broke out their rations and water, and discussed their first kill. They decided to keep hidden for another hour, then close on the next tank a few neighborhoods over. If they survived, they'd return to the culvert and hide out until the following night. Then, under cover of darkness, they could return to the bunker for chow and additional missiles.

Chapter 48

Incheon, South Korea, December 12th, 10:00 Hours

Tim's team had spent the hours since their short hop from Japan as productively as they could, using white boards that the South Korean Special Forces Command had thoughtfully included in their arrival package. There was a good selection of western and Asian food, plenty of hydration beverages, cots with blankets, eye covers—you name it, the Koreans had thought of it. Their arrival had also started in the best possible way: They'd not been shot down by trigger-happy ADA crews looking to smoke two ChiCom helicopters sneaking into their airspace.

The ROK SF headquarters was conveniently located in Incheon, and their special ops soldiers were modeled after the U.S. Green Berets. They had an impressive record dating back to their formation in 1958, and many had served in Vietnam. The 10,000 men who currently wore the black beret followed their motto: "Make the Impossible, Possible" approach like a ghost, strike like thunder, vanish like smoke." Tim was glad they were on the same side.

So far, Tim's Raiders had suggested small refinements to improve his hastily developed plan and, at least in theory, it was shaping into a first-class operation. The one thorny problem that so far had defied a solution was refueling the second helo; the plan called for two LZs—but one had fuel and one did not. The second helo would land in a clearing in a forest, and they didn't have enough gas to return to Incheon. Long-range tanks didn't supply enough fuel, either, and the mission needed the associated weight to carry personnel. At one point, everyone decided their heads needed a break, and they knocked off for half an hour and ate. Then everyone took their pills and enjoyed a solid six-hour power sleep; the refueling solution would have to wait. They would leave at dusk for Beijing—Operation Raider was nearly a go.

USS *North Carolina* (SSN-777) just east of Guam December 12th, 11:20 Hours

The Shark was proud of his crew: They were all business and had worked tirelessly during the boat's efficient speed run west. They'd recorded five kills on the first day of the ChiCom attack, and then spent an uneventful four days cruising at more than 20 knots to rendezvous northeast of Guam with *California* and *Connecticut.* Generally, American sub doctrine anticipated them operating alone—rather than in wolf packs like the German U-boats of World War II fame—but this time, COMSUBPAC wanted them coordinating their attacks against the multiple ChiCom threats. The enemy was on the verge of overrunning Taiwan, and the President had ordered all available forces to converge on their beleaguered friend to try to prevent their annihilation. They and many other boats would link up with the Nimitz task force, currently launching airstrikes from 500 miles east of Taiwan. Together, they would be a formidable powerhouse, capable of sinking most of the ChiCom submarine fleet around the island, and many of the ships in the strait. The *Nimitz* had dodged several ChiCom submarine attacks but, so far, the U.S. subs were making short work of the enemy boats. One ballistic missile attack had been launched against them, too, but they had escaped any serious damage. Since then the missile sites had been hit hard by the Allies cruise missiles and the attacks had nearly ceased.

The U.S. crews had been saddened to see the damage inflicted on Guam's submarine base, but it was a stark reminder of war and gave them additional focus. They re-armed and re-provisioned, then proceeded west. Their first assignment was to pick off the enemy boats known to be lurking north, east, and northeast of Taiwan. When that was completed, all U.S. subs south of Japan would launch their Tomahawk cruise missiles at mainland targets, then transition to the final mission—sinking every surface ship they could catch between the western side of the island and the mainland. They would not be involved in the Korean theater of operations. All Allied boats in Japanese and Korean waters were to assist the ROK/U.S. forces to halt the PLA advance down the peninsula.

Aiding both efforts were the fighter and bomber squadrons staging in Japan and Alaska. The Allied pilots had become proficient at pouncing on the Chinese fighters and lumbering transports, and their superior technology gave them decisive victories. The Navy air war gave the ROC army a fighting chance, while the Japanese, Korean, and U.S. Air Force planes did the same over Korea.

The Free Chinese Air Force had been annihilated the first day, but retreating ground forces were well dug into their long-established cave and tunnel systems in the highlands and mountains. They were basically holding their own as they prayed for help from abroad. They had vast stores of ammunition, food and water, and cleverly concealed artillery batteries that constantly harassed the advancing PLA. Untold numbers of civilians had died in the costal lowlands, and there was little left of those national guard units who couldn't retreat. Still, the Taiwanese national spirit was far from broken, and those still fighting believed they could win. Things were gradually improving for the Allies in the ocean war, but rolling back the mainland's ground invasion of their neighbors now seemed almost impossible.

5th Regimental HQ South of Haiphong, Vietnam

Captain Ly was in a somber mood when he reported to regimental headquarters. He was mourning his dead and wounded comrades, and their bravery and success in battle hadn't lessened his pain. He vowed to himself that, as soon as the war was over, he'd personally visit every one of his men's families, and tell them how their brave sons and husbands had died.

His driver parked under a large canopy of camo netting covering the huge headquarters tent, and Ly jumped out and told the young man to find himself something to eat. Ly had tried to clean up a bit, but knew he looked rough: His uniform was torn in several places, and he hadn't been able to fully wash the blood out, either. Some of it was his, some from his men that he dragged to safety, and some from the enemy soldiers he'd killed. He'd held two of his youngest soldiers as they died—and he promised each one that their lives would never be forgotten. He'd received great strength from their sacrifices, and he'd fought and directed his platoons like a man possessed.

Then suddenly it was over: A wounded one-star Chinese general on the beach ordered his men to cease fire, and called up that he wanted to surrender. Ly ordered a cease-fire and, after days of unimaginable noise, a terrible silence descended on the little stretch of sand dunes and one-foot waves. Those Chinese soldiers who could walk helped those who could only struggle along, and Vietnamese army medics began treating the wounded. The military police showed up an hour later and took charge of the prisoners. The general turned out to be a marine, and he and Ly could both speak enough English to make themselves understood. There wasn't much to say, but Ly asked the senior man how many had come ashore.

"About 3,000," replied the general morosely, "including our commander." He indicated a man with gold shoulder boards lying dead amid several others. Obviously, he'd been a brave man who led from the front.

Ly promised the general fair treatment of his survivors—there were less than 300 alive—including many who would shortly die. They were gradually taken away to one of the hastily constructed POW camps being erected across the northern provinces, and Vietnamese field hospitals were doing the best they could for the wounded. Early the next morning, a heavy bulldozer arrived on a trailer and, after all the identifications had been made of the enemy dead, their bodies were laid in a freshly dug and carefully marked trench, and then covered over. At some time in the future, their bodies could be exhumed and sent home. How that was done depended on which side won the war.

Ly entered the large green tent laid out as a typical headquarters, and he had to make his way around many small wooden desks and the bustle of a field command at war. He found the commander's "office" in the back corner, and checked in with the pretty lieutenant who was the colonel's gate-keeper. She gave him a sympathetic look, and told him to go on in. He pushed aside the canvas drape and stood before Senior Colonel (Dai Ta) Hien Le. "Captain Ly reporting as ordered, Colonel."

"Sit down, Ly," the colonel responded quietly when he saw the state of his young commander. He'd spoken with many of his company-grade and regimental officers since the war began, but many reports indicated that this one was special. He'd known Ly since he'd arrived from the academy—a young man thrilled with his first active-duty posting to the 5th Regiment. But, even then, when Hien served as the unit's XO, he sensed something different in Ly. He had the "it-factor" that set some leaders apart from their peers. Reports were still coming in of the incredible stand Ly's company had made on the beach—an ordinary infantry company fighting against 30 times their strength. They'd killed or captured most of a heavy brigade—and sank four LCACs armed with machine guns. They'd twice nearly run out of ammunition before being resupplied and, even as regimental commander, Colonel Hien had less than 50 soldiers to send as reinforcements. Ly had been wounded several times. At one point, he had left the questionable safety of the trench system to lead a few of his soldiers across open ground to stop an enemy flanking maneuver. It was one of the greatest stands in Vietnamese military history, and Colonel Hien knew it would inspire every patriot in the land.

Up on the border, the massed Vietnamese military had fought the PLA juggernaut to a crawl—and the war was shaping up as one of the notable resistance battles since Vietnam gained its independence from China 1,100 years before. They were in "bend-don't-break" mode, but it would take a miracle to keep the enemy from breaking through. He studied young Ly for a minute, then spoke kindly to this true hero—sorry that he had no time to celebrate this small but important victory. "I and the high command have learned of your company's stand, Ly. You and your men are a tribute to our nation!"

Ly didn't know what to say; he'd fought to exhaustion then barely slept since. Most of his men had been killed and he didn't feel very heroic. "Thank you, Colonel Hien," he responded quietly. "Eighty percent of my men are dead…"

"I know, Captain. And you are going to have to live with their sacrifices and honor their memories. You'll keep their deeds alive by leading other units and fighting on. For the rest of your life, you'll use the lessons of what you and they did to win. Effective immediately, you are promoted to Thieu Ta (major). I'm assigning you to Lieutenant Colonel Tra's newly formed 8th Battalion as his executive officer. Your company is temporarily dissolved until I can find soldiers to man it again, but your healthy survivors will join you and Tra now and, when others recover sufficiently, they'll join you, too. I'm sorry there is no time for you to visit your family, but we are going to win this war, and you are going to keep helping us do it! Good luck, Major Ly."

He then got up and moved around his desk to shake this remarkable young patriot's hand. What he'd done at the beach was both textbook and above the normal call of duty. The commanding general had already recommended him for the country's highest decoration: Hero of the Armed Forces (equivalent to America's Medal of Honor). But they would keep that quiet until the general was ready to make the announcement in a couple of days. A few in the regimental headquarters knew already but, for now, young Ly had enough on his plate.

"Thank you, Colonel. We will win..." After their firm handshake, Ly saluted his regimental commander, then pushed aside the canvas and nodded respectfully at the lieutenant. But, as he made his way the exit, everyone in the room rose and quietly applauded—and Major Ly didn't know why.

Korea, one mile south of the DMZ
December 12th, 14:20 Hours

Corporal Wei and Private Lao were still alive and still freezing, but at least they were part of their country's heroic advance to liberate and unify the Korean Peninsula. And it was infinitely better than being shot by an angry colonel in the aftermath of a spy scandal. They had been closely questioned as to why they let a foreign spy posing as an MSS major into the shipyard, but apparently their interrogators believed their story (which was true). However, they had been verbally reprimanded and sent to the Korean frontier as punishment, and there they'd serve out their time of national service. They had just barely settled into the routine of being freezing border sentries looking for NK defectors when out of the blue came a war. Their sergeant had jogged up to their cement lookout position a few days ago and told them to grab their gear and follow him. He led them to a line of APCs at the bottom of their small hill, and he told them they were to board the second one in line. After that, the column had crept forward for a few hundred yards and then waited for what they didn't know. Then came a fearful artillery barrage, and the soldiers were informed that a great war of liberation was under way. After the shelling stopped, their APC crossed one of the bridges across the Yalu River, and then the whole mechanized battalion had spread out and raced south.

That was a few days ago, and now all the two young soldiers had to worry about was their track being blown apart in the mine fields—supposedly destroyed by their own massed artillery. The mine fields were a death sentence rumored to extend across both sides of the border between China and North Korea, and between North Korea and South Korea, but they weren't the only threat: The two soldiers also feared the Allied air strikes—from the forces their political officer said didn't exist. Yet they had proof: American planes had already destroyed several of their regiment's tanks and other vehicles, and Wei and Lao were scared theirs would be next. The two young men also occasionally whispered about a secondary worry: Their girlfriends back in Dalian might forget their commitments of enduring loyalty during their boyfriends' unexpected absence, and would warm up to other guys. But compared to dying on this God-forsaken frozen battlefield, that eventuality was trivial by comparison.

"Dismount and attack!" came the shouted order from their squad sergeant manning the 7.62 mm coaxial machine gun in the cupola overhead. All six enlisted men scrambled out the back of their ZBD-04A infantry fighting vehicle and down the lowered ramp onto the frozen ground. They split into two groups of three, and dashed around both sides of their protective steel box—leaving their temporary home to face whatever was next. The open space in front of them looked like ploughed farmland, but more recently it had been torn apart by the heaviest artillery barrage in PLA history. The mines had exploded on contact (many sympathetically detonated by the ripple effect that became a thousand smaller blasts) so very few remained. But the deafening noise was still constant as shells arched overhead toward targets farther south. All the two friends could do was join the hundreds of others charging forward through the breach—a two-mile wide corridor just past the old north/south border. Their immediate fear was stepping on an unexploded mine, but chattering machine guns in the distance could cut them down, too. It was also freezing cold, and the chill penetrated their winter gear. Yet they stumbled forward as best they could: Pot holes were everywhere and men tripped and fell, but they got up again and zig-zagged forward toward the dubious safety of the next bushy fence line some 50 yards to their front.

Wei and Lao made it to the line of broken trees and piles of torn-up cyclone fence that marked the South Koreans' next line of defense. They paused with the rest of the battalion and surveyed another no man's land, and hoped it also had been cleared of mines. The Imjin River was behind them now, and the great city of Seoul ahead somewhere, but the PLA would have to get through a million ROK soldiers to reach it. Both men ducked and then dove for the ground as the unmistakable sound of bullets whizzed around them, kicking up bits of snow, rock, and icy dirt. The awful sound of screams from their wounded comrades reminded them to keep their faces pressed against the snow.

"Forward, men!" they heard the junior officers and NCOs repeatedly shout, and more artillery shells began landing on the barrier a few hundred yards ahead. Hundreds of frightened men got to their feet as their own light machine guns raked the South Korean positions, and the APC's small cannons and heavy machine guns joined the battle.

Finally, after ten nerve-wracking minutes of three-second run-and-drops, the two men reached the next just-vacated enemy trench system, and rolled down into its relative safety. The South Koreans had abandoned it and retreated south, and their dead lay everywhere. But since they were no longer a threat, they were largely ignored. Wei and Lao looked at each other with wonder: They were still alive! It was all that mattered for the moment. Everyone quickly checked each enemy body for signs of life or booby traps, then paused with hundreds of others to catch their breath and let the medics do their thing. Surprisingly, Wei noticed several North Koreans had mixed into the PLA platoons—something that seemed strange to him because two days ago the two sides were desperate enemies trying their level-best to slaughter each other. Apparently, the NKs had changed sides. Everyone grabbed their canteens and took healthy sips, and waited as the tracks moved forward behind them. Then, before anyone was ready, orders were shouted to advance again.

Chapter 49

Aloft northeast of Taipei
December 12th, 15:15 Hours

U.S. Navy Lieutenant Lance "Link" Buckland clicked his comms button to get the attention of his wingman, Lieutenant JG Mike "Brick" Fogerty, and motioned "look down." They were members of Fighter Squadron VFA-14 (Tophatters) assigned to Carrier Air Wing 17 (CVW-17) flying off the USS *Nimitz*. Below them was a formation of six ChiCom PLAAF Shaanxi Y-9 turboprop transports—no doubt ferrying troops to the battle on Taiwan. Lance had the lead, and there were no top-cover escorting fighters on his threat scope but he figured, after today, the over-confident ChiComs would send fighter escorts. No matter. The Tophatters had been shooting down enemy fighters, bombers, transports—anything that flew—for longer than any of the current members' parents had been alive.

This flight of two was on station because of circumstance: The Tophatters had departed from Lemoore Naval Air Station for a regularly scheduled WestPac cruise on the *Nimitz*. When the war began, the two had been flying top cover to protect the carrier, but now they were engaged in long-range combat patrols. Their job was to locate and destroy enemy planes.

Link kicked his FA-18E Super Hornet into a sharp left bank and dove on the unsuspecting formation—2,000 feet below and three miles distant. He got a good tone in his helmet and fired two AIM-9 Sidewinder air-to-air missiles. "Fox One, Fox Two!" he announced, then he peeled off and gained altitude so Brick could get in his licks, too. His wingman fired his missiles and joined him a few seconds later, then they banked sharply to make a second pass.

Before them was an incredible sight: Four transports were falling in slow-motion, partially afire and windmilling toward the deep blue water 10,000 feet below. He felt somewhat bad for the troops inside, but they had only their aggressive government to blame. The two surviving Y-9s panicked and separated, and were diving toward the surface that they logically considered safer. It appeared to the two U.S. Navy pilots that the Y-9s were racing their stricken comrades to the ocean's surface, but there was no escaping the focused Tophatters. The two FA-18s separated and lined up until they each had good tones and punched off one more Sidewinder each. Seconds later, their third kills were spinning downward—unable to fly with one wing blown off. One by one they hit the water with a tremendous splash, but soon even the small fires on the surface blinked out. There couldn't have been any survivors.

The two fighters regained their initial altitude, and continued on their assigned patrol. This was the tenth mission for both men, and both had been admitted into the special fraternity of "Aces"–those military pilots who'd shot down at least five enemy planes.

Incheon, South Korea, 16:00 Hours

"Raider" LTC David Chen had suggested the nuance that the team needed to get both helos refueled prior to the return trip from Beijing: Since they would settle into two LZs that were close to each other, the first helo could simply lift off after the mission and proceed at a reduced speed for the flight home. The second would then hop over to the vacated pad and, since the aircraft and uniforms were identical, and the ground crew could be alerted to the momentary arrival of a second aircraft, it would seem natural. The Chinese had adopted a strategy of "hiding in plain sight" and, in the big picture, turn-about was fair play.

Tim made a final check of his equipment as he listened to the simple elegance of his XO's suggestion, then kidded Chen that, so far, Delta had earned one more point than the SEALs. Soon the rest of the team surfaced from their REM sleep and got their own acts together. They'd board the helos in 30 minutes for the three-and-a-half-hour flight north.

The "Olympic Site" Conference Room
Beijing, 15:35 Hours

President Han of the People's Republic entered the spacious room later than his scheduled arrival time of three in the afternoon. Han's luncheon with senior CCP leaders had gone reasonably well but long, and he hadn't liked some of their insinuations that the PLA was behind schedule enough to endanger the greater operation. But now he had a different audience, and had to adjust accordingly.

“Good afternoon, Comrades,” he began pleasantly, “I will give a short general update on our progress across all theaters of operation, then I’ll welcome your questions and comments.” The hundred faces were intently focused which, though expected, was always a bit unnerving. Han proceeded to speak for several minutes, delivering a summary of what he’d learned that morning, plus the couple of updates he’d received since. Then he leaned back in his chair, took a measured sip of tea, and asked, “What are your questions?”

A sea of hands went up so he selected a safe deputy secretary from the Ministry of Heavy Industry, whose military son he’d recently approved for transfer out of the forward battle area.

“General Secretary Han, is the PLA having any supply chain problems? If so, what can we do to help?”

Han always loved softball questions to set the tone for the group. “Thank you, Comrade, and the answer is yes, to a certain extent. In order to subdue such a vast land mass, we’ve had to expend absolute mountains of ammunition and burn millions of gallons of fuel. But, thanks to long-range preparation by our logisticians, the forces are well-supplied and equipped. But the key to future success is to transition to local sources for every consumable—except maybe certain types of ammunition that we alone would have in our inventories. We hope to complete this part of our multi-faceted operation as soon as possible. As you know, besides unification with Taiwan, the purpose of Operation Unity is to identify and move resources from the conquered countries to the motherland, but our field army will consume what they need from these stores first.” It was a good honest answer to strengthen trust. A more junior member asked for recognition. Han knew his boss to be reliable so he risked acknowledging his assistant deputy.

“Thank you, Comrade General Secretary. I have a son on *Dragon’s Wing* who landed in Vietnam. I haven’t heard any news about the mission or his welfare, and his mother and I would appreciate an update. Our son is a proud PLAN marine!”

Uh, oh. This was a problematic question because this father hadn't been notified yet—or the media briefed—that the ship had been sunk outside the harbor. Better let a military guy answer this one. "Well, we are all grateful to hear of your son's valiant service, Comrade. Let me ask Rear Admiral Song to give you the particulars."

Han's military aide stood and moved to one of the side microphones. He looked serious and addressed the expectant father directly. "Comrade Assistant Deputy Minister, if you'll give me your son's name, I will have an aide reach out to his unit to discover his status. However, I can tell you that *Dragon's Wing* was torpedoed a short distance from a beach and most of the marines and crew had to come ashore in landing craft or rafts. The good news is that the mothership was so close to shore that many actually swam to the nearby beach. We last heard they were fighting with great heroism against a superior force of thousands of Vietnamese soldiers but were, nevertheless, advancing with great courage. That is all I know at this time." He felt for this father—he had two sons captaining ships in the cross-Taiwan Straits operation, and he worried about them constantly. He hated lying to this patriotic father, too, but there were greater issues here than comforting one parent. He knew about the slaughter at the beachhead, and that their boy was probably dead, but he'd find out and let the parents know privately. The PLA military police were working with the PAP to identify the families of deceased servicemen and move them to secluded hotels and military barracks where they could grieve out of public sight. They'd be sent home after the war if they promised to follow the party line.

"Thank you, Admiral," the ADM responded, clearly shaken by what he'd just heard. He hoped his son was okay. It would be hard to share this news with his mother tonight; she'd been pestering him for information since the war began. "I would greatly appreciate any update that you can give. Our family will be most grateful."

Han realized that, in that one brief exchange, the whole mood of the room had dropped precipitously. Now he had to take back the lead and buck up their morale. Keeping everyone in any large group on track was the constant burden of leadership. "In any war we are faced with these personal heartbreaks—and every son and daughter of China is precious to all of us. I can only say that I hope with all my being that your son is unhurt, and will be returned to your family as a hero. Now what are some other questions?" A hand went up.

"Comrade General Secretary, my daughter is a PLAAF lieutenant on *Dragon's Fire*. We heard that the ship has been sunk in the port of San Diego, in California. Our family has not heard anything about her, either. Is there some way the Ministry of Defense can get us lists of those injured or missing so our families don't worry? My wife is nearly beside herself."

This is not going the way I want: People have to focus on winning the war, and not on worrying about loved ones! We need to be on the same page in our efforts to become the world's only superpower. Enough of these whiny questions. "Yes, Comrade, that is a good idea. I'll mention it to Marshal Tai when I see him at a meeting tonight. Well, speaking of meetings, I must move to the next one. I hope my update has encouraged all of you that the war progresses steadily, and that we are generally on schedule." He rose to signal the meeting was over, and caught many by surprise. They all jumped to their feet as he trooped out with his usual gaggle of aides and bodyguards, and headed toward the elevators and the parking garage upstairs. He couldn't wait to get home—he needed a solid nap before facing Tai's briefing later on.

Incheon, Korea 17:30 Hours

Tim buckled in, wondering if he'd forgotten anything. The Japanese special operations staff had provided his team with PLA cold weather gear—and the raiders had brought small arms of their choosing. They also had two light mortars with ten rounds each, plus water and ammo, and the assortment of small items every soldier takes to the field. Each had a couple of energy bars, but they were not planning on fighting for more than a few minutes—precision timing was everything in this op, and they' be vulnerable throughout. The four Japanese Air Self-Defense Force pilots had the helo's transponders tuned to the local Korean frequency, but would switch over when they heard the first ADA chirps as they approached Chinese airspace. The team had stowed their personal gear next to their seats—and given the brevity of preparation, Tim figured they were about as ready as could be expected. They were all seasoned special operators, and several had made suggestions that improved both the efficiency of the mission and its survivability.

It got dark early in northern latitudes, so Tim decided to leave early. The weather folks had been tracking a storm bearing down on the Chinese capital from the Mongolian steppes—a complication that would be a mixed bag at best. The snow would mask their movements, but any accompanying winds could knock the helos around and it would impair visibility throughout. Then, once they landed, everyone would have trouble with orientation. *Oh, well, we'll just deal with eventualities as they come.*

Tim had just received the passwords they would need on the ground—a necessity because they changed daily. This information was a gift from the National Security Agency that had been focusing on the PLA's frequencies since the war began. The agency had acres of underground computers, and it was rumored that there were more Crays in the NSA's multi-story subterranean lair at Fort Meade than in the rest of the world combined.

The helos were pulled out onto the edge of the curtain to warm up, and five minutes later the Korean Air Force operators in the tower gave them clearance: "Korean Air, flight of two, you are cleared for take-off on Runway R25. Winds are north/northwest at eight." The two heavy PLA helos rolled past some parked airplanes until they reached the lift-off area, then gently lifted into the darkening sky. There were no lights anywhere: All of South Korea was under a strict war-time blackout.

The two aircraft initially headed out over the shallow bay that General Douglas MacArthur's invasion force had used to surprise the NK army in September of 1950. The helos banked south, then east in an arching turn so it would look on radar as if they were heading for southern Korea or Japan. Then, after five minutes in a normal traffic corridor—which everyone hoped would lull any curious ChiCom operators into ignoring them—they slowly sank until they were well off everyone's scopes. Then the dangerous flying began: The pilots turned the aircraft around, lined up in a simple trail formation about 1,000 yards apart, and began their journey north at just ten feet above the calm winter sea. They headed up the middle of the Yellow Sea using night-vision goggles, and would maintain the same low-level path until they were far enough up the Korean Peninsula to be well behind the PLA's line of advance. Then they would turn northeast and cross the North Korean coastline with their proper frequency squawking to let everyone know who they were.

They'd check in with the local flight controllers; at that point, they'd become a normal war-time pair of PLA Special Forces helos returning from a mission at the front. They would fly in the open at the altitude directed by the ground controllers, and would follow the assigned vector azimuth to their announced destination. At some point they'd drop out of sight again, but timing would be tight. However, with all the air traffic whizzing to and from every spot on the compass, their disappearance off some overworked controller's scope shouldn't be overly noted. At least that was the theory.

White House Situation Room
Washington, DC, 05:00 Hours

Spence hadn't slept much again; the anticipation of an impactful retaliation raid this early in the war was as dramatic for him as he believed the Doolittle Raid had been for President Franklin Roosevelt. He had kept the circle of those with the need to know small, but since others might offer key operational advice, he'd invited the full war cabinet to watch the raid once it was underway. He parked himself in his usual seat and was joined by his Vice President, the Secretaries of State, Defense, and Homeland Security, and the Director of National Intelligence—who brought in the Director of the Central Intelligence Agency and his operations director. Admiral Simms and the Joint Chiefs were there, as was John Laughton. Add in Korean, Japanese, and Chinese Mandarin translators from the NSA, and the room was nicely full. It was also locked down so no critical operational intelligence would leak out.

This was a joint CIA/DoD operation, but the NSA was monitoring the entire spectrum of communications, and everyone could follow along by watching the designated satellite feed. The two helos were using a known PLA frequency, and the translator was there to keep it real. The WHSR technicians working in an alcove were joined by an additional tech from the United States Special Operations Command (USSOCOM) and one from the NSA.

Spence gratefully took his first sip of doctored coffee and studied the display on the main screen. Clearly visible in the darkness were two helicopter icons flying in trail formation, and the data indicated they were close enough to the ocean surface to make him nervous. It was easy for the infrared-equipped satellite to pick out the warmer aircraft above the colder Yellow Sea, and he could tell everyone was concentrating because the room was quiet except for occasional whispers from the technicians near the door. A smaller screen showed the Korean Peninsula in a broader feed, and it was dark on both sides of the 38th Parallel. Superimposed outlines of the countries were necessary points of reference; the macro-view included tiny graphics to indicate opposing forces' locations.

After some nervous time-killing conversations as the satellite tracked the slow-moving helos, Spence noticed they were closing in on the critical point south of Dalian City where they'd rise and check in with the local air traffic authorities. Everything hinged on the teams being accepted and inserted into the busy airspace on their way to the capital. "General Simms, would you please let us know what we're seeing?"

"Certainly, Mr. President. The larger screen allows us to see the relationship between the two Koreas and China to the north, and Russia to the northeast. Japan is at the bottom of the screen. The two helicopters took off from Japan yesterday and landed at an airport on the edge of Incheon on the western South Korean coastline." He indicated these various geographic points with a handheld laser. "They spent today refining their operational details and getting to know each other, and then slept for few hours—which we consider vital before an operation like this." The admiral noticed the Secretary of State's hand go up. "Yes, Mr. Secretary?"

"How do they sleep with such tension?"

"The medical personnel issue special sleeping pills that put them into REM dreamland for about six hours. They are left alone, because startling them is disorienting."

"Oh, my…" *What won't these military types think of next?* Jack had never much cared for the warrior class, but he appreciated the fact that his department's negotiations went a lot smoother with the implied power lying quietly behind every negotiation.

For his part, Admiral Simms was happy to answer such questions: *If you didn't know something, ask.* He'd learned a lot in his career by asking questions—especially when others were afraid to look stupid. Knowledge at every level could save lives and he'd preached it for 40 years. As far as this operation went, he had to hand it to that agency guy who suggested it: It was bold, brilliant, out of the box—and just might work. If not, they lost 25 great Allied special operators—irreplaceable in one sense—but they were the risk-takers and he had to invest their lives dearly to achieve great things. Once again, he was grateful that President Stilwell had the courage and clarity of vision to trust talented people who could deliver amazing results.

He continued. "The two helos were contributed by the Japanese Air Force, and how they obtained these two ChiCom aircraft is a bit foggy." Several around the room smiled at that—their ally wasn't saying. "Nevertheless, they are perfect for this requirement: They are big, are a normal part of the ChiCom inventory, and each can carry 20 personnel in a pinch. Their course will take them across the Bohai Sea, and then they'll proceed about 100 miles inland to northern Beijing where they'll separate just about here," he indicated a place on the map just outside the capital's ring road. "They'll perform two complementary operations, and return by the same route. During their egress they'll be known to the air traffic folks, and we've factored that into the operation. I'm sure you have questions, and I'll answer them as best I can." There were many questions.

Aboard the lead helicopter, ten miles south of Dalian City

Tim glanced at his watch as the pilots gradually brought the helo up. They were about half way to their objective, and would soon be noticed by air traffic control. They'd also wake up the air defense batteries that could ruin their whole day. Just then, he heard the command pilot check in with the local military grid; the pilot's Mandarin was flawless.

"Dalian Air Force Traffic, this is Army 212, flight of two, returning from the front. We have wounded aboard. Request immediate vector to Beijing Military Hospital, North." The command pilot heard some sputtering as the startled operator suddenly discovered them on his screen.

"Army 212, Air Control Area Seven didn't alert us that you were coming. You must land at Dalian PLAAF airfield to confirm your identity!"

"I have 12 wounded Siberian Tigers aboard. If we land now, some will die. Our colonel will then come visit you…" The pilot guessed that special operators were the same everywhere. He heard some static, then the controller came back on.

"Army 212, you are cleared to Beijing air traffic control, North. Maintain 2,000 at two nine zero. Good luck!"

"Two thousand at two nine zero, control. 212 out." And that was it. If the ChiComs scrambled attack helos, they'd be shot down in minutes. The command pilot exchanged looks with his co-pilot and then back at the American dressed as a PAP colonel sitting in the jump seat. Life favors the bold—and they'd just caught a break.

White House Situation Room

Admiral Simms had been sweating it out for ten minutes, trying to look cool and encouraging. But he alone in the room knew that this was the first and most difficult part of the whole operation: If the pilots hadn't been able to essentially bluff their way past the first air controller, the mission was over. But they'd been accepted into the traffic pattern, and would be okay until they had to deal with a large approaching storm: They had another hour to kill before the weather closed in and things got exciting. He felt like a cop on a stake-out.

Aboard "Tiger One" above Northeastern Beijing, 20:35 Hours

Sitting in the jump seat between, but a bit behind the pilots, Tim had a clear view of the circular sweep of the radar scope situated on the central display panel and, unfortunately, it graphically showed the heavy winter storm they'd hoped to beat. It was less than ten miles away and rapidly bearing down on the city from the northwest, and it would definitely complicate their operation. The heavy radar return contained a mixture of pink and white streaks—which meant snow and freezing rain—and both made flying difficult and dangerous. Their destination was already enveloped by the leading edge of the storm, so the pilots would have to find their LZs and land in deteriorating conditions. Tim had been impressed by these guys so far—they were obviously crack pilots that reminded him of the 160th Aviation (Special Operations) pilots he'd flown with out of Fort Campbell.

Their approach over the Bohai Sea had been routine, despite the large number of aircraft in the area; another screen displayed the location and altitude of all aircraft within 20 miles, and the command pilot regularly spoke with one ATC after another. Just then the co-pilot turned around with his mic covered and informed him in passable Mandarin, "We're ducking under the radar now." Tim gave him a thumb's up, then he turned back to his team in the cabin; each man looked more comfortable in his seat than Tim expected. He twirled his finger—the universal sign to gear up.

The two helos didn't dive straight down—that would have attracted attention—but rather they gradually settled as if descending toward their requested landing at the hospital. As soon as they were well under the sweep of local radar, they changed course and headed directly west. They were skirting the ring road around northern Beijing and would land in about 15 hair-raising minutes. The first snowflakes hit the canopy and Tim felt the pilots begin to fight the buffeting of the oncoming storm. Along they flew over the vast spread of city buildings below—over the occasional twinkling lights still visible even in the general blackout. Soon these too disappeared and everyone's lives depended on the pilot's technical abilities. The Raiders were flying on instruments only and, as they moved away from the city skyscrapers and into the outlying areas, Tim believed it was God's providence that kept them from fire-balling into the low buildings and trees that dotted the rolling landscape. Soon the terrain below them would transition from flat to hilly, but the pilots were ready for that, too. Tim felt an uneasy sensation in his stomach and tightened his gut as they bounced along. *Okay, here we go.*

Chapter 50

Estate of General Secretary Han

Two members of the estate's regular contingent of security guards were patrolling about 100 yards inside the tree line north of the helicopter landing pad. Four others were in the guard shack trying to keep warm. Ten others were keeping watch on the southern perimeter, and the visiting dignitaries' chauffeurs and security cadres were hovering in the large parking area west of the main house. The last four sentries were fighting the cold at the main entrance gate, located a few hundred yards down the narrow canyon and east of the large residence. The sprawling complex was located on a fairly flat area that had been further flattened by engineers, and it was protected from the elements by hills that rose on three sides—a "box canyon," in ranchers' terms. Han's guests had been checked through earlier so the security personnel were quite relaxed.

Heavy snow was swirling everywhere, and the occasional blast of freezing rain was generally making life miserable for everyone outside. It was dark and cold and, with just a few top-hooded lights to aid the sentries' rounds, most had switched to night-vision goggles. The whole landscape looked barren and ghostly, and the outside detail envied everyone inside the luxurious multi-building estate who were warm and toasty. These freezing ones often thought about their president's guests and the sumptuous food and drink they enjoyed, but they didn't feel sorry for themselves: A dangerous war was raging across a hundred million square miles of land and sea, and all they had to do was keep a sharp lookout for (probably) non-existent dangers. President Han was far away from any foreign threats, and overseas the PLA was slaughtering every enemy's forces. They heard the daily broadcasts and were happy for their countrymen's successes—and glad they were safe and sound in Mother China! The sentries knew the People's Armed Police kept close tabs on any domestic threats, so the sentries weren't worried about that, either. The president's current meeting was due to wrap up in an hour or so and then the estate's regular security contingent would get to divide the leftover food and drink. That would be a nice end to a bitterly cold night shift.

Suddenly the handheld radio crackled inside the guard shack and, startled, the senior sergeant in charge grabbed it and listened.

"This is People's Police Helicopter Unit Number One. Landing pad security officer, acknowledge immediately!"

The booming command scared the living daylights out of the four guards—kicking back and chatting about the war without a care in the world. And, though they were a type of elite troops themselves, everyone was afraid of the PAP cadres who could arrest anyone at any time for any reason. "Sir, NCOIC Guo at your service!"

"Prepare the landing pad now! Roll back that netting and turn on the lights—and get your people ready to assist us as directed. Notify all your perimeter guards at once!" Major Suzuki, flying Raider One, had used his most intimidating voice—dangerous enough to scare anyone in a top-down society.

"Immediately, Comrade Pilot!" Sergeant First Class Guo then barked orders more forcefully than needed because even he was afraid of these intimidating policemen. One of his men flicked four toggle switches and the landing pad was suddenly bathed in light. The forest was lit up for 50 meters in every direction—reflecting off the snow on the ground and off the boughs of the evergreens. The whole scene was transformed into a fairy land, and the perimeter guards had to rip off their NVGs before they were blinded by its intensity. SFC Guo then pulled down a fist-sized lever, and the camo netting quickly rolled back from the helo pad. The four pulled on their soft caps, and hustled outside into the swirling snow. They saw firsthand that the wind was shaking the trees, and the storm made the opening in the middle of the forest look like a real-life snow globe.

Major Suzuki confirmed his final approach to his colleagues in the second helo; Raider Two had peeled off and was now three-quarters of mile to the south, curving around the far side of the tree-lined hill that separated the estate's front driveway from their intended LZ. They would land in a clearing beyond the southern boundary of the estate, and their job was to provide both a diversion and a threat that would support the activities of Raider One.

They'd also eliminate the southern boundary guards, plus any security cadres or others in the front driveway; noisily removing them in a firefight would greatly motivate Han and his guests to cooperate.

Suzuki needed all of his 15 years of flying experience to make his approach up the forested canyon: He was flying just above the trees in a buffeting storm—and dealing with snow and darkness in a place he'd never been. But he was highly skilled and ready for the supreme challenge of his life.

Just then his co-pilot, Captain Ogawa, exclaimed, "Major, there it is!"

Sure enough, through rapidly flashing wiper blades, the brightly illuminated landing pad and amphitheater-like circular opening in the forest gradually became visible. The pad had been scraped into a perfect oval—more than wide enough for any type of helicopter and, within seconds, both pilots spotted armed men waiting next to a cylindrical fuel bowser. Everything looked exactly like the satellite photos they'd studied earlier, and precise GPS coordinates had enabled them to arrive within feet of their destination.

Major Suzuki brought the powerful helo in smoothly in spite of the blustery conditions, and swung the aircraft around before landing so they were facing down-canyon for take-off. Raider One settled smoothly, and Suzuki's adrenaline began to bleed off. *I've done my job—now it's up to the snake-eaters.*

Sergeant Guo and his men had dashed to the landing pad, and were nervously wondering what was going on. PAP helicopters didn't just drop out of the sky, but they weren't unheard of, either. The president received Minister Ti regularly, and sometimes she came in her personal helo. But he'd never known any police to arrive unannounced at night—especially when the minister was already inside. Maybe it had something to do with the war? Nevertheless, he would be as helpful as he could and, hopefully, if anything was amiss, he wouldn't catch hell from the self-important military and police types who inspected his unit almost weekly. He watched the helo flare and land, and immediately the door flew open. Out jumped a string of tough-looking commando-types wearing camouflage uniforms and scary-looking streaked paint on their faces. The first man approached with a powerful gait, and Guo could see by the uniforms that this first man was a full colonel in the PAP while the rest were PLA Special Forces. They all looked mean and had a variety of automatic rifles at the ready.

* * *

Inside his warm and secure bunker, GS Han was enjoying the evening's summary delivered by Marshal Tai—a much better presentation than those he'd given before. Han was pleased that the PLA division rampaging through Laos had finally penetrated far enough south to swing east and threaten Vietnam's left flank. Perhaps that would finally break the deadlock that was the only failure of the war. Additional progress on the other fronts seemed to justify the original plan devised by Bao and Dang, both of whom were in attendance to help Tai. Han sensed his PLA commander had gotten the message regarding the inadequacy of previous updates, and tonight's upbeat briefing was filled with useful facts and seemed transparent. Han commented, "So, gentlemen, your summaries seem to validate the earlier premise that the six Dragons in America, Japan, and Australia, did, in fact, buy us the extra time needed on the mainland?"

"Yes, Comrade Han," responded Marshal Tai, answering for his team. "Our progress is fully enveloping our Asian targets, and the Allies cannot mount enough effective counter-strikes to stop us. Their efforts are limited to harassment from their formidable air power and surviving submarines, but that was expected. For them to negate our conquests, they would have to mount a long-distance invasion of the Asian mainland—now impossible since their navies have been severely degraded. They can launch a few missiles, but our factories are working around the clock to replace our own missile inventories. We can rain death on the western Pacific for thousands of miles and, in a few days, we will commence our second wave of strikes against Japan. That will deny the Americans the secondary airports they are using now. It is a no-win outcome for the Allies. We have already achieved 90 percent of our goals, and we'll consolidate our gains in every country within the next two weeks. We are pouring troops into every area that needs reinforcement, and the PLA is steadily overwhelming enemy opposition."

"Well, that is gratifying, Comrade Marshal…just don't let up now!"

"Comrade Han, the PLA is relentless—solely focused on complete enemy capitulation!"

"That's good news indeed. Now, I'd like to hear your strategy for extracting our Dragon forces from the six foreign ports. I heard many heartfelt stories earlier today from Party leaders who have children on those missions, and I need to give them hope. These patriotic families knew their children were exempt, yet the youth bravely insisted on serving. We owe them a lot. Perhaps our distinguished Foreign Minister can address this issue, too?" It was a topic dear to everyone in the room, so they began a lively discussion around timing of a negotiated withdrawal. They had the Allies over a barrel and could dictate terms that complemented their operations in Asia.

* * *

Tim was doing his best to deliver a one-man shock-and-awe campaign to the surprised and worried sergeant. He strode past the NCO nearly bellowing: "I am People's Police Colonel Song…the president's life is in jeopardy—where are your officers?" Before the man could reply, Tim suddenly stopped in his tracks, an intentional psychological trick he'd been taught at the Farm: It raised the discomfiture of trailing subordinates when they bumped into the senior. As expected, the nervous sergeant collided with him and was mortified and began to stutter. Tim ignored him and commanded, "Sergeant, lead the way to the escape tunnel now!"

"Yes, Comrade Colonel! Follow me!" The man dashed ahead—barking orders at his confused cadres. They quickly covered the 50 yards to the small building Betty had spotted on the satellite photo—now partially lit by the glare of the landing pad's lighting.

Tim and his ten team members followed at a jog, gratified that the operation was unfolding as planned. Twenty feet inside a scraggly tree line, the imposing wings of a ten-foot-high cement building loomed. The structure looked to Tim like the old ammo storage bunkers he had seen at Camp Lejeune some years earlier, and he was sure it could survive a direct hit from a fairly large bomb. It was also cleverly concealed in the contour of a fold in the terrain, and he admired, not for the first time, that his mentor in Langley was a gifted professional. The helo pad was behind him, and through the snowfall he could see the main buildings of the estate—constructed in a cluster down a gentle forested incline about a quarter mile to the south. A few dim lights shone here and there, but would be nearly impossible to spot from above. Behind him, Tim heard his XO give the execute order to Raider Two, but he doubted the sergeant would notice or care. In the distance, Tim heard the change in the rotor's pitch as the helo dropped behind the low hill that separated the front drive from the second LZ.

The sergeant halted the group in front of big metal doors, and their erstwhile guide reached for a phone built into the cement wall. "What are you doing, Sergeant?" Tim challenged.

"Colonel, I need permission from the major inside to open this end!"

"Open the door under my authority!" Tim demanded, feigning anger and raising his machine gun with a touch of menace.

"Immediately, Colonel! Sorry for the delay. It's our SOP!"

"No time for SOPs tonight, Sergeant…get that door open immediately!" Just then they all heard the first mortar round shatter the night as it exploded on the far edge of the estate's front driveway/parking area. Then a second round followed a second later—landing in the middle of the driveway itself. Team Two was walking the rounds toward the main building where the leaders were meeting, and shrapnel was blasting holes in some of the limos and cutting down the guards and drivers like grain stalks. The next two rounds hit the porch of the main house itself. "Move, soldier! The traitors are already here!"

The sergeant worked the combo lock frantically, wondering what traitors the colonel was talking about. He was truly frightened now, and barked another order that caused several of his men to spring to action. They grabbed the heavy metal doors and pulled them open as far as they would go. The tunnel was brightly lit and sloped down at a comfortable angle.

"Stay here and guard this entrance with your lives, Sergeant; you are protecting the motherland and our president!" Tim saw the guards fan out in a protective half-circle outside the tunnel door. Then he and his men jogged down the tunnel toward the next steel door 400 yards away. The passage was wide enough for a Hummer or similar vehicle to navigate and, as they neared the terminal end, a line of sturdy-looking electric carts waited in a neat line.

Inside his bunker, Han had just started listening to Foreign Minister Wu's idea for diplomatically disengaging from the six international harbors when, suddenly, he felt an unusual rumble, followed immediately by another, and then by many in succession directly above. Momentarily some smoky dust wafted down through the elevator doors and into his pristine sanctuary, and everyone jerked their heads around to see what was going on. Just then there was a commotion at the end of the main hall that led to the communications room and the never-used exit ramp. Those heavy metal doors flew open with a loud bang—the first time any of them had heard them do so. Han and his colleagues jumped in their seats. Dumbfounded, the president just stared open-mouthed as several heavily armed military commandos rushed into the room. The major who was head of his nightly security detail reached for his sidearm, but the leader of the group lashed out with a lateral hand strike to the man's neck and he dropped like a stone.

Then the leader announced in a loud and breathless voice, "President Han, Marshal Tai, I am Colonel Song of the People's Armed Police!" Tim turned to face Minister Ti, who would have been his organizational leader. "Please, Minister Ti, verify to our President that you know me personally, and my long record of service to the motherland!"

As Tim expected, Ti was shocked to the core, and was additionally alarmed that she didn't recognize this intruder in PAP dress, covered with face paint. But at least she could confirm that his uniform was correct, and that his manner was deferential and precise as she demanded in her tightly run bureaucracy. She also didn't want to look ignorant in a crisis in the presence of the General Secretary and the others. "Yes, Colonel Song, of course I recognize you. What is happening?"

Tim turned back toward Han, who looked as bewildered as the rest. "Honored leaders, the PAP has discovered a vile coup against the Party—and an assassination attempt against you, President Han, and you, Marshal Tai! I have brought a loyal detachment of Siberian Tigers with me who are known to Marshal Tai. More are on the way. Lieutenant Colonel Cheng, show President Han and Marshal Tai the photo of the traitor leading this evil plot! Honored leaders, you can already hear the intense fighting that has broken out in the front driveway, and it is typical of other fighting throughout the country. The traitor's agents are trying to displace your leadership and take command of Mother China!"

Dramatically, Tim stepped aside to allow his XO to move forward—theatrically extracting the damming evidence from his tunic as he approached the General Secretary of the CCP. He held it down between the two most senior men in the

PRC who were sitting next to one another, and they both gasped and looked directly at General Wing sitting a few chairs away.

"This man is the traitor, Comrade General Secretary! Is he here among you tonight—sitting as a serpent among the protectors of our sacred Party?" Tim was really laying it on thick, but his faux indignation was doing the trick. All he needed was for Han to point an accusing finger at Wing, whom he had spotted the second he entered the room, and everything would follow accordingly. He got more than he needed when Han and Tai both pointed fingers at the shocked MSS minister—rising to his feet and emphatically shaking his head in denial.

"Arrest him!" Han demanded. "He's the traitor!"

Tai then shouted in outrage, "How could you do this, Wing?"

Han then bellowed at Ti, who had that deer-in-the-headlights look: "Ti, I know you and Wing have an immoral relationship—surely you must be part of this vile coup, too!"

"No, Comrade Han, I swear complete loyalty to you and the Party!" She was practically in tears as conflicting emotions tore through her soul. But she was not going down with anyone, and clawed back to the high ground. "General Wing, I denounce you!" she shouted at him, and turned to her subordinate, "Colonel Song, I demand that you remove Minister Wing this instant!"

Wing's shock turned to anger in a half-second. He turned beet-red and screamed at no one in particular: "I'm not a traitor! Someone is setting me up! This is outrageous!" He tossed his chair to one side and lunged menacingly toward the nearest soldier, who he expected to cower in fear. But, instead of retreat, the soldier rudely flipped him onto his back, and then two others pounced on him as he struggled on the floor. Then Wing felt a sharp pain in his neck.

Tim saw his medic jab the needle into the general's neck and the powerful sedative took effect within seconds. Then he turned to back to the PLA commander, "Marshal Tai, we have sedated the traitor. Now, Sir, this complex is under heavy attack from the south. Mortar rounds are falling on the building above and the elevator is blocked. The entryway and front parking lot are under heavy small arms and machine gun fire, and the enemy force is advancing on this building. What are your orders, Sir? We have a helicopter standing by on the back helipad."

Tai thought fast. Their only chance of escape was the tunnel and helicopter. Thank the gods for the Siberian Tigers—they were the best special forces unit in the world. "Yes, Colonel, that is the best option. How many can you take?" *Me, Han, and young Kai, of course. The rest could wait.*

"Marshal Tai, it is a big aircraft; we can take all here plus your Siberian Tigers protective detail!" The most powerful military commander in China would have choked on his afternoon tea if he'd known who would be escorting him now—the real best special operators in the world.

Tai went into command mode: "Follow me, Comrade President, and everyone of ministerial rank! Everyone else stay here and protect the President's escape!" Then he dashed for the door and heard the rattle of banging chairs behind him as a herd of frightened people rushed to keep up. Tim's team just followed along carrying the limp Wing with them.

As the group entered the tunnel, Marshal Tai ordered everyone into the fully-charged electric four-seaters. Each had canvas canopies, and they looked like a row of golf carts on steroids. He asked Han to sit in the first one with himself as the driver, and waited politely as Minister Ti and Comrade Liu climbed into the back seats. Then he stomped on the pedal and it lurched and then silently shot up the ramp. The PAP colonel jumped onto the back bumper at the last second and clung to the canopy's frame. The remaining carts followed as quickly as they filled, and the inert General Wing was placed into the rear seat of the last one by two commandos. Team One also jumped onto the bumpers, and the last cart was half way up the tunnel before the lead one burst out into the bitter winter storm.

The shock of the freezing air hit them like a hammer, but everyone wore sweaters, and hoped the helo would be warm inside. The security sergeant ordered his men to jog next to the president's cart, and Tim spotted the refueling team moving back from the port on the side of the aircraft. One more box checked. The sergeant and his ground crew had done their jobs well. His men quickly hustled everyone aboard and they offered no resistance—no doubt aided by the cacophony of exploding mortar rounds and machine gunfire coming from the front of Han's estate. Fear had a way of motivating nearly everyone—especially people of continual privilege who'd never felt insecurity before.

They all took their seats according to rank and perceived importance, so the aircraft filled from front to back. It was very efficient. The young officer Tim guessed was Tai's aide was the last to board before the Team One members, and he took the last side-facing jump seat toward the back where he was out of the way. Tim had noticed him right off and thought he looked athletic, and therefore potentially dangerous. He contrasted with the rest of the passengers—all middle-age people used to power and having endless servants. Tim sized the young captain up as a warrior, and Tai wouldn't have him around if he weren't pretty tough and competent. He would bear watching, but at least he wore no sidearm. Tim commanded Sergeant Guo to prepare to refuel a second helo full of Tigers, then climbed aboard and gave Major Suzuki the thumbs-up. The engine revved and the command pilot pulled pitch; gracefully, the heavily laden helo rose into the stormy night.

However, on the far side of the front parking lot, Team Two had dispatched the last defender, and was preparing to leave. They had to get back over the hill to Raider Two, hop over to the helo pad to refuel, then catch up to Raider One. But just as they heard the lead helo power up and take off, a sniper they hadn't seen fired a round and hit Captain Charlie Woo in the right shoulder. The shock caused him to accidentally loose a short burst from his MP-5, and the bullets crossed the open space above the main house, and struck the rising helo's rotor blades. Raider One was just climbing past 30 feet when it was hit, and the bullet caused one blade to shatter. Suzuki had just nosed the big helo over for the flight back down the canyon, but as its composite blade splintered and ruined the aircraft's aerodynamics, it dropped like a rock. The men of Team Two could only watch in horror as the well-lit helo crashed into the heavy trees of the down-sloping forest.

Major Suzuki had no warning: One second, they were rising smoothly, and the next he felt a jolt followed by a mushy stick. The blades disintegrated overhead, causing catastrophic loss of lift, and they crashed into the trees. He jammed his foot on the pedal to keep from spinning, but his bird was dead. Propelled by their forward momentum, they just cascaded through the heavy branches at about 20 miles an hour, but were cushioned sufficiently to land smoothly and only slightly on the helo's left side. They hadn't fallen far enough to kill anyone, but screaming pandemonium broke out in the back.

Tim felt the jolt, too, but had little time to brace as that sickening feeling of a sudden drop passed through everyone on board. Three-point seatbelts saved everyone from serious injury, but now he was in an unexpected crisis and had to think fast—and remember to keep speaking Mandarin Chinese! "Siberian Tigers, help our distinguished leaders get out of this helicopter. It is full of fuel and might blow up." He said this slow enough so that everyone would understand the seriousness of their situation and not argue. He and Dave Chen muscled the right-hand door open and they clambered out first. Tim took stock of their predicament: He could see that the helo had smashed a corridor through several trees, but the way back up to the pad was manageable. The area was still bathed in light, and the sergeant and his men up by the pad had reacted well and were charging down to help. Just then Raider Two roared over and landed on the pad to refuel, and he saw his guys jump out and chase the guards down the uneven bank. Next steps were obvious: Get the VIPs on board the second helo, and then figure out everything else.

"Great news, Marshal Tai: Another Siberian Tiger unit has just arrived—they'll save President Han from the rebel assassins!"

Inside the helicopter, Han was unhurt but shaken. His immediate thought was that they were all going to die, but the trees had obviously softened the crash. He looked at Tai sitting next to him, and the man was a bit dazed but otherwise unhurt. Snow was wafting inside, but the freezing air helped everyone focus. He heard his rescue team leader's firm and encouraging voice and tried to take off his seatbelt. One of the commandos appeared at his side and hit the release, then helped him up and out the door of the tilting aircraft. Many willing hands assisted him and Tai to the forest floor, while others steadied him as he climbed up the slope. Another helicopter was there—a real comfort after his narrow escape. Something else for the memoir, he laughed to himself as he clambered over the broken limbs and shallow snow.

Within three minutes Tim and the team members had gotten everyone out of the crashed helo, and their line was moving steadily up the incline. Commandos and others helped the civilians into the second helo, while two of the refueling cadres pumped in precious fuel. Tim called out to his Raiders and they gathered together out of earshot.

Dave Chen had the only solution: “Only half of us can go with Han. The two Japanese pilots can’t stay behind because they will be noticed and compromise the team. We have to get out fast because the government will figure out what happened, and will be frantically looking for Han and company, with revenge the order of the day. Tim, you need to be the liaison at the other end. Therefore, it has to be some combination of us pure Chinese guys.” He was just matter of fact—they had little time to make life-and-death decisions. “Twelve must stay with me—who volunteers?” Immediately, everyone raised their hands, and he quickly sorted out those he perceived had closest-to-native language skills.

“Tim, we’ll head for the harbor and try to hijack a boat. It’s too far to hike out and airports have greater security. Good luck!”

The two men shook hands and Dave watched Tim and the others race up toward the pad. He then led his 12 commandos on what he hoped looked like an aggressive jog down the incline toward the estate—appearing to those in the helo like they were heading back to cover the president’s escape.

Tim shouted at the local security detail to protect the landing pad from the enemy agents, then jumped aboard when he heard the pilots bring Raider Two to full power. He saw Dave’s team disappear down the slope toward the front parking lot, and then his bird cleared the trees and plunged into the storm.

Dave reached the driveway and made a quick decision: The president’s limo and two others were not damaged, so they were the obvious choices of transportation. Not only would they provide the practical lift to the nearest port about 100 miles away; they were official cars with the presidential flag. There were several bodies lying in the drive, so they dragged them to one side and separated into the three limousines. One sported Han’s flag, one Wing’s, and one Foreign Minister Wu’s. Wing’s led the way and they roared down the hill and through the front gate. The guards there had rushed up the hill during the firefight and had all been killed. He didn’t expect their little convoy to be challenged until the word got out about the abduction: This was China, and they had three magic flags on their tank-like transportation.

Chapter 51

Inside Han's bunker

Left behind for lack of room, General Bao took charge of the two communications officers, the woozy major from the tunnel security team, four domestic staff, and the contingent of guards. He generally ignored Professor Dang, who was trying to puzzle out what he'd just witnessed. The sergeant in charge of the rear security team came down the ramp and quickly filled him in on the first helo crash and successful escape in the second aircraft, and that the PAP colonel had ordered them to guard the entrance to the ramp and the helo pad. Bao had noted that the fighting had stopped and didn't know what that meant, but he led his little force up the ramp, wondering what to do next. The Siberian Tigers left behind from the first helo had apparently headed for the fight in the front, but Bao didn't know if more would be coming to their rescue. They only had a few weapons, including the half-dozen rifles carried by the security team, plus a couple of pistols carried by the major and the communications lieutenant.

Bao cautiously led the way up to the tunnel's entrance, and all was eerily quiet—just the sergeant's men kneeling in a professional-looking semi-circle of heroic protection. The storm was raging and he peered through the swirling snow at the lighted helicopter pad, but there was no one in sight and no sounds of any firefight. He could also see the broken helo lying amidst the trees down the hill and it looked sadly abandoned. The devastation in the front drive must have been awesome from all the rumbling and dust that came down the elevator, but he was reluctant to investigate without a larger force. There were only a few domestic staff upstairs in Han's main house because his wife was downtown visiting friends, and he couldn't expect any help from them anyway. He'd been shocked to hear of Wing's coup attempt, but couldn't believe it had infected the military because their two cultures were quite separate. With no other course of action immediately apparent, he decided to bring in all the guards, lock the outside doors, and retreat to the communications room and place a call to his staff in the August 1st basement. They could tell him how pervasive the national coup was and, if they weren't too badly engaged, they might send up a helicopter to bring him back. The comms technician connected him, and then he had a very strange conversation.

Professor Dang was standing a few feet away, and heard Bao's side:

"Yes, this is General Bao—are you keeping the conspirators at bay?" He listened for a few seconds, then spoke again, this time more forcefully, "What do you mean, 'what conspirators?' There is a nation-wide coup attempt by MSS cadres. Minister Wing is under arrest and General Secretary Han and Marshal Tai are heading your way. They should be landing on the pad in minutes. Greet them properly. And be careful: The traitors may be lurking outside and waiting for the right opportunity to strike! Send a helicopter up here ASAP and bring me back to headquarters!"

Dang arched an eyebrow when he saw the puzzled look from the general, but he said nothing as they walked back into the main corridor. Bao then paused, looking thoughtful, then worry lines crossed his face as if he was contemplating something dreadful—then he suddenly stood rock-still. Then he startled the academic by shouting: "All of you, come with me!" He dashed back up the tunnel with a drawn pistol that he'd gotten from the sergeant. He crashed the doors open and sprinted around the nearest corner with surprising speed for someone in his late-fifties. The rest followed as best as best as they could, and they all disappeared down the slope on their way to the front drive.

Aboard Raider Two

The shaken civilian passengers were just starting to think clearly again. General Tai and President Han were sitting next to one another in seats just behind the command pilot, while Tim was sitting within arm's length of them in a sideways-facing fold-down seat behind the co-pilot. The jump seat was empty. The marshal's aide was sitting to Tim's left on the far side of the main door, while the remaining six awake civilians were mixed in with the commandos. General Wing was sound asleep, strapped into his seat in the second to last row next to Captain Woo, who had been patched up by the medic and would be okay. And the two extra Japanese pilots were directly behind them and hardest to see. The two ladies occupied the third to last seat. The commandos had disbursed themselves strategically to accomplish their next task.

"What happened when our helicopter tried to take off last time, Colonel?" asked Marshal Tai, trying to regain his situational awareness.

Tim kept in character and replied deferentially, "One of the rebels fired a burst at us, Comrade Marshal, and his rounds hit one or more of the rotor blades. They are made of composite material and shattered, so we were fortunate to be low and over trees. We also owe our lives to the Siberian Tiger leader who led his men on a suicide charge to fend off the traitor's assault so we could get away."

"Indeed, Colonel—and we are ever grateful for their sacrifice! I will see they are properly recognized." Tai said no more; he was shaken by the experience but wanted to maintain his composure until they could get to the August 1st Building's landing pad. It would be the safest place for him and Han until they could get a handle on the extent of Wing's coup and find out who else was involved. *I'm going to shoot a lot of traitors before dawn—the war could be lost because of this!*

When the men had transferred to the second helo, the team's medic made sure he grabbed a small bag and brought it along. It contained several syringes pre-loaded with fast-acting, long-term sedatives for their still-unaware captives. None of them had weapons (but Wing was carefully frisked to double-check). A firefight inside the helo could be disastrous. The raider sitting beside each civilian had a syringe ready; in the dark interior, it was easy to hold them unobserved. Tim casually looked around, gave a predetermined hand signal, and his men gently but firmly slid the needles into their seat-mates' arms and depressed the plunger to the base. The only potentially dangerous passenger was Marshal Tai's young aide, and PO3 Bob Loo, one of the Navy SEALs who'd intentionally chosen his seat next to the PLA captain, gently placed his pistol against the back of the man's head. He saw the young officer stiffen, but he offered no resistance or complaint.

"Ouch!" exclaimed Minister Ti when she felt a sharp jab in her arm. "Something just stuck me!" But her surprise and anger rapidly dissolved into oblivion. Several others exclaimed too in quick succession, but each quieted equally fast as the drugs took effect.

"Comrade General Secretary," spoke the medic soothingly as he hovered over the older man, "I am giving each of you an anti-nausea medicine. The pilots said the storm is really bad ahead and the turbulence will be awful." Then, before the most powerful man in the PRC could object, the medic plunged the sedative into his upper arm. Han initially startled, but before he could protest, his head slowly slumped forward against his restraint.

Marshal Tai witnessed this, but was in no mood for sedatives. He wanted to keep his wits about him as they faced this coup. "I don't need any medicine—I don't get airsick!"

Tim was sitting across from Marshal Tai and had drawn his pistol in the darkness. Every other captured civilian was asleep, and Tai's aide was under guard, so Tim briefly shone his web-gear-mounted mini flashlight on his gun and said, "Sorry, Marshal Tai, everyone gets the sedative."

The senior military man's head jerked around to confront this unheard-of defiance of his will, and he was instantly shocked into reality. "Who are you? Are you part of Wing's treachery?"

"Minister Wing's not a traitor, Marshal Tai. He's a psychopathic murderer, but otherwise loyal to the PRC. I, on the other hand, am an American intelligence officer, and my team is bringing you and your colleagues to Japan to appear before an international war crimes tribunal." Before his enemy could respond, Tim watched the medic plunge the needle into the senior soldier's deltoid muscle. After a brief struggle with the debilitating effects of the drug, the man's head lolled like the rest. Now all that remained was the young aide.

As Captain Kai watched the administration of the sedative, reality dawned. Despite the pistol pointing at his head, his initial thought was to try and take back control of the aircraft. However, he dismissed that thought in a flash when he considered the relative balance of power. Any brief success he had would be temporary, and it might cause the helo to crash and kill them all. He was in a no-win situation. He'd guessed that these Siberian Tigers were in actuality MSS agents and part of General Wing's conspiracy, and that the ever-devious MSS Minister had staged his entire arrest and drugging to facilitate the subsequent drama. It was textbook to say the least, and just the kind of ruse everyone would instantly buy. Now they were all being taken to MSS headquarters for probable execution. But his whirlwind of speculation sobered when the PAP colonel revealed himself as an American—an unexpected twist stranger than any Wing conspiracy. He listened with interest when the leader spoke directly to him.

"So, you are the marshal's aide. Do you want to spend the rest of journey asleep or awake?"

"Awake would be better," Kai responded evenly, wondering if the man was offering him a choice or just messing with him. He knew his options were otherwise limited anyway. If he jerked open the door and jumped, it just meant his death to no purpose, because everyone else was firmly belted in. He couldn't think of any scenario where his close-quarters combat skills would help the big picture, so he decided to just wait it out. The bottom line was that he knew the Americans were fair, and that he'd had no part in planning Han's crazy war. He'd also learned that several of his academy classmates had been killed and the losses had affected him deeply.

"We'll put zip ties on your hands, but obviously you have nothing to gain by fighting us. A crash at this altitude kills everyone and your country will be without its senior leaders."

"Yes, I accept that." Kai held up his hands so the soldier behind him could slip on the plastic ties, but he didn't cinch them too tight. Kai then switched to English; he'd spent a year in Australia, earning a Master's Degree in International Relations after graduating from the Defense University, and his language skills were passable. "An American team? Are you really a colonel in your military intelligence branch?"

Tim could see that this officer was unafraid but naturally curious, and there was no point in lying now; in fact, an honest exchange would keep him talking, and Tim might learn something useful. "No, I am a civilian. I volunteered for this mission because I thought it might hasten the end of the war. Where'd you learn English?"

Kai thought the man seemed honest, and he could afford to be; he held all the cards. Just then, the helo banked and dropped slightly as they hit a light-air pocket. They were out of the hills now and flying above the gently rolling areas north of the capital ring road, but the heavy weather was buffeting the relatively light helo from side to side. "After I attended our military college, I spent a year in Australia studying. I like the West and, for what it's worth, I didn't support the decision to go to war. However, I am a loyal patriot and will fight as I am ordered."

"We are in a world of patriots fighting as ordered. But there is objective truth, and your leaders blundered badly when they started a world war for selfish gain. Your country had a strong financial card to play in their negotiations with us and others, and they could have obtained any resources they wanted from the West. Force wasn't necessary. But if you have any say in the future when a new China emerges from this catastrophe, lobby for a defensive-minded military, and free and fair trade practices where every side wins."

"What you say is logical, and I don't disagree. But our Politburo doesn't think like that."

"Well, not to kick a dead horse, but your senior leaders are going to have to make some significant changes in the very near future. If they don't, more than a hundred million of your people will starve."

Kai realized the man was sincere and not spouting ideological propaganda, so he just shrugged his shoulders in the dark. Like most Chinese living in the PRC, he took the long view and would ride out the storm—literally and figuratively—and see what happened. He wondered how many of the captive leaders would be executed: Their decisions had killed hundreds of thousands of people in many countries, and the financial cost must be staggering—even astronomical. He hated the thought of his beloved homeland being the object of scorn and ridicule for generations. *How could they face their neighbors again?* He knew China could successfully resist any invasion and occupation, so they'd not be like Germany and Japan after World War II, but they would be largely ostracized. He shook his head at the irony: Without accepting future help from the West—the very thing that the Politburo hated and had led them to risk war in the first place—his people faced certain starvation and social upheaval would kill millions.

Tim watched this obviously fine young officer turn away in the dim light and look out the window. He felt for him on one level: On top of the world one minute, and a moment later confronted with failure and a dubious future. He guessed the man was only a few years younger, and it was painful to watch him process the implications of his predicament. It was a shocking and sudden turn-about for a dedicated soldier, and he wouldn't be Tai's aide unless his family was part of the senior tier of PRC society. But that was too bad; everyone had to adjust to China's new reality, and their transition would be witnessed by several billion people. The SEAL behind Kai put his pistol away, but didn't relax completely.

The helo bucked again, and Tim turned and watched the pilots wrestle with the controls. The good news was that they were moving east faster than the storm, and they'd be out of it in just over an hour. His greater concern now was Dave and the rest of the men he'd left behind.

In the command pilot's seat, Major Suzuki had taken over from the Raider Two pilot; not only was it his command prerogative, but he had far more experience. Admittedly, he'd lifted off with a bit of trepidation after the previous flight's disaster, and it had been a challenge to keep the helo stable as the storm knocked them around in the darkness. But, in the last few minutes, things were definitely smoothing out. They were racing along at more than 150 miles per hour, and the windshield wipers were fighting a losing battle against the snow and ice. But that was why all flyers practiced on instruments only. *Getting out of this slop couldn't happen soon enough.* However, Suzuki appreciated that they were invisible from the ground, and that they'd been readily accepted by now-familiar ATCs. Adding to their overall cloaking was the significant storm clutter on every radar screen that made them difficult to track.

They retraced their route over the spine of the Liaodong Peninsula and Dalian Harbor, and exchanged garbled conversations with the same controller they'd spoken with earlier. Their hand-off to the military controller monitoring the western Korean airspace and Yellow Sea went without a hitch, and a few minutes later Suzuki began his slow descent until he gradually vanished off everyone's scopes. He'd fly 50 feet above the highest wave crests until they cleared the storm, then dip lower. He figured they'd be in Incheon in about 90 minutes.

Tianjin Harbor Waterfront, 23:45 Hours

It had taken Dave Chen's mini-convoy of limousines just over two hours to navigate the 90 miles from Han's estate to the port. They'd accessed the northern Beijing ring road, and then branched off to Tianjin. They'd passed through the mostly blacked-out port city, then followed the signs to the harbor, but no one knew which end of the long row of docks and wharves belonged to the military. Their plan was straightforward, if not simple: Find a suitably fast navy or coast guard boat to highjack because it would have defensive weapons, then head for Incheon. They would be aided by the snowy darkness. The city and harbor were located on the western side of the Bohai Sea and, since it was the maritime gateway to the capital, there should be plenty of boats to steal.

The unusual sight of the president's motorcade driving along the docks had drawn many stares and, as word got out, people came out and clapped and waved, or just stood in awe. However, no one approached until the NCO driving the lead car spotted a pair of parked motorcycle cops. He slowed and shouted at them to lead the way to the military patrol boats. The shocked cops were happy to respond, and knew the vicinity well, so they kicked into high gear and led the way with sirens blaring. In less than five minutes, they motioned to the right and sure enough, a sleek-looking patrol boat was tied up alongside the quay.

"That's a Type 22 missile boat, Colonel!" whispered one of the SEALs in the back seat. "It's a twin-hulled lethal dart, extremely fast, armed to the teeth, and one of the best PT boats in the world!" Clearly the man was excited.

The team scrambled out of the three limos, and the cops just stared in disbelief at the commandos decked out in their military clothing and face paint, and carrying automatic weapons. Dave just hoped they looked intimidating enough to leave alone. He waved a "thank you" to the policemen, then looked over the railing and hailed the watch officer of the boat. The young naval officer was clearly surprised as he braced himself against the edge of the sleek cabin, holding steady as the storm surge banged his boat against the hard rubber protectors. Up close, the boat seemed perfect: It was a good hundred feet long, and looked very fast, like a bigger version of a classic American

PT boat. Dave asked permission to board, but didn't give the man time to object. He and the team streamed down the cement stairs from the top of the quay, and marched up the wooden gangway onto the boat. "I want to speak with the captain immediately!"

"Of course, Colonel, just one moment." The watch officer disappeared down a nearby ladder, and momentarily a surprised navy full lieutenant appeared and saluted.

"How may I help the Siberian Tigers, Colonel?" the captain asked. His watch officer had spotted the patches on the commandos' sleeves and recognized the distinctive crest.

"We need an emergency lift across the Bohai to the Liandong Peninsula: There is an MSS coup attempt and we have to capture the traitorous cadres there. Do you have enough fuel for that?"

The captain was about 30 years old, and he looked appropriately shocked. "Yes, Colonel, we have a full tank, but I need special authorization from the flotilla commander before I can take you."

"Sorry, Captain, but this is an emergency—a matter of state—and we don't know whom we can trust. Part of our other team has already rescued President Han and Marshal Tai and they are being taken by helicopter to PLA headquarters. Our mission has presidential authority. Make all preparations for getting under way, and tell your crew to ready their weapons!" Dave wondered how tough they'd have to get, but the storm had chased the curious locals back inside, so the area was deserted. If they had to commandeer the boat by force, they'd be out of sight of the public or other sailors. There were two enlisted men forward near a covered deck gun of some kind, but his team had subtly separated and could take them out with silenced pistols if necessary.

"This is most unusual, Colonel," protested the young officer—suddenly finding himself in the exact middle of a potential disagreement between two ego-driven senior officers.

"Nevertheless, make all preparations for a timely departure. We are going to apprehend or kill these rebels, with or without you as captain of this boat!" He fixed his best evil stare on the young officer and watched him capitulate. He felt for him: Being a company-grade officer in a field-grade officer's world was tough. The young officer saluted compliance, and gave rapid orders to the younger officer who, in turn, dashed off to rally the crew. A minute later, a dozen young sailors were running here and there as they pulled on heavy parkas, and they quickly readied their fore and aft deck guns and worked some dials on the boat's two ADA missile launchers. Others began casting off lines and generally getting ready. Seconds later, the engines rumbled to life and Dave thought they sounded powerful.

Looking around, he thought they'd gotten away free, but just then his ears picked up a bevy of distant sirens penetrating the storm's howl. As the noise got louder by the second, it was obvious that they'd been blown. The rest of the team heard the approaching danger, too, and quietly took up defensive positions behind equipment or just lay on the deck. The young ensign hovering nearby heard the sirens, and Dave shouted at him, "The traitors are coming, Ensign—tell your crew to prepare to repel boarders. Alert your captain!" *I sound like a pirate.*

Momentarily, the captain rushed out of the low bridge structure, "What is happening, Colonel?"

"It must be a contingent of MSS rebels, Captain. Bring your crew to their battle stations!" Dave watched the captain reinforce the ensign's orders; the sailors had already torn off the waterproof coverings of their dual-mounted heavy machine guns, but were still feeding belts of ammo into the breeches. Then they swung them toward the roadway and Dave was impressed; these boys knew their business.

Two things happened in rapid succession: Sailors began pushing the boat away from the dock, and several vehicles roared up above. Slammed doors and the sound of many boots alerted the boat that soldiers or policemen were nearing the edge of the quay. "There they are!" Dave shouted as two dozen People's Armed Policemen reached the railing and pointed automatic weapons down at the boat. "Fire at will!" His team cut loose with a torrent of automatic rifle fire, and the frightened sailors added steady bursts from their mounted guns. Together they mowed down the PAP cadres who'd hardly gotten off a shot. One short burst grazed one of the sailors, but that PAP officer was instantly blown back. None of the U.S. team was hurt.

The two big diesels roared to full power, and smelly exhaust fouled the pristine chill. The helmsman engaged the drive shaft because the boat was now well away from the dock, and the captain ordered emergency power. The sleek boat surged forward and executed the fastest exit of the harbor in history. Soon it was cutting through the water at 20 knots and gaining speed as it headed directly east into the open Bohai. Dave directed the captain to set a course for Dalian Harbor; that would force them around the peninsula. That was not their real destination, but he figured it would keep the crew focused for the time being. The team and the sailors kept their initial focus behind them, but the dock soon faded from sight, and it was apparent that there were no other threats. Now the sailors and Allied commandos were comrades in arms and had staved off a common enemy. They would remain that for the next few hours until the team would have to surprise their hosts but, until then, the storm enveloped the speeding boat. The seas were following and the swells low, so the captain steadily increased their speed to 25 knots until they tore across the tops of the waves.

Chapter 52

White House Situation Room, 11:50 Hours (local)

It had been a nerve-racking few hours for President Stilwell and his war cabinet: They'd been watching an uninterrupted satellite feed during the early part of the operation, and the graphics helped everyone understand the team's spatial progress until they reached Beijing. But once they'd disappeared under the circling bands of a ferocious winter storm, all communication ceased. One hour dragged by and became two, and Spence wasn't the only one beginning to fear the worst.

Raider Two, 23:50 Hours (same time)

Major Suzuki was elated when their helo emerged from the leading edge of the easterly-creeping storm, and he could again see the familiar sight of the undulating surface of the ocean. It was a beautiful night, with a pale half-moon reflecting off an uneasy sea. Relief flooded his spirit and the adrenaline pumps slackened. His co-pilot had composed a coded message to update the powers that be, and he reached up and popped the silver dollar-sized disk into their heavily-encrypted VHF radio. He hit a button and a micro-burst transmission shot up to the waiting satellite and then instantly downlinked to three places: To Incheon where their hosts would welcome them; to Japan where their "guests" would be debriefed and displayed to the world; and to the White House on the other side of the world. Three Allied leaders had a special need to know, and were anxiously awaiting the news. And, once the Chinese leaders arrived in Japan, they'd be held until their fate was determined by an international court of law.

White House Situation Room

Spence was terrible at killing time; he had to be busy doing something he considered important or he got both nervous and cranky. He'd made four trips up to the Oval Office on various pretexts just to escape the tension, and he'd swallowed as many anti-acid tablets as he had cups of coffee. *Please, Lord, let there be good news and this horrible war over!*

Everyone had his or her own ways of coping with the stress: Some drank coffee until their systems rebelled, some visited the small kitchen to munch on the same low-calorie pastries the President preferred in the morning, and others took turns in the Comms room (remembering to observe OPSEC protocols—operational security) to check in with their departments. Several were just returning from the restrooms when the main screen came alive again. "Look!" the President exclaimed, pointing to the big center screen, and the room came alive with anticipation.

"That's the symbol for Raider Two!" confirmed Admiral Simms, immediately worrying about the other half of the team.

"Only one helo, Admiral?" asked Edith Carmichael. She didn't miss much, and was worried about the mission in general. She was also privately concerned about her friend Betty, and about young Tim as well. She was privy to the mission details and knew he and the prisoners should be on the lead helo.

"Yes, Madam Director. But wait, there's a transmission coming through!"

"Put it up on the screen, Admiral," ordered the President. Spence hoped beyond hope that the miracle they'd prayed for was happening, but he'd also picked up on the fact of the single helo. Then he saw that the message was the greatest news:

"Raider Two to base. All guests aboard and sleeping. Raider One down, one minor casualty, different ETA. RTB SK 01:00 local. Nothing follows."

A cheer rose in the room. The helo would arrive in South Korea at one in the morning local, and the second team was coming home by a different route. Their quickly formed plan had pulled together military personnel from several Allied countries, and apparently pulled off one of the most audacious and important snatch-and-grabs in world history! Baker Halsey was reminded of Winston Churchill's "Few," who fought and defied the Germans during the Battle of Britain.

Incheon, South Korea
Saturday, December 13th, 01:23 Hours

Major Suzuki set the helo down gently at mid-point on the designated runway—thankfully bereft of any holes from enemy missiles—and then he taxied toward the silhouette of the U.S. Air Force C-17 Globemaster III hospital plane. As they got closer, he could see its tail ramp was down and interior illuminated by faint red lights. As soon as he shut off the main engines, the American mission commander who'd impressed one and all opened the helo's big waist door and slid it back, then stepped out and motioned the waiting medical teams forward. The rotors were still slowly turning when the Raiders lifted the first of their sleeping captives onto a military gurney and, one by one, the "patients" were quickly rolled up and into the flying hospital.

Tim motioned Captain Kai to exit because he was not expecting any trouble from him, and they waited side by side. There was no point humiliating the man and he seemed like a reasonable fellow. In any event, Tim had his sidearm if his evaluation proved wrong. He watched as all nine sleeping PRC leaders were moved into the big transport—as was Captain Woo, who was awake and enjoying the mild euphoria of his powerful morphine injection. Then he nodded to Kai to join the line of special operators who filed onto the plane and found jump seats for the short hop to Japan. Tim took a moment to climb back into the helo and shook hands with the four Japanese pilots: Without their brilliant flying, the operation would have been impossible. He agreed to hook up with Major Suzuki and the others next time he was in Japan. It was not an idle farewell: Their mutual respect was strong and would bring them together again and again as circumstances allowed. Tim stepped down onto the tarmac and jogged to the ramp, mindful of the state of war, and aware that they had to get off the ground as quickly as possible.

He was just settling into one of the ubiquitous red jump seats to grab 40 winks when a South Korean colonel in immaculately starched battle fatigues walked up. Tim stood up and shook his hand.

"Sir, would you please accompany me?" The man spoke perfect English and turned to lead the way.

No sleep tonight. Tim followed the older man up one of the narrow center aisles between the rows of vertical three-tiered medical bunks in the large bay, and he was amazed at the variety of medical machines attached to the bulkhead. It was clear that this large plane could bring dozens of wounded soldiers home from anywhere on the globe. The medical staffs on board these planes were the Angels of God, if you asked Tim—or especially if you asked any of the thousands of warriors who, because of these professionals, were alive in American beds instead of dead in overseas body bags. In typical modern combat, wounded warriors were treated in the field by medics, then evacuated by ground units or "dust-off" medical helicopters to field hospitals. Then, when stable enough to fly, they were transported back to stateside hospitals for appropriate treatment and thankful reunions with their families.

Tim followed the colonel forward to a separate and well-appointed space. A bulkhead formed a metal wall between it and the larger medical treatment area, and he correctly guessed that it was the doctors and nurses' lounge—absolutely necessary for long flights. But today it held one very special guest:

The colonel addressed his head of state, "Mr. President, may I introduce Colonel Duncan?"

President Kim of South Korea stood and greeted Tim warmly, "Greetings Colonel Duncan. On behalf of the Allied leadership, I offer my congratulations and profound thanks!"

Surprised, Tim nevertheless gathered himself, and thanked the South Korean president for his good wishes. He put on his best diplomat's hat and said how grateful his team was for the Korean military's enabling assistance. He also praised his Raiders—the men who did the heavy lifting. Then they were interrupted when the pilot announced over the intercom that everyone was to find their places and fasten their seatbelts, and moments later they felt the big plane begin to move. Tim wanted to be back with his men, but clearly President Kim wanted to hear about the mission. The short hop to Japan passed quickly as he relayed the details—including their near-disaster aboard Raider One. President Kim promised that his people would help rescue the Raiders still trying to find their way home.

As soon as the big transport gained altitude for its flight to Nagasaki, an unseen squadron of 12 South Korean Air Force F-16 fighters formed a protective escort around the perimeter. No Chinese fighters were getting near this particular aircraft tonight.

Nagasaki, Japan, 09:00 Hours

The C-17 was met in Japan by Colonel Gota and a platoon of his commandos, and they provided security as the prisoners were transported to a secure medical facility in a nearby secret location. The PRC leaders were taken to separate rooms where trusted medical personnel supervised the administration of the counteractive medication that would bring them slowly back to full consciousness. It took three hours to fully process each person, and they were treated with the full respect due their age and perceived health—as well as their status as national leaders. By noon, they were alert, shocked to say the least, and ready for their first of many interrogations attended by a representative of the International Criminal Court residing in The Hague, Netherlands.

Han was having a terrible time processing his new reality: He was in a sterile, windowless room with cement floor, walls, and ceiling. Physically he felt fine, but he was situationally disoriented and was barely able to recall his last half hour when the military unit rescued him from Wing's conspiracy. He vaguely remembered the first helicopter ride and the crash, then his extrication from the damaged aircraft and the short climb up the hill into the second helicopter. After that, everything was a blank. His first recollection after waking up was being surrounded by Japanese medical people conferring in their incomprehensible language. Now he was sitting behind a desk in a bare room, in a different but stylish new dark business suit with a red silk tie. *Am I dreaming?*

Watching him via CCTV cameras were several military, legal, and medical people who agreed he was healthy and psychologically adjusting to his new surroundings. They concurred that he could withstand the series of emotional shocks he'd be gently subjected to over the next few hours. But the authorities had to proceed because time was of the essence: Continuing military action was taking lives on many fronts. But, on the other hand, they had to do this right to maximize their leverage over this heretofore supremely powerful man; if he didn't cooperate, the whole effort was for naught.

Prime Minister Sato of Japan had welcomed President Kim, and both were speaking with the military's chief psychologist; she believed Han could handle a visit from the two international heads of state. "Honorable leaders, you can go in now and deliver your ultimatum. Just be aware that he's still confused."

The two leaders agreed and proceeded down the hall, accompanied by a translator and two technicians pushing a cart with a large-screen TV. Both heads of state spoke English, and they knew that Han did, too, but they wanted a Mandarin speaker just in case. They entered the room and walked to the table and watched Han carefully process his extraordinary new reality. The technicians pushed the cart to the side where all four men could see it clearly. Then the technicians hooked it up and left.

Han was stupefied. He'd understood that medical personnel had taken care of him, and he'd attributed his situation to another crash, but he didn't understand the Japanese aspect of his predicament, and no one would answer his questions. Now he was face to face with the leaders of Japan and South Korea—both of whom he knew fairly well because they had exchanged State visits. He stood up as an automatic diplomatic reflex—even as he had the unfolding realization that he was their prisoner.

"Sorry we have to meet under war-time conditions, President Han," said PM Sato. "You of course know President Kim of South Korea…" Though awkward, both offered their hands at the recommendation of the psychologist. Han had to be treated as a fellow head of state if they were to win his cooperation.

Han accepted the handshakes, and understood in his soul that he was no longer in charge of his fate: He hadn't experienced such feelings in many years. It was true he'd been in subordinate positions on his way up the Party ladder, but he'd been an absolute ruler for so long that any other situation seemed strange. He wondered what Fate had in store for him and his country—masked adroitly behind the too-polite mannerisms of the enemy leaders.

"Please sit down, President Han," beckoned President Kim. "We will briefly explain to you what happened, and tell you what we believe your options are. They are few, to put it bluntly." Kim was having a hard time being civil to this man who'd indirectly killed thousands of his countrymen, but he had to take the high road here to save millions more. At least the two Koreas would now be unified, the only silver lining in an otherwise disastrous conflict.

PM Sato spoke next, because the psychologist recommended that he and Kim keep the conversation flowing back and forth. "You were captured by a group of Allied commandos and flown first to Incheon and then here to Japan. You are in a secure government facility several stories underground, and you and your colleagues will be tried by the International Criminal Court, and then sentenced appropriately for the aggressive and unprovoked war you started. Their representatives are here and will bring their initial charges shortly. But be assured that you will receive objective legal representation—provided by experts from neutral European nations."

Han heard the simultaneous translation, but waved the man to silence. "I am fluent in English. Please continue." Then he watched President Kim pick up a handheld TV remote and power up the big screen. Within a few seconds, he was faced remotely by several American leaders sitting around a conference table. Included were President Stilwell and Vice President Mason—both of whom he had met—plus some others he recognized. All were stone-faced and staring daggers at him.

"President Han," spoke his American counterpart, "We meet again, unfortunately, in a time of war—a terrible reality started by your country without provocation from any of your neighbors or other members of the family of nations. Our purpose in meeting you today is to describe terms of cease-fire and return of your forces to the mainland. We expect the PRC to accept and implement our terms immediately, and to the letter. All the Allied countries you invaded have governments ruled by laws, and you and your senior colleagues will be treated according to ICC law and procedures. You are nine prisoners who will be tried as war criminals and will suffer the fate dictated by the ICC. Prime Minister Sato and President Kim will describe the specific terms: Your crimes are so grievous—crimes against humanity—that Allied leaders are in agreement that your cases will be expedited, and those found guilty will have their sentences carried out within the month. Now please listen to our two esteemed colleagues."

Han was stunned by the abruptness of the pronouncement and by its content, but he knew Stilwell wasn't bluffing. His great gamble had failed, and he had to face that fact and hope for the best. He didn't respond to the American President's comments, but instead turned and listened as the Japanese PM spoke again:

"President Han, you will continue to discharge your duties of office until your forces return to mainland Chinese borders. In effect, with a few exceptions, this is a return to the status quo ante. Two hours from now, you will face a televised audience comprised of the entire world, during which time you will read a statement accepting responsibility for the war. You will accept the list of ceasefire terms, and direct your military units of every kind to return home. The ICC will note your compliance, and your cooperation will be acknowledged during your trial."

Han was relieved. It certainly could have been much worse. His political instincts interpreted this opening condition as an escape from the firing squad, and that his country would retain its sovereignty. And it seemed that the CCP would survive as well. He couldn't know that this first component of the offer had been angrily discussed over the previous hours via conference calls between all the affected Allied leaders, and they had not been of one accord. Some had lobbied for much harsher penalties. But the heads of state, their chief military commanders, and diplomats finally agreed that—because mainland China still had massive military forces within its borders, any attempt to roll their invasion back by force of arms, let alone wage a nearly impossible war inside China's borders—it would cost too much in blood and treasure. They all accepted that trying to force an unconditional surrender of Mainland China—such as the Allies successfully did with Germany and Japan at the end of World War II—was a fool's errand. Outside of China, the Allies had great leverage; inside, almost none. They had to get the best deal possible, and giving Han hope was the key.

"Our second condition," stated President Kim, "requires you personally to surrender all your official positions in one week—the deadline for all PLA and MSS personnel in Asia to be back on Chinese soil. The other prisoners in our custody will be given different options. You are granted this one week of additional service to your people, partially to atone for the unprovoked aggression against your neighbors and trading partners. We also want to prevent more useless death and destruction. You will order your expeditionary forces to cease operations and to begin moving as rapidly as they can back to their points of departure. Those who entered the various countries by land may use any vehicle that does not have weapons on it—non-military cars or trucks, for example—for the return journey. Otherwise, they will walk back. The mileage is not too great, and every able-bodied soldier should be able to do so in less than a week. The troops may carry food, water, and pistols and rifles only; we're allowing these small arms to defend against massive reprisals. The affected governments will order their troops and peoples to allow uncontested passage along the way, but individuals or families may naturally try to take personal revenge."

It didn't take Han long to accept that he could live with these conditions, believing them to be better than fair. China was being forced back into prewar borders (what they meant by "status quo ante") with the loss of all their offensive equipment as partial payment for their aggression. Trillions of RMB wasted. But he knew these first conditions were only part of their demands.

"President Han," said President Stilwell, still staring at him from the TV screen, "all forces in port areas will stand down and stand fast until directed to the nearest airport. If this location is within walking distance, the soldiers can walk under the same provisions as above. If the distance is too far, they can use unarmed PLA vehicles, or local transportation will be provided. They will surrender their small arms at the base of the airplanes' passenger ramps. These troops will be flown home. Your wounded who are too badly injured to be transported home now will be treated by each country according to the rules of the Geneva Convention. When recovered sufficiently to travel, they will be flown home, too. All associated costs will be borne by the PRC."

Han nodded at the screen. It was a merciful set of conditions for surrender—and an obvious strategy to get his forces out of each country with the full cooperation of his troops. But he was sure there was another shoe, and that it would be dropped soon.

PM Sato spoke next. "Now, President Han, we come to righting the wrongs of this terrible conflict: First, each country will account for its dead and wounded under the general supervision of the International Red Cross and Red Crescent. The PRC will pay the families of the deceased or wounded soldiers, or civilians, 100,000 USD. This penalty will be paid in gold to the embassies of each country in Washington, DC. China will be forbidden to engage in international trade until these and designated additional penalties are paid."

These were outrageous demands! Han started fuming, but he exercised great self-control and didn't let them see his anger. Most of these dead or injured foreigners wouldn't see that kind of money in several lifetimes. *This is just a windfall for corrupt leaders and their cronies!* He just grunted reluctant compliance.

President Kim then delivered the even bigger blow that Han figured was coming: "President Han, the People's Republic of China will pay in gold, or other acceptable commodities, the entire reconstruction debt of every damaged building or thing in every country, to include the full costs of rebuilding the fleets of America, Japan, Taiwan, and the other countries that received war-related damage, plus reasonable interest. Timely payments based on your historical mining data will be used as a guide, and dispersals will be monitored by international observers. The debt will be paid over 20 years. Once the personal bodily harm payments have been delivered to each embassy as previously stated—because we know the PRC has sufficient reserves—China may engage in free and fair trade with the international community. That will continue as long as your country adheres to the aforementioned restitution schedule, but access to trading relationships will be suspended if the PRC falls behind its payment schedule."

At least I'll be long dead by then, Han mused inwardly. Out loud he said, "This will be a burden that will kill millions of my countrymen—it is too much to bear!"

Spence jumped into the conversation, "We will monitor this requirement, President Han. You cannot expect to destroy hundreds of billions of dollars' worth of state and personal property and not be held accountable. However, we have compassion for the ordinary people of China, and we will assist them with famine relief—but your government will pay reparations for this damnable war!" Spence felt his voice raising, and he forced himself to calm down. He didn't want to lose face in front of the others, nor hurt the larger cause.

Han had no leverage and didn't want to be executed, so he just replied neutrally, "Okay, what's next?"

President Kim spoke again, “Your forces in North Korea will withdraw in an orderly manner, handing over all captured forces and lands to the advancing South Korean army. Your troops will withdraw across the Yalu River and old border onto your side. What your successor does throughout the mainland is Chinese sovereign business. A week from now, the Kim family will be handed over to our representatives at the Chinese/Unified Korean border. We will decide what to do with them. The only good that will come out of this war for us will be the unification of our peninsula. We will establish a long-lasting peace, and help our northern countrymen live without fear of dictatorial oppression in a just society.”

“I’m glad we could be of service,” Han responded sarcastically. He saw Kim’s face color but the man didn’t respond. A long-term nightmare was coming to an end.

The PM saw this, too and jumped in to deflect a nasty confrontation. “President Han, the next order of business is world compensation for the coronavirus that has cost so many millions of lives and needless suffering. Your successor government will assume responsibility for payments to the families that died and were sickened, and for the expenses endured by the governments and companies that suffered. A payment schedule will be negotiated later, but will be significant.”

Han heard the term “successor” a second time and then it hit him like a hammer; his presidency was over, and he was to be kept out of his homeland. He realized he was personally finished, and that his country would never achieve its decades-long dream of becoming the dominant world power. At least, he knew that he and his generation of leaders had tried. They had essentially taken on the whole world. They had failed. The Party and China’s national sovereignty would survive, but without him. He didn’t know if the people would rise up and throw out the “successor government.” Probably not, if they had enough to eat.

President Stilwell spoke again, “While you are still president, you will deliver the aforementioned televised address to your forces and countrymen. It will be live and witnessed by the world, but will be in a respectful setting and you will not be humiliated in any way—beyond the larger context you cannot blame us for. You have an opportunity to do something good here, President

Han. Your colleagues have been briefed on our conversation here and will stand behind you during the broadcast. Only Minster Wing will be kept separate, and will shortly undergo more rigorous chemically-aided interrogations. We want to know the locations of his deployed spies and saboteurs. He knows his fate is grim, and he has been very uncooperative."

"That's all for now, President Han," summarized PM Sato. "You will take a one-hour break to prepare for your presentation. You will be able to familiarize yourself with the text, and the technicians will set up the live TV feeds. We could have pre-taped your speech, but we have decided to trust you."

Han looked at the monitor and at the two world leaders and replied, "I think you have been fair. I will read what I am given." He had no choice. Well, he did, but he wanted to die in peace and not at the end of a rope or in front of a wall. The big TV screen went blank, and the three leaders rose and shook hands again. They were very cold handshakes.

Chapter 53

24 nautical miles from Incheon, 09:40 Hours

Dave and his team had catnapped during the rough yet monotonous ten-hour voyage from Tianjin Harbor. As night gave way to day, they had dreaded the strafing jet that would send them to the bottom, but the planes never came and they could only thank the speed of the journey and diminishing overcast conditions that hid them throughout the journey. When they'd passed the logical point to turn into the Liandong Peninsula, his men had suddenly disarmed the captain and his crew but, after the initial shock and a brief tussle, they were secured below and seemed to accept their fate as prisoners of war.

Two SEALs on Dave's team knew how to operate boats at sea, and they took over navigation and operation of the sleek Type 22. If they'd had their choice of the entire ChiCom inventory, they'd have chosen this one; it was capable of 36 knots and they'd actually had fun bounding over the following crests—a thrill ride, to say the least. The boat had an excellent sweeping radar, and they had no encounters along the way. Now they were within an hour of Incheon Harbor and had to raise their counterparts in the South Korean military; after all they'd been through, it would be mighty embarrassing to be sunk by coastal missiles or SK aircraft. Dave checked in via uplink to Tim first, and their relieved mission commander assured them the Koreans would roll out the red carpet. The boat then turned directly into Incheon Bay, and the shallow draft of their catamaran helped them cross the historic waters at low tide—just as General MacArthur's invasion force had done in 1950.

White House Situation Room
December 12th, 21:40 Hours

Spence was elated. Even though he'd gotten mad during the exchange with Han, the hasty plan concocted by young Tim Duncan and "the Ladies" had been a truly inspired brainstorm. The impromptu team of commandos had pulled off a near-miracle. Just hours before, everyone thought they were in for a long and devastating war that would have changed the balance of world power, but the Chinese efforts had fizzled. Catastrophic damage had been done and many lives lost, but the end result for the living would be a more peaceful planet.

Going forward, Spence knew he faced recriminations because, like Pearl Harbor in 1941, the United States had not been suspicious enough of a dangerous potential foe. He had to bear some of that burden, and his countrymen and international friends had paid an awful price. America should have had its Navy and Air Force in the western Pacific—stationed on her islands and in the ports of her many friends—not tied up to piers in Seattle and San Diego. But that analysis was for later; now he had to manage the transition from war to peace, and he asked everyone to comment on what they'd observed during the video exchange with Presidents Han, Kim, and Sato.

The war cabinet was contemplative now that a cease-fire was just hours away. Admiral Simms had sent a warning order to American forces worldwide—a heads-up to prepare for the coming cease-fire. They would disengage as safely as their respective battlefield conditions allowed, and would not advance up the Korean Peninsula until the PLA began its orderly withdrawal. The Korean army would lead, and the U.S. ground forces would respectfully follow as asked. All Allied governments had been notified of the dramatic change of events, and of the broadcast that would soon take place. Sporadic fighting would naturally continue until all the smaller units got the word, and it was anticipated that some might not surrender or pull back. Those would be dealt with on a case-by-case basis. But, at least for the time being, most of the frontline units knew relief was on the way.

The Secretary of State raised an important issue: "Mr. President, just a practical matter: Should our consulate and embassy staffs in China be alerted, too? They should be ready in case of reprisals."

"I would think so, Jack. What do the rest of you think?"

"Yes, Mr. President," said Edith. "They need context to understand any changes that might occur around them. The local civil population may be extremely angry—at least unpredictable—and our diplomatic personnel and their families need to be ready for anything. The good news is that the local police have been keeping a watch on our scholars, teachers, tourists, and the like in various hotels." She had been alone in the Soviet Union when it fell apart, and it had been a very scary time.

"Mr. President," added VP Mason, "I recommend that Foreign Minister Wu and People's Armed Police Minister Ti be asked to connect with their respective ministries. They greatly influence those guarding all foreign citizens, plus the various Allied consulates throughout China."

"Good advice, Rebecca. Jack, can you teleconference with Wu? Take a translator and get him to notify the appropriate people in Beijing. Rebecca, can you and Edith do the same thing with Ti? I've heard she's a tough cookie, but you can do your long-distance best." The three immediately left the room and Jack assigned the ladies a translator from the pool.

The undisclosed prison site near Nagasaki
December 13th, 11:15 Hours

Foreign Minister Wu was sitting on his bed wondering about the future of his country. He had awakened earlier in a medical setting, and was initially confused by the Japanese faces in medical masks peering down at him. But, as he regained his senses, he realized that he felt fine, and remembered the disturbing events of the first and second helicopter rides. Then he heard a voice speaking Mandarin, and looked over to see a distinguished man in a business suit standing a few feet away, also wearing a face mask.

"Good morning, Foreign Secretary Wu. I am Sangiro Yamata, Japan's Deputy Minister of Foreign Affairs. We have met before during consultations in Beijing and Tokyo. You are our guest for the time being. How do you feel?" Yamata felt no ill will toward Wu. He was sure this man had been a voice of reason during the lead-up to war.

Wu was shocked but, in a way, felt quietness in his soul. He remembered meeting this diplomat before and knew him to be a man of peace and honor. "Yes, Minister Yamata. Can you tell me what has happened?"

Yamata had been given carte blanche to tell Wu everything, and did so. Then two orderlies helped the older man sit up and, after he regained his equilibrium, they also helped him transition to a comfortable chair. The two career diplomats chatted for a few minutes. Mr. Yamata excused himself while the orderlies helped the senior citizen into his new clothes. A few minutes later, they walked together down the hall to a room with a large screen TV. "Minister Wu, American Secretary of State Jack Madrid would like to speak with us." He saw this surprised Wu, but that was expected; the man was absorbing a lot of shocks in a short period of time. Yamata just hoped Wu's health was up to it.

Jack Madrid. Yes, I like him. Fair and appropriately direct. Trustworthy. Good long-term diplomat. Wu sat in the comfortable chair next to DM Yamata and looked expectantly at the screen. Momentarily it flickered on.

"My dear Foreign Minister—so sorry we have to meet long distance and under these circumstances. How is your health?" Jack liked this man, but was concerned about his generally frail appearance.

"I am in good health, Mr. Secretary. I, too, am sorry for all that has transpired over the last days—and during the preceding years. By now you know that our attack had been planned for some time."

"Yes, we know. But we do not blame you. I'm sure you tried your best to avert war. You have been briefed that General Secretary Han has agreed to a cease-fire. Chinese forces will pull back into the mainland—effecting a status quo ante. But we need your help: I am respectfully asking you to contact your office and inform them what has happened. All of us with citizens living in or visiting China are concerned about the safety of our people once news of the war's end becomes public. People will be angry at their losses and will lash out in unpredictable ways. Any ideas you have will be most appreciated."

Relieved in spite of his country's military and political disaster, Wu believed this saga would benefit China in the long run. He would do what he could to help now, and in the days to come. "Yes, I will contact my subordinates, as Mr. Yamata directs, and I'll do my best to ensure all international citizens' short-term protection and repatriation. I want nothing more than an enduring peace."

"President Stilwell was sure that we could count on you, Minister Wu. Now time is of the essence. We will speak again later and often."

They disconnected politely, then Wu followed the Japanese diplomat to another room containing a large and sophisticated bank of communications equipment. He was invited to sit in a central chair and given headphones.

Then a senior technician asked him in Mandarin what number he should dial. Presently, Wu was speaking with his deputy, who had a very hard time accepting what he was being told. After a few minutes, though, everyone understood and agreed to Wu's directive. Wu handed back the headphones.

As this little drama was playing out, his colleague who led the People's Armed Police was also having trouble accepting what she'd learned upon waking. She felt terribly vulnerable, and asked where Minister Wing was. She didn't like the vague answer she received from the female medical doctor—a military specialist who led the team attending her transition from drug-induced sleep to drug-induced wakefulness. She protested, "I demand to see my colleagues and General Secretary Han!" She was so stressed that her voice cracked.

Dr. Yukio Tanjiro was the product of a Japanese father and a Chinese mother—both medical doctors who had met in medical school in Tokyo. The brilliant couple had decided to marry and continue their life together in Japan, and their daughter had been born, raised, and educated there. Yukio was fluent in both languages plus English, and had been heavily recruited to serve in the Japanese Intelligence Agency. Known informally as the Pale Chrysanthemum, the shadow world of the Nippon clandestine service had agents in every country on earth. She had flown down from her office in Kyoto earlier that morning, and was leading the debrief of an obviously talented but complex and troubled woman. "Minister Ti, make no mistake as to your situation here; you are a prisoner of the Allied High Commission and will be charged with war crimes plus crimes against humanity. You are in big trouble!" She watched the woman cringe a bit as she processed the ominous threats, and believed that this lady had been raised as a princess in a closed society. She had never been told "no" and was a privileged elite who'd never known fear, so the changes she was experiencing were shocking, to say the least.

"I have been illegally kidnapped by terrorists—you must return me to China!" Ti demanded irrationally. *Oh, what will become of me? Where is Wing?*

"If you cooperate during the next few hours, you have something to offer the court. If you do not, your fate is certain, and you will be executed for war crimes. Trust me, the men who brought you here are the opposite of terrorists, and you will not be returning to China." Dr. Tanjiro could see the walls cracking; this brutal woman was truly scared, and she should be—her chance of escaping the hangman's noose was remote. But Yukio had to be careful with this woman, too: She was a known psychopath who was now psychologically vulnerable and believed to be unstable. In her current confinement, her mental state could degrade rapidly.

Ti was dazed and confused and saw no reasonable avenue of escape. She suddenly felt that she was facing certain death at the hands of these vicious pirates who were holding her prisoner. She was terrified, and changed her tone as she grasped for any straw that would save her. "I want to speak with my father," she demanded. Then she paused and asked with a voice of supplication, "What do you want me to do?"

Dr. Tanjiro heard the change, and knew the hook was set. "First, I will take you under guard to a nearby room where you will have a video chat with two very senior American leaders. They will give you instructions and I recommend that you not give them any reason to doubt your sincerity. They order people like you executed every day!" She knew this bit to be a lie, but Ti didn't know that—it was how she had conducted her life as a bully in the People's Republic.

"I will cooperate," Ti protested. But this stern woman just helped her to her feet and led her roughly down the hall. She was plunked into a hard metal chair in front of a large TV screen, and she wrapped her thin arms around her hospital gown. Dr. Tanjiro sat in the adjacent chair to translate if needed. Momentarily the screen flickered on.

"Minister Ti," said the first of two distinguished-looking women in business suits, sitting next to each other in a neutral room. They were speaking English, which Ti understood fairly well. "You have been a very bad person—bullying people for many years, and supporting this vile war! Now you will do as I say or your life will end badly!" Edith knew she was way over the top with her threat, but she needed to get inside this dangerous woman's head from the start. She had asked Rebecca if she could take the lead, and her old friend had readily agreed; rough stuff was not her thing. "My organization has been watching you for many years, Minister Ti. You are in serious trouble with the international community. Now you will show proper respect to Vice President Rebecca Mason of the United States!"

Ti had been shocked when she recognized the two women as the American Vice President and the U.S. intelligence chief. She couldn't remember the latter's title, but these women were heavyweights in American female political circles, and probably had the authority to order the executions of anyone they wanted. She was far more afraid of these women than Han or Tai—but no one was as frightening as her dear Wing. She longed for him to rescue her and comfort her, but she'd seen him drugged and dragged out of Han's bunker amid a flurry of lies, so she despaired of ever seeing him again. She'd even turned against him to save herself. Would he ever forgive her? "What do you want of me?" she asked as submissively as she could—the first time in her life to adopt a passive persona before anyone except her father and her lover.

"You will be taken to a communications room," responded VP Mason, deciding it was time for her to enter the conversation. "There you will communicate with your top senior deputies and order them to protect all foreign residents and visitors in the People's Republic. If anything happens to them, we are holding you personally responsible!"

Ti was dismayed, and asked plaintively, "What if I can't remember all those numbers? I usually have a secretary make those calls." She felt like a little bird caught in a trap. Then she heard the menacing intelligence chief proclaim alarming information:

"I'll give the radio operator the contact information for the top 75 members of your ministry, including their home numbers, cell phones, and girl or boy friends' numbers." Edith's sarcasm squashed any remaining resistance. "Your ministry will keep order, but they will no longer bully anyone!"

Ti was deflated. "It will be as you direct…" She watched in utter defeat as the screen suddenly went blank. The Japanese doctor took her arm again and led her to another room with the promised communications equipment. Ti began dictating numbers for the technician to call.

Rebecca and Edith headed back to the conference room where President Stilwell was waiting with the others.

"Couldn't have gone better, Edith," said the VP.

"I agree. That's one frightened woman!"

"She deserves that and more. I've read some of what she's done…" The two continued chatting quietly as they entered the conference room. The atmosphere was truly upbeat, a tremendous contrast from the previous days.

Nagasaki

Marshal Tai was also dealing with his own radical adjustments, but he'd come to the right conclusions faster than the others. He had also been led down to the communications room after his mostly one-way chat with Admiral Simms and, like Han, Tai accepted that they had tried and failed. He notified the PLA chain of command of the cease-fire and ordered all units to stand down within two hours. He further ordered them to listen for additional instructions that would be coming shortly. The war was over and they were all going home. He spoke with General Bao and was surprised that his subordinate had figured out what had happened. Bao was clearly saddened, but agreed to manage the headquarters until the Politburo appointed a new PLA commander.

Afterward, Tai was escorted to a larger room in the facility where he met his colleagues for the first time. As Han's scheduled address approached, they filed in a neat line behind their long-term supreme leader, who was sitting in a chair behind a desk. The Eight were no longer in charge of anything—it had been an emotionally crushing two hours that had radically changed their lives, and those of nearly everyone in the world. All of the prisoners wore impeccably tailored clothing and they just stood quietly looking straight ahead. Wing was being held separately, and his interrogators had already chemically extracted valuable information on the locations of many of his deeply placed agents. U.S. authorities were alerted to be on the lookout for Chaos Teams trying to exfiltrate across the Mexican border, and any of those apprehended would be charged with terrorism. The Mexican government was fully cooperating on their side, and were tracking down leads to any agent residing in or transiting through their country.

President Han Gaoli, in one of his last important acts as titular leader of the PRC, sat at the plain desk in his new suit, and spoke to his people: "Citizens of the People's Republic of China, I and the senior leaders standing behind me have been captured by the Allied military, and we are being held securely in an undisclosed location outside of China. Some of us will be moved to other countries in a few days to stand trial for war crimes and crimes against humanity. We are not being mistreated—in fact, we are being treated well. As president of our nation and General Secretary of our Party, it is my responsibility to bear the majority of the responsibility for China's invasion of our peaceful neighbors. We will pay the full reparations ordered, and we have been given reasonable terms of cease-fire and surrender. You will be informed about those details in the next few days.

"Of immediate importance, I am reinforcing the directive that all armed forces of the People's Liberation Army accept an immediate ceasefire. You will stand in place peacefully for the rest of this day, and tomorrow morning at first light, you will begin your return to China. You are not prisoners of war—just free Chinese soldiers returning to their homeland. If you are ground forces, you must abandon your fighting vehicles, including tanks and other vehicles with guns, but you may ride home in trucks or other vehicles without guns. If you can remove the guns from any vehicle, you may do so and use that vehicle as transportation. Otherwise, walk home to China using the same route you used to enter a few days ago. You may retain your small arms, including pistols and automatic rifles, but machine guns and anything larger must be left where you are now. The various countries in which you find yourselves have promised to refrain from attacking your columns, but you may defend yourselves if fired upon by locals of any kind. The international community is watching.

"All prisoners of war are to be set free by all sides. North Koreans are to be turned over to the South Korean military. If any of you are wounded but can still travel, then do so. Those too severely wounded to travel are to be left in the care of local medical professionals. I have been assured by the President of the United States that soldiers needing compassionate care will receive what they need from every country. Sea or airborne military and civilian cadres who landed in various ports are to gather at the waterfront or airfield where they landed. You will be directed by local authorities on when and how to return home. We will send unarmed transports to pick you up in Asian ports and airports—and American ships or aircraft will bring you home from U.S. ports. All affected governments have agreed to these non-negotiable terms.

"All transport ships currently assigned to the Taiwan campaign will immediately begin repatriating our forces back to the mainland. All PLA personnel will immediately move to the closest ports for repatriation. Leave all your equipment except small arms, as in other countries. All air assets will immediately return to their home airfields on the mainland. Those military and civilian personnel on the reconstructed islands in the East and South China Seas will vacate within one week. Take your personal items and official records with you—leave everything else behind.

"All of you will return home as honorable soldiers who did your best to complete your missions. You followed orders and any failure rests on me. Now you must obey this difficult order as I have directed. Once home, you will be the vanguard of a new China—from now on serving as a peaceful member of the family of nations. That is all." Han just sat there looking at the camera until its red light faded away. *So that is that: I have just brought on my people the greatest military and political disaster in our 5,000-year history.*

The August 1st Building, Beijing (same time)

Senior General Bao and Professor Dang were sitting together in Bao's basement office waiting for the broadcast. Marshal Tai had called earlier and notified them of the disaster, so nothing President Han said was a surprise. Bao had placed calls to senior staff, field commanders, and key military school leaders—giving all a heads-up about what was coming. The phone trees in China worked pretty well, so most Party members were alerted too, and they watched the horror show as it was unveiled. There was widespread dismay throughout the land. Both Bao and Dang were devastated that their otherwise brilliant plan had been undermined by Han's lax security. It was an epic failure. Both men were numb.

After some minutes of contemplation, Dang spoke first. "Well, General Bao, our plan worked to perfection until this unimaginable turn of events."

"Nevertheless, Professor, we need to pivot now, and prepare for what's next. We have to help the Politburo save our Party and country from mass hysteria and anger." His mind was working fast. The Allies' terms Tai had laid out allowed retention of Chinese territorial sovereignty, so all military forces within the country assumed a defensive posture. They were expected to assist forces returning home, and disburse them to help the police and PAP deal with any societal unrest.

"Agreed, General. What are your thoughts?"

"The first order of business is to confirm that all commands on our side of the border are helping returning soldiers. Many returnees will be wounded and will need efficient transportation to field hospitals or larger urban medical facilities. Those returning will need food, too, and transportation to their normal duty stations. I'll order all unarmed vehicles near the border areas to cross and help with repatriation." The two visionaries discussed as many relevant details as they could think of, and then made waves of additional calls.

Ten kilometers south of Lao Cai, Vietnam
December 13th, 16:12 Hours

First Lieutenant Kee and Sergeant First Class Ting were still alive—and, by some miracle, Ting was unscathed. The same could not be said for Kee, who'd been wounded superficially three times and was a real mess. He could still fight, and he hadn't stopped leading what remained of his sapper company as they fought their way through the small town of Lao Cai and a bit farther south. It had been dirty urban warfare, and they'd moved street to street against fierce opposition. On the second morning, his men had been decimated, but they had accomplished their principal mission: Removing the external explosives from beneath the Hong River Bridge—and crossing and keeping it intact so the massed columns behind his sappers could move south. But, by this afternoon on the sixth day of the war, there weren't many of his platoon left to learn about the ceasefire. When the two comrades heard the term "ceasefire," they thought the Vietnamese had surrendered. But it didn't take long before reality dawned: It was the PLA that had lost and now they were going home.

Kee thought back to the night before the assault, when he and Ting were lying on the hill above the bridge. They'd been expecting token resistance, but Kee, and probably the whole chain of command up to their Combined Corps three-star general, had been shocked at the number of hidden artillery batteries in the valleys and hills on the Vietnamese side. He had witnessed numerous PLAAF bomb runs and strafing missions—plus an even larger number of PLA artillery barrages and tank battles as they moved south. But resistance had been fearsome.

The Chinese soldiers had been chopped up from the first moments of the war, and many of the enemy forces hiding in deep caves and tunnels were still sneaking out at night and harassing the incoming columns of fresh troops. Kee's Sapper Platoon was essentially gone—only he, Ting, and five privates were left from the original 45 men. The rest were equally split between the dead and the wounded who'd been evacuated to the rear.

All that suffering and sacrifice! The two exhausted soldiers received the unthinkable orders passed down the echelons of command—first as a soldier rumor, then as confirmed orders from regimental HQ. The mighty PLA had lost; the war was over. The orders stated that the government had accomplished its goals and was now withdrawing, but the two comrades didn't believe this obvious propaganda hogwash, and were sickened by the news.

"What was the Politburo's goal, Ting? Kill several hundred thousand of our own soldiers and then go home?" He felt bitter and was on the verge of rebellion.

Ting was disgusted, too, but didn't want to get shot by his own commanding general for sedition or treason. "Let's not voice our disgust too loudly, Lieutenant. I want to return to my family alive." He was watching the younger officer carefully, while at the same time glancing around to see if anyone heard his remarks. But they were a safe distance from the nearest nest of new replacements.

"I know, Sergeant. I don't want to get you in trouble after all the close calls we've had. You saved me more than once and I'll be grateful the rest of my life." He'd been denying the pain from his three bullet grazes that had cut through the skin of his right thigh, right arm, and left rib cage: All were just a quarter centimeter deep but hurt like the devil, and he'd bled like a stuck pig. He hadn't changed clothes since the war began and he stunk, too. He was beginning to fear that his first two wounds were infected. His knees and elbows were raw—despite the hard plastic guards they all wore; he'd run flat out and dove onto hard surfaces so many times that it had taken its toll. And now this! No one could blame the army—it was disgusting politics at its worse!

An hour later, the two men hadn't moved, but something curious was happening: Silence had gradually replaced the steady drumbeat of war, and peace descended over the rolling hills and streams of wintry northern Vietnam. Men in various places began to stand up and look around. And, just a few hundred yards south of their position, close to the end of the main road of the small village they'd almost overrun, some two dozen Vietnamese soldiers appeared out of the bushes and just stood there. For what purpose? Kee wondered. Then the answer dawned: They're waiting for us to retreat so they can have their country back.

Just then, a young woman of about 20 came out of one of the ubiquitous roadside shops and walked up to the two dispirited soldiers with something in her hand. She stopped within arm's reach and just looked down at them with pity, then handed them each a local-label candy bar. Both men nodded their thanks but she just turned and walked away. Kee watched her close the door behind her and couldn't help but laugh derisively at the irony: *I came down here to get a wife and got a candy bar*. But there was no time to feel sorry for himself: Ting got his attention and pointed back north. A soldier with a large red-and-white flag was signaling: Assembly! The two tired soldiers looked nervously back at the enemy soldiers, but they were not pointing rifles or looking hostile. Slowly they got to their feet and began the long walk back to China.

Chapter 54

USS *North Carolina*

"Bridge, Comms. Message coming in, Sir."

Captain James (The Shark) Robinson walked the few paces to the communications room and read the message. The *North Carolina* and all other U.S. Navy submarines were ordered to periscope depth to receive new orders. *Wonder what that's about?* He returned to the attack center where he'd been observing a drill, and ordered the diving officer to come to the correct depth. "New orders," he said in a neutral voice to the XO and COB who were standing nearby with quizzical expressions.

Everyone on board heard the captain announce that they were heading topside to receive new orders, and they knew he would inform them if there was any news from home. It took the *North Carolina*, *California*, and *Connecticut*—paralleling each other since their rendezvous—about 20 minutes to rise close enough to the surface to raise their antennas. Several hundred sailors were curious as three multi-function masts rose above the cold sea to receive the burst transmission downlink from the satellite.

The Shark couldn't believe his eyes, and grabbed the mic: "Listen up, everyone, the war is over! The ChiComs have accepted cease-fire terms and are returning home!" A great cheer reverberated back and forth between the boat's open compartments. The news was unexpected in the extreme, but what joy! It was good news for all, but also produced a thousand questions—especially the biggest one for every deployed sailor: "When are we going home?" It was the same aboard every fleet submarine that had survived the first day of the war—and, as the news reached family members back home, they rejoiced and asked questions, too. Could it be that less than a week ago the U.S. Navy was 75 percent destroyed, and America and her allies had little chance of stopping the ChiCom advance?

The Shark then relayed the balance of the orders, none of which were "Eyes only-captain."

"We are ordered to continue west for as much time as it takes to secure American interests in the region, and to assist with evacuations as requests come in. But we should get some port leave soon. Our immediate job is to focus on our duties, and prepare for whatever comes next. Remember, everyone, there may be an enemy sub out there who hasn't gotten the word and, if we get sloppy, they could send us to the bottom. Keep your focus as if we are still at war! However, the word is the ChiCom military is pulling back into its original border points of departure but, because they did not surrender any of their homeland, we won't be entering their territorial waters. Their navy has been ordered to return home, and we are to let them pass. Just stay tuned—you have done an excellent job, but don't let your guard down now. We're going to finish this right! That is all."

Fifty animated conversations broke out as the crew began speculating on everything imaginable. The skipper couldn't blame them. He, the exec, and the chief of the boat just shook hands—they'd won an improbable victory and none of them knew why.

However, unnoticed by the rest of the crew, Seaman Melissa Janeway was throwing up in the women's head, as she had every day since the beginning of her second trimester. She cherished the skipper's announcement for her own special reason: Sooner than hoped, she'd be put ashore at an allied port where she could get some medical attention. Her growing baby needed prenatal vitamins and she was getting claustrophobic. She still hadn't told the baby's father, so Seaman Rob Tatter didn't know his life was about to change forever. She also didn't know if he'd want to marry her or not. They had put the cart before the submarine, and then the war had disrupted her hopes of leaving the boat at Pearl. So, for the moment, a young mother's life was very complicated.

On the outskirts of Manila
December 13th, 16:30 Hours

Major Ho couldn't believe his orders and asked for clarification. His brigade commander had just announced the dreadful news, and ordered all battalions to abandon their tanks and APCs and begin walking back to the port. *Dragon's Armor* had been damaged by the Philippine military's relentless counter-attacks during the first two days of the war, but the battalions assigned from the 62nd Division had gradually fanned out into a wide semi-circle and were pushing the enemy back. The defenders were still fighting with bravery and skill, and only reluctantly giving ground, and all of the battalion commanders who had entered the surrender pool on the first day had lost their bets. But it was clear that they'd eventually win—confidence buoyed by several airborne drops of men and supplies from the mainland. One of those light infantry units had captured the nearest airfield, and cargo planes were running the ADA gauntlet every night. The combined firepower delivered from Armor was awesome, and now his men were being ordered to abandon the ground they had fought for with their blood. Unthinkable!

Ho's brigade commander, Major General Ten, was nearly as distraught as his battalion commanders: He'd delivered the worst kind of news to angry subordinates who'd been winning battle after battle. "Men, this is a tragedy on many levels. You have performed brilliantly but politics has turned against us. General Secretary Han, Marshal Tai, and other key leaders allowed themselves to be captured by Allied commandos, and they are being held in an undisclosed location, probably in Korea or Japan. Senior General Jin is the deputy commander of the PLA and he has transmitted the president's orders. It seems everyone in the world knows the situation because of a TV broadcast."

"General, we didn't see it because we were fighting for our lives!" said one of his battalion commanders.

"Yes, I agree that this is distasteful beyond what we could have ever expected. Overwhelming victory is being snatched from our grasp!" He had to caution himself against signaling that he was supporting rebellion. He would not countenance that from anyone. "But we are professional marines and PLA soldiers, and we will conduct ourselves accordingly. The cease-fire agreement stipulates that China has not surrendered, so we will return home as free men. We have a future and will continue to serve as we always have—defending our motherland!"

"General, with respect, is there not some option to continue the war here? We can hold out until a new government sends us reinforcements!"

"There is no new government! We have only one party and the Politburo has ordered us home. If we disobey, we will be considered traitors and executed! And I will personally shoot anyone who defies our Party leaders—is that clear?" He saw the life go out of his commanders—he'd just dashed any remaining hope of victory. *What a nightmare. At least I will return to my family and help keep law and order.* "Conduct yourselves as professionals. The world is watching, and more important, our own people are watching. When we get home, we will be expected to help keep the masses under control. Many of our people are starving and may riot. We have to keep the peace or millions of our own people may die!"

"General, will the barbarians attack China?" This from another commander.

"No, General Jin said the cease-fire terms indicate a status quo ante. We leave our fighting vehicles behind, but retain our small arms until we board planes or ships for home. Our frontier will be as before, minus some small islands, but you can expect some policy changes from the Politburo after this disaster..." *I'm not going to lie to the men I took into battle.*

There was nothing more to be said. The commanders dispersed and drove back to their units to deliver the horrid news—rumors of which were already spreading like wildfire. Soon, disgusted fighting soldiers climbed out of their tanks and tracks—some disobediently tossing in hand grenades before trotting away—and joined the hundreds of others walking silently back toward the port.

Major Ho didn't know it, but units from the Philippine Army had already begun to move into the mountains to continue the war as guerillas—as did the Philippine Scouts and the Americans who didn't surrender before the Bataan Death March in 1942. But this would soon change as word spread through their ranks. From village to village, phone calls, and even runners, proclaimed the wonderful news that the Chinese forces had accepted a ceasefire and were returning home. Even the Philippine Chairman of the Joint Chiefs didn't believe the rumor until he heard it from the Secretary of National Defense—who'd gotten confirmation from President Han himself. *Could the miracle be true?* Within hours, news of the victory was permeating Philippine society.

Japan (same time)

Tim had a personal reason to speak with Marshal Tai and Minister Ti and, after he explained why to Colonel Gota, the senior man gave him special permission to interview the two prisoners. He figured either the PLA, the PAP, or the MSS knew the facts related to Jen's disappearance, but the odious Wing was currently sleeping off his latest session with the Japanese medical/intelligence teams. So far, they'd twice shot him full of truth-revealing drugs, and his revelations made the debriefing team sick: Seasoned professionals were appalled at the amount of evil one man could do.

Tim figured Wing would be a dry hole, and was waiting with the PLA commander and his likeable aide for the arrival of Minister Ti. Momentarily, she was hustled in by two female guards, and Tim was surprised when he saw how disoriented and frightened she appeared. Her eyes darted about, and she looked on edge. He had been told that she'd not been roughed up, but she was probably so shocked by her change of status that she was falling apart. They sat informally around a table in a drab cement room with soft drinks and Japanese crackers on the table—Tim's own philosophy that, at least initially in any interrogation, you won more bees with honey than vinegar.

"Why am I here?" blurted Ti. She seemed on the verge of a breakdown, and Tim was starting to think her presence might be counter-productive. She sure wasn't living up to her fearsome reputation. Typical bully.

"I asked to speak with you because one of my fellow intelligence agents went missing some time ago. She was investigating the secret cavern in Dalian shipyard where your Dragon Fleet was being finished, and we never heard from her again. Please let me know any information you might have on her whereabouts." Then he reached over and selected a still-cold Diet Pepsi and popped the tab with a refreshing whoosh.

"I don't know anything about any agent! Let me go!" demanded a panicking Ti. She needed psychological help for sure.

"Please relax, Minister Ti. This is an informal meeting." He was close to signaling the guards hovering against the back wall.

"You kidnapped us—it is against international law!" She was shaking and her eyes were unfocused.

"Security," said Tim quietly, looking back at the two female guards. "Please escort Minister Ti back to her room." They quickly but gently hustled her out of the room. It had been agreed with the Japanese doctor in charge of the facility that they were to use the term "rooms" instead of "cells."

"Sorry, Colonel," interjected Tai, continuing to relate to the American as his PAP uniform had indicated. "I don't know anything, either. Ti would know—that's her area of responsibility. But, as you can see, she is having some kind of emotional breakdown. Wing might know, too—he had his hands in many pots." Personally, he was shocked at how quickly Ti had melted after a few hours of stress. *What a princess.* At least Wing deserved whatever he was getting—he was an arrogant psychopath and everyone hated him for the hatchet man he was. Tai immediately knew who the American officer was inquiring about, but he wasn't going to betray any confidences to him or any other interrogator if he could help it.

Tim just nodded; he'd expected these responses but felt he had to try. He wondered who knew...someone did—probably Wing. "Okay, Gentlemen. I resent what your government did to the world, but I also understand that soldiers do their duty. Thank you for coming. Now, please return to your rooms." With that he stood up and offered his hand. They were surprised but both shook firmly. They headed for the door with the older soldier taking the firm lead—retaining as much military bearing as circumstances and a suit of civilian clothes allowed. Soon he'd be forced to trade his newly tailored business suit for an unfamiliar and baggy orange jump suit, but there was no mistaking his lifetime in uniform. However, just as Captain Kai reached the threshold, he turned and raised his eyebrows. Tim interpreted his gesture as a signal, but he didn't react as the younger man exited, following his general. They'd be taken to separate rooms by different hallways, but Tim would recall him in a few minutes.

Tim waited in the conference room for about ten minutes, then asked the security guard to quietly invite Captain Kai back. His heart was racing because he felt the young man had some revelation about Jen. Optimism and despair wrestled for control of his spirit until Kai was ushered into the room and sat down. Tim asked the guard to step outside and close the door. "Okay, Captain Kai, you have my attention."

Kai had read this tall American as a good man, and when he'd asked about the missing agent, Kai had nearly jumped out of his skin. *Were they colleagues, or perhaps something more? If that impressive woman cared for this man, then he must be something special, too. And very dangerous.* But Kai felt the man's humanity and, at this point, he could see no useful purpose in covering up her capture and death. "Colonel, are you speaking about Major Lee of the MSS Second Directorate?" He saw his words register, and realized he had to tread carefully.

"Yes, she was my colleague. And, Captain Kai, I will tell you man to man that she was my fiancée. What do you know? And don't worry; I won't shoot the messenger."

"I am honored to tell you what I know, Colonel. But may I say with both great respect and regret that she is with the Ancestors. She died without pain, and by her own hand."

Tim had been ready for this news for a long time, but its confirmation was a knife in his soul. His life would forever be partitioned into before and after this moment. But he also believed this officer, and was grateful that God had sent someone honorable to give him the news. "I'm saddened, as you can understand, Captain, but grateful for your candid revelation—you risked a lot here. Please share whatever details you can." Then he listened to the retelling of Jen's last hours, and blessed their God who let her pass into Eternity with bravery, dignity, and honor.

Kai spoke sympathetically, "If you can get someone highly placed in your government to make the request, I will volunteer to see that her remains are sent home. I assume your government intends to keep our senior leaders here for trial, but that I will be sent home?"

"That's a reasonable guess, and I suspect that the Foreign Minister and the provincial leader Liu will be repatriated as well. But some, especially General Wing, may be tried and executed."

"Wing deserves it: He's a monster!"

"Well, he belongs to the Western legal system now. And that's way above my paygrade." He stood again, feeling a great sense of loss, but also filled with pride that Jen had invested her life serving God and her country until the last. He was grateful to Kai—a man of honor who'd treated an adversary with respect. They shook hands and went their separate ways.

Epilogue

Five days after the ceasefire began, President Spencer Stilwell of the United States and his counterparts from all the relevant countries met in Hawaii to decide what they wanted from the post-war world. Not every delegation in the "Honolulu Conference" was of the same accord. Some wanted punitive revenge that would isolate and bankrupt China forever, while others took the longer view that managed trade would yield both humanitarian loyalty and mutual benefit. The early decision to allow the defeated military members to keep their small arms probably saved thousands of lives on every side. Understandable retribution was on the hearts and minds of the occupied peoples, and there were several firefights as the PLA ground forces made their way home. However, most of the PLA was now back in China, with only the severely wounded still receiving treatment left behind.

The conference also determined the protocols for the upcoming trial of the captured leaders, and confirmed the method and amount of the reparation payments. Heated words were exchanged behind closed doors, but the leaders presented a fairly unified public façade. At the urging of President Stilwell, Foreign Minister Wu was sent home with Dr. Liu Keqiang and Sun Yuanchao (whom Wu) vouched for. It was accepted by the conference that these three were moderate voices who would promote future peace—a team of ambassadors who would heavily influence the Politburo as it wrestled through the results of the war and its aftermath. And, as it turned out, this move yielded benefits that were better than hoped: Nine of the top 100 members of the party were sacked in favor of known moderates, and Wu was elevated to serve as Vice President of the PRC. Best of all, Sun replaced Han, and essentially absorbed Han's life and material holdings. He and his wife moved into Han's repaired estate, and Han's wife moved into a nice retirement villa on Hainan Island. She would want for nothing and would live out her days in peace. She was also free to travel with a diplomatic passport and was allowed to visit her husband as she wished.

Liu wanted nothing of this reorganization, and returned to her normal life in the south. She was content with the new reality that the moderates were in the majority, and that the militants were rightly blamed for the war. There was a quiet purge that ousted the worst offenders at every level of both the CCP and the government, but everyone else in China's vast political structure just moved up one place.

The PLA's expeditionary force left a vast amount of equipment behind. There were also incredible losses from battle damage, including the ships, submarines, and aircraft destroyed in the five-day war. The cost was so extreme that even the financial gurus in the Ministry of Finance were having trouble tabulating how much State property had been wasted. The gold in the treasury was carefully inspected by several leaders led by Vice President Wu, and it was determined that it was only enough to pay their reparations for the first ten years of the 20-year payment schedule. The rest would have to come from their mines. Since the Allies had agreed to take other metals and minerals too, Wu believed they could pay their debts in full and on time. Adhering to this requirement was crucial for the future, because timely payments were the doorway to recommencing international trade—the lifeblood of China's factories and cities. Sun and Wu assured President Stilwell of the United States and other signatories of the "Honolulu Declaration" that the members of the Politburo would henceforth honor China's membership in the World Trade Organization by obeying its rules—both literally and in the spirit of the text.

General Bao could have been blamed for planning the war, but President Sun believed the country was better served by rewarding faithful service in the line of duty. Bao was promoted again—over many senior officers—and given command of the PLA. He was not made Minister of Defense, however—that position went to a former Minister of Agriculture who was an army veteran and a dedicated moderate.

Former Minister of Heavy Industry Lee Tuc Chang's sentence was commuted to time served, and he was returned to China and appointed the new Minister of State Security. About one-third of the deployed Chaos Teams made their way back to China, but the others were either killed during the war, or were arrested and still being held for trial. In some cases, they'd already been tried and executed by the countries they'd terrorized.

Minister Ti's former deputy became head of the PAP—and the main components of Ti's organization were separated out and reorganized into the previously independent departments they'd been before Han's consolidation. Sun also ordered that all police forces change their modus operandi: They were retrained to think more like servants of the people, rather than rulers. This change was well-received by the general population.

Professor Dang continued teaching at the National Defense University, and wrote a best-selling book that detailed the planning of "Operation Unity." He became much sought after on the lecture circuit—both in China and in western countries. He avoided neighboring Asian countries for obvious reasons.

Marshal Zhang left Beijing for the countryside, and raised prize chickens until his death from old age. He was afforded the usual State funeral, and his body was interred in the Hall of Heroes in the capital. Han's old friend, Li Gao Bang, moved into the provincial home of his only child, a daughter on the faculty of a local primary school. He and his wife watched over their two grandchildren and enjoyed their anonymity.

The fates of the other members of Han's "Eight" were varied: General Wing was finally encouraged by various means into giving up his network—and its breadth and depth shocked even those in the intelligence community who'd studied the reach of MSS's tentacles for a living. He was tried and executed in Japan, his legal proceedings conducted by an international tribunal from the ICC. Their unanimous verdict determined that he be hanged for crimes against humanity. Minister Ti was evaluated for some time, and it was determined by multiple psychiatrists that she was insane. She was committed to a psychiatric hospital in Japan where she would live out her life under heavy sedation.

General Tai and President Han were sentenced to life in prison, but the Japanese didn't want them in Japan—it was too close to the Chinese mainland. New Zealand offered a fine solution and the pair were flown to a secure yet comfortable prison on the North Island. The two saw each other daily and their wives visited monthly. Both were writing memoirs.

Captain Kai was promoted to major, and became Senior General Bao's aide de camp. He's still looking forward to his next opportunity to command soldiers, but at least he didn't have to spend any time in Tibet. However, he did fulfill his promise to Tim, and oversaw the respectful exhumation of

Jen's remains and their repatriation to the United States. The U.S. Air Force brought her flag-draped casket to Joint Base Andrews outside Washington, DC, and she was buried quietly but with full honors in Arlington Cemetery.

The Politburo of the People's Republic knew their economic future depended on international trade—meaning they had to make some domestic concessions to prove they were good world citizens. Within a few weeks of the CCP's restructuring, orders came down to dismantle the Uighur concentration camps, and to lift the restrictive laws that impacted their historical lifestyle and religion. The same was true of the Falun Gong and other sects, who were invited to leave the motherland for any country that would take them. The persecution of Protestant and Roman Catholic Christians all but ceased, and house churches were legalized. China's leaders were shocked to discover that nearly one hundred million of their countrymen were Believers. Abortion was outlawed except in cases of medical emergency, and families were allowed to determine their own family planning. Many women requested that the government-mandated IUDs be removed, and couples enjoyed choosing their own method of birth control.

Most galling of all to the Politburo's deposed radical hawks, Taiwan was recognized as an independent democratic republic. The Republic of China was accepted as a full member of the United Nations. Current member states voted 86 present in favor of recognition, while 14 percent abstained. The United States was first to exchange credentialed ambassadors with the world's newest independent republic. Mainland China's veto power and permanent membership on the Security Council was suspended for five years, pending compliance with the terms of the Honolulu Declaration.

On Taiwan, Sergeant Po was a true survivor: He and four of his ten-member squad were still alive when the fighting stopped. He was awarded the Republic of China's Medal of Outstanding Service (A-Level) and promoted. But he was a lifer NCO who only knew one kind of soldiering, and he was soon back with a new batch of "soft recruits," happily whipping them into shape. However, he did manage to win the heart of a young lady from his home town, and had to admit that domestic life wasn't as bad as he thought it would be.

Other survivors included Corporal Wei and Private Lao, who daily grew more convinced that their chain of command had lost its mind. They'd just crossed the old border into South Korea when their unit was ordered to stop, leave their track in place, and walk back to China in the numbing cold. So, when they got back to their border guard post, they turned in their weapons to the armory, deciding they'd had enough of the military. They deserted with thousands of others, and were last seen in a line of unarmed soldiers trudging south along the snowy road to Dalian.

Admiral Sun survived, too: He was held in a hangar at San Francisco Airport with the surviving members of his command but, after two weeks and the repatriation of all but his senior staff, Admiral Simms convinced President Stilwell to send him home. He was a military man, not a politician, and was not a war criminal. His return to his wife was a bonus: Her son had returned home safely the week before.

There were no Medals of Honor awarded to the United States military, but there were thousands of heroism and service medals presented to deserving personnel. The highest medals awarded were three Navy Crosses presented to Captain James "the Shark" Robinson, skipper of the USS *North Carolina*, Captain Richard Crandall "RC" Marsh, skipper of the USS *California*, and Captain Jim Kraft, skipper of the USS *Ashville*. And the Air Force pilots of the B-2 that sank the four Dragon ships were awarded Distinguished Flying Crosses.

One significant and unintended consequence of the war was to permanently diminish the place of large-deck aircraft carriers in the American Navy. In their place, smaller, faster carriers were built as quickly as they could be sent down the ways. With the advent of "carrier-killing" missiles, the age of the large-deck flattop gave way to the age of the submarine, much as the battleship had given way to the carrier two generations before. The Navy still needed "Airedales" but, as the service transitioned to F-35Bs, the catapult systems were not incorporated into the smaller decks. The few surviving large-deck carriers would be in service for decades, but would be utilized differently as tactics adjusted to the new reality. Submarines circumstantially became the number one superweapon, and the construction schedule for *Virginia*-class boats was doubled. Additionally, the new B-21 Raider bomber was fast-tracked to replace the ageing Spirits. And all branches of the military invested heavily in missile and drone technologies, as the lessons learned from the Third World War were implemented by a new generation of visionary warriors.

American civilians had fought the invading enemy in all four ports—using their personal firearms to harass the ChiComs in ways the military couldn't. Their extensive sacrifices and heroism were its own reward; they had saved their families, which was their only goal. Matty Benigni was one of these, and the family buried their brother/husband/father John with great mourning. And, as he'd promised himself, Matty called on Mrs. Chong and consoled her with stories of her husband's sacrificial service.

Many years after his prescient report, Reg Trammell got the recognition he deserved: He was brought into the Oval Office and introduced to President Stilwell by the Secretary of State. His family, plus his friend Tim, watched gratefully as President Stilwell awarded him the Presidential Medal of Freedom. He was promoted to Deputy Assistant Secretary of State for Asian Affairs, and moved up two floors to a corner office in the main building. His wife nearly fainted from joy. A few days later she quit her job, transferred the kids into one of the Beltway's elite private schools, and fully immersed herself in the mid-level DC social scene.

In contrast, Polly Armstrong was given the tongue-lashing of her life by Secretary Madrid, and he reassigned her to the embassy staff in Zambia. She was the "number three" there, and he assured her that a letter had been placed in her personnel file to ensure she would advance no further. On the day she walked out of her office at State, she had to face the humiliation of handing her keys to Reg—but typically, he was his usual polite self and wished her the best. He walked in and admired the view while his predecessor walked stiffly down the hall, avoiding eye contact with all concerned.

That afternoon, Polly did try to contact a certain senator, but he wouldn't take her call at the office. Frustrated, that evening she dialed his home number for the first time ever, but was surprised when the senator answered but asked her to speak with his wife. The lady seemed to know who she was, and quickly convinced Polly of two things: She was PNG in DC society, and was lucky to have the Zambia posting. Then the lady hung up. After an hour of feeling sorry for herself, Polly called her parents and announced her selection to serve in a plum field assignment in Africa.

That little corner of the larger drama ended when President Stilwell had a brief conversation with the senator the following day, and the long-serving member decided to retire immediately. He told his staff and the few reporters who showed up for his announcement that he'd been in DC long enough and needed to spend more time with his family. Upon their return to their home town a month later, his wife announced she was divorcing him. The family fortune he'd been enjoying for decades had come from her father, not his, and his "ex" devoted her new life to charity. The ex-senator moved to a smaller town on the other side of the state, lives on his government pension, and, he too, feels very sorry for himself.

Tim and Jen were worthy of being feted as national heroes, but the American people would never know their names or deeds. They'd lived their lives of service in the shadows of the clandestine world—a place where there were no banners and no bands. But Edith Carmichael and President Stilwell and a few others knew what they had done. A gathering of special invitees sat in near-reverence as Edith described Jen's service and mission in as much detail as was allowed, and the President gently slid the drape away from the newest star on the marble wall in CIA headquarters. Hers was the latest of the many who had given their lives in active agency service, and the retelling of her inspirational story would be remembered by those who needed to know. Her family just wept with quiet pride as they mourned their loss and heaven's gain.

The President thanked Tim during the unveiling and, in front of those assembled, gave him a copy of the letter he'd ordered placed in his permanent agency personnel file. His parents were there, too, and amazed to learn what their quiet scholarly son had been doing.

One more person received a letter of commendation that morning: Vice President Mason and Director Carmichael asked Betty to come to the podium and join them and the President. She was reluctant, to say the least, but nevertheless was pleased to be recognized for her part in Operation Raider: She had spotted Han's tunnel entrance, and her subsequent brainstorming with her newest disciple was described in glowing terms. Personally, she was thankful beyond words that Tim had survived. And, when you help save the world, you get to keep the corner office and retire when you want.

This chapter in American and world history ended on a positive note: Seaman Melissa Janeway was put ashore in Japan ten days after the ceasefire, and subsequently flown back to Pearl Harbor where she was assigned light duties befitting her condition. Captain Robinson accepted that this personnel move was in everyone's interest, and believed that the blessed process was conceived before the *North Carolina* started her patrol. When they finally returned to Pearl after long months at sea, he happily performed a marriage ceremony for Seaman and Mrs. Rob Tatter. And, a few weeks later, the navy's newest bundle of joy came loudly into the world.

Author's Afterword

In spite of the foregoing story, I don't think the People's Republic of China is going to invade California (though we should never let our guard down for any worse-case scenario). But they don't need to do that to deny us access to the western Pacific. Based on their statements and actions over many decades, I do think the PRC will try to force Taiwan to unite with the mainland—a nation they regard as a renegade province—and that they will use as much force as necessary as soon as they think they can get away with it. With this possibility hanging over a close friend and ally, the United States must decide what kind of relationship we want with this outpost of freedom—and our decision will have significant implications for our many friends in the region. Then, once decided, we must take such actions as are necessary to support our beliefs. In other words, we must establish a well thought-out philosophy to serve as a strong foundation for our policies.

For those of us who advocate a close relationship with Taiwan—including a mutual defense pact—what are our courses of action? We first have to establish such a pact, which alone may dissuade the PRC from unifying the "two Chinas" by force. But, since the CCP has built up its military forces to the point where they are considerably more formidable than ours in the immediate region—their missile technology is potentially overwhelming—our commitment may require active defensive warfare on Taiwan's behalf. And, the longer we wait, the stronger the People's Liberation Army becomes, and the greater their belief that they can win.

Given the context of an updated treaty with Taiwan, we should move our Pacific military forces westward into every friendly place that will host us. Currently, we have military liaison offices in every country mentioned in this book, plus significant forces serving with several regional allies. We don't need the bulk of our Pacific Fleet stationed in San Diego and Seattle; we need them in Japan, Taiwan, the Philippines, Australia, in our many Pacific island strongholds, and in the ports of our other regional friends. We need to continue to mend fences with the Philippines, and thankfully, we are again making port calls with our aircraft carriers and other ships in Vietnam. In the face of PRC aggression, we need to establish updated regional mutual-defense treaties with all our Pacific Rim allies, and station our diverse military forces accordingly. This will give the PRC pause, and is our greatest deterrent against war. The CCP believes that "power comes through the barrel of a gun" and, therefore, they respect our concept of "peace through strength."

My story's description of the PLA's missiles and other technologies is real—at least they exist in fact—but only they (and hopefully our intelligence agencies) know the real numbers. From open sources we know their missiles have surpassed the U.S. in quantity, and they have more surface ships and submarines in the western Pacific than we do—and that advantage increases the nearer one gets to PRC home waters. Our submarines are substantially better, but since the PLAN has 80 of them, and we only have part of our 70 boats in WestPac at any one time, they have the advantage of sheer numbers. They have 50 more surface ships than we do—all of which can fire a virtual cloud of the latest anti-ship missiles with longer ranges than ours. Our large and small deck carriers are the most numerous on the planet, but we are deployed everywhere, and they are vulnerable to PLA Rocket Force ballistic missile barrages. Our Navy fighters are much better than any of theirs but, if our carriers are sunk or severely damaged, our pilots will run out of fuel and crash into the ocean as our heroes did in World War II. Our Air Force fighters are similarly better, but they are also deployed across the globe. We need a lot more military aircraft, submarines, and surface ships bristling with the newest missiles—and we need them where the PLA takes note and steps back.

Our bombers are the most formidable on Earth, but I think most of my fellow citizens would be surprised at how few we can deploy at any one time. Only 18 B-2 Spirits exist that can fly combat missions. Our B-52s have been upgraded, but they are 1950s platforms, and only 58 are in active service—plus another 18 in the active reserves, and 12 in long-term storage. Our B-1s are incredible, but of the 60 or so in our inventory (according to a Popular Mechanics article dated June 6, 2019), only 10 of them were fully operational at that time. More of them are probably mission-capable today, but that means the total U.S. bomber force is approximately 100 aircraft. The good news is that there are active plans to field a new fleet of advanced bombers to serve during the 50 middle years of the 21st Century. The bad news is that the first of these B-21 Raiders are not scheduled to enter active duty until the 2026-2027 timeframe.

Our Air Force F-22 Raptors are the best in the world, but that program was cancelled due to high cost. Of the existing 186 airplanes, only 123 are operational. The rest are used for training and parts. Navy fighters include the F/A-18s that came into service almost 40 years ago, and several hundred are still in active service, but they will be phased out as our newest fighters (the F-35s) are phased in. Our allies use both aircraft, which helps, but the combined available number of first-line fighters is still less than 1,000 worldwide. Therefore, at any one time, few of our military aircraft are anywhere near Taiwan, which is only 100 miles from the mainland. Based on objective facts, the island would be overrun before we could make a difference. Taiwan has less than 300 fighters while, in contrast, China has 1,200—and the PLAAF is building or purchasing newer squadrons as fast as they can.

Our current situation in the Pacific is eerily similar to the 1930s and 1940s when fascist Germany and Imperial Japan were steadily taking over Europe and the western Pacific, respectively. We have to guard ourselves against thinking that China is just a big Iraq—the last nation-state we fought against and beat handily. We and coalition forces had every advantage in that war, and we would have few when fighting China. The PRC would be the most challenging foe we have encountered since World War II. Their advantages include vast numbers of people to conscript into their military; a naval war that would be fought in their home waters; near parity with us in technology; and a distinct advantage in advanced missiles that can sink our ships and shoot down our airplanes. We could lose such a war.

We have to decide very soon if our friends in Taiwan (and our other friends in Asia) are valued enough to fight for. If we decide the answer is "no," China has already won. If we decide "yes," then let's not pretend we can win with the current balance of forces. If we don't inform ourselves of the looming dangers posed by the ever more powerful and focused CCP, we deserve our fate. A good place to start informing ourselves about the dangerous realities posed by modern China is the following short list of books. They present facts and scholarly opinions regarding modern Chinese intentions and capabilities. I've also included two works on the history of the attack on Pearl Harbor, and two on World War II in general.

Suggested Reading

On China:

Chang, Gordon G., *The Great U.S.-China Tech War*, New York: Encounter Books, 2020

Navarro, Peter, *Crouching Tiger: What China's Militarism Means for the World*, New York: Prometheus Books, 2015

Pillsbury, Michael, *The Hundred-Year Marathon: China's Secret Strategy to Replace America as the Global Superpower*, New York: Henry Holt and Company, 2015

Ward, Jonathan D.T., *China's Vision of Victory and Why America Must Win*, Atlas Publishing and Media Company LLC, 2019

Yoshihara, Toshi and Holmes, James R., *Red Star over the Pacific: China's Rise and the Challenge to U.S. Maritime Strategy*, Annapolis, MD: Naval Institute Press, 2010

On Imperial Japan's attack on Pearl Harbor:

Farago, Ladislas, *The Broken Seal: "Operation Magic" and the Secret Road to Pearl Harbor*, New York: Random House, 1968

Prange, Gordon W., with Dillon, Katherine V., and Goldstein, Donald M., *At Dawn We Slept: The Untold Story of Pearl Harbor*, New York: McGraw-Hill, 1981

On the World Wars:

Hanson, Victor Davis, *The Second World Wars: How the First Global Conflict was Fought and Won*, New York: Basic Books, 2017

Tohmatsu, Haruo, and Willmott, H. P., *A Gathering Darkness: The Coming of War to the Far East and the Pacific 1921-1942*, Lanham, MD: SR Books, 2004

www.ingramcontent.com/pod-product-compliance
Lightning Source LLC
LaVergne TN
LVHW020039110826
845155LV00029B/554

* 9 7 8 1 9 4 8 0 3 5 8 3 5 *